The Seducer

The Seducer

Jan Kjærstad

Translated from the Norwegian
by Barbara J. Haveland

THE OVERLOOK PRESS
Woodstock & New York

First published in the United States in 2006 by
The Overlook Press, Peter Mayer Publishers, Inc.
New York, Woodstock, and London

NEW YORK:
141 Wooster Street
New York, NY 10012

WOODSTOCK:
One Overlook Drive
Woodstock, NY 12498
www.overlookpress.com
[for individual orders, bulk and special sales, contact our Woodstock office]

This translation was partially financed by Norla, Oslo.

Cataloging-in-Publication Data is available from the Library of Congress

Manufactured in the United States of America
FIRST EDITION
ISBN 1-58567-765-5 (hc)
ISBN 1-58567-868-6 (pb)
2 4 6 8 10 9 7 5 3 1

Publisher's Foreword

We make no secret of the fact that the novel the reader now holds in his or her hand proved to be something of a headache for the judges of our major competition to find the best biographical novel. Not only was this manuscript the most topical – and by far the most controversial – of all the many manuscripts submitted, but when, after lengthy deliberation, the judges did decide to present the award to this novel and opened the envelope containing the winning name, they found that the author preferred to remain anonymous and that any eventual prize-money, and any other fees, were to be paid into a bank account in the name of a small but well-known humanitarian organization.

The question of literary merit aside, that we the publishers have had to consider whether the manuscript ought, in fact, to be published in book form, in line with the other two prize winners, was due, of course, to the extraordinary and much publicized events which form the basis for the novel – and, even more so, the grim sequel to said events of which, by the way, no mention is made in the novel. The fact that this book *has* been published serves, not least, as a reminder that in Britain freedom of speech is a constitutional right. Nonetheless, in an effort to forestall any unnecessary debate, we would like to point out that the publishing house's legal advisors have gone through the manuscript, and, since a number of names which appear in this novel correspond to those of real people, copies of the manuscript have been passed to those individuals who might feel injured or offended by its content. We would like to make it clear that in every case — although for quite different and sometimes surprising reasons, to be sure — they have given their permission for this book to be published.

Although the following account is founded on biographical facts, the validity of which can be checked by anyone so minded, it is just as manifestly a *novel*, allowing all of the liberties and the possibilities offered by that genre. We the publishers wish to emphasize that this is, in the final analysis, a piece of fiction, the 'truth' of which it will be up to the reader to decide.

A brief *notandum*: several of the judges remarked on a certain linguistic inconsistency in the manuscript. We the publishers have not, however, made any alterations to the text, other than the correction of purely orthographical errors, not because the author is unknown but because in the case of such competitions we elect to publish the manuscripts as they stand.

The Seducer

The Big Bang

Let me tell you another story. Although I do not know whether that is possible, not after all that has been written and said, but at any rate let me try. I have balked at it for long enough, I admit. I have put it off and put it off. But I have to do it. Knowing full well that this will sound unutterably provocative and appallingly high-flown, I will be straight about it: I do it not only for myself but for the whole of Norway.

I realize there are many people who believe they know everything there is to know about Jonas Wergeland, inasmuch as he has risen to heights of fame which very few, if any, Norwegians have ever come close to attaining and been subjected to so much media exposure that his person, his soul as it were, has been laid open as strikingly and in as much detail as those ingenious fold-out illustrations of the human body presented for our delectation in today's encyclopaedias. But it is for that very reason, precisely *because* so many people have formed such hard-and-fast opinions about Jonas Wergeland, or Jonas *Hansen* Wergeland as his critics liked to call him, that it is tempting, even at this point, to say *something* about those sides of his character which have never come to public attention and which should serve to shed considerable new light on the man: Jonas Wergeland as the Norwegian Tuareg, Jonas Wergeland as a disciple of the *Kama Sutra*, as champion of the Comoro Islands and, not least, as lifesaver.

But to begin *in medias res*, as they say, or in what I prefer to call 'the big white patch', representing as it does a stretch of terrain of which Jonas Wergeland – all of his fantastic journeys notwithstanding – was totally ignorant, and which he would spend the remainder of his life endeavouring to chart.

It all started with Wergeland asking the taxi driver, who had been stealing curious, almost incredulous, glances at him in his rear-view mirror all the way into town, to stop at the shopping centre, just where Trondheimsveien crosses Bergensveien, a spot where Jonas had stood on countless occasions, contemplating the way in which all roads in the world are connected. Although he could not have said exactly why, Jonas wanted to walk the last bit of the way to the house, possibly because the light that evening was so enchanting; or because it was spring, the air smelled of spring, spring to the very marrow; or because he was glad that the plane journey was over, filled with a sense of relief at having cheated Fate yet again. Which brings me to another fact known to very few: how much Jonas Wergeland, globetrotter, hates flying.

Wergeland was returning home from the World's Fair in Seville, but he was now making his way across ground which, for him, had every bit as much to offer as any World's Fair, representing as it did that spot on the Earth's crust which was closest to his heart. He strolled along, wheeling his lightweight suitcase behind him; breathing in the spring air as he let his eye wander over the climbing frame in his old kindergarten and beyond that to the stream down in the dip: the Alna, a stream up the banks of which he and Nefertiti had made countless expeditions, with Colonel Eriksen on a leash and an airgun over the shoulder, in search of its beginnings, which had long posed a mystery as great as the sources of the Nile once did. He walked past the old Tango-Thorvaldsen shoe shop, to which annual visits had had to be made: a sore trial to Jonas these, both because his mother could never make up her mind and because the shoes were always too big, agonizingly so, even after they were long worn out. It was spring, the air smelled of spring to the very marrow, and Jonas passed Wolfgang Michaelsen's villa where he could almost hear the swooshing of the Märklin trains over the tracks of what must have been the biggest model railway in Northern Europe. Jonas strolled along, trailing his suitcase, smelling, listening, drawing the air deep down into his lungs; seeing in the twilight the coltsfoot, like tiny sparks of yellow growing along the side of the road and up the slope towards Rosenborg Woods, which they had used to call 'Transylvania', because they had had to cut across this bit of ground after the spine-chilling Dracula films they saw, far too young, at film shows in the People's Palace. It was spring, the air smelled of spring, and Jonas was feeling extraordinarily fit and well, free, thanks to the air, thanks to the fact that the plane journey was over, or perhaps because straight ahead of him he had the low blocks of flats where he had grown up, or because on the other side of the road he could see his own house, popularly referred to as Villa Wergeland, sitting under the imposing granite face of Ravnkollen, in such a way that he sometimes felt protected, sometimes threatened by the very bedrock of Norway.

Jonas Wergeland turned in through the gate, trailing his suitcase. It was spring, the hillside smelled of spring, as did the air. It had that edge to it, Jonas noted: chill but bordering on the mild. He felt light, full of anticipation; he was happy, genuinely glad at heart to be home. The only thing causing him a twinge of unease was a touch of incipient nausea as if he might have eaten something dodgy on the plane.

He rang the bell, just in case anyone was home. No one came to the door. He let himself in, left his bag of duty-free and his suitcase in the hall before wandering into his office and sifting through the considerable pile of mail that had accumulated. Many of the letters were from people he did not know. Fan mail. He picked up the bundle of letters to read in the living room, to enjoy them, have a good laugh and roll his eyes at the weird notions that people had, their clumsy questions, then it occurred to him that he had better play back the messages on his answering machine. The first was from Axel Stranger: 'If your Grace would be so good as to call me. Concerning a trivial matter which cannot wait: namely the future of mankind.'

Jonas could not help but laugh, switched it off, he could listen to his messages later, now he just wanted to relax, open some of the precious booty from his duty-free bag, stretch out on the sofa, listen to music, look at a couple of letters, let his mind wander. He glanced towards the door of Kristin's room. The bed was neatly made, cuddly toys and dolls all in a row; he concluded that she must still be with her grandmother, down at Hvaler.

Jonas headed for the living room with a smile on his lips, flicking through the bundle of letters in his hand, inspecting the handwriting on one while wondering what sort of music he should play. He was relieved to be back home, he was filled with a great sense of contentment: a feeling that might be described, to use a rather lofty word, as peace.

So there he stood, with one hand on the handle of the living-room door, Jonas Wergeland, the first artist of note in his field in Norway, the man with a silver thread running down his spine, balls of gold and, as someone put it in a newspaper article, a brain as sharp and polished as a great diamond; Jonas Wergeland stood there, feeling well pleased. Behind him lay a successful trip, one which had, what is more, given rise to a number of original ideas of which the people of Norway would reap the benefit in the not-too-distant future. And he had every reason to feel pleased with himself, no one could blame him for that; anyone in his shoes would have been pleased with themselves. Jonas Wergeland did not only have everything, he *was* everything, one might even go so far as to say that he ranked second only to the king. No wonder then that for many years he had referred to himself, in his head, as the Duke.

Jonas Wergeland stood with his hand on the handle of the living-room door in his own home and was instantly conscious of the metal itself, its coldness; he contemplated the brass, the little scratches on the surface. Again he was aware of that vague but distinct nausea, a surge of nausea. Suddenly he remembered the three loaves lying on the kitchen worktop, the fact that there had been no smell of new-baked bread when he walked in.

Jonas Wergeland stood with his hand on the door-handle and was filled all at once with a desire to stay just there for a long, long while, had no wish to enter the room, stood there knowing, like someone who has stepped on a mine, that he would be blown sky-high the moment he raised his foot. But he had to. He took stock as it were, recapitulating the whole of his remarkable career in the blink of an eye as if he knew he was about to suffer a dreadful loss of memory, before turning the handle, opening the door and pulling up short on the threshold. The first thing he noticed was a distinct smell, the sort that hangs in a room where

Everything Flows

Once more he was thrown into the vortex, as they picked up speed and were drawn relentlessly onwards into the next stretch of rapids to suddenly find themselves caught up in an inferno of white water and whirlpools as if they were riding a tidal wave or had been swept away by an avalanche, and it was all happening too fast, Jonas felt, far too fast, he had no time to latch onto the details and already had that feeling of nausea, that ghastly nausea that always hit him when he had flown too high, when everything was reduced to the grotesque. Jonas Wergeland sat, soaked to the skin, in a frail rubber dinghy with more or less sheer walls of rock flying past on either side: concentrating, amid all the thoughts whirling around in his head, solely on keeping a tight grip on the rope running around the rim, while flattening himself against the bottom like a terrified bird in the nest. Everybody has to die sometime, he thought to himself, and now it's my turn.

Jonas cursed himself for being there, crouched on his knees as if in prayer, hanging on for dear life on this ride with death, at the bottom of a narrow gorge with only a thin layer of rubber between him and the rapids' seething embrace, when he could have been lounging on the hotel terrace, sipping a highball and contemplating the weird assortment of hotel guests from every corner of the globe, maybe picking out an Ellington number on the piano, drawing applause from lethargic Swedish aid workers in desperate need of a bit of R and R. Or he could have done something sensible and, above all, perfectly safe, and taken a walk up to the dusty, neglected museum to gen up on the geology and history of the region, in a room right next door to Livingstone's letters and measuring instruments and his partially mauled coat.

the television has been left on for days on end. Then his eye fell on the picture of Buddha, before alighting on the figure lying on the living-room floor, a woman. She looked as though she was asleep, but Jonas knew she was not sleeping.

So there he stood, Jonas Wergeland, as so often before, at the end of a long, hard journey, a wave of nausea building up inside him, on the threshold of his own living room, in the most famous villa in Grorud. And I might as well reveal right here and now that here lies the heart of my story: Jonas Wergeland, standing in a room with a dead woman, caught in the colossal psychological big bang that gave birth to the universe which, in the following account, I intend to explore.

For those who do not know, I ought perhaps to add that the woman on the floor was none other than his wife.

But instead, on an October morning in the mid-eighties, he had dutifully presented himself at the pool along with the others, to be briefed by a sun-bronzed smart-arse who took full advantage of the rather tense atmosphere, dishing out flippant bits of advice and telling macabre jokes, about the fearsome 'stoppers', for instance: a sort of vertical wave, usually occurring at the bottom of a stretch of rapids, which could drag a man under and keep him down there for ages. So it was with some misgivings that Jonas had filed along behind the others later on, as they clambered down the steep path to the bottom of the gorge through which the Zambezi continued its seething progress after the falls, zigzagging through deep and uncannily narrow canyons. The light was dazzling, the air as full of powerful odours as a chemist's shop and humming with insect life. Halfway down the native bearers made tea for them and even sang a few songs, seeing to it that the party acquired a little local colour into the bargain.

Down by the river itself, at the point where they were to board the rafts, Jonas stood for a moment listening to the roar of the falls farther up, millions of litres per second thundering downwards into an inferno of a chasm, a phenomenon so daunting and yet so fascinating that he could see why some of the natives imbued it with divine significance, believing this to be the wellspring of the world. And indeed they were surrounded by a strange almost unreal landscape which left one with the very distinct impression that man had no business here, that this was a paradise for plants and animals and the little lizards in particular.

After yet another nerve-racking pep talk, delivered in the calmer part of the basin, they slipped slowly into the mainstream. 'No way back!' some wit called out as the raft picked up speed, heading down the river, which closed in relentlessly as they approached the first stretch of rapids, and right then and there Jonas knew, as one often does in the seconds after making a fatal decision, that he should not have done this, that this trip was bound to end in disaster.

There were six rafts going down together, seven people in each one, including the man at the oars who, in theory, was supposed to be an experienced oarsman. Jonas looked at their man, a not particularly muscular-looking African wearing a sly grin, and felt far from reassured. Not only that, but the rubber raft seemed somewhat the worse for wear; and the grubby yellow lifejackets they were wearing did not exactly inspire much confidence either. Jonas had a suspicion that the whole lot dated from the Second World War and had been bought on the cheap. And here I would just like to add that the sort of modern innovations which are to be found nowadays up north, in the sheltered and strictly regulated confines of Scandinavia, helmets and wetsuits and the like, were of course quite unthinkable in these parts, and indeed would have been considered utterly ridiculous.

Jonas was sitting right at the back, along with a female journalist and a photographer with his camera in a waterproof bag. On a scale of one to six these rapids were classed as a five, and thus they attracted enthusiasts from all over the world eager to try all their hearts could take of white-water rafting and daredevil games with the elements. Jonas held on tight, seeing a wave rising up dangerously high in the air ahead of them; he even took time to wonder for a moment how this could be possible, how could a killer wave shoot right up in the air like that, like a geyser, or appear to be heading straight for them, in the middle of a deep river, but his musings were cut short when the oarsman – who, thought Jonas, must be off his head – steered straight at the wave while the three at the front threw themselves forward into the column of water, then the raft was gliding up and over as if going over a big bump, while they whooped ecstatically, thereby revealing the whole object of the tour: to have fun, to flirt with danger, to switch off from some dull office job in Amsterdam or Singapore or Cape Town. According to their instructions, the three at the back, where Jonas huddled, were supposed to keep the raft level, but Jonas had no thought for anything but to hang on tight, gripping the rope running round the rim as if it were an umbilical cord of sorts, the only thing tying him to life; then, almost instinctively, he hurled a primal scream at the precipitous cliff faces, a howl that was totally drowned out by the deafening racket, or fury, of the river waters.

Jonas knew there was no way this could ever turn out well. He had to ask himself whether this whole stupid exercise, casting himself out into the fiercest rapids in the world, might not simply be the manifestation of a covert death wish, or a means of escape, that he in fact had no desire to get under way with the venture which was to alter his whole career: that he could not face the thought of all those heated discussions, not to say arguments and hard-nosed deliberations over everything from budgets to people that would have to be gone through before he could have any hope of realizing the mammoth project he had in mind. On one quieter stretch, where the terrain also opened out, seeming to allow him a breathing space, oxygen for his brain, he thought not without some qualms of all the months of planning that lay ahead of him were he to pull it off: the colossal amount of groundwork, not forgetting all the jealousy, the backbiting and intrigue he would have to put up with. So perhaps this expedition was a final test, he thought, as everything closed in and the raft was once more caught up in foaming white waters that raced between sheer rock-faces, sweeping them along the bottom of a deep gorge, because if he made it through this, survived this ride between what looked like an endless run of rocky islets ready at any minute to close up and mash him to a pulp, as in some ancient Greek epic – except that nothing would have time to close up here, with everything moving at such a crazy speed – then he might even have some chance of overcoming the Norwegian rock-face, that massive hurdle denoted by lack of imagination and pettiness and an unwillingness to think big, all of which were so much the hallmark of the management team responsible for evaluating the project to which he was now, down here, about to put the finishing touches. That may also have been why he seemed to be constantly on the lookout for something on the dark cliffs speeding past, without really knowing what: an answer, a sign.

In any case he soon lost track of what his motive might have been, since it was all he could do just to hold on tight, just to be scared, so terrified that he became more and more convinced that this white speck, these white specks of boiling water, this endless roiling would be the death of him, that at some point his good fortune was bound to desert him, that good fortune which had saved his bacon in countless tricky situations in the most bizarre parts of the world: looking down the throat of a polar bear in

Greenland; on a ledge ten storeys above the ground in Manhattan; in the Sahara, lying on his back in the sand with a sword at his throat. Jonas Wergeland recognized that characteristic feeling of nausea which never failed, a sure sign that things were about to go wrong, badly wrong; that this was where his luck ran out; he was going to die here, in a sort of existential toilet: one pull on the chain and you were flushed away in a swirl of water. No good spouting paraphrases here on Darwin's revolutionary view of a term of a hundred of million years or any of the other argumentations which he had collected in a little red book and which had smoothed his path up the ladder of success. Here, between these cliffs, at this pace, all words were laid to earth, or rather, were washed away by the water. So Jonas was scared to death, assailed by regret, but it was too late, he knew that someone was going to be tossed out into those lethal rapids, and he had a nasty sickening feeling that that someone would be him. I know I have to go sometime, he thought, but why does it have to be in such an utterly ridiculous hair-raising fashion?

I know it is hard to believe that Jonas Wergeland, so famed for his consummate sang-froid and prodigious self-assurance, for his courage in fact, could have been so afraid or had such morbid thoughts, but without in any way meaning to boast, let me make it clear once and for all, that my acquaintanceship with this man Jonas Wergeland is of a sort that I cannot expect anyone to understand, nor do I see any reason to elaborate upon it, but it does enable me briefly to recap on the following facts: Jonas Wergeland is sitting in a sixteen-foot rubber raft, racing down the rapids on the Zambezi river, knowing that someone, and most probably he himself, is going to fall in, and he is so terrified that not only is he shitting his pants and jumping out of his skin and so on and so forth – he is so appallingly frightened that, for some of the time at least, he is not really there; his mind deserts him, is out there floating on another plane, with the result that he actually succeeds, albeit involuntarily, in doing what one sometimes tries to do, although with no success, at the dentist's, namely to think of something else entirely as the drill bores in towards the nerve in a tooth.

The Great Discoveries

Of all Jonas Wergeland's more or less epic journeys, of all his, to
varying extents, hazardous voyages of discovery, there was one
which never palled, which stood as the most heroic, gruelling,
groundbreaking and, not least, perilous, journey he had ever
embarked upon: a journey to the interior of Østfold. This journey he made as a boy, together with Nefertiti of course and, at
the moment when he set out, it ought to be said that they, or
rather he, Jonas, considered this expedition to be just about as
daring as sailing over Niagara Falls in a barrel, and consequently,
after this, after they came back 'to life' as it were, he knew that
anything was possible. From that point of view, Jonas could be
said to have got the hackneyed theme of 'young man sets out to
see the world' out of the way at the tender age of eight. Thanks
to Aunt Laura, a lady given to chalk-white makeup, voluminous
shawls and enigmatic hats, Jonas was familiar with such places as
Isfahan and Bukhara, but in Jonas Wergeland's life it was that
journey to the interior of Østfold which blew his childhood
universe apart.

But first let me say something about this childhood universe
as it pertained to Jonas Wergeland. Philosophers and scientists
are forever trying to come up with something smart to say about
the nature of life – take, for example, all that artful talk about
the world in a grain of sand. Not that I have any intention of
depriving anyone of the illusion of being able to discover new
'truths', but if I might just point out that this is something
which every child experiences, even if many of them do in time
succeed, by the most amazing feat of erasure, in suppressing
such insights. Every child inhabits all of history and all of geography in the most natural way possible. What those speculators

in the meaning-of-life industry grope their way towards time and again are, in other words, merely scraps of a lost childhood.

Jonas Wergeland and his friend through thick and – even more so – thin, Nefertiti Falck, grew up in Grorud, on a community housing development with the fine-sounding name of Solhaug – Sunnyhills – six low blocks of flats sitting at the top of Hagelundveien. Here, in the north-east corner of Oslo, within a relatively small area, the whole history of Norway was exposed to view. Here lay the forest where people could live as hunters and gatherers; here, on the farms around Ammerud, one could see the shepherd and the sewer, the whole of peasant society in the flesh. And behind the blocks of flats ran Bergensveien, bearing witness to a burgeoning commercial trade, not to mention highwaymen a little further up around Røverkollen – Robbers' Hill; Norway as an industrial nation could be studied at close quarters, both in the quarries alongside Trondheimsveien and in the textile factories along the banks of the River Alna. Grorud was one of the few places which provided an almost perfect illustration of the saying: 'Town and land, hand in hand'. And during Jonas's formative years, the new service industries also began to shoot sky-high, quite literally, in the shape of garish supermarkets and, not least, the Grorud shopping centre with its Babel tower block, all twelve storeys of it, with, most importantly – a real fairground attraction this – a lift. All history was there, in one small patch of ground. No one told them this, but they took it in, so to speak, with mother's milk, through play.

And when it came to geography, Grorud was, like all other places in Norway, a result of the creative movement of the glaciers with its rivers and lakes, its fertile soil in valleys nestling between hills and steep mountainsides. The stark, almost vertical, granite face of Ravnkollen, rising up directly behind Solhaug, was a particularly dominant topographical feature, a sort of magnified version of the Berlin Wall which their mothers strictly forbade them to scale – in vain of course. Thanks to the childish imagination, the wide world, too, was to be found in nucleus in these few square kilometres: jungle, prairie, Sherwood Forest – you name it – it was all there, in miniature. In the world of childhood there is always a Timbuktu, some sort of outer limit and a

Mount Everest, posing the ultimate challenge. Even the Victoria Falls were in principal anticipated at Grorud in the 'waterfall' down in the stream; for a child, a three-foot cascade is good enough.

On a day in mid-May, in the year in which Gagarin broke the space barrier in his own way, Jonas and Nefertiti embarked upon their great expedition to inner Østfold. It all began when Nefertiti's father received a letter, the envelope plastered with foreign stamps and in fact addressed to an aunt whom everyone believed to be somewhere abroad. Nefertiti's parents only had a rough idea of where she had previously lived and since the letter did not look all that important they laid it on one side, with the result that Nefertiti, who had a feeling that her aunt had returned home and that they would be able to locate her, decided to deliver the letter personally. But when Nefertiti mentioned the name of the place to Jonas he was all against the idea, since to him it sounded as alien and, not least, as daunting as any exotic name from the unreal frames of the comic strips. 'There's adventure to be found wherever you go,' said Nefertiti, 'and we can't spend all our lives sitting on our backsides in Grorud, can we?'

So there he was, on the train, and it was strange how well Jonas was to remember that trip, the sharpness of every detail, especially from the point where the track branched, after Ski station, and headed off into the complete unknown: up to then the only place he had ever taken the train to was Frederikstad. He always remembered that expedition into inner Østfold more clearly than, let's say, his trip to Shanghai: the moment, for example, when they crossed the River Glomma, having left behind them stations with such outlandish names as Kråkstad, Tomter and Spydeberg, and Nefertiti brought out a mouth organ. But Nefertiti did not play 'Oh, My Darling Clementine' or any other such tired old evergreen. No, she played 'Morning Glory' by Duke Ellington, no less, and she played that intricate melody beautifully on a gold, chromatic mouth organ, while they rolled along tracks flanked on both sides by black fields on which the first shoots were just starting to show; either that or spring-green meadows dotted with yellow flowers, and one with a whole herd of horses galloping across it and a gleaming white church in the background, like something Edward Hopper might have painted. She played so well, so divinely, that Jonas was able to take her cap round and collect a whole six kroner in jingling coins before they passed Mysen.

Now at this point I really ought to say something about Nefertiti, although nothing can really do her justice. She was the same age as Jonas, but unlike him, the mere sight of an ant could prompt her to point out that the ants had already evolved into at least ten thousand different species while at the same time asking Jonas why the life of human beings should be governed to such an extent by sight and sound whereas ants went wholly by taste and smell, a chemical form of communication; or she might ask what Jonas thought of a world that revolved around the woman, the female. Nefertiti had an unusually shaped head which she always concealed under a cloth cap; it was so uncommonly long at the back that Jonas sometimes wondered whether she might be from another planet. Her clothes and her appearance were pretty ordinary apart from the fact that she always wore her hair in plaits, had pearl studs in her ears and boasted the longest eyelashes in the world. These aside, Nefertiti's most distinctive feature was her inexhaustible imagination, which ensured that no matter what she thought of or made, it was always different. She could make paper airplanes shaped like the Concorde of the future that glided endlessly through the air; she knocked together carts that made the kids from Leirhaug, the development down the road, scratch their heads and made rafts the like of which Huckleberry Finn would never have dreamed possible.

Jonas Wergeland's first stroke of genius, albeit unbeknownst to himself, was to choose a girl as his best friend. It was Nefertiti who taught him that women are, first and foremost, teachers, then mistresses – and above all that when you come right down to it, the female is a very different and, more to the point, a much more fascinating creature than the male.

They alighted at Rakkestad, sniffed the scent of a sawmill on the other side of the railway track before walking up to the crossroads, where they stood with their backs to the Co-op, the sort of shop where you could buy anything, absolutely anything, from paintbrushes to three sorts of syrup, but which has, of course, since been pulled down, every last brick of it – in true Roman fashion, one might say – to be replaced, as in so many other places, by a standardized box of a petrol station.

So here we have Jonas and Nefertiti standing between the Central Hotel and The Corner, gazing down Storgata like two cowboys coming to a lawless town and wondering whether they dare take the chance of riding through it. Which was perhaps not all that surprising, since Rakkestad, like so many small villages the world over, does give the impression of being the sort of place one instinctively suspects to be populated by an assortment of weirdoes – people who lie in their sickbeds keeping a precise tally of their whooping-cough fits and severity of same – and the sort of half-witted, hillbilly characters who are just itching to blow you away, sitting at their windows with loaded shotguns, dribbling tobacco juice and leering and muttering under their breath all the while. In those days, before you came to Grandgården and on the same side, there was a kiosk known simply as 'Langeland' and right outside this Jonas and Nefertiti ran into three pretty hefty boys of their own age. One of them was bouncing a football, a rather battered lace-up football, while another, who was missing his front teeth, was fiddling with a formidable-looking catapult. Despite a warning nudge in the arm from Jonas, Nefertiti boldly asked them the way to Haugli General Store. The boys laughed. Did they know her aunt? 'Sh'isnæ hame,' laughed the boys, thereby erecting a language barrier that felt no less great than the one experienced by Jonas at a later date, when he heard the Bedouins talking among themselves at the foot of Jebel Musa. A sly grin spread across the face of the boy with the catapult, as he picked up a rather sharp-looking stone from the pavement and fitted it into the leather sling.

Jonas, who had had his doubts about the trip from the very start, had plagued Nefertiti to at least let him bring his new gun, which could take several strips of caps at once, thus making a bigger bang, but Nefertiti had laughed at him: 'Why don't you take some glass beads and copper wire and be done with it?' she said. 'Or the Bible?'

The boy with no front teeth had raised the catapult into what could only be called a menacing position when Nefertiti did something unexpected: she pulled out a yo-yo which Jonas had never seen before. She shot the yo-yo out into the air in such a way that it knocked the catapult out of the boy's hand, caught it on the rebound, much like catching a boomerang, and then, before they had time to collect themselves, she proceeded to do the most amazing tricks with that yo-yo, leaving the boys standing there open-mouthed like kids at a circus – and, may I add, this performance of Nefertiti's really *was* quite unique, this being long before the days of Coca-Cola yo-yos, when almost every self-respecting kid could do 'Around the World', 'Rock the Baby' and 'Walkin' the Dog'.

As soon as she was done, Nefertiti invited the boys into the kiosk and stood them a small cola each and a pack of a new brand of chewing gum that came with a transfer inside the wrapper. Then she put a coin in the jukebox and played 'Apache' by the Shadows as if wishing to show, through the natives' own music as it were, that she came in peace. Thus, yet another well-known scene was enacted: that in which travellers in a foreign land find themselves surrounded by hostile individuals and someone, usually a professor, saves the situation by suddenly breaking into the tribe's own language. Because Nefertiti actually did start to talk like them. Jonas could not believe his ears as he stood there watching her waving her arms about and hearing her use words and expressions such as 'bags 'n' bags' and 'right guid' as well as even more obscure phrases such as 'ah dinnae think sae' and 'disnae maitter a doaken', while the Shadows provided a dramatic backdrop of sound.

'Haugli General Store's a bit further down Storgata,' said Nefertiti when she came over to him afterwards.

The last stage of the journey went without a hitch, the boys even accompanied them a bit of the way, they were on their way down to Mjørud Grove in any case. Before they said goodbye, Nefertiti juggled the football about a bit, rounding off by bringing it to rest at the base of her neck, while the boys muttered something about 'Jinker' Jensen, star of Brann FC. And I would say that it was here, at this point, on Storgata in Rakkestad, while the boys were saying something to Nefertiti about 'awfie nice' and 'nae bother attaw', that Jonas Wergeland lost his fear of the unknown and acquired the fundamental belief that most people are to be trusted. And also, almost as important, he realized that Norway was an infinitely mysterious land, a land full of white patches.

This last, this sensation of having entered unknown territory, was only reinforced by his meeting with Nefertiti's great-aunt, who was overjoyed to receive the letter and invited them into her little cottage on the banks of the River Rakkestad, also an ideal spot for punting or fishing for bream, perch and pike. And it was here, on a terrace in Rakkestad, surrounded by birdsong and the humming of insects, while they drank squash and ate fresh-baked raisin buns which Nefertiti had had the foresight to purchase in Dahl's pastry shop, that her aunt produced a stereoscope, a marvellous instrument new to Jonas, and showed them pictures from all over the world, pictures in black and white which were a wonder of depth and inviting landscapes. Jonas Wergeland would never forget that afternoon when he sat on the terrace in inner Østfold and, instead of seeing the embankment on the other side of the River Rakkestad, saw the Arc de Triomphe in Paris, the Great Pyramid of Cheops in Egypt and Sugar Loaf in Rio de Janeiro.

'From Rakkestad I could see the whole world,' Jonas Wergeland was later to say.

Nefertiti's aunt had been a missionary, most recently in Madagascar, and when they were finished looking at the pictures she told them not only about Tananrive but also about the even more distant country of China, where she herself had been, and the mighty rivers that run through it. She did not say much about the missionary work as such because she knew that children do not really see the point in that, but she took them into the house and showed them a map hanging on the living-room wall. Of all that Jonas saw and experienced that day, this map was the one thing which branded itself most indelibly on his memory; it was a map of the world, with lines running from Norway to all of those parts of the globe where Norwegian missionary organizations were active, their stations indicated by red pins, and in truth there were no small number of lines radiating from Norway and ending in a red pin. To Jonas, those lines seemed to extend to nigh on every country in the world, and he stood for ages just gaping at this evidence of the area encompassed by Norwegian missionaries, the host of rays and red pins, as if Norway were the centre of a red sun enlightening the whole world. Now and again a train rumbled past on the embankment outside, on the other side of the River Rakkestad, as if to show that here, too, they were linked to every part of the world.

At Rakkestad, Jonas learned that there was a Norway outside of Norway, and thus he could be said to have broken the space barrier twice that day – not only did he break free of the world of his childhood, he also broke free of Norway. And standing there in that living room gazing at the map of the world covered in all those red pins, he struggled to grasp an idea which obviously, at the age he then was, he did not manage to formulate clearly in his mind, but which he would spend much of his life endeavouring to confirm: that every country contains the whole world. And that the whole world contains something of Norway.

Opera of the Waters

So, how do the pieces of a life fit together?

Jonas Wergeland was shooting down seething rapids on a rubber raft, terrified out of his wits and staring at rock-faces, so ominously close, and waves that shot straight up into the air around them, as if someone were setting off dynamite down below: a situation so unnerving that he despised himself deeply and fervently, for, although he loved to travel, he hated putting himself at risk, hated the idea of being an adventurer, a daredevil. A lion, for example, was something he preferred to observe from a tall, four-wheel drive safari truck in the company of a bunch of camera-clicking Germans and most certainly not while creeping through the bush with a rifle in his hand.

In any case, the trip had been planned and this destination chosen largely because this was one of the few places on the map of the world on which he had not stuck a red pin to denote some sort of personal conquest, and also because he believed the majesty of the place would lend him inspiration in the final stages of preparations for his new project. And right from the start Jonas felt good there, liked being there, in the middle of what had, more than a century before, been a white patch on the map, which is to say the European map, in a place named after a white explorer which will – as everyone knows – at some point acquire a new name. It was Nefertiti's great-aunt who first told them about Livingstone – Livingstone with his Bible and his bag of medicines, Livingstone with his left arm scarred from an encounter with a lion, Livingstone, the living stone, proof that everything does move about, even stones, Livingstone who ventured into deepest, darkest Africa, just took a run at it and jumped right in and found those smoking, thundering Falls, which were not of course called the Victoria Falls back then; a waterfall on an almost inconceivable scale, lying at the heart of one of the whitest patches on the map. Which only goes to show that one will always discover something, and not only that but something magnificent, if only the goal and the drive are great enough.

The visit had begun well, too, and Jonas had really taken to the place: the hotel with the odd-sounding Kololo name, the countryside, the climate and, not least, the sight of that mighty waterfall; all of these conspired to provide exactly the right setting, the boost he needed, as he sat there on the terrace, with the roar of the falls in his ears, a sun-downer in his hand and a notebook on his lap, putting the finishing touches to his ambitious project, *Thinking Big*.

It was at just such a twilight hour, as Jonas sat deep in thought on the hotel terrace, that Veronika Røed, daughter of Sir William, walked in as if it were the most natural thing in the world, wearing the most exquisitely eye-catching little number, dazzlingly beautiful, too beautiful, and greeted him as if they had just bumped into one another on Karl Johans gate in Oslo. It was all such a coincidence and was to have such fateful consequences that it could have been one of those melodramatic chance encounters resorted to in operas. Because this was, of course, Veronika Røed, the journalist, already famed for her daring, cutting-edge features from foreign parts, who, after the standard opening gambits as to why and how come, peppered with the latest news of the family, had asked whether Jonas would like to come on the rafting trip down the Zambezi which they – that is to say Veronika Røed and her photographer, a nondescript character in aviator shades and a sort of paramilitary uniform with loads of pockets – had planned for the following morning. And in a fit of curiosity and bravado, and possibly cowardice, he had said yes.

And now there he sat, wishing – too late – that he had never come and realizing that she was going to be the death of him after all, Veronika Røed; that in the end she would succeed in doing what she had tried to do time and again: kill him off. Jonas thought fleetingly of a wife and a small child, but the thought was swept away, caught by the current, the foaming eddies, along with all thoughts to do with the purpose of the trip, recharging his batteries and getting things into perspective before facing the biggest test of his whole life. And now there he was, soaking wet, hanging on to a rope, trapped in a totally confined space, in a claustrophobically narrow corridor of black basalt with not a single fork, no chance to do what he had been so intent on doing all his life – choose another direction, make a detour, cut across – because here he was being hurled straight ahead, taken from A to Z by the fastest means possible, and he knew he was going to die, a notion as absurd and ironic as the possibility of Fridtjof Nansen dying in the midst of preparations for his journey across Greenland.

They were heading for a so-called 'a-b-c' run, a long stretch of rapids in three stages. The oarsman yelled at Jonas and Veronika and the photographer that they were going to have to be better at shifting their weight when he gave the word. Things started to move dangerously fast; the raft pitched and juddered. Jonas felt as if he were in the middle of a hurricane surrounded by an incessant roaring. He fiddled with his life-jacket, which did not look all that reliable, a fact which one nervous individual had pointed out repeatedly back on the river bank. Jonas was conscious of his own adrenalin surging as fiercely as the waters around him. There was a smell of water, of moisture, water against warm hillsides, the smell of sweat from the man at the oars, from all of them, or from the rock-face itself. Spray was constantly flying up, everyone was sopping wet, the air around them resounded, white foam against black rock, a deafening thunder, applause from hell.

And then something happened which, oddly enough, in spite of the risk and the foolhardiness and, if I might add, the stupidity of such ventures, almost never happens on these expeditions: someone fell into the water, right at the top of the second of the three almost continuous falls, and it took a moment for it to register with an incredulous Jonas Wergeland that it was not, in fact, him. The accident occurred as they took a wave the wrong way, and the raft was flipped aside as if by a giant hand.

For one perverse, protracted second, as he clung to the rope and saw, nay, studied this person being flung overboard, how in midair the face of the individual in question went rigid with shock, how the limbs spread-eagled, Jonas contemplated the vast and quite incredible power contained within water.

The previous day he had been up by the Victoria Falls, overlooking the sheer drop into the long, narrow gorge at Knife Edge Point, a rocky outcrop every bit as grim as its name suggests, admiring the mile-wide mass of water plummeting down into the depths and feeling, of all things, as if he were confronted with a gigantic organ, possibly because of the mighty roar and the almost palpable pressure on his chest from the wall of water.

He was making a quick sketch in his notebook, concentrating mainly on capturing the sweep of the cascade – not an easy task with the paper continually being spattered by spray – when an African man approached him and inquired politely as to whether Jonas was Norwegian, pointing as he did so at the plastic bag in which Jonas was carrying his shirt and a camera and which – quite coincidentally and yet most aptly, considering that they were standing next to a rock-face curtained by water – happened to come from the Steen & Strøm, literally 'Stone & Stream', department store in Oslo. In all probability it was the 'ø' which had aroused the African gentleman's suspicions.

The man, who was there with his family, all of them eminently well-dressed, the wife in high-heels, formally introduced himself and informed Jonas that he was a manager with Zesco, the Zambia Electricity Supply Corporation, and, after they had exchanged a few preliminary remarks from which Jonas gathered that he was here faced with a highly educated man, the Zambian asked, with not a little pride, whether Jonas had visited Kafue. As it transpired that Jonas had not visited Kafue and, to the man's astonishment, knew nothing about the place, he went on to describe in some detail the six turbines supplied to the power station there by the Norwegian company Kværner Brug.

'I have been to Norway,' the man said, as if anxious to change the subject for Jonas's sake, and again he pointed to the carrier bag. 'I attended a festival of the sun. And I thought the Norwegians were a Christian people,' he laughed.

Jonas had no idea what he was talking about.

'This man told me about Odin,' said the man.

'That was a long time ago,' said Jonas.

'But it's a locomotive,' said the other.

Jonas still did not know what he was talking about.

'I've visited the Opera at Rjukan,' said the man.

'I think you must be mistaken,' said Jonas. 'There's no opera at Rjukan.'

The Zambian was starting to bridle, thinking Jonas was making fun of him, but as he went on to explain, Jonas began to get the picture. The man had been to Oslo in the mid-seventies, on a visit to Kværner with a Swedish consultant to check on orders for Kafue and Zambia, and while he was there a hospitable, cosmopolitan Norwegian engineer had invited him to his cottage at Rjukan in Telemark. In the course of this memorable trip to the mountains, in March no less, the Zambian had the opportunity, among other things, to look over the Såheim power station, popularly known as the Opera House, with its old towers built out of blocks of granite. It was this same exceptionally kindly Norwegian engineer who had told his visitor from abroad about Odin, one of the little steam engines used on the steep branch-line from Rjukan to the Vemork plant. 'But of all the things I saw in Norway, nothing impressed me as much as Samuel Eyde,' the Zambian exclaimed with real warmth as he stood there next to Jonas at Knife Edge Point in the spray from the mighty Victoria Falls. In Rjukan, he said, he had seen a statue of Sam Eyde, and the Norwegian engineer had told him about this far-sighted Norwegian who had been astute enough to recognize the potential of the power inherent in waterfalls for the growth of Norwegian trade and industry and who, in years to come, was also to establish that cornerstone of the nation's business sector, Norsk Hydro.

'What a pity Sam Eyde wasn't African, and that he didn't start up here a hundred years ago,' said the Zambian with a little smile and went on to deliver one of the most crucial lines Jonas Wergeland was to hear in his adult life. 'The course of history might have been quite different if he had.'

The man walked over to his family, but Jonas stayed where he was, thinking about what the African had said. Not the part about the Kværner turbines at Kafue – he had known nothing about these, an example of Norwegian engineering know-how in the middle of Africa – or about the power station in Norway so beautiful that it had been dubbed 'the Opera', a name which could perhaps be justified by the fact that the song of the turbines sounded so operatic. No, Jonas Wergeland was considering the name of Sam Eyde. He knew the name, of course, but had never really understood its import. For a moment, this name seemed so full of meaning that it was as if Jonas had come across a severed limb, something belonging to him, something he had lost, a finger, a hand. Eyde. Water. Eyde and water. Water as opera. Water as work, an entire industrial plant.

And now here he was, in the thick of those rushing waters himself, surrounded by all that ineffable power, power capable of lighting up a whole country; or, he thought, in the middle of an opera, because this is a truly Valkyrian ride, not to mention pure soap opera. All of the geographical features around them, the rocky gorge, the glimpses of trees two hundred metres above them, were reminiscent of a stage set, seeming almost too theatrical, too extravagant to have anything to do with reality.

It was Veronika Røed who had been tipped into the water, who had forgotten to hang on when they collided with that wave at the top of the middle stretch. She was probably pondering how best to describe this hazardous ride in her piece for the newspaper; looking for a metaphor, something along the lines of 'a lifeboat down a bobsleigh run'.

Despite the ceasefire of sorts that had been in force, Veronika Røed was a lifelong enemy, and so, terrified as he was, Jonas could not help but feel a frisson of malicious glee at the sight of this woman and the wide-eyed expression on her face as she was hurled up and out, in an arc, arms and legs outstretched, as if this were an act of revenge devised by him personally: a horrid and involved plot which entailed him getting roped into something from which he would normally run a mile. But even while, in some malevolent corner of his mind, he was crowing with delight, he could not help but see how she was instantly dragged under by the roaring waters and stayed under for so long that she was gasping for breath and evidently in a bad way when, thanks to her life-jacket, she bobbed into view now and again amidst the foam, heading down the rapids.

At this point events took yet another dramatic turn: at the foot of the rapids, at a slight bend in the river, with everyone screaming at once and no one hearing a word, just as their own boat, which was the last in the convoy, was drawn relentlessly towards the next set of falls, Veronika Røed was sucked into a whirlpool; and even though the man at the oars – also filled with disbelief and furious with this bloody tourist who wasn't even capable of holding on – struggled frantically to manoeuvre the boat against the current towards her, or at any rate towards the shore, it was clear to all of them that they were going to be swept away and no one could say what then would become of Veronika Røed, who was caught in this whirlpool and, what is more, looked likely to lose consciousness at any minute.

Six people remained on board, and Jonas knew that someone was going to have to jump in soon, and he wondered who it would be even while searching, out of the corner of his eye as it were, for something, a sign, although he had no idea what, knowing only that someone was going to have to jump in, and he knew it would have to be him, he was going to be forced to jump in and save his worst enemy, a woman for whom, in his heart of hearts, he felt the most profound contempt; for her and her family and all they stood for. Jonas could not think straight, he felt sick, sick to the very core of his being, sick with fear, sick with indecision, sick with indignation at having allowed himself to become mixed up in this singularly tricky situation; a murderous form of blackmail offering only one alternative.

Jonas Wergeland jumped into the water, felt how he was promptly dragged under, thinking deep inside himself, in some corner of his mind, that this is too bloody much. So she managed it after all, he thought: by sacrificing herself, by dying in order to trick him into jumping in, he too would die in the heart of darkest Africa.

Rattus Norvegicus

Uncle William, or Sir William, as everyone in Jonas's family called him on account of an incurable weakness for expensive blazers and flamboyant silk cravats, had been in Africa, a fact that he never failed to mention as if it were an alibi for some crime about which no one had inquired. During the eventful dinner party, much talked about within the family thereafter, when Jonas and his sister Rakel went to the length of poisoning Sir William, the latter seized his chance the minute they sat down at the table, having already consumed a couple of generous pre-dinner highballs. 'Did I ever tell you, our kid,' he said, 'about the time I met Haile Selassie?'

'Our kid' was none other than Haakon Hansen, Jonas's father, who had just risen from the piano where he had been improvising a lovely little prelude to dinner aimed also at tempering Sir William's dissatisfaction with their cheap whisky. He merely smiled back, not without a trace of concern: after all, here was his brother, together with his children, honouring them with one of his very rare visits. Now he was just waiting for his brother to start up his constant refrain: 'I never could see why a dyed-in-the-wool heathen like you didn't become a concert pianist, that way at least you'd have made a bit of money.'

But it never came. Sir William had more than enough to do, holding forth about Haile Selassie as if he were the world's leading authority on Ethiopia, a personal friend of the emperor who had personally witnessed the skinny little monarch feeding the lions and leopards, not to mention the black panther, in the course of his regular morning constitutional. Not that Sir William did not have an excellent excuse for making this his topic for the evening, since the emperor had just died, a prisoner in his own palace. 'D'you remember when we visited Addis Ababa, Veronika,' he said, addressing his daughter, 'and we saw St George's Cathedral, where Haile Selassie was crowned?'

Veronika made some inconsequential, corroborative reply, but Sir William was not listening. Veronika, attractive, almost *too* attractive, and the same age as Jonas, had just started her studies at the institution which was to lay the foundations for her sensational career: the College of Journalism.

Uncle William went on pontificating about Haile Selassie – about his fantastic memory and his gratitude to loyal servants – realizing to his delight that he had come up with the perfect subject with which to dominate the dinner party, better in fact than the optional extras on his latest Mercedes, or his meetings with the prime minister, so he talked in glowing terms of Haile Selassie. Encouraged by the fact that no one was interrupting him, he launched into a long account of how the emperor had resisted Mussolini's invasion of his country, growing more and more animated as he went on, like those mediocre actors who never land a leading role and so, in an effort to get even, elevate every social gathering to a stage upon which they blow their trumpet loud and long all evening, delivering endless monologues broken only by their own hoots of laughter.

The Brothers Grimm, who had not been to Africa, sat facing one another, wearing impeccable, almost identical suits and lending a strange symmetry to the table. Their names were Preben and Stephan, and Jonas recalled with a shudder his uncle incessantly cheering them on when they holidayed together on Hvaler as boys, whether they were diving, fishing or kicking a football about: Perfect, Preben! Splendid, Stephan! Rakel called them the Brothers Grimm because they were so ugly and because they had once ruined a fabulous doll's house belonging to her. Rakel never forgave anyone for ruining a fairy-tale.

Now, however, the Brothers Grimm said hardly a word. In Sir William's presence even these two inveterate egotists were relegated to walk-on parts. They had to content themselves with laughing or making little comments – when, that is, they were not blatantly inspecting the backs of the cutlery for hallmarks or sniggering eloquently at one another over the cheap crystal glasses. The Brothers Grimm were pushing thirty, but they were still just big kids, something which went some way to explaining why they were the first – and by that I mean at least a year ahead of everybody else – to have mobile telephones, pagers, laptop computers, Time Managers, fax machines, SUVs and the like. Fix & Fax Ltd., as Rakel said when speaking of their business dealings.

They were sitting in the dining room of the new villa. The large windows looked out onto Bergensveien, the town and a September day in the mid-seventies. Before dinner, Sir William and his three children had been shown around the house, which really was a very different story from the three-room flat in one of the low blocks of flats across the road. Only the picture in the bathroom, Theodor Kittelsen's *Soria Moria Castle* remained the same. Sir William had run a curious eye over the place and a finger along the mantelpiece merely to ascertain with obvious disapproval Åse and Haakon Hansen's relaxed approach to housework. For his own part, after his divorce he had employed someone to keep house for him. He banged a wall here and there or admired the pleasing blend of wood, tile and Persian rugs, these last a generous gift from Aunt Laura, who had most firmly declined the invitation to dinner. Even now, as he relentlessly continued his soliloquy on the emperor of Ethiopia, spouting assertions which no one was in a position to check, Sir William's eye roved the room, taking in the full suite of dining-room furniture, all in pine, as if he could not believe what he was seeing: that his younger brother finally had his own house.

Jonas sat fiddling with the tablecloth and gazing out of the window as his uncle launched into a long, involved story to do with Haile Selassie's reforms and his building projects, in which he gave the impression that this diminutive monarch had more or less single-handedly raised Ethiopia out of the Stone Age and into the twentieth century, even though Sir William knew very well that the emperor was a despot of the first order who had clung to power any way he could and had vast sums of money salted away in foreign bank accounts, while his land lay fallow and his people ate sand. Suddenly, Jonas's uncle turned to his hostess. 'By the way, Åse, where's your mother?' he asked artlessly. 'Still playing war games over in Oscars gate?' The Brothers Grimm obviously got a great kick out of this question. Sir William was referring to Jonas's grandmother who had, for long spells in her life, adopted the persona of Winston Churchill.

Jonas's mother did not turn a hair, just sat there, smiling her little half-smile, as if now, as always, she knew something that no one else knew. In fact, she set some store by her brother-in-law's lack of social nous, not least because his rude remarks usually provided fodder for weeks of amusing conversation with her husband.

Jonas felt much the same. There was something about his uncle's creatively poisonous tongue which fascinated him, that ability to spend a whole evening going on and on about what a brilliant diplomat Haile Selassie was simply to prevent anyone else from getting a word in edgewise: a manifest demonstration of power quite in the spirit of the old emperor himself.

Rakel, on the other hand, had had enough of their uncle and had decided to shut him up more or less as an experiment, to see whether such a thing was even possible. She had hatched a plan to which Jonas was party, more out of principle than out of hate. Rakel believed it was time their uncle was given a taste of his own medicine: poison. So when she now appeared in the kitchen doorway wreathed in delicious smells, only these two, sister and brother, were aware that, all going well, this evening was liable to turn out rather differently than their uncle imagined.

The dishes were set on the table, thus forcing Sir William to stem his own stream of rhetoric: a mishmash of facts about Ethiopia, about all the intrigue which had sadly toppled the emperor from his throne the previous year, and snide remarks about Norwegian radicals who did not know the first thing about Africa, these aimed mainly at Jonas's brother Daniel, one year his senior, 'Red Daniel' as he was known in those days. His brother, however, having been on the receiving end before, had been wise enough to make himself scarce that Sunday. Besides, he hated 'such petty bourgeois affairs'.

Rakel had taken a lot of trouble over dinner, preparing *filet de boeuf en croûte* with a mushroom stuffing. Sir William smacked his lips at the very sight of the laden serving dish, and Rakel flashed Jonas a look of encouragement before she started slicing into the pastry, revealing what lay inside, the slices of beef interspersed with the mushrooms – this last being, obviously, the vital ingredient. Rakel passed round the bowl of salad, but had the dinner guests hand their plates to her to help them to the meat. That way she could make sure that her uncle was given the correct portion of mushrooms. If all went according to plan, in a little while he would have more to think about than sitting there like an emperor on his throne, dispensing spiteful remarks. Buddha was just about the only one to be exempt from his insinuations. He simply sat there, wearing his inscrutable smile and seeming to rise far above the verbal ructions round about him.

'I remember how cheap fillet steak was in Nairobi,' said Sir William after sampling the food. 'Cost next to nothing – and quite out of this world. We'll never have meat like that again.'

The reason for my dwelling at such length on Sir William is, of course, that this man happens to personify a crucial element in the story of Jonas Wergeland's life. Sir William is not merely an uncle, Sir William is Norway, disguised in a blue blazer and gold cravat, a *nouveau riche* upstart. To Jonas, Sir William represented the very key to vital chapters in his nation's most recent history. So when his uncle sat there, droning on and on about Emperor Haile Selassie, wearing an expression of superiority, authority and moral infallibility, in Jonas's eyes it might just as well have been Norway sitting there talking.

Sir William had lived and worked in Kenya for three years and, speaking of this, I would like, if I may, to insert here a brief discourse on Norway. I am, as I am sure some of you will already have guessed, not Norwegian. I am an objective observer. I do not know what I would have to say to shake a Norwegian out of his fixed ideas about his nation's history, but I might perhaps say that Norway and the sudden prosperity experienced by this country during the second half of the twentieth century could, in fact, be likened to the Netherlands – that, too, a small country bounded by the North Sea – and its almost unbelievable heyday during the seventeenth century. But unlike the Netherlands, Norway has been able to rake in the fruits of the rest of the world *without* – and this is the amazing thing – armed intervention, so that its people, almost unseen by the international community, have been able to sit back and revel in the riches which have poured into the country and which they themselves have, so to speak, merely processed, not altogether unlike a rat stowing away on a ship laden to the gunwales with food. Nor, I should perhaps point out in parenthesis, has Norway experienced any flourishing of the arts in conjunction with this material surfeit, as was the case in the Netherlands – and I suppose there is some justice in that. Little good does it do for an overexcited journalist once to have described Jonas Wergeland as the Rembrandt of his medium, on account of his innovative use of colour and wealth of detail.

I would like, in other words, to defend a point of view which holds *luck* to be the key factor in the history of Norway in the twentieth century; and when I say luck, I do not just mean the fluke by which, by being in the right place, at the right time, a nation quite unexpectedly finds itself enjoying a golden age. I am also thinking of the sort of good fortune which makes it possible to commit a crime and not be punished for it: crime *without* punishment, to twist the words of one of Russia's greatest writers. And I have asked myself – please do take this as being well-meant, as a working hypothesis – whether it might not be this self-same good fortune, or the suppression of such, that has turned the Norwegian people so clearly into a nation of spoiled children, to the point where they have utterly lost sight of one of the most important facets of human nature: a sense for the tragic.

Sir William – who had studied civil engineering at the Norwegian Technical College, as it then was, in Trondheim – was the embodiment of this same combination of luck and criminal tendencies, of what one might call the 'lucky sod' syndrome. In the mid-sixties he had signed up as a so-called expert with the newly established and extremely lucrative undertaking that went by the name, not to say alias, of Norwegian Development Aid. So Sir William belonged, in fact, to the first generation of Norwegians to leave the country as perfectly ordinary Norwegian citizens and to come back rolling in money – not so much helping others as helping themselves, as Rakel put it – so much so that they could go right out and buy a better car or build a bigger house, the latter also necessary in order to have room for all those enormous zebra hides and rugs, all the chests and weapons, lion-claw necklaces and stuffed baby crocodiles, drums and stone figurines, the whole of Africa reduced to bric-à-brac, as if their stay there had been one long safari, several years of tourism, with the Norwegian state footing the bill. It was his time as an aid worker in Kenya that did for Sir William, although he had evinced incipient signs of snobbery early on: as, for example, when he exchanged his original surname for that of Rød, a place near Hvaler, and as if that weren't enough had added an extra letter, giving Røed. But it was in Africa that he really had the chance to be on top in both material and social terms, where he could savour to the full the pleasure of belonging to a social elite with people bowing and scraping to you both in your own home and at the office. So by the time Sir William returned home, ironically enough from a commission entrusted to him by the Norwegian state, all of his socialist upbringing with its ideals of equality and distribution of goods had been about as thoroughly undermined as it could possibly be.

And yet the most amazing thing, and the reason why Jonas always kept a very close eye on Sir William in case he should inadvertently let slip some clue to the mystery, was that this long sojourn in a poverty-stricken African country had not instilled in him a greater sense of humility and gratitude. Instead, Sir William could sit there and talk as if he were the world's greatest expert on Africa, when, that is, he was not pouring scorn on Norway as if intent in some way upon renouncing his country's excellent infrastructure and relatively well-developed democracy in favour of a misgoverned dictatorship on the verge of collapse simply because it accorded such paradisiacal privileges to people of his (i.e. Sir William's) calibre. Sir William did not return home, as did the individuals in Jonas Wergeland's television series *Thinking Big*, intellectually enriched; he came home laden with prejudices, even more narrow-minded than before – and, not only that, but espousing a baffling brand of morality which amounted, basically, to straining at a gnat and swallowing a camel. He could, for instance, never understand – indeed it was quite beyond his powers of comprehension – how his brother, Jonas's father, could have chosen a profession in which the chances of making any real money were so slim.

And it was for this reason that he reluctantly concluded his peroration on Emperor Haile Selassie with a sort of prophetic pronouncement to the effect that tomorrow's Ethiopia was going to go down the toilet and only then deigned to congratulate his brother on his new villa: 'Splendid house, our kid, splendid,' he said, glancing around. And even though Sir William earned five times as much as Jonas's father and lived in a mansion, he could not quite conceal yet another character trait which he had honed to perfection while mixing with the other foreigners in Kenya: envy. 'But where the hell did you get the money for it,' he asked. 'Did you rob a bank? Or have people suddenly started paying you for creating an atmosphere in their church?'

'Winston Churchill helped us,' said Jonas.

'No, it was art,' Haakon Hansen said, his fingers fluttering fretfully along the edge of the table as if longing for the piano keys. 'I know you'll find this hard to believe, William, but we came by the money through art.'

'It's not exactly what you'd call a prime location, is it?' one of the Brothers Grimm chipped in.

'The fact that it's Grorud knocks half a million off the price,' added the other.

Jonas's mother just sat and smiled, shaking her head ever so slightly, as if she were shocked but was nonetheless having an uncommonly good time and would not have missed this for the world.

The mention of art prompted Veronika to turn the conversation to an exhibition which was currently the subject of fierce debate in the newspapers: a move which led Sir William, after screwing up his face at the red wine, to make a show of his interest in the arts by proclaiming how appallingly bad the artist in question, a woman, was, while his tirade only served to betray the fact that he had not even seen the exhibition.

As their uncle took a forkful of the poisonous mushrooms and popped them into his mouth, causing Rakel to look down at her plate, a sly smile on her face, he asked, apropos this artist, if it were not the case that Jonas knew her and if it were not in fact the case that he had even gone out with her. 'That would be just like you,' he remarked, turning to Jonas. 'You never did have any ambition.'

Journey to the
Centre of the Night

The name of the woman to whom Sir William was referring was Dagny M., and Jonas had met her one Sunday at Katten, a popular bathing spot on the shores of Oslo Fjord, after his last dip of the year. Jonas Wergeland was, as we know, a keen swimmer. He had been sitting on the rocks, gazing out across the water, overcome by a strange melancholy, when he became conscious that someone was watching him – no, *staring* at him – and when he looked up she did not take her eyes off him but simply went on staring as intensely as if she were capturing him on film. The fact that she had strawberry-blond hair barely registered with Jonas, and he took no note at all of what she was wearing although that was pretty much par for the course: Jonas Wergeland seldom latched on to more than one feature of a person and in Dagny M.'s case this feature was her eyes, which is to say that piercing *look*. She had also made up her face in a striking manner which deliberately drew attention to her eyes, and that in itself was remarkable enough, this being the seventies and makeup not exactly what one could call a top priority with women of her age.

Jonas rose to his feet and walked up towards the road towards the bus stop and noticed nothing until she was right alongside him. He saw that she was also wearing nail polish and an unusual shade of lipstick and that her eyes were not green, as one might have thought and as the newspapers would often have it, but blue, very blue, brilliant blue eyes. 'You'd better come with me,' she said.

Only then, walking up the slope towards Mosseveien, did Jonas recognize that sign which he reckoned to be just about fail-safe: a shiver creeping slowly from his tail-bone to the back of his neck, to leave a tingling sensation between his shoulder blades as if a silver thread running up his spine had been gently warmed up. And so he did not hesitate to follow her. To say no would have been tantamount to refusing a very precious gift.

She took him to an old Swiss-style villa sitting on the hill above the road, with a magnificent view of the fjord. She wanted, quite simply, to paint him, have him to model for her, that is. The fact that she was an artist made no impact on Jonas, but he might have been surprised had he known how famous she would one day become. Dagny M. had a very rare gift: she was a trailblazer who would receive much acclaim in the course of her life, not to mention many international honours, for her groundbreaking works, and many people believed that she alone had saved Norwegian art from utter mediocrity and provincialism at a time when even criticism of new Norwegian art tended to be pretty poor, as was demonstrated, not least, by the embarrassingly judgemental response to her first exhibition.

'Would you mind undressing?' she said. So he took off his clothes, asked no questions. 'Underpants, too,' she said. He took off his underpants, and Dagny M. spent a long time studying his member, unashamedly, with a rapture that she made no attempt to conceal and which quite confirmed one of Aunt Laura's favourite sayings, that the cock is a work of art.

'Sit over there,' she said, pointing to a chair. She worked feverishly for about an hour. Jonas had the feeling that she hardly looked at him or, if she did look at him, her glance flickered over his genitals rather than his face and the rest of his body. From the chair he could look out of the window at the scenery and the fjord. The light began to fade. He gazed down on the calm waters showing between the trees and the roofs of the houses and noted the lovely lines formed by the beach and the Nesodden peninsula farther out, an observation that gave him pause: never before had he taken pleasure in a landscape for the line of it.

'Come back in a week's time,' she said with her back to him.

And Jonas came back. They exchanged no more than a word or two before he got undressed and sat down on the chair. She worked intently, glancing up now and again, glancing at his member. He came back each week for three months. She worked just as intently each time. He liked sitting there even though he did not understand how she could take so long to complete just one canvas. But he enjoyed being painted, it made him feel good, a bit like having his hair cut. He liked feeling her eye on him, liked being studied, appreciated. And he liked looking out of the window at the scenery, the trees and the rooftops, the fjord down below, the lines formed where the water met the shore. She always stopped when the light waned, when the clouds were stained red, and the water turned pure-white.

They said little to one another. She told him none of the things that would later be revealed in biographies of her life: that she had been plagued by illness, especially as a child; that she had fought a personal battle against angst, nerves; had led a footloose existence, wandering around Europe. She simply painted, feverishly, looking up now and again to feast her eyes on his penis.

The room could hardly have been described as a studio. Only the smell betrayed the presence of the paints, the tubes and bottles laid out on the little table next to the easel. Other than that, the room was neat and tidy and bore more resemblance to an office, possibly an architect's office, what with the couple of slanted drawing boards and the filing cabinets with their shallow drawers for charts and drawings. Sometimes one had a feeling in this room of being on the bridge of a ship or in a control tower, due not least to the view and the massive and complex hi-fi system arranged on the floor under the tall windows, with its array of lights. To Jonas's great delight Dagny M. listened to opera while she worked and during those months only once did she smile, when Jonas suddenly began to sing along, at the top of his voice, to '*Deh vieni all finestra, o mio tesoro*' from Mozart's *Don Giovanni*.

Autumn came, and the days grew darker. Outside the windows of the studio the landscape had fallen into a soft minor key as Jonas called it in his head. He was still in the habit of contemplating, with an interest as great and as freshly-aroused, the purplish hues outside, the tops of the pine trees, the winding coastline and now and again the column of moonlight on the water, as if his optic nerves underwent a change while she painted him. As the weeks progressed, more and more sketches were hung on the walls, sketches of which he could not make head nor tail, but in which he occasionally thought he recognized the shapes of airplanes, snow-castles, propellers and suchlike, sometimes just vague outlines which moved him to guess, to make associations: a scarab, a truck, a row of organ pipes, a caricature of Mao Tse Tung, penises of different shapes and sizes. Eventually these sketches came to form a frieze on the wall, a decorative feature, a sum which had nothing to do with the individual pictures.

Then, one evening, she was finished. The full moon hung outside the window, and a vibrant column of gold stretched across the waters of Oslo Fjord. She did not say that she was finished, she simply came across to him and kissed him without hesitation. She kissed him passionately, consummately, kissing him in such a way that they melted together in the dark, without faces, without lips, and he felt her kiss, her tongue, touch something at the very heart of him.

They kissed in the darkness, while she steered him around the floor as if in a dance. She stopped, took his head between her hands. Outside, the pine trees loomed dark-blue. She was as tall as he, she curved her head round, kissed the back of his neck lingeringly,.wrapped him in her hair, kissed him, gently bit him.

She pulled out a mattress, unrolled it and took off her clothes before purposefully laying him down on it and, as she did so, he realized how prepared he actually was, how *ready*, as if in painting him she had been priming him mentally to be made love to. And Dagny M. truly intended to make love to him. She pinned up her hair with two paintbrushes, Japanese-style, and sat astride him. She was wet, had saved up three months' worth of moist lust, and now she let it ooze down over him, began to run her vulva over his body as if it were a sponge and she were washing him. Jonas felt as if she had gone from painting on a canvas to painting him, with a damp brush, a form of body-painting, decorating him, executing quirky little strokes this way and that like a ritual almost, as if she were intent on transforming him, recreating him or getting him to remember something, something of which he had only dreamed once upon a time. Dagny M. took her vulva on a long journey across his body, took her time, left tracks, lines, let her movements describe a pattern which she repeated again and again, drew her wet pubic hair across his thighs, his stomach, up to his nipples, made circling movements with her sex, moistened his skin, from head to toe. Jonas lay there and allowed himself to be slowly rocked, brushed, into another state of mind.

Then she guided him inside her, enfolded him, and even in the heat of the moment Jonas noted that she had a classic mare yoni, a vagina so delightful that as they made love in the dark he began to see colours, dramatic pictures which were, nonetheless, nothing but colours, large planes of colour flowing past one another or blending together, colours he had never seen before. It was as if he were on a journey through colours and shapes, going in all directions at once, and he wanted only for this journey to last, for her to go on and on making love to him, every bit as passionately, while the darkness glowed with colour.

He was jolted out of this state, or perception, by the orgasm which began to shake her, first gently then with greater and greater force, and yet so infinitely removed from all the clichéd notions of orgasm, while her face exhibited surprise, disbelief almost, as if she herself could not comprehend it, such forces, such pleasure coursing through her body or as if she had suspected that it was bound to come to this, at the end of a long journey which, for once, surpassed even the most optimistic expectations, but hardly dared, even so, to embrace this experience, this overwhelming ecstasy when first it made its full force felt.

And since he, too, had in a way returned to consciousness, he let himself slide the last bit of the way into unconditional surrender, and here, in Dagny M's house, overlooking a purple landscape with the moon dripping gold onto the fjord, Jonas Wergeland did something he had never done before: he screamed out loud as he came, a scream that set waves of different colours rippling around his body, layer upon layer of them.

Although they only made love that one time, for both of them this proved to be a momentous event. Dagny M. was struck by a desire and a passion the likes of which she would never know again, a sense of euphoria which filled her the moment she lowered herself down onto him and did not leave her until long after she had climbed off him, a thrill and a warmth which were totally new to her and which relegated her orgasm to an almost incidental part of the pleasure. There may be those who imagine that I am exaggerating, but that is how it was and that is how it would be for all of those women who lowered themselves down onto Jonas Wergeland's – I might as well say it now – quite exceptional penis. The very memory of this act of lovemaking was enough to make these women's hearts beat faster and render them numb with desire, even as they were filled with a huge sense of loss, as if Jonas Wergeland had established a utopia which, they knew in their heart of hearts, they would never find again.

At the tail end of that long night, in the grey light of dawn, Jonas was allowed to see the picture, a picture which surprised him because it depicted only his face and because he was struck by the magnetism of the portrait as if becoming aware for the first time of his own charisma. His face looked like a map, limned in the colours of the atlas and marked with routes, lines, tracks: a face which presented the whole intricate network of stories which went to make up his life while at the same time capturing many of the other faces he owned, colours laid one on top of the other, hidden levels, levels of which he knew nothing, had only an inkling, and thanks to his gift, the ability to know a good work of art when he saw it, Jonas realized right away that this was a fine, no, a masterly picture.

'Why did I have to pose in the nude?' he asked.

'Because the face is a part of the body,' she replied.

Only a day or so later Jonas felt an irresistible urge to draw. He had done some drawing before but only every once in a while. But as soon as he picked up the pencil he could tell that something had changed; he was aware of a facility that had not been there before, the pencil even *sat* better between his fingers, as if he had been doing this all his life. And when he drew the first line on the paper he could see that even this line was quite different from anything else he could remember: sure, significant, not to say creative, it went its own way, and he experienced, not least, the pleasure of executing this line, the pencil point on the grain of the paper, the infinite potential of that line to become a part of anything whatsoever. So he drew, drew for a long time, and sketches grew beneath his fingers, amazing figures which showed him that he was on the trail of a considerable and untapped innate talent, and it would be no exaggeration to say that Jonas Wergeland – at long last – realized his dream of becoming an architect thanks to his encounter with Dagny M.

Rattrap

Dagny M.'s exhibition had been the talk of the arts scene in the high summer, a furore which gave rise to all manner of inquiry and analysis in the press, all of it dominated by philistine celebrities, and panel discussions on television in which those few who could actually wield a brush were drowned out by all of the other windbags. It had been a long time since Jonas had visited an exhibition, now that his grandmother had wound down her activities as a patron of the arts, but he did make a point, not surprisingly, of taking in Dagny M.'s controversial debut, although he chose to ignore the invitation to the opening. He spent a whole morning at the Art Society keenly surveying walls hung with what one might call travel pictures, or perhaps it would be better to say: pictures which had travelled – vague, hazy monuments and antique buildings, possibly in ruins, canvases covered in layer upon layer of colour, colours which seemed quite, quite new, shimmering and yet triggering associations with aircraft aluminium and railway-carriage panels and bearing such titles as *Caravan of Dreams* and *Hadrian's Trail*.

'There was one portrait there, not particularly flattering,' said Veronika, while Jonas, utterly hypnotized, studied the way in which she stuck her tongue far out to meet the food as if wishing to satisfy herself as to the taste long before the contents of the fork entered her mouth – if, that is, it was not an indication of her forked tongue, her viperish streak or her duplicity. 'A face caked with brushstrokes and paint splotches,' she went on. '*Journey over J.W.* it was called. That wouldn't have had anything to do with you, would it, Jonas?'

'It might have,' said Jonas.

'Well, you always did have bloody awful taste,' said Sir William, to Jonas's satisfaction stuffing another forkful of deadly mushrooms into his mouth. 'This is delicious, Rakel. I really think marriage has been the making of you.' And the food truly was worth remarking on; if anyone had served *filet de boeuf en croûte* at a family get-together when Jonas was a boy it would have been considered every bit as bizarre as those dishes said to have been served in Ancient Rome, where whole roasted oxen were slit open and live birds flew out.

There was one reason, and one reason only, for Sir William's ridicule of Dagny M. and, through her, Jonas: that reviewers had slated her exhibition. In fact, they had well and truly torn it to shreds, as they say. And as far as Jonas Wergeland was concerned, this just about summed up his uncle, that is to say Norway, in the guise of an expensive blazer and a flamboyant silk cravat: that it was quite beyond his grasp that a painter who had received bad reviews might, nonetheless, be good.

All in all Sir William had the ability constantly to amaze Jonas and fill his head with questions and thus was forever challenging his notions of what was actually possible. His uncle lived up on the hill next to the Heming sports stadium, on Gråkammen – 'the best part of the west side' as he put it – in a house where the books were arranged by colour and the pictures on the walls purchased by an interior designer with a flair for harmonious tonal schemes. Whenever Jonas visited this part of town there were two things in particular which fascinated him: one was the garages, which spoke of an interest, totally alien to Jonas, in all things sporty, crammed with everything from dozens of pairs of slalom skis to obscure accoutrements for sailboats and even, now and again, a real live horse. The other was the rooms of the houses, so stuffed with traditional rustic furniture that Jonas could not help thinking that every stick of old furniture from every Norwegian farmhouse for centuries must have found its way to this area around Holmenkollen Heights. Jonas had been given some little insight into the enigma which was Sir William on the day his uncle opened the door of an age-old rose-painted cabinet to show off his new set of golf clubs.

'Well all I can say is, buying one of those pictures would be a really rotten investment,' said one of the Brothers Grimm.

'There's absolutely no way of knowing what those daubs are supposed to represent,' said Sir William, who had happened across a couple of reproductions in the newspapers. 'A dose of realism would have worked wonders there.'

'Realism ought to be defined as the opposite of art,' retorted Jonas quick as a flash, and suddenly all eyes were on him. 'The only thing which could save realism from being something other than an empty word would be if all people had the same idea and were of the same opinion on absolutely everything.' Although he did not say so, Jonas was quoting the French painter Eugène Delacroix, from an entry in his diary for 22 February 1860, if anyone is interested.

'Yes well, you always were so bloody smart,' said Sir William. 'I don't know where you get it all from. Funny that you've never amounted to anything.' Jonas dropped his eyes and bit his lip. This was one of his uncle's favourite hobbyhorses: belittling Jonas for his shilly-shallying, harping on about him being 'a perpetual student', quizzing him, cross-examining him on how things were going with his music studies, his plans for the College of Architecture, while Veronika and the Brothers Grimm hugged themselves with malicious glee. 'You'll never get beyond the bloody Entrance Exam,' he confined himself to saying. 'Pity you had to get such a prize wimp for a son, our kid,' he said to Jonas's father.

I do not intend to delve much deeper in my attempt to describe Jonas Wergeland's uncle and his three children, not that it does not, for all its brevity, say something about these people, but because Jonas – who is, after all, my main concern – did not really know these relatives, a fact which never ceased to intrigue him, all through his life. Take, for example, the Brothers Grimm at the dinner table, plying their toothpicks so one could be forgiven for thinking that they were afraid that even the tiniest morsel stuck between their teeth would be regarded as a blot on their immaculate facade. Jonas never did discover what they did, whether they were in shipping or property or what, whether they were speculators or in business in some way. All he knew was that they belonged to the ranks of the paper brokers, people who made their money by ways other than through the production of goods and who could make a fortune simply by being in possession of the right currency at the right time. The Brothers Grimm did not move stones or steel about, they moved money; they did 'light labour', as Rakel called it, 'legitimate fraud'. For this reason these two also seemed abstract in Jonas's eyes, and every time the two families were together it was this particular aspect of them he studied, his relatives' indeterminacy, their indefinable contours, their extraordinary impenetrability, their limp handshakes which somehow made him feel as if he were shaking hands with a shadow.

At this point in the dinner Jonas asked his sister, as they had agreed and just by the way, as it were, whether she had also put into the stuffing some of those other mushrooms, the little ones which they had not been too sure about and had been meaning to have an expert to look at, just out of interest. Rakel replied, resisting the temptation to glance in Sir William's direction, that yes, she had used them, but what harm could it do, there were so few of them.

Sir William's eyes flickered ever so slightly. He had not realized that they had picked the mushrooms themselves, and he had been thinking they tasted a bit odd, but he pushed this thought away, not wanting to let Dagny M. off the hook so easily: 'D'you know what I call people like her? Parasites. Living off the rest of us. It's a disgrace. Who pays for her oil? Daylight robbery if you ask me. Grants and all that. She doesn't know how lucky she is to live in Norway.' Sir William knocked back half a glass of red wine, made a face. 'God-awful bilge water,' he muttered.

'Has it never occurred to you,' Jonas said, 'that *you* are actually stealing the oil from which you make such a packet?' He just threw the comment in purely on instinct; he knew nothing for sure. Sir William just laughed, did not even bother to reply.

But Jonas Wergeland was actually onto something here: an important point. While people in Norway were ranting and raving about the EEC, the really crucial moves were, as always, being made on the quiet: in this case, the setting up of Statoil, Norway's very own government-run oil company. Jonas's casual accusation was prompted by the fact that Sir William was now working for Statoil, in fact not only working for them, but practically running the company, one reason why he was also toying with the idea of selling the house on Gråkammen and moving to Stavanger for good. And here I would like to insert my second little discourse on the subject of Norway and its good fortune, the 'lucky sod' syndrome, this time as it relates to the nation's oil. It was just around this time that Norway, believe it or not, suddenly and inconceivably began to show the highest level of economic growth in Europe, and it started to dawn on people what fabulous wealth the oil represented, so great that fairytale metaphors were all they had to fall back on, talk of the Ash Lad and the like, in endeavouring to explain what was going on. You see it was not only that Norway, due to its situation on the outskirts of Europe, was able to share in the more or less blatant tapping of resources in other parts of the world without getting its fingers dirty, as it were; in addition Norway discovered oil, thereby adding – if you will forgive me – yet another unspoken crime to its national record.

Which brings me back to the Netherlands and its golden age, since it was thanks to the father of international law, Hugo Grotius, who wrote that 'the sea is common to all, being so boundless that it cannot be the property of any one nation', that the oceans were for so long considered to be mankind's common heritage until, that is, in the wake of the Second World War, certain countries demanded greater disposition rights over their part of the Continental shelf. But the Norwegians were slow to catch on, thinking, as usual, mainly about fish, and I can safely say, without treading on too many toes, that there was a distinct dearth of expertise, interest and, above all, imagination. In the fifties, when the Norwegian Institute for Geological Surveys received an inquiry from the Ministry of Foreign Affairs as to the commercial potential for the nation of the Norwegian Continental shelf, back came a reply which was both short and to the point, a classic example of professional incompetence: 'Any possibility of finding coal, oil or sulphur on the Continental shelf bordering the Norwegian coastline can be ruled out.' Not until 1962 when, as luck would have it, foreign oil companies contacted the Norwegian authorities, did it occur to anyone that there might be something afoot, and shortly afterwards an Order in Council was issued, establishing Norway's rights to its part of the Continental shelf. A couple of years later Norway entered into delimitation agreements with Great Britain and Denmark and had the luck of the devil once again – I almost said it goes without saying – when the median line principle was introduced, although this was by no means a matter of course, thus securing for Norway, among other things, the rich EcoFisk field. All this thanks to luck and a handful of prescient and, above all, open-minded public servants, first and foremost among them the then Parliamentary Under-Secretary, Jens Evensen. The Netherlands may have had Hugo Grotius, but Norway boasts its own legal brain in Evensen. It would not be at all unreasonable if every Norwegian, out of sheer gratitude, were to have a bust of Jens Evensen displayed in their home.

And what were the gains from this? The gains were colossal; the gains were so high that they transcend the bounds of even the most chauvinistic imagination. In terms of geographical area, Norway is about the sixtieth largest country in the world. But take into account the area of the sea now coming under Norwegian dominion and suddenly only eleven countries in the world exceed it in size. Nowadays Norway lays claim to a section of the Continental shelf four times as great as its mainland, corresponding to one third of the entire European shelf – in other words, Norway has secured control over untold resources.

So what does this tell us? It tells us that the most improbable things happen all the time without anyone being aware of it.

The 'nationalization' of the sea and the seabed represents the most radical carving up of geographical areas and commodities since colonial times, and this is a point which never ceases to amaze me: in a country where people will march and protest against just about everything under the sun not one single citizen opened their mouth to question the gigantic area gain which fell straight into Norway's lap thanks to the efforts of others and, in fact, this phenomenal expansion of Norway has not so much as figured on the public agenda. Unbelievable! I say again: Unbelievable! It may be that Norwegians will take exception to

my use of the word 'crime' and indeed think it quite fair that
Norway should receive such a big slice of the cake and equally
fair that fifty-five countries in the world, to all intents and purposes, receive nothing at all, thus proving that we have long since
realized Peer Gynt's motto: 'be sufficient unto oneself.'
Nonetheless if I might be so bold as to remind the reader of how
these days everyone laughs at the Tordesilla treaty, signed at the
end of the fifteenth century, under the terms of which Spain and
Portugal simply split the Atlantic Ocean and thereby the world,
between themselves. If we are to learn anything from history
then we ought perhaps to question whether anyone today would
view the nationalization of the continental shelf in the same
light. In any case, I do not mean to preach, I merely want to
point to luck as being the key factor in modern Norwegian
history.

Dinner at the new villa in Grorud was drawing to a close. Sir
William was looking a touch glassy about the forehead and
seemed remarkably preoccupied with the heavy ring on his little
finger, set with a blue, not black, stone which, to Jonas's mind
spoke of sorcery, of his uncle's penchant for secret societies or
perhaps rather his amazing luck. Jonas was just about to press on
to the next phase of their plan when Veronika unexpectedly
came to his aid: 'Am I right in thinking,' she said, sounding a
mite anxious, 'that some mushrooms can be confused with fly-
agaric, especially when they're small?'

'That's right,' said Jonas. 'Weird, isn't it, how the poisonous
ones grow right next to the edible ones?'

'How can you actually tell if you've been poisoned?' asked
Veronika, trying to sound casual, but with a note in her voice
which betrayed that she, too, had eaten a couple of mouthfuls of
the stuffing that had been intended solely for Sir William.

'Well, nausea for starters,' said Jonas. 'I've heard it can come
on pretty quickly.' He cast a sidelong glance at Rakel, who was
having trouble keeping her face straight.

And that, basically, was all it took. There was one ghastly
moment when Sir William realized that he had eaten fly-agaric
and that one of the most lethal of all poisonous fungi was being
absorbed by his intestine, thence to pass into his bloodstream. Sir

William was in a bad way, he felt a wave of nausea building up inside him. To some extent he had good reason for thinking he had been poisoned inasmuch as Rakel had given him a very generous portion of stuffing. Granted, it had contained nothing but harmless mushrooms, but it had been laced with a substance procured from a pharmacist acquaintance of Rakel's which made the stuffing taste a bit odd and acted as a mild, but undeniable, emetic.

Sir William rose to his feet, white as a sheet, and started to walk, to stagger towards the bathroom. 'Is something the matter, Uncle William?' Rakel asked. 'Shut your mouth, Rakel, and just get out of my way or I'll smash your face in, you bloody bitch, damn whore!' Sir William was almost weeping with rage, but he was also scared stiff; brutishly he knocked a couple of chairs out of his way en route to the bathroom, making it abundantly plain that beneath the veneer of a modern lifestyle dominated by information and science, by expertise on Africa and oil technology, by higher education and every conceivable material advantage, that under all of this lurked primitive forces which, when given outlet, were ruthless in their ferocity.

Sir William made a dash for the bathroom, clearly nauseated, ashen-faced; and since in his haste and his desperation he forgot to shut the door behind him everyone could see him crouched under Kittelsen's picture of Soria Moria Castle, spewing out chunks of beef and pastry and mushrooms which he happened to believe to be fly-agaric, all mixed up with red wine; some of it landing on the white tiles, some going into the pan. And even while kneeling there, or hanging over the lavatory pan, he still had the presence of mind to curse his brother's damnable family, who had always wanted to do away with him, who weren't even fit to tie his shoelaces and who, if he lived through this, would never see his shoes again either.

It was not the knowledge that the symptoms of fly-agaric poisoning should have made themselves felt much later which aroused Veronika's suspicions, but the strained expression on Rakel's and Jonas's faces, which could be put down to triumph at having done what they set out to do, tinged with disappointment at not having succeeded in shutting up Sir William. Not even with a mouth full of vomit did he stop talking.

Veronika eyed them accusingly, especially Jonas – a look he remembered well, expressing as it did such unequivocal sorrow over the fact that Jonas was still alive. It was a look he had seen at least twice before in his life and was to see again at least once more.

Buddha was the only one who had not risen, he sat and observed the whole performance with a smile on his face.

Sir William yelled from the bathroom, where he knelt in a pool of his own mucilaginous vomit, whipped into a panic by the power of psychosomatic suggestion. He roared for someone to ring for an ambulance, or no, that there wasn't time and at that, he came out, spattered with vomit and yelling that one of his sons would have to drive him to casualty, drive like blazes, it wasn't all that far away, thank heavens, bloody family, rotten sods, c'mon Preben, here's the key, step on it, lad. They barged their way out.

What Jonas Wergeland liked best about the whole evening was a little detail that caught his eye as his uncle tottered past him: a speck of vomit smack in the middle of the badge on the breast-pocket of his expensive blazer.

Jonas stood on the front steps as his uncle and his three children threw themselves into the Mercedes with one of the Brothers Grimm at the wheel. The last they heard was a 'Perfect, Preben', so even on this occasion Sir William did in fact have the last word.

Jonas shook his head before going back to the bathroom and pulling the plug, watching the vomit partially disappearing in a swirl of water.

The White Patch

Jonas was convinced that he was going to be dragged under and drowned in the swirling water right at the very outset of his reckless rescue attempt but instead found himself being pushed back to the surface as if in an elevator, gasping for breath, his first, totally disoriented thought being that he was being swept towards the rapids into which he could see the stern of the raft disappearing, before he eventually managed, by dint of a few powerful, instinctive strokes to get himself out of the mainstream and in to the bank, if you could call it a bank since it was no more than the foot of a slide covered in boulders and scree offering little or no purchase.

Both Jonas's knees were grazed, but he scrambled and scrabbled his way across the rocks, clawing his way back upriver until he came level with the whirlpool in which Veronika Røed was being spun round and round, at which point, as if playing for time, he dredged up an observation on the literally cliff-hanging scenery, this gigantic zigzagging cleft in the rock, a geologist's El Dorado, until his eyes were once more drawn, mesmerized, to the whirlpool with a woman in its embrace, and he thought fleetingly of everything from maelstroms seething round a reversing boat to how as a small boy he was so fascinated by washing machines.

So what now? Jonas stood at the water's edge gazing at the whirlpool, which seemed somehow to form a little countercurrent; he caught himself delighting in this phenomenon, the sight of a circle in the middle of the line, unnatural almost. He had to do something, but he was paralysed, standing at the bottom of a gloomy ravine listening to the interminable rush of water, the same sound as that of a television when there's nothing on and the volume is turned up, a smell like that of explosive gases. He stood on the bank, black basalt cliffs to front and back of him, the sky like a blue band high above, but he did not look up, he looked down, held spellbound by the whirlpool at his feet, the circle of water and the face at the outer edge of the circle, a woman's face, a cousin's face, he had to jump in, pull her ashore, revive her; but if he jumped in he, too, might become stuck in that circle, be swept round and round along with her, his lifelong, detested foe; but still a face, an individual who would be done for if he, Jonas, did not jump in, take the risk, and still he stood there, staring at that face, that pale phizog being spun round and round by the current and he was struck by how white it was, almost as white as the water, a white speck among other white specks, a face, an entire undiscovered continent, and it was for this face that he was obliged to jump in, even though it belonged to someone whom he despised.

Jonas Wergeland hesitated, for one second, two seconds, on the banks of the Zambezi; this was a question of values, it all came down to faith, a leap, to being out of one's depth, with those fabled 70,000 fathoms of water beneath you, and those rapids truly *were* immensely deep; deep beyond imagining almost, inasmuch as those impatient waters had for thousands of years been forced to go into depth rather than take the broader approach.

He had to leap into the depths, but he held back, held back even when he saw that she was gasping for breath and was not, in fact, unconscious, as he had thought. She was struggling to keep her head above water, he saw this and still he wavered, in a quandary, because here he was at the very zenith of his career, about to embark on his life's work, presented with a tremendous opportunity to rouse his fellow-countrymen, to teach them how to think big, so why on Earth should he die trying to save his worst enemy?

Jonas stood wavering on the banks of the Zambezi, suddenly conscious of a Duke Ellington melody pounding away at the back of his mind, one which might have been there all along, like an accompaniment that was only now getting through to him, much the way that you rarely notice the soundtrack of an action movie. Jonas considered the face being swept round and round by the water while a snatch of Duke Ellington's 'Cotton Tail' came and went in his mind. He stood there with Ben Webster's swirling saxophone and Jimmi Blanton's pulsating bass riffs in his head, stood there while the melody played over and over again, such an incredible driving beat, that too a whirlpool; he stood on the bank, soaked by spray and shivering, because the sun did not penetrate to the bottom of the ravine, remembering, out of nowhere, a snow cave, the cold; remembering a propeller, again all-awhirl, the pain in his legs and, even so, her face, because she was lying in the water in such a way that her face was all he could see, as if it were just a face floating there, a white speck which seemed in a way to be beaming upon him like an icon, something sacred, and when he did finally jump in it was primarily in order to save that face.

Jonas was in the water, struck once more by the mighty forces at work here, buffeted about as if caught on the fringes of an avalanche; he worked his way towards the whirlpool, musn't get too close, barely touch it, like a tangent; as in a nightmare he pictured how he could be caught up in it, how he could get stuck there, to die along with her, Veronika, two bodies going round and round for ever.

He was very close, saw her face drift past, more yellow than white now, felt those forces, watery muscles, tiny hands clutching at him; maybe, the thought flashed through his mind, this is the hub for which he had always been searching, these tremendous forces, a hub completely hidden away at the bottom of a ravine between black basalt walls, an utterly desolate spot, a counter-current with a face caught in a whirlpool. Veronika glided past again, Jonas gathered himself, swam as close as he dared, conscious of a propeller slicing lethally right next to him, reached out a hand and managed to catch hold of an arm, heaved, swam backwards for all he was worth, and he actually managed it: pulled Veronika Røed out of the whirlpool, took her in tow and floundered towards the bank then hauled her up onto it.

She was breathing, she was conscious, retching, spluttering, her eyes were open, she looked at Jonas as if she could not believe what those same eyes were telling her, that this man, her cousin, had saved her life; she said not a word, did not have the breath to say anything, anyway. Jonas was just relieved that he did not have to give her mouth-to-mouth resuscitation, was aware of a terrible pain in one knee, an old injury acting up, an injury sustained in the greatest collision of his life, and even at that moment his mind was elsewhere. He had seen something, could not remember what, only that it was important, absolutely crucial, he must have caught sight of it just as he jumped into the water, remembered only that it was important, looked around, looked down, looked up, up the length of the cliff on the other side of the river and then he spotted it: a little fir tree growing straight out of the rock-face, a tiny green tuft amid all the black, it was a wonder it could grow there at all, and he realized that this was what he had been on the lookout for throughout the trip, this one detail that could transform a life, something even more important than the fact of having saved someone's life, and right then and there he knew with absolute certainty that he could do it, he could win through and realize his grand vision.

They were going to have to go back into the water, clamber a little way down the bank before swimming out and drifting with the current over the next stretch of rapids to the pool where the others were waiting for them in the raft. He was no longer afraid. It was going to be all right. He knew it would be all right. Veronika had regained her breath, was half-sitting, staring into space. Jonas knew it would be all right. The others were waiting. It wouldn't be too much of a problem to drift over the rapids on their backs. It would be all right. His project too was going to work out just fine. He knew it. He would get there. He would see it through even if he had to take on the whole of NRK, the Norwegian Broadcasting Corporation, single-handed. He took Veronika's hand and pulled her to her feet. They clambered down the bank a little way before once more plunging into the foaming waters.

Pyramid Playing

Jonas Wergeland had originally intended to open the programme on Ole Bull with the central character, in the shape of Normann Vaage, standing by a waterfall, playing one of his hell-for-leather compositions: a nod, so to speak, in the direction of the myth of the Fossgrimen, the fiddle-playing sprite of the falls, and the magic of the fiddlers of old. This sequence would also have fitted in beautifully with a cut to pictures of the green-patinated statue of Ole Bull set amid the fountains in the lovely gardens outside the Hotel Norge in Bergen, after which they could pan up to the peaks of Fløyen and Ulriken and the landscape of western Norway which supposedly meant so much to Ole Bull.

That it did not turn out this way was due not only to Jonas Wergeland's decision, following one of the basic principles behind the series, to set the key scene in each programme in a foreign location, which meant dispensing with most of the hackneyed images associated with Ole Bull – old Bergen, the family home in Valestrand and, not least, the quite fascinating jumble of a house on the island of Lysøen, a monument to his hectic travels – but also to the fact that at the planning stage Jonas had asked the same question of Ole Bornemann Bull as he asked of all his other chosen subjects: what is the story at the heart of this person's life? And in Bull's case, Jonas Wergeland replied as follows: Ole Bull's story is that of a man who travelled the world over in search of the perfect sounding-board for the Norwegian tone. And this Ole Bull found at the top of the Great Pyramid of Cheops.

Now it could be argued that this scene, too – Ole Bull atop the seventh wonder of the world on his 66th birthday – has been pretty much done to death, but when it came to a choice between this and a scene from Oleana in a small valley in the Allegheny Mountains of Pennsylvania, Jonas opted for Egypt, prompted not only by the fact that this scene could have been made for television but also by another, underlying, motive: the chance of finally getting to see Cairo, one of the few capitals in the world he had not visited. In this respect, Jonas Wergeland falls neatly into line with all the other individuals who have had NRK foot the bill for their own private jaunts abroad.

The greatest challenge was, therefore, to come up with a ploy which would breathe fresh life into the Cheops scene, and this Jonas achieved by alternating vertical shots of the pyramid with a frenetic, panorama sequence which actually constituted the programme's main leitmotif, depicting Ole Bull travelling the length and breadth of Europe like a sort of musical Casanova in his English-built coach. Thus the programme darted back and forth between a young Ole Bull on his helter-skelter tour of the concert halls of Europe, large and small, and an elderly Ole Bull climbing the Great Pyramid of Cheops. For the scenes of the perpetual progress from one city to the next, from Paris to Trieste, from Cadiz to Riga, Jonas alternated between exterior shots of the coach, with eight fine horses between the traces, and shots of the interior, specially fitted out as a sleeping chamber in which Ole Bull and his manservant could spend the night – all of this filmed on one of the avenues in Frognerparken in Oslo and interspersed with shots from the concerts, where the set – a more or less faithful reproduction built in the studio of the concert hall in Bologna, scene of what was possibly the most important concert of his career – remained the same throughout with various different backdrops representing Florence or St Petersburg simply and quite openly being dropped into place, and Ole Bull always giving a solo performance of the coda, rich in musical pyrotechnics and bravura flourishes, from his own, not particularly well-known, but tempestuous composition 'Polacca guerriera' – possibly inspired by the eruption of Mount Vesuvius – thus giving the viewers the impression of a constant repetition of the same elements: the massive coach racing full tilt across the same stretch of country; Bull in his seat, the same impatient expression on his face; the same concert hall, the same audience, the same music, the same ovations, the same ladies weeping, the same gifts, flowers and jewellery, brooches and snuff boxes inlaid with precious stones, then the carriage again, charging on through dust, mud, snow, rain, then the concert hall and so on and so forth, broken only by Bull as an old man, shot in slow motion, negotiating the massive stone blocks of the Great Pyramid, the sound of his breathing and his heartbeat amplified, dominating the soundtrack. It was said of this programme that the shaking of the carriage eventually transmitted itself to the armchairs of the viewers at home and that every time the old man was seen laboriously ascending the pyramid they were on the edge of their seats, almost as if they were watching a thriller as if, even though they knew the outcome, they were not sure whether he really would make it.

The middle segment of the programme was given over to the regular spot in which Jonas Wergeland himself, in modern dress, stepped onto the set to interview the central character. Much of the series' popularity could be put down to this part of the programme, thanks to Wergeland's unique television presence and the extremely artful way in which the interview revealed certain less well-known aspects of the hero's character. Thus, in this programme, Jonas Wergeland sat halfway up the Great Pyramid, talking to a clearly exhausted and exaggeratedly aged Ole Bull – looking like a burnt-out Casanova, to pursue the metaphor – with Bull replying as animatedly and as eloquently as was apparently his wont to the questions Jonas Wergeland put to him regarding his Arabian horses, his attempt to commit suicide by jumping into the Seine, that duel with rapiers – did that really happen? – his weakness for casinos, his affair with opera singer Maria Malibran, his two marriages, and is it true, Ole Bull, that you were offered the post of general with the Spanish army? They then went on to talk about his music, about Torgeir Augundsson, the Lad from Myllar, about the Norwegian airs, their unique character, and, above all, about Ole Bull's great passion: violins – from his first, a Santo Seraphino, by way of all the others, among them an Amati *grand patron*, a Stradivarius, a Guarnerius – or was it three? – to the pride of them all which he now cradled in his arms, caressing it as if it were a baby, a

Gasparo da Salò with the carved angel head at the top of the neck and the delicate zigzag border on the fingerboard. From this Wergeland switched to asking Ole Bull, halfway up the Great Pyramid of Cheops, how his instruments were constructed, got him to explain how the bridges were made lower and flatter so that he could play all of the strings at once and why he used an especially long, rigid, heavy bow, after which Ole Bull demonstrated his finesse on the violin in a brilliant sequence – with close-ups of a real violinist's hands, of course – in which the viewers were given a taste of Bull's matchless polyphonies and inimitable cantabile, his pizzicatos and trills and harmonics, together with a mind-boggling staccato technique which could conjure up 350 notes with one stroke of the bow, before the musician rounded off with imitations of everything from birds twittering to the wind sighing in the tops of the birch trees, from waterfalls to the crackle of lightning.

For his own part, Jonas Wergeland was happiest with the ending – perhaps because they had been the first foreign television crew for many years to be granted permission, without bribing anyone, to film at the top of the Great Pyramid of Cheops, which says much for Jonas Wergeland's rare gift for seducing people. They had gone so far over the top in this scene that it teetered on the very brink of pure parody. Norman Vaage, clad in a copy of Ole Bull's concert dress, looked magnificent standing on the top of the pyramid in the sunset next to a fluttering Norwegian flag, overlooking Cairo and the Nile and the desert, playing, or supposedly playing 'The Saeter Girl's Sunday' with such a passionate expression on his face and such theatrical gestures and such power that anyone would have thought he was trying to bring down the Great Pyramid the way the Hebrews had done farther east with the walls of Jericho. The diamonds set in to the tip of the bow, sparkled in the light and the music, that melancholy Norwegian melody, was so irredeemably unctuous, going as far as it decently could without slipping over into an unadulterated gypsy serenade, while Ole Bull, alias Normann Vaage, finished off – or so it seemed to the viewers – by releasing a white dove from the violin case. In addition, the Bedouin extras had been encouraged to act even more awestruck than the story would have it, if that were possible, which is to say that they fell to their knees as if bewitched, exclaiming 'Allah, Allah!' In Jonas Wergeland's version even the camels knelt before him.

Jonas realized, of course, that Ole Bull had to be viewed in the light of the nineteenth-century concert tradition, whereby the performer was very much an improviser, creating the music as he went along; nonetheless Jonas wanted also to leave some room for those critical voices which hold that Ole Bull was more of a buffoon and a conjuror than a musician, not to say composer, of real standing and maintain that Bull had to resort to cheap tricks and bravura displays for want of genuine virtuosity. And here Wergeland was alluding to a particularly Norwegian syndrome: that in Norway one can at best be a virtuoso but never creative and certainly never innovative – as exemplified by Ole Bull, who could have been one of the truly great musicians but who possibly let this opportunity slip by not taking lessons, so that one cannot but agree with Franz Liszt when that temperamental gentleman declared in the midst of a private contretemps that the name of Ole Bull would have been forgotten by Europe when the world was still paying homage to his, Liszt's, memory. Nevertheless Jonas Wergeland succeeded in highlighting Bull's greatest gift to the Norwegian people, both in his own day and today: his innate ability to kindle excitement in others. There were many viewers who felt that Ole Bull not only conquered Cheops but also the heart of the Norwegian people. Ole Bull's was a fine, uplifting story, a fairy tale to his contemporaries, the first and greatest red-letter day of their lives, as Bjørnstjerne Bjørnson – for once – so aptly put it, a Norwegian who played a whole night long in the Colosseum in the moonlight and proved that even an insignificant little country such as Norway could make its mark in the big wide world: a fact which to this very day the nation finds it hard to comprehend, with the result that they have to go to the length of creating advertising campaigns costing millions of kroner, taking out full pages in the newspapers to persuade more Norwegians that they are as good as the rest of the world.

Although Jonas Wergeland had long since become used to the power of television, he could still be surprised by its unforeseen consequences. After the programme on Ole Bull people rushed out in droves to buy the soundtrack from it, which included 'Polacca guerriera', the relatively unknown piece by Bull that had run like a deep, irresistible undercurrent throughout the programme. It was also gratifying to note that this record had been made by a young Norwegian musician – the same violinist whom Jonas Wergeland had used in the programme – so this was just one of many examples of the way in which, through his television series, Jonas Wergeland played his part in promoting many talented artists, thus triggering a wave of creativity within many areas of the Norwegian arts scene.

Cleopatra's Nose

And now, not to something before or after this, but *above* it all. I mentioned an old injury to Jonas Wergeland's knee. One of life's paradoxes is that things happen and yet we refuse to accept that they do just happen, by which I mean that we go around brooding over how and why this or that could happen, someone falling into a river, someone having to jump in, even years after the actual event when life has long since moved on, and on this score we would appear to have inexhaustible reserves of energy, so much so that generation after generation will sit down and brood, for example, over what might have happened had it not rained on the day before the battle of Waterloo. And it is every bit as pointless to go around wondering how Jonas Wergeland's story would have turned out if only he had been paying more attention to where he was going or at any rate if he had not fallen head over heels for Margrete's nose.

It was their wheels which brought them together. This was in fifth grade, a first encounter which was to give rise to quite a little local legend, there having been so many witnesses. It was springtime, with coltsfoot growing on all the banks and a strong whiff of bonfires in the air, a sign, if you like, that this was a season when things could easily be set aflame. Jonas came wheeling down from Bergensveien, from the housing estate of the new middle-class; Margrete was riding over from Teppabakken, Grorud's answer to Holmenkoll–Heights, if one can refer to that area of fine old houses in such terms. As I say, there they were, riding along at a fair lick, coming from opposite directions and both set to turn in through the same, relatively narrow, school gate. It was bound to end in disaster.

It suddenly occurs to me, my theme here being that of collision, that it may have been a little thoughtless of me just to set
this wheel of stories, all that has gone before, spinning without
any sort of a preface or explanation. I ought to have introduced
myself, I know, but I am very much afraid that this would only
lead to misunderstanding. For some, this tale would thus be lent
too much authority; it would lose all credibility in the eyes of
others. My own popularity is, after all, plummeting, and – this
much I can say – I am now so much *persona non grata* that a lot
of people have declared me to be dead. I must, therefore, choose
my words with care. I am who I am. More than that I cannot say.

I could of course have gone about this in some other way, but
eager as I am to get my views across, I have no choice but to settle
for a level – adopt a genre, style, call it what you will – which is
totally alien to me and which cannot help but make the story as
a whole seem somewhat unsatisfactory, not to say slapdash,
something which is not helped by the fact that I happen to be
putting this in writing, a medium so far removed from that over
which Jonas Wergeland exercised such supreme command, and
using the Roman alphabet to boot. Not only that, but I originally
wrote it in Norwegian, a language spoken – in some cases better
than others – by around four or five million people. Here I would
like to take the opportunity to apologize for those linguistic
errors and idiosyncrasies which were bound to crop up in the
original and just as inevitably be carried over into this rendering,
not to mention all of the – doubtless unwarranted – analytical
passages. I would be the first to admit that I can in no way be said
to have mastered all the stylistic levels of the Norwegian language. Nonetheless, I have – this, too, I confess – regarded the
writing of this manuscript as a challenging experiment.

It is of course no coincidence that out of all the people in the
world I should have chosen Jonas Wergeland, and apart from my
obvious, aforementioned motive – that of wishing to say something to the Norwegian people and even to influence them in
some way – I make no secret of the fact that I am curious: that,
more than anything else, the driving force behind the writing of
this story has been wonder. After all, how is it possible? How did
all this come about? And how can so many scurrilous and untrue
things be said about one man?

In other words, I want to see justice done. I do not come from Norway. I see things differently. I am capable of taking the broader view, of seeing Norway from above, with all the necessary detachment. And since Jonas Wergeland's gift is that of being able to consider phenomena from a different angle it seems only fair that his life, too, should be presented from another and less biased slant than that taken by most people to date – not least by bringing to light certain events known to very few, such as the collision with Margrete.

But enough of that. I promise not to go on and on about my own motives. This is not meant to be about me, for one thing because I know how averse Norwegians are to self-conscious narratives and, for another, because the essential idea behind this project, if I dare use such a word, is my own deep secret.

In conclusion let me, for the sake of honesty, endeavour to forestall the irritation which is bound, in any event, to be felt: I do not intend to reveal my identity because I do not believe in such a concept as 'identity'. I would therefore ask that this 'I', whom you will find breaking into the narrative now and again, be taken for what it is: the one telling the story. Of that there should be no doubt, not least when it comes to the host of anonymous and to some extent dubious stories about Jonas Wergeland doing the rounds; always, no matter how well concealed it may be, someone is telling the story.

As I am now: at the moment when, as I say, Jonas and Margrete came riding down the road from opposite directions, the one as cocksure and uncompromising as the other, with the result that two universes – one could go so far as to say that – collided right outside the school gate in an honest-to-goodness starburst. They collided because, as Jonas said, he assumed that any ordinary lamebrain of a girl would give way to a boy, while she, naturally, was grumbling about this ill-mannered twit who didn't even know to let a lady go first: what one might call a severe difference of opinion. And it was not only their bikes that collided; they collided, boy and girl, on their bikes.

I must be allowed to say a little bit about bicycles, since they play no small part in Jonas Wergeland's life and because bikes occupy a very special place in people's memories – just think of the palpable thrill that runs through the body at the memory of the drag when a dynamo is flipped in against a tyre. And, even more than the bike itself, what one remembers are all the accessories and trimmings. In fact, I would go so far as to say that for many people the status seeking that has since manifested itself in having as many letters and digits as possible after the name of a car had its beginnings right here. I could mention at random the different types of handlebars, not least the so-called 'speedway' handlebars which were all the rage for some time and which, if I remember correctly, were even banned, in keeping with the Norwegian fondness for every possible sort of safeguard, and which boasted such features as luminous handgrips with little nubs that pressed into the palm of your hand, and gears – source of such stories as, for example, how Frankenstein pedalled up the steep slope of Badedamsbakken in 'third', *sitting down* – and a speedometer, an item which in Jonas's day was long a rarity, owned only by boys like Wolfgang Michaelsen, not to mention a lamp of the type that had two little yellow lights on either side of the big one, like fog-lights, and last but not least, the obligatory bell, which the really cool guys replaced with a beauty of a horn. Then you had the wide variety of different saddles, foremost among them the banana seat, motorbike-style, which suddenly became the in thing, and the accompanying cross-country tyres; and who could forget those mud-flaps emblazoned with an 'N', as if one were all set to cycle across Europe? Anything else? Oh yes, the tool kit on the carrier with its carefully stowed contents, anticipating the suitcase-packing problem in that everything had to be slotted into exactly the right place or the lid wouldn't close. This fastened with a little padlock, available in various colours, and came complete with minute keys; which in turn brings me on to the advent of the combination lock, with a cat's eye on the knob, and the hunt for the most baffling combination, which was engraved on a little copy of the lock itself and which, for some, represented their first encounter with the recursive element in life. Lastly, I ought to mention all the badges for sticking onto the mudguard, and the pennant, its rod vibrating so delightfully; and then, of course, the flags and foxtails that made you feel like the Shah of Persia as you rode around the blocks of flats. But one of the most interesting features in this connection was the trimming of the wheel-spokes, first with empty cigarette packs: Ascot, Speed, Jolly, Blue Master and, above all, Monte Carlo, the menthol Virginia cigarette that came in three varieties – yellow, red and black – adorned with little paintings which today seem quite exotic, like works of art from a bygone age, and later with triangles formed out of fuse-wire, which is to say copper wire of the sort insulated with different coloured plastic.

I take this opportunity to fire off – the word 'fire' being most apt here – a few remarks on the mystique attached to copper wire, inasmuch as Grorud was at this time experiencing something of a mini-revolution. It was as if Le Corbusier had suddenly been given free rein with the building of what were, by the standards of the day, the monumental concrete piles of the Grorud shopping centre and the new subway station, which in both cases entailed the blowing away of a lot of rock. A few parochial reactionaries were, as one might expect, sceptical about the new buildings, which rose up on the spot where the chapel and the Masonic Lodge and the corner shop had once stood, but Jonas and his chums welcomed this development with open arms; in the wake of the building boom the boys could go treasure-hunting, overcoming all sorts of inadequate barriers and – often illegally and on occasion at some risk – following the copper wire, like Ariadne's thread, through a labyrinth of dynamited rubble and the fumes from explosive gases until they came to the coil at the end, with any luck lying close to a rubber mat. A few enigmatic exceptions, usually a future pillar of society like Daniel, Jonas's brother, removed the plastic and sold the copper by the kilo to a scrap dealer, but for most of the boys the wire was a status symbol, a figment, which was of value only because they were all agreed on it – not unlike the Africans and their glass beads, the Polynesians and their shells – and which rose in value the rarer the colour of the plastic. Obviously I do not tell you all of this merely as a digression, but because I wish to underline the fact that the local community was undergoing drastic changes and, hence, to suggest that this might, unconsciously, have had an effect on Jonas such that he was, in other words, primed for a personal explosion, for a radical reconstruction of his inner being.

The first thing a dazed Jonas Wergeland saw after the collision, once he began to grasp what had happened, was his bicycle wheel with its elaborate trimming – perhaps because he knew that his whole life would be spent wrestling with the mystique of the wheel, with the circle, with the hub – and not only that but one of the lengths of copper wire wrapped round the spokes had come undone and was now pointing straight at Margrete, thus directing attention to a charge of dynamite greater than anything Jonas could have known.

So there they lay, he on top and she underneath him – a prophetic touch this – with the whole school standing round them, half-curious, half-gloating, all but cheering, in fact. They were curious because no one had ever laid eyes on this girl before, which was hardly surprising since her last school had been some distance away, in Bangkok to be precise, where she had attended the International School, and this was her first day at Grorud School. And they were gloating because Jonas Wergeland had fallen flat on his face and was at long last going to get his comeuppance for defying the ban on cycling to school. No one knew, of course, that Margrete hadn't passed her cycling proficiency test either and was, therefore, Jonas's partner in crime. Her full name was Margrete Boeck, a surname Jonas at first pronounced as 'book' until she informed him that it ought to be pronounced 'boak'. The more spiteful referred to her, possibly because of their head-on collision, as 'buck'.

Once Jonas had gathered his wits, he noticed that his mirror was also smashed, a brand-new mirror with a transparent red rim, and that made him really mad. But then he caught sight of Margrete's nose and he was done for. Embedded in Margrete's nose, just alongside one of her nostrils, was a tiny sliver of mirror and, I might as well tell you right now, this left a scar on her nose, a scar which would always remind both of them of this incident, of what can happen when no one is prepared to give way. But right at that minute the sliver of mirror was still embedded there, and Jonas could not take his eyes off it. It looked so much like those tiny jewels which people in India wear in their noses, and this added an entirely new dimension to the girl lying underneath him, something foreign, something goddess-like.

Margrete was the first and she would be the last.

She shook him off and pulled herself to her feet, put a hand to her nose and winced as she removed the sliver of glass, causing the blood to well up, and when she saw the blood on her fingers she subjected him to a torrent of verbal abuse that he would not forget in a hurry:

'You nearly killed me, you dirty goddamn red-faced son of a bitch, you stinking crazy big-cheeked stupid rat, you google-eyed cowardly bloody bastard son of a bitch – idiot!'

Shocked as he was, Jonas could not but admire her perfect English pronunciation, having wrestled with English for nigh on a year and still being more interested in the pretty English mistress's provocative way of dressing, not least her skin-tight sweaters which came, in a way, to symbolize the expanding, forward-looking possibilities presented by the English language, something that was also being brought home to him now, when he was being given a proper dressing down by a strange girl and did not understand one word of it. The worst of it was that he could not get up, because of his knee, which must have taken a knock with the result that, as this stream of invective poured over him, he stayed where he was in front of her, on one knee, as if he were proposing.

I ought perhaps to add, for anyone who has not yet guessed it, that this is the woman who is lying dead – those with no respect for the gravity of the situation might say 'knocked down' – on the floor at Jonas Wergeland's feet at this moment, which is to say the moment which I have chosen to form the hub of this spinning narrative in which I keep picking spokes at random, something which I can do because I know that all of the spokes run from the outer rim to the centre and that chronology is not the same as causality. Anyone wishing to understand Jonas Wergeland's life will first have to dispense with the belief that the passage of time says anything about cause and effect.

Someone took care of Margrete and walked her up to the main school building, while others tried to pick up her bike. It turned out, however, that the front wheels of the two bikes had inexplicably become locked together, rather like those rings that conjurors' use in their acts. And while people pulled and tugged at the bikes, Jonas saw how the rear wheel began to turn, slowly, round and round, both in motion and standing still, all decked out with an intricate pattern of copper wire and cigarette packs, the eye drawn in particular to the Monte Carlo pack, the 'Mona Lisa' of cigarette packs, a woman's head on the outer rim of the roulette wheel.

Someone has put some coltsfoot in a jar on the living-room table and you stand in the doorway and stare and stare. Coltsfoot. Of all things. A dead woman and coltsfoot, you think, and in your mind's eye you see that nightmare image, or hear it, feel it, a wheel, you think, the wheel just turning round and round, and getting nowhere, you think, a wheel simply spinning in mid-air, just a circle, an endless repetition; so who, you ask, as you have asked so many times before, who then, you ask, is turning the wheel; what, you ask, what lies at the hub of the wheel, because it was wheels that brought you together and she bled that first time too, blood first and last, you think, and coltsfoot, so he was right, that old writer, when he said that all the paths of love are strewn with flowers and blood, flowers and blood.

You stand there, a bundle of fan mail in your hand, you stand in the doorway and stare and you have this terrible feeling of nausea, as if you had eaten fly-agaric, as if you were about to throw up an entire life, turn yourself inside out, you think, and you look at the body, and you see that this sight, this landscape in the guise of a human figure, forces you to address a question regarding the way things hang together, one from which you have always shied away, the broad brushstrokes, you think, simplification and you only just manage to stop yourself from throwing up, and you gaze out of the big windows overlooking Bergensveien and Ammerud Meadows and the town and you think that you must remember what the weather is like, that this is important, because it's a lovely day, you think, and it's spring, you remember, and already quite mild, you think, and you would like to have known exactly what the temperature was, as if this would explain everything, change everything, and in the gloom you can see that the sky over the city is deep-blue and perfectly clear and you stand for a long time considering this light, the band of yellow at the very bottom, the light late in the evening, the light between winter and summer, a light found nowhere else in the world, you think, a light so indescribably beautiful it hurts, you think, and I would be the last to reproach you for not picking up the phone right there and then, but instead summoning every ounce of intuitive energy to prevent your own body from going to pieces, from falling to the floor like a flat expanse of invisible molecules, nor would I blame you, as others no doubt would, for the fact that you put down the bundle of letters and walk or somehow get yourself over to the shelf in the living room on which the hi-fi looms.

Mechanically you press the buttons that bring the black boxes to life, you savour the vibrant thud from the loudspeakers, like a heartbeat, you think, and you flick through the row of CDs, more or less at random and pull out a CD, and you lift it out of its holder, you study the disc, seeing how it shines, like a miniature sun you think, or no, it strikes you that it looks like a wheel, shot with rainbows, you think and you lay it in the tray in the CD player and pick up the remote control, select the track you want and fall into a more abstract reflection on the feel of the tiny rubber button on the remote control, its perfect pressure on the thumb, and you try to isolate this pleasure and you think also of something else, something vague, a cordless connection, but it eludes you and you hear, or listen intently to, the electronic whisper for the tenth of a second it takes the CD player to aim the laser beam at the correct spot, a bit like a memory at work, you think, as now, you think, faced with a dead body, you think, and you hear the music pouring out, Johann Sebastian Bach, you think, as if surprised by the organ music which fills the room, a fugue, you think, and you sit down in the armchair and shut your eyes, and your throat feels as if someone were squeezing it gently while subjecting your eyes to a dose of teargas and you have to swallow and you have to wipe your eyes, more than once, and you listen to the music, not because it is the antithesis of the thing on the floor, a dead wife, but because you are trying to identify that inexplicable something which links the notes together, if it is not the swell of the organ, you think, the very breath of life behind the music, you think, feeling in acute need of oxygen, as if you had just surfaced after almost being drowned in a whirlpool.

So there you sit, Jonas Wergeland; Norway's answer to Dick Fosbury, turtle hunter, one of the few people to have played the biggest organ in the world, and you are listening to this fugue by Johann Sebastian Bach because you have to stop your body from falling apart and you gaze round about you, your mind a blank, and you cannot remember who you are, and you would not believe it if anyone, at this moment, were to come up to you and tell you that you were a big celebrity, you would deny it, no way, you would shout, you're Jonas Hansen, an ordinary man from Grorud, except that you are not, because you are Jonas Wergeland, a top-notch actor, and you stand up, to be met by your own reflection in the mirror on the wall opposite, a gift from Aunt Laura, you think, an antique mirror in an exquisite frame, you think, with a glass that distorts the features, making you wonder who owns this face with the lost eyes, and this prompts you instantly and quite automatically to make a face, as you some-times do when you catch yourself in the monitor in the studio, and the sight of this contorted expression on your own face lifts you out of the situation so that you are viewing it from the out-side, as if from a new angle, you think, because even now, at this moment, you cannot help looking for new angles, because out-side it is spring, late evening and mild, with an enchanting deep-blue sky, not to mention a pale-yellow band on the horizon, you think, and you can see that there are many sides to this situation, that it may even deal a cut to the eye that could put all of your life in a new light, you think, and you stand outside yourself, seeing yourself from a distance, as shocked, grief-stricken, bewildered to the point of breakdown, and seeing yourself from the outside like this, in the mirror, you see your grief laid bare and suddenly you see the funny side of the situation, in the midst of this tragedy you see yourself in absurd caricature, and you contort your features again, make another face and, as you do so, unconsciously you do something else, with your little finger, a sign of profound emotional upheaval, you think, a trick you

picked up, something a great actor once did during a performance at the National Theatre, as a way of showing that his world
was tumbling down about his ears. And this puts you in mind of
Gabriel, and your thoughts stay with Gabriel as your eye returns
to the body on the floor, and you think of Gabriel, and you think
of the question that has been niggling at you: did he really
believe such things?

The Turtles

Gabriel had been there to meet him, as usual, on the beach and rowed him out, with long, practised strokes to the boat. A stiff breeze was blowing from the south-east. Jonas had a suspicion that Gabriel had been at the bottle already since, instead of going below to the saloon, he immediately proceeded to climb the rigging like a strip of a lad: 'Blow, winds, and crack your cheeks! rage! blow!' he bellowed across the water, his coat flapping about him. 'You cataracts and hurricanoes, spout till you have drench'd our steeples, drown'd the cocks!' Jonas sat down on one of the deck lockers, not taking his eyes off Gabriel, who was now standing on a ratline far above. 'Once, in the China Sea, I shot a pirate right where you're sitting,' Gabriel yelled down at him. 'By the way, did I ever show you the teeth marks left in the jib boom by that killer whale we ran into off the west coast of Canada?'

When he eventually came down, Gabriel decided to walk the manrope. Jonas rushed across to support him. 'Are you going to come away with me next summer?' Gabriel asked. He was always going on about it. 'Let's leave this bloody, stick-in-the-mud country behind,' he said, just about falling overboard – though a nice cool dip might have done him good. Gabriel Sand belonged to that quite unique breed of hot-headed dreamers who are dead set on following the route taken by Ulysses around the Mediterranean or sailing to Vinland, via Greenland, in the wake of the Vikings, and it went without saying that he had a mind to solve the mystery of the Bermuda triangle. 'At least come as far as the Galapagos Islands,' he said. 'I've always dreamed of being able to prove that Darwin made a fatal error out there. Let's go back to that crossroads and find the other path, the one Darwin could have taken but didn't. Two hundred years from now, m'lad,

Darwin'll be as out-of-date as those idiots who thought the Earth was flat!'

'But what would take its place?' Jonas felt obliged to ask.

'That's what we've got to find out, you great ninny!' Gabriel's gold tooth flashed. 'Maybe we're descended from sea horses. I've always had a soft spot for sea horses. In any case we could take a look at the turtles down there, big as VW Beetles they are.'

It was a real tonic to be onboard Gabriel's boat. Jonas was in, or rather: yawning his way through, his second year at high school. At least once a week he took the ferry across to the Nesodden peninsula, going on from there by bus, then by row-boat to the *Norge,* as Gabriel had been presumptuous enough to name his boat because, in his eyes at least, it was indeed a royal barge. It was moored to a buoy far out in Vindfanger Bay, due north from Drøbak, on a level with Oscarsborg, and just the sight of it was enough to make Jonas relax, to breathe out: its graceful lines and splendid rigging, the intricate and yet eminently practical tracery of rope, block and tackle. The *Norge* was an old lifeboat, and Jonas felt that it had saved his life, too.

That Jonas Wergeland always maintained that Oslo Cathedral School where, then as now, you virtually had to fight for a place, was a highly overrated and uninspiring school, says more about Jonas Wergeland than it does about the school. The way Jonas saw it, in all of his time at high school there was only one bright spot: Axel Stranger, a kindred spirit who made it, psychologically at least, easier to yawn one's way through classes. Strange as it may seem, Jonas did not learn a thing at high school and yet his marks were excellent, a fact which in everything except the science subjects could largely be attributed to a little red book, the fragmentary contents of which he had memorized inside and out. From this he could quote, in writing or verbally – and only rarely let it be known that he was, in fact, quoting – provocative opinions on just about everything: realism as viewed by the painter Eugène Delacroix, for instance; and thus, by paraphrasing briefly or at length or, if necessary, juggling quotations about to create the most unexpected and explosive combinations, he contrived to both impress and startle his teachers.

That was one way of getting through a class. The other was by going hunting for turtles. Jonas had taken the idea from an intriguing feature which crops up again and again in a number of ancient mythologies: the idea that the world rests on the back of a huge turtle. Hunting for turtles therefore involved seeking out the foundations upon which their teachers' theories rested, the hub around which all their teaching revolved, for always, beneath the plainest, most solid facts, there lay a fiction, a turtle as big as a VW Beetle.

So let us sit in on a lesson with form 2MFb at Oslo Cathedral School. The class is in the middle of a history lesson and the teacher is Mr Osen, a newly-appointed member of the teaching staff, straight out of university, young and cocky, with a first-class degree and a brand spanking new PhD gained on the strength of a thesis entitled *Wage Labour and the Rise of the Class System in Norway, 1870-1921*. Girls in bulky white Aran sweaters had a particular tendency to fall like flies for Mr Osen, and, I might add, there were a whole lot of girls in bulky white Aran sweaters at Jonas's school in those days. Rumours that during the same year in which he had defended his thesis, in the glorious year of 1968, Osen had been living in Paris did no harm either, since this made him what would later be termed a true-blue sixty-eighter, or 'sixty-niner' as Axel re-christened them due to their insistence on free love, their substantial contribution to the divorce statistics and, as Axel saw it, their preferred position when it came to sex and, later on, in their various positions in daily life in which they continued, as it were, to suck up to one another and lick one another's arses.

But to return to Mr Osen. Osen was a smart teacher: a bit wet behind the ears, maybe, but very, very smart. Our lesson deals with the subject of 1848, another great revolutionary year, and Osen has come up with a teaching ploy that, to his mind at least, is little short of brilliant. Although this class is bright enough, they are simply far too dependent on the textbook; what they lack, Osen feels, is *understanding*, by which, without realizing it, he actually means *belief*. But how to give these pupils, and not least these girls in white Aran sweaters, some insight into the mighty wheels that drive history forward?

Mr Osen begins not by sitting down at, but casually draping himself *over*, his lectern and asking, deadpan, whether anyone can cite the reasons for the revolution of 1848, whereupon the pupils, and in particular the girls in white Aran sweaters, several of whom are disturbingly sweet, reel off stock phrases from the textbooks on everything from population overspill and urbanization to a lack of democratic influence and unemployment, all of which is fair enough, thinks Olsen, but dear, oh dear, so generalized, so abstract, so devoid of any fundamental *understanding* – and, I might add: *belief*. So what does Osen do? Osen gets down, no, he doesn't get down, he vaults down off the lectern, as pumped full of adrenalin as a gymnast completing his routine on the pommel horse, and proceeds to rummage in his briefcase. Then he sets up one of those little steam engines, the sort of toy which Jonas remembers from his childhood and which are usually found in the homes of children whose fathers are engineers or something of the sort, Wolfgang Michaelsen, of course, had one, and now here is Osen rigging up his little steam engine on the top of the lectern, as eagerly as any child, and indeed this was his own old plaything, so Osen is a dab hand at this, dropping small fuel tablets into the drawer underneath the gleaming boiler which he has filled with water and firing it up, a hectic flush in his cheeks, forgetting all about his PhD because this is a brilliant idea, thinks Osen, as he straightens up, something this class will never forget; the little steam engine chuffing along while he, Mr Osen, *Dr* Osen, delivers a lecture on the driving forces behind historical events and on 1848, *pumping*, so to speak, the information into those sponge-like brains, causing a totally fresh insight into history to permeate like steam through porous walls. It would have been an unmitigated triumph, had it not been for those two blasted know-it-alls sitting one behind the other in the row nearest the wall. Axel Stranger and Jonas Wergeland were sniggering, and if there is one thing a teacher hates it is pupils sniggering like that.

Axel and Jonas most certainly are sniggering. They had soon figured where all this was leading, as had the rest of the class come to that, so when Osen eventually reaches his conclusion that the steam engine was the main driving force behind the

revolution of 1848; referring to the steam engine as 'quite literally, one of the wheels upon which history ran', it comes as an
anticlimax, despite the fact that Osen, as he makes this pronouncement, gestures with a flourish, rather like a conjuror, at
the steam engine, the wheels of which, thanks to a piston mechanism, are now whirring and running across the top of the desk,
so perfect in every detail that it is all Osen can do not to blow
the whistle.

Axel turns to Jonas with a look of exasperation. Jonas nods
and raises his hand.

Now it ought to be said that Mr Osen was a tough nut. There
were times when their teachers' assertions were so utterly lacking in any well-reasoned foundation that they presented no sort
of challenge whatsoever. As when their physics teacher had the
effrontery to state that it would never be possible to prove
whether quarks did or did not exist, or their chemistry teacher
obdurately maintained that no one would ever succeed in mapping out the human genome. This testified to such an infinite
disdain for the inherent potential of human beings, for good or
ill, to be forever expanding their knowledge that Jonas and Axel
could respond in only one way: by getting up and leaving the
class, pleading a sudden – joint – attack of depression.

They occasionally had to resort to other tactics to save themselves from falling asleep, as when, instead of demanding exactly
what was laid down in the syllabus, they insisted on *more* than the
set syllabus, thus sending many a teacher just about round the
bend. 'Please sir, could you tell us a bit more about Gödel?' asked
Axel when the maths teacher was careless enough to let slip a
remark about that scholar, perhaps simply wanting to impress
them. And if the poor teacher did happen to know a little about
the, if I may say so, extremely interesting and notable mathematician and logician, Kurt Gödel; if he, for example, vaguely
remembered something about Gödel's proof, some recollection
from his long distant days at university and possibly went so far
as to resort to the blackboard, Axel would simply keep on at him,
asking Sir please to elaborate on everything he said or wrote on
the board, much as an analyst will latch on to the last few words
a patient utters and ask him to tell him more about that, until the

teacher was standing there stuttering and stammering and having to admit that this was beyond his grasp: a fact which, ironically enough, in this instance illustrates Gödel's statement that fundamental questions are impossible to determine. To which Axel solemnly replies: 'Yes but sir, this is important. I believe I speak for the whole class in asking you to provide us with more information on Gödel in our next maths period.' The majority of teachers weighed their words very carefully when teaching 2MFb.

But these teachers were not to be pitied, nor were they robbed of any of their self-confidence. I would remind you that we are talking here of Oslo Cathedral School, Norway's élite school *par excellence*, an institution which, in spite of everything, prided itself on the quality of its teaching staff. And no one need feel sorry for Mr Osen PhD, with his thesis on *Wage Labour and the Rise of the Class System in Norway, 1870-1921*, when Jonas put up his hand to protest, and Jonas was protesting not only, like Axel, at Mr Osen's cocksureness; he was also protesting because such a system, in which all of the pieces fall neatly into place – illustrated, what is more, by a wheel spinning in mid-air – was so monstrous that it made him feel physically sick.

'This stuff about the steam engine is all very well, sir, but whatever happened, one might ask, to an element such as "the spirit"?' It is only a slight exaggeration to say that, at the word 'spirit', Mr Osen recoils like a vampire confronted with a crucifix. 'I would just like to remind you of what the historian Jacob Burckhardt says in that celebrated work *Die Kultur der Renaissance in Italien*,' Jonas goes on, 'in the first chapter of the third section, which deals with the Renaissance attitude to antiquity.' As you can see, this was one of those occasions when Jonas Wergeland revealed the source of his quotation, and to listen to him anyone would have thought that he had just finished reading this relatively demanding work, in an early edition, printed in Gothic at that, just sailed through it, and not, as was in fact the case, simply memorized a piece from his little red notebook, one which was five lines longer than the part he had cited: 'Here,' says Jonas, 'Burckhardt asserts that it was not the revival of antiquity alone, but as much the spirit of the Italian people,

which led to the spread of the Renaissance throughout the western world. Would you then, sir, rule out the possibility that the
spirit of the French people, for example, had some bearing on
the events of 1848?'

As I say, Osen was a tough nut, and so Osen simply ignores the
question or rather, he is so nettled by the mere *mention* of Jacob
Burckhardt's name that he snorts, a snort which is, to be sure,
drowned out by the chuffing of the steam engine.

Then it is time for Axel to take over: 'But sir, what about the
minds of the people? What about the theories that had been
making themselves felt in Europe for fifty to sixty years?' he says
or all but shouts. 'Theories propounded by, for example,
Diderot, Montesquieu, Voltaire and Rousseau? Do they count
for nothing, sir? Or do you perhaps believe that Diderot, too,
came about as a consequence of the French Revolution? Or,' and
here Axel points to the toy on the top of the desk, 'of the steam
engine?'

Then the thing that Osen fears most happens: the class bursts
out laughing, even the girls in the white Aran sweaters laugh.
And at this moment Osen thinks back with longing – and this
makes it possible to forgive him – to when he was a boy, to the
Christmas when he was given this toy, so long before all the years
at university, all the toiling away at *Wage Labour and the Rise of
the Class System in Norway, 1870-1921*; Osen thinks of how, that
first Christmas Day, he put the steam engine through its paces
for his chums and they had stared, all agog, at this marvel which,
for a short time, put Osen – the boy Osen, that is – in the for him
unwonted position of being the centre of attention: a marvel
which was not a steam engine – they had not the faintest idea
what this thing might be used for, that it was a model of something which actually existed – but a miraculous object, a sort of
perpetuum mobile, and what mattered was the gleam of the paint-
work, the tooting of the whistle, the smoke issuing from the
funnel. It was pure magic, a pure enigma, much like history.

Axel had long since spotted the turtle in Mr Osen's lesson –
and it was one of the truly big turtles of the day: dialectic
materialism. And since Axel Stranger was extremely interested
in causal relationships, a mania which would also come to

determine his choice of profession, he now rises to his feet, as if to mark the solemnity of the moment, and says: 'History requires *good*stories, sir. What you have not grasped is that dialectic materialism is a really *rotten*story.' And at that he delivers a lengthy and pretty impassioned diatribe against dialectic materialism in which he succeeds quite brilliantly in mastering such dogmatic and deadly concepts as 'the forces of productivity' and 'means of production' and 'basis' and 'superstructure' in such a way that he not only takes up the fight but actually goes into the attack on Osen's home ground, where the goal is defended by Karl Marx and his foreword to *A Critique of Political Economy*. That Axel thus dismisses dialectic materialism's answer to the not exactly trifling question as to what factors have contributed most to the transformation of human society, could be put down neither to his being an uncritical idealist or a wish on his part to return to the primary school's subjective, storybook style of teaching, but to a demand for fewer bombastic theories and a more nuanced approach – in other words, have the steam engine, by all means, but not just that. 'You might at least put a well-thumbed volume from Diderot's encyclopaedia alongside that bloody steam engine, eh sir?'

And it is here that Mr Osen makes his fatal blunder: he tries to accommodate Axel's views and as a result, particularly after a swift and elegant parry from Axel, he loses himself in a hopeless rigmarole of vulgar Marxist jargon: living proof, if you like, that no Norwegian is ever capable of absorbing more than the most simplified version of any theory from the outside world, just as turtles from along the coast of Mexico are doomed to die on those occasions when they stray into the Gulf Stream and end up in Norwegian waters.

Axel, on the other hand, is in his element. It would have been fair enough if Olsen had simply trotted out Engels' fine-honed version of dialectic materialism, even though that, too, is now so utterly banal, since anyone with an ounce of sense has long since recognized the relationship between technology, ownership structures and civilization. But what Osen is advocating with his little steam engine really is going too far, a ludicrous brand of determinism. 'So you see, sir, what I cannot accept about this theory of yours,' says Axel, 'is, first of all, that it denies the significance to history of conscious human acts, which is, in itself, quite absurd; and secondly it states that human beings act solely from motives which spring from material concerns, something which, quite honestly, sir, goes against everything experience tells us.'

So ends this history class with 2MFb at Oslo Cathedral School, and it ends with a teacher packing away his boyhood steam engine and a pupil, right to the last, following one pointed remark with another until, as the school bell rings he strategically gets in the final word, as he concludes by saying that the interesting thing about Watt's steam engine was not what it gave rise to but what had given rise to *it*. In other words, whether it had been an angel or a devil that had given Watt and the others the idea.

So much for high school. But right now it was recess for Jonas. He was on board a little gem of a lifeboat, a slice of Norwegian history if you like.

It was now quite dark. Out in the channel they could see the lights on the odd boat. Gabriel came over to the locker on which Jonas was sitting and put an arm round him. Was Jonas hungry? How would he like to taste a speciality from London's West End?

They crossed to the hatch and climbed down the ladder. Gabriel was one of the few people with an old boat of this kind who had not installed an engine. Instead he talked about the wind: of the wind as cause and effect, of caprice and unpredictability. And of humility. 'The wind is always there,' he said. 'But it's only when you start to sail that you really become aware of it.'

Jonas settled himself in the saloon and lit the paraffin lamp, while Gabriel went into the galley to make his West End speciality. Jonas liked being in the saloon, he felt happier in that saloon than almost anywhere else, he liked the smell, liked the light and above all else he liked the stories which inhabited that room. On one of the bulkheads hung a bookshelf constructed in such a way that the books, all of them plays, would not fall out when the seas ran high.

The food was served up, the same as always, corned beef and tomatoes. And whisky. In ship's mugs.

To those who know Gabriel Sand it will come as no surprise when I say that not everyone was so enamoured of his boat as Jonas Wergeland. In fact, that very evening certain characters of a more vindictive nature were making their way down to the bay and a waiting rowboat, sharp knives in pockets.

On board the *Norge* Gabriel raised his mug: 'Did I ever tell you about my time on the Marquesas Islands, when I swam in the most wonderful lagoon I've ever come across on this Earth? It lay between the legs of the princess Aroari.'

All Roads Lead to ...

Jonas Wergeland took a relaxed attitude to sex, thanks to his family. No talk here of rather strained or diffident conversations about the birds and bees. Not a bit of it, there was no beating about the bush in that house. All boys have some older girl whom they idolize like a goddess; their own local Brigitte Bardot or whomever the times may have elevated to that position. Jonas and Daniel had their own sister, Rakel, and you didn't get many of her to the pound, that was for sure. With her six years head start on them Rakel was of invaluable help to the two brothers, rather like an icebreaker clearing a passage through which they could sail.

While Jonas and Daniel had their noses buried in comic strips depicting the Wild West, the Second World War or Walt Disney's more or less amazing world, Rakel had already delved deep into the Arabia of the Middle Ages as she was introduced to it in the *Arabian Nights*, in a splendid edition given to her, of course, by Aunt Laura. No Bobbsey Twins or Nancy Drew for Rakel; nothing but the *Arabian Nights* would do, and it may have been for this reason that Jonas acquired such an early distrust of any and all forms of reading, seeing that he was soon to discover what an alarming effect books can have on a person.

After only the first couple of volumes something happened to Rakel's eyes, her eyelids drooped slightly, giving her a character-istic *veiled* look, and she viewed the world as if constantly intent on seducing everything and everyone in it. From then on, the brothers did not remember their sister as Rakel, but by turns as Emerald or Princess Full Moon or the Serpent Queen; when, that is, she was not being some far more complex character such as Tauaddud or Kutt-el-Kulub or Menar es-Sena. Their sister switched identities, taking on the parts of the various and pretty complex characters in a way that was quite awe-inspiring; to the point where she not only took to wearing a bewildering variety of imaginative costumes, but *demanded* to be addressed by the correct name: 'I beg your pardon,' she was liable to say indignantly if someone happened to forget. 'My name is Sobeida,' referring to the caliph's favourite wife, assuming that Sobeida was the role model of the moment. Jonas never did figure out whether these changes of character had some bearing on the way his sister saw the world: whether she lived her life, as it were, according to the stories she was reading – breaking into song after reading about Maimoune, for example – or whether it was the things that happened to her in real life that sent her in search of new role models from the tales, so that she might, for instance, only come across the doughty Princess Abrisa after having had a fight with some boy. This was Jonas's earliest encounter with the question of cause and effect, and he had a suspicion that there was no easy answer. The point I am trying to make, however, is that Rakel's sense for the erotic and its significance can be traced to the *Arabian Nights*.

One of the most unforgettable lessons in life, that concerning the turtle of existence itself, Jonas and Daniel learned when their sister was fifteen years old and they were eight and nine respectively. 'Today boys, I'm going to teach you about the centre of the world. Okay, trousers down!'

I think it might be as well to express, once and for all, my wonder at how touchy Norwegians are when it comes to sex, not least as a reminder of the background against which this little scenario of ours is played out. I think one can safely say that Norway is not one of those countries where sexuality has been most openly discussed, hence the tendency in this land to resort, at the drop of a hat, to antiquated pornography laws. Around this time, a couple of years later, that is, the censor took the step of cutting out thirty-two metres of Ingmar Bergman's not exactly insignificant film *The Silence*, and it made no difference that these scenes happened to be crucial to the film as a whole, because they were of a sexual nature. As far as I know, Norway must also have been the only country in the world in which people seriously debated whether the miniskirt could have a detrimental effect on efficiency in the workplace and even today, posters depicting young ladies modelling underwear can provoke front-page headlines in the newspapers and so much debate you'd think the security of the nation was at stake. As for what Norway did to the writer Agnar Mykle, I would rather not go into that at all.

Rakel, on the other hand, had an unorthodox, one might say an un-Norwegian, approach to sexuality. She was very advanced for her years. She knew that the body was an instrument, and one which had to be mastered as quickly as possible; her matter-of-fact approach went hand in hand with an experimental, not to say humorous, view of the whole thing. Jonas found it hard to forget the time when she got the new vicar at Grorud, the one they had for bible study, into such a state that he was all set to give up his calling, or at any rate to move to another diocese. It happened one Sunday during church service and, as usual, there were only a handful of people in the church. Jonas and Rakel were sitting upstairs in the gallery, Rakel because she liked to observe the vicars from above, Jonas because he liked to watch his father playing. Their mother, if anyone is wondering, never accompanied them to church, she much preferred to lie in the bathtub at home with one of her seven lovers.

In the middle of the sermon, while their father was relaxing with a copy of the *National Geographic* in his office, and Jonas was sitting on the organ bench pretending to be driving the biggest racing car in the world and keeping half an eye on what was going on in the rest of the church through the nifty mirror fixed to the side of the organ, he noticed that his sister was unbuttoning her blouse and then, suddenly, there she was, sitting naked from the waist up; her breasts, which were already well-developed for her age, pointing straight down at the young vicar who, as he raised his eyes – possibly looking for inspiration, quite clearly lost the thread of his sermon; at best, his thoughts may have turned to 'The Song of Solomon' and the verses in which two breasts are compared to two young roe-deer feeding among the lilies. After this incident, the young vicar gave Rakel a wide berth whenever they happened to meet.

The order to her brothers to drop their trousers stemmed, on Rakel's side, from pure compassion. She was, after all, related to these two kids and felt, at any rate now and again, a certain responsibility for their upbringing. 'Okay Mutt and Jeff, now the fact is that I *don't* want you to be caught with your pants down later,' she said. 'So allow me to give you a basic introduction to anatomy.'

Most boys first learn about the nature and the secrets of the sexual organs through vague rumours and thereafter from more or less appropriate and abstract handbooks. But here, once and for all, Jonas and Daniel were given a concrete demonstration at close quarters. 'These, boys, are called the testicles,' she said, squeezing their balls lightly. 'The pouch they hang in is called the scrotum. With me so far?' She gave them that heavy-lidded, seductive look of hers which did not, in fact, betray any hint of lust, it simply *was* the way she looked at them. 'Scrotum,' the boys muttered. 'A very delicate arrangement, guard it well. Have you heard of jock-straps?' They were doing just fine as long as they stuck to pointing and naming, it became a bit more tricky when she rolled the foreskin back from the head of Jonas's penis and it rose up to its, for his age, decent length, thus presenting his sister with the perfect cue for a brief lecture on the influx of blood and fungal growths. 'D'you know what "wanking" means?' They nodded. They weren't that dumb.

This proved to be just the beginning. Their sister now proceeded to take off her own trousers and underpants and lie down on the bed. 'Sit there,' she said, pointing to the foot of the bed. They did as they were told, whereupon Rakel spread her legs to reveal the number-one talking point among boys which, for that very reason, seemed to Jonas to look rather like a keyhole, while at the same time he was surprised by how little hair there was and how much flesh. Then their sister moistened her middle finger and ran it down the length of her slit, causing the outer lips to fold back on themselves as if she were unzipping them, thus revealing the underlying substance of her genitals in all its prosaic reality, and you can take it from me that Jonas's and Daniel's hearts were pounding as hard as those of Howard Carter and his team the first time they shone their torches into Tutankhamun's tomb. 'No need to blush, boys. There's a first time for every-thing.' Their sister regarded them from under lowered lids. 'Now listen carefully,' she said. 'In the years to come you're going to hear a lot of weird things about the meaning and the purpose of life. Most of it is utter bullshit. I'm going to say this once and once only, so pay attention: for you boys, for men in general in fact, it all comes down to just one thing.' She pointed between her thighs. Instinctively the brothers nodded as one. 'There might be many a detour and plenty of smokescreens, but at the end of the day all roads lead to just one place,' she said. 'And this is it.'

After this rather philosophical preamble the lesson switched to a more practical level, with a review of all the different parts, their names and their function, all of this while a pungent odour pervaded the room. 'And this, boys,' she said, towards the end of the demonstration, 'is the clitoris. Clitoris means "shut away", because its hidden behind this fold of skin. And the sig-nificance of this vital feature seems to be pretty well hidden as far as most men are concerned. But remember: with a woman, reverse logic applies: our secrets lie on the outside, not on the inside, as men believe. So I'm telling you now: stick to the out-side.'

That was the day on which Jonas realized that the female is an outsider with a feel for the marginal. Later in life he would often speculate as to what the clitoris of life might be, and it was thanks largely to women like Rakel that he always sought the essence of things on the periphery and not in the centre.

Rakel also told her brothers that they should never charge at the clitoris like a bull at a gate, but that when the time was ripe they should proceed with the greatest caution and sensitivity and, above all, take their time. 'You've heard of Aladdin's Lamp? Well it's the same with a woman, rub her the right way and after-wards she will do the most magical things to you.' Due to its dis-passionate and scientific nature, this session never came anywhere near what is known as incest. In all respects it repre-sented an informative lecture on the female anatomy – a de-mythologizing, if you like – which gave Jonas and Daniel a good head start on other boys of their age and left them forever in their sister's debt. Jonas and Daniel did not have a great deal in common, but their sister meant more to both of them than almost anyone else.

Jonas told no one about Rakel's lesson, with one exception. The following day he and Nefertiti set off to try out a kite which they had built to Nefertiti's design and which Jonas had bet they would never get off the ground. While they were unravelling the cord at the top of the hill, Jonas told her what had occurred. 'Did she also tell you about Bartholin's lymph glands?' said Nefertiti, fluttering her long eyelashes.

'What're they?'

The kite flew into the air and hung silhouetted against the sky like a spirit out of a fairy tale. Nefertiti sent it into a dive towards the hilltop before deftly levelling it out and making it loop-the-loop a couple of times. She passed the cord to Jonas. 'A sort of irrigation system,' she said.

It took a lot to impress Nefertiti.

In the weeks that followed, when Jonas thought of Rakel presenting her genitals to them, as it were, it was the totally fragmentary, detached aspect of it which struck him; it took such a long time to digest all the talk about the woman's pleasure and other such advanced concepts. He had been treated to a demonstration of an object which, even though to begin with he had no idea what it was for, seemed as fascinating and alluring and complex as Wolfgang Michaelsen's little steam engine.

Rakel was, in many ways, the most intelligent and original member of the family. There were many things in life which Jonas found it hard to understand, but possibly the greatest mystery was how Rakel should have ended up the way she did. As a housewife. Married to a long-distance lorry driver – a great guy, but still. Or maybe it was only natural: that a woman who had spent so much of her life immersed in fairy tales, so intense, so full of energy; who had eyed the world so seductively for so many years, was bound to end up being totally ordinary, like a space probe that has burned out its booster rockets getting itself out of the Earth's atmosphere and was now drifting quietly in orbit. Because it ought to be said: Rakel may have become invisible, blended in, so to speak, with the bedrock of Norway, but Jonas could not think of many people who were happier than she, and in Rakel's case this was no empty platitude – no matter how much Jonas tried to explain it away, what Rakel had was *genuine* enviable happiness, utter contentment.

20,000 Leagues Under the Sea

The whole point of being human, as Gabriel told Jonas again and again, was to take over the direction of one's own life. Why allow yourself to be defined by others. Be a king, for Christ's sake! Did Jonas hear what he was saying? You had to pose your own questions, set your own terms! And at this point Gabriel invariably flung his arms wide, gesturing to the bulkheads surrounding them and reverently declared, his intonation perfect: 'I could be bounded in a nutshell and count myself a king of infinite space.'

Jonas Wergeland had never sailed – to sea, that is – on Gabriel's boat, and yet his visits onboard the old lifeboat, securely tethered to its buoy not far from the shore, riding at its moorings as they say, represented a voyage of sorts around the world and, in terms of enlightenment, an endless continuation of the journey to inner Østfold. Just to sit below decks there in the saloon was enough, in a room the air of which was unlike that of any other, as if you could smell the scents of all the places at which that boat had docked or dropped anchor. 'From Drøbak I circled the globe a dozen times,' Jonas used to say.

The chief feature of that room was Gabriel Sand himself, in his ancient dark suit, complete with waistcoat, watch-chain and all, an outfit so totally out of date that it actually lent him a style all his own, a dash of a bygone nobility which went well, in a way, with his gift of the gab. Gabriel could talk and talk about everything and anything, all night long, non-stop, his flow of words punctuated only by the odd slice of tomato or a chunk of corned beef, or Jonas chucking another log into the stove; Gabriel could produce some object – a shell from the Society Islands, say, and spend hours telling the story of it. Jonas leaned back on his

bench and listened, fascinated as much by Gabriel's gold eye-
tooth glinting in the gloom as he talked, like a sort of beacon in
this ocean of yarns and assertions, predictions and curses,
because in between his yarns Gabriel would suddenly start to
rant and rave, usually in English, so that Jonas never knew
whether he was quoting lines from some play or what; although
he did learn the correct pronunciation of a host of rare and not
always quite proper English words which would later earn Jonas
much baffled admiration when he come out with them in English
class. As a rule, though, Gabriel tended to do his grousing in
Norwegian, and what the devil was he doing in this pettifogging
little country anyway and why in hell's name wasn't he in
Martinique or on the Charing Cross Road.

Gabriel Sand was going to have more reason for complaint,
seeing that he was now onboard a boat which was about to set
out, that evening, on a most dramatic and quite unintentional
voyage, inasmuch as someone was very shortly going to cut its
moorings and, as if that weren't bad enough, the *Skipper
Clement*, the ferry which at that time used to set sail for Frederikshavn at 10 p.m., was just pulling out of Oslo harbour.

There was no end of curiosities onboard the *Norge*. On one
bulkhead hung a barometer which always read 'fair weather' and
next to the bookshelf, in the place of honour, hung a weathered
playbill from the twenties advertising a performance at the
Regent Theatre, King's Cross with Gabriel's name right up
there alongside John Gielgud's, no less. Sitting in state in the
for'ard cabin, in a corner which Jonas could see from the saloon,
was what Jonas had first taken to be a puppet theatre but which
proved to be an old television, or at least the outer shell of one,
with a skull sitting inside it, like a test card for death or some
obscure sacred relic. 'News, that's the religion of today,' Gabriel
was fond of saying, 'especially when it has to do with war or
death.' Gabriel sniffed at people who thought religion had died
out, people who could not see that its significance was steadily
increasing; that the age of crusades was only just beginning. And
here he was: talking, mark you, about genuine religious conflicts
and not the shite that went on in Northern Ireland, where religion was no more than a cover for something else. No, what he

was talking about was the bizarre tension between Christians and Muslims that everybody seemed to think belonged to the Dark Ages, not realizing that Muhammad's boys were only warming up and would soon be making their comeback, more terrible than ever before. 'Here, Jonas, have another drop of whisky, won't do you no harm, lad.'

Next to the gold tooth, what Jonas noticed were Gabriel's eyes, they had such a heavy look about them, almost as if he were drugged. Not only that, but one of his eyes contrasted sharply with the other due to an ugly scar running along the underside of the eyebrow.

In Gabriel's opinion, the anti-metaphysical attitude of the Norwegian socialists was particularly risible. Their thinking seemed to stop at the bridge over Svindesund, at the border with Sweden, they simply could not conceive of the possibility that the yen for some divine element in everyday life might well up again, more strongly than at present, even in Norway. And what did Jonas think of these Marxists, setting the agenda with their extreme views these days? You'd think that'd be enough to make everybody realize that religion wasn't dead. 'These Norwegian Marxist-Leninists, they're no better than any of those religious cults with their head-shrinkin',' said Gabriel. 'The only difference bein' that it's their own heads they're shrinkin'.'

As you can see, Gabriel Sand was a talker – 'blabbermouth' would be too flippant a word. When Gabriel talked it seemed always to be a necessity, like the shark which has to keep on swimming and swimming to save from sinking, because it has no air sacs. Not that Jonas had anything against Gabriel's talking. He loved to sit there listening to him, occasionally helping himself to some more corned beef and tomatoes or pouring himself another drop of whisky, well watered down, while at the same time taking in the creak of the rigging, of the gaff, and the occasional gentle wallow as they were nudged by the wash from boats out in the channel. But first and foremost there was Gabriel and Gabriel's talk of everything under the sun, all night long, because it was at night that they had their talks; at best, Jonas would manage a couple of hours sleep in one of the bunks before Gabriel rowed him back to the shore the next morning and Jonas headed back, dozy, and yet somehow elated, on the Nesodden ferry. And on the way in to Oslo harbour and the Town Hall; on the way to the Cathedral School and classes that all but lulled him to sleep – if, that is, Axel was not all geared up for some madcap turtle hunt – Jonas thought about the things Gabriel had talked about, such as the tenability of the doctrine of predestination or dinosaur skeletons in Colorado; or else the drift of the continents towards and away from one another, or the eclectic ideology of ancient Chinese philosophy.

What Jonas learned onboard Gabriel's boat was not facts. When you came right down to it, Jonas learned just one thing: to feel wonder. But if, when sitting below decks in the saloon, Jonas felt himself to be down in the depths of the ocean, his very first university was situated on high, in a loft, in fact. And the person who really introduced him to the art of make-believe, that gift which was to set its stamp most clearly on his career and on which, like a turtle, his creativity rested was, of course, Nefertiti.

All of the two- and three-storey blocks of flats on the Solhaug estate had their own communal loft. This was in the days when, naïvely perhaps, people would happily store their belongings alongside those of their neighbours. The loft belonging to Jonas's staircase was a real Aladdin's Cave and a favourite hangout of Jonas and Nefertiti, not least because of an old gramophone which played seventy-eights and which really came into its own again after an overjoyed Nefertiti discovered the box of Duke Ellington records which Jonas's mother had inherited from Uncle Lauritz and simply stowed away in the loft. Nefertiti was, of course, well acquainted with Duke Ellington and his intricate opus and as good as insisted that Jonas listen to and learn from these discs, which showed how even the simplest of melodies could be turned into a pyrotechnical display of tonal variations and rhythmic finesses. 'It was Duke Ellington who taught me that the arrangement is all,' as Jonas said in one interview. After playing through the whole pile several times, Jonas discovered that there were some numbers which swung more than others, swung to set you rocking from top to toe, and Nefertiti informed him that this was the 1940 band in which the man who made all the difference, from 'Jack the Bear' onwards, was bass player Jimmy Blanton, working away like a propeller under all the rest, driving the whole thing forward with a reckless and unprecedented energy.

One day Nefertiti came with a parcel for Jonas. Inside he found a red box which he opened, to lay eyes for the first time on his Hohner chromatic mouth organ, nestling in gleaming blue velvet, its plate beautifully engraved. Nefertiti could already play the mouth organ and, thanks to her enthusiasm and fantastic flair for teaching the right way to hold the instrument, how to play the individual notes, use the slide button and generally get the hang of the instrument, as well as the breathing technique and a pretty neat hand vibrato, it was not long before Jonas, too, could carry a decent tune, enabling them to perform several of Ellington's catchy melodies together, the pièce de résistance in their repertoire being 'Concerto for Cootie', with the one instrument answering the other, just like the orchestra on the record. There was only one number which they never really mastered, the mind-blowing 'Cotton Tail' which called for the sort of technique not even Nefertiti could command. They tried and they tried, and it became a sort of goal in life for them, one day to get it right.

Thanks to Nefertiti, Jonas did not become a cellar sort of person, though he might have been so inclined. Instead, psychologically speaking, he became a loft person. That loft was a props cupboard in which every single object could be a springboard for the most breathtaking flights of fancy. It was in this loft, in a block of flats in Solhaug, Grorud that Jonas Wergeland learned to see the potential in the little details; realized that every object, even the very smallest, was full of possibilities around which the imagination could weave a tale. There was nothing to beat those imaginary journeys in the loft. All Nefertiti needed was a suitcase, some old clothes, an earthenware vase, a Christmas-tree stand, a spade – and hey presto! – they could be anywhere. The only things they ever took from the outside were provisions in the form of dried apricots, nomad food as was only right and proper, drawn from Nefertiti's apparently endless supply at home. Other than that they had all they needed. Some sheets served for Tibet, starting point for a gruelling hunt for the

Abominable Snowman; one solitary tarnished mirror became the great glittering palace of Versailles; a shattered pot was enough for the momentous discovery of ancient scrolls hidden in sealed clay jars at the back of deep grottoes; a small rug and a brass pot sparked off an intrepid visit to Mecca disguised as Muslims – all of this to the accompaniment of Duke Ellington's magical orchestra, more particularly the 1940 band with Ben Webster and that wizard Jimmy Blanton: 'Ko-Ko', 'Conga Brava', 'Sepia Panorama', 'The Flaming Sword'. The way Jonas saw it, it was no accident that Duke Ellington would later release records that spoke of journeys, albums such as *Far East Suite* and *Latin American Suite*. One particular day, when 'Echoes of the Jungle' was making the dust in the loft dance, Nefertiti unearthed a moth-eaten fox-fur stole, which provided the inspiration for a lengthy safari. Along the way she taught Jonas, among other things, that chimpanzees have a language all their own and that '*Nn ga kak*' meant 'I'm hungry', a phrase which she had actually tried out on a visit to Copenhagen Zoo, whereupon the chimp had promptly handed her a banana. Again, up there in the loft, a pair of sandals had taken them to Ancient Rome, to warn Caesar, and I need hardly say that this was long before American film director Steven Spielberg showed all children that time-travelling of this sort can have the direst consequences. And in the evenings, in the autumn especially, all they had to do was open the trapdoor in the roof to observe the full moon through a pair of binoculars with shattered lenses, though this did not hinder their loft, now metamorphosed into a space ship, from making a nice soft landing, shortly afterwards, on the surface of the moon.

Nefertiti's imagination knew no bounds; where she was concerned even a cowpat could represent an entire universe, be translated into pearls of wisdom, pure gold. As I said, Jonas Wergeland's first stroke of genius was to choose Nefertiti as his best friend. He knew all along that it could not last, that she was clearly too good for this world.

To some extent Jonas felt that his nights on board the *Norge*, Gabriel's boat, constituted a continuation of that first university, of those travels among linen bags and mothballs and all the old

magazines, their subject matter as antiquated and absorbing as
any *Codex Sinaiticus*. The loft had been replaced by the saloon in
which Gabriel lit the paraffin lamp when the light filtering
through the skylight began to fade and, instead of dried apricots,
there were now corned beef and slices of tomato like little red
wheels. Besides emitting a fine soft light, the paraffin lamp hanging from the ceiling also gave off a particular smell, and this
odour mingled with the scent of the tar used for impregnating
the hull, a scent which pervaded the boat; like incense, stimulating the memory, reminding Jonas of one of the best parts of his
life: his grandfather – his father's father, that is – and the stories
he told.

In many ways, all of Gabriel's yarn spinning came down to
just one long story. No matter what he happened to be talking
about it was liable to end up as the 'Tale of the Chance of the
Unlikely'. Gabriel could open a newspaper and in just about
every column he would come upon grotesque examples of
inanity and narrow-mindedness. 'People just can't see further
than their own noses,' he said. 'Here's some so-called expert stating categorically that unemployment is a thing of the past in
Norway. I ask you! Chuck another log in that stove will you,
Jonas. That sort of senile stupidity fair makes my blood run cold.
How can people go around thinking that the world just stands
still? Every bloody time somebody or other sets another world
record, in speed-skating or athletics or whatever, we're told that
this one'll never be broken. Where's the historical perspective in
that? And now heaven help me if they aren't running down that
poor sod of a composer again. I'll bet you anything those same
people will be writing articles praising him to the skies ten or fifteen years from now, the day he's given the key to some grace-
and-favour residence. It's a bloody disgrace, so it is. Oy! Wake
up, lad!'

What Gabriel did not know was that, under cover of darkness,
someone had glided soundlessly up to the buoy and sliced
through their mooring, setting the boat adrift. There were plenty
of people who had no time for Gabriel and his ranting, especially
not when he stood on the deck, and certainly not in the middle of
the night, roaring his opinions to the four winds.

'What's wrong with the world?' Gabriel asked, his gold tooth gleaming, while Jonas lay back, enthralled, drinking in this phantasmagorical display, worthy of another Don Quixote; to him these tirades were a thing of beauty in themselves, like exercises in inventiveness, stretching the mind. 'People don't believe in the improbable. That the most unlikely things can happen,' said Gabriel, turning his rather heavy eyes on Jonas, the one rendered different by the scar under the brow seeming to gaze into another world. 'For instance, if I were to say that a second-rate movie star might one day become president of the United States, people would kill themselves laughing. Damn right, they would. Even though it's only a matter of time. The society they have over there, that's the way things are going. We see the most unlikely things happening round about us all the time and yet somehow we manage to negate that such things could happen again. Pretty good, eh? Take the Berlin Wall, for instance, and all the people who think that *that*'s always going to be there.'

I would ask you to bear in mind here that the sixties were just giving way to the seventies; bear in mind, too, that the *Skipper Clement* was on course for Frederikshavn and would very shortly have to pass through the very narrow channel into which Gabriel's boat was now drifting, a stretch of water which, by the way, happened to be one of the most renowned in the history of Norway, for it is here on the seabed that the rusting hulk of the German battle-cruiser *Blücher* lies, testifying to the fact that something which no one would have thought possible did actually happen once, and in Norway at that.

But in the saloon, beneath a paraffin lamp, in the warmth from the wood stove, Gabriel was fulminating over this singular forgetfulness. Folk even forgot actual historical events. How could they? They neatly forgot, for instance, the disparities between ethnic groups living side by side in the same country. What was Jonas laughing at? By Christ, it was no laughing matter. How long, for example, did he think the Soviet Union was going to last, hm? Or what about some of these countries in the Balkans? They were only cobbled together willy-nilly anyway. 'It's only a matter of time,' said Gabriel, 'before the whole kit 'n caboodle blows sky-high. I'm telling you, Jonas: use your imagination.'

Sometimes Gabriel's lectures took their outset in the boat itself, not least when he came to the subject of the Norwegian national character. Then he was liable to get up, duck inside one of the bunks and treat Jonas to a description of the inner skin of the hull, the pinewood lining and the outer shell overlaying this, the oak timbers; of the double frames and the 'crooked knee-timbers', launching off from this into expositions on everything from Viking ships and Norwegian prefabs to dragon-head patterns and the lumber trade with England. The first time Jonas came across the name of Colin Archer was in the middle of a discourse on the stave church at Lom.

Polar Opposite of the Nervous System

Every programme in the *Thinking Big* series generated sacks of letters to the editors of newspapers all over Norway as if an entire nation had suddenly rediscovered the art of putting their thoughts into writing, and the longer the series ran, the bigger the pile of letters grew. Most of those who wrote in were, of course, positive, and indeed in some cases praised it to the skies, thanking Jonas Wergeland in superlatives for opening their eyes to these unique individuals and in the process giving them a renewed self-confidence and pride in being Norwegian. A few correspondents were, however, more critical, and the programme which provoked the greatest volume of disappointed and irate letters was that on Fridtjof Nansen. 'It is quite outrageous,' wrote one viewer, speaking of course 'on behalf of many', 'that a television programme about Fritjof Nansen, our national hero, should not say one word about, nor show one picture of the *Fram*, Colin Archer's masterpiece of a vessel, this Columbus egg which was the absolute prerequisite for Nansen's greatest triumphs. To present a profile of Nansen's life without including the *Fram* is like profiling Ole Bull without his violin.'

And precisely because so many Norwegians had such a fixed idea, an almost stylized, romanticized image of Nansen, Jonas Wergeland's biggest problem had been how to use the prism inside his head to refract and break up the powerful light emitted by Nansen and thus arrive at the spectrum or the story which would reveal more clearly than anything else all the facets and the depths of his character, some less well-known aspect, preferably having nothing to do with crossing icy wastes on skis, or polar bears or cheering crowds on the quayside at Christiania. And

Jonas found this story: that of a man who stood on a chill plain and wept in front of a group of mothers.

But there was also a simpler explanation for the absence of anything to do with Nansen's polar endeavours: Jonas Wergeland hated snow and ice. He hated skiing. So, even though he had to shoot some scenes by the river Glomma in the south-east of the country in wintertime, this was still less off-putting than having to film on location a lot further north.

The programme's key scene, for those who may not remember it, depicted an incident which took place during the horrific famine in Soviet Russia in 1921, the most terrible disaster since the Black Death and a situation which became truly precarious after a pitiless drought-ridden summer left the valley of the Volga and large parts of the Ukraine utterly parched, putting twenty million people – some reports said thirty-five million – under threat of death by starvation. Fridtjof Nansen, who was already involved in relief work with prisoners of war and refugees, undertook to lead the rescue mission, for one reason because, as he said, it was his *duty*, and because he knew he could help, he had faith, he was in fact a land apart, accepted by all the parties involved, and this is what brings him – Fridtjof Nansen, a Norwegian in a broad-brimmed hat, in the wake of his famous speech to the League of Nations assembly in which he appealed to the most elementary humanitarian instincts and deplored their dismissive attitude – into the very midst of that heart-rending tragedy on the banks of the Volga where, despite all the Russian intriguing, over the next couple of years he would be instrumental in saving the lives of possibly twelve to thirteen million people while being decried by heartless individuals, his fellow Norwegians among them, for aiding the Bolsheviks. Fridtjof Nansen, in Norway regarded primarily as a sportsman of sorts, but in Europe as a nation in himself, travels from district to district, observing the situation, while on the steppes the winter begins to make itself felt; he sees how people first slaughter dogs and cats and, when that source dries up, eat the thatch from the roofs of their outhouses or pulverized bones and horses' hooves; in some places they resorted to the graveyards, digging up bodies simply in order to have something in their stomachs, everywhere he looks there are wasted faces and children with swollen bellies. Fridtjof Nansen, hard-bitten polar explorer, travels on, from place to place; around him people are eating grass and earth and it is here, in a small village on the banks of the Volga that Nansen finds himself surrounded by mothers lifting their children up to him to let him see how famished they are, and he has to turn them away, because there is not enough bread to go round; it is standing here, in his heavy overcoat with the fur collar and the familiar broad-brimmed hat, here, faced with these mothers with their starving children in their arms and no food to give them, that he breaks down and dissolves into tears. And this was the scene which Jonas Wergeland spun out and spun out, shots of the powerful body shaken by sobs, the valiant hero and the tears streaming and streaming.

When it came to the regular spot when Jonas stepped onto the set to talk to his central character, in this case it was more to offer comfort, since Nansen, in the shape of Normann Vaage, was so distressed that Jonas's tentative inquiries as to what he had written about the Eskimos and how he felt about having an asteroid called after him, were simply dismissed as if they had nothing to do with him. By centring everything around this scene Jonas also managed to bring out an aspect of Nansen's character which he felt that a lot of people overlooked: his melancholia, his introversion, his depressive personality. In Jonas Wergeland's version of Nansen's story, tears took the place of skis.

It must also be said that at no time have more people in Norway shed tears at one and the same time as when this programme was shown. Not because the images deliberately set out to elicit such a reaction, but because in its simple and fundamental clash between the moral obligation and the agonizing sense of impotence, it had something of the same heart-rending effect as the pictures from the horrendous famine in Ethiopia and Somalia in the eighties – and this despite the fact that it was a dramatized incident from a distant chapter in history.

But what I have presented here is really only a pale outline of the programme, and I ought at the very least to say that it did also contain other elements, the most telling of these being a shot that cut from the scene by the Volga, from a close-up of Nansen's eyes, to a scene with him as a young man sitting hunched over a microscope, studying nerve fibres: this too a voyage of discovery of sorts, inasmuch as the hunt for the axons and cells of the nervous system led out into the great unknown, with the aim, as he himself put it, of discovering the wellspring of thought, the hidden secret of life. To Jonas Wergeland, this nervous system represented the very key to Nansen's life, so much so that Jonas tended to construe his journey across Greenland on skis as an expedition by Nansen into his own emotional life, and Nansen's oceanographic surveys, particularly those relating to the currents, as an attempt to chart the central nervous system of the ocean. Jonas Wergeland also made much of the image of the young curator of zoology, newly returned from a crucial visit to Italy where he had learned various scientific processes, including how to dye preparations, studying the nervous system of invertebrates under the microscope – a study which was to bear fruit in his controversial and only belatedly acclaimed thesis *The Structure and Combination of the Histological Elements of the Central Nervous System*, which showed, among other things, how the nerve fibres split to form a 'T'-shape having once penetrated to the innermost root of the spinal cord. A smooth crosscut between the Volga scene and this laboratory scene was achieved by dissolving the shot of the nerve fibres under the microscope into that of the starving mass of humanity.

In every programme in the *Thinking Big* series, Jonas Wergeland focussed on one prop, one detail which epitomized some vital characteristic of the hero in question. In Ole Bull's case, it was the diamond set into his violin bow; with Fritjof Nansen it was the microscope – and positively *not* the sextant.

The most audacious feature of this programme, however, and one which only the experts and those with a particular interest in the subject picked up on, were certain technical experiments. One of these concerned the Northern Lights which are not, of course, found in the Ukraine but which were in fact the aurora borealis, as Nansen himself had so often described them: drifting, shifting clouds of light, a silvery, iridescent haze, shimmering ripples and tongues of flame expanding and contracting in a restless chase across the firmament before melting away with what sounded like 'the sigh of a departing spirit'. Jonas Wergeland's team had filmed actual Northern Lights with a special-effects camera, using time-lapse photography to make the action more dramatic. Then, in the lab, with the aid of an optical printer and masking, they had projected this onto the sky above a weeping Nansen. In this way the Northern Lights were likened to nerve fibres which caused the whole sequence to vibrate or, if you like, the shimmering sky to become the image of Fridtjof Nansen's inner being.

The other special effect had to do with the sound of pack ice. Nansen was fascinated by the devastating power of the ice. The way he depicted it, it began with a thunderous roar, like a distant earthquake, after which it started to screech and snap all around you, and the ice cracked and shot up on all sides, with a boom like cannon-fire. The audio team endeavoured to create this particular sound by mixing synthesized creaking noises with sound effects, i.e. real sounds, from crushed ice: the sound you get when you drop fresh ice-cubes into a glass of water, those little *cracking noises*. This sound of pack ice was exactly what Jonas Wergeland was looking for in the scene in which Nansen stands there weeping with the Northern Lights flaring across the sky; gradually they increased it in volume until many viewers actually felt as if they were being *squeezed*. Some said later that they had squirmed in their armchairs, others that a long shudder ran down their spine, the sort induced by someone running a fingernail across a blackboard. Whatever else they may have felt, the majority were struck, in the scene in which Nansen stood on that steppe beneath a sky scintillating with Northern Lights, weeping before a group of mothers and their starving children, by a sense of primitive forces at work, a sense that something was about to split wide open, to be crushed and dragged under. Those viewers who could not see that the *Fram* was there in that programme were quite simply lacking in imagination.

So the programme on Fridtjof Nansen also had to do with cold and ice – not least in human terms, with a global spirit that was sick unto death, as Nansen said in the speech he made on being presented with the Nobel Prize – a fact which Jonas

Wergeland intimated most strikingly by concluding the pro-gramme with a close-up of Nansen's eyes, showing the tears frozen to the skin.

A Cut to the Eye

There they were, on board the old lifeboat, renamed the *Norge*, where Gabriel Sand was now talking about acting, 'the least understood of all the creative arts'. He demonstrated, for example, after fixing his eyes on the deck for thirty seconds, how he could turn on the tears and when Jonas looked impressed he said: 'It's you who sees the weeping and the emotion; all I do is squeeze out a couple of tears.'

As if to underline this illusion, or the air of magic, he lit a cigarette and was soon wreathed in coils of smoke which took on an unwonted movement and dimension in the light of the paraffin lamp. 'So what do you plan to do after high school?' he asked.

'Study architecture,' said Jonas, not really knowing why, although he had an idea that the urge to do so dated back to walks around Oslo as a boy, when there were certain buildings which he never tired of seeing: the Town Hall in all its massive symmetry and the Art Centre with its so-called 'golden mean', but more than anything else, due to the fact that his father often took him down to the harbour to look at the boats, there was Lars Backer's exquisite Restaurant Skansen, a revelation in terms of functionalist form which for some reason the people of Oslo allowed the powers that be to raze to the ground – as I say: the most unlikely things are forever happening.

'Rubbish!' said Gabriel. 'Be an actor! Build castles in the air, not on the ground. Create illusions inside people's heads. They'll outlast structures that'll be pulled down before you know it anyway.'

The cigarette smoke enveloped him like a swirling veil; it might have been a stage-effect, the only thing lacking was for him to go through to the for'ard cabin and fetch the skull ensconced in the shell of the television. Gabriel smoked Camels as if to betoken his nomadic existence, and Jonas recalled how he and Nefertiti had sometimes bought liquorice cigarettes that came in the most gorgeous packet with a copy of the Camel logo on the front. The camel picture also happened to rank above all others when it came to the cigarette packs they fixed to the spokes of their bike wheels, possibly because it was so rare and hence lent a lot of prestige, as well as being squashy, which meant that they had to glue it onto a piece of cardboard. Seeing Gabriel with his pack of Camels, Jonas had a feeling of being back there, a feeling that everything went in a circle, round and round, like a wheel of fortune.

'What makes you think I should be an actor?' Jonas asked, lifting his mug of whisky.

'To be who you are. Why not follow it through?'

'I can't quite see myself on a stage playing some part.' The very idea made Jonas laugh.

'Don't say that, lad.' Gabriel was vehement now, brandishing his cigarette like a conductor's baton. 'Every one of us invents and plays as many different parts in our daily lives as we need in order to be taken seriously. Just look at yourself. I mean, it's ridiculous to think that each person should be stuck with just one persona.'

'I'm not with you.'

'What I'm saying is that every human being has many sides to their character,' said Gabriel. 'See, any one of us could go off our heads at any time, it just so happens that, for some reason, we don't.' Gabriel squinted at Jonas with his two mismatched eyes. 'I'll never forget my dear friend Niels Bohr,' he went on as if something vital had just occurred to him. 'A man of vision who gave one of the most momentous speeches of the twentieth century, at a physicists' congress in Como, in '27 that must have been, in which he introduced the world to the theory of *complementarity*, working from the basic principle that light appears to exist both in particle and in wave form. So don't you ever forget, Jonas, that there's more than one side to a human being; just like light, we contain the potential for both particles and waves. At the very least. Imagine the possibilities! All you have to do is take your pick. So: be an actor!'

Out in the galley, some pickle jars chinked together as a couple of waves – one might almost think Gabriel had ordered them up specially – caused the boat to roll a little more than usual, but neither of them turned a hair. In an act of sheer genius Fridtjof Nansen had once let his boat drift with the ice. Now it was Gabriel's boat that was drifting, although this was far from being part of some grand plan but an act of sabotage. The boat drifted on, without the two on board, snug and warm down below in the saloon, noticing a thing. They had no idea that they would soon be right out in the middle of the shipping lane and even less idea that the *Skipper Clement*, more like a small town than a ferry, was heading straight for them.

Gabriel was no longer in the theatre, but he could look back on what had been a remarkable career. After leaving school he had followed his English mother when she moved back to London, where he soon found himself caught up in the theatrical scene, and it was here, among other things, that he formed a firm friendship with the actor John Gielgud, who was the same age as himself. More than once Gabriel had described Gielgud's inimitable interpretation of Hamlet – *not* the much-vaunted production at the New Theatre in 1934 but the one staged in 1930 at the Old Vic, the best *Hamlet* ever, according to Gabriel, making Jonas laugh with his imitation of Gielgud's way of speaking, in which 'Words, words, words,' came out as 'Wirds, wirds, wirds.'

Every person has their own quintessential story, one which says more about who they are than any other. Gabriel Sand's was a classic story, albeit with the odd twist or two; in the early twenties John Gielgud had persuaded him to take part in a production of Shakespeare's *Romeo and Juliet* to be staged at a little theatre near King's Cross – the competition for parts was fierce, but even so, after only one audition, Gabriel was signed up.

Just for the fun of it, and to show Jonas that he could still remember it, Gabriel did the first half of the balcony scene for him, taking both Romeo's and Juliet's parts; he played it any number of different ways, to show what a wealth of techniques an actor has at his disposal: everything from diction and tempo to pauses and posing. For Jonas, it was a bit like when his father played the organ and showed him how he could make a tune sound different by switching to a different register. One version Gabriel did as a parody so outrageous that it put Jonas in mind of Norwegian actors, those few he had seen.

Gabriel stood on the deck with a bookshelf at his back and a paraffin lamp as his only spotlight and truly *became* another person, or rather a whole host of other people, and even in his antiquated suit and without a single prop he *was* Juliet, to the life, and then, in the warm light that glinted softly off his gold tooth and the watch-chain draped across his stomach, he suddenly played the balcony scene in a way which left Jonas convinced that Romeo and Juliet *wanted* to die and, thereafter, by dint of only a few minor alterations, forced Jonas to change his mind completely and believe that it was all down to the hand of fate. More than just about anything else, what he admired was Gabriel's beautiful English; it was perfect, spoken like a true native. Jonas never witnessed better theatre than in the saloon of an old lifeboat, on a stage that reeked of tar and whisky, birch logs and Camel cigarettes.

In the London production Gabriel had played, not Romeo, but his friend Mercutio. To cut a long story short, the cause of all the drama – off-stage, that is – was that Gabriel, by all accounts an incorrigible satyr, had seduced and bedded the girl-friend of one of the other actors, something he had not given a second thought, such goings-on being not exactly unknown in those circles. In any case the rehearsals went smoothly, with no confrontation of any sort. But his injured fellow-actor, who, as luck would have it, was playing the part of 'the furious Tybalt' and, as such, his adversary in the play as well, had other plans.

'I knew on the first night that something was wrong,' said Gabriel. 'Bloke had this really crazy look in his eyes. And at the beginning of the third act, in the sword fight that breaks out between Mercutio and Tybalt, where Mercutio is meant, right enough, to be mortally wounded, I suddenly realized that this man really *was* out to kill me, right there on the stage: that way he could get away with saying that it had been a regrettable accident. Oh, you should have been there! He fenced like a madman, using a needle-sharp rapier – no foil. I had to use every trick I knew to fight him off. And the audience – well, of course, they were thrilled, shouting "Bravo, bravo!" They'd never seen such a fierce or realistic swordfight. After the performance John Gielgud told me he'd only ever seen one man fence better than me, a young actor by the name of Laurence Olivier.'

The fight had grown more and more frenzied, with his opponent becoming ever more frantic in his efforts to deal Gabriel the *coup de grace* – a truly fatal blow, that is. Gabriel was at his wit's end by the time Gielgud, who was playing Romeo, decided, thank heavens, that the fight had gone on long enough and stepped in, as he was supposed to do in any case in the play, to stop them. This allowed Gabriel to stagger back and die, without actually being fatally wounded. It was as he was about to deliver his final lines, beginning with 'Ay, ay, a scratch, a scratch,' that he realized that Tybalt, his adversary that is, the boyfriend of the woman he had seduced, had nonetheless managed to deal him a rather nasty wound over one eye, drawing blood – to the delight of the audience who assumed that this was merely a splendidly lifelike stage effect.

It was at this point that Gabriel had his threefold revelation: Firstly, he saw quite clearly how he, Mercutio, constituted the very nub of the play – and later in life, this perception would lead to his bringing a fresh motivation to every part he played, inasmuch as he worked from the premise that the entire play centred on that one part, no matter how small the part might be.

Secondly and more significantly, Gabriel gained a fresh insight into the *chain* of cause and effect: it suddenly dawned on him that he had not slept with that woman because he was attracted to her but in order to avenge the cut to his eye. As if the latter had come first.

And finally, perhaps even more importantly: as Gabriel is about to deliver the line about his hurt being neither so deep as a well, nor so wide as a church-door; but 'tis enough, 'twill serve – just as he says these words he sees something down in the auditorium which makes him think that that cut must also have opened a flap in his consciousness, created a new aperture into his inner self, because down in the auditorium he sees hundreds of people all with his own face, just dressed differently, and this leads him, with a sort of existential Eureka!, to the realization that he is manifold, that he contains a multitude of different personas within himself – all at once.

'From then on I saw the world through different eyes,' said Gabriel. 'And it made me a better actor. I remember all the arguments we had, John Gielgud and I, up in his flat, about those old theories that say you have to forget yourself on stage, as if we have this nucleus inside us, this individuality which constitutes our self and which will always get in the way of all the other roles we try to play. On this point, I always maintained – so strongly that I don't think John ever forgot it – that, on the contrary, I *was* those other roles; that the potential for all of them was already there, inherent in me, it was only a matter of unearthing it.'

While Gabriel's boat, the *Norge*, floated more or less motionless out in the sea lane, thanks to the tug-of-war between wind and current, and the *Skipper Clement* was drawing level with Oscarsborg, packed to the gunwales with people who were already having a high old time, letting their hair down, as if the ferry to Denmark were a stage-set on which they were expected to assume roles other than those they played in everyday life, Gabriel rose and went out to the galley.

Jonas thought he had gone out for more corned beef to replenish the plate on whose white china only a couple of slices of tomato lay in splendid isolation; instead Gabriel came back with an onion which he promptly and ostentatiously proceeded to peel, having first taken a long swig of whisky.

'Few things annoy me more than Ibsen's metaphor of Peer Gynt and the onion,' he said. 'It's a poor look-out when an author comes up with a bad analogy, but it's even worse when such an analogy is given credence and adopted as some sort of moral guideline, not to mention being elevated to the status of a kind of national emblem. Who in the world would expect to find a kernel in an onion? I mean, it's nothing but a bundle of *leaves*! Botanically speaking, it's the absolute height of nonsense! If it's a kernel he's looking for, then Peer Gynt ought at least to look at the rootstock or at the part to which the very innermost leaf is attached, the onion base, the point of growth, which is definitely

not found in the middle of an onion.' Gabriel snorted and commenced to remove layer after layer from the onion, laying them
side by side on the plate in front of them while illustrating that
Ibsen's metaphor was enough to make you weep, wiping away
the tears with a voluminous blue handkerchief. The most annoying thing about Ibsen was that he believed he was presenting a
negative image of a human being, when in fact it was a positive
image. Quite phenomenal. We *were* all these layers. What was
wrong with that? To be oneself, which was what Ibsen was
always going on about, actually meant accepting that people had
many sides to their character and that it was the *sum* of these that
was the kernel. 'The greatest freedom, the very hallmark of
mankind,' said Gabriel, 'is the freedom, at any time, to reinvent
oneself, by drawing on all of one's potential. That's why you
ought to be an actor, Jonas. To gain a clearer understanding of
this. Reinvent yourself. Be a king. Be a duke!'

It was during the months following Gabriel's reflections in
this vein that Jonas found himself taking a fresh view of the portrait of himself as a one-year-old, which hung in the hall at
home, the sort of portrait that was very popular in the fifties, presenting forty-eight different images of Jonas, each one just
slightly different from the others, in one frame.

Now, however, he was on board an old lifeboat, examining a
row of onion layers arrayed on a plate, before finally looking up
to meet the eye of an old actor, well-oiled by now, who lit another
Camel and was soon enveloped in a cocoon of smoke. 'Be a duke,'
he repeated, but Jonas had lost the thread, he had caught a whiff
of danger, although he could not have said what it might be: a
drifting iceberg perhaps, or the *Skipper Clement*, now only a few
hundred metres away from them in the darkness and looking,
from the shore, like a resplendent floating palace.

Aqua Vita

The mere prospect of it, the very façade of the organ was enough to take anyone's breath away – without a doubt the most impressive Jonas had ever seen, with over one hundred burnished ornamental pipes. Standing there on its platform at the far end of the concert hall, fifteen metres high, it looked more like a little palace of pure silver. It was in fact the biggest tracker-action organ in the world, with 10,500 pipes, five manuals plus pedals and 127 stops – it almost beggared belief.

It was late in the afternoon, the guided tours were over for the day, and Jonas had been allowed into the famous building 'as a special favour' – Jonas Wergeland was frequently granted such privileges – by a Mr White, or 'Edward' as he insisted that Jonas call him, who actually claimed to know Ronald Sharp, the man who had built the organ. Mr White was kindness itself, he could not do enough for Jonas; a connoisseur of Linie Aquavit, that nectar of the gods from the other side of the world; a Norwegian and a man of some standing at that, Mr White had discovered that Jonas worked for Norwegian television and that he was on his way to New Zealand to do a programme on islanders of Norwegian descent.

Jonas seated himself on the organ bench before, or rather enclosed within, an enormous console, complete with a television monitor placed high up on the console and the facility for taping the music. It was like sitting deep inside a power station, linked up to a huge waterfall. Jonas set the registers as best he could, and his thoughts went to his father as he located the Principal in this masterpiece, although there were a lot of stops he had never heard of – Gamba, Schwebung, Unda Maris and – what was that: Vox Humana. He wisely left the couplers alone, likewise the combination buttons with their amazing capacity for electronic storage. Instead he began to play and was as captivated as always by the profusion of sound that poured out at the touch of his fingers and toes. Jonas Wergeland may not have been the only Norwegian to play the Grand Organ in Sydney Opera House, but he was the only Norwegian ever to play Duke Ellington on it.

So how do the pieces of a life fit together? In but one way?

Jonas thought of the road from Grorud Church to this place, an ocean of a difference, an ocean between them, and it struck him that he was starting to become a bit blasé, perhaps because this overwhelming compression of the world in terms of time and space no longer left any room for excitement or dreams. In the toilet of the flat in Solhaug when he was a boy there hung a reproduction of Theodor Kittelsen's painting of Soria Moria Castle, a glimmer of gold on the horizon. 'A long, long way off, he saw something glittering and gleaming.' Jonas always used to think, when he was sitting on the toilet, that this picture was all about travelling, probably because the boy in the foreground had a knapsack on his back and a staff in his hand, but also because the toilet contained another special feature, a small bookshelf filled with copies of the *National Geographic*, the only publication, other than newspapers, which their father read. Jonas also used to leaf through these and it was here, in the toilet of a flat in Solhaug that he made his first journeys into the realms of imagination, accompanied by the churning motors of his bowels, as he browsed through issues containing features entitled 'My Life in Forbidden Lhasa' or 'The Great Barrier Reef' or 'To the Land of the Head-hunters', and even if he could make no sense of the headlines, he read all he needed to and more in the wonderful pictures. So already, here, the solid foundations of his mistrust of the written word – or, not mistrust but a firm belief that words were superfluous – were being laid, because the pictures said it all: weird and wonderful painted faces, giant clams that could snap shut around a diver's foot and the golden roofs of the mausoleums of the seven Dalai Lamas at the top of the Potala Palace – 'A long, long way off he saw something glittering and gleaming.'

Jonas had also thought of his father earlier that Sunday when he took a walk along the harbour front from Harbour Bridge to Pier One, the old wharf buildings recently converted into specialist shops and aromatic seafood restaurants – just as was happening all over the world in the eighties. Jonas eyed the crabs in their boxes, the selection of oysters on their beds of ice, the yachts and ferries out in the bay; felt happy to wander aimlessly, almost surprised that no one turned to look back at him as people were forever doing in Oslo.

Jonas strolled on down Darling Harbour, making for that part of the city at the very head of the bay which, within just a few years, would be transformed into a huge leisure area complete with aquariums and a maritime museum, and suddenly, as he was walking along Hickson Road, enjoying the fine weather, the unfamiliar surroundings, his eye was caught by something familiar, something akin to a Norwegian flag: the funnel on one of the ships at the quayside, black with two white rings, denoting that this was a Wilhelmsen ship. His paternal grandfather had been a sailor and Jonas knew all the different funnel markings by heart before he learned his alphabet. He followed the wire fence until he came to a gate which offered a good view of the ship and there he noticed a man coming down the gangplank, a man with a blissful expression on his face who, on reaching the gate, stopped in front of Jonas, obviously bursting to tell him something.

This, of course, was Mr White, Edward, and he could hardly believe his luck when he discovered that Jonas was in fact Norwegian. Eagerly he told Jonas, as if anxious to persuade him that they were related, that his great-grandfather had signed on with the first Wilhelmsen ship to call at Sydney, in 1895, the *Tiger* she was called – imagine that, incredible isn't it? – which had sailed to Vladivostok with a cargo of railway sleepers before carrying on to Sydney, where she had taken on a cargo of hides for Europe. Did Jonas know that Wilhelm Wilhelmsen himself had been second mate on that ship; that same Wilhelm later to be known only as 'the Captain', who took over the running of the shipping line on the death of his brother Halfdan? Did Jonas happen to know anything about this Wilhelm Wilhelmsen?

'There was this one time in the Mediterranean, in Marseille,' said Jonas, taking it on the run, remembering something his grandfather had told him. 'It was the first time Wilhelm Wilhelmsen, "the Captain" that is, had ever been served black olives. He tasted one, then he said: "Who the hell's been pissing on these grapes?"'

Mr White doubled up with laughter, he was Sydney's most appreciative listener, welcoming anything that came from Norway, that day at any rate. Because Mr White had just been allowed to come onboard the Wilhelmsen ship and been shown the sealed containers which held the Linie Aquavit in its old sherry casks, a nigh-on religious experience, since he had once been treated to a glass of Norwegian Linie Aquavit by a sailor but could not credit the story of its odd ageing process, 135 days at sea, well, he refused point-blank to believe it – imagine, a drink that involves a journey! – until this very day when he had seen the story substantiated so conclusively that he could remember everything his guide had told him about the whole of that long, involved voyage around the world, every single port. 'I swear,' he said, 'that from this day on I'll never drink anything but Linie Aquavit. Where can I get hold of it?'

When Jonas promptly promised to arrange this for him and wrote down the man's address on the back of a receipt for a newly-consumed plate of oysters, nothing would do but that Mr White invite Jonas over to the Opera House, where he happened to occupy a top administrative post, and there was nothing Jonas would have liked better, he had in fact been planning to visit Sydney's famous landmark the following day; he had, after all, dabbled in architecture himself and had frequently come across pictures of that renowned exterior, which simply cried out for metaphors, from copulating turtles to a ship in full sail. What he did not realize was that the building also housed a Soria Moria castle, a gigantic organ. As Nefertiti said: 'There's adventure to be found wherever you go.'

The instant he laid eyes on the organ, Jonas was struck, as he never ceased to be on his travels, by a sense of rediscovering something that he had lost, a part of himself, and in this case, because of the façade, he was reminded of a rib, a feeling so strong that he clutched at his breast. He wasted no time in asking whether it would be possible to try the organ, and, thanks to Mr White and Linie Aquavit, on that day nothing was impossible.

Whenever he sat down at an organ, Jonas's thoughts turned to his father. I am not sure whether I have mentioned this, but Jonas had a wonderful father. Haakon Hansen may not have talked as much to his son as other fathers did, but he played for him a lot and this alternative upbringing, as Jonas himself called it, was to be of far-reaching significance in his life. 'I was reared on the organ bench,' he used to say.

Jonas loved to watch his father play, especially his feet, the way his shoes seemed to skip over the pedals of their own accord with the most fantastic dexterity, flicking back and forth from heel to toe, the one crossing over the other, as if in a dance, or a proper little puppet-show. One time, Jonas was allowed to paint faces on his father's shoes, creating one good and one bad shoe which fought when his father's feet flew over the pedals, a battle in which good and evil seemed constantly to take turns at having the upper hand.

Although Jonas found it hard to explain, his father's playing had a way of firing his imagination. All fathers loom large in their children's lives, even Freud figured out that much, and Haakon Hansen was not just a big man in Jonas's eyes, he was the Ruler of the World. From the organ bench he held sway over the world with this complex machine of his; the register settings were actually top-secret orders sent out to his assistants. All of this was confirmed for Jonas when he saw how people reacted: no matter how much of an atheist Haakon Hansen may have been, he played with such feeling that it brought tears to their eyes.

There was one story in particular which had offered Jonas a glimpse into his father's world: as a little boy he had accompanied his father to a funeral outside of Grorud – funerals in the surrounding area presented a welcome source of extra income for an organist – and afterwards they had driven down to the harbour in his father's Opel Caravan for a look at the boats, as they did whenever his father played at a funeral and Jonas came along to act as a counterweight. More often than not they would head down towards the *Blenheim*, the passenger ferry to England which berthed just below Akershus Fort; if Jonas had tried once he had tried a hundred times to draw the elegant lines of that ship, the funnel especially, and he never tired of it. Late that afternoon they had passed beneath the monstrous cranes and strolled all the way out to the end of the quayside, down to Vippetangen, when suddenly two men jumped out from behind a shed and started to beat up Jonas's father, two men in overalls, big, burly characters. Haakon Hansen did not have a hope, no chance to make a run for it even; they knocked him to the ground, hauled him back onto his feet then threw him to the ground again, kicked him in the chest and legs, spat on him, grabbed him by the lapels and pulled him upright so that one of them could hold him while the other punched him in the stomach and never a word spoken. Jonas stood there, looking on, screaming and howling, but they paid him no mind; it all seemed so totally senseless, an act of pure malice, either that or some ghastly misunderstanding. Jonas had never experienced anything so awful as to stand there watching his father being beaten until the blood spurted from his nose; the only sounds the awful *thunk* of punches and kicks and his father's groans, for it was not just a father who was being roughed up before his very eyes, but the Ruler of the World.

What surprised him was his father's reaction. When the two thugs finally made off, he struggled to his feet, took Jonas's hand and led him back to the car, *smiling* all the while and saying over and over again: 'They didn't touch my fingers, thank God, they didn't touch my fingers.' As if everything was fine because they had not broken his fingers. Jonas cried and cried. They climbed into the Caravan and his father managed to drive, not to the casualty department, but to Grorud Church, where he dragged himself up to the organ with several broken ribs and a face covered in cuts and bruises. Jonas noticed blood on the keys and that his father had lost at least one tooth, because he kept on smiling, muttering, 'Thank God, thank God'; and he played; he played a piece that Jonas had never heard before, the music filling the church to bursting point; Jonas had no idea whether it was an improvised piece or what, only that it swelled, surged, rose and fell, going on and on as if his father were trying to press this senseless violence into some sort of pattern, refusing to accept that it might have been a random act. For a while, possibly because of the wind, the organ seemed to be puffing and panting, making Jonas think that his father was fighting some huge creature, a prehistoric monster, an impression which was further enhanced by the Gothic lettering on the stops, before the music suddenly slipped over into a more serene phase, calm and yet somehow weary, and eventually ran out into '*Leid milde ljos*' in a strange, unfamiliar arrangement involving harmonies which seemed, to Jonas's ears to verge on the impossible.

Later Jonas realized that this therapy, or whatever you want to call it, had been as much for his benefit. If there is one thing that children, especially boys, find hard to bear, it is injustice, the idea that wickedness can go unpunished. Which is why they read *The Count of Monte Cristo* and devour hundreds of stories about the lone avenger who returns to punish the bad guys and reward the good. It was this very way of thinking that his father had negated, as it were, at the organ, the entire chain of cause and effect; he lifted the whole thing onto another plane where – and Jonas was in no doubt about this – those brutal thugs got what they deserved. In this way the organ music also wiped away Jonas's horrific experience, and he would, strangely enough, always remember this incident as something positive.

By the time his father had finished playing, his wounds seemed to have healed – his face no longer looked the slightest bit battered, the tooth was still missing, that was all. So what was life all about? That barbaric attack or the organ music?

Now here was Jonas Wergeland sitting at an organ himself, the biggest organ in the world, just about as far from Grorud Church as he could get. And at the thought of that bloody, yet positive, episode he experiences – right there, in Sydney, beneath a facade of gleaming ornamental pipes reminiscent of a gigantic, glittering mirror – some of the same feeling, as if it had been handed down to him – in other words, he catches a glimpse of another way of thinking, an inkling of hidden links, lines criss-crossing one another. He is playing, of all things, '*Ved Rondane*' by Edvard Grieg, a song his father often played at funerals. Jonas finds the 'Tutti' button, plays the last part full out, producing cascades of sound that are, nonetheless, enigmatic. A bit like reproducing the song of the whales, he thinks, playing as he is with the sea right outside so that these notes could be carried all around the world by the life-giving water, even to Norway, like the lines on the map of the Wilhelmsen line's sailing routes that hung on the wall of his grandfather's outdoor privy, down by the shore on the island of Hvaler.

He finished off and turned around to find Mr White in tears.

'Is something the matter?' Jonas asked.

Mr. White shook his head. 'Play something else,' he said. 'Please play something else.'

Jonas Wergeland sits back down at the manuals of the Opera House's Grand Organ and plays '*Leid milde ljos*' in an arrangement based on harmonies borrowed from Duke Ellington. And halfway through this enchanting hymn, Jonas feels the Opera House slide into the water, transformed into a mighty ship.

To Be or Not To Be

The night was overcast and quite, quite dark, with no moon. Gabriel was so drunk that his eyes kept falling shut. Jonas glanced from the barometer with its pointer stuck on 'fair weather' to an inclinometer, also broken. He was just about to get up and take *Peer Gynt* down from the bookshelf to check whether Ibsen, Norway's national poet, really had been so misguided as to speak of the 'kernel' of an onion when he realized that something was wrong, something was very wrong.

It may seem hard to believe, in the normal way of looking at things, I mean, but I beg you please to believe me when I say that Jonas Wergeland received a warning in the form of a stanza of organ music, a little phrase from '*Leid milde ljos*' which seemed to Jonas to be carried across the water and resonate off the hull of the boat.

Jonas raced up onto the deck to find himself confronted by the *Skipper Clement*, although of course he did not know the vessel's name, only that it was huge, an absolutely colossal ship – there are those who may remember this elegant Danish ferry with its characteristic elongated funnel and its name in white letters amidships – and not only that, but that it was headed straight for them. Jonas's first, albeit irrational, thought was that here was another vessel called the *Norge* about to go down, like that last one during the war, as if history were repeating itself; another circle; he hated circles, and yet he stayed put, held spellbound by the sight, which was indeed a beautiful one, indescribably beautiful, this ship that was almost on top of them, too big, too bright, too close, he had not the faintest idea what was going on here, this was not a boat but a swirling circle, it was an opera, a floating organ, it was Improbability itself once more taking probable form.

'Light the lamps!' he screamed to Gabriel down below. No reply from the saloon. 'Where the hell's the switch?' yelled Jonas. He leapt down onto the well-deck, fumbled about, panic-stricken, looking for a switch.

No, he heard Gabriel saying down in the saloon, he only had paraffin lanterns, and they'd have to be prepared first. Why'd he ask? Were they going for a sail? Jonas peered down through the hatch and caught a glimpse of Gabriel standing in the glow of the paraffin lamp, pouring himself some more whisky then peering at the fob watch which he had pulled out of his waistcoat pocket as if wishing to confirm that the collision would take place at exactly the right moment.

The danger was, to say the least of it, overhanging. Jonas could almost see the bow towering above him like the posters one saw in so many Norwegian homes, picturing ships head-on. Jonas dashed across to the foghorn and cranked the handle like mad – that, too, was out of order. 'Bloody hell, Gabriel, when did you last sail this thing?' he had the presence of mind to say, or mutter to himself, as if even there, even then, he had come up with another angle that shed light on unknown sides of the character of the *Norge*'s owner. Jonas noted the life buoy hanging on the mizzen shroud; another second and the bow would be rushing down on, or rather *slicing through*, them. Then he remembered a lamp, just at the bottom of the hatchway, outside the toilet. He slid down the ladder, found it, up onto the deck, batteries were bound to be dead, or the bulb gone, but no, it worked and even gave off a good strong light. He aimed the beam at the ship, remembering something from his childhood, the joy of a new torch, the thrill when the light hit a wall a long way off, a sense of power, but here, a torch against a colossal steel plough; he felt a right fool, managed to angle the beam upwards at the *Skipper Clement* at the very moment that the bridge disappeared from view, and the ship was transformed into pure hull, pure bow, pure steel, pure death.

Jonas saw the bow of the ship veer slowly, so infinitely slowly and only very slightly but just enough to prevent it from cleaving the *Norge* in two, and as it did so the *Skipper Clement* sounded its siren, a long, deep note from the ship's horn as if from the bass pipes of an organ but in this case amplified to such a fearful extent that the sound alone looked likely to send them to the bottom.

Just before Jonas lit the lamp, Gabriel had appeared on the deck, with his coat on as if he had been thinking of going ashore to a party. He did not seem at all surprised or startled by the sight of the mountainous bow slicing through the water towards them. 'No, they cannot touch me for coining; I am the king himself,' he roared at the ferry. Then, once Jonas had succeeded in sending the life-saving signal and the bow had veered aside, he tore off his coat and leapt, or rather staggered to the rail and drew himself up like a matador with his cape, seeming almost to flick the huge vessel away, yelling 'Olé!' and hooting with laughter as the hull swished past, almost soundlessly, a rustling whisper, only a few feet away from them.

So entranced was Jonas by this vast black wall which simply went on gliding and gliding past them as if there were no end to it, that he had to hang on tight to the mizzen shroud, to the life buoy. How wonderful! he thought. The merest whisper. A black wall swishing past, right alongside them. A black wall strung with glittering holes. To Jonas it seemed like another universe ploughing past. Another possibility entirely. A sort of tangent to the circle of real life.

Then all at once it was gone. In place of the black wall they saw the lights on the other side of the fjord. They were floating in a vacuum, in an all-engulfing hush which only gradually allowed room for sounds, enabling them once more to hear the wind and the creaking of the rigging. The *Skipper Clement* was already a long way off, a shimmering layer cake, unreal, as if it had never been.

As luck would have it, a cabin cruiser came along, on its way to Fagerstrand, and gave them a tow back into the bay, where they tied up once again to the buoy from which the severed end of the mooring rope trailed in the water. They climbed down into the saloon. Sat a long time in silence. The stove was smoking, there was a smell of gunpowder, as after an explosion. 'More whisky?' said Gabriel. Jonas rejected the offer with a wave of his hand, that was the last thing he needed right now.

'Well lad, you saved my life back there, I'd say,' Gabriel said at length. 'For that you deserve a reward.' It was as if he had woken up, become another person. He looked at the skylight, not at Jonas. 'I said you should become an actor. Forget that. Where'd I put my mug? What I'm going to say to you now is the most obvious thing in the world, so obvious that folk just don't see it.' Gabriel took a swig from his mug. 'Television, that's the future, lad. Damn right it is. Television. It came to me a couple of years back. The day my TV went on the blink.' He pointed into the forecabin where the old television, stripped of its innards formed a 3D frame for the skull. 'I went in to Drøbak. Not a soul to be seen. They were all inside watching TV. Watching the royal wedding – Sonja and Harald. D'you know what? That day marked a revolution in Norway. A social revolution. An entire nation synchronized, sitting in armchairs in front of a screen. A watershed in the history of mankind! And what's television? Light, lad. Light. Take it from me: before too long television is going to be as important as sunlight.' Gabriel lifted his empty dish and raised it heavenwards. 'Give us this day our daily bread,' he said without realizing of course that in so doing he was anticipating the dishes which many Norwegians would eventually have fixed to their house walls or roofs.

Jonas had no idea what Gabriel was on about, he had never taken much interest in television. Granted, his family had, like so many others in Norway, bought a television for the sake of watching the 1964 Winter Olympics, and his father in particular had felt that it had been well worth the money, and then some, just to see the three Norwegian speed-skaters step up onto the podium after the 5,000 metres. Other than that, though, his parents didn't watch much television. Jonas had only vague memories of the programmes from his childhood: one of the *Falcon Club* programmes with Rolf Riktor, a couple of episodes of *The Saint*, the odd evening with Gunnar Haarberg and *Double Your Money* and of course the fish during the interval, which were possibly the most interesting part of the whole thing, inasmuch as the television was suddenly transformed into an aquarium. To be honest, he found it boring. Before they acquired a television of their own, he used to watch *Robin Hood* on a neighbour's television which had a sheet of plastic in front of the screen. This plastic sheet was split up into three horizontal panels, blue at the top, reddish-brown then green, supposedly to give the illusion of colour television, and everybody would clap enthusiastically when the three colours actually matched the picture, more or less, which is to say for the five seconds each evening when a shot of some scenery appeared on the screen. Years later, this would still be Jonas's impression: that television only matched reality for a handful of seconds every night.

Nonetheless, Jonas understood that television represented something important, though he could not have put it into words, something tremendous that had an effect on people's daily lives. There was one time when he had been visiting a friend who lived in a villa on a hill facing one of the new twelve-storey tower blocks in Ammerud, which meant that they could see into something like 250 living rooms. It was a Saturday evening, dark outside, and Jonas could not figure out what the blue light was that he kept seeing. To begin with he had thought it must be some sort of mass psychosis: that all these people had suddenly felt the urge to sit under a sunlamp. This sight was to stay with him, this image of a modern Norwegian society in which almost all of its inhabitants were stuck in front of a television screen, as if they believed that it gave off some life-giving, or at any rate, vital radiation.

Gabriel stood up and came over to him: 'So to put it simply, Jonas, what I want to say to you, as a reward for your heroic action with that torch this evening is: start with television. You could do the trendy thing and start with computers or something along those lines. Forget it. Television is the future.'

Gabriel then proceeded to deliver a lengthy lecture, astonishingly lucid considering the amount of alcohol he had taken on board, or maybe because of that, on all the possibilities presented by television, from which I will confine myself, here, to quoting his assertion that television broadcasting and the products it could create, all of which had to do with symbols or information – remember that word, Jonas: information! – would have as much of an impact on the society of the future as the steam engine had had in the past, and not only that, but that these days, it was as much a matter of mental as of material resources, knowledge-based enterprises, a fact which filled Gabriel with optimism since it offered everybody an equal chance and, hence, the opportunity for Norway, this tuppenny-ha'penny country to make its mark on the world. 'It's no longer a matter of luck, m'lad, of who just happens to have the waterfalls or the oil, oh, no, what's in demand these days is creativity, whatever country has the people with the greatest imagination.'

Gabriel walked through to the forecabin and came back with the empty shell of the television with the skull inside it and set it on the table. 'Shell within shell,' he said, picking up the death's-head. 'Layer within layer.' Jonas was almost expecting: 'Alas, poor Yorick!' or, at the very least 'To be or not to be', but Gabriel's face grew grave, and he said very softly: 'Sure he that made us with such large discourse, looking before and after, gave us not that capability and god-like reason to fust in us unus'd.' And with that he crossed over to the ladder, tossed the skull out of the hatch with a basketball player's flick of the wrist, an act which was followed by a faint splash.

'If you want to direct the course of events, this is the new stage,' said Gabriel, pointing to the empty box of the television, which truly did resemble a miniature stage. 'Being an actor is, after all, a particle option. Remember what I said? About my friend Niels Bohr? That people, like all matter, can take the form of either particles or waves? Okay. Now listen: to start with television, that would be something different, something new, a wave option. A chance to explore all the different inexplicable ways in which people can be influenced. A chance to make some totally new discoveries about cause and effect.'

With one firm blow, Gabriel loosened and removed the base of the television then slid the box over Jonas's head, bringing it to rest on his shoulders. 'There. I hereby crown you. Jonas, it's time to reinvent yourself. Be a duke, be a king!' Gabriel eyed his handiwork with satisfaction: Jonas's face looking out of a television set. 'Set your sights on television, lad. Dare to take that giant leap!'

Thus Jonas Wergeland made his first appearance on television.

Quantum Leap

The area championships' meet was being held, for once, at the Grorud sports ground and not at Jordal Stadium, and Jonas Wergeland was getting ready for his last shot at the high jump. The bar was set at a utopian 1.60 metres. Clear that, and he was area champion – against all the odds.

Jonas was far from being the best in his age group, but sometimes luck was with him. Like today. From the minute he stepped out onto the field to warm up he had been feeling in incredibly good form, as if he were on pep pills. This was confirmed in the 100 metres when he beat his personal best by half a second to take third place; it was almost unbelievable. His trainer, surprised and disconcerted, came over to congratulate him, gabbling something about new training programmes and a free place on the tour to Finland.

The event at which Jonas really excelled, though, was the high jump, as he had discovered while still a small boy, when he and Nefertiti used to play on the sports field that the big boys had made all by themselves down by the stream that ran below the Solhaug estate – a pitch which was as legendary among all the local children as any Olympic arena. This sports field was a wonder to behold, with proper goals and nets, albeit handball size, and both a long-jump pit – boards and all – and a high-jump set-up. In one corner of the field was a shed where they kept such lethal pieces of equipment as javelins, discuses and shot, and which also acted, it has to be said, as a good hiding place for more suspect items: condoms in circular yellow packs, for instance, and a girlie mag, its pages gradually yellowed by wind and weather. When it came to the high jump, there was no talk here of simply scissor-jumping ingenuously over the bar; they also used a pole and even though many a suicidal attempt at a dive-straddle jump was made none of these could compare to the breathtaking flights made by the odd few with the aid of the bamboo pole – this last exotic enough in itself to lend the field an air of being part international arena, part South Sea island. Then again, there was nothing quite like being seven or eight years old and slinging oneself six feet into the air, sky-high so it seemed, on the end of a pliant bamboo pole, to land on a not very big and not exactly soft mound, sending the sawdust flying.

But this is for real, or at least more so, and Jonas Wergeland prepares for the decisive jump, for his one big chance to become area champion. He eyes the bar, one metre and sixty centimetres above the ground; it's high, he's never jumped that high, but he knows what Gabriel Sand, the old actor, will come to say to him, note my choice of words, will come to say to him, because they have not yet met, but they will meet and those things which will happen are already inherent in him, carried within him even now, so he knows that Gabriel Sand is going to tell him about the wave potential of human beings, about all the things we are but which we do not exploit because they seem so hard to fathom. Jonas knows that anything is possible, even the most unlikely things, when human beings have the muscle power to leap over a house, a fact which has been proved scientifically, in other words: the *potential* is there.

Jonas Wergeland also had something else going for him; that spring he had met Nina H., one of the greatest track-and-field athletes in the whole of the Grorud valley, in the whole of Norway, for that matter. They had been confirmed together in Grorud Church and had come to know one another well, very well, during confirmation classes in which the vicar placed particular emphasis on the seventh commandment and all the ins and outs of sexual morality, though this of course merely added a bit of spice to what were, otherwise, pretty deadly classes and, paradoxically, titillated those young confirmation candidates more than was good for them. To begin with, before they ever spoke to one another, Jonas had noticed how Nina H. glanced in his direction more than once, especially when the vicar referred, in his dry, roundabout fashion, to the untold perils and temptations of puberty, and Jonas felt that shiver which ran slowly from the base of his spine all the way up to the back of his neck, leaving an inexplicable tingling sensation between his shoulder-blades.

Like Nina H., Jonas was a member of the athletics side of Grorud Sports Club, which moved its training activities in the spring from the gym to the sports ground across the road, and it was here, one rainy training night when only a handful had shown up, that Jonas and Nina H. found themselves the only two left in the clubhouse. Nina showed such promise and was considered so trustworthy that she had her own key to the changing rooms. Jonas had showered and was sitting naked on one of the wooden benches, digging sand out of his spikes when Nina H. walked into the boys' changing room, wrapped only in a towel. She said not a word, maybe smiled a little smile, before going down on her knees in front of him and stroking his thighs while she gazed into his eyes. 'Just relax,' she said. Then she gently cupped her hand around his 'lingam', as Jonas would have put it, seeming almost to weigh his penis in her palm, apparently rather surprised both by its consistency and its lightness, when in fact she was enraptured, studying the lines of his penis, its shape and proportions, following the course of every vein, taking in every irregularity in such a way that Jonas understood what his Aunt Laura was getting at with her pithy assertion: a good cock is worth its weight in gold. Nina H. looked as though she had found a treasure map, the sort they used to etch into walrus tusks in olden days.

Seeing the way she stuck out her tongue just a little before putting her lips to the head of his penis, Jonas could not help thinking of their confirmation, the sight of her at the altar rail in exactly the same position, on her knees, her eyes half-closed, how lovely she had looked. She wasn't religious, he was pretty sure about that, and yet she had an air of expectancy about her, as if she knew that this was a solemn moment, that it was right, no matter what, that it had to do with life, rites of passage, a leap marked by something symbolic; now her hands were round his hips, in a room pungent with sweat, and her lips and tongue were doing things he had never imagined possible, things for which even his sister's anatomy lessons had in no way prepared him, and he felt his body swelling as her tongue fluttered around the ridge of his glans, how his muscles suddenly bore witness to resources of energy unknown to him, and when he came, when the semen spurted out in great warm jets over her lips, and she even opened her mouth to swallow some of it, as if it really were a blessing or at any rate a fortifying drink of some sort, he could not stop himself from thinking of how she had opened her mouth in just that way, with her tongue protruding slightly, to receive the wafer from between the vicar's fingers; and even when his conscience instinctively started sending out blasphemy signals and quashing this comparison, he realized that this, what she was now doing to him, what she was now giving him, ought also to be seen as a sacrament, and I – even I – would be the last to object to that.

Their game did not stop there, however; they switched places as if intent on taking their confirmation classes a stage further or, better, taking up a matter they had not previously touched upon. Now it was Jonas's turn to kneel in worship, he ran his fingers over Nina H.'s long, muscular legs, remembering that that was the first thing he had noticed about her, her thighs, showing under skin-tight jeans, because she was a runner; Jonas had even stood watching in admiration sometimes when she was practising tempo runs on the curves, contemplating her marvellous stride, the look on her face which intimated that it might not be the idea of competing which drew women to take part in athletics but the mystical element; at any rate it was an aesthetic delight to see those long legs propelling her body forward so swiftly, the very lift of the knee, the springiness, the flexing of the tendons, while at the same time he felt there was something erotic about the sight, an idea which is not so far out when you think that the Chinese, for example, when they wish to declare their love, say 'I have seen a woman's foot.' Nina H. had long been a member of the distinguished 1,000 Club, and her room at home was bedecked with silver, so I assume that most Norwegians, at least, will know exactly whose legs Jonas Wergeland was now crouched between, legs which it would later be said ought to be insured with Lloyds, and will recall her triumphs in the 100 metres hurdles, not least the race she ran and the gold medal she won at the European Championships in the mid-seventies, the most beautiful race ever run on European soil, as one ecstatic journalist described it. And now here he was, Jonas Wergeland, on his knees in a changing room redolent of countless boys and their united efforts and dreams of gold, his face pressed between those legs which would at a later date be regarded as nigh on public property and his tongue buried deep in certain far more private and unknown parts of her anatomy. The fissure between the labia majora and minora has been compared, not without some justification – at any rate if one thinks of the opening up of new possibilities – to the physicists' fission of the atom, and Jonas truly did have a sense of something explosive inside him, an urge, an appetite, which had been totally missing from his sister's pragmatic demonstration and which gave him the chance to try out a skill which also vouchsafed a glimpse into the heart of creation, deep-red secrets. Rakel had at least explained to them that not all women's genitals were the same shape or size – far from it – and as far as Jonas could tell, Nina H. had, according to his own terminology, a splendid example of a gazelle yoni, as seemed only natural, considering her particular discipline; a tight vagina which clamped itself around his finger like a suckling mouth, a soft vice, as if her vagina, too, had benefited from all the training to which she had subjected her body. This was Jonas's main impression, kneeling there between Nina H.'s perfect legs, surrounded by a scent reminiscent of damp sawdust, that this thing, this place which his tongue was exploring was, first and foremost, a muscle; or rather, not a muscle, but a source of potential energy which, if he tapped into it, would boost his own body's performance, like a pole when you made a jump. And as if to assure himself of a share in this flood of vitality, he flicked his tongue still harder, until Nina H. raised her arms, grasped the hooks above her head, pulled herself up and hung, almost suspended in mid-air, while she came and came and came again, her athletic body writhing as if she were doing a split jump, with a smile on her face and her eyes closed, so that Jonas looking up, saw her for the first time, with her arms raised above her head and that smile of relief, as he was to see her time and again on television in later years, when she broke through the tape, almost always coming first.

So Jonas Wergeland knew it was little coincidence that he should now find himself here on the field, only a week after the occurrence in the changing-room, simply bursting with energy. It was his turn to jump. No one could have guessed that they were about to witness something quite exceptional; in Norway sensational moments in athletics tend to be very few and far between. Not that I mean to make fun of Norwegian pole-vaulting, but I need only remind you of Audun Boysen and a Norwegian record in the 800 metres which was to remain unbeaten for half a generation, and that a Norwegian is likely to win an Olympic gold in athletics only once every 40 to 50 years.

So it was not as if anyone were expecting anything, nor was Jonas himself really prepared for what was about to happen, mainly because he still favoured the scissors technique, a bit more old-fashioned than the dive-straddle but far less dangerous when you are having to land on all manner of rock-hard mats, so Jonas concentrated on his ritual – in the high jump the ritual is half the point, or half the fun, even on the sports field down by the stream at Solhaug they had performed the craziest rituals prior to jumping, and it was most important that one followed the same procedure every time, as in church, so Jonas slowly removed his track-suit, jogged back and forth, stretched a bit, checked that the bar was sitting properly, flexed, checked his start mark, did a trial run-up, gave his limbs a shake, loosening up, flexed again, did a couple of high-kicks, knowing that he was annoying the life out of the other competitors, particularly the guy who was going to win if Jonas knocked down the bar, since he had already jumped successfully at a lower height, the jammy bugger, so Jonas had to clear it, *he* might not even believe he could do it, but there was something about his body, an unaccountable litheness, the itch to jump. He stood still, glanced over at Grorud Church, the tall spire, retreated into himself, shutting out his surroundings, shutting out the sounds, shutting out even Nina H., who was over there by the curve in the track, leaning on the fence and watching; he knew that this was it, this was the decisive jump – no, not a jump, but a *leap*. Jonas took the measure of the run with his eye, several times, swore at that bar to stay put, measured the run again and again brushed back his hair, brushed back his hair once more, heard some guy sighing with exasperation and yet did not hear him, broke into a trot, took a few short strides then picked up speed, more speed, full speed, heading towards the bar from the right side, taking long strides now, knew he was looking good, knew he was looking fantastic; standing outside of himself, looking on, even while he was running, relishing the image of himself; he was on the move and standing outside of himself at one and the same time, running in an arc towards the bar, sensing that this would give him greater momentum, jumped like a tangent striking out from a semicircle and there, right there, in that tenth of a second when he came down with everything he had on his left foot – he always planted with his left foot, for the simple reason that most people planted with the right, and he was Jonas Wergeland who would take a different approach to most other people whenever he could – just as he brought that foot down, abruptly compressing himself, as a writer will do in a fine poem, he heard a cry break through his film of concentration, 'Come on, Jonas!!', and instinctively he turned to see who was shouting, almost losing his balance, almost going over on to his back, so that his body actually twisted and he flew over the bar left shoulder first and, as if that were not enough, he flew over the bar back first, or at least that was how it seemed to the spectators who were all set to burst out laughing, except that their laughter was nipped in the bud as they saw Jonas Wergeland jumping over, way over, 1.60 to become area champion, a feat which prompted Nina H. to call out again, exultantly, as if she were lying beside him on the pile of foam-rubber mats: 'Fantastic, Jonas!'

Jonas was a star for a day or two, and people talked about it for weeks; shook their heads as they described how this crazy guy had jumped 'backwards'; shook their heads, that is, until they saw the American Dick Fosbury on television during the Olympic Games in Mexico City that same summer, taking the gold in the high jump with the selfsame technique which Jonas, albeit by accident, had demonstrated on the Grorud sports ground. That Jonas Wergeland would later be described as a pioneer will come as no surprise to anyone who saw him do the Fosbury flop long before anyone else in Norway.

Jonas did not know it yet, but he was now on the track of his unique penis.

And now you are making another leap, an impossible leap in which everything gets twisted and you land involuntarily, with a stab of pain, as if you had landed wrongly, here, here in this room, thirty square metres of it and it might as well be a galaxy, in which someone is playing Johann Sebastian Bach's celestial music on the organ, and I understand why you do not make that call, why the thought of picking up the phone simply does not enter your head, why you stand stock-still in that room with a dead wife and let the seconds pass, you even cast the occasional glance at your wristwatch, an exclusive make, a present, you think, it must have been a present, you think, and you remember, wondering as you do so from what corner of your mind the memory has surfaced, the stopwatch you were in the habit of using on the skating rink, that blissful sense of being in control, the significance of every second magnified, tenths of a second and, most important of all: the ability to stop the hand, stop time, break the circle, and you look down at your wrist-watch to find, to your surprise almost, that time continues to pass, regardless of the sight before you; you see the second hand moving forward in tiny jerks as if every second were a minuscule impossible leap, and you think that surely one of these small leaps ought also to be capable of flicking things back to the way they were, much like yanking a dislocated joint back into place, you think, or sending things off in another direction, the way the bow of the *Skipper Clement* abruptly altered course, you think, knowing all the time that this thing here, this body on the floor, springs from something else entirely, that time has nothing to do with cause and effect.

So there you stand, Jonas Wergeland, connoisseur of art, the bomber's last victim, son of a mother who had seven lovers, and you notice the fireplace, notice that someone has had a fire going, Margrete often lit a fire, you think, she liked having a blaze as big as a bonfire in the grate when she was reading a book, because bonfires and stories went hand-in-hand she said, and you see that she must have been reading not that long ago, because there is a book on the coffee table in front of the sofa, and you sniff the air in the room as if the smells might actually reveal something, give you a clue, and you catch a whiff from the fireplace, a suggestion of smoke and dead embers and you detect the vaguely stuffy odour of synthetic materials, of dust on electronic equipment in use, warm plastic, and you feel so hopeless, as if this mélange of scents is telling you that you are looking here at something, a constellation of old and new, which you will never understand.

But just as you are about to resign yourself to the inevitable, it comes to you, as pain turns to perception, that it has something to do with burglars, a break-in, you think, and Margrete has surprised them, you think, how stupid can you get, you think, why couldn't you just let them take whatever they wanted, you suddenly find yourself shouting at the dead woman, and for a few seconds you even expect an answer, an explanation, because you know how gullible Margrete is, how ingenuous, you never could fathom that naïve, trusting side of her, bordering on stupidity, you think and you picture the scene: Margrete, standing in the doorway and asking, politely no doubt, what they were up to, as if she could make the burglars see reason, you think, and you picture what happens next, aching inside, and now there she is, stone dead, on the floor in a pool of congealing blood.

You look round the room, notice the picture of Buddha, and you have to strain your eyes in the gloom simply to ascertain that nothing is missing, everything is where it should be, including the more valuable pieces, you think, the silver, stuff that would be easy to sell, so what in hell were they after, you think, what's the most valuable thing in the house, you wonder, and in a flash you see it all: the pictures, you think, the paintings in the dining-room, four perfect gems, these days one was forever reading about such cases, stealing to order, some unknown collector, you think, some madman, with a few pieces of his own personal jigsaw puzzle missing, some loony who didn't want to sell them, only to keep them locked away in some room, so the thieves knew what to go for, you think, your rare early paintings by famous artists and you start towards the dining-room, to confirm what you already know, feeling grief momentarily replaced by anger, but the sight on the floor pulls you up short, as if you were about to trip over a huge turtle.

Now you remember, a ripple across the smooth surface of your mind, you are an artist, you were born with a silver thread running up your spine and you have been an artist all your days; you are glad to have rediscovered your identity and you are struck by the distinctive light in the room, as dark as a Rembrandt, you think, even as you take in, afresh, the magical Nordic spring evening outside the windows, the deep-blue sky and the yellow band on the horizon which will soon be gone and you look at the little jar of coltsfoot on the table and you look at Margrete and you notice the way the light from the lone lamp lends an odd, yellowish sheen to her skin, and you see how the two small, gold earrings positively glow in the semi-darkness, and you see the red, you don't want to see it, but you see it, the red patch, carmine red, you think, like blood, you think, and you are struck by a sensation which surprises you, shocks you almost, and yet you cannot deny it: a feeling of standing in the middle of a work of art which fills you with a sneaking sense of pleasure, one might almost say glee, in the midst of the pain, in the midst of the agony, and you recognize this as a unique and precious moment in your life, endowing you with clear-sightedness and awareness as only great art can.

You stare and stare, endeavouring to spin out this feeling, but it does not last because the music has come to an end and the cobweb, the imperfect safety net woven by the organ music, snaps, not even the biggest organ in the world can help you now and once more you find yourself, after a far too foolhardy leap, a hard fall, standing in the middle of the living room in your own home, stunned, blank, desolate, and you gaze around the room in despair, searching for some detail, like the little chunk of reddish sandstone on the bookshelf, something capable of lifting you out of all of this, taking you on an imaginary journey, you think, to Ayers Rock, Australia, you think, anywhere at all, you think, and again you glance down at the second hand, as if this were your only fixed point, the only spoke in a fragile wheel, you see the second hand suddenly transformed into a propeller, a propeller slicing into your body, cutting you up, carving you into tiny chunks that float, drift off, going their separate ways, and you have been tortured by this sensation long enough, your body is racked by convulsive sobs, and you try to think, but you cannot bear to think and so for the moment you will have to postpone a vague idea of going through to the dining-room to see how many paintings the burglars have taken.

The Connoisseur

Jonas was eight years old. It was late April, one of those classic, longed for April days buzzing with regenerative energy. The pavements were dry and inviting and one could almost see, or feel in one's bones, that the trees in Studenterlunden were working fit to burst to rid themselves of their black, spiky appearance; that the green, that mentally invigorating green, was straining against its thin sheaths. It was hardly coincidental that Jonas Wergeland should have discovered his gift on just such an incomparable spring day, a day simply zinging with light and latent colour.

Jonas and his grandmother were walking from Oscars gate down through Slottsparken. Jonas had swapped his winter boots for thin-soled shoes and had the same delightful sensation of lightness which he imagined a creature must have when it sheds its skin. Feeling as though he had hundreds of tiny springs in the sole of each shoe he headed straight for that magical spot on the corner of Karl Johans gate which went by the name of Studenten, where they sold ice creams in every imaginable form and colour; a place heavy with the tropical aromas of vanilla and bananas and the most obvious point to make for when one had just switched from winter boots to light spring shoes, so much so, in fact, that Jonas could tell that his *shoes* themselves were all set on going there, but his grandmother was resolutely pulling him in the opposite direction, towards Fridtjof Nansens plass and the twin towers of the town hall. 'Business before pleasure,' she said firmly.

Is this the most crucial story in Jonas Wergeland's life?

Shortly afterwards they found themselves inside the Society of Artists building, in a bright, white room, its four walls lined with paintings, and the room itself crowded with people not only because it was a Saturday but because this was the opening of the first exhibition by a young Norwegian painter. Jonas stood quite still, listening to the hum of voices and watching the people circling the room expectantly, as if this – their clothes, their facial expressions – were more interesting than the works of art. 'What do you think?' his grandmother whispered. Jonas had been expecting to be bored out of his skull, but as he ran an eye more or less unconsciously over the walls it was caught and held by one painting, as if some sort of visual glue were preventing his eye from moving on.

'It was a royal-blue egg cup that made me aware of the silver thread running down my spine,' Jonas was later to say.

Standing there, looking at this picture, Jonas felt a shiver run through him – or, not a shiver, but a faint and yet quite distinct tickling sensation that worked its way slowly from his tailbone to the nape of his neck; a very pleasant, almost erotic, sensation which finally concentrated at a point between his shoulder-blades.

'That one over there is . . . nice,' he said, pointing.

I would ask you to bear with me for dwelling for a moment on this painting, seeing that it does, after all, represent a watershed in Jonas Wergeland's life. This was far from being anything in the nature of 'Bridal Procession in Hardanger' or any of those other large-scale, hyper-realistic canvases to which children are usually so readily drawn; this was an unassuming little picture, a still life: a bright-blue egg cup sitting on a blue table set against a green wall, with a pear lying next to it on a yellow napkin. So simple and yet so complex. Jonas moved a little closer, thinking that it must be the violet field, a triangle stretching out – cryptically – behind the eggcup, that had seized his attention, or maybe it was the pale-blue brushstroke directly below the pear. Jonas stood there, growing more and more fascinated, endeavouring to take in the very palpability of the picture, the thick layers of paint, the play of light and shade on the yellow napkin and, as he let his eye wander over the picture as a whole, how all of the colours fell into the same scale, most of them broken by white, rendered lighter: a tonal effect which caused the canvas to come alive and glow with a tremendous – and here he searched for a word he never used but which now, confronted with this picture, seemed perfectly natural – beauty.

'I'll buy it,' said his grandmother, already making towards the office. Which is how Jørgine Wergeland became one of the first people in Norway to acquire a painting by Jens Johannessen, an artist who would in years to come be highly esteemed and frequently described as one of the foremost painters, if not *the* foremost painter of his generation and who, on several occasions – and I admit he has a point – has asserted that the railings surrounding Norwegian art need to be torn down, and soon. Not only that, with this purchase Jonas's grandmother sparked off a veritable landslide, with Johannessen's paintings selling unexpectedly well, so well in fact that the elderly painter Henrik Sørensen, who would sometimes buy a picture in order to encourage a young artist, had to go home empty-handed, having turned up somewhat late in the day, clad in his ubiquitous grey coat.

As far as Jonas Wergeland's grandmother and her background is concerned, I regret that I needs must confine myself to presenting a few facts. Jonas's maternal grandmother and grandfather came from Gardermoen in Ullensaker county, but after the death of his grandfather, Oscar, during the war, Jørgine Wergeland moved to Oslo where she took up residence in Oscars gate, for no other reason than that she felt this was something her husband would have appreciated. I should perhaps also mention that this flat in Oscars gate was a fair-sized one, his grandmother having arrived in the city with a tidy sum of money in her handbag, although thereby hangs another tale entirely. The main point, so far as this story is concerned, is that in the years immediately after the war, as well as being an erstwhile smallholder or, as she herself used to say, a country bumpkin, Jonas's grandmother adopted two other personalities. She quite simply became Winston Churchill, just as she also became a patron of the arts and collector, with the result that every time Jonas visited her, he was filled with the same sense of eager expectation. When she opened the door would she be an ordinary grandmother, given to talking about the old days at Gardermoen, tending the cattle, his grandfather's shoemaking skills; or would she be Winston Churchill, making the V-sign and mumbling on about his dramatic escape from a prisoner-of-war camp during the Boer War, an account peppered with a host of colourful words, although where she had picked those up Jonas had no idea; or would she, as she ushered him into the long hallway of the flat, get straight to the point, asking him, all businesslike, whether he had seen any paintings by a young man called Håkon Bleken? 'With such a washed-out name,' she would say, 'that man must have a terrible hankering for colour!'

To Jonas Wergeland's credit, it must be said that, like his mother, he did not regard these multiple personalities as a sign of madness, as most other people did – people who did their utmost to have her locked up in an institution. To Jonas's mind, Jørgine was the perfect grandmother, with three deep creases in her brow which were constantly changing, rather like the trigrams, those three broken parallel lines found in the Chinese book of wisdom and divination, the *I Ching*; a grandmother who could be feeding the ducks one day, rambling on about this and that, to turn, the next day, into an astute, single-minded, steely patron of the arts. Not to mention her Churchill days, which were, for Jonas, absolute gala performances but which I regret I cannot go into here. What I would just like to make clear is that, all unwittingly, Jonas learned a very important lesson from his grandmother: that the inner nature of a human being is not as easily mapped out as all that, and that it is, in essence, pretty much unfathomable.

From the flat in Oscars gate, it was only a short walk for Jørgine Wergeland to a dimly-lit, smoke-filled establishment on Uranieborgveien called Restaurant Krølle, at that time a favourite haunt of many Oslo artists, writers and other nonconformist individualists who in later life would look back on those dingy premises with their hideous wrought-iron fittings and greasy walls with a good deal of nostalgia and indeed regarded it as one of their most important seats of learning; and it was here, in these subsequently so legendary surroundings – far more so than Theatercaféen – by listening in to the passionate discussions conducted over the beer glasses, that Jonas's grandmother picked up tips about promising young painters who would be prepared to sell their pictures for next to nothing, or a bottle of cheap whisky come to that. I know of many people who recall the old lady with the three deep and shifting creases in her brow as an eccentric feature of Krølle's – just ask the poet Stein Mehren, who spent several hours one evening conducting an evenly-matched conversation with Jonas's grandmother on the subject of non-figurative art, after which she generously – and this was most unusual for her patron of the arts persona – treated the gifted young poet to two of the house's traditional *smørbrød*: one with meatballs and one with bacon and egg.

It was after one of these long evenings among Krølle's Bohemian patrons that Jørgine invited Jonas to accompany her to a tenement in Gabels gate. They climbed right up to the top floor then made their way to the end of the airing loft where she knocked at the most Spartan of doors with a washbasin outside it. The door was opened by a young man with features which Jonas would instinctively have described as Roman; at first it looked like he might turn them away, but Jørgine Wergeland persuaded or as good as bullied him into eventually, rather apprehensively, allowing them to step inside a room, not very big, which seemed to Jonas to reek more of horse than of turpentine. This little room, with two skylights and a ladder leading to a sleeping platform, was home to the painter, his wife and their small baby. Jonas found it hard to imagine that anyone could live in such conditions, but maybe it was all part and parcel of being an artist who had, according to his grandmother, already had his pictures turned down several times for the Autumn Exhibition.

The painter told them that he had just returned from a visit to the royal stables, which were quite close by, where he had been making some sketches. A large anatomical model of a horse, with all of the musculature clearly defined, was set up on a big, home-made table. Out of the blue, Jørgine asked whether she could buy a couple of his paintings, and the young man with the Roman features, realizing that in the face of such perseverance there was nothing for it but to give in, nodded towards the wall on which his pictures, the majority of them quite small, were hung.

Jørgine Wergeland promptly proceeded to inspect the canvases and motioned to Jonas to take a look at them too.

And again . . . there was no mistaking it: when Jonas's eye fell on the picture on the easel, he had the feeling of a soft feather, 'as if from an angel's wing', being run all the way up his spine and coming to rest at the nape of his neck, making his hair stand on end and wringing a shudder from him. Jonas Wergeland would never find it possible to put this inner *frisson* into words and far be it from me to try, all I will say is that it had nothing to do with having a trained eye, nor was it subject to the taste of a particular day and age, or one specific place – he would later experience exactly the same thing when faced with works of art, old and new, from every corner of the globe, from Egyptian sculptures to acrylic paintings by the aborigines. Jonas Wergeland simply had an innate appreciation of perspective, balance, proportion, the play of colour – I am deliberately generalizing here, reluctant as I am to be drawn into pointless debates as to what makes for a good work of art.

The canvas on the easel depicted a group of horses and riders, with a large mirror in the background in which the riders were seen reflected, all executed in earth tones: ochre, umber, sienna, a tinge of Indian lake, but although the main impression was of brown, Jonas's eye was immediately caught by a shimmering light underlying the sombre, muted hues, a golden sheen which seemed to speak of an invisible energy. 'From the royal stables,' the painter said kindly, somewhat surprised by Jonas's absorption in the painting, going on to add: 'The horse is the one animal most closely akin to man.' When Jonas stepped right up close to the painting he noticed a number of unaccountably fine brush-strokes on the hindquarters of one of the horses, which, incredible as it may sound, offered him a glimpse into another dimension.

Jørgine needed only to look at Jonas. His face said it all. At the age of eight, Jonas Wergeland was an art connoisseur. He had no idea how this had come about, it just happened: he had a Geiger counter inside him that was triggered by fine works of art. He also picked out a landscape for his grandmother: 'from Torvø' they were later informed.

'I'll take them,' Jørgine announced without further ado. She counted out 1200 kroner and laid the banknotes on the table next to some blue jars. Jonas had the idea that the painter thought this was too much, that he was almost embarrassed. 'But you haven't signed them,' she said.

He signed the pictures. 'Frantz W.,' it said in ochre with a touch of white, this being long before the days when Widerberg opted for a palette of pure primary colours, simplified his name to Frans and became one of Norway's most highly acclaimed and best-selling painters, his pictures becoming so ubiquitous in the form of prints, calendars and posters in thousands of homes that they were well on the way to becoming archetypes in themselves, every bit as much as the archetypes he endeavoured to portray.

Later in life Jonas would wonder whether he had possessed this gift for evaluating pictures from infancy. However that may be, it was when he was with his grandmother that he became aware of it, and there is no doubt that here we see the roots of what many regard as Norway's greatest television talent of all time, namely, the ability to be able to tell right away when a picture is good, or *could be* good, or a scene, for that matter, in those instances where the pictures were to be shown on a screen. And, I might add, in years to come Jonas Wergeland would also make use of his remarkable inbuilt antenna when taking his exceedingly selective and *very* fruitful pick of Norway's women.

But at the age of eight this tingling between his shoulder-blades was not something to which he gave much thought – in any case he had no idea what use he could make of it, in real life as it were. In time his grandmother's interest in art also petered out, and she concentrated instead on perfecting her life as Winston Churchill, particularly in the years following the great man's death as if, at long last and with some relief, she could be the only Churchill alive. But during the years when his grandmother's art collecting was at its height, Jonas simply allowed her to take advantage of him, making no objection, obediently singling out a picture here and a picture there, perhaps because these gallery visits always wound up, as a reward, at the Studenten ice cream parlour. From that point of view, Jonas Wergeland was as easy to please as a sniffer dog when it is given a titbit for having sniffed out some concealed substance that it alone was capable of finding. When you come right down to it, and when you are only eight years old, there is nothing to beat that work of art known as a banana split, served in a bowl shaped like a half-moon, in that childhood paradise on the corner of Karl Johans gate, a place which even smelled as heaven must smell: of halved bananas, chopped almonds, strawberry jam and hot chocolate.

The Strangest Thing

I could, with some justification, say that it was the connoisseur in Jonas Wergeland who first discovered Margrete Boeck since here too – although he had no notion why it should happen when he looked at a girl, and one with a sliver of glass stuck in her nostril at that – he was conscious of a quite indisputable tingle between his shoulder-blades. A few days later there could be no doubt about it: Jonas was in love, and this was *the* great love, that 'once in a lifetime' when the nerves are given an extra turn of the screw, and you are knocked almost senseless by emotion, wandering the face of the Earth like one great feeling encased in skin.

There is nothing, absolutely nothing, to touch that first real falling in love. Take the most glorified romantic experiences of adult life – and none of them bears the remotest resemblance to the incandescent quality, not to say supernatural dimensions, that are the mark of that first breathtaking love. And the thing I like most about this phenomenon is that, at this stage of their lives, boys, even the most ruthless careerists in the making, actually take time and exercise patience so that the innocent path from a girl's fingertips to those indescribable square centimetres between her thighs can take, say, a whole year. This is due not only to a becoming shyness and lack of self-assurance, it owes as much to an awareness, stemming from a God-given natural instinct, of the unique and never-to-be-repeated nature of this experience, which leads them to do all they can to prolong the delight. Incredible as it may sound, even boys of this age realize that love is more than just a physical thing, that above all else it has to do with longing.

After the fatal – or felicitous, depending on how you look at it – bicycle crash of the spring, Jonas gradually became more and

more infatuated with Margrete, the new girl who established
herself in record time as the kingpin of her class, not least after
they finished reading a tear-jerker of a story from their school
reader, written by Dikken Zwilgmeyer, about a poor girl whom
everybody teased and who finally died, whereupon Margrete
thumped her desk with her fist and declared that nobody had any
bloody right to go writing such a load of sentimental rubbish.
And so, following the accepted procedure, a few weeks after the
beginning of sixth grade, and following a summer break during
which Jonas had done little else but lie flat on his back on Hvaler,
just thinking and thinking and *thinking* about her – while the
Beatles' 'Can't Buy Me Love' played on the transistor radio and
not even a heated summer debate regarding topless bathing suits
could take his mind off her – he dispatched a chum to speak to
one of Margrete's girlfriends, a middleman, not unlike the sort
employed in matters of diplomacy, and let it be known that he
was 'nuts about her', as the parlance of the day had it, as if it
were generally recognized that love and madness are adjoining
rooms with extremely porous walls. And then it was merely a
matter of waiting, with his blood racing through his veins at
twice its normal speed, until Margrete's friend came back, after
the obligatory and fairly protracted pause for thought to
announce that, okay, Margrete wouldn't mind going out with
Jonas.

With that, Jonas Wergeland was swept off into the most intox-
icating months of his life, days and weeks which would later
come to seem like a unique blend of intensity, hyped-up emotions and, above all, magic because, from the day and hour that
Margrete said yes, the whole world simply stretched out at his
feet like a red carpet, or perhaps I should say a Persian carpet.
Nothing, absolutely nothing, could go wrong.

So there they are, on an autumn day in Grorud, Jonas
Wergeland and Margrete Boeck, strolling through a wood like
golden amber on their way up to Lilloseter, where Jonas treats
them both to, of all things, beef stew and root beer as if to mark
the end of childhood. It is on the way down, when they are just
about level with Aurevann Lake, its smooth waters mirroring the
golden-yellow woods, that Margrete, with a deliberately casual

swing of her arm, finds his hand for the first time and they hold hands, the concrete proof that a boy and a girl are actually going steady, and she continues to hold his hand, triumphantly, boldly, all the way past Steinbruvannet and down past the blocks of flats on Bergensveien, where they are observed by quite a few of their classmates, and the word is out once and for all: it's official, they are going steady, they are a couple, they are sweethearts.

I know it is banal and that I am repeating myself, but it is nonetheless necessary to restate the fact: you can take the most sublime act of love – and the list, as I am sure most people would admit, is extremely short – and compare it with the first time you felt the fingers of a person of the opposite sex curl round your own fingers and, not least, the *thrill* of those seconds, and we all know which one would come out the winner. I think I am safe in saying that many people would give a great deal to be able to relive that moment, the first time one holds hands with a child-hood sweetheart, making contact not only with the palm of a small hand but with an ocean of strange warm feelings.

Jonas soon becomes aware that he is unbeatable. He plays what they call 'pigeon rings', more rightly known as 's's and c's', the classic game being 'ten plus ten', so called because of the way the rings can be neatly linked together to form a 'tenner' bunch in which the finely-tuned shooter bunch stands out, sprawled across the tarmac like a streamlined sports car, but Jonas also plays 'fifty-fifty' with huge bunches that fly across the play-ground; he never misses, can hit anything, the trick being to sight along the left foot; corridors full of schoolchildren looking on, the first-graders in particular in open-mouthed awe of daredev-ils who would risk staking five rings on one game, one shot; gasp-ing every time his chain slams with hair-raising precision into the other guy's bunch from the most impossible distances; he wins tons of these multi-coloured plastic rings that were all the rage, collectors' items back then, tosses them to the first-graders like small change to beggars, he can afford it, because he is unbeat-able, he is a wizard, jumps the triple, hovering in mid-air as if Mercury himself had loaned him his winged shoes; becomes the first man to cover the distance between the two white marker lines in the playground in six strides, an amazing feat, and in rounders he comes *this close* to doing what no one in the whole history of the school has yet managed to do, the unattainable mythical dream, to break a window in the pavilion at the far end, striking the ball in a way that would have drawn an approving nod from Babe Ruth himself.

Meanwhile, he goes around holding hands with Margrete, it is enough just to hold hands, a joy that transcends all else, simply to hold hands, hold her unique hand, a lucky rabbit's foot, during recess, or to walk hand-in-hand with her across Trondheimsveien to Tallaksen's, where they alternate between buying such exotic delights as peanuts in their shells, two nuts in one shell, just like them, and Sweet Mint chewing gum, its wrapper printed with hearts, which they blow up into enormous pink balloons that will never burst, that are in danger of carrying them heavenwards. Even in a situation where the odds are stacked against him, Jonas manages to turn it to his advantage: a dinner at the home of Mr and Mrs Gjermund Boeck when Margrete's mother appears dressed in what is, to Jonas's mind, a hideous Mary Quant outfit, black and white with an ultra-short skirt, and otherwise blends into the background, thus making her father seem that much more predominant, red in the face and sporting a gaudy Hawaiian shirt. Having instantly sized Jonas up as a potentially subversive element within the family's well-ordered dictatorship, he makes a point of delivering a long and, Jonas has to admit, impassioned speech on the necessity of bombing Vietnam – bloody Communist swine – back to the Stone Age and then some before – and this is where, by sheer coincidence, Jonas's luck turns – putting on a record by Duke Ellington, thereby giving Jonas the opportunity to make a few tentative remarks on Jimmy Blanton's all too early demise and deliver a brief panegyric on alto-sax player Johnny Hodges's solo on 'It Don't Mean a Thing', with the result that the urbane Gjermund Boeck settles back on the sofa, somewhat impressed, thinking damned if he isn't starting to take to the boy.

This is followed by the slow progression of a drama wrapped in the great political dramas – both domestic and international – all of which are, of course, totally irrelevant as far as our young players are concerned: namely, the physical drama being played out between Jonas and Margrete. It is New Year's Eve, under the relatively close supervision of a friend's parents, and as the corks on the champagne-soda bottles pop, she *embraces* him; she, Margrete, opens wide her foreign-made beige cape like a gate and pulls him to her, hugs him tight against her lovely blue dress for several seconds, so tightly that he can feel her body, her curves, her bone-structure, that combination of hard and soft, against his own body and wishes that they could stand like this forever, wrapped inside a beige cape, on a New Year's Eve, on a veranda, breast to breast, in a close embrace that would never be broken, until at last he lifts her into the air while, in a fit of pagan ecstasy, the people of Norway blow millions of kroner on painting the skies around them red and green and yellow.

But it had to end, because it was winter and, even though Jonas has never bowed to the national imperative as regards skiing, hates snow in fact, he goes skiing with Margrete, dons that most laughable article of clothing, knickerbockers – referred to in Norwegian, even more laughably, simply as *knickers* – and this he endures only because she is even more hopeless on skis than him, if that were possible – Bangkok not exactly being renowned for its skiing – and, what is more, because she looks so beautiful skiing, or trudging along, past Sørskogen, in an old grey anorak, with frost on her hair and eyebrows, to sit at Sinober, with glowing cheeks and fathomless blue eyes, drinking hot blackcurrant. Jonas not only endures it; by some miracle he actually manages, for the first time ever, to stay upright going down the lethal slopes to Movatn Lake, outdoing himself in swerving elegantly around those blasted dogs that are always liable to show up when you least expect it, in the middle of the track, on the worst bends, because all of a sudden he is a wizard, unbeatable, even on skis, a fact which they celebrate by hugging one another again, right out there in the forest, surrounded by snow and ice, as if wishing to check whether it really is true, or as good as the last time, or to see if they can make the snow on the trees melt just by standing underneath them for long enough, breast to breast, arms around one another, skis and poles entangled.

It was as if Jonas's luck transmitted itself to the nation as a whole that winter. Take, for instance, the time when he and

Margrete went to watch the speed-skating at Bislett, and Per Ivar – Per Ivar Moe, that is – won the world championship: Per Ivar of Oslo Skating Club, the man with the vaguely Mongolian features whom Jonas had even seen once, putting up a neon sign at Grorud shopping centre. They stand there, Margrete leaning back against Jonas's chest, and watch Per Ivar skimming round in a dazzlingly white track top, a white knight, with people shouting 'Moe, Moe, Moe' and not, as one might think, 'Mao, Mao, Mao' like a people on the other side of the world, although here, too, in Norway, there is talk of a revolution, a skating revolution, stage-managed by a man called Stein Johnson, and I would like to make it clear that this was an extraordinary event, inasmuch as it was the first and only occasion on which Jonas Wergeland allowed himself to be swept away by a crowd and even go so far as to roar like a man possessed. It was during the ecstatic singing of 'Victory is Ours' that Margrete, without warning, took his head between her hands and kissed him, right there and then, in the middle of Bislett stadium, an arena that reeks of chauvinism and Norwegian triumphs: and not only Norwegian, come to that – in the summer of that year the Australian Ron Clarke would set a new world record there, in the 10,000 metres, during an international tournament, the first man to do it in under twenty-eight minutes, so Jonas could not help but feel, when that day came around, that it was owing to their presence there, their kiss, months earlier; that they had, as it were, blessed the stadium, left it sprinkled with magic dust or something of the sort. After all, it is not every Norwegian who can say he was kissed for the first time at Bislett stadium to the strains of 'Victory is Ours' during a tournament in which a Norwegian athlete won the day.

At least, Jonas *thought* he had been kissed because they were still only in the first phase of kissing, the very nature of the kiss being prolonged, like a menu with lots and lots of courses until they reached what is termed 'French kissing', a form which, I venture to point out, is by no means regarded as the supreme kissing experience, or main course, in all parts of the world but which certainly in Grorud, at that age represented the ultimate thrill, regarded almost as a status symbol; everyone knew that the record was held by Hansie and Randy Ruth who had French-kissed non-stop for forty minutes and then some. In other words, what Jonas discovered – at a time when he was still unbeatable, a wizard, so much so that if he came by some lads throwing snow-balls at the ridge of a relatively high gable-end, he needed only to make one single snowball because he *knew* that it would hit the apex of the gable dead-on and not only that: he would strike it slantwise, effectively blocking it off and leaving no loophole for the others – what he, or they, discovered was the tongue's place in the mouth and that it could be used for more than talking: an avenue which they spent months exploring, even when they lay entwined and laughing in a snowdrift after being forced off the track by others in the gang during some pretty foolhardy sledge rides from Lilloseter down to the barrier at Ammerud, where the lethal iced-over snow of late winter sent sparks flying from the runners. Not only did they discover the tongue they discovered the ears and the throat and the back of the neck, and every time was like the first.

Then spring came to Grorud, with melting snow and kids building dams in the streets, the slap of skipping ropes and hop-scotch squares chalked out on dry patches of tarmac; snotty toddlers in wellingtons parked in the sandpits with diggers and bulldozers and the air smelling as only spring air can. Jonas was riding a wave of success, winning fabulous sums of money at pitch-and-toss, five øre coins or sometimes one kroner, zooming through the air like remote-controlled flying saucers, gluing themselves to the line or sticking to the penknife, coming up heads time and time again. He was a wizard; he was unbeatable. He sat in a wicker chair in Grorud cinema, and it was here, during a film entitled *Home From the Hill* starring Robert Mitchum, that Jonas gently, very, very gently, laid his hand on Margrete's thigh for the first time, and when she did not react, negatively I mean; when she did not turn a hair but just sat there with her eyes fixed on a nonchalant Robert Mitchum, Jonas stroked her thigh gently, but anything but nonchalantly, back and forth, and when she did not make any objection to this either Jonas had to let his hand lie still to save her from hearing the pounding of his heart.

For a couple of warm weeks at the beginning of June they spent their time by the pool at Badedammen with Margrete's new portable Bambino record-player, listening to *Beatles for Sale*, and it was here, in a spot that they had all to themselves, towards the end of the day when they are lying stretched out, replete with sunshine, swimming, custard creams and orangeade, that a girl who just happens to be wearing the most gorgeous yellow bikini in the whole world runs her hand for the first time over Jonas Wergeland's body, and he is struck by something he has never noticed: that the skin of the human body is made up of about a million erogenous zones, that the skin is one vast and quivering sexual organ which all but bursts at the touch of her hand.

The Sunday before Midsummer's Eve, a summer gala day, organized by the Grorud School boys' brass band, is held in Sangerparken on the banks of Badedammen: cheering crowds and a procession of lorries decorated with flowers and lilac and birch leaves and packed with kids in fancy-dress, transformed into a crowd of cowboys and indians, gypsies and pirates – a proper carnival with a real community spirit and, above all, a truly *festive* spirit which leaves the slightly hysterical and forced Norwegian attempts in the early eighties to imitate the Latin Americans totally in the shade – with the band playing and the choir singing among the trunks of the pine trees and Jonas sweeping the board on the shooting range, raising the rifle and planting each of the five red-flighted little darts smack in the middle of their respective targets, making Margrete, standing at his side in a white summer frock, laugh: laugh at her boyfriend who is a sharpshooter and he didn't even know it, he is a wizard, he is unbeatable, scoring a bull's-eye so many times that the man in charge of the booth has to call a halt because Jonas has the aim of a Zen master or is just so happy that he could hit a target in the dark. Then, with their arms laden with daft prizes, they wander across to the dance-floor where, some years previously, Jonas's sister Rakel had danced to the music of Big Chief's jazz band with none other than Roald Aas on the day she was crowned Grorud's gala queen: Roald Aas, who won the gold medal in the 1500 metres at the Olympics in Squaw Valley and

who, more to the point as far as Jonas's sister was concerned, was
as dashing as a prince from the *Arabian Nights*. But right now it
is Five-Times Nilsen and Tango-Thorvaldsen who are strutting
their stuff up on the bandstand, the latter regarding this as the
highlight of the year since it not only gives him the chance to
show off the latest fashion in gents shoes but he also gets to
dance with every lady from Hukenveien all the way down to
Grorud station, a route followed roughly now by Jonas and Margrete before they stop at the top of Teppabakken. And it is here,
on a bright summer evening, while they are kissing behind the
church after the local gala day celebrations, that Jonas Wergeland
ventures to slip his hand down inside her pants; and at this point,
when it comes to this occurrence behind the church, up against
those solid blocks of Grorud granite, with Jonas's light and fleeting brush of Margrete's vulva – and I deliberately use such a
high-flown word as vulva – that I opt out because there are no
words and no metaphors to cover this: every boy's first fingertip
contact with a girl's vulva. There is a limit to my omniscience
and this is it, so I will have to leave them to drift onwards, Jonas
and Margrete, hand in hand, towards the last days of school
and the green report cards, in which Jonas is given nothing but
M's for merit without having lifted a finger as if this were a
comment on the whole of that one, long delicious experience:
mmmmmmmmmmm.

The Cathedral Builder

There was, of course, a great temptation to build the programme on Gustav Vigeland around the series of sculptures depicting love in all of its widely differing phases found in Vigelandsparken in the Frogner district of Oslo; and in particular around the Monolith itself, in the pale-grey granite of which both the first tentative advance and copulation's greedy embrace find form. Just *how* tempting this was for Jonas Wergeland can be appreciated only by one privy to a certain occurrence – a boy leaning against the granite wall of a church with his hand on the most intimate part of a girl's anatomy – in other words, one who can see the connection, as it were, between stone and stone.

Wergeland did, however, retain the notion of something sacred by basing the whole programme on Vigeland's visit to Lincoln Cathedral in England. Around the turn of the century Vigeland was involved in the restoration of Nidaros Cathedral in Trondheim, creating sculptures in the Gothic style, and it was largely on account of this work that he set off on an extensive tour of France and England to study the great cathedrals and, more especially, their decoration. The interesting thing about this spell abroad is that it encompasses some of the most productive months in Vigeland's life as is indeed evident from the sketches, around 1500 of them, which he made during the course of the trip. To Jonas it seemed that the Gothic architecture not only fired Vigeland's imagination, sparking off a whole host of ideas and schemes, but in fact provided the key to an understanding of the man and his most significant work: Vigeland Park. In his programme Jonas took this angle to the extreme by implying that all of Vigeland's subsequent work might conceivably have first seen the light of day in Lincoln.

The pivotal sequence, to which the programme kept returning, therefore showed Gustav Vigeland in the late August of
1901 sitting in the midst of Lincoln's mighty cathedral, peering
through a pair of binoculars at the various figures on the walls
and up under the roof, dwelling especially on the little angels in
the choir as if these could lend him inspiration; with Wergeland
cutting in the odd black-and-white still from Nidaros Cathedral
and Vigeland's sculptures there. By this means, Jonas also gave
some sense of a comparison between the two cathedrals in
Lincoln and Trondheim which served, in a way, to illustrate an
inherent Norwegian characteristic, something to do with the
scale: how everything in Norway is smaller and how everything
in Norway is merely an imitation of something else. There
were those who maintained – unjustly – that by juxtaposing a
Norwegian cathedral and an English cathedral in this way Jonas
also succeeded in expressing some of his own feelings about the
relationship between Gustav Vigeland and, say, an artist of the
stature of August Rodin.

For the greater part of the programme, however, Vigeland was
seen sitting in Lincoln Cathedral, his binoculars resting on his
stomach, drawing – drawing and drawing like a man possessed as
if this Gothic interior were acting as a catalyst for his genius,
giving rise to a torrent of ideas. Jonas had a steady stream of
people pass by Vigeland as he sat there in the middle of the
cathedral – children, adolescents, men and women, adults with
children, old folk – and showed, with close-ups of the sketch
pad, how Vigeland drew them or took his outset in them, and
how each and every one formed the rudiments of some well-
known figure, which Jonas demonstrated by dissolving from the
sketch to the finished sculpture as it can be seen in Vigelandsparken or elsewhere. Jonas was particularly pleased with
the moment when the church organ suddenly surged into life,
whereupon Vigeland promptly began to sketch out, as if in a
trance, the outlines of his great fountain, the one now standing
at the centre of the park.

In this, the main body of the programme, Jonas also introduced an experimental ploy which was to crop up throughout
the series, a spot which he called 'Cross-Connections', the idea

being that, one way or another, the central character always crossed paths with one or more of the subjects of other programmes, which was often an 'impossible' person. This was Jonas Wergeland's way of alluding to influences that run counter to conventional ways of thinking. Thus in the programme on Vigeland he had both Henrik Ibsen and Edvard Grieg – both in the masterly guise of Normann Vaage, of course – stroll past Vigeland as he sat there in the heart of the cathedral with his binoculars resting on his stomach, whereupon Vigeland, this time working with clay, working like magic – the speed of execution achieved by trick photography – promptly proceeded to model busts of them, as indeed he did in real life. But Wergeland also had the subject of another programme come wandering anachronistically past, to be reproduced in bust form, namely the fashion designer Per Spook, who also exchanged a few remarks with Vigeland regarding the significance of the sketch and the idea of the mannequin as sculpture in motion, together with a few words on the subject of permanence and transience.

Jonas Wergeland's prime aim with this programme was, nonetheless, to show how the whole of Vigelandsparken was nothing less than a secularised cathedral. If there was one thing Vigeland had learned on his 'Gothic tour', from standing in all of those vast cathedrals, it was the way in which each individual element merged into the greater whole.

During the planning stages Jonas himself was surprised, so surprised that he could hardly credit it, by how much the park had in common with a Gothic church, and Lincoln Cathedral in particular; how the strict axial design of the park could easily be interpreted as an echo of the long church building. By dint of a slow dissolve, to the strains of organ music, from an aerial shot of the interior of Lincoln Cathedral to an aerial shot of Vigeland Park, filmed from a helicopter, the viewer's eyes were opened to the similarity between the two and to the image of the park as a perfect open-air cathedral in which the great wrought-iron gates at the main entrance correspond to the front door of Lincoln cathedral or, possibly more correctly, the translucent stained glass window above the door; the bridge representing the nave of the church and the Children's Playground, a side-chapel of sorts.

At the intersection of Lincoln's transept and choir one finds the organ and in the park this corresponds perfectly with the fountain, encircled, what is more, by a labyrinthine design of the sort found inlaid in the floors of medieval churches. But what about the Monolith? Besides being akin to a tower, the Monolith and the circular steps leading up to it are exactly like the high altar in the choir of the cathedral, the only difference being that people have taken the place of the angels. The Wheel of Life behind this could possibly be likened to the east window in the choir or perhaps an altarpiece. Jonas even found an echo of the Lincoln Imp, the grotesque little carving on one of the cathedral pillars, in Vigeland's serpentine figures on the pillars by the bridge. So for Jonas Wergeland, Vigelandsparken suddenly became a church without walls or roof, a cathedral built around everyday life, in which man is seen depicted at all of life's sometimes weird and wonderful stages, with the Monolith speaking of a bond between this man and the universe.

The main point of this comparison was, however, to illustrate the hidden Gothic element in the Vigeland Park sculptures: the very thing which, as far as Jonas was concerned, gave them the necessary twist and precluded any naturalistic misapprehension whereby Vigeland would be credited with an all too facile imitative zeal. The more walks Jonas took through Vigeland's park, through that fantastical setting, especially at night in winter, the more he was struck by the wry aspect of many of the sculptures, individual figures and groups; there were times in fact when, in their vulgarity, one might almost say brutality, they all but tipped over into caricature or grotesquerie, not least when viewed as a whole, giving as they did the impression of a swarming mass. If there was one thing Vigeland's sculptures were not, it was smooth and lifelike. Instead they were so rough that in the groups of stone figures you could almost see the marks of the chisel. By and large, Vigeland's style was – like the Gothic – not all that remarkable; it was more the substance and the feeling behind it that hit one in the eye, most of it – again like the Gothic – extremely naïve, such that it spoke straight to the heart. For Jonas, this Gothic touch saved the park as a whole from appearing pompous and stiff. Instead its strength lay in the profusion of images; the park acquired the air of a fable and as such it also functioned as a springboard for the imagination of the strolling onlooker.

I have to admit that Gustav Vigeland is, to put it mildly, not one of my favourite sculptors, but I believe that Jonas Wergeland acquitted himself very well in the difficult, not to say impossible, task of saying something thought-provoking about Vigelandsparken, considering the enormous popularity, the almost banal place this artist occupies in the hearts of most Norwegians, as was proved quite conclusively some years back when the theft of a small and in itself not particularly exceptional sculpture caused as much of a stir as an average-sized natural disaster. Although the park is a popular tourist attraction, I venture to point out that by no means all foreign visitors find it as fascinating; in fact a few have even gone so far as to say that Vigelandsparken is the sort of complex that Albert Speer might have built for Hitler had the Germans not lost the war.

Precisely in order to reflect the varying, sometimes eccentric, notions of his heroes in all of his programmes, Jonas Wergeland ran a spot which he called 'Three Off the Street', in many ways a comic spot in which, apparently at random, he stopped three foreigners – played by the same three actors throughout the series – and tested their knowledge of the programme's subject. In the Vigeland programme, the first person Jonas stopped, next to the Wheel of Life, was a 'Japanese tourist' hung about with all the paraphernalia of his photography fetish, who declared in broken Norwegian that Vigeland must have been a Buddhist, for one thing because he was so adamant in his assertion that life was a circle and for another because he had created the entire park in the form of a stupa. Had Jonas by any chance seen Borobudur?

Next came a 'Dane', a typical academic, who talked non-stop while trying in vain to find his way through the labyrinth in front of the fountain and fervently asserted that Vigeland was, first and foremost, a writer and that no one had written better about art than he. He then proceeded to read, or rather recite from memory, some caustic passages, truly amazing, from Vigeland's letters: on the way in which dim-witted art critics misinterpreted the Icelandic-Danish sculptor Bertel Thorvaldsen, and on the quite unique power of Phidias's sculptures for the Parthenon on the Acropolis. Had Jonas ever heard anything like it? Could anyone possibly put it better?

Finally, Jonas Wergeland approached an 'Italian lady', an excessively sensual character, who was standing on the bridge fondling the penis of one of the bronze statues, shiny from the touch of many fingers. After a volley of Italian adjectives she explained that what she really liked best of all about Vigeland were his utterly amazing, almost perverted, figures of fable, the majority of them no more than plastic sketches; she then went on to reel them off, from the woman leaning draped over the back of a panther with her head in its mouth to the rearing ox with two naked women tied by their hair to its horns, while shots of these figures were, needless to say, being flashed onto the screen.

Thus the programme of this, in the eyes of so many Norwegians, monumental artist concluded with an image of Vigeland as a minimalist, with those small, fabulous figures testifying to Vigeland's true gift: his indomitable restless imagination.

Personally I find it a little odd – and odd is just the word for it – that Jonas Wergeland did not somehow or other manage to slip in the fact that, in Vigeland's work, love consists mainly of pain, and that he did not include his own favourite sculpture; because I can tell you right here and now that his favourite, or rather his raw spot, among all of Vigeland's works is the one entitled 'Orpheus and Eurydice', which depicts a man on his knees, reaching out at full stretch for a woman who is slipping out of his arms. Jonas could never look at this sculpture without thinking of Margrete and the incident on a certain skating rink, an incident which also brought him close to what Vigeland attempted to portray in the relief entitled 'Hell': a representation of the suffering of man in all its phases.

The Bomber Man Cometh

The summer holidays came and went, they moved up into seventh grade, and still Jonas Wergeland went around hand in hand with Margrete Boeck, so aglow with something that went beyond mere happiness that even the teachers on playground duty had to smile and give their bunches of keys an extra rattle behind their backs. So Jonas's sense of being a wizard, of being unbeatable, was every bit as strong, a fact which he proved, not least, by doubling every single record set on the pinball machine in Gro Snack Bar, again together with Margrete, one button each. Jonas wondered whether it was the attraction between him and her that produced the reversed magnetic field which was responsible for the fact that the gleaming ball-bearing simply would not drop through the hole at the bottom and looked set to go on dancing between the rubber bands of the targets for ever, while the machine pinged and flashed, and the digit counters whirled round so fast that the machine seemed on the point of breaking down or exploding. They celebrated their pinball wizardry by treating themselves to ice cream cones or small bottles of Coke with straws and putting more coins in the jukebox so they could listen to 'Rock'n'roll Music' or 'Eight Days a Week' ringing out over the Formica-topped tables of the little snack bar on Trondheimsveien yet again, with that wonderful, slightly fuzzy sound that only a jukebox can make, while they laughed up their sleeves at the bigger lads showing off outside, revving up their Tempo motorbikes for the benefit of a bunch of girls with beehive hairdos and about a pound of chewing gum all-told between their teeth.

The autumn sped past, as always, with election day and – to the extent that they took any note of it – an epoch-making victory for the Conservatives; with scrumping for apples, in which Jonas's daring reached new heights when he actually managed to pinch two beautiful green apples from the garden of the ever-vigilant and not exactly mild-mannered 'Hawkeye' Larsen; and dark evenings with a nip in the air, ideal for long goodbyes, closely entwined with your back against the granite blocks of Grorud Church.

Jonas Wergeland and Margrete Boeck were the most loving couple in the Grorud Valley, and there was nothing, absolutely nothing to suggest that the sand was running out of the hourglass of their bliss or, perhaps I ought to say, the last ball-bearing would soon drop down the hole between the two bottom flippers. Then came the fateful day at the skating rink. Suddenly it was over, and in all probability it was the abrupt, almost explosive, way that it ended that led Jonas to pin the blame on the Oslo bomber.

For those who have forgotten, or did not experience it, I feel I ought to say something about this phantom or whatever one wants to call him, who terrorized the citizens of Oslo during the year in which Jonas and Margrete drifted about, almost weightless with love; an individual, soon known simply by the thriller-style name of 'the bomber', who shook Norway's capital to its foundations from February right through the spring by setting cunning and lethal booby-traps in various parts of Oslo so that no one felt safe, not even in Grorud, and an entire populace went around in fear, keeping their eyes peeled for strings tied to gates, stretched across footpaths or between cars and lifting their feet good and high in dark alleyways. I believe that this period represents a milestone in the consciousness of many Oslo folk inasmuch as the bomber unwittingly induced in them a peculiarly existential state of mind in which each step they took was a leap in the dark that might bring them down on his deadly spider's web. The one thing that we all know, deep down, was suddenly a concrete reality: one false step, and life would never be the same again.

But this possibility – the chance of getting a shower of shrapnel in your back at any minute – did not scare Jonas and Margrete; on the contrary, it only enhanced their happiness as if their romance were flourishing during wartime or under a state of emergency. And then, just as unexpectedly, Oslo was rid of wires and explosives. The police thought the man must be dead.

Winter set in brutally early – this alone should perhaps have served as a warning to Jonas, but at the end of November, with the temperature at an all-time low of minus sixteen degrees, he presented Margrete with a rolled-gold locket on which Aunt Laura had engraved an exquisitely lettered 'Jonas' as if this piece of jewellery could shield them from the cold or exert some sort of white magic that would make her his forever. One evening when they were propped up against the church wall, their arms wrapped tightly around one another to keep warm, he hung it around her neck like a medal and said: 'Gold in love'.

And then what happens? The bomber returns, that's what – the bomber strikes again. Just when Jonas is thinking that he could not be any happier, he trips over an invisible cord, one of the bomber's tripwires; except that this particular wire is not reported in any newspaper, and neither is the shattering explosion. But for years afterwards Jonas Wergeland was to be haunted by the memory of the bomber and the thought of that day.

It was an evening just before Christmas, and they were at the ice rink. Jonas cherished, as I said earlier, something approaching a hatred of winter, the only part of it he could stand was the skating and not only because Roald Aas had danced with his sister. There was something about the sheen of the ice, particularly under the floodlights in the evening, which fascinated him; and something about going round the turns, feeling the centrifugal force. He also liked the atmosphere in the cloakroom of the clubhouse, where you could buy beef broth, hot and strong, from the guy who spent the rest of his time swanning about, collecting entrance money in a bag like the ones used by the bus conductors, leaving you with the impression that you were going on a journey. I ought also to mention that all of this took place during what was a golden era in Norwegian skating history, a time when Norwegian skaters had to fight over the three places on the winners' podium, and boys – incredible as it may seem today – wanted racing skates for Christmas.

They had just finished playing a game of tag on the inner rink, the girls with white covers over their figure-skates with most of them wearing those helmet-shaped crocheted hats which were all the rage that year and never again, when Jonas – in a fit of hubris or, more correctly, in his eagerness to show Margrete that there is at least one winter sport that he is good at – hits on the idea of doing the 5,000 metres, and, as if that weren't enough, he challenges a guy from the Labour Skating Club, who happens to glide by at that moment, using an ostentatious catlike technique.

The guy from the LSC is only too pleased to take Jonas on, is happy to get a bit of practice; he grins at Jonas's presumption; grins at Margrete, who doesn't seem too wild about the idea of this race, as they get off their marks in the 5,000 metres, a bit of an improvised start, since they are both skating in the same lane. After setting a pretty stiff pace in the first lap, the boy from LSC glances over his shoulder, to find to his surprise that Jonas is still on his tail; he does not know that Jonas is a wizard, unbeatable, and that Jonas really *can* skate, that he even likes to skate, practises a gently swaying style and has long since become so fast that he can skate right round a turn without taking any ordinary strokes in between; he remembers the first time he got the stride right all the way round, the feeling of breaking the sound barrier. The rink staff have started playing music over the loudspeakers, they have put on the autumn's new release, the Beatles' *Help* album, and it will take the boys almost as long to do the twelve and a half laps of the 5,000 metres as it takes to play the first side of the album. They skim on across the ice, Jonas ten metres behind the LSC guy. Jonas knows he has to take it easy, make each move with the minimum of effort – *And now my life is changed in oh, so many ways, my independence seems to vanish in the haze* – they are skating almost in step, gliding smoothly, swinging round the turns, the other guy in his smart green and black club colours, the letters on his back, close-fitting 'devil' cap and skin-tight top, Jonas in a weird, amateurish – but nonetheless lucky – outfit: knickerbockers like those worn by cross-country skier Harald Grønningen, a jersey knitted by Rakel in a pattern similar to the one in which alpine skier Stein Eriksen was often photographed and a dark-blue woollen hat with a little white bobble of the sort worn by ski-jumpers, most notably by Toralf Engan. Even Jonas's clothing testifies to the fact that he is unbeatable, a wizard, as he glides round and round, staying loose to prevent stiffening up, both hands behind his back, he glances towards the gang of girls standing in a cluster on the inner rink – *Were you telling lies? Ah, the night before* – knows that they are watching, sees Margrete – *Was I so unwise? Ah, the night before* – Jonas Wergeland is doing the 5,000 metres on the Grorud circuit, he cannot put a foot wrong, although he really isn't in the right form for this, but he finds his form nonetheless, has no trouble maintaining his speed, he's a wizard, unbeatable, he hardly needs to try, it's as if the glare of the floodlights were propelling him round; he swings his right arm out towards the entrance, relishes the sense of physical control, tilts his weight over to take full advantage of the curve, feels the centrifugal force helping him round and into the next long stretch, skates lap after lap under the floodlights, gliding from side to side, perfectly balanced – *Gather round all you clowns, let me hear you say, 'Hey, you've got to hide your love away'* – shaves the verge of snow on the turns, glides on and on, as one of the girls takes a few dance steps towards them on her figure-skates and shouts 'Come on, Jonas!'; he revels in the feel of the skate blade on the smooth ice, freshly sprayed, the crisp crackle; he makes the most of each glide, knows that he must not push it, endeavours to keep his push-off soft but springy, is starting to feel the air tearing at his lungs, can tell it won't be long before his back is begging to be allowed to straighten up – *oh, yes, you told me, you don't want my lovin' any more, that's when it hurt me, and feeling like this I just can't go on any more* – skates on and on, pushing off, catching sight of his own tracks in the ice, it's like something is wrong, he has lost his way, gone round in circles, but he is still ten metres behind, lap after lap, knows that the other guy ought to be in better form, but Jonas is skating on willpower, dredging up strength from way down in the basement, as the jargon has it, catches a whiff of beef broth, glances at Margrete in the midst of the cluster of girls, locks onto the heels of the LSC guy, notes that his opponent's stride is shortening, he is looking down at the tips of his skates, a bad sign according to radio commentator

Knut Bjørnsen; one more lap and Jonas is breathing down his neck – *I don't wanna say that I've been unhappy with you, but as from today, well, I've seen somebody that's new* – it's all very well to say that Jonas ought to have realized that the songs which are ringing out across the ice, especially when taken as whole, could never bode well. Then, just as he passes his opponent in the crossover lane, exhausted, but happy and proud, only half a lap from the finish, with the Beatles chanting out the message, loud and clear – *you're gonna lose that girl, yes, yes, you're gonna lose that girl, you're gonna looooooooooooose that girl* – some sixth sense tells Jonas Wergeland that this is going to go wrong, even though he is going to win, beating the LSC guy – who cannot believe his eyes – by ten metres. Jonas is coming out of the final turn, which he skims round beautifully, one arm swinging loose, picturing himself in the Classic Norwegian Position. And what, you may ask, exactly is the Classic Norwegian Position? Well, the Classic Norwegian Position is that assumed by Knut Johannesen, pictured on the turn in the 10,000 metres at the Olympics in Squaw Valley in 1960, when he took the gold and set a new world record, wearing that timeless white jersey with the Norwegian flag over the heart, and with his body – thanks mainly to the line of his right leg – extending upwards from the ice to form a perfect diagonal, an image which is to many Norwegians what the statue of a discus thrower is to the Greeks: it doesn't get any more beautiful or more aesthetically pleasing than that – and just as Jonas is picturing himself being photographed in the Classic Norwegian Position, he catches a glimpse of Margrete walking off through the gate, and then she is gone.

Yes, Margrete was gone. Later, Jonas felt sure that it was all the fault of the circle. The repetition. That this repetition was a kind of death. As if by letting himself be manipulated into whirling round and round like that he had unscrewed something

Margrete is gone, and while Jonas is standing by the gate, trying to regain his breath, Margrete's chum comes over – like an angel of death, he thinks to himself, even before she gets to him – picking her way because of her skate guards: 'Margrete's breaking it off,' she says.

Jonas stands there, watching the steam from his own breath. Then he says, the way one does, amazingly, manage to say at such moments: 'What do I care?' For years he was to wonder how he could have come up with such an inane choice of words. 'What do I care?'

What do you do when you are desperate?

Jonas's mind is a complete blank. All he can do is to skate gracefully backwards, concentrate solely on skating gracefully backwards, perhaps unconsciously wishing to turn back the clock. But so intent is he on displaying the utmost grace in the art of skating backwards that he does not see the chunk of ice on the surface of the rink, just as Per Ivar Moe did not see the sliver of soap some weeks later in Deventer: a booby trap of ice which causes him to come crashing down, as badly as it is possible to crash on skates. Charlie Chaplin could not have done it better: first the frantic skittering, faster and faster, in a futile attempt to regain his balance, and then the finale, the dreadful fall, where you just manage to adopt a perfectly horizontal position in midair before coming down on the rock-hard ice, and every single part of the back side of your body seems to take a battering as your head and heels both hit the ice at once.

And finally: the explosion. The back of Jonas's head slams into the ice so hard that a myriad shards of light, a whole universe of starbursts, come racing towards him and through him, a bit like the effect used in a film to give the illusion of travelling faster than the speed of light. When he emerges on the other side he is convinced that his spine has been shattered and that the silver thread – although what bloody good is a silver thread to him now, anyway? – has been severed.

For a long time Jonas just lies there, as if he were dead, he *is* dead, his eyes closed, while the chill from the ice spreads throughout his body, a not unpleasant sensation. He only wishes that he could put himself into deep-freeze and that someone would wake him up when the world has become less crazy and bewildering.

For a long time Jonas lies there, chilled to the marrow, listening to the mawkish strains of 'Yesterday' pouring out of the loudspeakers right above his head with the result that he would come to hate that song, felt like crying every time heard it. And, as most of you will no doubt appreciate, he had to endure listening to that song many a time over the years. To cut a long story short: Jonas Wergeland was never a great Beatles fan.

Margrete was gone. Margrete was the first and the last. And it was on account of Margrete that Jonas Wergeland killed his mother's seven lovers.

Beyond the EEC

What do you do when you are desperate?

Jonas Wergeland blamed the American cartoonist Carl Barks for his trip to Timbuktu. As a child there were few things Jonas loved more than the final frames of Barks's inimitable stories, in which Donald Duck, alone or, for instance, with his friend Gyro Gearloose the inventor – usually drawn in silhouette – would be seen hightailing it to Timbuktu, or quite simply find themselves in Timbuktu after the most hair-raising scandals and disasters have become a fact. The whole point is to get as far away as possible, to someplace where no one knows you.

There are times when we all yearn to be far, far away and in the autumn of 1972, Jonas Wergeland yearned to be far, far away. This was due not so much to Carl Barks as the need to get away from the circus surrounding the EEC referendum, which, to Jonas's mind, not only dulled the wits but also turned the heads of the Norwegian people for several months; suddenly the derogatory term 'parish-pump politics' seemed to cover the reality of the situation perfectly. The country was bursting at the seams with loudspeakers and public meetings; there were stands on every street corner, demonstrations at every turn, leaflets through letterboxes, posters on every telegraph pole, bad political ditties on the radio and hysterical debates on television. Ideologies became muddled up, and no one noticed; in the same breath candidates could profess both radical politics and conservative values or vice-versa. As far as Jonas was concerned there was nothing to choose between the 'Yes' and the 'No' camps for stupidity, so when he made his escape, it was not from yes or no but from dogmatism, or perhaps he was acting on an intuition that, despite all the shouting, the issues which these people were debating were of little consequence, as would later be confirmed. While the full battery of spotlights and microphones was trained on the tackling and hard play that surrounded any standpoint taken on the EEC, the crucial decisions, the ones which would *really* determine Norway's immediate future, were made in the shadows and on the quiet, under the direction of people like Sir William. The foundations of Norway the oil nation were being laid without anyone asking the Norwegian people.

It is easy for me, who can indulge in the luxury of being a dis-interested party, to say that Norway in the late summer of 1972 was an admirable example of a democracy in full flower. For Jonas Wergeland, however, this was a time when an entire country was stage-managed like a media event and, what was worse, one that wasn't even entertaining. Where others saw a debate, Jonas saw only a welter of emotions camouflaged as rational argument, where they would have done better to dish out clubs instead of pamphlets. In actual fact, the thought of travelling to Timbuktu had never entered Jonas's head before, but once it was there it had become almost a compulsion. And thanks to Charles Darwin's *The Origin of Species* he could simply pack his bag and go.

I suppose I ought to mention in parenthesis here that travelling to Timbuktu nowadays is, of course, no big deal: not like it was for the first Europeans who actually paid with their lives, either on the way there or merely because they were unfortunate enough to reach there, travellers who suffered the most appalling hardships and only survived the desert by slitting open their veins and drinking their own blood, eating lizards and chewing on their leather belts. A trip to Timbuktu today, on the other hand, is not that arduous or dramatic and requires little more in terms of organization than taking the underground from Oslo's Central Station to the suburb of Stovner, the main difference being the need for a visa and a couple of vaccinations. So I do not intend to waste any space on the journey as such but simply let Jonas Wergeland follow David Attenborough's example and pop up on the scene.

When Jonas Wergeland arrived in Timbuktu, in Mali, a country where people die earlier and earn less than just about anywhere else on Earth, he was, unlike the first Europeans to reach the place, not disappointed. Those explorers had been expecting to find a pulsating city awash with gold and ostrich feathers and leopard skins, with rulers who surrounded themselves with seductive dancers and jesters whose voices emanated from their armpits. Instead, what they found was a tiny huddle of mud huts, about as rich and exciting as the remains of a sand castle once the tide has come in; a town which had nothing left of its legendary past but its name.

But Timbuktu fulfilled all of Jonas's expectations simply because he had none. Added to which, for some hours, as they were driving out to it from Kabara, the town was enveloped in a cloud of sand because of the wind. Timbuktu was not even there. Jonas was over the moon. He was travelling into a mist, an uncharted nebula. The cloud of sand reinforced his conviction that he was not visiting a town, but a *word*, a name which marked the limits of the real world.

And he was not disappointed, not even when the wind died down, and the sand settled. Timbuktu gave the impression not only of utter disillusionment with the myths that surrounded it but also of a bleakness and a monotony unlike anything Jonas had ever come across before with its stark light and its homogeneous low, square buildings linked together in a way that put him in mind of a Cubist painting or gave him a feeling of having landed in the middle of an experiment, at some outer limit (or on some far frontier). No doubt about it, he thought, here was a place, a spot, where it must be possible to come up with a new angle. On Norway, on his own life. Because this was of course, for anyone who has not yet figured it out, the subconscious motive for his trip to Timbuktu: the search for enlightenment. If Timbuktu were the hub of the world – how would the world look then?

So what Jonas did in Timbuktu was *think*, or search. He wandered up and down the sandy streets lost in thought, back and forth between sun-baked mud huts that changed colour in the course of the day, turning from white and beige to brown and ochre; he did not notice the children who gave him funny looks, the chickens and the goats, the donkeys and the camels, the stench of their droppings; he was so thoroughly engrossed in an attempt to push his thoughts as far as he humanly could. Only occasionally did he seem to come to himself, surrounded by flies, outside one of the massive dark-brown wooden doors, intricately carved and studded with nails and hung on heavy iron hinges, running his fingers over a gash left there, although he did not know it, by a Tuareg sword. The door itself seemed to give him some inkling of both the difficulty and the possibility of reaching new domains of perception.

He thought and thought on into the evening and, indeed, into the night, in dreams. For the record I ought to mention that this was before Sofitel opened their hotel in the town, and Jonas was therefore staying at one of those hostels to be found all over this part of Africa, primarily geared towards travelling civil servants.

During the day he would be out walking again, and of all the images I have of Jonas Wergeland, this is possibly the one of which I am most fond; the one which I wish the people of Norway could set alongside his rather more glamorous public image because this, too, is Jonas Wergeland: a young man walking up and down the run-down streets of Timbuktu, utterly absorbed in his own thoughts. Jonas strolls from the main market to the meat market while thinking about Norway, what sort of a country Norway is; he wanders from the old fort to the camels' watering-hole, wondering what sort of a person he is; he meanders through the Tuareg quarter and down to the town well, wondering what he should do next, after graduating from high school; he walks from the Djinguereber Mosque to the famed Sankoré Mosque, which looks like a gingerbread tower studded with cloves, thinking of Axel and how he wants to study biochemistry; he saunters from a group of ramshackle huts, little more than termite-hills, to the house in which René Caillié, the first European to come out of Timbuktu alive, had stayed, and thinks of Margrete, always Margrete; wondering what has become of her; he wanders from the coffee house where a little group is playing some board game, to the 'palaver tree' under which the old men sit, chewing cola nuts and passing the time of day; for one second, just one second, he also thinks of the EEC.

At night he lies in the cool hostel room, a bowl of dates next to the divan, and lets his thoughts mingle with his dreams.

One night, when he had woken up and could not get back to sleep, he pulled on his jacket, draped a blanket over his shoulders and went outside. He took the path leading into the desert and soon found himself some way to the north of Timbuktu, out among the sand dunes that rolled in towards the town like ocean waves.

On a whim he plonked himself down in the sand, thoughtfully scooped up a handful of the fine grains and put them down on another spot. Behind him he could make out the low, featureless skyline of Timbuktu. A heap of mud in the middle of a desert. A gingerbread town. Not that it gave one any reason to feel superior. This part of the world had seen governments come and go long before the birth of Christ – while Norway still languished in the obscurity of the Stone Age. And Timbuktu, older than Oslo, had once been the first city of Mali and the Songhai Empire, vast states that stretched from the Atlantic Ocean to the Sudan. At the end of the fifteenth century this bustling metropolis was said to have been ringed by trees and have a population of some 50,000. It was also commonly acknowledged to have been a centre for Muslim scholarship, boasting three universities and several collections of priceless manuscripts. Timbuktu's story told of greatness one day, a sand-hill the next.

He sat in the desert, wrapped in a blanket, looking up at the stars; he could hardly believe his eyes, there seemed to be so many of them, so close and so bright. He gazed out across the sand dunes, was struck by how quiet it was, how overwhelmingly . . . empty, how . . . endless. With his hand he moved sand from one spot to another, thinking to himself that in terms of the big picture he was changing the desert, changing the world.

Then, all of a sudden, as if in answer to a question he had never managed to ask, he was lying flat out on the sand – with a sword at his throat. Terror-stricken though he was, this somewhat absurd concrete manifestation of an existential choice was not lost on him; he even had time to wonder that anyone could move that quietly, make themselves so invisible. He realized that they were Tuaregs, three of them, recognized them by the lengths of cloth wound round their heads, leaving only their eyes visible.

They dragged him to his feet and led him further into the desert, until they came to a camp nestling between two high sand dunes. It is easy to see how Jonas, whose knowledge of deserts had for the most part been gleaned from Carl Bark's comic strips, could have imagined that these Tuaregs must be attached to one of the caravans that brought in salt from Taoudénit, when in fact they belonged to the Kel Intasar tribe, nomads who had gravitated towards Timbuktu because of a drought of Old Testament proportions which would come to a head over the next two years and which was already taking its toll on their way of life.

Jonas had no idea what his crime might be. He wondered whether he had desecrated one of their holy places. Or worse: that they took him for one of those idealistic aid workers who drilled wells to develop the deserts, thus ruining the ecological balance, or forced them to settle in one place and become farmers instead of nomads. Or worse still: they thought he was French and were out to take their revenge for almost half a century of ruthless oppression.

The man who still had his sword out of its leather sheath and pointed at Jonas motioned to him to stop next to a fire on the outskirts of the camp. Jonas noticed a number of small fires dotted here and there in the sand, also some cattle, some goats and, of course, camels lying here and there, although not very many. People were sitting outside the entrances to their tents. The general impression was one of poverty, of a myth exploded. Where were the dark lords of the desert, riding high on their white camels, rulers of the wind, the very epitome of dignity and pride? Jonas could tell that something was very wrong when such people as these huddled on the fringes of the desert over which they had reigned for thousands of years.

He held out all the banknotes he had on him as if begging some sort of indulgence. Three pairs of eyes merely looked him through the slits in their headdresses, *looked*, full of contempt. The cloth wound round their heads seemed glossy, metallic. They said something, evidently asking him a question. Jonas had not the foggiest notion what they were jabbering on about, knew only that he was in a tight spot, a very tight spot. Suddenly he remembered that Alexander Gordon Laing, one of the first Europeans to reach Timbuktu in the nineteenth century, was killed by Tuaregs. One of the men was armed with a dagger embossed with silver and brass. It might well be that these three were of noble blood, members of the warrior caste. Again they said something, their tone aggressive. What language were they speaking – Tamashek, Arabic, Hausa? Or just such bad French he could not understand it? Or maybe it was Bambara? Weren't there any teenagers here who spoke French?

How, he wondered, as two scrawny dogs came over to sniff at him, could he explain to them that he had come to gain a little leeway for himself in terms of time and space; that he wanted to find out what it was like to be Jonas Wergeland stuck in the middle of Timbuktu's mud heap: that he had left Norway and 1972 because he had suddenly found that country and that time so unutterably claustrophobic, stifling in its imperative insistence on what was important. He was looking for an angle in the sand, a filter of stars. Right then it occurred to him what a fitting view of the EEC this offered – here, in the desert, with a double-edged sword at one's throat: How much did the EEC matter, really? Or Europe as a whole, come to that?

Jonas tries to say 'Norway', that he is Norwegian as if this fact alone would automatically result in the removal of the sword tip from his throat; as if Norway were synonymous with innocence, harmlessness, neutrality. Jonas Wergeland sits in the desert, under the stars, outside the town of Timbuktu in Mali and says 'Norway . . . I am Norwegian' in every language he knows, slowly, distinctly, while the eyes that stare at him through the slits in the indigo headdresses remain impassive; the Tuaregs have never heard of Norway.

Jonas shoots a glance at one of the tents, sees a woman busying herself with a brass pot, sees another woman crushing something in a mortar. At that same instant he has a vision of Norway cut off from the world, as Mali was in the seventeenth century. The previous day in a coffeehouse, his musings had been interrupted by an eager young African who had told him something of Mali's history, how Timbuktu had hung on to its position of power for as long as it remained a crossroads for the trade in salt and gold, for the caravans and the ships travelling up and down the Niger, and how its decline owed less to open hostility from neighbouring countries than to the shifting of the trade routes. Long-distance trading declined drastically with a drop in the demand for gold on the other side of the Sahara, following the Spanish colonization of South America – added to which, the Portuguese had switched to trading across the Atlantic. Both these factors effectively strangled trade in the Sahara. Once again Mali was closed-off. A backwater. The final blow, delivered by the ever-greater influence of the French in that region, came with the rerouting of the last remnants of trade to Senegal and the towns on the coast. In a coffeehouse in the mud-hut city of Timbuktu, Jonas Wergeland learned something about relativity, about the mighty hand of history and how important it was not to become isolated, not to wind up on the fringes of international trade. Today, he thought, Norway is a wealthy country. Tomorrow, or a few hundred years from now, it could be another Mali, or as poor as Norway itself was just a few hundred years ago.

The camels kneeling in the sand started to growl, signalling, so it seemed, that the situation was coming to a head. A hand fumbled at Jonas's throat as if searching for an identity tag, still taking him for a French mercenary. One of the other Tuaregs went through his jacket pockets and pulled out a battered paperback, *Aku-Aku*, Thor Heyerdahl's book about Easter Island. Jonas's travel reading. The Tuareg obviously knew the Roman alphabet. He sounded out 'Hey-er-dahl'.

This one word worked like a charm, like Sinbad's 'Open Sesame'. Jonas heard the name spoken and saw a new light come into the eyes surrounding him. The book and the name Heyerdahl were like salt, worth their weight in gold. The sword was slipped back into the leather scabbard.

'Kon-Tiki,' said one.

'Ra,' said another.

They repeated the names 'Aku-Aku', 'Kon-Tiki', 'Ra' and 'Heyerdahl'. Again and again the words were murmured like mantras: 'Ra . . . Ra . . . Ra'. To Jonas it sounded like they are giving three cheers: 'Hip, hip, hur-rah!'

At last they had hit upon a common language. It was as if the name Heyerdahl had also given the nomads back their hope, as if for a moment their dignity, their innate pride had been restored to them.

I know it seems incredible, that Thor Heyerdahl's name should have been known here, in the heart of the wilderness of the Sahel, by men who had probably never seen the sea, even though the caravans might well have brought kinsmen of theirs to the Moroccan coast, starting-point for the voyage of the *Ra*. It is true, nonetheless, and says more about Thor Heyerdahl's exploits and how widely known, how unbelievably well known, he is than about the curiosity of the Tuaregs. To some degree this can, of course, be put down to the fact that Heyerdahl is, like them, a nomad: a man with an instinct and an eye for the great travel routes, for the connections in which no one else believes.

This put a whole new slant on things. All of a sudden Jonas was their guest, and he was led, amid loud proclamations, to a fire in front of one of the goatskin tents where he was served a glass of sweet mint tea from a silver jug. Jonas sat there holding the warm glass, and it came to him: he was a nomad, would always be a nomad. Everything had changed, was suddenly beautiful. Orange flames in an inky landscape silhouetted against a deep-blue sky. Stars right above his head. He still could not understand what they said, but he could tell that they were giving him the VIP treatment and that he ought to return the compliment in some way. He wished he had his mouth organ with him so he could have played something for them: Duke Ellington's 'Morning Glory', for instance. What he did have in his pocket, however, was a crystal prism, a good-luck charm given to him by a friend, a dear childhood friend who had shown him how light turned into something quite different when it struck the facets of the prism. He handed the piece of glass, a symbolic gift, to the Tuareg whom he took to be the leader before being escorted back to the town by two boys.

When Jonas Wergeland returned to Timbuktu on the morning of Tuesday 26 September 1972 the bread ovens were already lit. He stood for some time watching the flames dancing inside the ovens, shivering slightly as he breathed in the smell of the bread. He had always liked the smell of fresh-baked bread. Back home in Norway, the people had pronounced their verdict on the matter of the EEC, quite oblivious to the trials to which Jonas Wergeland had been subjected.

Osiris

They were on the steamship jetty when it happened, one of those summer days filled with the sound of a thousand seagull cries, low tide and a dead calm, and a sea so smooth that the skerries could be seen mirrored in it. Colours were at their most intense in the afternoon light: the white of the houses, the red of the sheds along the quayside, the green of the lyme-grass; and the planks of the yawls gleamed like burnished gold. The air smelled of seaweed, of blue clay, of salt water. Jonas was six years old and had just learned to swim.

The high point of the day was the arrival of the *Hvaler*, a trusty old workhorse of a coaster which was in fact celebrating its centenary just around this time. Even as a grown man, Jonas could still recall every detail of that boat, right down to the smell down in the saloon, the judder of the engine and, not least, the noise it made, which could be heard half a mile away. The jetty, not the biggest of its kind, was packed with people, as it always was in those days when a coastal steamer was entertainment in itself. The majority were only there to check out what manner of funny-looking summer visitors would step ashore – their luggage was a dead giveaway – or which of the local residents had been over to Fredrikstad to buy new wallpaper. For a child, the mere fact of having a line thrown to you could make your day. Jonas, clad only in a pair of shorts, was there on the jetty with his cousin Veronika, who was already strikingly pretty, *too* pretty. They were standing roughly halfway along the jetty when Jonas suddenly became aware that the crowd seemed to be pushing them towards the edge, towards the boat which was now reversing out of the dock.

So how do the pieces of a life fit together?

Apropos the rationale for Jonas's trip to Timbuktu, I apologize for oversimplifying. As always, there was at least one other, complex, reason. If anyone were to ask why Jonas Wergeland became a nomad, I could just as easily say he was searching for himself. And I mean that quite literally; he was searching for his arm or his hip, if, that is, he was not searching, purely and simply, for his head. This also explains why he was so delighted with the little leather pouch the Tuaregs gave him to hang around his neck, ornamented with a yellow and emerald-green motif representing the print of a sandal, to symbolize a man. Jonas felt as if he had found a foot, a limb that he had once lost.

You see: Jonas Wergeland was, in fact, carved up, dismembered, as a child.

It happened on that selfsame glorious summer's day when the crowd, by dint of an incomprehensible conjunction of forces, a sort of parallelogram of forces, nudged him closer and closer to the very edge of the jetty until he was right up against one of the posts, and there he stood, staring down into the foaming water, at the seething whirlpools generated as the boat struggled to reverse out. In this part of the sound the current was exceptionally strong, and sometimes the crew had to make two or even three attempts, at full throttle, before they succeeded in bringing the boat round with the bow pointing towards Fredrikstad.

Jonas is gazing down into the boiling white waters, right out on the very edge of the jetty, almost mesmerized by the whirlpools, the way one can be mesmerized by the eyes of a snake – and then it happens: he is actually pushed in, down into those awful, frothing circles, not far from the stern of the boat and its fearsome propeller. Jonas's first, spontaneous thought is that it is the mass that has pushed him in. So if anyone should wonder where Jonas Wergeland's contempt for the masses springs from, the source of his oft-repeated assertion that the masses stunt the individual, now you know; it dates from that jetty on Hvaler where he quite literally became a victim of the power of the masses, the awe-inspiring energy which is always there, lying latent, in a crowd of people.

Jonas has only just learned to swim, he tries frantically to swim out of the way, but he can feel himself being dragged backwards, relentlessly, towards the propeller; he kicks and thrashes for all he is worth, but it does no good. There is a swishing, almost metallic sound in his ears, growing louder and louder, and already, on the brink of death, he feels the sharp pain of his feet being sliced off.

It was such a paradox, this whole incident, since up to that point in Jonas Wergeland's life summer holidays on the island out in the mouth of the fjord had been associated with uninterrupted happiness. The stories of most people's lives include a chapter entitled 'In the Realms of Adventure', and for Jonas this chapter was set – in two senses since it related both to being caught up in an adventure story and listening to adventure stories – in his father's childhood home on Hvaler, one of the islands lying to the south of Fredrikstad, level with the Swedish border and overlooking the open sea. Here, in an old white house, in an atmosphere that would have to be described in a children's song, not to sound banal, Jonas spent all his holidays as a boy. He experienced those summers with such an intensity that he *knew*, each morning when he awoke, that everything that happened that day would stay with him, that one day he would sit in an old folks' home, looking back on, and shedding tears over, events that had gone straight to the heart of him with no detours: a beauty and a setting of such sunlit clarity that even a child who has never given any thought to such things instinctively understands that he is, as it were, establishing a bedrock within himself. And at the centre of this scene was his grandfather, exactly like a figure in some National Romantic painting, scratching the stomach of a grey tabby cat with the toe of his shoe.

People today have – if you will forgive me – such a narrow one-dimensional concept of the significance of the family, that I am not sure whether I should say anything at all about the part played in Jonas Wergeland's life by his grandparents. Permit me, at any rate, to highlight one of the more general aspects in the form of a statement. The whole purpose of grandparents is to supply the fairy-tale element; they are the trainers of a child's imagination. Not that they absolutely have to tell stories; in many cases it is enough for them to *be there*, like Jonas's grandmother, because they are, in themselves, a story.

Jonas never knew his paternal grandmother, but his father's father, Omar Hansen, lived long enough to fulfil his function in his grandson's life. What Jonas remembered best about his grandfather was the fine creases at the corners of his eyes, radiating towards his temples when he screwed up his eyes, and he almost always had his eyes screwed up, as if he were constantly on the look-out for something that lay beyond what he saw around him all the time, something which Jonas fancied must be a sort of hidden story or a Story of Stories. In this, Jonas was not far off the mark, for Omar Hansen was a Platonist when it came to stories, believing as he did that every history, no matter how good, was only a pale shadow of a better story. Hence the reason that Jonas's grandfather was perpetually brimming over with stories as if he were hoping that if he just went on telling them for long enough, or mixing up enough tales, some underlying story would eventually be revealed. In actual fact, I think Omar Hansen must have been the closest one can get in Norway to a rhapsody, a man with whole strings of stories committed to memory.

So for Jonas summer holidays consisted of a grandfather sitting in a blue kitchen with copper-hung walls and shelves lined with white jars inscribed with neat black lettering, telling a mish-mash of tall tales and true ones while cleaning fish or cutting plugs of tobacco. 'Just imagine, Jonas,' he would say, 'if you were living ten or twelve thousand years ago and were one of the first folk to come to Norway after the Ice Age. You'd have sailed right across here, so you would. You see, back then our island was under the sea, so you would have come ashore farther inland, up at Høgnipen, for example.' Summer holidays were a grandfather in a rowboat, two big fists curled around the oars and fine creases around the eyes, a grandfather who taught Jonas how to haul in a net and lift the flatfish over the gunwale while at the same time pointing out the huge cairn on the crest of the island and saying something about his great-grandfather having dug up both the king and the bronze-age treasure that had lain underneath it: an exercise in inventiveness, both the quiet morning on the waters of the fjord and these stimulating stories.

Or they went for strolls, hand-in-hand, Jonas and his grandfather, through the dense belt of pine trees that stretched across the island, walking on a carpet of pine needles between tall golden trunks and beneath swaying treetops, while his grand-father talked of the old days, of the herring fishing, of men falling from the masts, of the village shop and Harry Hansen's boatyard that was bewitched – and had Jonas ever heard the one about Lanky Arnold and the cherry tree? Or it might be the story of the customs men and the terrible blunder they made the time they tried to catch those smugglers from Sweden; or the mis-sionary who used to preach at the village hall, only to be irre-sistibly tempted into the paths of sin and, thence, eternal damnation, by one of the island's bonny lasses.

But always, first and last, there would be these two, Jonas and his grandfather, sitting on the smooth scoured rocks overlooking the open sea, where his grandfather had to bellow out his stories like another Demosthenes, to be heard above the roar of the breakers. What Jonas liked best of all was that his grandfather commenced all of his stories with the words: 'Just imagine, Jonas, if you were . . . ' thus making Jonas himself the hero of every tale, no matter whether it was about maelstroms and sunken treasure, or mermaids, white whales and submerged reefs, or Tordenskjold's victory at Dynekilen, not to mention lifeboats and great acts of heroism: just imagine if you were steering the pilot-boat, Jonas – can you picture it? – out there, heading for Koster to meet the *Peter Wessel*, or a spine-chilling tale of shipwrecks, see those banks over there, that's right, there, where the surf is crashing something wicked, just imagine if you had gone off course one stormy night. The *Store-Karl* went down just there, you know. I was just a lad, saw the whole thing from Rokka, there was nothing anybody could do. And all the while his grandfather would be peering out to sea, with those fine creases around his eyes, as if he could make out another story, just over the horizon.

Omar Hansen had been a sailor, and hence a lot of his mate-rial was drawn from the sea. The parlour was like a gallery filled with small pictures of ships, painted with a fine brush, and down in the outside privy hung a sheet of cardboard from an old cal-endar showing the sailing routes of the Wilhelmsen line, white lines on a dark-blue chart: a little like a star chart brought down to sea level. Jonas never tired of sitting there, frequently along with his grandfather, on the seat that offered the better view of the shore and the sea when you left the door open, with the wind tickling at your backside. Only later did it dawn on Jonas that *that* was why his father read the *National Geographic* in the toilet at home in the town: not because he had a yen to go travelling but as a means of recalling his childhood, the sensual delights of an outside privy: that view, the scenery, an open door and a shimmering sea – and, now and again, most wondrous of all, the sound of rain falling softly on the grass.

So, as I say, this unhinging accident – Jonas falling into the water between the jetty and a reversing boat – in no way fitted with the usual summer routine: a glimpse of hell in the midst of paradise.

Jonas is floundering helplessly in the water, aware that he is being drawn towards the propeller. Then, just as he feels an excruciating stab of pain and is quite sure that his feet have been chopped off, it hits him that it was Veronika, his cousin, who had given him the crucial nudge; he had noticed her standing close beside him as the crowd pushed them towards the edge, knew she was right behind him when he was standing up against the post, gazing spellbound at the eddies swirling around the reversing coaster. Would you believe it? Veronika had pushed him in; cool as you like, how mean can you be, he thinks, and now he is going to die, is *already* dead, because at that moment he is struck by an utterly convincing feeling that his head alone is left floating and thinking, in a sea of red, while the rest of his body has been chopped up into little pieces that are now drifting off in all directions; and in the midst of his mortal panic he has a vision of parts of his anatomy being washed ashore in the most widely divergent parts of the world: some ribs in Sydney, his heart in the Gulf of Aqaba, a hand off Buenos Aires, an ear on the east coast of Greenland because he is already dead, dismembered, so he believes, just as the metallic swooshing dies away. Someone has managed to signal to the people onboard to stop the engine; he hears a splash, feels someone getting an arm round him, feels himself being held up, being lifted, and he is back on the jetty where, to his surprise, he realizes that he is in one piece and that the smarting of the skin on his thighs stems from jellyfish stings.

The first face he sees is Veronika's, a sight which prompts him to blurt out a weak and incredulous 'Jesus Christ, Veronika'. And only those who have read this far will guess that what Jonas is actually saying, even though he does not have the words with which to verbalize this perception, is: 'So this is how you thank me for saving your life on the Zambezi?'

Jonas was in a state of shock, for a few minutes he also lost his memory and did not know who he was. And even after he gradually began to recover and could think clearly, he had a bewildered look about him, as if in some way he still was not sure who he was. His grandfather was more aware of this than anyone else and tried in his own way to undo the harm: day after day he sat on a rock overlooking the open sea and told Jonas who he was; in other words, he put Jonas back together. While the breakers rolled slowly in towards the rocks, Omar Hansen peered out to sea and told a never-ending stream of stories: just imagine, Jonas, if you were walking down by the docks in Sydney – Omar Hansen had been to Sydney himself and knew the city well – or, just imagine, Jonas, if you were a sailor going ashore in Buenos Aires, there's a street there, by the way, called Avenida de Mayo, an adventure in itself . . . All in all, Jonas's grandfather's storytelling was more intense than usual; he really gave it everything he had, dragging up one gripping yarn after the other. Imagine, Jonas, listen to this, Jonas: important episodes, mainly involving the people of the island, distant relations, Uncle Melankton, a genius; his grandfather sat by the sea with the breakers crashing at their feet, fine creases around his eyes, and told stories to this small boy who suddenly seemed so scared, so pale, as if the water had washed away the tan he took on so easily in the summer. But pale or not, Jonas listened; and it was here, on a rock by the sea that Jonas Wergeland learned – by which I mean, he understood later – that the stories his grandfather told him might be more than a diversion or an amusement, a way of passing the time. That they represented something utterly fundamental, something on which his whole existence depended, that they built him up in the same way as food did.

Even though Omar Hansen did his utmost, to the point where he almost caught a glimpse of the Story behind the stories, and even though Jonas could see with his own eyes that he was all there, he never rid himself of the feeling that, psychologically speaking, he truly *had* been chopped into pieces, the way you see on those wall-charts showing cuts of beef, and that his dismembered limbs had been swept off by the currents and scattered across the world.

So when Jonas Wergeland travelled abroad to Timbuktu for example, he was really going in search of himself.

The Magic Penis

One limb which, fortunately for Jonas Wergeland, came to no harm either that time on Hvaler or later in life, was the one between his legs. Apparently there is a local museum, somewhere in France, where Napoleon's testicles are preserved for posterity in a glass jar, and I seriously believe that plans ought to be made now for doing the same with Jonas Wergeland's golden balls so that some day their secret may be disclosed, much as the brains of certain geniuses have been examined in order to see whether they are folded differently from the norm. I have already given some hint of what I am getting at here, so I might as well come right out with it: Jonas Wergeland had a magic penis.

Jonas must have had some notion of his amazing good fortune after that confirmation act of fellatio – and his subsequent clearing of the high-jump bar backwards – but the true 24-carat quality of his balls was not brought home to him until he came into contact with girls who were prepared to wrap themselves around him in other, more radical, ways. So when he found himself lying in a daze on the floor of the old library in Oslo Cathedral School, with the aforementioned member throbbingly erect, he was in no doubt whatsoever; he knew that he was in possession of a wonderful gift: in other words, that anything could happen when Christine A. completed the manoeuvre on which she had begun, lowering herself down onto him or, as Jonas thought to himself, slowly burying his lingam in her warm, smooth yoni.

Is that possible – I mean, for a penis to have quite exceptional qualities? I know that I am touching here on a subject most people find more fascinating than they care to admit. You need only look at those inane, yet nonetheless increasingly popular newspaper columns dispensing advice on sexual matters; all those useless experts, so devoid of fantasy – and 'devoid of fantasy' is, in this instance, a well-considered term of abuse – who imagine themselves to be divine authorities in this sphere. I apologize for allowing my inherent sang-froid and forbearance to desert me, but if these people had the gumption, just now and again, to raise their blinkered eyes and look at the answers they come up with from . . . oh, just a couple of decades into the future, ten to one they would choose their words with much more care and humility, not to mention irony. I would like to set at rest the minds of all those who have had their doubts as to the substance of such dogmatic utterances – all credit to you – on losing one's virginity, on impotence, on jealousy and vaginal orgasms by stating that they are for the most part a load of inconsequential claptrap churned out at a random point in time in some quite specific part of the world. Swallow rubbish like that and you will certainly have no difficulty in accepting the notion of a magic penis.

Over the years Jonas would often wonder what it was about his organ that put him in this, in two senses, fortunate position, and since it could not possibly have anything to do with size or staying power, he thought it must be down to its *form*. When he inspected his member, particularly during the transition from limp to erect state – an activity in which all boys regularly indulge – he began to suspect that it had something to do with a bit of a curve, possibly in conjunction with the hint of a spiral form, not unlike the horn of a kudu for anyone who has ever seen one of those: that it was this which drove women wild, not least when they sat astride him, in which position they claimed to experience 'an utterly divine pleasure' as one woman put it – although, for the record, I feel bound to object to that adjective – or that he 'hit the G-spot dead-on' as another, more feminist-minded girl breathlessly informed him back in the days when there was a lot of talk about this particular phenomenon: a pure fiction, of course, if that is of any comfort to those women who have hunted for it in vain. As it happens, it was these comments on the source of the magic which gave Jonas Wergeland his first inkling of form as the be-all and end-all.

Early in the spring of his second year at high school Jonas became better acquainted with a girl in the class above him:

Christine A., a girl with a delicate tracery of blue veins at her temples who was notorious for having an almost daunting gift for mathematics, a gift she would go on to develop, after graduating from high school, at various foreign universities, among them the world-renowned Institute for Advanced Studies at Princeton, where she was a protégé of the pioneering Norwegian mathematician Atle Selberg – in fact, in the mid-eighties the Norwegian television network NRK did a programme on her which Jonas watched with an interest that spoke to his colleagues of something more than mere professional curiosity.

Jonas, on the other hand, had no head for maths. Quite frankly, he *hated* maths, mainly because this subject persisted in remaining a closed book to him. There are two types of people in this world: those who understand the paradox of Achilles and the tortoise and those who do not. Jonas belonged most definitely to the latter group. He simply could not grasp why Achilles could never catch up with the tortoise, let alone understand such totally senseless conceptions as incommensurable quantities, irrational numbers and periodic decimal fractions. Geometry he could cope with, set theory too, at a pinch, but algebra . . . as far as Jonas was concerned algebra made about as much sense as 'abracadabra'. His little red book was of no use when it came to mathematics, not even James Clerk Maxwell's pithy warning as to the dangers of limited knowledge. That his marks reflected this shortcoming was the result not of laziness but sheer incomprehension.

Christina A. was not one of those razor-sharp minds who can add up quicker in their head than anyone else could with a sliderule, or who laughed at their teacher's pathetic blackboard antics; she was a deep thinker, her strength lay in posing unexpected questions, perceiving connections between different sets of problems, turning things on their head in the style of one of her heroes, the Dutch mathematician L.E.J. Brouwer. Nor was she an out-and-out pragmatist, as a type, I mean. She took just as great an interest in other subjects, not least Norwegian. The school magazine ran a colourful portrait of her in which she was pictured against a blackboard covered in transcendent and elliptical functions, while the best part of the interview was taken up with her talking about authors such as Julio Cortázar and Iris Murdoch, names quite unknown to Jonas.

Christine A. was also a monitor in the reading room in which Jonas could be found dutifully dashing off his homework before class. More than once he had felt her eyes on him when she thought he wasn't looking, and he had long since been alerted to her indubitably high calibre by that little, aesthetic lightning bolt between his shoulder blades. Once, on walking past her and noticing that the sheet of paper in front of her was covered in figures and letters, he was tempted to say: 'Beats me how you can be bothered with anything so abstract.'

'What makes you think it's so abstract?' she asked.

'Algebra's all Greek to me,' said Jonas.

'Well, I could start by telling you that the word itself actually comes from the Arabic,' she said. 'And see here . . . ' She drew a six. 'Six is a *perfect* number. D'you think that's abstract?' Jonas thought it looked like a hard-on. 'If it weren't for numbers, for mathematics, mankind would still be stuck in the Stone Age,' said Christine A., and when the school bell chose just that moment to ring she coolly asked him to wait behind.

When everyone, even the keenest chess players, had gone off to their classrooms she ushered him out of the room and led him, by the hand almost, up the stairs, past the gilt-lettered memorial plaques and the portraits of famous pupils, which always gave Jonas the feeling of being in a mausoleum, to the second floor where she let them in to room thirty-seven – one number that would come to hold some relevance for Jonas – where the school's collection of antiquarian books was housed. Books for borrowing were also kept here, hence the reason that Christina A. had a key. Having little or no knowledge of these all-but secret chambers, Jonas stood for a moment running his eye around a room in which every available inch of wall space was taken up by bookshelves containing thousands of what looked like very old books indeed, with hide bindings in every shade of brown and spines of dull gold with patches of scuffed red showing here and there. Jonas could take books or leave them, but this quite took his breath away. The general impression, induced mainly by the galleries running round the three sides not overlooking the playground, with their stairs and iron railings, combined with the dust and the stuffy atmosphere, was of a set for a Gothic horror movie.

Christine A. pulled out an old book bound in parchment. 'Feel this,' she said. '*Arithmetica Universalis*," Jonas read. Written by one Isaac Newton. An edition from 1732, if he read the Roman numerals aright. 'Take a look inside,' she said. Jonas leafed through the book, running his eye over words in Latin and rows of numbers with the odd set of brackets here and there; he could not help but find it beautiful. Christine A. produced another heavy volume bound in pale calfskin from a safe. Jonas opened it. 'Ionnis Keppleri, *Harmonices Mundi*,' he read, fingering the thick rag paper. 'Kepler's Third Law,' she said. 'A first edition from 1619.' He pored over the text, the profusion of beautiful illustrations, the geometric drawings; ran his fingers over the letters, the indentations in the paper. 'This must be worth a fair bit,' said Jonas. 'A quarter of a million kroner," said Christine A. 'Still think it's abstract?'

Jonas could hardly believe it. Here he was, in his own school, in a room he had never entered before, surrounded by books worth twenty-five to thirty million kroner: smouldering gold lettering on every side. Then, with consummate self-assurance, Christine A. wrapped her arms around him and kissed him long, until his body was red-hot and it struck him that this was not only a storehouse for books but also the storehouse of a power station producing an unknown form of energy.

'Would you like me to show you something even more valuable?' she asked and drew him up the stairs to the gallery where another, internal, stairway led up to the third floor and another store of books, through the wall from the music room where an indomitable singing teacher was endeavouring, yet again, to make dozy pupils sing 'Stabat Mater' in four-part harmony. The room lay in semi-darkness. Christine A. moved right up close to him, stood there with those translucent temples making him feel that the brain must be the body's most erogenous zone, before resolutely pulling him down onto the floor among piles of old books and making love to him far into the next period – and, I might say, beyond that into the realms of mathematics. While his

form was in a maths class, struggling with digital roots and
potency, he was lying on the third floor, under a roof that sloped
down to meet the windows, being tutored, in much more cogent
fashion, in digital roots and potency. So it is no exaggeration to
say that it was Christine A. who finally set mathematics into the
right context for Jonas Wergeland, who showed him the relationship between mathematics and life.

The moment she lowered herself down onto him, Jonas could
tell that she had what he would have called a mathematical yoni:
for one thing, because she gave him a sense of being in close
touch with an equation, full of unknowns, and – even more so –
because she promptly began to execute geometric figures over
his pelvis, using his penis as a sort of compass point, as if from
that spot she were attempting to shift the Earth. After a while she
turned to concentrating on figures of eight, the most incredibly
delightful rotations that put Jonas in mind of a book he owned in
which it said: 'This position can only be mastered by dint of
much practice.' She sat astride him, executing these figures of
eight with such virtuosity and for so long that Jonas caught a
glimpse of himself from the outside; of himself there, in that
room, among the dull gold of the book spines, an image which
reminded him of the pictures on his grandfather's biscuit boxes
depicting a man holding a biscuit box bearing the same picture
of a man holding a biscuit box and so on, further and further in.
Not only that, she also seemed to be screwing him upwards
towards some lofty lookout point from which, just before she
stopped in order to take pleasure in her own orgasm, he had a
fleeting impression of gazing upon infinity itself.

I ought perhaps to mention that Jonas Wergeland was one of
only a handful to obtain an A in his final maths exam, something
which no one would have bet on the year before. It was as if, after
that period with Christine A. in a storehouse full of learned
tomes, Jonas suddenly got the picture, saw the point in looking
for known or unknown quantities. All at once everything seemed
so clear, even Achilles and the tortoise, which was, of course, a
variant of the problem of infinity. The whole of this 'aha' experience was something akin to a key that simply needed to be
given an extra little turn for the lock to click open.

This incident provided Jonas with quite unmistakeable proof of his penis's magic properties. For while he could always explain away other such occurrences – convince himself that he had a latent talent for drawing, for example, or athletics – in his heart of hearts he knew that if there was one thing he was not, it was a mathematician.

The Killing of the Seven Lovers

But to get back, or on – depending on how you look at it – to that traumatic evening at the ice rink when Margrete walked out of his life and Jonas was left lying shattered, in the fullest sense of that word, on the ice under floodlighting that somehow only served to enhance the sense of disaster (or to make the disaster seem that much worse). Lying there, flat on his back, Jonas felt the physical pain gradually ebb, partly thanks to the numbing chill seeping up from the ice and through his body and, not least, his crotch, making the skin of his scrotum shrivel and turn thick as a walnut shell; and his balls, those precious balls, drew themselves up into his pelvic regions as if going into permanent hibernation.

Only one thing to do now, he thought: head for Timbuktu.

On top of that, as if the weather, too, was conspiring against him, that winter proved to be a very hard one, with average temperatures lower than in any other winter on record. The ice lay dauntingly thick on Oslo Fjord, and heavy falls of snow transformed the Grorud landscape into a claustrophobic maze of tall frozen banks through which Jonas stumbled, kicking chunks of ice as hard as he could. For Jonas's grief also had its aggressive side, which explains why he became King of the Castle – which is to say, of the enormous mound of snow in the playground – for the first and last time, knocking other kids off like some terrible Little John. In a way he was still unbeatable, but it was in the wrong way.

The situation was not improved by a letter he tried to write to Margrete – the very fact that he resorted to the written word shows just how desperate he was. He spent ages on it, searching for words, wanting to say something out of the ordinary. 'Your

yoni is like a hidden fruit,' was one of the phrases which he
penned, rather tentatively, although really quite pleased with the
formulation, before rounding off a string of clumsy sentences
with a cry for help, purely a strategic move, a quote from that
detested duo Lennon and McCartney: he knew what a sucker she
was for them.

And what happens? What thanks does he receive for this bold
baring of his soul?

An unsuspecting Jonas steps out into the playground at the
lunch recess and there, neatly ranged on the steps are just about
all of the girls in Margrete's class, killing themselves laughing
and singing – no, not singing, bawling out: '*Help me if you can
I'm feeling down*,' and so on and so forth, and as if that weren't
enough, they proceed to trail after him in a body, screeching out
the refrain over and over again, sending it echoing around the
playground for everyone, including the teachers on playground
duty and, indeed, the whole of Grorud, to hear.

Jonas refused to accept that there might be a connection,
refused to believe that it was true, but it was: Margrete had read
his letter out loud to her class, standing on a chair as if it were a
huge joke: a letter in which he had left himself totally exposed,
stripped bare, as it were. He walks around the playground with a
troop of screeching girls on his tail, shooting sidelong glances at
her, much as a wrongfully condemned man or a torture victim
will eye his executioner and only then, seeing her standing alone
on the steps, cruel and proud – she even meets his eye – does he
see, bitterly disappointed and humiliated though he is, why he is
so utterly infatuated with her. It is not something external, nothing like that at all. It is her inner radiance.

'Want to feel my yoni?' yells one of the boldest girls, eliciting
a barrage of delighted giggles from her sisters. Jonas squirmed
his way through the lunch recess, walking an endless gauntlet of
smirking faces. For a whole week, people would burst out laughing whenever he so much as showed his face.

Things did not look as if they could get any worse. But they
could, and they did. Jonas learned what it felt like to be kicked
when you are down: Margrete went away. She just disappeared.
It was one thing to call it off, quite another to go away. All

hope definitively gone, Jonas felt in acute need of a heart transplant.

What do you do when you are desperate?

You can take yourself off to Timbuktu, but you can also kill your mother's seven lovers.

Is such a thing possible? Jonas's mother with seven lovers? Was that why she went around with that crooked little smile on her face, looking as though she knew something no one else knew? Bear in mind that this was in the sixties, in Norway, Oslo, Solhaug: a few score families and everybody as good as knowing everybody else's business; a community so transparent that the walls might have been made of glass, where each and every household knew about it the minute Mrs Bogerud received a letter from Hong Kong or the Myhres went to the length of acquiring something as unbelievably extravagant as a toaster. Bear in mind, too, that Jonas's mother, Åse Hansen was a no-nonsense sort of a woman with both feet planted firmly on the ground and that she worked – although I'm not sure whether I mentioned it – for the most prosaic of companies, Grorud Iron-mongers Ltd, a rock-solid concern manufacturing hardware in brass and steel under the ambitious leadership of the Bratz brothers, one of whom even held the post of Minister for Trade and Industry for a while – down by the station, and there she stood on an assembly line, coming into daily contact with such concrete items as door hinges, doorknobs and Tip Tight window fastenings. How did all this square with anything as unheard of as a whole bevy of lovers?

It was true. Jonas's mother did have seven ardent lovers and all thanks to her brother, Uncle Lauritz. Jonas's only recollection of his uncle was of a rather exotic character, a man in a dark-blue uniform with four gold stripes on his sleeves, a fragrant-smelling figure with sleek black hair, a monsoon, an eminently enigmatic wind which blew in across the temperate climate of their everyday life from time to time. Uncle Lauritz, jazz-lover, belonged to that legendary generation of pilots trained in Canada who served in World War II before going on to join the Norwegian national airline DNL, later to become part of SAS. Every now and again, when the occasion called for it, Uncle Lauritz had presented

Jonas's father with a bottle of aftershave lotion – different brands, all with names redolent of southern climes or heroic myths – the contents of which his father used only sparingly, possibly because he set such great store by them, or because aftershave was not his style. So they were left to sit on a shelf in the tall old-fashioned oak cabinet in the bathroom year after year, long after Uncle Lauritz had ceased to blow in over Grorud like some exotic wind: seven beautiful bottles, each displaying its own fine lines and containing its own golden and distinct perfumed liquid.

As a boy, one of Jonas's favourite ploys when he went to the grocer's with his mother was to sneak open the bottles of rum, vanilla and almond essence and sniff their delicious aromas as avidly as any hopeless slave to opium. Likewise, he often stood and admired the seven bottles in the bathroom cabinet, running his fingers over their elegant lines, picturing them to himself as elementary forms of some sort as he unscrewed the tops and inhaled their scents. I do not propose to launch into a long spiel concerning the evanescent nature of scent, nor to shake anyone's belief in the objectivity of our sense of smell by citing the surprisingly varied preferences shown in different eras and by different peoples where perfumes are concerned, let me simply say that Jonas thought they smelled – oh, quite heavenly, so heavenly that the story of the three wise men and the word 'myrrh' automatically sprang to mind. The seven bottles of imported aftershave lotion were also costly by the standards of the day, amounting to little short of a treasure house in a bathroom belonging to perfectly ordinary, hard-working social democrats.

Only on special occasions, those times when he shaved again in the evening, did Jonas's father splash a few drops on his cheeks, selecting one of the bottles on the shelf at random, and so it came about that his mother used to joke to the children that she had seven different lovers who came to her and whom she could only tell apart in the darkness by their scent. 'Last night I had a visit from Alfredo from Capri,' she might say at the breakfast table, smiling her crooked smile. Jonas always thought how wonderful it must be . . . to be seduced, night after night, by a different scent each time.

We all know how traumatic puberty can be. Personally, I rather like this contrivance on the part of Mother Nature and am frequently amused by what people are liable to say or do during this period, not least in terms of irrational rebellious acts. All too many individuals are too quick to shrug off the irreplaceable perspectives on life afforded by this hormonally charged time – the most ungrateful of them even go so far as to consider the phase as a necessary evil. In any event, Jonas Wergeland also committed his share of rebellious acts during puberty and one of the earliest of these, the one closest to my own heart, due to its shocking, almost primitive originality, happened to involve his mother's seven lovers.

Without any warning, Margrete had vanished without trace, and eventually Jonas discovered the reason why: she had gone abroad. Her father the diplomat, Gjermund Boeck, had been assigned to a new post, on the other side of the world no less. This at least provided Jonas with a sorely needed scapegoat: Margrete's father. Had it not been for him, blasted fiend that he was, Jonas would at least have been able to *see* Margrete. To say that Jonas hated Gjermund Boeck merely scrapes the surface of his volcano of emotions. As a last cruel cut, Jonas found out about Mr Boeck's 'kidnapping' as he referred to it in his mind, just as the World Skiing Championships were getting under way in Oslo, a competition in which another Gjermund, namely Gjermund Eggen, was to become a new national hero, winning three gold medals and ensuring that for months afterwards, Jonas could not go anywhere without hearing or seeing that despised Christian name, even in an advertisement for root beer.

During this time, while Jonas was wandering about, not with a thorn in his flesh but with a thorn in his heart, his parents could have shown a little more consideration. Jonas had, as I have said, a wonderful father, and there never was a wiser mother than Åse Hansen; besides which, there was that crooked little smile of hers, adding to everything, joys as well as sorrows, the essential, ironic grain of salt. But faced with Jonas's wretchedness, they were at a complete loss, which may explain their tactlessness and why, one evening as Jonas was standing in the bathroom doorway his father let fly a thoughtless remark from his chair in the living:

'Take it easy, Jonas, you'll soon forget her, I'm sure.' Just at that moment his mother happened to come in from the kitchen. At sight of her son's pale drawn face, she almost lost her temper and came out with a cliché which, by the very fact of it being a cliché, hurt Jonas that much more deeply: 'Pull yourself together, boy! Nobody ever died of a broken heart!'

I admit that mothers are a mystery to me, not least their knack for making the most infamous remarks in delicate situations where really the only thing to do is to tread carefully and remember that silence is golden: a knack that might almost be likened to the sow's tendency to eat her own young. Neither his mother nor his father really understood Jonas's inner turmoil at all; they had, in other words, forgotten their own adolescence, the peaks and the abysses. They simply did not see that for a thirteen-year-old, losing someone whose hand you could hold, someone to press their lips against yours, was a disaster on a par with World War I; they did not realize that an entire inner landscape had been laid waste, suddenly and senselessly.

So what do you do when you are desperate? Or, to put it another way, how heavy is love?

Jonas stands in the bathroom doorway, contemplating the tall, narrow ton-weight of the oak cabinet rearing up between the washbasin and the toilet, the only piece of furniture his mother had brought with her from her childhood home in Gardermoen; and there, more importantly, are the seven bottles of precious aftershave lotion, ranged along the uppermost shelf. Jonas grips the sides of the doorway, his parents' words ringing in his ears; he feels grief and fury melding, endowing him with a strength of untold dimensions, so great that he makes up his mind to throw that bloody great junk heap of a cabinet out of the bathroom window, a little peephole no more than thirty centimetres square. After all, if man has the muscle power to jump over a building, surely it must also be possible to lift a tall massive cabinet about as heavy as a piano and chuck it out of a window that is too small. After all, the most unlikely things are forever happening. With that, he strides resolutely across to the cabinet, gets his arms round it and actually manages to lift this colossal chunk of oak off the floor, as if he were pulling the Norwegian national tree itself up by the roots and not only that; with a savage roar he also succeeds in throwing, or somehow ramming, the cabinet into the tiny square window high up in the wall: a wonderful cathartic moment as he feels the agonizing implosion transformed into an explosion, the result being that the cabinet crashes into the wall with an infernal bang, shattering the shelf of *National Geographics* before smashing to the floor, where every article of glass shatters into a million pieces, and Jonas goes on seething for a few seconds more over everything and anything, not least the fact that he did not manage to *hurl* that cabinet through the little peephole hard enough to send bricks flying in all directions.

Inasmuch as the bathroom in many ways was the flat's holy of holies, a chamber of dreams both for his mother and his father, Jonas had the great satisfaction of feeling that with this gesture of protest he had killed two birds with one stone. Years of *National Geographics* lay scattered across the floor, littered with broken glass and spattered with a good few decilitres of scent. Jonas, on the other hand, was safe; the crisis had passed: his destructive energy had, as it were, been burnt off.

How heavy is love? At least 150 kilos I would say. For some days afterwards, Jonas was painfully aware that he had strained himself badly. But better to have aching kidneys than an aching heart. And in any case: it is not every day one has the satisfaction of killing seven lovers with one lethal blow.

What Price Beauty

The bathroom in the new villa was of course quite a different story. It had a red fired-brick floor complete with under-floor heating, gleaming white tiles on the walls with a chequered border in ultramarine designed by Aunt Laura and copied, according to her, from the dome of a mosque in Samarkand. Everything was bigger – the bath, the washbasin, the whole room in fact – which meant that there was also space for a shower cabinet and this, together with the ferns, quite a little rain-forest of them, lent the bathroom an air of sheer luxury, an impression which Jonas crowned by installing a bidet when he took over the house. There were times, sitting on the toilet, when Jonas fell to contemplating the astonishingly rapid rate of social change in twentieth-century Norway: the leap from his grandfather's naturally aromatic outside privy on Hvaler, by way of the tiny bathroom in the block of flats at Solhaug, to this sumptuous, one might almost say international, chamber in the new house with its generous expanse of mirror and fittings worthy of any number of design awards – the equivalent of making the leap from Stone Age to Atomic Age within a couple of generations. It should be said, however, that they did retain the shelf of *National Geographic*s, the only difference being that the old scent-spattered copies had been replaced by newer issues. Theodor Kittelesen's picture of Soria Moria Castle also hung in its place on the wall, clearly visible from the toilet seat. Which reminds me that I never did finish the story of Jonas and his grandmother and their activities within the Norwegian fine-art market: a story which has both a moral and a happy ending.

Åse and Haakon Hansen had been on the look-out for some time for a bigger house, although they still had ample room where they were even after Buddha came along, Rakel having left home around the same time. But they had fallen prey to that dream common to all Norwegians: the dream of a house of one's own, as if the fact of no longer having to live through the wall from anyone else represented the last lap on the road to happiness, a legacy of sorts from the days when every Norwegian inhabited his own valley with high hills between him and his nearest neighbours. Which is why, when a plot of land on the other side of Bergensveien came their way, only a stone's throw from the block of flats in which they lived, they jumped at the chance and hence – typically – were only just starting to realize their dream of having their own house as Jonas and Daniel, too, were about to leave the nest.

Jonas's parents hired an architect to draw up plans for a simple house, a house they could afford, but even this proved to be beyond their means. The building, which extended upwards and outwards and would later be dubbed 'Villa Wergeland', looked like remaining as out of reach as Soria Moria Castle, to stick with Kittelsen for the moment, the building costs proving to be far greater than anyone had expected – double in fact. Unlike the men behind a number of subsequent, much publicized Norwegian building projects, however, Åse and Haakon Hansen discovered this at an early stage. They obtained a number of estimates from an obliging builder, at no obligation, and very quickly figured out that such an outlay was more than they could afford.

One Sunday when the whole family was, for once, having dinner together in the flat at Solhaug – cold roast pork as usual on such occasions – Jonas's father explained the situation to the children, with a lot of fiddling and fidgeting, and announced that sadly they would have to shelve their plans for a house of their own. At that very moment, while all of them were feeling pretty glum and even Åse's crooked smile had been wiped off, the doorbell rang and there stood Jonas's grandmother, Jørgine Wergeland, who had long since read the signs in telephone conversations with her daughter.

It had been a while since any of them had seen her. Jørgine had gone through a lengthy spell of being Winston Churchill – a magnificent Winston Churchill, I might add – but the word was that in recent years she had gone back to being herself, which is to say an ordinary, one-time farmer's wife from Gardermoen sitting reminiscing in the kitchen in Oscars gate or down by the pond in Slottsparken, chatting away quite normally to other old folk.

'Dearie me, you're a right cheery-looking lot!' Jonas's grandmother wasted no time. She asked them to sit themselves down in the sofa nook, she asked for a glass of port, she asked them all to relax.

Then she laid a cheque on the table, made out to Jonas's mother, Åse Hansen.

'There you go, and good luck to you.' She raised the glass of port, winked at them all, even Buddha, who was gazing in wonder at the three deep creases in her forehead.

Jonas's mother was completely nonplussed. 'That's an awful lot of money,' was all she said.

'True, but then what would I do with it?' said his grandmother.

'But how did you come by it, mother? You haven't been doing anything illegal, have you?'

So Jørgine told them the story of 'the young businessman' who had rung her doorbell one day and asked to see her pictures. Jonas had all but forgotten the paintings that he had helped to collect. As recently as his first year in high school he had called in on his grandmother a couple of times after classes; he particularly remembered one visit to the Art Centre, occasioned by a biennale of works by young Nordic painters which had caused quite a stir, when he had persuaded his grandmother to buy a couple of early works by painters as diverse as Bjørn Carlsen and Odd Nerdrum, before celebrating a job well done not, as previously, with a visit to the Studenten ice cream parlour but with dinner – meatballs and stewed cabbage – at Restaurant Krølle, where his grandmother, clearly very much at home, impressed on Jonas the importance of only buying pictures by artists who were endeavouring to break new ground. 'Like Knut Rose,' she said, thinking of the boldly coloured paintings by him which she had acquired in the late sixties, prompted, needless to say, by that unerring tingling between Jonas's shoulder-blades.

This 'young businessman', as Jørgine called him, wandered from room to room of the big flat in Oscars gate in a daze, hardly crediting what he was seeing; over the years Jonas's grandmother had hung the walls with an impressive collection of works by young Norwegian artists, together with a few pictures from the fifties by Jakob Weidemann and Inger Sitter and a couple of Munch lithographs. When he had regained his breath he made Jørgine an offer on the spot for the whole collection. A very generous offer. More than it was worth. A lot more, by Jørgine's reckoning. He insisted. She asked him to let her think it over. The following day she took him up on his offer, sold the whole lot, apart from four pictures which she later gave to Jonas, as a special thank-you to him.

'Here's the money,' said Jonas's grandmother, 'and now I'll take a little more port, if you don't mind. Åse, stop looking so worried.' Suddenly Jonas saw his grandmother as level-headed countrywoman, triumphant Churchill and wealthy patron of the arts all rolled into one; these three facets of her personality seemed to have synthesized into a greater whole, or perhaps only now were they seeing the real Jørgine Wergeland. 'With this money you'll be able to build that new house,' she said. 'Now that's not so bad, is it?'

No, it was not so bad, and thus Jonas learned that the price of beauty, too, is constantly rising and that it can be converted into something concrete: a fine little brick-built house nestling under the reddish-brown granite face of Ravnkollen, for example. Jonas's family always maintained that their house had been built by artists: by a bricklayer named Widerberg, a joiner named Rose and a plumber named Johannessen.

I might also add that Jonas's grandmother most definitely did not need too feel bad about her 'young businessman'. He had immediately recognized the value of Jørgine Wergeland's unique collection of experimental works by young artists, the majority painted at a stage when they were in the process of breaking away from teachers and traditions and trying out new ways of painting. In other words, this man had a 'nose', and a nose for fine art at that. Before the seventies were out, Jens Johannessen, Frans Widerberg and Knut Rose – to name but three – would all, in their turn, score major successes as exhibitors at the Bergen Arts Festival and representing Norway at the Biennale in Venice. More to the point, however, is the fact that the 'young business-man' had detected something which escaped the attention of all but a few at that time: namely the first signs of what would later be referred to as the 'yuppie decade', which began to manifest itself towards the end of the seventies. Suddenly, works of art were fetching unprecedented sums of money – not only because they represented an investment and a speculative venture but also because they actually accorded the buyer a certain cachet. For instance, at the height of this wave, a picture by the not particularly inspiring, late nineteenth-century artist Erik Werenski-old was sold at auction for two and a half million kroner, and even a painter from our own century such as Kai Fjell could command prices of up to two million kroner for a picture. So even if, with a few exceptions, each of Jørgine Wergeland's paintings on its own might not have been representative of such massive price increases, as a *whole*, as a collection, they constituted a very attractive proposition. Thus, when the time was right, her 'young businessman' was able, in his turn, to sell the collection to another 'young businessman' at a price three times greater than the exorbitant price he himself had paid.

If it is any consolation, I should just say that there is bound to come a day when the general public will enjoy these pictures, when this second, or a third, 'young businessman' is getting on in years and decides to do penance for his sins by building a magnificent art gallery as an annexe to the empire he has established almost solely by picking up the phone and saying 'sell' or 'buy'.

What is more to the point, as far as our story is concerned, is that his grandmother's transaction opened Jonas Wergeland's eyes to the fact that this spine-tingling sensation of his could, as it were, be turned into hard cash. In which case he saw no reason why it should not someday be possible to trade in his own collection for something he truly dreamed of. You see, Jonas Wergeland did not collect paintings, he collected women.

And now you are standing in the Villa Wergeland, paid for, years ago, by your grandmother's paintings, and you remember that you were on your way to the dining-room, and now you do actually walk through to the dining-room to check if the paintings are gone, if they have been stolen, and you do not need to switch on the light because you can see that the pictures are still there, they seem almost to shine in the dark, with a glow several layers thick, paintings you once singled out yourself, but what good does that do now, you think, what's the use of a silver thread running down your spine now, you think, what the fuck use is art to anyone anyway, you think, and you trail back into the living room and you see the picture of Buddha and once again you are confronted with Margrete, dead, on the floor, and you have the urge to bend down and take her in your arms, hold her like a little child, tight against you, like a sculpture by Gustav Vigeland you think, man with a woman in his arms, you think, but you do not do so, you merely look and look, at her face, always that face you think, do you remember how I managed to ski all the way down the hills to Movatn, you ask out loud, all the way without falling once, for the first time, you say out loud, looking and looking at her, feeling your eyes fill with tears, the ache in your throat, a sword, you think, a sword at my throat you think, and now you are finally going to be chopped up and your limbs scattered around this room, as if across a vast, barren desert, you think.

Your eye falls on the bowl on the side table, filled with fruit, like an oasis you think, looking at the oranges and remembering how Margrete would peel an orange, slowly, in awe almost, and how she would split it up into wedges, 'boats' she called them, eyeing each one lingeringly, holding it up to the light as if it were a work of wonder, you think, before putting it into her mouth, and you remember how she savoured, really savoured, every boat, you think, and the word 'boat' pulls you up short, makes you think of a boat reversing, and you hear a whooshing sound, like water seething around the stern of a reversing boat and you listen, intently, until it fades, dropping to no more than a faint hum, or radiation, and again you are struck by the distinct odour of electronic equipment in use and of some gently heated synthetic material, mingling with the smell of charred logs and ashes, and you walk round the corner to find a television set, switched on, but with the sound turned down, and at first you cannot think what a television is doing here, or what a television is, anyone would think you had never seen such a contrivance before, but it reminds you of something and you lift your eyes to the row of blue transparent jars on the shelf above it, as if these were every bit as important, because these are Margrete's jars and there are seven of them, just like in the fairytales, you think, and you have a mind to knock them to the floor, in protest against something or other, but you do not, you merely look at them, at the delicate, transparent blue in the dim light and gradually it comes back to you, what it is, that machine sitting below the blue jars, what it is used for, pictures, you think, a screen you sit and look at, you think, and something slowly dawns on you, the way it does when you gradually begin to recognize someone who has said hello to you only once they eventually say their name, and the machine is switched on, you think, surprised, it must have been on all the time, you think, even as Margrete was dying, you think, as if this holds the key to it all, and you stand there looking, looking and looking, but you cannot make head nor tail of the images, neither what they represent or how they hang together.

So there you stand, Jonas Wergeland, brother to the polar bear, champion of the Perfume Islands, darling of the Norwegian people, in front of a television set, and you vaguely remember that you actually have cashed in on your collection of paintings, no, not paintings, you think, something else, you cannot remember what, only that you have exchanged it for something that has to do with this screen in front of you, these images, without sound, the chance to be behind these images, or *to be* these images, you think, and now you realize, as things become clearer, that it is the evening news flashing across the screen, and you recognize the newsreader, you are sure you have spoken to him sometime, you think, and there is something about these images, dramatic items from different countries that fills you with a desperate need to learn everything that has been happening in the world that day, and you think to yourself that if you can do that, you will also find the one detail which will explain everything, why you are standing here, looking at a dead body, you think, and from then on you will actually be enormously keen to know what went on in the world on that particular day, during those minutes when you wandered about in a daze or stood riveted in front of the evening news on TV, events at home and abroad, soundless, and there is something about these images, from society, as it were, from the world outside these windows, you think, which triggers a memory of who you are, one of the other people you are, because you are many people, you think, you are also a politician, you think, once you even climbed a flagpole for a cause, you think, and you were, no, you are still, deeply concerned with how you, an insignificant little individual, could step in and have some effect on the big decisions taken by a community in which almost no one shows their face and almost everyone is faceless, and you stand there, in a living room with a dead body lying next to you, and you gaze at a silent television screen showing a report of the more scandalous sort, some exposé or other, some outraged face speaking into a microphone held obligingly to his lips by a disembodied hand, and you remember that you too have made television programmes, a lot of programmes, you think, presenting Norwegian society from unusual angles, and you know that people were hit, hard, when they least expected it, struck by a ball that shot off at an angle, often more than one angle, like a billiard ball, you think, and you know you have shocked people, no more, aroused hate, you think, and you turn from the television screen to Margrete, dead on the floor, and you realize that any Norwegian citizen could be behind this, it could be anyone, even the Oslo bomber, you think, someone who's sick in the head, or simply someone who hates being provoked, hates these all too revealing, all too unforeseen angles.

Strike the Christian Cross from your Flag

Always this: to find a different angle from anyone else. Like the time he took the stairs two at a time to come breathlessly to a halt outside the door of the corner room on the third floor and, quivering more with impatience than nerves, managed to pick the lock – he, Jonas Wergeland, the Duke, on the hunt for new angles.

He crosses to the window, shaped like the upper half of a circle. A half-moon. How apt. It is early in the morning, before first period, and Jonas is standing in the dusty flag-loft of Oslo Cathedral School with a length of fabric rolled up under his arm and his heart pounding in his chest. These are the days of student revolt and like so many others Jonas Wergeland means to hoist a flag – but not the usual flag.

The horizontal flag-pole was anchored inside the room itself, running through the wall just below the window; it put Jonas in mind of a jib-boom and made him feel as if he were standing in the bow of a lifeboat, all ready to do great deeds. But what he saw outside, or down below, was not the sea, but the cemetery.

Oslo Cathedral School was tucked away in one corner of the huge Rikshospital complex and Jonas actually felt more like a patient than a pupil: a patient who was constantly being given the wrong diagnosis. To be brutally frank, Jonas would have regarded his three years at this high school, all mentions of which were invariably punctuated by such epithets as 'venerable' or 'steeped in tradition' or 'charming', as seriously damaging to his mental health, had it not been for the fact that it lay just across the street from Our Saviour's cemetery. For it was there that he had met Axel.

During the lunch-break on one of his first days at the
Cathedral School, following an almost destructive impulse,
Jonas had slipped through the wrought-iron gates of the cemetery. Despite the beautiful August weather, he was feeling
thoroughly depressed and shuddered to think what the three
years ahead of him held in store in terms of tedium and, worse,
unsatisfied curiosity. Jonas cursed himself and the whim that had
led him to this 'august' school in the heart of the city.

Gloomily he made his way between the rows of graves, and it
was while he was walking along, kicking up the gravel, his eyes
fixed on the ground, that he heard a familiar sound, a sound so
familiar that at first he could not figure out what it was. He
walked faster, straightened his shoulders, headed towards the
sound, some faint notes played on an instrument he ought to
know better than any other. The music was coming from someone hidden behind the leafy foliage surrounding one of the
graves in the Grove of Honour. And there, sitting between two
striking weeping beeches, on the grave of none other than Bjørnstjerne Bjørnson, was Axel Stranger.

Anyone familiar with Our Saviour's cemetery in Oslo will
know that Bjørnstjerne Bjørnson's grave is marked with a flat
stone of red granite. The actual concept – a flag, yes, yet another
flag – is really rather grotesque, but the monument itself makes
a perfect place to sit; in summer the stone is lovely and warm
and, as I mentioned, well screened by thick foliage. Axel had
resorted to this spot to read. Oddly enough Jonas, who rarely
opened a work of fiction, tended to choose friends who were
readers. Nefertiti and Margrete were also readers. Lying on the
granite next to Axel was Halldor Laxness' *Veveren fra Kashmir*,
a battered copy from Deichman's Library.

On seeing Jonas, Axel finished the tune he was playing, the
title of which had finally come to Jonas: 'In a Sentimental
Mood' from Duke Ellington's inexhaustible repertoire. Without
a word, Jonas put out his hand, and the mouth organ was placed
in his palm like a relay baton. It was exactly the same as his own,
a Hohner Chromonica, well used, with a dent in the casing.
Jonas raised it to his lips and played 'Sophisticated Lady', not
altogether satisfied with his performance, it was a long time

since he had played, but he got through it. His face deadpan, Axel took back the instrument and proceeded to play – without wiping it on his trouser-leg first, which Jonas promptly took as a vote of confidence – 'I Got It Bad and That Ain't Good' with such virtuosity and such feeling that it sent shivers up Jonas's spine, forcing him to swallow several times. Never had anyone brought out the aching melancholy of that tune so well, no one in Ellington's own orchestra come to that, not even Johnny Hodges. And as Axel played, Jonas felt something loosen its grip on him. Nefertiti. Or rather, he felt as if he were letting go of one hand and clasping another, a new hand. And it is as if Nefertiti herself was there beside him, giving this new friendship her blessing.

'Christ Almighty,' said Axel. He slipped the mouth organ into his jacket pocket, ran a hand through his tousled locks and squinted up at the sun. 'What a shower.'

Jonas knew what he was referring to. Their class. Not because they were so all-fired clever. Nor because so many of them were the children of pillars of society who before too long would themselves constitute a disproportionately large slice of Norway's highly visible élite. It was because they were such bloody conformists. Even their radicalism was conformist; their very rebelliousness followed the fashion, usually of an earlier era, so they could ponce about in their fathers' berets and their grandfathers' black waistcoats, reading Sartre, like Jonas's cousin Veronika – who, it went without saying, was also a pupil at the school. It reeked to high heaven of opportunist opposition.

'And those *teachers*.' Axel made a face.

'Aye hope you awll rrree-alayze what sawrrrt of school you arrre attending.' Jonas did a perfect imitation of the headmaster.

'I knew it the minute I saw you,' said Axel. 'I could tell by your shoes. You were a wanderer. You were the only one.'

Jonas had also noticed Axel. It's always the way. You home in on one another almost as soon as you walk through the school gates: like ants, it's all down to chemistry, even in a crowd of several hundred. It might be a look, a laugh – in Jonas and Axel's case it was their shoes. Both wore a particular type of sturdy, thick-soled black brogue, well polished. And they were dressed almost identically in white cotton shirts, buttoned to the neck, dark tweed jackets and baggy trousers of a good quality; in other words, what I would call timeless clothes – clothes that never reflect the current fashion, no matter how much or how often that may change.

'Where did you learn to play like that?' Axel asked.

'From a girl.'

'And Duke Ellington?'

'The same.'

'Looks like we've both been lucky,' Axel said. 'To run into originals in a world full of imitators.' Otherwise, Axel's most distinctive feature was his hair, a thick black mop that at times looked so wild that it could have been mistaken for the Rasta dreadlocks of a later date.

They made many a visit to Our Saviour's cemetery during their three years at the Cathedral School. While other pupils headed for the town centre at lunchtime, going all the way down to the Studenten ice cream parlour, wolfed down stacks of *millefeuilles* in the neighbourhood teashops, sneaked into the Rikshospital canteen or wandered along to Ringstrøm's second-hand bookshop to rummage through the boxes set out on the street, Jonas and Axel took refuge among the stone monuments on the other side of Ullevålsveien, where the graves of famous Norwegian men and women provided them with a place to relax between two spells of dreary school work. 'During lunch-breaks at the Cath, I mixed with a lot of interesting people,' Jonas would later say. In the classroom they went hunting for turtles; at lunchtime they sat or lay stretched out in the Grove of Honour and played the mouth organ, their eyes resting on the top of a lovely copper beech or a majestic horse chestnut. Jonas taught Axel the arrangements for two mouth organs that Nefertiti had taught him, first and foremost their *pièce de résistance*: 'Concerto for Cootie'. They really made that number swing, so magnificently that on occasion they ended up being chased by the caretaker. 'Don't you have any respect for the dead?' he would holler, waving his fist at them. 'Vandals!'

Jonas and Axel would have been more inclined to say that they were 'honouring the dead'.

They had their favourite graves. The grassy slope alongside Edvard Munch's memorial plaque was just right for 'Morning Glory', Olaf Bull's beautiful grave with its tall undressed stones lent a unique resonance to 'Never No Lament', perfect for two mouth organs, while they did honour to composer Johan Svendsen's lofty obelisk, fittingly enough, with 'It Don't Mean A Thing If It Ain't Got That Swing'.

There were not too many Norwegian students who could be tested in a Norwegian literature class on the serpentine influence of Sigurd Hoel and then go out, slip a red stocking cap over the head of said gentleman atop his gravestone and play that lovely Ellington number 'The Girl In My Dreams Tries To Look Like You', finding in this a welcome safety-valve, a way of letting off steam. Axel in particular, having the handicap of being a reader, was forever getting into arguments with their Norwegian teacher, not least because this Norwegian teacher was an advocate of a turtle with an especially tough shell, a commonly held theory known as 'realism', with the accent on mimesis, imitation and so-called reliable sources – reliable in relation to what? Axel would ask – which their Norwegian teacher would put into practice by claiming, cool as you like, without dropping his gaze for a second, without blushing, without stammering, that the novel *The Fire* by Tarjei Vesaas, coming between the two highly acclaimed works *The Birds* and *The Ice Palace*, was no good. The best one could hope for, according to Axel, was that he had merely gleaned this opinion from orthodox contemporary book reviews. At worst, he had actually read *Brannen* himself and meant what he said. Either that or the Norwegian teacher would drive Axel to despair by claiming that the experiments carried out by Johan Borgen later in his career had little to offer compared to his earlier, far more traditional work: a viewpoint so monstrous that Axel could not even laugh it off. One day, incensed by an argument he had had with this teacher on the subject of what a damnably overrated writer Henrik Ibsen was and why in hell such a senile old fool should be allowed to take up so many of their vital Norwegian classes, Axel stormed out in a rage and peed on Ibsen's tombstone, the obelisk in the Grove of Honour: a traditionalist's phallus, according to Axel, a stinking corpse in the hold. There are many ways of making a protest. Axel replaced the catchword of the day – 'Peace!' – with his own alternative: 'Piss!' For those of you who might feel offended by this, I would, if I may, like to say a few words in Axel's defence. His reaction was prompted by a great love of literature, so great – not to say excessive – that he could often be moved to tears by the things he read, a trait which Jonas never understood. To be honest, he never really could comprehend those members of the human race who were readers.

As I say, there are many ways of making a protest: there was Jonas Wergeland, in the flag-loft of Oslo Cathedral School, all set to hoist a flag. He opened the middle of the three panels in the arched window and considered the white pole sticking surprisingly far out into midair, as much as five metres maybe, and the rope toggle which, as ill luck would have it, must have been tugged loose by wind and weather and had slid a good way down the pole. He was going to have to shin out onto it, not far, but the very thought was enough to leave him paralysed.

Is this the most crucial story in Jonas Wergeland's life?

He has to do it. He has made up his mind. He is Jonas Wergeland, the Duke, on the hunt for fresh angles. He forces himself not to look down at Ullevålsveien as he crawls carefully, very carefully out of the window and stretches out, even more carefully if that is possible, along the pole. Like a bowsprit, he thinks, even as he feels it give under him; it is a wooden pole, the mere thought that it might be rotten brings him out in a sweat and, worse, moves him to look down, inducing an attack of vertigo; half of him wants to let go, the other half is hanging on for dear life. A woman glances up at him in astonishment but does not stop. She must think that Jonas is some sort of chameleon, or that a high-school student clinging to a flagpole sticking straight out into the air thirty feet above the ground is a perfectly normal sight in these rebellious times. Jonas looks down on the cemetery, fantasizing as to what they will write on his tombstone, but he makes it, grabs hold of the line, undoes it one-handed and crawls backwards to safety.

Jonas unfurled his length of fabric, fixed it to the rope and hoisted it out onto the pole. It looked great, really . . . exotic.

What would people on the street below think? That a new embassy had been established on Ullevålsveien?

The flag fluttered beautifully in the breeze. It was green, with a white half-moon and four small stars.

Jonas slung his rucksack over his shoulder, slipped back out of the flag-loft door and produced a little sliver of metal which he wedged into the lock – an old and effective trick. In any case, it was a good solid door, not to be broken down just like that.

There were still twenty minutes to go until first period and more, much more, to be done before then.

The Rise and Fall
of the Roman Empire

Jonas Wergeland did not, in fact, have a fear of heights but a fear of outlooks or overviews. This was something he was also plagued with on his countless visits to Torggata Baths, where time and again he had sworn that he was going to dive from the five-metre platform only, just as often, to have to back down, feeling dizzy, almost nauseated. Which is to say it was not the height as such that petrified him, so that his feet refused to take those last few crucial centimetres towards the edge, but the image of the pool from above, that bird's-eye view which turned the familiar surroundings into something alien and ghastly with all the detail of the hall erased and the people in the water suddenly being deprived of their facial features to become creatures of another sort, frogs executing meaningless movements.

During the summer they larked around in the lakes among the hills and forests just outside of town. But Nefertiti loved to swim in the winter, too, and so she had introduced Jonas to Torggata Baths. They used to take the yellow and green Grorud bus to the bridge at Møllergata and invariably popped round to the Central Fire Station to see whether the turntable ladder truck was out, or to Deichman's Library if Nefertiti had books to return, before running on down to the baths. Nefertiti was like a seal in the water. Jonas would look on admiringly as she spun round like a wheel, dived straight to the bottom and cavorted about down there or when she did the most amazing somersaults from the springboard, breaking the surface perfectly, just like the lady on the Brynild liquorice pastilles pack.

Not to put too fine a point on it, as far as Jonas and Nefertiti were concerned, Torggata Baths was a holy place. The bus-stop in Grorud was just outside the grocer's shop, so they always picked up a couple of bottles of Mekka, a brand of chocolate milk produced by the Norwegian United Dairies at that time, a brown bottle with a silver top, as if to illustrate the fact that they were setting out on a pilgrimage of sorts: that, like the Muslims, they considered the cleansing of the body a solemn affair. I know that to this day there are many people living along Trondheimsveien who remember those two children on the bus in the winter-time, sipping devoutly from their Mekka bottles and playing the odd Duke Ellington number on chromatic mouth organs, the most charming duets.

It was not only that the Torggata Baths had something of a religious air about them; throughout his life Jonas was to associate them with the concept of socialism owing to the sense of equality fostered by those chlorine-scented halls: the fact that no one could tell the difference between a Spartacus and a Caligula. Right from the time in the loft in the block of flats in Solhaug when Neferitit, wrapped in a sheet, had told him about the Romans and their *thermae*, those huge bathing establishments of which all that remains today are ruins that might have been tailor-made for open-air opera productions, Jonas had been fascinated by public baths. When you came right down to it there was something un-Norwegian about Torggata Baths. As Jonas was walking up the broad steps leading to the palatial entrance, the word that always came into his mind was 'Europe'.

From another point of view, too, Torggata Baths was a memorable spot; it was here that Jonas met his mentor Gabriel Sand, during the winter when Jonas was in eighth grade to be precise.

As usual, Jonas had been hovering in the vicinity of the platform up in the gallery, desperately wanting to have a shot at diving off it, when a bunch of bigger lads came running up, almost as if they had sensed his fear, and made to chuck him off.

All of a sudden there he was, Gabriel Sand, a total stranger to Jonas, a most unlikely figure in a thick, black terrycloth robe with a white towel draped around his neck. He only had to *look* at the other boys for them to let go of Jonas and promptly beat a retreat, fearfully and apologetically, backing away, bowing and scraping, as if they had just been caught red-handed in the midst of some prank by their headmaster at school.

Jonas studies Gabriel long and hard before he thinks of something to say: 'You know that priests are the servants of the imagination, that their power stems from their being able to make the masses believe the most incredible things?'

He waves a hand in the direction of Gabriel in his black robe topped off by the white towel and then towards the stairs down which the boys have disappeared, as though implying that he thinks Gabriel looks like a priest and that he must have worked a conjuring trick, some sleight of hand, like Mandrake the Magician, causing the riff-raff to vanish into thin air.

Even Gabriel could not know that Jonas was quoting here, or rather, had plucked a gem from the little red book in which he had begun to note down certain passages, in this instance some sentences from Charles Baudelaire's *Oeuvres posthumes et correspondances inédites*, fortunately translated between the lines in Jonas's edition. Nonetheless, Gabriel was impressed by a boy who could not have been any more than fourteen coming out with such a statement. I think I can safely say that Gabriel Sand would never have invited Jonas into his changing-room had it not been for that covert aphorism from Baudelaire.

I can see how, for example, people might forget the lovely El Dorado cinema rotunda, sadly demolished in 1985, and how it looked, but that anyone, even older residents of Oslo, could succeed in actually erasing the old interior of Torggata Baths from their memories is quite beyond me. I am happy to say that Jonas Wergeland never forgot that establishment but cherished it as one of his fondest memories. Later, when confronted with some fine construction, such as the stations of the Moscow underground, those sunken palaces, he would mutter to himself: 'By Jove, this could almost be Torggata Baths.'

As soon as he set foot in the vestibule, with its ticket office like a little glasshouse built into the wall, he was faced with an interior fit for a king. But it was not until he was older that Jonas explored the secrets of its nethermost regions which, besides a medicinal department featuring mud-baths and massage, housed a little-frequented Turkish bath; three vaulted chambers filled with hot air, like three little chapels ranged one after the other, and a small pool room with four stout pillars, one in each corner;

black floor and white marble on the walls. This was a place where for next to nothing every Norwegian could transcend time and space and be ruler of the world for a day.

As a small boy, Jonas frequented the first and second floors – not only the bathhouse and the big pool, that vast colonnaded hall with the electric lamps hanging from the ceiling and daylight streaming in through the tall windows on either side through which, in the afternoons, the sunlight fell straight onto the green surface of the water – but also, what seemed to him at that time nothing short of a miracle: the sauna. Jonas Wergeland had never seen a sauna before he visited Torggata baths, and for him, with the chill that never seemed to leave his bones, it was a blessing – that was the very word that popped into his head – to be able to sit there, in a golden-yellow sauna, in the middle of winter, in Oslo, and sweat and get really warm 'right to the soul', as he said to himself. Afterwards he could take himself off to a cooling-down room which had showers and a nice little pool, and at the side of this pool – in front of the two marble massage benches in the alcove further back – there was, wonder of wonders, a copy of a small statue from Florence, no less: a boy holding a dolphin which spouted a jet of water into the pool. Finally one could retire to the rest room, settle back in a deckchair and flick through a newspaper, take a breather before getting dressed.

There was nothing to beat Torggata Baths. With its copper, its marble and mahogany; with its elaborate tile-work, the exquisite patterns on floor and walls and, not least, its deckchairs, it was a real-life Utopia, open to all.

Then, in 1981, they closed the baths. From a purely personal point of view I am happy to say that I have no reason to become all het up about such a trivial matter, but I admit it is a mystery to me that more citizens of Oslo were not driven to protest against this move. A lot of people still bear a grudge against the yuppies, and Jonas hated them because they, or it would be truer to say, their spirit, reduced Torggata Baths to a collection of chic boutiques, chi-chi restaurants and snooty squash courts – and a scaled down Turkish bath that no one knew about. But the real crime, as I see it, is not what the yuppies did to the old interior but that the yuppie way of thinking, the fixation with money and

indiscriminate profiteering, should have gained the upper hand
in the city council, in the people's own democratic decision-
making processes. So it was in fact the people themselves, and
not the yuppies, who showed just how short the distance is
between two apparently opposite poles – a public baths and what
it became: a limited partnership.

Jonas did not see any of this, but he saw how sad Buddha was.
Jonas often took Buddha with him to Torggata, and he loved the
place even more than Jonas. He did not think it was anywhere near
so much fun to swim in the sterile new Nordtvedt Baths where
the all-round experience offered by Torggata, a treat on many
different planes, was supplanted by sheer function, pure keep-fit.
Not that I have anything against that, but if you ask me, the clo-
sure of the old Torggata Baths represents the real divide between
Oslo as a social democracy and Oslo as a town run according to
the slick, one-dimensional principles of neo-capitalism. Until
then, even the conservative parties had upheld the basic social-
democratic principles. I would go so far as to say that 1981 and the
demise of Torggata Baths mark the end of a golden age for twentieth-century Norway inasmuch as social democracy was no
longer an ideal and a set of values but a hollow system of government, little more than a vacuous accounting firm.

But I am supposed to be telling you about the first time Jonas
met Gabriel Sand, and I am not so far off the track as one might
think. You see, Gabriel invited Jonas into the most wonderful
corner of all in the old Torggata baths: the changing rooms up
on the galleries, little cubby-holes with walls of glazed tile and
doors of fine reddish-brown mahogany that put Jonas in mind of
the classy speedboats he saw down on Hvaler, belonging to ship-
owners or visitors from the island of Hankø, select summer
haunt of Norway's *beau monde*.

Jonas was feeling not a little bewitched by this man who had
shown up out of the blue and saved his skin, and when Gabriel
reached his own cubicle and motioned to Jonas to follow him –
the man had not yet said one word – Jonas did not hesitate but
stepped right inside the cramped changing room, where a pinstripe suit hung neatly from a hook, and sat down on the bench,
after which Gabriel promptly closed the door by lowering that

wooden bar, which some readers may remember, into place across it. Jonas was not at all afraid, though; there was something about this elderly man which inspired confidence, an air of authority – maybe it had something to do with the scar beneath one eyebrow, like a badge of honour, a sign of valour. On the bench between them stood a matte-green bottle and a small blue tin: 'Foie gras', Jonas read on the side of it. 'Would you like some goose-liver pâté?' It was the first time Gabriel had opened his mouth. 'Some champagne?' Jonas declined the offer, sat there in his swimming trunks looking round about him. There was something about Gabriel, his clothes, a gold pocket-watch, the food, a pack of Camel cigarettes, that made him feel as if he were in a little cabin, as if this man lived here, cramped, but cosy. 'Have you ever noticed how mahogany has an air of the exotic about it?' said Gabriel. 'The very word "mahogany" makes you feel you could talk the language of Jamaica.'

'What's your name?' Jonas asked.

'That question is of little consequence to one who abhors all outward appearance but seeks the profound, the hidden, those things worth knowing.' This answer seemed to echo around the cubicle, and Jonas thought it smacked of recitation. Gabriel smiled, and for the first time, in the dim light, Jonas caught the glint of his gold tooth.

'My name is Gabriel,' he said. 'And I'm on the run from my wife.' With that he launched into a long and occasionally frenzied tale that made Jonas laugh out loud more than once, about a dragon of a wife who forced him to seek sanctuary here, to enjoy forbidden fruit.

Then, having consumed the last of the pâté and the wine, he said, 'So you guessed it, then.'

'How do you mean?' said Jonas.

'That I'm a priest, albeit a retired one.' Gabriel regarded him with what Jonas would have called 'soft' eyes and made a gesture that seemed, in the most amazing way, to extend the cubicle into a church and the food to a sacrament. Although Jonas did not realize it, he was witnessing acting at its best. It would be a long time before he discovered that Gabriel Sand was not a priest and neither did he have a wife. 'Tell me. Have you tried diving from the five-metre here?' Gabriel asked, changing the subject without any preamble.

Jonas told him about his fear of such an undertaking.

Gabriel opened the door: 'Off you go and dive,' he said, making it sound almost like a biblical commandment.

'I can't,' said Jonas. 'I really can't.'

Quietly Gabriel explained that it was all psychological. Why couldn't Jonas imagine that he was Samuel Lee, Olympic diving champion in 1948 and 1952? And again Gabriel broke into a fantastic account of how the Korean-American Sammy Lee, later to become a doctor and otologist, had taught himself to dive, all lies from beginning to end, but Jonas did not know that, he allowed himself be carried away, and who can blame him? That tale was the storytelling equivalent of a reverse dive with one and half somersaults and a triple twist.

'I'm not Sammy Lee,' said Jonas.

'Oh, yes you are. What's so unlikely in that? A lot more unlikely things have happened in this world than that you should, for three seconds, be Sammy Lee. Remember, your bodies are composed of exactly the same matter.'

Jonas walks up to the platform at one end of the hall, imagining that he is Dr Samuel Lee, two times Olympic champion in high diving. Samuel Lee at the age of fourteen. There is nothing to hinder him, the pool below is clear. Jonas covers the last few centimetres, curls his toes over the edge and imagines that he is Samuel Lee, senses the twists and somersaults and, not least, the *joy of swooping*, residing inside his body, in some chamber unknown to him. Jonas gazes down at the surface of the pool and imagines that he is Sammy Lee. He launches himself off in a perfect swallow dive; Sammy Lee could hardly have done it better. Not until he is in the pool, so overjoyed that he is gulping water, does Jonas become Jonas again.

'Well done,' said Gabriel moments later, when Jonas stood before him once more, like a soldier who has just carried out an order. 'You've broken a barrier today. Dared to make a leap. We're going to be good mates, that's for sure.' He took a long look at Jonas, nodded approvingly before saying, 'By the way, I've got this lifeboat. I could do with a crewman to accompany me on a voyage 20,000 leagues under the sea.'

Isfahan

Aunt Laura's flat looked like a bazaar. Where the walls were not covered in oriental rugs they were hung with objects made of copper and brass, and crawling around the floor was a leopard-tortoise with little gems affixed to its shell. Jonas had the feeling that the tortoise was forever going round in circles and that time stood still at Aunt Laura's.

Apart from Torggata Baths, nowhere in Oslo had a more edifying influence on Jonas Wergeland's imagination than Aunt Laura's flat.

To gain a deeper insight into this unique world I would recommend the following experiment: make a cup of tea, preferably one of the rarer varieties, put on 'Isfahan' from Duke Ellington's *The Far East Suite* and settle back into a pile of soft cushions. Then shut your eyes and listen to the mellow lazy horns of Duke Ellington's seductive orchestra, inhale the scent of, say, China tea while running your fingers over the cool silk of the cushion covers. Try also to imagine how Billy Strayhorn's wonderfully languorous melody would sound in a room where the music was muted by an untold number of thick rugs and the sound of hammer-blows on soft precious metals mingled with Johnny Hodges' haunting saxophone solo. That was Aunt Laura's flat. Every child has his own Ali Baba's cave, and this was Jonas's.

Jonas's family was blessed with many weird and wonderful characters, and Aunt Laura, his father's sister, was one of them: with black-lined eyelids and blood-red lipstick in an almost chalk-white face, and a flair for shawls and hats seldom met with in grey ascetic Oslo. All in all, Aunt Laura belonged to that microscopic band of Norwegians who could have stepped straight onto the set of a Fellini film. She had trained as a

goldsmith and lived alone in a tenement in Tøyen on the east side
of the city. After working initially for a reputable but dull company with showrooms on Karl Johans gate, his aunt had gone
into business for herself, setting up a workshop in the flat, at the
far end of the living room. And she was doing very nicely; she
had built up a devoted clientele who positively outbid one
another for the pieces she made, *objets d'art* which gradually
began to acquire the status of cult objects, and *provocative* ones
at that.

When Jonas's aunt's work-lamp was not switched on, the
room lay bathed in a dim light that opened it up, creating vast
distances. The rugs became windows onto evocative shadowy
landscapes, and the copper and brass on the walls and the silver
on the workbench glowed mysteriously. To Jonas that room
seemed transformed into a firmament in which the glints in the
metal were stars, and the patterns of the rugs hinted at the tales
that lay tucked away within those faint points of light. In this
room, Jonas Wergeland was told stories the like of which few
other children in Norway would ever hear.

Aunt Laura was a collector, she collected rugs, and in order to
track down new rugs she was forever out travelling – so often that
she spent more time abroad, particularly in the Middle East
and Central Asia, than at home. Jonas's aunt was an expert on
Oriental rugs, one of a tiny handful of people who took a pride
in being able to differentiate between a Bergama, a Ghiordes or
a Kemurju-Kulah rug and who could give you a complete run-
down on the symbolism of the 'boteh' motif and all its regional
variations at the drop of a hat. She had, however, only one criterion, albeit a most exacting one, when it came to choosing rugs
for herself; they had to inspire her.

Jonas was fascinated by those rugs on the walls which, if he
turned round quick and only looked at them with half an eye, all
looked exactly the same, but which were in reality all quite different just as no two crystals of snow are alike. Jonas remembered the day when he was lying among the pile of soft cushions
on the sofa, with a cup of tea to hand, and his aunt – sitting at her
workbench behind the hanging drill, the lathe and the saw-frame
– first told him about the greatest of all the rug-makers: nomads

endowed with such exceptional powers of recall and imagination that they might carry as many as two hundred carpet designs in their heads, down to the smallest detail, and these they would sing out, knot by knot, to the rug-knotters in village after village. 'Actually they were a bit like your grandfather,' his aunt said.

For Jonas, the greatest revelation came when Aunt Laura put down her work, positioned herself next to one of the rugs – rather like his geography teacher when he pulled down one of the big maps in the classroom – and showed him how each rug could contain a story, a legend and sometimes more than one, all of which she recounted while pointing out the different features of each rug. It was not only the technique involved that left Jonas all agog, the idea that even the simplest story could be made up of millions of knots, thus saying something about the complex and underrated art of weaving a tale, tying several threads together, as it were; it was as much the fact that the rug, this symmetrical, stylized, almost abstract pattern of shapes and colours, suddenly seemed to come *alive* before his very eyes, like a film.

I am not telling you all of this just for the sake of it. I do have my reasons. You see, these rugs gave Jonas his earliest insight into the way a single image could harbour infinite possibilities, and thus they came to form a model for the television images he himself was to create, images rich in ornament, in repetition and minute variation. But, above all else, these rugs taught him that an image does not need to *resemble* the thing it represents: that to some extent you could tie it up to reality however you pleased.

Jonas could never get enough of this: the aroma of tea and his aunt standing by the wall, pointing and explaining, bracelets jingling; her inky eyelids and chalk-white face against a background of soft woollen surfaces that glowed with all the colours of the rainbow: red, blue and, loveliest of all, the golden-yellow of emperors and pistachio green, the prophet's colour.

Taking this velvety herbarium as her outset, Aunt Laura taught him how to tell the different flowers apart: roses, carnations, tulips and irises – and this here is a lotus flower in its classic Persian form, lovely, isn't it? Then there were the inanimate objects: pots, combs, lamps, pillars and, of course, every creature from Noah's Ark, from parrots and peacocks to gazelles and horses, and there was a scorpion – and this here, this square with legs, is a spider. That much Jonas could make out for himself, but what he did not know was that all of these things also possessed their own symbolic significance. Thus the scorpion stood for courage, while the spider guarded against bad luck. Other things were not so easily made out, like the scarab or, favourites of Jonas's, the tortoises. The lions' heads looked like diamonds, and many of the rosettes put one in mind of multi-faceted gems as if elaborate pieces of jewellery had been hung in front of the rugs. Some things defied recognition, like clouds, while others could have been interpreted in a number of ways. Take, for example, this almond shape here, his aunt said. On this rug it was a leaf on Buddha's sacred tree, while on that rug over there it was a face. What Jonas liked best of all were the fabulous creatures, whimsical figures that his aunt would point to, telling him that this was a dragon or a chimera, a phoenix, a winged horse – sheer magic, a bunch of different coloured knots and you had a sea-monster.

Jonas became a great admirer of such creativity: of the way the rugs stimulated the imagination. You were out on the steppes in your simple tent, unrolled a rectangle of wool and – hey presto! – found yourself in a sacred place. Even as a small child, Jonas Wergeland had been sceptical, to the point of nausea, of over-simplification, but with these rugs it was not a matter of simplification, but of a twisting, a splitting, as when light was refracted by a prism, breaking up into its separate and surprising components. The rugs were not an imitation but a *transformation* or an unveiling of real life; you saw the world from another angle, thanks to one small detail: a knot. In this way the rugs represented an attempt to reach beyond the world or to reflect the world in a totally new way. After all, said his aunt, there weren't many holy places that could simply be rolled up and tucked under your arm.

Only later did Jonas realize that this was what had inspired his aunt's endeavour to capture the entire world in a piece of jewellery, a piece which would only become a reality if she could find the one detail in the world that embodied the world. 'There's a legend,' Jonas's aunt told him on one occasion, her bracelets jingling, 'that tells of a flower so perfect and so beautiful that if anyone were to find it and pick it, the world would disappear.'

It was at such times, lying on his back among silken cushions with his eyes resting on the rugs while his aunt sat working, surrounded by her graving tools, round burs and chasing punches, that Jonas used to beg her to tell him the tale of Princess Li Lai's lovers. At such times the word 'no' never passed Aunt Laura's lips, even though some people would no doubt consider this tale unsuitable for children. 'In Xanadu,' she said, 'Princess Li Lai received another suitor in her cool palace, for she had yet to find one who could make love to her as she desired, one who would make love to her until she saw a turtle with a shell that looked like a face. On this day, the one who had come to woo her was the calligrapher Lu Xan, and he did not waste any time but carried her to the bed and immediately proceeded to make love to her. Right from the start, Lu Xan concentrated on the layers of lips enfolding her sex as if they were fine paper on which he was resolved to write. The princess felt his delicate member moving in strange, swift flicks across her lips, lines in a rhythmic dance, first from side to side then up and down then in arcs from left to right, stroke after stroke, patiently and at length, and as he made love to her more and more urgently, now sweeping his penis from the outskirts of her sex towards the centre, Princess Li Lai felt a warm glow begin to spread through her body as if she had moved out into the sunshine and were walking through a landscape which Lu Xan the calligrapher was slowly inscribing in her path, with bamboo groves and fold upon fold of mountains, seeming to go on forever. And as Lu Xan executed a few swift studied strokes with his member, the princess came to a river which suddenly overflowed its banks and swept her away, and she floated off, floated and floated in a warm stream that flowed faster and faster, swelled up and caressed her body, more and more powerfully, until she was thrown onto the bank where a troop of hares ran off in fright and soon all she could hear was the sound of their galloping paws, like heartbeats, and she opened her eyes and she saw a hare with the features of a human face that gradually changed into that of Lu Xan the calligrapher, the lover now lying looking down at her, and she thanked him, but asked him to leave, because she had not yet seen a turtle with a shell that resembled a face, and Princess Li Lai was sure that there must be a better way to be made love to.'

After a tale such as that, Jonas would lie on the sofa for a long time without saying a word. Complete silence reigned in the room, apart from the scratching or tapping sounds from his aunt's workbench, which had also accompanied the story. When his aunt switched off the lamp, and Jonas looked round, he caught the glow of gold in the corner: soft but intense, magnetic, as if all of the remaining light were being drawn to that fragment of metal and, indeed, as if that one point could soak up everything, the whole world.

'Tell me about Samarkand,' he would say just before he left. It had become a ritual. He knew his aunt had been to Samarkand, and he asked the same thing every time.

'As for Samarkand and what I found there, that I can never tell you,' said Aunt Laura. 'You will have to go there yourself.'

Cities in Belgium

Jonas Wergeland is writing a's in his copybook. He knows that he is involved in a solemn undertaking; he knows intuitively that this is a privilege, this fact of being able to sit here writing a's. He had covered his copybook himself with the most fabulous waxed paper, carefully selected from the host of rolls in the stationer's, in the most uncommon pattern possible. On the front is a label bearing his name, a label like the ones his mother stuck on the jam jars, as if to show that this book, this memory, has to be stored away, preserved in his recollection. Jonas dips his pen in the inkwell, a cheap plastic pen: black at the end where he fixed the nib and with a pale-blue shaft. Jonas writes another row of a's, relishing the pressure of nib on paper, watches the wet ink slowly soaking into the fibres and drying, the tiny particles on the white surface bringing it home to him that writing is something concrete and palpable, a bit like his aunt engraving silver, he writes as neatly as he can – *a a a a a a a* – like a sigh of delight, something ecstatic, then draws a border. Borders are tricky, but there has to be a border. Jonas realizes that borders are important; they are ornamentation, they are a sign that the letters are not only letters but also something more, something beautiful: decoration or symbols harbouring a significance that extends far beyond the sound of 'a' or the word in which the letter appears. Jonas writes a's, small characters that are like windows, openings onto other rooms, possibilities he has never seen before. The teacher comes over, she draws a lovely flower – Jonas has never seen such a lovely flower – in the bottom corner. Although his a's are far from perfect and the borders are a bit crooked, she draws a make-believe flower as if to show that this – these a's and borders – are as furrows ploughed in fertile soil in which almost anything can be made to grow.

Jonas Wergeland had not always been so sceptical of school. High school was one thing, elementary school was quite another. Where high school had represented a closing off, elementary school constituted an opening up. To the boy Jonas, those first years at elementary school were as exciting as the rugs in Aunt Laura's flat, which is just about the greatest compliment a school could be paid: they were doors leading to wonderful rooms.

In Jonas Wergeland's life there were only two sorts of school: the good and the indifferent. Elementary school was good, while junior high, high school and university were all indifferent. One could go so far as to say that Jonas Wergeland only ever had an elementary-school education, since this was the only public institution to teach him anything – the rest of his education he took care of himself.

Bearing in mind the fashion these days in literary circles for depicting the first years at school as a child's worst nightmare, with teachers outdoing one another in acts of calculated terrorism, and pupils lying awake at night twisting their eiderdown covers into knots and muttering the most unlikely things to themselves, usually in Latin, I would like to present another, slightly different picture, not least because, from where I stand, it seems a mite strange, excuse me for saying so, that so many Norwegians – oddly enough, almost invariably people who have done very well for themselves – are forever whingeing about childhood and schooldays when one considers the less than idyllic conditions in schools in other parts of the world, where something as basic as a blank sheet of paper is like gold.

What I am saying is that when it comes to Jonas Wergeland's elementary school, to Grorud School, you have to dispense with all the horror stories found in books and newspapers. Grorud School was no different from other state elementary schools of that time. It looked exactly as a school should: a great mastodon of a brick building with such standard features as drinking fountains with holes that you could press your finger over and send jets of water shooting sky-high, not to mention right in the face of some poor first-grader; a shed behind which to sneak a quick puff and lavatories in the basement where the girls could share their acquired knowledge in secret, and the boys, just as secretly, could spurt out their semen after catching an unbearably arousing peek of the English teacher's bra between two of her blouse buttons.

As far as Jonas was concerned, elementary school had nothing to do with the search for truth; it was a place where one was presented with certain fundamental options. The most important lesson, or gift, he received there was an awareness of the infinite number of things about which he would never be any the wiser.

Jonas's first-grade teacher was related to the poet and churchman Anders Hovden, and she taught her pupils a number of Hovden's, permit me to say, very beautiful songs. Jonas loved to stand beside his desk, like a little candle burning in the night, to use a metaphor often attributed to young schoolchildren, singing '*Fagert er landet*' along with the rest of the class. And what did this song teach him? It taught him that language is music, that there is more to words than their superficial significance; there is sound and rhythm. The fact is, you see, that Jonas did not understand the half of what he was singing at the top of his voice, singing out loud and clear, because it is written in Norway's other language: *nynorsk*. But he loved this tune, the way these words fell one after the other, '*soli ho sprett og ho glader*'; more than anything else this '*soli ho sprett og ho glader*' was an enigma, beautiful and incomprehensible, of which he never tired, that and the first lines of the second verse: '*Likjest vårt folk i mager jord/skjelvende blomen på bøen*'. Then there was another one, '*Handi hans far min*', just as beautiful with its totally unfathomable lines, '*Fekk ho sin svip av den tungføre år i andror so mang ei stund*', which sounded so wonderful that you had to rise up on to your tiptoes and shut your eyes. No one had to tell Jonas that words were objects containing layer upon layer of deep secrets. Indeed, after this, the whole dispute over the Norwegian language, or *languages*, was beyond Jonas – a fact I throw in, in the full knowledge of the, to an outsider, almost farcical fights that Norwegians will get into over the New Norwegian question. New Norwegian was a language which Jonas would have liked to have learned, had not so many teachers, with their cramming and fanaticism, eventually rendered this a lost cause.

Of course, it always helped to be in the same class as Nefertiti, who knew that nothing of what they learned could be taken
for granted, that the bulk of it was based on arbitrary, histori-
cally and geographically determined attitudes and information
and was, therefore – to their teacher's understandable consternation – forever addressing herself to the most bizarre questions
and pursuits. She could, for example, spend a while gazing at
her blotting paper and then, prompted by this, suddenly get to
her feet, unasked, and tell the class how a guy called Leonardo
da Vinci used to make notes using mirror writing, just think –
mirror writing! Whereupon every member of the class would
turn to studying his or her own blotting paper. Either that or she
might draw a picture of Jesus in the garden of Gethsemane and
when the teacher, not the one, it should be said, with the Anders
Hovden hymns, asked with ill-concealed annoyance why in the
world she had the trees casting purple shadows, Nefertiti would
reply without so much as looking up: 'Because Gauguin did it
that way.' Again she might sit for a whole hour staring at her
pencil and ruler to finally, at the end of the class, raise her hand
and say, 'Please Miss, why do we only use twelve centimetres of
the eighteen-centimetre pencils we buy?' Now Miss had never
given this much thought – and who can blame her? But then
Nefertiti would say: 'I think it's really stupid that we have to
throw six centimetres away.' 'What makes you say that?' Miss
felt moved to ask although she feared the worst. To which
Nefertiti replied, 'Because the annual global production of pencils stands at fourteen billion, which means that 20,000 trees are
felled every year just to fill our rubbish bins.' As I say, Nefertiti
was one of a kind. Jonas knew, and it saddened his heart, that
she was too good for this world, that she had a head as fragile as
terracotta.

Speaking of trees, the woodwork room was, not surprisingly, a
glorious fund of substance and smells. Jonas so enjoyed his first
encounter with a plane – the resistance offered by the wood, and
the transparent wood shavings – that he planed what was meant
to be a chopping board right down to a spindly stick. When the
teacher asked what he was doing, he pointed to the coiling shavings and asked if he could take them home. As for handwork,
generally regarded as a girls' subject, this was, if possible, even

more fun. Jonas never quite grasped how, with the aid of two needles and a length of wool, one could in principle create a never-ending garment, not to mention the difference between plain and purl; right away Jonas had to try, out of sheer curiosity, to knit a scarf using nothing but purl stitches.

This was the elementary school where Jonas Wergeland learned something, an idyllic place where details were left undisturbed and could be appreciated one by one for the miracles they were. Because it was the *opening up* of subjects that Jonas found fascinating, the door that was flung wide, allowing you to simply run right in and dive head first into whatever seemed most interesting at the time, things that others might consider a load of old rubbish – just like the Ash Lad or like, well, a child. This was before the time when individual details were forged into iron-hard systems that then had to be swotted up and churned out at an exam; this was before teachers started talking about the great concepts and theories, before anyone told you that the rainbow's pretty colours were actually white light.

This was, therefore, still in the days when, in a magical science lab packed with cupboards full of mysterious objects and gas taps on the desks – that alone! – the teacher might well bring out an odd-looking piece of equipment known as an electrostatic machine. And what then? Well, he would ask a pupil to step up onto an insulated stool and hold the black drum while he, the teacher that is, spun the glass disc, causing it to rub against two leather flaps before, with a dramatic flourish, switching off the light and making great sparks jump between it and the pupil's nose, like some wizard from Camelot. Or take the device known as a 'tellurion': a revolving model of the Earth and the Moon. Jonas did not know it, but his subsequent fascination with the planet Pluto had its beginnings here.

Best of all, however, were the geography lessons. Nothing at elementary school came as a greater revelation than the blank maps that were handed out from time to time, sheets marked only with the outline of a country, forming a delightful starting point for a sort of personal migration or voyage of discovery on which you yourself could give names to an as yet unknown continent: rivers, mountains, cities. You learned geography in the fullest sense of that word; you described the world.

Perhaps this is the most important experience in Jonas Wergeland's life, inasmuch as years later he would attempt to make television that was as exciting as those first years at school, when everything was as fresh as the morning dew and full of blank pages, to return to a metaphor with which Norwegians are familiar; when the taste-buds were still sharp, the possibilities legion; when details were still details, the world still the world and not a theory of the world. This was, of course, a Utopian ideal, but Jonas Wergeland did try in his series *Thinking Big*, to tell the stories of Fridtjof Nansen and others as if the viewers had never heard of them and as if the viewers knew nothing of the workings of television. Jonas Wergeland tried, in other words, to achieve the impossible aim of creating television programmes based on the assumption that no Norwegian had ever seen television before.

And now, for the benefit of my non-Norwegian readers, a brief but necessary foray into Norwegian literature, to a novel by Alexander Kielland entitled *Poison*, a bitter denunciation of the late nineteenth-century grammar-school system and of mindless mechanical learning by rote: see another boy, a boy named Marius sitting in a geography class where he is being driven to despair by a teacher demanding of his pupils that they reel off the names of cities in Belgium, more cities in Belgium, more cities in Belgium . . .

Then see this boy, Jonas Wergeland, being handed a blank map of the Netherlands, Belgium and Luxembourg, plotting in the cities according to his own sweet will: Brussels, Antwerp, Liège, Brugge. He knows it is alright if he puts them in the wrong places, it doesn't matter, he's creating the world. There's only one thing wrong with this set-up: there are too few cities in Belgium and so Jonas has to come up with some other names. And since this is in fifth grade, his teacher does not say a word; instead she permits herself a little smile. And may they live forever, all those schoolmistresses who teach children to sing 'Fagert er landet' and smile at the things children will come up with and who do not try to correct anything, even when it involves a subject as touchy, in Norwegian terms, as cities in Belgium.

Norwegian Wood

Then see this boy, a high-school student now, jogging along the corridor on the third floor of Oslo Cathedral School, past the main stairway, still no pupils, jogging on over to the metal ladder bolted to the left-hand wall, climbing the ladder, pushing open a hatch in the ceiling and coming up into the dark and dirty attic, where he locates and opens another hatch or rather a skylight this time, and clambers out onto the roof which, to his relief, is flat.

Jonas shoots a glance at the green, verdigrised onion dome across from him, surprised by how different everything looks from this angle, before cautiously wriggling over to a thick cable running from this roof to the roof of the old rectory. He opens his rucksack and pulls out another flag which, by dint of a nifty homemade pulley contraption, he manages to run out onto the cable, bringing the flag to a halt at the lowest point, where it hangs fluttering directly above the schoolyard.

There it hung, high in the sky, suspended in midair: the flag of a foreign country, green, with a white crescent moon and four stars. I have not yet said which flag it was. I dare say that very few people would be able to identify it anyway, and even fewer back then, since it had only been in use for a few years and was not officially adopted until the end of the seventies. Jonas regarded the length of bunting, feeling, in fact, rather solemn, the way he did when the Olympic medals were presented. He ventured a wary peek over the edge. More and more pupils were streaming through the gates into the schoolyard, and they all spotted it, stopped and pointed, baffled, as if the flag were some tropical bird, an impossibility. The rector, too, had come out, stood with his hands at his sides, peering up into the air. Jonas almost felt sorry for him. The rector was easily riled.

One aspect of Jonas Wergeland's life that is rarely touched on concerns his attitude towards the great existential question: What to do? And here I am thinking, as the phrase suggests, along political lines: of the exceedingly banal, yet exceedingly complex question as to what, as an individual, one can do to make the world – neither more nor less than that – a better, a more just place. In due course Jonas would celebrate both Grotius Day and Michelangelo Day with great pomp and ceremony, but during his time at high school, as with so many others, this huge question could still fill him with an almost abstract lethargy, bordering on loathing. Then suddenly one day he shook off his almost normal and necessary apathy, looked this mind-boggling challenge straight in the eye and, from a wealth of options, chose as his cause the Comoro Islands, that tiny island kingdom in the Indian Ocean, north of Madagascar; more as a symbol of his willingness to lend a helping hand, naturally; as a sort of sop to his self-respect rather than out of any illusion that he could be of real help. And it has to be said to Jonas Wergeland's credit that he chose a country and a cause that very few people cared about. I would go so far as to say that Jonas Wergeland was the only person in Norway around 1970 to speak up for the Comoro Islands, this being a time when, of all the conflicts big and small being waged throughout the world, the people of Norway concentrated – to all intents and purposes – all visible opposition on two things: the EEC and the war in Vietnam.

So it was the Comorian flag that Jonas had unfurled for the edification of his schoolfellows and anyone else who happened to be walking along Ullevålsveien that morning. In those days, as I am sure many readers will remember, the actual idea of hoisting a flag was nothing new, but the flag of the Comoro Islands was hoisted in only one school in Norway or in the whole of Europe, come to that: Oslo Cathedral School. So from that point of view – considering the school's reputation as the Alma Mater of original thinkers – one might say that the rector had no real reason to be as upset or as enraged as he actually was.

I realize that some of you are growing impatient, but here's the point: how did Jonas Wergeland learn about the Comoro Islands?

It all started on a train: on the Oslo-Bergen line to be precise. From the minute the train pulled out of the station Jonas had been gazing at the man sitting diagonally opposite him – and who could blame him? The man was a Negro. That's right, a Negro in Norway. Now I use the word 'Negro' and not 'black' or 'African' simply because the word used in Norway at this time by everybody, even the socialists, was *neger*: literally 'Negro' or, I am afraid, 'nigger'. There were not many Negroes to be found in Norway in the late sixties and this particular Negro was, what is more, clad in the most peculiar, not to say downright comical, outfit. The real eye-catcher was a brand-new, gaudily patterned sweater of the sort sold in the souvenir shops attached to the big hotels; and even though it was only the beginning of November and not especially cold, on his head he wore an enormous fur hat, the sort commonly referred to in Norway as a *bjørnefitte* – literally a 'bear twat' – with the ear flaps hanging down.

Jonas could not take his eyes off this man, who had spent the whole time staring curiously or wonderingly, one might almost say 'goggle-eyed', out of the carriage window, the sort of window that cannot possibly be opened, never mind the fact that there was a sign warning passengers not to lean out of it. But Jonas was sure that if the window *had* been open, the Negro would have been leaning out of it; it seemed as if he just could not get enough of the sights he was seeing through the window, he had hardly so much as glanced around the compartment, not even when the refreshments trolley came past, with its bitter coffee and rubbery cheese slices which, by the way, I believe should be sampled by anyone who wishes to learn something about Norwegians, about their high cost of living and their astonishing eating habits: food that defies all comparison – this railway fare, at any rate – unless it be with the character-building meals consumed in ancient Sparta.

The train was halfway between Hønefoss and Nesbyen, and the man was still staring out of the window, looking possibly even more dumbfounded than before, well-nigh enraptured – staring out at the pine forest. Jonas had never seen anyone gaze in such wonder at a pine forest. It was as though the man found it impossible to take in the mass of pine trunks, and Jonas even began to feel a little bit proud of the Norwegian forests, of the fact that pine and fir trees could fill a Negro with such awe. Jonas fancied that the man must be sitting there lost in thoughts of Viking ships and stave churches and the like as the train chugged on through the pine trees. Eventually, the Negro began to shake his head, slowly, again and again, before finally murmuring something that Jonas had to strain to catch: 'Even the woods are safe here.' The Negro went on shaking his head, smiling incredulously at the wall of trees and softly repeated: 'Yeah, even the woods are safe here.'

Now Jonas's curiosity was well and truly aroused. I should also say that Jonas was no more racially prejudiced than most Norwegians and besides, one of his heroes, Duke Ellington was a coloured American. But there was something about the lips of this man – an honest-to-goodness Bantu, if I may say so – that put him far closer to the epitome of the term 'Negro': they were big, absolutely enormous, like a caricature.

'What are you doing in Norway?' Jonas asked in English. 'Are you a sportsman?' The last summer Olympics were still fresh in Jonas's mind with memories of Tommy Smith's and John Carlos's black, gloved fists held high and Bob Beamons's unbelievable long jumps.

The man shook his head. 'Are you a jazz musician?' Jonas asked, not without some hope.

'I'm a refugee.'

'Are you from Africa?'

The man laughed. 'Africa is a big place,' he said.

'From Biafra?' Thanks to the nightmarish pictures that had been in the news in recent years, this was one of the few African countries that Jonas could name.

'An older struggle,' the man replied.

At this point Jonas gave up, although even with his lack of interest in international conflicts, he might have come up with the answer had he given it a bit of thought. All he saw was a Negro, and to him a Negro meant an African, and to him Africa was Africa, not a collection of different countries. Africa was one big country inhabited by black Negroes who all looked alike.

The man explained politely that he came from South Africa but that, after having been imprisoned for some years, he had run away and lived for a while in Dar-Es-Salaam before he was given the chance to come to Norway. He had been offered a place at university here, he explained, a scholarship. He was studying medicine – yes, medicine, he repeated when he saw the expression on Jonas's face, in a way that made Jonas realize that he must have to tell everyone twice. Now he was on his way to Bergen to visit friends – maybe the same people who had given him the sweater, which he was now wearing, Jonas thought, purely out of politeness.

It was this man, whose name was Isaac and who today – although Jonas does not know it – is a well-known figure in the United Nations, who, in the course of a long conversation, not without the odd neurotic note to it, had happened to mention the Comoro Islands to Jonas, one of his forefathers having hailed from there. This was just by the way, a word, a name tossed into a lengthy conversation covering subjects that were considerably more grim and disturbing, a conversation in which Jonas learned for the first time of incidents and atrocities which have since been described so often, to diminishing effect, that most people have become totally immune to them. But thanks to Jonas's sense for detail and, even more so, to his utter ignorance of *Les Comores* – he actually thought this was a place on the African mainland – he had remembered the islands and subsequently picked up odd bits and pieces of information here and there until eventually he knew quite a bit about the country.

This was, however, a long-term result of the meeting with Isaac. Initially, what Jonas could not get out of his mind was the sight of this African, tricked out in a Norwegian sweater, sitting on a Norwegian train and gazing in disbelief, or rapture, out of the window at a Norwegian pine forest, murmuring that 'even the woods are safe here' as if he could hardly believe his eyes or his senses.

There is an old literary ploy that involves allowing one's own country to be depicted by foreigners. For example by putting a Chinese in Berlin and having this Chinese describe life in Berlin so that everything is suddenly seen with a fresh eye often from such an alien perspective that familiar things appear quite laughable. And for Jonas Wergeland that one sentence, 'Even the woods are safe here', had just such an impact, one that deserved a whole book to itself. It was not only laughable; it was shocking.

Even before he alighted from the train in Bergen – in the sunshine, just to underline what an almost unnaturally idyllic place Norway was – where the Negro, Isaac that is, would stand for a long time simply peering round about him, out over the fjord, up at the mountains, in that gaudy sweater, with the fur hat pulled well down over his ears, Jonas knew that he would never be able to imagine what life was like in the continent from which his travelling companion came or understand one whit of his predicament: having to flee from country to country, never feeling safe, knowing that you could be shot or thrown into prison any time at all, for anything at all, and that once you were in prison the worst imaginable evil could befall you. Or you might escape being shot or thrown into prison only to starve to death instead. And if you chose to run off into the forest, into the jungle or bush, you were not a lot safer, what with bloodthirsty animals, snakes, venomous insects – in fact a natural world that was in itself murderous, a sort of impenetrability.

It suddenly dawned on Jonas Wergeland – and not only because the sun was shining on Bergen or because a certain area of that town happened to go by that name – that he was living in a paradise. It may sound absurd, to think that a young Norwegian should not have tumbled to this fact before now, but very few young Norwegians are aware of it at all, ever. Only then, at the thought of an African clad in a travesty of a Norwegian sweater and an incongruous fur hat, gazing at a pine forest – something which had never held any emotional associations for Jonas – while shaking his head and murmuring 'Even the woods are safe here', did Jonas Wergeland realize what an incredibly safe country Norway is, what a bewilderingly secure, quite incomprehensibly safe country he inhabited. All at once Jonas Wergeland saw that he lived in a land so inherently safe that anyone who had ever been in danger simply would not believe it. And, Jonas thought later, maybe that was the real reason why the

Negro had pulled his fur hat, that enormous bear's twat, closer about his head: not because it was cold but in order to keep his wits about him. In Norway you could, by accident of course, be run over by a truck, it's true, but you could stroll into the densest forest or out into what Norwegians describe as their wildest wilds and feel sure that no harm would come to you. The most dangerous thing in a Norwegian forest was the adder, its bite about as lethal as a mosquito's.

There were times, when out travelling, that Jonas neglected to say that he lived in Norway – which is to say in that place so totally devoid of real need and real insecurity. There were times abroad, if the situation were critical or catastrophic enough, when Jonas Wergeland had to resort to a lot of double-talk to save disclosing his nationality.

As far as that goes, Jonas Wergeland could have hoisted any flag at all over the schoolyard – as long as it came from a country that was not a part of the West.

Ultima Thule

So how do the pieces of a life fit together? Or, to put it another way, do they fit together at all?

They had finished filming, and Jonas could tell right away that the shots from the area around Myggbukta would be good: the old, derelict sealing and weather station, huts lined inside with musk-ox hides, and of course the spectacular landscape round about; in fact just being confronted with that Arctic landscape in the comfort of your own living-room would be enough to take your breath away. The purpose of the shoot had been to afford a glimpse of a sealer's life, and after a hectic week's filming the NRK team had footage of just about everything: dog teams, with a camera fixed low down on the sled; hares, foxes, musk ox, seal, walrus – the only thing lacking was a polar bear. This sequence was to form part of a programme on the all but forgotten annex-ation of Eastern Greenland by Norway in the early thirties, a programme which caused a justifiable stir and gave rise to much, occasionally heated, debate in the press when it was shown on Norwegian television screens – understandably, seeing that the Norwegian people have every reason to want to forget this embarrassing episode, an example of a brand of polar imperial-ism to which Norway has never cared to admit. Not unexpect-edly, it ended in bitter defeat for the Norwegians when the case was brought before the International Court of Justice in The Hague.

The film team were now in Scoresbysund, further down the coast, where they had been taking shots of the Danish base, the opposite pole in this dispute. And it was here, in this small hunt-ing and fishing community with its little, red-painted wooden houses and racks draped with all manner of hides hung to dry, a sort of polar Timbuktu inhabited by Inuits, Danish troops and several hundred howling dogs straining at stout tethers, in a muddy street, that Jonas ran into Jørn Rasmussen, an elderly, one-time hunter now working for the Greenland Trade Department. And since this unexpected friendship was struck up, almost symbolically just as the ice on the fjord began to break up – the high point of the year – Jørn Rasmussen promptly suggested, nay, more or less demanded, that Jonas should come with him to one of the sealer's huts up the fjord. And all credit to Jonas Wergeland, he never let such a chance pass him by. So the team left by helicopter for Mestersvig, to take a Twin Otter from there to Iceland, while Jonas stayed on for a few more days as a guest of the Dane.

Just twenty-four hours later, Jonas was sitting in a tiny sealer's hut in the heart of the East Greenland national park, at the mouth of one of the narrow arms of the fjord. They had arrived there in a boat that looked like a shark, sailing between the ice floes with the sea birds whirling overhead. To begin with, the country around then had been wide and open, but then another landscape hove in sight; one which, to put it mildly, Jonas would never forget: white, black and blue. Ice, rock and sea. A landscape so monumental and at the same time so desolate and so elementary that it reminded Jonas – of all things – of a desert, not least because of the stark light. Again he had a feeling of having reached some outer limit, the very periphery of the humanly possible, or the beginning of something totally alien to him. The glaciers especially, plunging into the sea, the chill breath from a sheer wall of blue ice, made him shudder, even while he felt drawn to it, as if the blue cast itself held some vital secret.

Jonas Wergeland found himself in the heart of the wildest landscape he had ever seen. The simple wooden hut lay a hundred metres from the beach and was totally covered in tar-paper, both roof and walls. Behind the hut the mountain reared straight up 1,000 metres into the air, and beyond it jagged rugged peaks soared to 2,000 metres. Despite the primitive conditions, Jonas felt happy there from the word go. He was to spend two whole days and nights out here in the wilderness, in a borrowed sleeping-bag, together with Jørn Rasmussen, some kegs of aquavit and, not least, several kilos of freshly boiled seal-meat, large chunks of meat running with fat and juices, served steaming hot on dented tin plates – with no other accompaniment but salt and mustard.

On their first morning there, Rasmussen stepped outside and opened a box that had aroused Jonas's curiosity early on. Out came, of all things, a portable battery-operated stereo system complete with two speakers, an anachronistic sight when set against the rude hut and the timeless terrain. This was a ritual, the Dane explained while he mounted the system on the wall of the hut: each year when the ice in the fjord broke up he came here. And what did he do? Jonas asked. Just a minute, Rasmussen said, pulling a tape out of his anorak pocket. The weather was beautiful, they had had fine weather for some time, a permanent ridge of high pressure and dazzlingly bright all day long.

All at once the air was filled with the sound of opera music. Mighty music. And the strange thing, thought Jonas, was that this music – majestic, in many ways wild – suited, nay, echoed the landscape. And suddenly the country round about them seemed like a stage-set, the whole of this vast landscape had about it something of the unreality and beauty of a stage, artificially lit and with scenery built on illusions. They sat with their backs against the wall of the hut, each on his battered chair and listened to opera. They were well wrapped up, and the sun was heating up nicely. Not far from them, about a kilometre away, there was a glacier, with an icefall of at least twenty metres, plummeting straight down into the sea. Behind it lay a couple of nunataks, like two gigantic black horns on the glacier's smooth, snow-white brow. They sat listening to opera music and saw how the ice glittered, every shade of white and blue. Jonas had been seized by his old dread of ice, of being crushed by ice, the minute he caught sight of Eastern Greenland from the plane, but the fear had gradually faded and now he could rest his eyes on the wall of ice without the thought of hell once crossing his mind. Rasmussen looked at Jonas, nodded, smiled, raised a cup of black coffee chased with a dash of something stronger. Jonas recognized the music. It was Wagner – 'what else?' he thought. It was Wagner, *Tristan and Isolde*, and it was Kirsten Flagstad singing her celebrated *Liebestod*, Kirsten Flagstad's voice that was being hurled across the landscape at the all-embracing ice-cap and at the icefall rearing straight out of the fjord directly in front of them, where they sat with their backs against the tar-paper of the hut wall, with woollen plaids over their legs and warming cups of coffee in their hands. 'I knew you'd like it,' said Rasmussen. 'That's why I invited you.'

And then it happened: the glacier right in front of them calved. A colossal, an unbelievably huge chunk simply broke off and slid into the sea, sending spray shooting high into the air. It all happened with such ineffable slowness that they had time to take it in, to comprehend and memorize the shock, and only after the sight had, as it were, been absorbed, did the sound reach their ears, like a clap of thunder increasing in volume behind Kirsten Flagstad's voice and Wagner's music, a tremendous roar and an echo that reverberated off the mountainsides. Jonas had the distinct impression, no, he was positive that it was Kirsten Flagstad's voice – and not the sun or the surging of the sea – that had sliced off this massive chunk of ice; that Kirsten Flagstad's voice had sent a shiver running through it, causing the glacier to calve out of sheer delight.

Only later, when the music had been turned off and they were sitting there with their backs to the wall of the hut, surrounded by a silence so palpable that it was in itself an experience, did Jonas ask Rasmussen why exactly he had played *Tristan and Isolde*. It was clear to Jonas that this was the role that had been assigned to him, that he was supposed to ask, just at this moment, and then had to listen, and he was not meant to say anything, because Rasmussen simply needed to tell this story at regular intervals, about once a year, and preferably around the time when the glaciers were calving, so he could say that it was love that split the ice apart and because this was the most uplifting time of the year and, hence, the best time for anyone wishing to contemplate their sad fate, shed a tear or two and pour an extra drop of aquavit into their coffee. This was how Jonas Wergeland heard his story, while they sat side by side, leaning back against the wall of the hut, with their eyes on the enormous iceberg slowly drifting down the fjord like another *Flying Dutchman*; a story so heartbreaking and in many ways so unlikely that I reserve the right to remain silent – some stories are even sadder than the myth of Tristan and Isolde. In any event, Rasmussen's story ended with a self-imposed hermit-like existence, 'in a climate as cold as the chill that struck at my heart,' as he put it, where not even the most death-defying Valkyrie riding across the ice with nine semi-wild huskies harnessed to the sled could make him forget.

'I heard Kirsten Flagstad at the Metropolitan in '52,' he said. 'I've never wept as much.'

'You mean you heard her sing just after?' Jonas asked, his eyes fixed on the iceberg as it floated off over the smooth waters of the fjord, chiselled as a sculpture, marble on mirror.

'A week later. I had two tickets, but I had to go alone.'

'And then you came here?'

'Then I came here.'

Jonas Wergeland would later cherish the theory, in his heart of hearts, that it must have been Kirsten Flagstad's voice, possibly certain overtones in it, that had drawn the polar bear to it, seeing that it happened that very same evening, when he had to make a visit to the toilet, and when the chances of running into a bear at that time of year, in that region, were microscopic. Rasmussen had not even told him to remember the Mauser, normally as obvious an accessory as a toilet roll.

It was a typical outdoor privy, apart from the fact that the door was missing. As far as Jonas was concerned that was all to the good, he could sit and look out at the shore and the fjord just as he had done as a boy at his grandfather's place on Hvaler. It was bright as day outside, totally calm, and the landscape suffused with colours the like of which he had never seen before: supernatural hues. Out on the fjord drifted icebergs, miniature palaces. He could not help but think of Kittelsen's picture in the bathroom at home; 'A long, long way off he saw something glittering and gleaming.'

Just a few seconds later, as he was getting up from the toilet, he heard a shuffling sound and before he had time to think that it might be a fox, a broad – a gigantic – head appeared in the doorway, filling it completely. It was a polar bear. Jonas could not believe that a polar bear could move so quietly.

I think I can say – and I have given this a lot of thought – that Jonas Wergeland was faced here with the most dangerous opponent of his life. Jonas Wergeland stood with his trousers round his ankles, nose to nose with a polar bear. Tuaregs are one thing; a massive animal, half a ton of it, with eyeteeth befitting the biggest carnivore on dry land, is something else again. Jonas had heard – they heard a lot of stories during the shoot – that the polar bear was totally unpredictable at close quarters, that nine times out of ten it would attack; it has to be a long way off if you are to have any chance of scaring it away. But this polar bear was close, really close. Jonas tried, of all things, to look it straight in the eye. The polar bear tilted its head slightly, unsure. Suddenly it snapped its teeth together, five or six quick, dry snaps. If there were one time in Jonas Wergeland's life when you could employ the phrase 'and his blood froze', this would be it. But at the same time he was thinking, because his mind was running the whole time, in wild leaps and little circles, how quickly things could happen; you sit on the toilet, you take a crap, you look out over the shore and the fjord, for once you take time to enjoy being alive – and then you're dead.

The polar bear stretched its neck all the way through the door, and this Jonas saw, as with the glacier calving, in ultra slow motion; or as when he used the remote control to flick through sequences in video films, studying certain scenes frame by frame and always being amazed by how many shots there were; now not only did he see a polar bear's head coming at him, he saw the black nose, the expressionless, coal-black eyes, saw the ears – like a teddy bear's, the thought flashed through his mind – saw every hair in the fur around its snout but also, or at one and the same time, he saw the landscape behind it: the shore, the fjord, the blocks and floes of ice – and again, like marble over a mirrored surface, infinitely beautiful – the mountains, the colours, those unbelievable pastel hues, and not only that, but also the wooden planks around the door, how weather-beaten they were, how big the cracks were, the hole where a knot had fallen out, a hole that drew the eye, giving him the urge – as the last thing he did – to put his eye to that aperture, to see what slice of life this would afford him, but instead what Jonas saw was the black snout and that mouth closing in on his crotch, because that was exactly what the polar bear was aiming at, and a second later Jonas actually felt its snout nudge his penis. For one fleeting moment, for the first and only time in his life, Jonas experienced that phenomenon which the late, great Sigmund Freud expended so much of his energy and imagination on explaining: the fear of castration.

The polar bear blew down its nose, a snort that struck Jonas as sounding so loud in the silence that the word 'inny-dick' which they had used to shout at one another in fun as kids, suddenly became a reality. On the point of passing out, Jonas nonetheless managed to register that the polar bear had pulled back, turned round and was galloping off towards the beach. Jonas could hardly believe what his eyes were telling him: that the polar bear was running away. He thought this must be something he was seeing through a knothole on the other side of death's door, the outcome of some sort of parallel occurrence: an alternative course of events that never actually took place. Jonas stood with his trousers round his ankles and watched the polar bear bounding down to the beach, turning its head to look at him every now and again before it jumped into the water and swam off. Jonas followed it with his eyes until he could no longer see it between the icebergs, marble gliding over a mirrored surface.

Only then did he dare to look down at his benumbed body as if he could not believe that his member was still intact. For years Jonas would wonder what could have scared the bear away, and he thought to begin with that it must have had something to do with his penis's magic quality, a distinct odour. Later he came to the conclusion that the polar bear had spared him quite simply because it saw that they were brothers; they were both nomads.

So how do the pieces of a life fit together? What determines the course of a life?

Two months after Jonas returned safe and sound to Norway, Margrete discovered to her surprise that she was pregnant, even though she had been using contraception. Jonas felt sure that the polar bear must have scared extra life into his sperm cells, enabling them to defy all resistance.

Tabriz

Aunt Laura's flat looked like a bazaar. Where the walls were not covered in oriental rugs they were hung with objects made of copper and brass, and crawling around the floor was a leopard tortoise with little gems affixed to its shell. Jonas had the feeling that the tortoise was forever going round in circles and that time stood still at Aunt Laura's.

When Jonas paid her a visit, his aunt would serve teas with names he never could remember and saw him settled among the pile of cushions on the sofa before she took her own seat at the far end of the room, in the corner that bristled with buffers and gas cylinders and draw-plates and plate rollers, not to mention a mysterious old safe. Jonas loved to sneak peeks at the bench at which his aunt sat and worked as she talked, as if the things she shaped out of gold and silver and the stories she told were all part of the same process.

Aunt Laura often spoke of her travels, and as time went on Jonas found that, once again, the sequence of cause and effect had become mixed up. His aunt did not go out travelling, as he had first thought, because of the rugs; it would be truer to say that the travelling was the cause; the rugs were merely an excuse. 'My rugs have taken me all around the world,' his aunt would say or: 'These rugs form forty doors and every rug opens the door onto a journey.' But Jonas saw no contradiction in this because when you came right down to it, as with the rugs, his aunt's travels represented a search for stories – indeed, they made a grand story in themselves.

Aunt Laura's secret *beau idéal* was Ibn Battuta, one of the greatest nomadic spirits of all time, born in Tangier at the beginning of the fourteenth century. Her eyes lit up when she mentioned Ibn Battuta's name so that to begin with Jonas thought he must be an old and particularly fierce-burning flame. Tucked away like a treasure in an exquisitely carved chest, his aunt kept the French four-volume edition of Ibn Battuta's *Rihlah*, and every now and again, usually when she was in a good mood, she would take out one of the volumes and leaf through it, stopping here and there, her blood-red lips curving into a smile, as if at some sudden recollection, before she laid the book back in the chest. Afterwards she would recite fragments from it to Jonas so that eventually he was able to reconstruct the whole story of Ibn Battuta's overwhelming urge to travel, a passion he believed that God himself had instilled in him. Indeed, he had set himself the goal of visiting all of the world's most renowned mosques, and because Ibn Battuta followed the rule never to take the same road twice, his travels led him to every part of the known world of the Middle Ages, from West Africa to China – Jonas particularly enjoyed hearing the different names for all the cities: al-Iskandariya for Alexandria, Misr for Cairo, Bait al-Muqaddas for Jerusalem. And wherever he went, through the secretary to whom he dictated the story of his travels, Ibn Battuta recounted little tales and anecdotes about people and places, from historical facts to where they grew the best melons and apricots, either that or he would quote homages made by poets to certain spots, or describe a rhinoceros for the benefit of his contemporaries. But first and last Ibn Battuta described all of the mosques, as, for example, when he devoted ten pages to the Umayyad mosque in Damascus with its three slender minarets, hailing it as one of the most beautiful buildings in the world.

Aunt Laura, too, had a particular penchant for mosques on account, as she put it, of their perfect balance between the masculine and the feminine, the minarets and the dome. She could sit for hours, telling Jonas how the small towns looked from a distance, the line of their rooftops against the sky, bows and lances, 'or, if you like,' she would say, 'phalluses and breasts in perfect harmony as if in defiance of the suppressed sexuality of Muslim society.'

The truth of it is, however, that Jonas's aunt went travelling to see minarets of quite another order, sacred objects of a much more down-to-earth sort. Not to beat about the bush: she travelled abroad to see all the penises in the world. And as time went on she made no secret of it either. If there was one thing Jonas liked about Aunt Laura it was that she said things straight out, quite unabashed, unlike other adults. And like Ibn Battuta she had also kept a record of her travels in the form of a bundle of highly unusual sketchbooks.

On one occasion, Aunt Laura drew the erect penis of a man lying on his back, viewed from the side, and showed Jonas how much it had in common with a mosque: the scrotum as the soft, rounded dome and the shaft itself as a proud minaret. So in fact it was here, in a flat in Tøyen, on the east side of Oslo, surrounded by Oriental rugs and precious metals, that Jonas first learned that he had a sacred object between his legs. And this might well explain – it's just a thought, mind you – why a polar bear would one day back away from Jonas Wergeland's genitals: out of respect for the divine.

One evening, when Aunt Laura had finished soldering the join on a cylinder of silver that she had bent into a circle, with the faint smell of gas still lingering in the room, she told Jonas about Ibn Battuta's description of the Ali ibn Abi Talib mosque in the town of Al-Basra, which had seven minarets, one of which trembled when the name of Ali ibn Abi Talib was spoken out loud. Ibn Battuta had tried this for himself and seen how the minaret shook. Aunt Laura turned her white face to look at Jonas as if weighing up whether he was mature enough to hear the truth. Then she said, 'In the same way you can make a cock tremble by whispering certain words.' And Jonas realized that, like Ibn Battuta, she must have put this to the test.

In connection with his visit to Mecca, his aunt went on, Ibn Battuta had described the Black Stone and how kissing this 'affords a pleasure that is especially good for the mouth'. Ibn Battuta regarded the stone as God's hand on Earth, which meant that kissing it was actually synonymous with touching the hand of God. Again Jonas's aunt scrutinized him from under inky eyelids, to see whether he could cope with what came next: namely, that she had found the same to be true of penises, that they were like antennae of a sort, tuned in to the celestial. 'Some kiss the Black Stone in the Kaaba, others kiss stones in kaabas of another sort,' she said.

To be absolutely frank, so passionately obsessed was Aunt Laura with the male organ that rugs were not all she collected on her long and arduous journeys; she collected penises too. That is to say, she drew them. Jonas's aunt had sketchbooks full of penises, all shapes and sizes. If, prior to this, Jonas had imagined that a cock was just a cock, much as a layman cannot tell the difference between Oriental rugs, then his misconceptions on this score were put straight with a vengeance at Aunt Laura's. 'Just as with the goldsmith's craft, it all comes down to the tools,' she said.

It was at such times that his aunt would pour more tea and bring in a brass salver of fruit on which a banana might be lying, graphically arranged between two plums, before she sat down next to Jonas on the sofa and showed him her sketchbooks, or travel journals as she called them, from every corner of the globe; turning their pages with fingers adorned with rings the like of which Jonas had never seen: spirals and little facets that gleamed and flashed among the drawings of all the penises she had come across in different societies. Later in life, Jonas would wonder whether his aunt might have had some deeper purpose with all of this. While in olden days there were people, phrenologists, who believed that they could tell something about a person's temperament by measuring the skull, Aunt Laura's study of the penis's countless physiognomic aspects may have sprung from a theory that this said everything about what these men were like as people: how intelligent they were, for example.

However that may be, as his aunt leafed through her journals, with her bracelets jingling, Jonas beheld penises of every length and thickness, pointed and stubby, and in their various states: limp, erect and ejaculating. There were also sketches of individual details, as if each part of the organ were deserving of a study in itself: the pubic hair, for example. When it came to the foreskin, Jonas was particularly intrigued by certain peoples who, according to his aunt, arranged the skin in folds like a sort of drapery – in direct contrast, in other words, to all those men who were circumcised. In one sketch of the glans his aunt had depicted it as a helmet, in others as the wing cases of a beetle and as a scarab. Or it might be the scrotum, covered in a labyrinthine pattern of wrinkles, which made it look like a piece of coral or a brain. On some pages his aunt had executed detailed studies of the furrow that divides the scrotum in two; on others she had captured the head of the penis from in front, like a Cyclops. Jonas also came across some sketches of ejaculating penises which resembled nothing so much as rough drawings for fountains.

But the majority of the sketches depicted what in good Anglo-Saxon is called a 'hard-on', as if this posed the truly creative challenge. Aunt Laura was especially interested in the compar-isons which a hard-on invited. Some resembled horses' heads, the neck and the head, or the whole of a horse's forebody, others were like dolphins and snakes. 'I ran into this one in Brazil,' said Aunt Laura, pointing to one which, owing to the pronounced ruff around the glans, had the look of a Triceratops dinosaur about it. Jonas saw other penises reminiscent of asparagus, tulips, various sorts of mushroom and a sprouting onion. Or shaped like large loaves. Or bones, clubs and flagpoles. There were even some flutes and bejewelled sceptres. Some were streamlined as rockets. In other cases his aunt had given her imagination free rein and drawn penises as telescopes, light-houses, antlers, curling trunks or as the top of a champagne bottle, complete with cork. Some of the drawings had been coloured, with the result that in one instance the penis looked like a large, glossy purple aubergine, in another a pillar of ivory etched with fine blue lines and one last as an old tree trunk, gnarled and twisted.

Jonas liked these single-minded studies, the emphasis on a solitary detail: the attempt to reflect the nature of sexuality from such a strange, such a bizarre angle. But there is no getting away from the fact that he also became much more aware of the organ between his own legs, at the very time when, to stick to Aunt Laura's analogy, he was in the process of changing from a plant-eater into a beast of prey.

Those sketches which Jonas found most fascinating bore no resemblance to anything; they were utterly original figments of the imagination. Just as with the rugs, Jonas saw that you could depict reality any way you liked. Occasionally these sketches formed a series of metamorphoses, progressing from a recognizable penis to a piece of jewellery.

Did Jonas want some more tea? His aunt filled his cup before getting up and going over to her workbench at the far end of the room where she began to tidy away her soldering iron, files and emery paper, the grinding paste and buffs. It was high time men started to take their member seriously, learned to control it, his aunt said as she hung tongs and scissors in their places among the multitude of tools, a whole ironmongery on the wall. Had Jonas heard of those women who can smoke a cigarette with their vagina and pick up coins with their labia? Why shouldn't boys be able to do something equally accomplished? Aunt Laura then proceeded to tell Jonas about men she had met who, by controlling their muscles, could make their penises point in different directions. And take them from erect state and back to limp, quick as you like, by sheer willpower. She had met men who could beat a drum with their penises, without using their hands. 'Just imagine what such a man could do to you!' she said, and her bracelets were given an extra jingle, although Jonas found it hard to picture this. On Bali she had come upon a group who could masturbate and hit a coin five metres away with their semen, just the way Jonas's grandfather could hit the spittoon from a good way off, she added. And then there were the Tibetans who were able to hold onto their semen. All Norwegians could learn something from that, said Aunt Laura as she switched off the light, giving the room over once more to the dim light that Jonas loved so well.

For a long time silence reigned. Jonas ran his eye along the walls, from rug to rug, and he had the idea that the patterns were moving, alive. 'Tell me more of the story about Princess Li Lai,' he asked.

'In Xanadu,' said Aunt Laura after first pouring herself another cup of tea, 'Princess Li Lai received another suitor in her cool palace, in the innermost room in which she had shut herself away for many years, for she had yet to find one who could make love to her as she desired, one who would make love to her until she saw a turtle with the image of a face on its shell.

The one who had come to woo her on this occasion was the celebrated jade-carver Taw Maw and he did not waste any time, but carried her to the bed and immediately proceeded to make love to her. Taw Maw concentrated solely on her clitoris, as if it were a rare stone which he had resolved to shape into an ornament. The princess felt his stiff member begin to rub against her clitoris, felt as if he were gently drilling and sawing, rubbing and rubbing. And as he made love to her, more and more urgently and passionately, Princess Li Lai felt this rubbing filling her with a warm glow as if she had stepped out into the sunshine and were walking through a landscape that Taw Maw the jade carver was slowly filing in her path, with vaguely transparent trees and fold upon fold of mountains that seemed to go on forever, and as she came to a river it suddenly overflowed its banks and swept her away, and she floated off as if caught up in a tidal wave, floated and floated in a warm stream that flowed faster and faster, more and more powerfully, until the princess was thrown onto the bank and she noticed a bridge nearby. This she walked across and it brought her to a plateau at the foot of a mountain, and while Taw Maw the jade carver made love to her ever more vigorously with his hard member, boring and filing, rubbing and rubbing, making fine movements born of long experience, she felt her legs carrying her towards the mountain, faster and faster, until she was raised up, climbed and climbed, drifted upwards and when she reached the top of the mountain she felt a stab of pain and she realized that a dragon had lifted her in its claws, and this discovery filled her with such a raging fury that she flew at the creature, punching, kicking, biting, yelling, quite beside herself, until she managed to claw a hole in its skin, and it blew apart with an explosion, a bang that caused her to open her eyes. And there she saw the face of the jade carver Taw Maw which, just for an instant, bore the features of a dragon. And she thanked him but asked him to leave, because she had not yet seen a turtle with a shell that resembled a face, and she was sure that there must be a better way to be made love to.'

Jonas lay back among the soft cushions, gazing at one of the rugs on the wall, trying to remember what the different figures

represented. For a long time he lay there, feeling a little mesmerized, partly by the glow of all the metals round about him.
He shut his eyes, heard the jingling as his aunt moved about the
room.

'Tell me what you found in Samarkand,' he said at last, just
before he left. He always had to try.

'As for Samarkand and what I found there, that I can never tell
you,' she said. 'You will have to go there yourself.'

Rhetorica Norvegica

Now and again, when he was lying among the soft, silken cushions in Aunt Laura's flat, Jonas had the feeling that there were stories *inside* him, all packed up tightly in some way, like parachutes just waiting to be released, to unfold; and sometimes he tried to take a peek inside or work loose a corner of these prospective stories, in advance as it were. So it was that later Jonas found on several occasions that he was already familiar with a situation when it occurred, as if somehow he were simply living out a story, a script that he had rehearsed. This was the feeling he had about his acquaintanceship with Anne B.

Jonas Wergeland always maintained – almost as if excusing himself – that he had enrolled in Oslo Cathedral School because Grorud Valley High had become so overcrowded that classes had to be staggered. In actual fact, he changed schools to save having to see his brother Daniel, with whom he had been on less than friendly terms for some time, and in hopes of meeting people from other backgrounds. This latter wish was fulfilled with a vengeance. For Jonas, his years at the Cathedral School amounted more to an encounter with the secret face of Norway than to learning such things as the periodic table or Old Norwegian.

To take one example: one evening Jonas Wergeland attended a party given by one of the girls in his class, Anne B., who lived in an elegant town house in one of the most exclusive streets on the west side, only a stone's throw from spots Jonas knew well, Majorstua and the streets around Frogner swimming pool, and yet it was another world. In fact the whole experience was vaguely reminiscent of the main attraction at the overcrowded Frogner pool when Jonas was a boy: the windows in the big pool through which the swimmers and divers could be viewed from an unexpected angle – something which, as one might expect, appealed greatly to Jonas. Nor is there any hiding the fact that it was something of a turn-on to see the girls from below, spreading their legs and kicking out, with no idea that they were being watched, even if some of the most audacious did swim down and make faces through the glass, their hair swirling Medusa-like around their heads.

That Jonas found Anne B.'s party to be very different from parties in Grorud, rather like a peek into a strange aquarium, had nothing to do with the material aspect, with which Norwegians tend to be so obsessed, but more with the actual *tone* of the evening. In other words, what impressed Jonas was not so much the fact that Anne B. lived in a house with a fireplace in the kitchen, five bedrooms and furniture bought from shops he had never heard of, not to mention original works of art on the walls, pictures that actually seemed to give pleasure; Jonas was more impressed by the way Anne B.'s guests – Jonas being the only one from their class – were welcomed, with some formality, by her parents, both of whom were doctors; and not only that, but that her parents joined the party for the first half-hour and conversed – it is the only word for it – with their daughter's guests quite as a matter of course as if these young people were their equals, their very close friends.

To top it all, early on in the evening Jonas had been complimented – again it is the only word for it – by Anne B. who told him he was looking great, and this she did while he was scanning a bookshelf lined with the standard 'classics' and chewing on the first olive he had ever tasted, fished from the bottom of a dry martini. Thereafter, Anne B. gave him a hug which left him in no doubt, nor did she intend to leave him in any doubt, that she was inviting him to more thoroughgoing embraces when he felt ready for it. In other words, she displayed a directness, an ease of manner and, not least, a self-assurance never before encountered by Jonas among girls of his own age.

And finally there was the dinner, or not so much the dinner as the atmosphere around the dinner table. And again I must emphasize that I am not talking here of anything as banal as the fact that they were waited on by a maid or that it was a three-course dinner with a bewildering array of cutlery – phenomena it would be all too easy to joke about and which would really only serve to obscure the main point. It was the actual manner in which the dinner party was conducted that amazed Jonas. The fact that people carried on a *conversation*. There was no yelling, no loud music; they talked, animatedly, but quite quietly, while records of pieces by Bellman and Taube played softly in the background, as if even the *Tafelmusik* were designed to add a mildly philosophical note to the proceedings.

And what did they talk about? As far as Jonas was concerned this was the most staggering part of all. For although they touched on most topics, from the theatre to glacier trekking, at all times politics ran like a red thread through the conversation and, even more staggering, it dealt not so much with specific issues of the day but with values and principles. So in between comments on the moon-landing or Woodstock, these teenagers discussed politics as a concept, neither more nor less. Jonas was all ears. Not that he felt inferior – Jonas Wergeland never felt inferior – but this was something different, almost unheard of: teenagers sitting at a table, discussing how social democracy could avoid becoming just another form of totalitarian regime, while the courses were served and cleared away and their glasses were kept topped up with wine and mineral water, a product new to Jonas. Even after a break, during which one of the boys rose to his feet and made a speech to Anne B., and a very original and witty one, at that; a speech which he rounded off by reciting a poem, and not just any old rubbish, but a poem by a relatively obscure writer called Charles Bukowski, a most unusual poem about what it was like to make love to a panther – even after that, the red thread of socialism as a concept was picked up yet again. Just before the dessert, a couple of these young people, neither of whom had seemed anything out of the ordinary to Jonas, presented a somewhat tentative but perfectly lucid discussion of the pros and cons of democratic socialism: 'a system based on compromises between different sets of mutually restrictive values' as one of them put it. Both were taken up with the idea that freedom and equality could not exist side by side. Eventually, the discussion, or conversation, crystallized into a candid question as to whether a social democracy along Scandinavian lines, with its almost fanatical obsession with equality, would render a society epitomized by its diversity impossible and hence, in the end, stifle the growth of new ideas.

Jonas loved it. He loved the crossfire of long, searching arguments mingled with poetry about lovemaking and panthers, all to the hushed accompaniment of Carl Michael Bellman; Jonas loved it not least because these animated expositions were leavened with just the right degree of uncertainty and, most importantly: irony, elements which saved them from seeming pretentious. Nor did Jonas have any problem holding his own. On a couple of occasions he even came up with paraphrased quotations from his little red book, including one from John Stuart Mill's *On Liberty*, from the very last page as it happens, as to how a state that dwarfs its citizens so that they will become more docile instruments, even in order to do good, will find that no great thing can be accomplished with small men. This sparked off a pretty fierce debate on the question of unduly far-reaching state control, concern for the underprivileged as opposed to new industry and the need to take responsibility for one's own life, a discussion in which the girls were the most vehemently vocal and took the greatest exception to Jonas's indirect criticism – unintentional though it was – of the welfare state.

Who were these people? Anne B., whom Jonas was seated next to at dinner, told him in her slightly husky voice that many of them were, like herself, members of Labour Youth while the rest were just friends. Although this may not have come as a shock to Jonas, it did serve as a sharp reminder that the Labour Party not only represented the workers but also this affluent, academic stratum of Norwegian society and their children, sophisticated teenagers who ate three-course dinners while discussing everything under the sun, who were active members of Amnesty International, who had hiked the length and breadth of Jotunheimen and knew the first three pages of *A Farewell to Arms* by heart, in English, not because it was part of their schoolwork but because they thought 'Hemingway wrote so divinely' – and beneath all this, or besides, they had it in them to stand at a gathering and sing 'when I see a red flag flapping on a bright and clear spring day' with feeling, mark you, real feeling. Once again Jonas was reminded of, and had to concur with, Gabriel's theory of the multifaceted individual. Jonas could not bring himself to condemn this little circle, not least because they were at least endeavouring to find a third way, and being a young Labourite was not exactly the most opportunist option at a time when the majority of so-called politically-aware teenagers either joined the Young Socialists or the Young Conservatives. In the years that followed, Jonas was to find Labour Youth more amazing by far than the Young Socialists, later the Norwegian Marxist-Leninist Party. To Jonas's mind, it was Labour Youth and not the Marxist-Leninist Party that was the real miracle.

After dinner, when they had once again fallen into conversation, this time in smaller groups, liberally supplied with expensive whisky and brandy, Jonas asked one of the girls, Guro, about this whole Labour Party business, whether it wasn't 'a complete dead loss in our day and age'. And it was during the course of her long explanation of why she was a member of Labour Youth, peppered with many an 'at this moment in time' and 'we, for our part', that realization dawned on Jonas: up to that point he had regarded these conversations as a casual flirt with political standpoints, little more than a mode of cultivated, not to say civil, conversation, but now he saw that many of the young people round about him actually were genuinely committed and had aspirations to a political career. The Young Socialist phenomenon was a mere flash in the pan but the Norwegian Labour Party was a party with a future, this girl Guro told Jonas, thereby revealing that such a sense of commitment was rooted not only in youthful idealism but also and to as great an extent in a rational plan of attack and a certain cynicism – and, indeed, no small lust for power. Or did Jonas really believe, Guro asked, handing him a glass of brandy, that future generations would be likely to compare a radical trade unionist like Tron Øgrim and a prime minister of Einar Gerhardsen's standing – a pigeon dropping and a monument?

At one point during the party, while he was standing listening to a brief lecture, quite brilliant, on the extent to which a democratic system could ever gain control of the economic market

forces, Jonas was struck by a sense of being in solitary confine-
ment, or a sort of prison camp, like the one at Grini during the
war, where all the leaders of the future sat biding their time while
madmen played havoc with the country.

On the return of Anne B.'s parents – they, too, Labour supporters, Jonas learned – they had a drink with the young people,
a drink which Mr B. mixed in a cocktail shaker, and again stayed
for half an hour of polite conversation before retiring to the first
floor. Immediately afterwards, as her guests were starting to
leave, Anne B. asked Jonas if he would not stay behind, in fact
she told him straight out that she would like him to spend the
night there – in her bed. She did not beat about the bush; her
gaze did not waver. Jonas muttered something about her parents,
but she said it was okay with her parents. It was *okay* with her
parents? Jonas repeated incredulously. 'And I'm on the Pill, of
course,' said Anne B. 'Mum advised me to start taking it last
year.' As I say, Jonas was here faced with a side of Norwegian
society he had not known existed: second and third generation
Labour supporters, fathers who mixed their drinks in a shaker
and mothers who could coolly tell their seventeen-year-old
daughters that they ought to consider using contraception.

So Jonas stayed. And when he climbed into her bed, naked,
she boldly proceeded to stroke his body while she went on talking, remarking on the party guests, or commenting on what he
had said about doing great things in a country of small men,
saying that it was well said, that that was what she liked about
him, that he could come out with such statements, even though
she didn't agree, the Scandinavian society had to be regarded as
a social experiment, nowhere near finished. Anne B. carried on
talking in this vein, one might almost say arguing, while she
caressed him, stroking his skin, as if they were two sides of the
same coin, caresses both, and Jonas had nothing against this, it
did not get in the way of anything at all, just made it that much
more erotic. She had, he noticed, a huge yoni; one by one his fingers slid inside it as he fondled her, an elephant yoni, large and
wet like an open mouth, but he had no difficulty in filling her
when she sat astride him, a position she choose both to illustrate
her freedom of will, her deliberate decision on that particular

night to choose him, and because she wanted to set the pace, starting out slowly and lingeringly, as if she could not quite believe that she had actually found a cock that could fill her completely; but then she was not to know that Jonas Wergeland had a magic penis, a penis that could become thicker or thinner, shorter or longer as required, like a zoom lens; she was not to know that Jonas Wergeland could fill any vagina exactly as that vagina longed to be filled, perfectly, to give a pleasure second to none, so to begin with she moved slowly, tentatively, still talking all the while, pursuing her line of argument, which involved a number of objections to Jonas's quote from John Stuart Mill and which amounted, on the whole, to a discourse on finding the right *balance*, she said, accentuating the word 'balance' first one way, then another, while she rocked back and forth on top of him, soon starting to ride him faster and faster, bearing down harder, and he felt something happening to his body, felt it opening up, becoming receptive to something or other, something that was starting to take shape inside his head, new ideas, filling him with energy, even as she was talking to him and making love to him, both at once, and he loved it, he loved her voice, that slightly husky voice, as if she were forever talking, never gave her voice a rest, he loved the stream of words, the long sentences in which sub-clauses wove in and out of sub-clauses, while she never once lost the main thread of the sentence; he felt his own thoughts starting to turn in the same insistent way, the same way as she was making love to him, short, sharp thrusts alternating with longer, more rhythmic strokes, breathtakingly wonderful and stimulating, for her too, and as she approached a climax she could no longer keep her sentences in order, a fact which manifested itself first of all in her statements, in the way that her sub-clauses no longer hung together; and thereafter became more and more marked by sudden leaps and unfinished sentences, running out into disconnected preambles and such rhetorical expressions as 'it is resoundingly clear' and 'quite the reverse' until at last she was reduced to firing off single words and, in the long pauses between, her pelvis worked more and more frenetically until she stiffened with something that reached him only as a little gasp escaping her lips, a barely audible exclamation mark, after which he drove inside her as if giving her a standing ovation, as much for her long, oratorical performance as for the exceptionally fast, almost relentless, pace at which she had made love to him. And I hardly need add that it was this same strong-willed woman who – after changing her surname and taking her degree in socio-economics, it's true – is now the leader of her party; a woman who, I warrant you, will leave behind her not a pigeon dropping, but an enduring memorial, a towering monument in Norwegian politics.

Smoke Without Fire

Not long after the party at Anne B's, Jonas noticed that his manner, when discussing political issues, was different, smoother somehow, the words seemed to simply flow from his lips as if a totally new rhetorical organ had taken up residence inside him and was now demanding to be heard. For someone who had never been very good at putting his thoughts into words, suddenly he had a mind that worked like lightning – he could plan what he was going to say later in his argumentation *even while* he was actually making a point – and not only that, he found he had such a fantastic grasp of the actual sentence construction that he could easily depart from his main sentence and embroil himself in an intricate web of sub-clauses, only then – elegantly and without losing the thread for a second, with fresh cogency and weight, so it seemed – to complete his main sentence, like snapping shut a heavy lock. Jonas Wergeland overpowered others with such sentences, throwing out coils of words like a lasso with which he could not only catch and rope them in but also force them to the ground and bind them hand and foot.

I would like to stress that this discovery of other sides of himself did not, as some might think, have anything to do with sucking up a talent from another person, to allude, notwithstanding, to the requisite sexual element. It was much more as though Jonas Wergeland were quite naturally open to a continual metamorphosis, or rather: expansion. Jonas knew, especially after he met Gabriel Sand, that he was many people and the women he met merely helped him, by dint of a sort of hook-up, to give vent to these other sides of his character – including those he had not been aware of before. Often this new skill would create a need; at other times it turned out to be most opportune, as was the case with Jonas's new command of language, which he had plenty of opportunity to display in the hours following his demonstration on behalf of the Comoro Islands.

When the students streamed out into the schoolyard after the first period, one of the fire department's splendid turntable ladder trucks was just swinging in through the gates. It *looked* more dramatic than it was. There was no fire at the Cathedral School, although symbolically speaking one could perhaps say that the fire brigade had been called out by one of those 'burning hearts' of which the poet speaks; there was a fire on a flagpole at the Cathedral School. Jonas had also jammed the bolt on the skylight, and the rector, in a blend of desperation and rage, had called the Central Fire Station on Arne Garborgs plass and explained his problem; and since one has to assume that there were no other fires, real fires, raging elsewhere in the city and since it was not that far away, the duty officers agreed to do him this 'favour' and promptly dispatched a turntable ladder truck to the school to bring down the two flags, both the one on the pole jutting out over Ullevålsveien and the one on the cable above the schoolyard – 'those pirate flags' as the rector put it as if buccaneers had made an attempt to board his school.

It was a strange sight, and Jonas suddenly found himself wishing that Nefertiti could have seen it, not only because the demonstration had been very much in Nefertiti's spirit but because it was the same turntable ladder truck that they had so often stopped to admire on their way to Torggata Baths. Jonas was downright proud to be the cause of such a singular to-do: the fire engine in the middle of the schoolyard and the ladder with a man in uniform at the top of it, sweating and straining to undo Jonas's ingenious pulley contraption from the cable and so 'lower' the green flag of the Comoros, now fluttering over Norwegian soil for the first time.

By lunch-time that same day, long before the rector had completed his assiduous and vengeful hunt for the sinner, which would in due course require Jonas to draw on all of his newly won rhetorical skills, Jonas got into an almighty row with the school's resident Young Socialists, who had long since figured out that Jonas Wergeland, that exasperating, swell-headed provocateur, had to be the man behind this weird demonstration, a demonstration which, even before they learned the motives behind it, they regarded as a deplorable act of heresy. And it was here, in a school shed, during the subsequent discussion, that Jonas Wergeland put the Cath's Young Socialists so firmly in their place that for a long time afterwards students at the school, or at any rate those who heard about it and spread the rumours, found it hard to take the Young Socialists and their policies seriously.

Jonas, knowing as he did that attack is the best form of defence, began by asking what they knew about the Comoro Islands, these characters who spoke with such absolute certainty about the sorry state of the world, of imperialism and the class struggle in general – and, he added triumphantly, the necessity of a good education, not least for the cadres, among whose number these Cath Socialists counted themselves. This immediately gave rise to a lot of shifty looks in the Young Socialist ranks because of course they did not know the first thing about the Comoro Islands. Then, before they could gather themselves together, Jonas smartly fired off a round of questions, first of a geographical nature – what were the names of the four main islands, what was the capital called and what did they associate with the name 'Kartala' and suchlike – before switching to questions which he answered himself as he went along, regarding the current economic situation and social conditions in the Comoros. What did they export? What did they import? What was the average life expectancy? And by dint of these questions and answers he succeeded, quite cunningly, in presenting a picture of the tremendous poverty on the islands and the horrendous political decisions that had led the kingdom to the point where everything centred on vanilla pods, cloves and ylang-ylang essence for the perfume industry, leaving the people in abject poverty with no agriculture to feed them, which, and here he played his trump card, brought him to the question of who – who! – was to blame for this appalling misrule or, to put it another way, which country had been the colonial power, and indeed still looked upon the Comoros as its own overseas territory? And he stared hard at these faces, surprisingly many of which sported glasses with black frames, wreathed in greasy hair, with FNL badges stuck directly under their chins as if it were some sort of fashion, or a uniform, but none of which could supply the answer: France. That's right dammit: France, the most cynical of all countries when it came to its activities outside its own borders, making the English look like out-and-out humanists by comparison when it came to foreign policy and the building of infrastructures in their colonies. It really was incredible, that these guys, these Young Socialists, didn't know about France and the Comoro Islands, seeing as how, when you came right down to it, France was also at the bottom of that unscrupulous conflict in Vietnam, which the Young Socialists were supposed to be such experts on, going on about it as if they had personally spent at least a year fighting in the jungle.

There stood Jonas Wergeland – in the schoolyard of Oslo Cathedral School, in that shed in which the students could shelter in foul weather – generating, aptly enough, a veritable storm of arguments and critical questions and harangues that made those poor, and in their own eyes, radical and politically conscious Young Socialists cower as if seeking shelter from a thunderstorm. And Jonas had not yet come to his *pièce de résistance*, namely, to ask, to no avail, of course, whether they could outline the political situation in the Comoro Islands. And you can take it from me, gaining any sort of overview of the political situation in the Comoros at that time was no easy task. But Jonas really let them have it, he inundated those ignorant, so-called activists with facts about the traditional Comorian parties, the UDC, the RDCP and the UMMA, also known as the 'greens', the 'whites and the 'white-oranges', and thereafter on MOLINACO, PEC, PASCO and ASEC, all of whom were in opposition, more or less socialist and illegal, as well as the conservative MPM. Jonas rained these acronyms, a whole alphabet of them, down on their heads, only rarely giving the full French designations of the abbreviations, letting these Young Socialists see just what it was like to hear someone talking political double Dutch. But the worst, or the best, of it was that at this point Jonas Wergeland truly did have mastery of this bewildering mishmash of different political constellations and standpoints as to whether they should forge even stronger ties with France, or fight for full independence – a mishmash that would have formed a fantastic breeding ground for support groups from all manner of factions – and, I might add: a lot of entertainment – if only more Norwegians had taken an interest in the Comoro Islands. And believe me: it took some doing for a Norwegian to differentiate between Mouzaoir Abdallah and Ahmed Abdallah, or tell the difference between Saïd Mohamed Cheikh, Prince Saïd Ibrahim and Prince Saïd Mohamed Jaffar.

But it did not stop there: Jonas Wergeland also succeeded, thanks to his newly acquired command of the rhetorical devices – by which I mean not necessarily the classic form but a pawky Norwegian, social-democratic variant – in delivering all of this in the form of outrageously convoluted arguments involving sentence constructions verging on a complexity comparable only to that of the larger molecules in organic chemistry – while at the same time hammering home rebukes and stressing points with such expressions as 'it must be resoundingly clear' and 'quite the reverse' – bringing the whole thing to a conclusion with a question shaped as a calculated complaint, while in a vacant corner of his mind he sent his grateful thanks to Anne B., whom he had spied over by the stairs leading to the girls' gym, as to why in the world every radical in Norway had to fight for the same cause. Why did they all have to flock like sheep around the Vietnam banner? Surely there were other countries deserving of our solidarity and our attention, countries that were struggling to rid themselves of the yoke of colonialism? How could people who called themselves revolutionaries and who were supposedly fighting for the Third World not know shit about the Comoro Islands? It was a fucking revolutionary disgrace! Jonas flung out an arm, taking in all those FNL badges not to mention Mao badges and all sorts of other badges: some of these guys had chests like kids in the school band with a lot of jamborees under their belts or old Soviet soldiers celebrating a national holiday. In that shelter in the schoolyard of Oslo Cathedral School, Jonas closed his fiery speech on the Comoro Islands with an indirect denunciation of his schoolfellows' apathy, their *superficiality*, their blinkered outlook – which of course led one to suspect that it was not Vietnam, say, that mattered to them; they were not interested in the world, they were interested only in power, in manipulating. Vietnam was simply an excuse to flaunt themselves and their ironclad egos; the actual object of their hate was neither here not there. So in closing let me just add, for the record, that Jonas's thundering denunciation was in no wise prompted by a reckless urge to heap abuse on the superficial commitment and political narcissism of Norwegian youth. At that moment Jonas Wergeland *was* the Comoro Islands champion in Norway, right then it was important to him, more important than anything else, that the students at the Cath should be told about this island kingdom in the Indian Ocean.

I ought of course to tell you how things went, in the years that followed, with this fervent commitment to the Comoros. In the autumn of 1976, Jonas received a letter from none other than President Ali Soilih, who had toppled the new state's first president, Ahmed Abdallah, from power the previous January. And in this odd letter Ali Soilih, the utopian dreamer who initiated a most peculiar Maoist-cum-Socialist experiment on the islands, *thanked* Jonas Wergeland for his efforts on behalf of the Comoro Islands' cause in Scandinavia and maintained that his fight up there in the north had been an inspiration to those fighting for full independence, which, as far as at least three out of the four islands were concerned, had been achieved in 1975. This letter meant such a lot to Jonas Wergeland that he had it framed, like a diploma, and showed it off whenever anyone accused him of lacking political awareness. How Ali Soilih found out that Jonas Wergeland had hoisted the Comorian flag in a school in far-off Norway was a mystery to Jonas and everyone else, and even though there is a very simple explanation I am not going to disclose it here and risk ruining the best part of this tale.

Because from there on, it is the usual story: of a commitment that gradually peters out. In Jonas Wergeland's defence it should be said that he tried, he tried very hard to follow future developments in the Comoro Islands. Jonas did his best, somewhat resignedly, to keep track of the new parties and alliances that sprang up after his raising of the flag: the PUIC, FNU, UDZIMA, FNUK-UNIKOM and FD, to name but a few of the permutations of initials that Jonas found increasingly abstract. He valiantly endeavoured to keep abreast and still more valiantly to understand what was going on down there on those islands in the Indian Ocean: the power struggles and political proclamations. Not least, he tried to understand the employment and the presence of foreign mercenaries, primarily French, in various coups d'états. It almost became something of a hobby, rather like stamp collecting; Jonas Wergeland collected piece after piece of an African reality, the only thing being that the more pieces he accumulated the less he understood any of it. The Comoro Islands actually afforded an angle onto the whole African dilemma, lying as they did off the continent, like a lens through which the mainland could be viewed. The whole gamut of depressing factors was to be found there: a mixed-bag of ethnic groups, a ruinous colonial past, overpopulation, extreme poverty, food shortages, high infant mortality rate, low life expectancy, illiteracy, one-sided exports, political intrigue, governmental chaos, coups, abortive utopian socialism, mercenaries, the Muslim syndrome: a disheartening sum which in the end Jonas found impossible to add up. Or perhaps it was simply that he could not figure it out, not even after the mathematical breakthrough that brought him insight into equations involving several unknowns, the problem of infinity. Sometime in the mid-eighties – and, quite honestly, who can blame him? – Jonas Wergeland gave up, mind reeling, battered and bruised by incomprehensible facts. He threw in the towel. The Comoro Islands and Africa won on a technical knock-out.

But as far as his debate with the Young Socialists as a high-school student, in the schoolyard, in that shed was concerned – *that* Jonas won. And it is important, as it was for Jonas Wergeland, to feel at least at one point in your life that you have an overview and that, perhaps precisely because of that overview, you manage to light on a cause that has not been taken up by everyone else. So even though, in the long run, the Comoro Islands affair ended in defeat, for Jonas Wergeland it represented unequivocal proof – as witness the letter from Ali Soilih – that it does actually pay to step in and do something to change the world. In those terms, Jonas Wergeland's fight for the Comoro Islands was a glorious victory and, if I may say so, an example worth emulating.

The Hub

With a few exceptions – one of which I have already mentioned – Jonas Wergeland had the best of all possible childhoods, a childhood so happy that its end was bound to come as a shock. There comes a day when, as one writer put it, the bubble of childhood bursts, and for Jonas that day came with Nefertiti's death. Of course Jonas had always known that Nefertiti was too good for this world, but even so, when she died he was not prepared for it. In short, he fell apart. He took ill, became so ill that he had to be taken to hospital. Jonas Wergeland was sick right to the marrow and so cold that he thought he would never be warm again. The doctors at the hospital did not know what to make of it: a ten-year-old who languished in bed, pale and wan, and kept throwing up, vomiting fits for which they could find no cause, a boy with a body temperature well nigh as low as that encountered only in people who had miraculously survived record lengths of time in extreme cold. And one thing they would not have understood anyway, even if there had been gauges to measure that sort of thing, was Jonas's feeling of being totally out of joint, of lying there like a carcass that had been chopped limb from limb. Jonas had only one thing to hold onto: a crystal prism which he clenched tightly in his fist and did not let go of, not even when he was at his sickest.

Jonas's father was considered by many people to be a rather distrait and distant character. Where other fathers dreamed of cars and BMWs, Haakon Hansen dreamed of Bach and BWVs. Even Jonas had the feeling, when he was alone in the church listening to his father's improvisations on the organ, that his father was endeavouring to *create* worlds, or a zone of his own, where he could be alone. But when Jonas came home from the hospital, still no more than a shadow of himself, Haakon Hansen showed that he did notice what was going on around him. And one day in late August, when Jonas came home from school, pale and miserable, and did not even want the egg and tomato sandwiches that had been carefully prepared for him, his father suggested – without the slightest bit of fiddling – that they should take a look at the new organ in Grorud Church. Okay, Jonas muttered, fingering the prism in his pocket, why not; there was something about his father's fluttering fingers that made it impossible for him to say no.

From the moment they stepped inside the church and his father ranged himself alongside the altar rail and proudly pointed up at the gleaming new case, 'based on a Principal 8 and an Octave bass 8', Jonas noticed, to his surprise, that his nausea was starting to subside. Behind the organ's glittering façade wooden slats fanned out in rays, making Jonas feel for a moment like the boy in Kittelsen's picture; 'A long, long way off he saw something glittering and gleaming.'

Up in the organ-loft his father was a whirlwind of activity, dashing hither and thither and telling Jonas about this new organ from the manufacturers in Snertingdal, really big, with twenty-nine voices and three manuals, with a tracker action and electric–action stop controls. 'Almost 2,000 pipes, Jonas – imagine that!' And excited though his father was, Jonas noticed that his hands had steadied, ceased their fluttering, as they always did around an organ. 'Amazing,' his father said again and again, pointing to couplers, mixtures and buttons for free combinations. 'Isn't that amazing?'

But it was in the office, behind the organ, when his father went to fetch his music, that the truly amazing feature was revealed, when Jonas opened a small door. Where did that lead? Had it been there before? Jonas asked. That was the door to the chest, his father told him. Did Jonas want to take a look? He opened the door and they passed through a little room containing the blower and the bellows before his father opened yet another door, leading to the chest itself. 'Go on in,' his father said when Jonas hung back on the threshold. 'This here's kind of like the engine-room of the nave, if you know what I mean.'

I make no secret of the fact that the experience which awaited Jonas Wergeland here is one that I hold infinitely dear – the mere fact of being able to write about this episode makes this whole undertaking worth the effort, or perhaps I should say the trouble. For once, however, I must apologize for the fact that I have no choice but to describe it in the crude and narrow terms that this form and this language, which is to say this role that I have taken upon myself, dictate.

Jonas stepped across the threshold and promptly found himself inside the heart of the instrument, surrounded by pipes of all sizes, the largest sixteen feet tall, set at several different levels. It was a large room, or a little house, with other small houses inside the main house, boxes and walls. 'What's that over there?' Jonas asked, whispering, as if he were inside a shrine, pointing as he did so at something he took to be a little organ in itself. 'That's the swell,' his father said. Jonas went on gazing round about in disbelief, he did not know what to make of it all, but he liked it instantly; it was not, in fact, unlike the engine-room of a ship, possibly because of the steep and narrow steps leading up to ledges, and all the bridges one could walk along between the pipes.

'Can I sit here while you play?' Jonas asked.

'Aye, aye cap'n! Full speed ahead!' his father replied and went out.

Jonas heard his father settling himself on the stool in front of the console and leafing through his music. Then something strange happened; his father switched on the organ, which is to say the electricity that powered the blower, and Jonas heard, no he *felt* the space around him being filled with air, how the air streamed into the valves. It was like being in the countryside, in the wind, a warm wind. Jonas sat there, savouring this whooshing, and the clicking of the stops, noticing that already he was not as cold and that he was starting to relax, as if there were some strange accord between his father's manipulation of the organ and his own nervous system.

Then his father started to play. Johann Sebastian Bach. Haakon Hansen was never in any doubt. If anyone could help his son, it would be Johann Sebastian Bach. To Jonas, ensconced inside the organ chest, it sounded wonderful. Like hearing the music from within himself. He was *inside* the music, he was float- ing on it. His body became a pipe, or rather, every bone became a pipe, and since every bone was a pipe and since Bach's music is more coherent than any other music, joining things up, Jonas felt his father's playing putting him back together, reassembling his dismembered limbs, and there came a point when Jonas had the sensation, like a tremor running through him from top to toe, that his body had become whole once more; and since the music was surging around him in the most beautiful way, he started to cry, very softly.

Later Jonas came to the conclusion that the organ had saved him. Or his father, or Bach, depending on how you looked at it. That the weight of his grief over Nefertiti had been punctured: lightened by the air that generated that music. That autumn, as if he were attending a course of treatment, at least a couple of times a week after his last class at school, Jonas would head straight across the road to the granite church, where he shut him- self up inside the organ chest and let his father play for him. To begin with he would sometimes break into the music. 'Which note does this pipe play?' he was liable to call from inside the organ. 'What does it look like?' his father would call back. Then he would try first one then another until Jonas learned which note, on which manual, at which pitch, through the network of linkages, produced a sound from that particular pipe. The pipes connected to the pedals were situated in an especially out-of-the- way spot. Jonas wormed his way around the chest, up steps, bal- ancing on crossbeams, inspecting every pipe made of tin, or rather of an alloy of which tin was the main component; inspected the square wooden pipes, the group of copper pipes in the centre, all the minuscule pipes smaller than piccolos. Occa- sionally he amused himself by pulling on the sliders, thus creat- ing notes over and above those his father was playing, like a spirit inside the machine.

But what Jonas found most interesting about the organ was the fact that, while keys were positioned side by side on the man- uals, their pipes did not sit side by side inside the organ so, for example, a C and a C sharp, which were right next to one another

on the keyboard, could be almost two and a half metres apart
inside the chest. When his father played all twelve notes on a
scale, they would sound from all around the inside of the organ,
especially when he coupled down voices from other manuals.
Jonas loved it, made his father do it again and again, slowly, while
his ears tried to follow the notes as they swelled out into the air
around him. Jonas more than loved it; he almost went down on
his knees in the face of this unexpected and totally different
chain of cause and effect, looking upon it as a gift, this glimpse
of another form of logic, one which – and this was the comforting thing – was connected to the logic outside, on the manuals, as
if they were two parallel but different universes.

His father sat patiently on the organ stool, obeying the slightest hint, and this he did with pleasure because he knew that this
finding out how the organ worked was in itself a kind of therapy:
to discover that something so apparently complex did nonetheless make sense. So it was with hopes steadily rising that he
allowed his son to crawl about in there, like an organ-builder's
apprentice, mapping out pipes and abstracts, complying with
Jonas's wish to hear all the voices one after another without a
murmur and making not the slightest objection when his son
declared that he thought the Cromorne sounded best played on
the Choir, together with the Bassoon played on the pedals.

In due course Jonas learned a lot about the organ, including
the fact that it was *alive*, that notes sounded different from one
day to the next. Just as he learned that when he pulled out the
stop that said 'Mixture 3 fagot', it came across loud and strong,
like the last verse of a hymn, and it occurred to him that it was
the same with people: now and again you might be in a 'Mixture
3 fagot' mood, but that the usual tone tended to be that of the
'Principal', the keynote of the Hauptwerk. For his own part,
Jonas felt like a 'Reed', barely audible.

As time went on, however, Jonas slipped inside the organ chest
simply to listen. He had found a broad plank, almost like a bunk,
in the midst of the maze of pipes and there he would lie as if at
the heart of an incredible machine – had he read Hermann Hesse
he might have said glass bead game – for hours on end, week in,
week out, month after month, letting his father play Bach for

him until he could feel the music permeating his body like a medicine; or perhaps it was more that, having first put his body together, only now, with the help of time, could his father blow life into it. One day Jonas had the idea of taking the crystal prism – his most treasured possession at that time – from his pocket and placing it on his brow, and it was then, while he lay there as if on a bunk in the middle of the organ, with the prism on his brow and his father playing Bach, that he saw, felt in every bone in his body, possibly because the prism broke up the music in such a way that the brain apprehended it differently, that he was lying inside the very engine of existence. Because again, beneath everything else, this was what troubled him: the wheel. Why did Nefertiti die? Who turned the wheel? Who or what sat at the hub of the wheel? And as he lay there, Jonas realized that he himself was at the centre of the wheel, that he was lying still, and yet he was in motion. And lying there, at the centre of something he did not understand, with a prism on his brow that refracted the light and created a little rainbow somewhere out of eyeshot, Jonas was aware that he was slowly being healed.

No wonder then that Jonas Wergeland conceived a very special affection for organs, after lying for half a year on his back, listening to that blend of air and sound, the creaking of the sliders and clicking of the stops, while gazing at the swell, the little house, seeing how the little doors were opened and closed as his father regulated the volume with his foot and how the abstracts, trackers and tracker wires, all the filigree network surrounding him, moved in time with the movements of his father's fingers. Of all the pieces of jewellery Jonas Wergeland saw in his life, Aunt Laura's included, none was more beautiful than the organ with its tin and lead, its copper and ebony, against a backing of pine. Jonas was never fazed by computers and their microchips, not even the control room at NRK could impress someone who had seen an organ from the inside: the world, as it were, from the wrong side.

For a long time Jonas believed it was Nefertiti's death that had driven him into the organ chest, but the real cause lay, of course, in the future. Not until he was a grown man, looking back over a long distance, did Jonas understand that his time inside the organ had equipped him for experiences and ordeals that were to come later in life.

But already that autumn Jonas had grasped that, in the little door in his father's office, the one leading, that is, to the organ chest, he had found an unusual and original angle on life as a whole. Later, when faced with any apparently complex phenomenon, he would always look for this little back door, this entrance that would take him to the backside or the inside and provide him with a totally different viewpoint. 'Crawl inside the organ,' he would say to himself. So when, for example, Jonas stumbled across the Comoro Islands, he knew right away that this could be one of those rare angles that would lead him to the backside of a complexity, like someone taking you behind a grand building and showing you that it is a flat on a film set.

In later life Jonas Wergeland held the belief that everyone should have the chance to crawl inside an organ chest, even if none of them could enjoy the same privilege as himself: to be able to lie inside an organ while your own father sets the world to rights with his playing in a church built of granite, the stone of your childhood.

Bukhara

Aunt Laura's flat looked like a bazaar. Where the walls were not covered in oriental rugs, they were hung with objects made of copper and brass; and crawling around the floor was a leopard-tortoise with little gems affixed to its shell. Jonas had the feeling that the tortoise was forever going round in circles and that time stood still at Aunt Laura's.

One day, Jonas was allowed to look on while his aunt cast a little head out of gold, and what intrigued him more than anything else – more than the complicated gravity casting technique – was the way she transformed four old wedding rings into molten gold in the crucible with the aid of a gas-gun, before pouring it into the mould. There was something about that molten gold that he would never forget, a colour and a sheen which he occasionally thought he detected in certain uncommonly good pictures. This was one of Jonas's favourite occupations: to watch his aunt working, often wearing a leather apron like a blacksmith, in that corner of the room which had the look of a proper little industrial plant. Jonas found it hard to believe that you needed so many tools to make something so small.

Having cleaned and polished the gold head his aunt asked Jonas to fetch the tortoise, which was crawling about the floor. She studied it long and hard, from all angles, before he was allowed to set it back on the floor. And for anyone who has not yet guessed as much, it was, of course, Aunt Laura who first told Jonas the old Chinese tale about the world resting on the back of an ancient creature, Ao, a huge turtle; a tale which Jonas later recounted to Axel and which inspired their hunt for their teachers' underlying and often shaky propositions.

In many ways, his visits to Aunt Laura's flat were akin to crawling inside the organ, although in the one instance Jonas had to lie on a hard wooden plank, while in the other he sank back onto soft silk cushions. In June 1964, the same year, strangely enough, when the James Bond film *From Russia With Love* went on general release in Norway, Nikita Khrushchev paid a visit to that country and while he was there Werna Gerhardsen, wife of the Norwegian prime minister, invited the first lady of the Soviet Union to pay a call on one of her neighbours in the Tøyen tenement where she lived, so that Madame Khrushchev could meet 'a typical Norwegian family' and see how they lived – the whole thing duly covered by the national press, naturally. Jonas often thought, laughing to himself, what a sensation it would have caused if the two first ladies and the whole entourage of reporters had rung the wrong doorbell and called instead on Aunt Laura, who happened to live in the same building as Prime Minister Gerhardsen. To some extent, however, he decided on reflection, it would not have been so bad, because in many ways Aunt Laura's flat provided a different and necessary angle on Norwegian society. And there were times, when he was lying on his back on the sofa in Tøyen with a bowl of pistachio nuts on his chest, that Jonas saw it all so clearly: It was Einar Gerdharsen's flat, right over his head, that was unreal and these things round about him, including Aunt Laura with a lump of gold on the anvil, that was the true Norway.

The flat's unique character also owed something to the absence of a television. 'What do I want with a television when I have forty screens in my living room, and every one of them presenting a wonderful story?' Aunt Laura would say, pointing to the rugs on the walls around her. Jonas knew what she meant; he liked lying on the sofa, taking in one rug after another. If you tired of one – its colours, its patterns – you only had to let your eye move on. Although he did not know it, in this Jonas was anticipating the possibility that would be open to television viewers of the future, to switch from one channel to another using a remote control.

Aunt Laura was totally absorbed in her work at the bench at the far end of the room, and Jonas had gone over to pour her some more tea – as usual he had no idea what sort of tea it was, but it smelled good. His aunt was correcting the lineaments of the little gold heart ever so carefully with a graver. It was a fine sight, his aunt with her black-lined eyes and blood-red mouth bent over gold and silver, hand moving purposefully and surely. As a small boy Jonas had been allowed to sit alongside her and play with tongs and a piece of silver plate and was thus able to experience for himself the solemn, almost sensual feeling of bending the silver. He could sympathize with his aunt's love and respect for these malleable metals, their durability: silver and, even more so, gold, metal of the gods, metal of the sun.

Jonas left the teapot with his aunt and went back to the sofa, where he sank down into the pile of cushions with one of his aunt's sketchbooks, her 'travel journals' in his hands. He opened it at random and was promptly confronted with something that made him start: drawings of penises covered in rings, or with little swellings like warts. 'What's that?' he asked, curious and a little afraid, holding up the book. Aunt Laura barely glanced up from under her black-lined eyelids then quietly went on working, quite unperturbed, on the gold head, while she explained to Jonas that in many societies, even in the West, men pierced holes in their members for rings and little metal rods. 'If, for example, you have a pin stuck through the head of the penis, it's known as *ampallang*,' his aunt said matter-of-factly. 'And if you have a ring, preferably of gold and set with small precious stones, through the skin at the side of the scrotum, that's called *hafada*.' As for the lumpy penises, those swellings he saw there, those were pearls, surgically inserted under the skin. Her aunt looked up at him. What was he making faces for? Why couldn't men wear pins and pearls on their penises? They stuck them in their ties, didn't they?

Jonas was not only making faces, he could virtually feel his own testicles smarting. Nonetheless, for the first time he perceived a connection between his aunt's collection of penises and their aspects, those sketchbooks, and her jewellery, because it was clear that in some way all of those different organs, both with and without rings, inspired her.

'You know the penis is a piece of jewellery,' Aunt Laura said. 'These men have simply taken that to its logical conclusion. I've said it before, and I'll say it again: the cock is a work of art.' As I say, Aunt Laura was not one for mincing her words.

Through all his comings and goings in the flat in Tøyen, Jonas gradually came to see that not only the rugs and the travelling but also these penises amounted to one and the same thing. As with the rugs and the travelling, when you came right down to it, this collection of penises also testified to the search for a good tale. The idea that the penis truly did contain a story, possibly concerning the secret of sexuality, had often occurred to Jonas when his aunt sat next to him on the sofa and showed him, with a pencil held between fingers adorned with spirals of gold, how this simple form harboured no end of possibilities.

His aunt switched off the lamp at the back of the room. She was finished working, and Jonas was allowed to see the result. On the bench was a silver cylinder, rounded at one end, sitting on a base of oxidized copper, or rather: you had to slide the base *over* the cylinder. No one needed to tell Jonas that he was looking at a lingam and a yoni. 'But take a closer look,' his aunt said. 'See what you can do with the cylinder.' And this was the surprise, because when Jonas lifted off the top, he found what looked like a large diamond, though it was in fact a chunk of crystal, cut into an oval, and faceted. Jonas tilted it and saw how beautifully the dim light was refracted by the glass as if through a prism. 'Give it a shake,' Aunt Laura said, her blood-red lips smiling eagerly. When Jonas shook the crystal, out slid four little feet and a head of gold, in much the same way as one of those Transformer toys that would appear in the shops a few decades later, and suddenly Jonas realized what it was: a turtle. He laughed. 'Great stuff, Auntie!'

'This is my turtle,' said Aunt Laura, kissing him on the cheek. 'The turtle that lies at the bottom of everything.'

Jonas stood there admiring his aunt's work, popping the cylinder through the copper base, noting how neatly they slotted together, taking the top off the silver cylinder, shaking the crystal. Amazing. A silver penis. Ejaculating a turtle with a golden head. And only then – with that silver cylinder and crystal turtle in his hand – did Jonas understand what a lovely, nay, nigh-on perfect story this was. As if all of his aunt's rugs and travels had been shaped, reworked into a piece of jewellery.

Later, Jonas lay back down on the sofa, in the pile of soft cushions, with a cup of sweet-scented tea on the table next to him. His aunt moved about the room, tidying up, bracelets jingling; she put the sketchbooks back in the chest alongside the precious four-volume edition of Ibn Battuta's *Rihlah*. The room lay in shadow, the rugs on the walls became windows onto fabulous landscapes and when Jonas turned his head he could see the lingam on the workbench in the corner drawing all the light around it and storing it in the silver.

'Tell me more about Princess Li-Lai,' Jonas asked.

And at such times the word 'no' never passed Aunt Laura's lips. 'In Xanadu,' she said, 'Princess Li Lai received another suitor in her cool palace, in the innermost room in which she had shut herself away for many years because she had not yet found one who could make love to her until she saw a turtle with a shell that looked like a face. The one who had come to woo her on this occasion was the celebrated rug-maker, Kara Bagh, and he did not waste any time either but carried her to the bed where he immediately proceeded to make love to her. Kara Bagh concentrated solely on her insides as if she contained a multitude of threads which he was resolved to knot into a rug. The princess thought she could feel his member growing hard and soft by turns and how he alternated between long strokes and short, close-knit twists and turns deep inside her as if he were knotting something that was attached to the very tip of his penis. And as he made love to her, ever more strangely, with the most surprising movements, in the oddest patterns, Princess Li Lai felt these touches filling her with a warm glow as if she had stepped out into the sunshine and were walking through a landscape that Kara Bagh the rug-maker slowly created in her path, knot by knot, with vegetation in glowing colours and high mountains in wild formations stretching away behind and beyond one another, seeming to go on forever, and as she came to a river it suddenly overflowed its banks and swept her away, and she floated off, as if caught up in a tidal wave, a delicious pressure against her body, floated and floated in a warm stream that flowed faster and faster, harder and harder, until she was thrown onto the bank, and there she caught sight of a bridge nearby. She crossed this and it brought her to a plateau at the foot of a mountain, and while Kara Bagh the rug-maker made love to her ever more vigorously with his alternately hard and soft member, with long and short strokes, with knots and loose threads, the princess felt her legs carrying her towards the mountain, more and more swiftly, until she was lifted up, rose higher and higher, drifted, and when she reached the top of the mountain Kara Bagh made love to her in patterns so rare and with actions so studied that she lost her balance and toppled over the edge of the cliff and fell and fell and fell through the air, as if being set free, heavy, replete, until she came once again to a stretch of water, went on sinking, sank and sank, a glorious, all-embracing feeling, an endless sinking, until suddenly she had a sense of climbing, even while she went on sinking, climbed and sank, sank and climbed as if she were being expanded in all directions, liberated from without and from within, achieving consummate insight, immaculate stillness, a rainbow of light and then she broke the surface again, shot through with warmth and discovered that she was being carried by a large turtle, lying on her stomach on its back, and Princess Li Lai saw, on the instant, that the shell looked like a face, the selfsame face that she gazed down on when she opened her eyes, the face of Kara Bagh the rug-maker for, unknown to her, he had changed position, so that she now lay on top of him. And she thanked him and asked him to stay because she was sure that this must be the best way to be made love to. "What did you do to me?" Princess Li Lai asked. And great was her astonishment when Kara Bagh told her that he had not been inside her at all. For, as he said later: "No man can reach the innermost depths of a woman with his member.'"

Often, perhaps too often, in novels, one reads of young men being seduced by their voluptuous aunts; an aunt, for example, with a pale face, a lot of kohl around her eyes and blood-red lipstick. Jonas Wergeland was not, however, seduced by his aunt's body but by her stories. Many things in Jonas Wergeland's life

would have been different had he not spent so much time surrounded by rugs and copper in Aunt Laura's flat.

'Tell me about Samarkand,' he said at last, as always, just
before he left.

'As for Samarkand and what I found there, that I can never tell
you,' she said. 'You will have to go there yourself.'

Opium of the People

Allow me to introduce Nora Næss, resident of the town of Bryne in the Jæren area of south-west Norway, a teacher, married to a man who works out in the North Sea, two children, own house. A perfectly ordinary, middle-aged Norwegian woman, exactly like Nanna Norheim in Bærum or Nina Narum in Tromsø. On the evening on which NRK TV showed the first programme in Jonas Wergeland's series *Thinking Big*, Nora Næss had not really been intending to watch television; she pressed the button more or less out of habit, without checking to see what was on, because she was in the dinette, ironing tablecloths and could just as well have something to look up at now and again, something to break the monotony of the job. And then suddenly there was this amazing programme. First she glanced up more often than usual, possibly for a little longer, then she started watching more and more and ironing less and less until eventually, without taking her eyes off the screen, she pulled the plug of the iron out of the socket, sat down on the sofa and watched television as if she had never watched television before. Or, as she confided to her friend, and the odd thing is that Nanna Norheim and Nina Narum both confided almost the same thing to their friends: 'To be honest, I felt as though I was being made love to. I mean it. And as the programme was coming to a close I could feel myself swelling up with pleasure.'

Now of course this should not be taken too literally. What Nora Næss – likewise Nanna Norheim and Nina Narum – wished to convey was, first and foremost, a sense of being taken seriously: a sense of gratitude that someone had fondled her of all people, her eyes, her ears, all of her senses, not least her intellect, giving her a sort of all-embracing sense that this concerned her, concerned her to such a degree that it gave her goosebumps.

So over the months that followed Nora made sure, as did Nanna and Nina, that she saw all of the programmes in the series; in fact she not only saw them, she *lived* them, she video-taped them and watched them again, more than once, really *watched* them. For the first time, thanks to Jonas Wergeland's television series, Nora Næss thought of herself as a viewer, or rather as a *seer* in the true sense of that word, a visionary. Because, although she found it hard to put into words, she had seen something *new*, something important, something she had never seen before which filled her with a positive energy and moved her to watch the programmes yet again, such that she was constantly discovering aspects and details that she had missed on previous occasions while at the same time spotting more of the similarities and devices that cropped up again and again; thus she was continually expanding her grasp of the common thread linking all of the programmes. 'They're like gems within a larger gem,' as she put it, not knowing that Nanna Norheim and Nina Narum had said pretty much the same thing. She talked about those programmes, really felt a need to speak to someone after viewing them, and since others had the same urge, they discussed them in the staff room or outside the local shop or in each others' homes. Nora Næss also talked to her husband about them, in case anyone thinks there were problems on that front. He had seen the first two programmes out in the North Sea and was every bit as hooked on them as she; in fact they actually believed, both of them, that their relationship was somehow strengthened by the series.

I am telling you this in order to make it clear that there is no way that Jonas Wergeland's series, *Thinking Big*, can be condensed into words; what is more, in resumé it seems banal and rather dull. I would like therefore to take this opportunity to apologize for my earlier accounts of it, because the series' success, if that is the right word, is impossible to explain. Mind you, media experts have for a long time been producing big fat treatises in which they have attempted to analyse why and how these programmes had such an impact, but apart from citing those factors which were patently obvious, such as the high professional standard, the sophisticated technical quality, they had to admit defeat and resort instead to drawing parallels with poetry, not to mention mysticism and talk of 'the unutterable'. A few did keep their feet on the ground and venture to highlight Jonas Wergeland's voice 'which has the same appeal as that of a prime minister, a national father-figure', some spoke of his knack for composing pictures while others pointed to the original viewpoints, the actual angle of attack, and still others latched onto his personal presence in the programmes, the intensity of his expression – all this without, of course, a single person mentioning anything about a silver thread in his spine, a crystal prism in his head or balls of gold. No one has yet been able to say anything about the cause, only about what an almost narcotic effect the series had on large sections of the Norwegian viewing public.

How could such a thing happen? When Jonas Wergeland started working in television, he simply *had* the gift. Everyone who met him while he was learning his craft – not just mastering the technical side but making a close study of the very best television productions from around the world, from Britain in particular – was struck by his obvious rapport with the camera, a creativity within the medium that could only be described as an innate talent. Even after the programmes he made in the early eighties, viewers like Nora Næss were exclaiming 'God, that was terrific' as if, after twenty years of watching television, they had had their first encounter with great television, one which instantly threw other programmes into relief for them. All at once, people like Nora Næss from the town of Bryne over in Jæren, saw how bland and, above all else, how dull, all of those other programmes were, even on Saturday evenings. You see it is easy to forget that Jonas Wergeland's programmes also provided entertainment, with knobs on. And in the midst of this entertainment, while people were thoroughly enjoying themselves, he tore conventions apart, reflecting things from totally unexpected angles, accentuating details in the bigger picture that left people like Nora Næss agape at the picture as a whole. Consequently, Jonas Wergeland also found on several occasions, precisely because the form of the programmes put across the subject matter in an unusual and striking fashion, that he was setting the agenda for other media – saw how the newspapers in particular tended to follow up his programmes with long, probing articles.

Even so, Jonas Wergeland was also astonished by the tremendous impact of *Thinking Big*, which he thought could perhaps be put down to the fact that it was produced as a series, with the programmes being shown at two-week intervals for almost a year, and that in this way they had a cumulative effect. However that may be, he did in fact succeed in realizing the concept of the title, borrowed from Henrik Ibsen who, in his application for a writer's grant wrote that he would fight for 'that vocation that is for me the most important and the most necessary in Norway, that of arousing the Nation and encouraging it to think big'. It really was quite remarkable. For nigh on a year not only Nora Næss and Nanna Norheim and Nina Narum but virtually the entire population of Norway went around thinking big. It has been said that people *walked* differently in Norway that year, with straighter backs. It was quite an achievement – and let me add: a mystery unequalled in the history of Norway. For one brief moment, Jonas Wergeland lifted a whole nation a few centimetres above, or out of, its accustomed ways of thinking.

It should be said, however, that this phenomenon is unlikely ever to be repeated, inasmuch as Jonas Wergeland's series was shown during the heyday of public broadcasting; when money was not only made available for serious programmes of this sort but when it was still also possible to gather an entire nation in front of the television screen at one time, a time which will soon be looked back on with nostalgia, just as there are many now who recall how certain radio broadcasts could command the ears of the whole country in the fifties.

Even so, none of the bosses at NRK, broadcasters to the nation, had any idea what was going on. They were quite simply not prepared. To be honest, it was so totally unlikely that such a concept, a series of programmes about famous Norwegian men and women, should score a hit with the general public at all. But for a year, via the television screen, Jonas Wergeland held a whole nation mesmerized; towards the end, if you remember, it became almost a mass psychosis – it was not only Nora Næss and Nanna Norheim and Nina Narum who sat glued to the screen but everyone with eyes to see, so to speak, as if it were the final episode in some long-running detective series or the lead-in to a disclosure that would directly affect their own lives. After each programme the NRK switchboard was inundated with calls from people who did not want to complain but simply to give vent to their heart-felt enthusiasm, who wanted Jonas Wergeland's telephone number, wanted his address, or those of the actors, Normann Vaage and Ella Strand; or who were insisting that the pro-gramme be repeated, at once, as soon as possible. People bom-barded the newspapers with spontaneous and frank communications of all kinds. In one ecstatic letter an impotent man declared that watching the programmes had revived his sex life.

They had even less idea of the more long-term effect. Not only was the series showered with awards, including the Prix Italia – for the programme on Armauer Hansen – other countries also evinced an exceptionally voracious interest with the result that a number of television networks bought all or part of the series, even some Third World countries were anxious to screen a few of the programmes. Teachers wrote candid articles in which they described how the series had given them a shot in the arm. Company directors and others spoke out in the newspapers and at seminars, claiming that the series had inspired them. From the lectern in Stortinget, the Norwegian parliament, politicians announced that these programmes had boosted the self-confidence of the nation as a whole.

Again: why? And again: not one study has succeeded in solv-ing the mystery.

Throughout Norway people like Nora Næs from the town of Bryne in Jæren watched those programmes over and over again, and not only that: Nora Næss bought records of music she had never heard, she borrowed books from the libraries, biographies, novels as if the programmes were by no means finished when she switched off the television; she visited museums and galleries, she went to see hitherto unknown films and, during a trip to Oslo, she took out her old figure-skates and went out on the ice for the first time in twenty-five years, together with her daugh-ter; she made excursions to parts of Norway she had never seen, she even travelled abroad several times. Jonas Wergeland received hundreds of postcards, addressed to NRK, from Cairo and the Great Pyramid of Cheops, from Bihar in India, from Stamford Bridge in England. Nora Næss sent him a card showing Saint Peter's in Rome. 'I felt as if I was being seduced,' she told a friend, in strictest confidence, some time later. 'Of being taken by the hand and led somewhere I had never been.'

And in her heart of hearts Nora Næss could not deny, any more than Nanna Norheim and Nina Narum could, that she eventually became as obsessed with Jonas Wergeland as she was with those celebrated Norwegian men and women. Ultimately, she watched and interpreted the stories of the individuals featured in the television series as extracts from Jonas Wergeland's own life, with the result that the more she learned about those other people the more she wanted to know about Jonas Wergeland. And so, in spite of this unique and in many ways *historic* television project, not even Jonas Wergeland was able to prevent the whole thing, in the end, from revolving around him personally.

So there you stand, watching television, amazed in a way by images following images, a soundless flickering, and you stare and you stare at this screen that has won you so much acclaim, a glittering career, you think, doubly so, you think, and one that has led you here, to this bewildered room, and you place your finger on the 'off' button while watching images that become more and more baffling the longer you gaze at them, and you click the button, you see the colours fade to black while the set crackles with static, and you feel as if you had switched off yourself, that your life is finished, a pointless programme, you think, and now it is over, you think.

You look at the seven blue jars on the shelf above the set as if they were another programme, a more significant programme, because they remind you of something, Margrete, you think, and you turn back round the corner, to be met by the sight of her figure on the floor, on its back, as if in total surrender, you think, betrayed, you think, and again you are struck by that uncontrollable urge just to collapse, and you look at the Persian rug over by the window between the two armchairs, a Bukhara, you think, or a Sehna, you think, you would not mind collapsing onto that, that's for sure, onto that rug, disappearing into that pattern, that landscape, to come out in some other land, and you long for your aunt's dimly-lit flat, for a pile of soft cushions and a time when life was one long story, and you look back at Margrete and only now do you see, or *wish* to see, that she is lying on a polar-bear skin, and you look and you look, and you cannot figure out what it is doing here, the polar bear, a brother, you think, it doesn't fit, you think, it feels like a betrayal, you think, as if someone had returned evil for good, and you look at the picture of Buddha, then your eye goes back to the skin and you see only the skin, the red blood against the white skin, as if the bear had been shot, you think, or as if it had been in a fight, you think, between an animal and a human being, you think, and again you look at Margrete, and you feel like screaming *a a a a a* for so long that it will cover all the a's you wrote in your copybook in first grade and all the a's you have written since, to no good purpose, you think.

So there you stand, Jonas Wergeland, disciple of the *Kama Sutra*, opera lover, climber of Jebel Musa, in the centre of your own living room with an inaudible scream in your ears, and you try to listen, and you think to yourself that this is important, the sounds, that the cause may lie here, and you think that you must remember the sounds, cherish them, and you listen intently, stand stock-still in the middle of the room with your eyes fixed on Margrete's dead body, and you listen, and you hear a car drive by further down the road, and you hear, or think you hear, a mouth organ far in the distance, if it isn't a siren, a fire engine you think, something that could save you, you think, and you cross the room and press the remote control, filling the room once more with Johann Sebastian Bach's fugue, and you think that you would like to crawl inside the organ chest again, you want to be healed, you want to be brought to life, you think, another life, you think, a life far from this room, you think.

You stand there looking at the body of your dead wife, looking and looking, and you don't know why the tears always have to well up when you hear this music, and you notice how the tears distort your vision, and you fumble in your pocket for something, a prism, before you remember that you have given it away, and you think to yourself that you will never manage to find another angle here, break up the sight before you, veer out of the big picture and into the detail, impossible, you think, impossible in the face of all this blood, you think, so I can see, or at least I try to understand, more than anyone else, why you do not walk across to the telephone, why you do not call the police, why instead you go into the bathroom, why you feel a frantic need to wash yourself, or not wash, but rinse yourself, and you pull off your clothes, toss them in all directions, knock over one of the ferns before climbing into the shower cabinet, turning on the water and shutting your eyes, you let the water stream down over you, turning the hot tap further and further, as if it could never be hot enough for you, for ages you stand there, without reaching for the soap, just letting the hot water stream down over you, until at last you turn it off and step out into a bathroom now filled with steam, like the old Torggata Baths you think, and you stand at the washbasin, and you gaze into a mirror that has misted over and you gaze at all of Margrete's things on the shelf, at the bath salts, and you remember how Margrete loved taking a bath, how she loved to have the water scalding hot, like the Japanese you think, how much she enjoyed it, how she had this unique capacity for enjoying everything, turning any ordinary day into unadulterated pleasure, you think, and you gaze at all the other strange bottles and jars that are hers, were hers, and you open a perfume bottle, and you sniff, inhale, and suddenly you remember a whole lot of things connected with this scent, and you feel as if your head is beginning to mist over, like the mirror, and you know you are close to passing out, and you hang onto the washbasin and think to yourself that you had better do something sensible, so you pick up your electric razor, the good one, better than the little one in your suitcase, and you start to shave, shaving in exactly the same way as always, doing your best to follow the same pattern as always, as if the simple force of habit, the pedantry of it, could be the saving of you at this moment, keep chaos at arm's length, or possibly because right now it seems important to consider how you look, in case a television team should show up. 'How did you feel when you entered the room?' you think, the sort of question put to sports' stars, and you go on shaving for so long that the mirror clears and you see your own face, and you pick up a bottle of aftershave to pour a few drops onto your palm, and you think of your mother's seven lovers, and at the thought of the seven lovers you begin to have some inkling of who you are, as if all this time you had been trying to suppress the knowledge.

You walk back through to the living room, naked, and you remember who you are, it's being naked that does it, you think, and all at once a name from the bundle of letters comes into your head, the letters you glanced at when you came home, and naked you walk across to the antique bureau where you left the letters and again you flick through them, and you find it, and you read the sender's name, a woman's name, you think, the name of a very famous woman, you think, and you remember those women whom you have loved and who have loved you, heartily, you think, deeply, you think, and who have given you of their abundance, and you turn towards Margrete with the letter in your hand, naked, and you realize that one of them, one of these women, might be behind Margrete's death, one who refuses to let go of you, who still loves you, and you think of your golden balls, and it's only to be expected, you think, that one day they would be your downfall.

Jonas Wergeland is nine years old. It is late at night and he wakes with a tightness around his balls.

I doubt if I need to remind anyone of the sexual frustrations of pre-pubertal boys and the ways they find of letting off steam. Some play rather artful games of 'doctors and nurses'. Others can make do with reading the small ads in the newspaper, under the heading of 'Health and Hygiene', or uttering the name 'Mount of Venus' with all its connotations of scaled peaks and astronomical mysteries. Some run a tremulous felt tip along the side of the transformer station under cover of darkness, making up smutty rhymes ending in 'pussy', 'Lucy' and 'juicy', while others run a black market in condoms stolen from unwitting fathers. Some turn up in triumph at school with a stuffy sex manual discovered in an old dusty box in a far corner of the cellar, while others concoct myths about Mamma Banana, the girl who lives in the Swiss villa across from the flats, who was said to be so randy that every night, if no boys showed up, she had to stick an Ice Pole up 'you know where' to cool herself down, and we're talking a fifty-øre Ice Pole at that. When Jonas Wergeland was a boy there were even some who plucked up the courage to club together for a pretty harmless girlie magazine, playing a nerve-racking game of poker to decide who would go into the shop, with sweaty palms and a tongue like lead, to buy it, so they could read it on the sly behind the garages and learn how even the most dauntingly pale and unimaginably ugly women – sporting light-green eye-shadow and weird hair-dos – could get you seriously worked up and leave you with friction burns on your foreskin.

While we are on this subject, it might be tempting to air a few home truths about psychologists, but since they are after all no greater charlatans than anyone else, I will confine myself to lamenting the fact that members of this profession have ruined many people's chances of understanding what I am now about to tell you about Jonas Wergeland. I could, of course, be underestimating the average Norwegian, but I fear that not a few of them have gone along with the speculative and oft-repeated old bromide about sexual insecurity springing from some suppressed fear conceived in childhood. If this is true, then I would just like to say that on this score Jonas Wergeland was more fortunate than other children of his age – and that is a gross understatement. Not only did he have a sister who deemed it her almost sacred calling to enlighten her brothers when the first sweet itch made its puzzling presence felt in their groins – he also had parents who, one year later, were responsible for dispelling any last shreds of doubt planted by all the scaremongering that surrounded sex. Thanks to his parents, Jonas followed the development of his genitals with eager anticipation.

Jonas Wergeland experienced something that many another child before him has experienced, and this incident so crucial to his relaxed – some might say profligate – attitude to sex, occurred on a perfectly ordinary Wednesday evening. Until that day, Jonas had never given much thought to his mother's and father's private life, far less their nocturnal activities; as far as he was concerned, his parents were two regular individuals, much loved of course, but nonetheless just normal people living the usual sort of Norwegian life, their days made up of a combination of factors that could be counted on the fingers of both hands.

As I say, plenty of people have had the same experience; it was late, after 11.00 and all the children were asleep. Jonas woke up bursting for the toilet. He shinned down from his bunk-bed by dint of an impressive technique not unlike a fireman sliding down his pole or, according to Rakel, asleep in the next room, like Elvis in the scene where he sings 'Jailhouse Rock' in the film of the same name. The biggest hindrance was posed by Daniel's collection of revolvers and rifles and accompanying belts, as well as cowboy hats and waistcoats adorned with gleaming sheriff's stars, all slung around the bedpost, enough equipment to fit out a whole Western. Jonas tiptoed across the room, the walls of which were adorned with pennants, a dartboard, Jonas's drawings and Daniel's innumerable diplomas, not to mention the best of all – the cards from Uncle Lauritz: during his lifetime, Uncle Lauritz had sent them postcards from all the destinations flown to by SAS, with the result that eventually half of one wall was papered with brightly coloured cards from such cities as Istanbul, Tel Aviv and Cairo, to name one route of which Uncle Lauritz was especially fond – and these, both the scenes they depicted and the terse notes on the back, whetted the imagination and the wanderlust of Jonas in particular, as much as the copies of the *National Geographic* in the toilet did. Dotted here and there among the cards were also photographs of the planes with which Uncle Lauritz had conquered the world, the four-engine, propeller-driven DC-6B and DC-7C and, Jonas's favourite, a plane which Uncle Lauritz unfortunately barely had the chance to try out: that quite indescribably elegant jet, the Caravelle, with lines that left a tingling sensation between the shoulder-blades.

Jonas trod softly across the room, almost without opening his eyes, as if reluctant to leave slumber behind, groped for the door-handle; aware, even with his eyes closed, of the object lying on the chest of drawers right next to the door, more because of the energy it gave off. Jonas had found a ball-bearing from the hub of a bicycle wheel and for reasons he did not quite understand it had become something sacred to him, a sort of portable altar, not because the ball-bearing looked so nice with its little circle of little steel balls, almost like a piece of jewellery, but because there was a mystique about it which in some unaccountable way exerted a strong attraction on him.

Jonas opened the door, softly still, moving more or less by feel; crept through the kitchen and into the bathroom, where he did the needful. It was when he was on his way back, in the hall, that he heard a vague murmur from the living room, the door of which was standing slightly ajar, so he stopped, because something was wrong, but what was it that was wrong? There was too little talking, almost no sound at all, and the words being murmured were too soft.

One of the things which Jonas Wergeland liked best about his parents and which he came to admire even more when he reached adulthood himself, indeed regarded as something of a mystery, was their supreme talent for quiet conversation, their unbelievable mastery of 'the fine art of small talk'. This was Åse and Haakon's fondest pursuit: to sit each in their chair in the living room and talk the evening away, which is to say: those evenings when both were at home, since Jonas's father had his church duties, and his mother was active in any number of societies that Jonas never could make head nor tail of, although he could tell that his mother had a greater need for social contact than his father. But those evenings together truly were special occasions, something his father underlined by shaving again after dinner and splashing a few drops of foreign aftershave on his cheeks. On the wall of the living room hung a cuckoo clock, a source of much amusement to the children, until the day when Daniel, possibly in a premature act of rebellion against paternal authority, shot off both the cuckoo and the little man who played 'O mein Papa' with his catapult. Jonas's mother was in the habit of setting this cuckoo clock an hour slow, something which Jonas was sure she did out of principle, so that she and his father could talk on for an extra hour every evening with a clear conscience.

As Jonas grew older and was allowed to stay up longer, he used to sit between them, on the rug, building with Lego. He loved to sit there surrounded by the hum of their conversation, constructing buildings out of Lego bricks, endeavouring to exhaust all the possibilities for the sorts of houses you could build with the same number of bricks, as if he had already tumbled to the fact that you only had a limited number of basic forms to play with, and that life consisted of shuffling these about. In a way he felt that his mother and father were engaged in something similar, because they talked a lot about the same things, over and over again, but always in new patterns and variations, thus ensuring that the conversation was always interesting and exciting, and – the banal subject matter notwithstanding – rather like an everyday version of Plato's dialogues. Only when he let Nefertiti help in with the building, did this theory collapse, because even with the same Lego bricks as he had, she could build houses he would never have dreamed possible, lifting them up to the lamp to show him how the secret of the construction derived from light and shade; houses which, if anyone should be wondering, helped

sow the seeds of Jonas Wergeland's ambition to become an
architect.

But as a rule Jonas lay alone on the rug between his parents,
listening with half an ear to the hum of their voices, their laughter, which seemed to act as a spur to his invention; his mother
talking about her work at the Grorud Ironmongery, and his
father about things he had seen and heard in Grorud Church,
and for Jonas there was something about this very contrast
between the church on the hill next to the school and the factory
in the valley alongside the railway line that made his parents the
perfect conversationalists, giving them an ocean of topics on
which to draw. He revelled in it, lying there between them, listening to the way they talked, also about those things on which
they disagreed, little arguments, although the tone never varied;
the way they jumped from one topic to another, without needing
to use a newspaper as a springboard, talking about people they
knew and events in the surrounding community, anything and
everything, but still much in the same vein, a mesh of this and
that, building into a web – and, by some sort of alchemy, into
something precious. Jonas noticed that his father's fluttering
hands steadied when he was talking to his mother, just as they
did at the organ as if here, too, in these conversations in which
they could come up with endless variations on a theme, he was
practising a kind of *Kunst der Fuge*. The week before had, as it
happens, been a little out of the ordinary, with a more serious
note creeping into the hum of voices, and Jonas, lying on the
rug between his parents, striving to build a house he had never
built before, had repeatedly picked up such words as 'Cuba' and
'rockets'.

Now Jonas stood in the hall listening, eyes open, stood there
gazing at the picture hanging above the black bakelite telephone
of himself as a one-year-old in forty-eight different poses.
Something was wrong, there was too little talk going on, too low,
in the living room. He was just about to go in and investigate but
stopped short as he moved into a position, or perhaps I should
say adopted an angle, from which the chink in the door afforded
him a view of another corner of the room, and there he stayed,
looking and looking. Jonas saw the textured wallpaper, he saw the

cuckoo clock that always ran slow, he saw the Negro lady on the wall, with the gold rings in her ears and around her neck – later to become a collector's item – and he saw the two curving chairs with their distinctly functionalist design, noticed them above all else, because they were empty; his parents were not sitting in their respective chairs, talking about this and that, weaving something precious together, they were lying naked on the rug – bare-naked as children would say – and not only that but in a funny position. Jonas stood in the shadows and watched, not with fear, but with tremulous wonder; he had a feeling that here, too, they were weaving something, something beautiful, precious. He realized that what his parents were doing was something that made you blissfully happy, and if he had not induced this from anything else, then he could tell from the look on his father's face: his father had the same look on his face as he had when Knut Johannesen skated the 10,000 metres at the Olympics in Squaw Valley, a race I mentioned in passing at an earlier – which is to say chronologically later – point. Jonas never forgot that moment or that look. He and Daniel had walked into the room, each clutching a paper cornet of liquorice pipes, all set to listen to *Children's Hour*, the absolute high point of the week, primarily on account of the serial. But it was not the *Children's Hour* signature tune that issued from the radio. Instead of 'And now it's time for *Children's Hour*' they heard the almost hysterical voice of sports commentator Oddvar Foss, telling the Norwegian people about this fantastic race on the other side of the Atlantic, a race which Jonas found nowhere near as fascinating as observing the look on his father's face – and let me just add that Haakon Hansen was a true skating aficionado, a real fan, like so many others at that time. Jonas Wergeland belonged, in other words, to the last generation of Norwegian children to grow up with their fathers' ardent, nigh-on pathological, passion for skating. So Jonas stood there, observing his father's face as Johannesen skated circuit after circuit on the other side of the world, and he could see that his father was over the moon, that he could not really believe this was happening, that Johannesen was about to do the distance in under sixteen minutes, a feat regarded as bounding on the impossible. Jonas stood there spellbound, watching as his father's face was further transformed, passing into an expression that spoke of utter, almost divine, rapture, to culminate in what Jonas was later to define as the 'Face of Bliss' – not so surprisingly, perhaps, seeing that Johannesen, when he crossed the finishing line, had beaten the record set by Hjallis in 1951, a record that the pundits had claimed could never be broken, by an incredible forty-six seconds. And it was this very expression, the Face of Bliss, that Jonas's father was wearing now as he made to love to Jonas's mother, in a sort of Olympic event, you might say: making circuit after circuit.

Jonas stood in the hall, at the living-room door, and watched and watched, feeling rather solemn, filled with awe. There was something about these smooth, effortless actions, the semblance of perfection and, not least, the juncture of his parents' pelvises that gave Jonas the idea that this, too, had to do with a ball-bearing, a hub, something sitting at the centre, around which everything else miraculously revolved.

The Happy Few

I am sure a lot of people will find it hard to identify with this leit-motiv in Jonas Wergeland's attitude to sex: the idea that love-making was something which lifted him up into another sphere – please note, I did not say a *higher* sphere. Going by what I have related so far regarding Jonas Wergeland's liaisons with women and, even more so, by the speculations that certain sections of the media have seen fit to print, a great many would probably maintain that he was a Casanova of the first water. I know that I am faced here with a nigh-on impossible task – after all we are talking both of sexuality and of shaking the hard and fast views of the average Norwegian – but since I have set out to present an alternative picture of a life which most people feel they already know inside out, I see it as my plain duty to state that Jonas Wergeland was a highly moral, an admirably moral person – at any rate where sex was concerned. I would even go so far as to say that very few men in Jonas Wergeland's position would have been able to lead as upright a life as he did, especially when one thinks of what I have, perhaps rather casually, referred to as his 'magic penis' and the demonstrable gains he derived from the sexual act.

There are, of course, plenty of stories doing the rounds about Jonas Wergeland's irresistible attraction for women. It is no exaggeration to say that, had he so desired, he could have slept with a thousand women. He chose, however, only a select few: those who set the signal bell in his spine jangling. I can reveal that over the years Jonas received a lot of very flattering offers from well-equipped, gifted women who had heard glowing reports of him in those instances where Jonas's chosen women were unable to keep their mouths shut – not so surprising, perhaps, when one considers what an impression he made on them and the pleasure he gave them. Jonas declined all of these offers without a second thought and without regarding it as any sort of a sacrifice.

At the most felicitous point his life, in collaboration with Lorenzo da Ponte, Wolfgang Amadeus Mozart wrote the opera *Don Giovanni*, a work which, oddly enough, has a certain role to play in Jonas Wergeland's life – albeit only as a backdrop. In one of the opening scenes of this opera there is a very entertaining sequence in which Leporello, Don Juan's servant, reels off to Donna Elvira a list of all the many women to whom his master has made love. The list covers women from many different countries and in the refrain Leporello makes much of the fact that in Spain alone his master has slept with one thousand and three women. Now Don Juan is, of course, more of a *beau idéal* than an actual historical figure, but for the record I would just like to mention that in later life the French writer Georges Simenon claimed to have bedded no less than 10,000 women, an assertion which his wife later dismissed as an idle boast: according to her he could not possibly have slept with more than twelve hundred. Mind you, twelve hundred is not bad. I mean, in suchlike cases I could well understand if anyone were to start sounding off about loose morals.

I believe a brief discourse on the difference between Don Juan as he is traditionally depicted and Jonas Wergeland would be in order here, seeing that so many have been so ready to cite this symbolic figure when speaking of that life which I have set myself the task of writing, or rather *rewriting* – and let me say yet again: as far as I am concerned Jonas Wergeland is nigh on the negation of Don Juan.

After all, what is Don Juan's chief characteristic? That's right: unmitigated lust, a desire that has about it both a demonic element and a touch of deceit. Even as Don Juan is making love to one woman, he is thinking about the next one. His lovemaking is exclusively sensual and utterly faithless; Don Juan does not love one, but all. And, that being so, he makes no demands on the object of his desire other than that it must be female – age and looks do not really come into it – and thus every act of love becomes the same as the one before, a mechanical exercise devoid of any greater substance, devoid of any variety. In other words, Don Juan possesses an enumerative superficiality or abstraction which is best expressed through music.

Jonas Wergeland's lovemaking, on the other hand, is spiritual, if I may be permitted to use such a high-flown word; I might even use an adjective like 'chivalrous', with its connotations of faithfulness. Women are not, as in Don Juan's case, everyday events; to Jonas Wergeland they are red-letter occasions, unique occurrences. With Don Juan, it is his lust in itself, that sensual energy, which women find so seductive; with Jonas Wergeland it is his face, his enigmatic expression, that draws women to him, with the result that all of these women would give different reasons for their interest in him, and not one of them would use the word 'seduction'.

Note also that Jonas Wergeland never did anything to win his women; one could say that he made no move in their direction. It was the women who came, or were drawn, to him. We are looking, therefore, at a form of seduction that has nothing to do with desperate changes of identity or coaxing and cajoling under balconies. One might say that it was the women who *took* Jonas. He, for his part, remained passive.

Nor was Jonas what you would call a satyr, a man with an inordinate sex drive. When he fell, or allowed himself to fall, for these women, it was not because his libido ran away with him but because he detected something precious in all of them. For Jonas Wergeland, sexual desire had less to do with sex than with enlightenment.

Some people might feel that I am skirting the issue here. What they want to know is exactly how many women were there in Jonas Wergeland's life? I am afraid, however, that this may come as something of an anticlimax: apart from Margrete – the first and the last – there were twenty-three women in Jonas Wergeland's life, no more and no less. And not 'were' but 'are'. They stayed with him, even after they had, in bodily form, left him. And I am not counting mothers, aunts or sisters. There were twenty-three *lovers* in Jonas Wergeland's life. And since none of them were married, or involved with anyone else when

Jonas met them, I believe this effectively puts paid to the notion that Jonas Wergeland was 'a wanton libertine with no moral scruples' as a certain woman journalist found it expedient to write on one occasion.

Jonas Wergeland never boasted about his 'conquests'. He never once spoke of them to anyone else. And later, when he saw these women on television – sooner or later almost all of them appeared on television – he did not laugh or make fun of them or think of how the microphone into which they were speaking – or over which they were leaning – reminded him of what they had once done to his genitalia. He watched as if awestruck, adoring them and filled with gratitude for what they had meant to him. For even though he knew – he was not, after all, one for false modesty – what he had given these women, Jonas Wergeland never forgot that he was also deeply indebted to them.

Hell

What did Jonas Wergeland look for in a woman? Or, to put it another way, why did he get that tingling between his shoulder-blades on encountering a select few members of the opposite sex? Is there an explanation that goes beyond all the usual clichés concerning the randy male and basic instincts?

Thanks to my – how shall I put it? – unique position, I am able to cite an incident that offers one possible answer to this question. And again it concerns Jonas's fateful cousin, Veronika Røed.

The year in which Jonas was born, Professor Ole Hallesby made a speech, broadcast on the radio, in which he sent the following, not exactly entertaining, thought into thousands of homes: 'You know that if you dropped dead this instant you would go straight to Hell.' This sparked off the much renowned 'Hell debate' as it was called – yet another one of those exchanges that exposes diverting sides of the Norwegian national character. I am not, however, going to succumb to the temptation to comment on this, merely to state that in due course Jonas Wergeland came to side with Hallesby; he knew there was a Hell.

Jonas always said that he was a cold-blooded creature. Even as a child he evinced an inveterate mistrust of winter and, more particularly, the Norwegian *cultivation* of this season; it was the cold, more than the snow, that got to him. No matter how many layers of clothes, or how thick the layers, his mother wrapped him in, even when tucked up nice and snug inside a sheepskin sleeping-bag with layer upon layer of blankets on top, he still seemed to shiver and shake. Later, Jonas would also belie the boast that all Norwegians are natural born skiers. He hated those strips of wood that the others had such a whale of a time sliding about on, not to mention all the sticky, messy business of waxing the things. All of the children at Solhaug, except Jonas, cheered when the first snowflakes began to fall; within seconds out came the skis and sledges, the skimmer-boards, the little toy ski-jumpers that you could bend at the waist and the plastic bob-sleighs with lead weights in the runners. All winter long, Daniel and the other boys – and the girls for that matter – were hard at it building ingenious bottle slides; hanging onto the backs of cars (strictly illegal) rolling about in the snow and making whole hosts of snow-angels, while at the same time carrying on endless snowball fights with lethal clumps of ice as ammunition. And after all of this, they would come running in, looking like snow-men, gleefully rosy-cheeked, leaving puddles in the hallways and filling the flats with the stink of wet wool. Jonas viewed with aloof distaste all the pointless hassle of winding disgusting strips of insulating tape round ice-hockey sticks, not to mention dodg-ing deadly pucks, all the time spent building staggeringly high ski-jump slopes, devising new waxing combinations to make jumping skis go faster, practising hazardous downhill turns, and all just to end up with broken legs and grazed faces. As they grew older Jonas looked on with growing disbelief as Daniel and his other chums wasted all of their free time on making long cross-country expeditions across Lillomarka just to obtain another stamp in their orienteering cards against some place name printed in red, green or black, thus winning themselves useless little yellow badges bearing a picture of a Birchleg, a legendary Viking skier; it wasn't long before Daniel had an anorak covered in them, and he posed as proudly as another Oscar Mathisen for his father with the camera. Jonas rolled his eyes every time his brother barged breathlessly through the front door, drooling from the corner of his mouth and with a trail of blood-tinged snot running from his nose, yelling delightedly that he had set a new personal record out and back on the cross-country trail to Lilloseter.

For his own part, Jonas Wergeland did his best to confine his winter activities to the unavoidable trip to and from school, as far as possible he even avoided looking out of the window. The rest of the time he sat, or reclined, in a sort of hibernation, with his back against the radiator, reading comics and listening to Duke Ellington, first and foremost the so-called jungle numbers, full of weird sound effects, from the Cotton Club days: 'East St Louis Toodle-Oo' with Bubber Miley's and Joe 'Tricky Sam' Nanton's mournful, muted wah-wahs and wild, growling trumpets and trombones, 'The Mooch' with Sonny Greer's gongs and pounding, galloping tom-toms; and 'Haunted Nights' with Teddy Bunns's delicate wistful guitar solo – all in all, a sound so theatrical and exaggeratedly primitive that it provided the perfect accompaniment to the comics he read. Jonas was convinced that he and Duke Ellington shared the same loathing of wet woollen mittens and great, clodhopping, leather ski boots with ice-caked laces, that both he and Duke Ellington abhorred itchy long-johns and ludicrous string vests; all in all, there was something about the red-hot rhythms of 'Jungle Nights in Harlem' that told him Duke Ellington must detest everything that so much as smacked of ice and snow as deeply and fervently as he did – and this, although Jonas could not have known it, was true enough; Duke Ellington even hated fresh air, so much so that he never opened a window. But to return to Jonas, all winter long he sat with his back propped up against the radiator, longing for spring.

One of the few things he could stand to do, however, was to build snow-houses – something which can of course be put down to the architectural leanings he was later to display. It did no harm either that snow-houses were easier fashioned when the snow was wet, which is to say when the temperature had crept up above zero. One construction in particular was to brand itself into, or more correctly become frozen solid in, Jonas's memory. One March, during a mild spell, he and Nefertiti built an imposing palace on the slope running down to the stream, where the snow lay several metres deep. By using shovels to hollow out the inside and by rolling snowballs, they were able to build both up the way and down, creating several floors and criss-crossing passages. Nefertiti had sketched out the plan beforehand, and she and Jonas had made a trial model out of white Lego with Nefertiti explaining that this was a somewhat simplified version of the palace of King Minos on Crete. Jonas's only happy memories of winter at Solhaug up to then were of him and Nefertiti sitting in spacious white rooms made of snow with a candle burning in the centre, eating dried apricots while Nefertiti told him about the catacombs in Rome, the cave paintings in grottoes in the South of France and about Elephanta in India, fabulous temples hacked out of the mountain.

One Sunday at the end of March, Sir William's family had paid them a visit, and in a rash moment – he cursed himself later – Jonas had taken Veronika down to their masterpiece on the hillside. They crawled up and down passages which were sagging badly due to the thaw that had set in, only just managing to squeeze through the narrowest spots. In the largest room Jonas lit a stub of candle, and they sat there, silently, self-consciously, watching the light sparkling on the smooth walls. Below-zero temperatures over the past few nights had frozen the whole palace rock-hard.

Afterwards, they rolled snowballs in the wet snow outside, bowling them down the slope until they were gigantic, so big that tufts of grass came to light in their tracks, making Jonas want to roll up that whole carpet of snow and get a head-start on spring. He was actually well under way with this attempt to change the seasons when his father's whistle sounded from a veranda somewhere out of sight, calling them in to dinner. 'Hang on a minute,' Jonas said to his cousin. 'I'll just get the candle.' He crawled in through the little opening in the sagging snow palace.

I am sure the reader has long since guessed what Veronika did: with a strength that would have left anyone speechless, she rolled one of the enormous snowballs the last bit of the way down the slope so that it wedged tight across the entrance to the snow-cave. And off she went.

It is not easy to explain a person like Veronika, a girl who was already so pretty that she was actually *too* pretty. Some people might use the word 'evil', but that really does not cover it. On the whole I prefer to say as little as possible about Veronika Røed; I do not intend to comment on her motives in this instance or in any other instance on which she tried to harm Jonas. More than enough has already been written about Veronika Røed and her convoluted merits.

This is meant to be a book about Jonas Wergeland. This is meant to be a book written on Jonas Wergeland's terms. At long last. He deserves it.

Back at the flat, where their dinner was already on the table, Veronika said that Jonas had run off and left her, she even managed to squeeze out a tear or two. And since Sir William had been smacking his lips demonstratively and impatiently for some time, Jonas's mother said that he was probably on his way and that they should just go ahead and start dinner without him: cold roast pork and brown gravy as always at such family gatherings.

The minute Jonas discovered that the entrance was sealed off, he knew that it was Veronika's doing. He tried to kick his way out, but it was no use, she had blocked the hole perfectly. Having run his hands along the solid ice walls more in discouragement than panic, Jonas crawled back to the big room, sat down resignedly in the centre and lit the candle stub, thinking to himself that he would be alright as long as the flame was burning. He sat gazing round about, sat in the centre of a circle, under a low dome. He was cold, even more so than usual, so cold that his whole body ached. It was worst around his groin, he could hardly feel a thing, his willy seemed to be turning into a little icicle. He cried for help, hearing how stifled his cry sounded, with no echo, like being under a quilt. The candle went out. He did not know whether this was because there was no air in the room or what. A faint, feeble light filtered through the roof. He knew he was going to die. He lay down, curled up foetus-like, lay there feeling one limb after another grow numb. He saw the glimmer of light beyond the walls gradually fading, like the glow of a Golden Fleece going out, conscious all the while of his mind being drained of images, going blank, totally white, like the room in which he lay.

See this boy, huddled inside a cave of ice which, when viewed from above, together with the passage to the outside, looks not unlike the womb and the birth canal. And I ask you: is this the Jonas Wergeland whom so many people feel they know; on whom a whole host of people have aired their views with such certainty? Know, at any rate, that this picture, these crystals of ice, are a prism, a magnifying glass, as good an instrument as any other through which to examine Jonas Wergeland's life.

And then? What happens next? Well, as always, our hero is saved by his best friend. When Jonas's mother began to suspect that something was wrong her first instinct was to go to Nefertiti. The latter pulled her cloth cap well down over her ears, immediately understanding the gravity of the situation. Jonas was not the sort to spend ages playing outside in wintertime. They instigated a search, called the neighbours, looked in the cellars, combed the area up around Eigiltomta, calling his name, hunted as far down as the shops on Trondheimsveien. By this time his mother was really worried, she was convinced that someone had abducted him, a six-year-old without an ounce of sense. Everybody joined in the hunt, even Veronika. Veronika, that astonishing child, searching with every semblance of zeal and earnestness. It was growing dark. Even Nefertiti, who was never afraid, was worried now, so desperate that she ran up to the gamekeeper's lodge on the other side of Bergensveien to borrow Colonel Eriksen.

Colonel Eriksen was a grey elkhound. He was actually called something boring, like Rocky or Rover, but Nefertiti had renamed him on the day when, by the most fantastic stroke of luck, he had almost bitten the balls of a vicious Rottweiler from further down Bergensveien that used to terrorize all the local kids, lunging menacingly on its chain and barking as fiendishly as the Fenris wolf. Colonel Eriksen, in case anyone is wondering, was the commander of Oscarsborg fortress out in Oslo fjord at the time of the sinking of the *Blücher*. Jonas and Nefertiti became particularly friendly with Colonel Eriksen and were occasionally allowed to take him for a walk or borrow him for expeditions up the river Alna.

It was one thing to lay low a monster of a dog, quite another to find Jonas Wergeland, a boy who hated snow and who was now, most improbably, shut up inside an airtight icebox. In addition to which, Colonel Eriksen was a very old dog; it was debatable whether he had any sense of smell left at all, but when Nefertiti let Colonel Eriksen sniff one of Jonas's mittens – a trick she had picked up from a Lassie film on one of her many visits to Grorud cinema with Jonas – the old dog seemed to come to life and started straining at his leash as if he were a champion tracker dog and not an ancient hound long since ready for the happy hunting grounds. What a cliff-hanger; worthy of any B-movie at the Grorud flicks: Jonas, all but buried alive under the ice with time most definitely not on his side, and Colonel Eriksen, dashing with amazing purposefulness across the flagpole green, nose to the snow, dragging Nefertiti behind him as if he had caught the scent of the phantom elk itself. Not until Colonel Eriksen, growing more and more frantic with excitement, had led Nefertiti to the slope beyond the green did the truth dawn on her, even though she would never have believed that Jonas would dare to go inside the sagging cave.

After ascertaining that the snowball had frozen solid across the entrance, Nefertiti left Colonel Eriksen making a heroic, but vain, attempt to dig his way through the ice with his blunt, old claws and went for help. After some backbreaking and pretty frantic digging the rescue party managed to pull Jonas out, in the nick of time as they say, just as he was about to fall into a deep slumber induced by the delicious warmth that was spreading throughout his body: in other words, before the cold turned him to ice. From then on, Jonas always imagined Hell to be like that ice-cave, and though he did not know it, on this score his thoughts more or less coincided with those of a number of authorities, including the great Dante himself who, in *The Divine Comedy*, makes the surprising assertion that Hell does not consist of fire. The nethermost circle in his inferno is of ice.

Veronika's reaction was that of most children. 'I didn't mean it,' she said and put on a display of such heartbroken and contrite sobbing that no one could be angry with her, least of all Sir William, who comforted his daughter in a manner that might have led one to suspect that he was sorry her plan had failed.

Jonas had been rescued, but the cold never lost its grip on him. 'Below the waist I'm cold as ice,' he would later say as a joke. So, to return to where we started: for the rest of his life he would be searching for warmth. And for Jonas Wergeland, there was nothing to match the warmth certain women transmitted to him when making love. So what he was looking for in a woman was, in fact, warmth: quite literally a fire at which to warm himself. Jonas Wergeland was chilled to the bone, and so he collected glowing coals, and like a member of some primeval civilization he never forgot that tending these coals and carrying them with one was the most important thing of all.

O Mio Tesoro

It was not unnatural that Jonas Wergeland should have run into Nina G. at Det Norske Opera. It happened right after the interval, while Don Giovanni, the Lord of Misrule, in the shape of a young Knut Skram, was kneeling under a balcony dressed in his servant's clothes, playing, or pretending to play a mandolin, while singing cajolingly to Donna Elvira's maid, begging her to come to the window: '*Deh vieni alla finestra, o mio tesoro*'. It was just at that moment, as Don Juan was proving that he would do anything to win a woman, even assume another identity – in the midst of this serenade, so outrageously absurd and yet so infinitely beautiful – that Jonas Wergeland became aware that someone was looking at him, or not looking but staring, drinking him in with their eyes. He turned, to be met by the gaze of a girl sitting a few seats away from him, on the row in front. The gaze was that of Nina G. and her eyes were as round and full of desire as the o's in '*O mio tesoro*'. Then she looked away, turning her eyes back to the stage, but even in the dark, that one glimpse was enough. Jonas could tell straight away, by the tremor running down his spine, that this girl evinced a rare capacity for bestowing warmth.

So how do the pieces of a life fit together? Like an organ in which the pipes sound from different corners even when the keys you are pressing are right next to one another?

Jonas had for many years been one of the youngest, not to say *the* youngest habitué of the Oslo jazz scene and, despite the fact that after 1965 jazz had gone into something of a slump, there were still a number of places one could frequent – which is to say that, apart from Friday nights at the newly-opened Beehive Club, Jonas basically had to sneak in to such places, aided and abetted by friends. One of the trickiest to gain entry to was the jazz club at the halls of residence in Sogn, although here, on the other hand, it was easy to blend into the crowd of students who sat there shaking their heads and slugging red wine, never knocking the ash off the cigarettes that dangled from the corners of their mouths. There has been a lot of talk about rock music and its detrimental effect on the hearing, but Jonas always felt that someone ought to have checked how all that shaking, and in many cases rotation of the head, had affected the 1968 generation, since he had the suspicion that so much drunken head-tossing in time, for example, to Arild Andersen's driving bass lines must have led to a sort of collective whiplash effect. Jonas eventually left the scene, however, not so much because he had witnessed so much inordinate and alarming 'digging' but more because the music as such lost its outsider quality, perhaps precisely because in the end the very 'freeness' of the melodies and the rhythms had become so utterly predictable. And so he had gone in search of something else, and what he found was *the opera*. Let me put it this way: not all that many young people frequented Den Norske Opera in the years after 1968, and certainly not those of a rebellious bent.

The first operas he saw were Verdi's *Falstaff* and Bizet's *Carmen*, but it was Wagner and *The Flying Dutchman* that really showed him he was on the right track and not, as some might think, because of the story: a man condemned to sail on and on forever. No, it had more to do with the utterly unbelievable, tempestuous music that set the dresses of the ladies in the red plush auditorium fluttering from the very first notes of the overture and, not least, a sumptuous Aase Nordmo Løvberg in the role of Senta. The way I see it, Jonas Wergeland must have been one of her biggest fans at that time. He was forever popping up to the second floor of the Stortorvet Inn, vainly hoping to catch a glimpse of her in the booth just inside the door where the opera singers hung out, watched over by a waiter named Nyhus whom the singers – as one might expect, with their sense for all things Italian – had dubbed 'Casanova'.

Jonas was captivated by the opera, the mere fact of being able to sit in that red auditorium, in the dark, and listen to a load of absolute claptrap swathed in bombastic music. To be honest, he liked it so much that he sometimes caught himself shaking his head exactly like some jazz freak, in a combination of incredulity and rapturous glee. It made his toes curl with delight to hear these bedizened characters giving vent in song to their passions and frustrations, particularly on those few occasions when the whole thing was sung in German. He could not get enough of it: the extravagant gestures, all of that totally unnatural set-up, with people dotted about the stage like chess pieces, singing, wailing of their intrigues; those passages in which the most hopelessly sentimental words were poured out with every last ounce of sincerity. Jonas sat there in the dark, wondering what it could be that moved him so deeply, and he came to the conclusion that it had to be a sort of pathos by proxy, that these people on the stage were going over the top for his sake, too, to save him having to do so in his own life. There was something about the artificiality of it all, the utter remoteness from reality that lent an air of fantastic comedy to these overdressed tableaux; the recitatives in particular were priceless. 'If you feel like an alien on this Earth then do something about it, go to the opera,' he told Axel. 'Experience the unreality of society taken to the extreme.' Jonas sat there in the dark, revelling in it with all his senses. The opera also heavily reinforced his decision to become the Duke, to tell his own story, independent of Norwegian daily life, *outside of* Norwegian society. Up and down the country people were sitting watching television or reading magazines or doing their homework or tinkering with the car or demonstrating against the USA. Here he sat, Jonas Wergeland, in his rightful surroundings, in a red plush auditorium ringing with ear-splitting song, in the centre of Oslo, in the centre of the nation's capital and yet so marvellously, liberatingly *outside*.

Naturally some of the Young Socialists at school got wind of it and spread the word about this appalling example of class betrayal: a Grorud lad at the *haute bourgeois* Opera House. During one fierce discussion in the schoolyard, in the shed yet again, not all that unlike an outdoor stage, when the Young Socialists asked whether he ought not to be making his points in song, one politically active girl had dared him to give a talk about

opera at a meeting of Owl, the Cathedral School debating society, and in the heat of the moment he had agreed. Owl could be
described as something of an intellectual sandpit, but it was,
even so, a well respected platform, at any rate until the Red Front
took over and turned the whole thing, as always, into a hopelessly
sectarian business. The most disparate figures had willingly
taken part in Owl meetings in their various capacities, people like
Reiulf Steen, Nils Christie and Berthold Grünfeldt, as well as a
high-flying Einar Forde, who made a passionate speech about
draft-dodging as a political statement, and the chief medical offi-
cer, Karl Evang, who talked about drugs and caused a furore by
handing out samples of various substances. In this forum, Jonas
had contemplated giving a talk entitled 'Opera as Socialism' –
working not from the inherently intriguing fact that the Opera
had taken over the old People's Theatre premises but from the
idea that opera, like socialism, wanted to change the real world,
while both socialist ideals and opera involved the necessary dash
of naivety and pathos.

Jonas was not, however, giving any thought to that right then,
sitting as he was in the balcony, in the third row, with Knut
Skram on bended knee down on the stage, Knut Skram with
whom he had once exchanged a word or two at the Stortorvet Inn
while the singer – already a star, in Norway at any rate – was displaying his partiality for *smørbrød* with cod roe. Now here was
that same Knut Skram, kneeling down on the stage, too young to
play Don Juan, but wearing a wig that gave him a balding pate,
being someone else entirely, singing in Italian, no one would
imagine that he had ever eaten *smørbrød* with cod roe in a Norwegian restaurant. Jonas was giving no thought whatsoever to
what he would do at the debating society meeting; he was too
busy just savouring the moment.

Even in the foyer, before the performance began, there had
been an extra buzz of excitement in the air, possibly because it
was just before Christmas. The whole thing reminded Jonas of
his first visits to the theatre with the school, the formality of such
occasions: the boys showing up with slicked-down hair and bow-
ties, and the girls looking almost unrecognizable, little ladies in
their best dresses with a drop of stupefying scent in the hollows

of their throats, none of which stopped them from chucking fruit drops at one another and flirting freely and outrageously during the interval, as if that were the real point of a visit to the theatre. And in the midst of it all one could not help but be seduced by the merry-go-round action of the revolving stage and the dreamy blue shimmer of the stage lighting, by something unreal which was nonetheless sheer magic: as if the lie went so far that it bit its own tail and became true.

So, too, with this. Jonas had had the time of his life from the minute the curtain went up to disclose a stairway, a balcony, some arches; simplified forms suggestive of Spanish architecture: in other words even this, even the scenery, was stylized, a clear sign that one had left reality and all need for credibility far behind and should prepare, for instance, to see the Commendatore and Don Giovanni crossing swords in time to the music. Amazing. Jonas had the urge to clap. A fight to the death in time to the music. How they must have had to rehearse that, Jonas thought. He gasped ecstatically when the Commendatore was mortally wounded and lay there singing as he died. Fabulous. Jonas had to restrain himself from shouting 'bravo!' The fact that the libretto was in Norwegian made it all the more hilarious. In *Don Giovanni* the serenade was the only piece sung in Italian. And it was at the very moment when Jonas was most enjoying being able to sit there in that scented atmosphere, watching a bedizened man lying dying on a stage and singing as he did so, that the whole perspective suddenly swung around, like a revolving stage and all of a sudden he realized that this opera, or any opera whatsoever, was not in fact an escape from reality; on the contrary, it held up a mirror to reality. That was the way life *was*; it was only that so few people had realized it. People fenced in time to the music and sang while they were dying. After this perceptual about-turn, Jonas viewed the rest of *Don Giovanni* as a masterful facsimile of all the melodramatic and banal aspects of life, with coincidences, masked faces and mistaken identities all the way. So when, only a moment after killing the Commendatore, Don Giovanni tried to seduce Donna Elvira, who for some strange reason he did not recognize, even though he had actually been married to her for a short time, Jonas no longer found any of this odd. Quite the reverse: he applauded this totally unlikely situation as a nigh-on perfect reflection of the society in which he lived with the result that the entire opera was transformed into passages of almost startling beauty. Not only Don Juan's duet with Zerlina, 'Give me your hand', in the scene where he gate-crashes the peasants' wedding, but also and to as great an extent the farcical, not to say pornographic, sequence in which Zerlina tried to appease her betrothed, Masetto, going down on all fours, wiggling her backside at him and singing 'Beat me, beat me' in such a way that even those members of the audience who had become totally, breathlessly, wrapped up in the story – such people do exist! – could not help but laugh.

To Jonas, even the interval took on a new dimension, becoming if possible an even more crucial part of the performance than in his schooldays, more like an *entr'acte* in which the audience unwittingly played the lead. Jonas stood at the bar, listening to the chatter, with people referring to the singers by their first names as if these were pivotal lines in the piece, and where even the merest snatch of conversation could cause him to see whole scenes, and even the music, in a new light, as when one elderly gentleman asked another elderly gentleman: 'Did you notice the lovely lady who was playing the cello?'

In any case, it was directly after the interval that Nina G. had prompted him to turn and presented him with a gaze or a face that was more than enough to trigger that tingling between his shoulder-blades. For the remainder of the second Act Jonas was acutely aware of her presence, like an additional layer to the music, or as a sort of bonus, over and above the pleasure of seeing Donna Elvira manage to confuse Don Giovanni, her beloved, with his servant, merely because they had swapped clothes. Jonas could not remember when he had seen a better piece of entertainment. What a way of looking at identity! You put on other clothes and – hey, presto! – even a woman who has been this man's mistress takes you for him! And throughout all the fun and games, which constituted, mark you, an uncannily accurate reflection of real life, out of the corner of his eye he could just make out the back of Nina G.'s head, although of course he did not know her name at that point. Not until the very end, in the scene in which the Statue, which is to say the dead Commendatore, complete with ashen-grey mask, appears at Don Giovanni's table, and the latter grasps his hand and bemoans its deathly chill – only then did Nina G. turn towards him again. They exchanged a long, lingering glance. Then she smiled. Jonas felt her warmth hit him like the breath of a warm dry wind, a pleasant contrast to Don Giovanni's cold end on the boards of the stage.

The director of this production had done away with the epilogue and its moralistic finger-wagging, and thus the opera finished right after the point when Don Giovanni, refusing point blank to repent of anything whatsoever, curled in on himself and, instead of having him engulfed in flame, a beam of light was shone only on his upper half, until he had sung his last words, after which he collapsed and the light went out. Despite, or perhaps precisely because of the absence of, any moral lecture, the audience went wild; they rose to their feet, shouted 'bravo!' and whistled in a manner more normally associated with sporting events as if this, with a handful of exceptions, exceedingly middle-class audience wholeheartedly approved of Don Giovanni's impenitence, a rebel to the last: a response which, to Jonas's mind, served as a fitting end to that exceptionally exuberant evening and the unusual view of things it had afforded him.

Jonas saw Nina G.'s back disappearing in the direction of the exit, but he took his time, considering whether to approach her in the cloakroom. When he emerged into the corridor and looked around for her, however, she was nowhere to be seen. I have already said that Jonas Wergeland never wooed or made any effort to win a girl. This, if only in his head, was the one exception and one which I ascribe to the whole mood of the evening – he was, after all, standing in Den Norske Opera. Jonas was all set to follow that girl, get down on one knee outside her window and sing a serenade. Strictly speaking, the mood he was in he could have done just about anything.

Georgica

One should not judge Jonas Wergeland too harshly for wanting all of his relationships, and indeed life in general at that time, to be like one big opera, full of drama and pathos and grandiose exaggeration all rounded off by a violent death to the singing of a long aria. So wisely is life ordered, however, that by the time he and Margrete were living together this had long been forgotten; nothing could have been more remote from life with Margrete than drama and pathos.

So what did life with Margrete consist of? Of baking bread, for one thing. Apart from watching his small daughter when she was sleeping or playing, nothing filled Jonas with greater contentment – a heavy warm feeling of well-being tinged with a sense of something eternal – than to watch Margrete baking bread.

Like now.

It is evening, spring, and still light outside. On the windowsill is an egg cup with some coltsfoot which in some strange way shed a yellow glow over the whole kitchen as if all the light has to pass through this point before spreading out into the room. Margrete is standing at the kitchen bench, baking; Jonas sits in a chair at the rough-hewn kitchen table just watching, watching his wife baking, in a pair of faded jeans and a dark-blue woollen sweater, barefoot, as if baking were a holiday of sorts, a pleasure similar to that of walking barefoot in the sand. Margrete has no time for bought bread; there's nothing worse, she says, tastes like sawdust. This makes Jonas laugh, but Margrete is serious: rotten bread makes for a rotten life, she says, so Jonas follows her with his eyes as she dabs at the water in the fireproof dish on the stove as if she had an in-built thermometer in her finger, then she crumbles the yeast into the liquid – never use dried yeast! she says – while Jonas sits there chuckling, closely following her every move, seeing how she prefers to blend the yeast liquid with a little wooden spoon, an ancient implement, wood is so gentle on the ingredients, she says, and metal gives the bread an after-taste. Jonas sits in the kitchen watching his wife as she adds a pinch of salt, working on instinct, always this, working on instinct, a little sugar too, as it happens. Jonas drinks in the sight of Margrete standing there barefoot, in a baggy dark-blue sweater, sleeves rolled up, pounding dried herbs from her own garden to a powder in an old mortar, no herb is quite as wonder-ful as basil, she says, sprinkling it over the yeast mixture before pouring in coarse-ground wholemeal flour, then wheat germ, about so much, there it is again: 'about so much'; he marvels at Margrete, seeing her sprinkling sunflower seeds into the bowl, one, no two, handfuls; adding linseeds that she has soaked in water beforehand so that they will swell and not steal moisture from the dough, oh, right, Jonas will try to remember that, sit-ting on a chair in a kitchen tinged yellow by a bunch of coltsfoot in a little egg cup, observing Margrete, observing, not least, her actions because, as Margrete is always saying: bread is culture, bread is the very keynote of a culture, she said, and never tired of telling him about other peoples, how they ground the grain, how they *danced* while the bread was baking. Jonas watches Mar-grete bustling about, barefoot, happy, watches as she demon-strates the most underrated aspect of the art of baking: the knack for dough. It was a mystery to him. No matter how carefully Jonas weighed and measured he never got it right or, at least, you got bread, but it was nowhere near as good as Margrete's. Mar-grete simply *had* the knack, and so Jonas sits there watching, trying to wrench the secret from her, how she does it, as if she were an alchemist. In fact he not only watches her, he marvels at her, savours the sight of her sifting the flour, because you should always *sift* the flour, even if it says on the pack that it's pre-sifted, to give the flour air, she always said; and Jonas likes the fact that she says the same thing every time, as if she does not think he will ever remember it because there is no way of proving it, it is just something she believes, has discovered for herself; Jonas likes to see the way she measures the flour out roughly, judging by eye as if it were a way of life, 'roughly', and how she dusts off the flour by clapping her hands over the sink as though applauding herself or the privilege of being able to bake one's own bread.

Every individual has their own story, and Margrete is no exception. They had been on a motoring holiday in Norway – Margrete, Jonas and Kristin. Kristin was just a baby at the time. And apropos Kristin, I ought perhaps to point out that I have deliberately excluded her from this account. I merely wish to make it known that Jonas Wergeland does have a child. Not everyone knows that.

They were driving along the side of a fjord somewhere in western Norway, surrounded by scenery that never ceased to amaze Jonas, a landscape that filled him with a constant urge to pinch himself to make sure that he wasn't dreaming. They were on their way to catch a ferry and they had plenty of time, Margrete liked to have plenty of time, especially in this case, because it was the last ferry of the day. They had stopped at a so-called home bakery by the roadside in one of those little hamlets, all of which look alike. It was on the way to catch that last ferry of the day, half an hour later, that Margrete, who was driving, asked Jonas to give her a bit of bread because she was hungry. So Jonas took the loaf of bread, a perfectly ordinary loaf of bread, or so it seemed, in a white paper bag and broke a corner off the end. No sooner had Margrete taken a bite and swallowed it than she slammed on the brakes, did what amounted to an emergency stop, making Jonas think that she must have spotted a sheep that he had not noticed, but there was no sheep on the road; she then executed a rather hazardous U-turn, tyres screeching, and proceeded to drive back the way they had come. But they'd never catch the ferry now, Jonas protested, looking at his watch. Who cares? Margrete had retorted, she simply *had* to talk to the person, the *genius*, who had baked that bread. Which is how they came to drive back to that small hamlet on the banks of a fjord in western Norway, where Margrete actually succeeded in tracking down the baker and having a long and animated conversation with him about bread, not least about what constituted the real hallmark of good bread, a point on which they were so perfectly in agreement that they all but hugged one another: you felt it in your stomach the next day, in the form of a lovely warm feeling. Bread ought to leave you with a sense of physical well-being, and it should go on feeling good, not just the day after, but the day after that and the day after that again, in fact strictly speaking it ought to get better and better. So of course they had to sample several different varieties of bread, while Margrete swapped recipes with the baker, or not so much recipes as *ideas* about bread, about wood-burning stoves and storing in *tiner*, the old-style bentwood boxes, and naturally they had to stay the night in that little hamlet, nestling amid scenery that took your breath away, as the baker's guests; everyone made a great fuss of them, and they had had such a lovely time because, as the baker was at pains to point out, there's nothing quite like good bread for helping a conversation along. Then he had gone off to spend the night baking, so the next morning they were able to drive off to the ferry not only with memories stocked with a fresh batch of stories but also a backseat packed so full of bread that there was hardly any room for Kristin. That was the closest one came to drama in Margrete Boeck's life.

Margrete loved bread. For once I am going to succumb to the exaggeration inherent in the word 'loved' because it would be incorrect to say that Margrete liked bread, she *loved* bread; her whole life represented a quest for the perfect loaf of bread. She was forever experimenting or trying out recipes she had picked up, and whenever she and Jonas travelled abroad, they spent half their time sampling different sorts of bread. While others went in search of the Holy Grail, Margrete went in search of the Perfect Bread. She was constant and insistent in her belief that good bread was the very essence of life itself; simply eating good bread was half the battle. Jonas laughed at this, but sometimes, when he could not sleep, he would get up and have a slice of Margrete's bread with wild raspberry jam and a glass of milk. More often than not he was asleep before his head touched the pillow.

So perhaps this is where it all begins, or ends, with this story: Jonas sitting on a chair in the kitchen, watching Margrete bake bread: mixing the dough with a wooden spoon, putting her whole body into it, a furrow of concern between her brows as if she knows that this is the crucial stage, so she sifts in a little more flour, making the dough smooth, *feeling* when the consistency is just right. Jonas sees how she feels it with her whole body, sees the rapturous expression on her face; she really works at it – 'opera', as it happens, can also mean 'work' – she dances as she works the dough, endowing the whole process with an erotic touch, while the smell of yeast, faintly acidic, fills the room; and Margrete mutters to herself, or to the dough, gives it one last turn before sprinkling some flour over it and leaving it to rise.

It is evening, spring, still light outside. On the windowsill sits an egg cup full of coltsfoot, staining the whole room with yellow. Margrete looks at him and laughs, why doesn't he treat her to one of those fabulously absurd quotations of his, she asks, and to please her he quotes something from Friedrich Schleiermacher, from *Über die Religion*, from the end of the second part, in which Schleiermacher asserts that ideas are paramount, the greatest and most essential element of human nature, and indeed that religion as such, the belief in God, is reliant on the direction such ideas take, at which Margrete laughs, she is the only person to actually laugh at his quotations, as if she could see right through him, his bluff with the twenty-odd quotations he had collected in his little red notebook, or regarded these 'pearls of wisdom', at best, as being self-evident. Nevertheless she comes over to him and strokes his cheek with a floury finger and gives him a hug, her dark-blue sweater is covered in spots of white and dusted with flour, like a dark sky full of nebulae – I am a universe, she was wont to say when he asked her why she sat quietly thinking, and she often sat quietly thinking, as if that were enough in itself, a colossal and precious deed, but now she is looking at the bowl on the worktop, because this is the most vital, the most exciting part of the whole process: the proving, *whether* the dough would rise, that was religion enough for Margrete, *truly* a test of the imagination, and she would jump with joy when it rose, there were few things she found more fascinating than the proving, those forces, organisms that saw to themselves once they had been set in motion, there was nothing you could do except stand humbly by and watch. There were times, odd occasions, when the dough did not rise, or when the bread somehow did not turn out well, although she could never figure out why. On such days, Margrete was all at sixes and sevens.

Sometimes they talked while the dough was rising, Margrete liked to talk about his work at NRK, kid him about it, ask him about people, intrigues at Broadcasting House, scandals, although she seldom watched television. She, on the other hand, said next to nothing about her own job as a consulting physician with the Oslo Health Board – not because her work was confidential but because she preferred to switch off from it when she came home. Or because there were other things she would rather talk about. Often she would tell Jonas little stories – the most marvellous flights of fancy – which he suspected had been plucked from books, that being Margrete's favourite pastime: reading. Which is to say, she did not read, she laid herself open to the writing. Other times, Margrete might take a bath while the dough was rising, she had an Archimedean affinity for bathtubs. If there was one thing that Jonas admired, and envied, in his wife it was her sense for what are known as 'the little things in life'. Margrete possessed a unique awareness of, and took a singular delight in, the things with which she surrounded herself: everything from an arrangement of flowers in a vase on the table in the living room to the toilet paper in the bathroom. 'You only have to look at something for long enough for it to become interesting,' she would say. And she had an even more exceptional gift for turning the daily round into a work of art; an expression such as 'the tedium of everyday life' was totally alien to her. To Margrete, every occurrence, even those that were repeated again and again, was a small miracle, a ceremony out of which she squeezed every drop of goodness. The way Jonas saw it, Margrete did for day-to-day life what Einstein had done for mass; she discovered, or disclosed, its energy. Those things which to others were blind routine, were for Margrete a whole succession of sensations: waking up, stretching, sniffing bodily odours, getting washed. Cutting her nails was a ritual in itself, a sort of minor engineering project. Getting dressed was like a ballet, not of pleasure but of concentration, as if her mind was constantly on the job, giving it great thought. After breakfast she would tune in to, take delight in, the workings of her bowels.

Margrete could even turn a trip into town on the subway into an eye-opening experience. She particularly enjoyed the gardens on the aboveground stretch between Risløkka and Økern, the way they changed with the seasons.

But more often than not they went through to the bedroom and made love. There was nothing quite like making love while the dough rose. Margrete pulled off jeans and a floury sweater and made love to him in a way she only did when she was baking bread, with firm hands and a tense expectancy, taking a long time over it – as long as it takes for a batch of dough to rise.

Afterwards, Margrete would go back to the kitchen and remove the tea towel from the bowl, proudly, as if unveiling a monument, because the dough had risen, and Jonas would sit back down on his chair and watch how she kneaded the dough, passionately almost, as if she were still making love, or touched by their lovemaking, before dividing it into portions, placing each one in an old baking tin brushed with olive oil to give the bread a nice crust. Jonas would sit and watch her, say something to her, usually something banal, something hopelessly, ineptly banal, that almost always expressed how much he loved her and which always caused her to send him a long, lingering look, to walk over to him, barefoot, pensively, while the loaves rested again. Then she would brush them with egg and put them in the oven. And he would not get up but would go on sitting there while the scent of Margrete's bread filled the kitchen and it grew dark outside, slowly, as it does when Norway is at its best.

Jonas especially liked to watch Margrete taking the finished loaves out of the baking tins and tapping them as if she were listening for just the right note. He took even greater enjoyment in seeing how happy, how truly happy she was when the bread was acceptable, although as far as she was concerned it could never be absolutely perfect. Occasionally he sat on, gazing at the loaves ranged on their rack, the sheen of the crust, how they almost seemed to glow, and he could not rid himself of the thought that this might be the Golden Fleece for which he had always been searching, that it might be that simple, that close at hand. In any case, the bread was precious to Margrete. She gave away loaves as Christmas presents, wrapped in tea towels and tied up with ribbon.

It is evening, spring, soon it will be dark outside. Kristin is asleep in her room. Jonas is already looking forward to breakfast, to Margrete's bread. To Jonas, this is happy married life: looking forward to breakfast. Jonas experienced many great and exciting things in his life, and yet given the choice, there was nothing to match breakfast with Margrete, her bread with wild raspberry jam and a glass of milk.

A First Reader

Now where was I? Ah yes, I was about to tell you how Jonas Wergeland caught, or rather, was held spellbound, by the sight of his parents in the act. In actual fact, however, it all started some months earlier, on the day on which Nefertiti hinted to Jonas that the piece of furniture which he referred to simply as 'the bookcase' actually contained treasures beyond price in more ways than one.

Jonas and Nefertiti were stretched out on the floor, playing and listening to Duke Ellington, 'Me and You' and 'So Far, So Good' and 'At a Dixie Roadside Diner' and Jimmy Blanton's swinging bass and, above all else, Ivie Anderson's lazy croon; Jonas thought he might be a little bit in love with Ivie Anderson who, according to Nefertiti, had had to give up singing because she was asthmatic and who had also happened to play a mean game of poker. Jonas and Nefertiti were playing with those plastic cowboy and Indian figures that had just come on to the market, with revolvers which, wonder of wonders, could be pulled out of holsters, and bows and arrows that could be detached from the hands. Nefertiti was always an Indian, she particularly liked showing Jonas how the Indians had attacked General Custer at the battle of Little Big Horn, occasionally telling him something about Red Indian customs and rituals, about their sand paintings for instance. Jonas was just in the act of chasing a couple of Indians all the way into the bookcase when Nefertiti's eyes suddenly widened and she took a book from the shelf. She blew the dust off it as if it were smoke from a revolver, opened it and nodded: 'This is very valuable,' she said. Jonas thought she was kidding. It was just an old book, nothing special about it. Nefertiti pulled out another one and said the same thing. This went on for some time.

At this point I ought perhaps to say something about Jonas's family's attitude to books. His parents did not read at all. Rakel had merely ploughed her way through the edition of the *Arabian Nights* given to her by Aunt Laura, and Daniel and Jonas read, or flicked through, nothing but comics. Their living room had been bare of bookshelves until the day when some boxes, quite a lot of them in fact, turned up from the western part of the country. Somebody in his mother's family had died, some fairly distant and childless relative; some other, even more distant, relative had divided up the estate and by sheer chance – that much I can divulge – the boxes of books were sent to Åse Hansen. This came as a complete surprise to Jonas's mother; nonetheless, she went out and bought some cheap bookcases and placed the books on them, mainly to brighten up the walls, a bit like wallpaper.

'Wow! This one ought to be locked up in a safe.' Nefertiti's eye were just about popping out of her head. Jonas looked on, mystified, as she moved the books around, arranging those she had pulled off the shelves in order, a couple of dozen volumes ranged in a row, leather spines embossed with faded gilt lettering. 'Jonas, these books are actually worth a fortune. Take good care of them.' She eyed him gravely as if this were a matter of a last will and testament, something she was bequeathing to him. As, of course, it was, although Jonas did not know it then. Nefertiti kept her eyes fixed on him until she was sure that her words had sunk in. Then they went on with their game. And Jonas did remember, although it would be many years before he acted more systematically on this tip.

When they were finished playing, and the cowboys and Indians had all been thrown together higgledy-piggledy in a cardboard box, a kind of impartial mass grave, Nefertiti took another book from a shelf higher up. 'You should take a look at this,' she said. 'It's valuable, too, albeit it in another way.'

Jonas opened the book and sounded out a few sentences in what seemed to be a funny sort of Norwegian: 'In the beginning, the Lord of Beings created men and women, and in the form of commandments in 100,000 chapters laid down rules for regulating their existence with regard to Dharma, Artha and Kama.' Was this old Norwegian, Jonas wanted to know. Nefertiti explained that it was Danish. Jonas turned to the title page: 'Ka-ma Sut-ra,' he read. 'It sounds a bit like a magic spell,' Jonas said. Nefertiti nodded. And without batting those long lashes once she gave him a brief run-down of the book's seven parts, recommending the second part in particular to Jonas as being not only diverting but also most informative. Jonas turned to the appropriate page, but when he saw that it was entitled 'On Sexual Union' he gave a start and made as if to put the book down. Nefertiti laughed at him and told him that it could be read in several ways; you could read it as a list of all the ways in which a man and a woman could have a nice time together, but you could also read it as transcriptions of all the many paths leading to the truth.

Over the next few days Jonas dipped into the book, and even though it was written in a rather dry vein, the sentences really set his imagination in ferment. 'On Biting' – what was that? 'Leaf of a blue lotus' – sounded a bit funny. 'When the woman places one of her legs on her lover's shoulder and stretches the other out and then places the latter on his shoulder and stretches out the other and continues to do so alternately, it is called the "splitting of the bamboo".' Mind-boggling. You might say that Vatsyayana, and not Thorbjørn Egner, was the author of Jonas's first reader. If the truth be told, the *Kama Sutra* was one of the few books that Jonas read from cover to cover, something which was bound to leave its mark. For a start his teacher had to give him a telling-off for writing certain words in the Danish way – *kvinder* instead of *kvinner* for 'women', for example.

A lot of strange things have been said about Jonas Wergeland, but there is one thing that no one can take from him; even if he did not understand much of it, his early encounter with the *Kama Sutra* left him with a very different attitude to sex from most men. What he had grasped – and this was, in essence, the most important lesson – was that sex was a solemn undertaking, something important, something to be contemplated with the greatest respect. Added to which, it was an inexhaustible subject, encapsulated in a work consisting of '100,000 chapters'. The art of love was, in other words, all embracing. Fortunately, or unfortunately, there was more to copulation than the vulgar simplicity of 'pussy and prick/together stick'; copulation was also about 'the art of making beds and spreading out cushions and covers for reclining', 'playing on musical glasses filled with water', 'quickness of hand or manual skill' and, not least, the 'solution of riddles, enigmas, covert speeches, verbal puzzles and enigmatic questions'. This last fitted with what Nefertiti had been getting at, and thanks to her Jonas would always associate sex with the search for truth. This being the case, it seemed only reasonable that the physical act of love should be difficult, calling, quite frankly, for a certain virtuosity. More than once, after the description of a sexual position, Jonas came upon the words: 'This position is learnt by practice only.' Jonas understood that in order to become a good lover you had to train; that when you came right down to it, it must be as hard as qualifying for the Olympic Games.

To Jonas, the Danish in which his edition of the *Kama Sutra* was written was like a very formal, slightly archaic Norwegian and for him, later in life, this was to remain the language of lovemaking. He always felt that there was something exalted and dignified about the act of love, with all those prepositive possessive pronouns and indefinite articles. Only weeks after those first reading sessions he noticed that in his head he had stopped using the standard word 'twat'. When it came to sexual terminology Jonas Wergeland preferred the Sanskrit.

Now in passing it ought to be said that the attitude of small boys towards that endlessly fascinating part of a woman's anatomy lying between her legs is nothing if not complex. One could, with some justification, bemoan the fact that men seem incapable of channelling the inventiveness and playful metaphorizing of their boyhoods into other areas later in life. Among Jonas's chums, comparisons – or the attempt to establish a sort of Kretschmer's typology of vaginas – were more often than not drawn from the dinner table or the animal kingdom as if the female genitals were a cross between a cold buffet and a zoo, or as if they could not make up their minds what was more thrilling: *looking* or *tasting*. If, for example, a girl was considered to be frigid – although, of course, it was always a case of pure guesswork, not to say wishful thinking – she would be said to have a 'chicken twat' as though all the boys had first-hand experience of what it felt like to stick their little peckers inside one of the ostensibly cold pale chickens in the window of Grorud Fish and Game. 'Orange twat' was the term given to the juicy ones or, more accurately, those girls who were imagined to be so; the treacherous types, the VD carriers, were 'shark twats'; dry sticks were 'juniper twats'; if they had their period they were 'strawberry twats', and the tight-arsed, impervious sort were 'nut twats'. The ideal was what they called a 'lamb twat' since almost all of them had been across to Ammerud meadows and experienced the strange and delightful sensation of having a lamb suck their fingers – I shall resist the temptation to make any comment on this, but if anyone feels inclined to laugh at these attempts to encapsulate the secrets of the female body in words, might I remind you that even such a world-class writer as Mallarmé was not above such a line of thought, comparing as he did a vagina to 'a pale-pink shell' as if it were an ornament to be displayed on a shelf the way Jonas's grandfather had done. In any event, it ought to be something of a challenge, I almost said in the name of women's liberation, to come up with something new to say on this topic, something more original, something more akin to the description of the vulva given in the ancient scriptures – 'like the print of a gazelle's hoof in the desert sand' – and, above all else, something more dignified. I might add that as a student Jonas himself made the following rather high-flown but nonetheless creditable attempt: 'Her sex was as unexplored and impenetrable as a distant spiral galaxy.'

In other words, while the other boys were going on about 'muffins' and 'beavers', Jonas opted for the more formal 'yoni': or rather, not so much formal as detached. Jonas thought in terms of elephant yonis, mare yonis and gazelle yonis. To some extent, from boyhood onwards, these outlandish terms elevated the sexual act onto a metaphysical and, not least, epistemological plane, if I may be allowed to use such lofty words, while at the same time vouchsafing him a glimpse of other, alternative, ways of comprehending reality – something which I, for obvious reasons, set great store by. If, later in life, Jonas was nonetheless pressurized into coming up with another, less obscure metaphor, he would only have one word for a vulva, quite simply because that was how he saw them all: as a thinking cap. All of the women who guided Jonas inside themselves had some influence on his way of thinking and in order to illustrate how they did so, I will now tell you the story of his second encounter with Nina G.

A Life of Harmony

As I said earlier, Jonas regarded his years at high school as an encounter with the hidden face of Norway. As luck would have it, for instance, he attended the nineteenth birthday party of one of his classmates, held not just anywhere, mind you, but in the Rococo Room of the Grand Hotel. In the early days at high school this classmate, who boasted four names rounded off by a 'Jr.', had seemed pretty ordinary – apart, that is, from a rather suspect green loden coat – but he had eventually given himself away with such remarks as 'Can't go into town with you, guys, I've got a flying lesson with Dad' or 'You'll have to come home and meet these two Oriental girls we've got working in the house.' It turned out that his parents were neighbours of Sir William up on Holmenkoll Heights, but they were not *nouveaux riches* like Sir William, they had inherited their fortune without having to lift a finger and they handled their status symbols in a casual often surprisingly devil-may-care manner.

For them, popping down to the Rococo Room was really just the urbane equivalent of a Saturday-night hop at the village hall, if not a less strenuous version of the only things that really interested them: sport and open-air pursuits. Incredible though it may seem, as much cachet was attached to a good slalom technique as to a seven-figure bank balance.

Here Jonas was brought face-to-face with Norway's moneyed class, that one per mil of the Norwegian population who could contemplate hiring the Rococo Room at the Grand and inviting 200 people for a party at the drop of a hat in the middle of January, for example. And even though this was a formal dinner with everyone in evening dress, these people managed, by dint of a sort of innate nonchalance, to give what were for Jonas the most unreal surroundings, the appearance of an ordinary, every-day living-room. After dinner there was dancing to the music of a grand orchestra, strings and all. With something approaching disbelief Jonas, clad in a borrowed suit, watched young people of his own age, and especially the girls in their fabulous gowns, gliding around the floor as if it were the most natural thing in the world, in a room that sparkled with gilt, and with a tapestry on the back wall forming a museological backdrop to the orches-tra – disbelief because these young people did not merely shuf-fle about, as Jonas was in the habit of doing, they glided, they floated across the floor in ballroom and Latin American dances, and they really *could* dance, adding nifty little variations of their own to the basic steps. Even so, they did not really seem to take it seriously, just as they did not take their wealth seriously, all but yawning as they danced, or with an affected fervour, giving Jonas an impression of something stylized, as if the whole set-up were a kind of opera, an enormous tableau. Jonas did not speak to anyone, he merely strolled about, nodding to this one or that; he really had nothing to talk to these people about, although they all seemed very nice. The plain fact was that they inhabited a totally different world. It was enough for Jonas simply to circulate and watch, to sit on red sofas and soak up the atmosphere – including, if the truth be told, a whiff of the odd joint – of a modern-day Norwegian ball, of a style that was totally vacuous. There was something about it all that was every bit as anachronistic, not to say comical, when compared to the world outside the windows, as all the rustic furniture with which these people filled their homes.

After midnight he suddenly began to feel very tired, because of the wine, he thought, although it might just as easily have been brought on by consternation. Nevertheless, he did not want to go home, he just needed to have a little nap.

And it was his search for a suitable spot to lay his head that brought him to the Mirror Restaurant, which was closed for the evening. He shut the glass door behind him and the sound of the music in the Rococo Room faded to a distant hubbub. He made a tour of the elegant restaurant, across the soft red carpet, beneath chandeliers reminiscent of huge and enigmatic glass plants; ran his eye over white-clothed tables and the mirrors that lined the walls, dim and mysterious, shades of a benighted Versailles. In one corner stood a grand piano draped with a black cover, like a misplaced Kaaba, a shrine. He lifted a corner of the cover, crawled under the piano and was instantly fast asleep.

He was woken by something falling on him, something light. It took a while for it to dawn on him what it was. Music. Music falling from above. Someone was playing the piano: quietly, gently. He turned his head and spied the hem of a dress and a foot on the soft pedal, one high-heeled shoe on its side next to it. He could hear no sound from the Rococo Room, had no idea what time it was. It was still pitch-dark at any rate. He lay quite still, wondering who this woman was who just sat there creating sounds, harmonies, on the piano: soft, muted sounds that ran together. As if it were raining notes. Because he could actually feel them on his body as if they were landing on him, or as if this were some sort of musical acupuncture, the light touch of note after note, soothing, immediately taking the edge off the beginnings of a hangover, filling him with a sense of well-being. She struck chord after chord, gradually building up into an alternative melody in which the notes were strung together in a more intricate fashion than in the main theme. She seemed to him to be making a voyage of discovery across the keys, into the unexplored realms of harmony, seeking out more and more new combinations, becoming more and more adventurous. Slowly the notes twisted into new patterns. A kaleidoscope for the ear. Original. He played the piano himself, knew that this was something else, something *radical*, the most bizarre sounds, making him think at one and the same time of Norway and of faraway places. Part of him wanted to see who was playing, another part simply wanted to lie there listening, enjoying. He lay there under the grand piano, surrounded by dark mirrors, beholding a sort of ribwork, four beams fanning out, like rays; he lay there, feeling the music created in the case above his head, infinitely beautiful music, making a tangible impression on his body, like vibrations, caresses. As if the piano itself were lying on top of him, making love to him.

'Who's that?'

'Me.'

'No, I mean who composed that?'

'I did.'

'It sounds . . . different somehow.'

'That may have something to do with you.'

Her voice had a strange note to it. He heard her get up, the rustling of fabric, layers and layers of fabric, then saw a face peering in at him. It was *her*, he ought to have guessed: the girl from the Opera House. She had been very late getting to the party in the Rococo Room. Jonas had not seen her, but she had seen him.

This was, of course, Nina G. Yes, *that* Nina G., a composer who in years to come would occupy the same position in the national consciousness as Arne Nordheim with innumerable international projects and commissions to her name, compositions premièred at ISCM festivals, a regular visitor to such avant-garde strongholds as IRCAM. By the time Jonas met her she was already displaying an experimental approach to music, but even Jonas could not have guessed that this rather shy, sedately dressed girl – a girl who, during the summer months, dusted off both the dialect and the national costume of her native region and worked as a guide at the Folk Museum, among the lofts and wooden storehouses – that this girl would become an acclaimed pioneer, in international terms at that, in the field of computer-based composition with a flat full of electronic equipment and advanced software. Most listeners, of course, perceived her music as a series of stringent constructions, but Jonas for one realized that they in fact represented powerful emotions expressed in an alternative form.

But this was Nina G. as she was then, and Jonas knew nothing about her when she grabbed hold of his legs, hauled him partway out from under the piano and tugged his trousers down to his knees, pulling off her own tights and knickers as she did so, but retaining the frothy layers of underskirt and dress. Then, with not a word said, she sat astride him and guided him inside her, laid her hands on top of the piano at the curve in its side and slowly began to rock back and forth.

As you can see, this accords with what I said in my little discourse on Jonas Wergeland's select group of women; it was they who took the initiative. Why? I have already mentioned that it was his face which they found seductive, but I suppose I ought to elaborate on this by saying that women have far more subtle reasons for finding a man attractive than is the case the other way round, so let me simply state, very generally, that when Nina G. settled herself on top of Jonas Wergeland, a boy who was a stranger to her, she was moved not so much by desire as by the knowledge, called it female intuition, that this was a unique opportunity, the sort of chance that comes along just once in a lifetime.

Jonas lay on a red carpet at the heart of the Grand Hotel, gazing up at the underside of a grand piano and listening to the rustle of dress fabric. Like lovemaking in an opera, extravagant, unreal, or so unreal that it became real. If he tilted his head back he could see a couple of the mirrors; how fine they looked in the darkness, how they seemed to live, to breathe. At one point she stopped her rocking, ducked down under the piano to him, found his ear, concentrated on it, letting her tongue caress it, running it round the auricle; she whispered something into it, laughed softly, groaned softly with pleasure at the coupling of their lower halves and to Jonas the whole world seemed to converge into just one sense, his hearing; with her tongue and the kisses to that organ she seemed to be opening his ear to new sounds as if she had removed a plug, enabling him to hear everything differently, not only the swishing of her dress and her breathing but also the sounds coming to his ears from beyond the walls, from the city, cars outside, a far-away voice, even the barely audible tinkling of her earrings. Jonas derived enormous pleasure from this; she seemed to him to make love in much the same way as she played the piano, a combination of something familiar and something new. She was sitting so high up on him and clenching her vaginal muscles so tightly around him that he felt as if she were pulling him, heaving him, towards a boundary and a little beyond, while at the same time drenching his ear in kisses, playing a carillon of sorts on those tiny bones in the labyrinth deep inside, whispering now and again or uttering sounds that were not words, but more like music emanating from her body and evoking a weird resonance inside him as if she were conducting his body, calling forth latent harmonies, making it thrum until it glowed.

The one thing which the women who made love to Jonas had in common was that they all instinctively sat astride him. This had nothing to do with a feminine urge to dominate, nor with the absurd concept of the 'new man'. Without going into the highly individual reasons for adopting this position, let me simply say that this was the position that Jonas himself preferred far above any other. For him, the pleasure seemed twice as great when these women sat on top of him. Jonas gave a lot of thought to why this should be, and he came to the conclusion that more than any other this position opened the door to the cognitive potential inherent in lovemaking; when he lay on his back like that, in some strange way his thoughts were set free. Not for nothing did the Arabs call this position 'the Archimedean screw'; this tallied with Jonas's own feeling that the Earth could be moved during lovemaking, from one single, fixed point.

As now, on a red carpet at the heart of the Grand Hotel. The instant his penis came into contact with her vagina and slipped inside, he was struck by a sense of a chemical change in his body; he was filled with energy, raised onto a higher plane, as if by a hydraulic system created by the friction between his penis and her vagina. From Aunt Laura's sketches he knew that the phallus formed a straight line running out from the curved form of the scrotum, like a tangent from a circle, and this was also how he regarded something of the potential inherent in his penis; by dint of this he could break out of the set cycles of thought and shoot off at a tangent that would lead to something quite different. Exactly as here, because as they built towards a climax, slowly, because he was doing his utmost to spin it out, holding back, he noticed that his thoughts were starting to travel along different lines than usual until they eventually flowed out into an idea, a vision almost, as to what he should do for Owl, the debating society. He had been asked to talk about the opera, but now it was quite clear in his mind: he would rather play. He knew just what he would do; he would play arias from the opera but using different harmonies, jazz chords, old refrains with new tonal variations. While Nina G. sat astride him, making gentle, rhythmic love to him, giving him greater and greater pleasure, since she was now gripping the edge of the piano case and was thus able to raise and lower herself gently and vary the depth of penetration, he strove to hold onto this dream, spin it out, postpone the climax, so that he could also *hear* how good it would sound.

And that concert at the Owl meeting a couple of weeks later did indeed prove to be a sensation, an event that was still being talked about at the school years later: how Jonas Wergeland, wearing a Persian-lamb hat of the sort worn by Theolonius Monk, jazzed up some well-known arias – opening with the stirring, seductive habanera from *Carmen*, '*L'amour est un oiseau rebelle*', in a tempo and an arrangement that rendered it almost unrecognizable; following this up with Senta's ballad from *The Flying Dutchman*, the wistful piece from Act II, '*Doch, dass der arme Mann noch Erlösung fände auf Erden*', and adding most tellingly in the transition to '*Ach, könntest du, bleicher Seeman, es finden*' some harmonies that sent chills up the audience's spines. Last but not least he had played Don Giovanni's and Zerlina's duet, '*Là ci darme la mano*', with a number of chords and springs from one key to another that made people gasp, partly because nobody could see how such a wealth of sound could be produced from one solitary piano. There were those who knew what they were talking about – and bear in mind that Jonas never made any effort to take this further – who believed Jonas Wergeland to be Norway's greatest jazz talent since Jan Garbarek. It was not that Nina G. *passed on* this gift, by osmosis as it were or, to be more specific, by way of her moist vagina; nonetheless, it was thanks to her that he could suddenly see, or *hear* this potential within himself. Through Nina G. he discovered a different and unknown gear in music.

But I am getting ahead of myself. Jonas Wergeland was still lying on his back, his upper half under a grand piano in the Mirror Restaurant of the Grand Hotel, aware that Nina G. had started to tense into a tremulous, increasingly vehement rhythm, and was uttering sounds which made it quite clear to him that she was approaching a peak, or heading *into* something; and so

eager was she, or so carried away, that just before she came, with
a soft, muffled whimper like a glissando from the high to the low
notes, she banged her head against the piano case, producing a
sound, faint, but nonetheless audible, that swelled up among the
dark mirrors and filled the room with a sort of fog of sound that
Jonas was to hear again long afterwards – he would have sworn
to it – built into one of her most famous pieces. And even though
he did not want the pleasure to end, he too had to succumb to his
orgasm, which he always dreaded slightly, or disliked because it
interrupted a marvellous train of thought, snuffing it out. Jonas
Wergeland could well understand why orgasm was known as 'the
little death'.

When We Dead Awaken

Speaking of death, that reminds me that I ought to tell you something known only to a handful of people.

At one point, Jonas Wergeland was told that he was going to die – the big death this time.

It happened while he was attending the College of Architecture, at a time, what is more, when he had just stumbled on an angle that really whetted his appetite for his studies on Louis Kahn and his stimulating ideas on the significance for a building of light and shade. Jonas had discovered something suspicious – one might almost say a shadow – in his body. He went to see a doctor. The doctor frowned and wasted no time in sending him for tests, X-rays; the pictures came back, the diagnosis was plain. I won't mention the word, everyone knows how rapidly such things progress, especially in the form that had struck Jonas. Jonas Wergeland was going to die; it was that simple, that inconceivable. You will have to excuse me. This entire episode invites so much sentimentality and pathos that I will have to keep this as short as possible. The main thing, surprisingly enough when one considers the terrible emotional upheaval experienced by Jonas Wergeland when other people died, is that he took the news calmly, with dignity, just as people are capable of altering their pattern of behaviour when the situation demands it, in time of war for example. Or, more radically: it might have seemed as if Jonas suddenly felt that he belonged to an alien civilization: one which took a very different view of death.

However, what is more interesting – cynical as that word may sound in such a context – for anyone wishing to gain some insight into Jonas Wergeland's life are the consequences which this news was to have. Jonas Wergeland was not the sort to just lie down and die. The doctor had given him a rough idea of how long he had, and Jonas was left wondering: What now? Meaning: How far can I get on whatever fuel I have left?

From time to time in newspaper profiles and interviews, one finds people coyly professing that even if they were told they were going to die soon, they would go on living their lives as normal. When, after saying the necessary farewells to the necessary people – not least after a long talk with Buddha – Jonas set out for the Sinai peninsula and Jebel Musa; he really was going on living as if nothing had happened, seeing that he had already had the trip half planned. There was no thought in Jonas's mind of legends of elephants dragging themselves off to their secret graveyard, nor of choosing a particularly spectacular setting in which to draw his last breath. And one thing is for sure: there was no religious motive behind it.

Shortly afterwards, by virtue of his usual efficiency and a last bit of help from Adam Smith's *The Wealth of Nations*, Jonas touched down in Israel, and without so much as a glance at Jerusalem, without stopping to stick his own little slip of paper into the Wailing Wall, he took the quickest route, a military one, that is, by way of the Gulf of Aqaba, to the southern tip of the Sinai Peninsula. The skeletons of trucks and a tank left him in no doubt that he was now traversing borders that were taut as a bowstring. And yet nothing could have worried him less than the thought that a major war might break out, right under his nose so to speak.

As I say, there is no subtle way of telling this. And I admit that this is one point in the story when I am tempted to reveal who I am, since certain things would then be easier to understand. I apologize for the fact that, under the circumstances, I have to make such a demonstrative secret of my identity.

Be that as it may: Jonas reached his destination in the afternoon. For some time they had been driving through a rugged landscape, barren, hot, its mountains like earthenware that has cracked after firing. That was fine by Jonas. It occurred to him that the wheel had come full circle; that this was the rock-face of his childhood, Ravnkollen, taken back to its origins: to rock, to light, to shade, to silence. They rounded a headland to finally find themselves at the entrance to Wadi Shuaib, and down in the dip, surrounded by torn and craggy massifs, lay St Catherine's Monastery, a cluster of buildings encircled by a stout wall like a little vessel, a lifeboat, a miraculous sign of human life, survivors in a sea of gigantic petrified waves.

Jonas approached the monastery alone. Outside the walls lay a garden, its cypress trees breaking the monotony of the rock. He listened to the distinctive sound of the surrounding countryside, a faint sough in the air. Some Bedouins from the Gebeliyah tribe came into view then disappeared through the wall, although Jonas could not see how. Moments later, however, a monk appeared and let Jonas in, after pointing inquiringly at the mountain and receiving a nod from Jonas in return. Beyond the gate, on the way to the guest wing, Jonas found a warren of buildings and narrow alleyways reminiscent of a Greek village. He noted that the church was constructed out of massive blocks of granite, exactly like that back home in Grorud. Again he was struck by a sense of homecoming, or of finding some part of himself, a vital part, perhaps his heart. Jonas followed close on the heels of the monk with no intention whatsoever of seeing the exceptional collection of icons or the priceless manuscripts in the library or the glittering church containing the relics of St Catherine, the most unbelievable richness and splendour in the heart of a scorched, dun-coloured wilderness; he barely knew of their existence, he had but one thought in his head: to reach the top of Jebel Musa. He could tell his strength was failing, was afraid he would not be up to it.

Is this the most crucial story in Jonas Wergeland's life?

He was shown into what looked like a monk's cell. White walls. A narrow slit of a window. Light and shade. He lay down on the simple bed. Needed to rest. Closed his eyes. Here, too, he was aware of a gentle, soughing sound. Father Makarios, who looked after the monastery's guests, came in; rotund, black hat and a coarse blue robe; a beard with an incipient tinge of grey. He set a bowl of olives on the table, some bread, a jug of wine. He walked over to the bed, looked down at Jonas, kindly, compassionately, stroked his brow. 'Rest,' he said in several languages. 'Just rest.'

At that war-fraught time, few people journeyed to the Sinai Peninsula and the spot which was traditionally considered to be the world's spiritual pole – from a Western point of view, that is – but it so happened that there was one other person lodged in the guest wing, a German social anthropologist, actually based at the Feirân oasis, who was making a study of the nomadic way of life and who promptly invited himself into Jonas's room – not because he was sick but because he was sickening for company – and sat down on the only chair. Jonas was feeling weak and wanted to rest, but the German wanted to talk. Primarily about Henrik Ibsen. Jonas had long since ceased to be amazed by total strangers, encountered in the most desolate spots on Earth, who, the minute he said where he came from, would suddenly reveal a passionate interest in something Norwegian. In a way it was, therefore, not so surprising that in the middle of the Sinai desert, standing at death's door, Jonas should be confronted with his most famous countryman.

Although Jonas was not really listening. He caught only fragments of a long opinionated monologue on Henrik Ibsen as a nomad. 'Well, what else would you call a man who had lived abroad for thirty years, but a nomad?' declared the German, popping an olive into his mouth. Or what would Jonas call someone who spent his whole life moving from one place to another and would never countenance the addition of any personal touches to his homes, with the possible exception of the odd painting? No buts about it: Ibsen was a man who never pitched his tent too firmly, said the German reverently. Did Jonas know that the famous playwright had to have the windows open while he was writing and that, besides taking his daily stroll, he also walked about while he was working? And Peer Gynt, an obvious self-portrait, what was he but a Bedouin in Norwegian national dress? Actually Ibsen was a lot like Moses, said the German, flinging out an arm, as if to encompass the countryside beyond those four walls: a man who had learned from nomads before going on to become an exacting prophet with strict moral precepts, exactly like Ibsen. And weren't they both obsessed with climbing to the tops of mountains to attain the ultimate insight? Or had Jonas forgotten Gerd in *Brand* – and at this the German spat out a stone and suddenly began to quote, triumphantly, in broken Norwegian – how she spoke of the Black Peak that 'pointed straight to Heaven!' And Irene in *When We Dead Awaken* who wanted to pass 'through all the mists. And all the way up to the pinnacle of that tower, that glows in the sunrise.' All that was missing here among the mountains of Sinai were huge masses of snow under which they could be buried, the German joked, on his way out the door at long last. 'By the way,' he said, 'have you seen the sepulchre?' He rolled his eyes. 'Piles and piles of skulls.'

Jonas shut his eyes and slept.

At three in the morning, while it was still dark and the monks were making their way to the first mass of the day, Jonas began the ascent. For breakfast he had had a grapefruit, that was all, a delicious grapefruit from the Feirân oasis, without feeling overly maudlin, even if the thought of a last supper did cross his mind. Father Makarios met him at the gate and handed him a little loaf of bread stamped with the image of St Catherine, strictly speaking only for communion use.

'How can you know if that really is God's mountain?' Jonas asked, pointing into the gloom, to where he could just make out the contours of the cliff face.

'Go up and sit there for a while and you will understand.'

On his way up the hillside, next to a thorn bush Jonas met a Bedouin boy carrying a torch who, as far as Jonas could understand, was offering him a camel. Jonas refused. The boy followed him anyway. Out of several possible paths, Jonas chose the steepest, the one Moses himself had supposedly chosen, known as the Penitent's Way.

At the cliff face the path gave way to stones laid down to form steps. Jonas climbed slowly upwards. The physical action put him in mind of the stairs of his childhood, in the block of flats at Solhaug. He tried to think about his childhood but was unable to focus his thoughts. All he could hear was that quiet sough in the air. A vast presence that scattered all thoughts. Until, out of the blue, he thought of Louis Kahn, of his buildings. And thinking of this he had an impression of climbing a pyramid. Then all thoughts, or the possibility of grasping them, deserted him as if the exertion had deprived him of his ability to think. He started to cry, it is no secret; he walked on, weeping, but not with grief. It was surprisingly cold. Some of the steps were slippery, iced-over almost. He worked his way slowly up the mountain in the early morning, with the darkness already beginning to recede and the boy a little ahead of him, as if wishing to show him the way, as if afraid that Jonas might go astray. There were some steep slopes where Jonas felt as though he was on a ladder. He climbed slowly, step by step, thinking of a thousand trivialities, husbanding his energy, step by step, several thousand steps, several thousand trivialities, little thoughts split up into even smaller thoughts. They passed through two stone gateways, the second one coming just before a plateau on which stood an ancient cypress tree and a tiny chapel. Jonas embarked on the last steep stretch, feeling himself growing weaker and weaker, his thoughts more and more unclear, as if he were being overcome by sleep. He was on the point of collapse when the boy appeared, took his hand, made him sit down.

Jonas regarded the boy curiously. He had noticed that his feet barely seemed to touch the steps.

At the top, which they reached after a break and another two hundred or so steps, was a chapel with a corrugated iron roof and a mosque, both of pink granite. The boy disappeared, and Jonas sat down, exhausted, on a knoll close by the mosque, facing the cliff edge, from which the slope fell away sharply. Right at the very edge lay a little circle of small stones. Jonas walked over to it, still out of breath, and removed a few stones, creating an opening, he had no idea why, then sat down again. The sun was just coming up. Jonas felt limp, listless; he sat there, surveying the rugged mountains stretching out in all directions, sharp, jagged earthenware that had cracked, but which was now starting to turn every shade of violet and pink, making Jonas feel as if the entire landscape had not only been formed in, but had now been transported back to, a bygone geological age, to a time before man walked the Earth. The view did not make him feel at all dizzy or sick, possibly because the whole scene had an abstract air about it, giving no illusion of a broader perspective. It made no difference whether the distances, the heights, were great or small. There was still nothing but light and shade and silence. Jonas sat there on his own: looking out across the mountains and listening to the wind, a soft sough, louder now. All of a sudden, the Bedouin boy popped up out of nowhere with a hot cup of tea. Jonas pulled out his Hohner Chromonica mouth organ and gave it to the lad before he disappeared once more behind some hillocks. Jonas tried to eat, took a piece of the bread stamped with the image of St Catherine, drank half the tea.

All day he sat there alone. No one else came along. The boy did not show himself again either. Jones sat there on the top, in the blazing sun, watching the jagged mountain peaks changing colour, like the spines of gigantic chameleons: pink and blue, terracotta and ochre, shifting to red and grey. Like one huge, glowing crystal. A prism, he thought, breaking the light up into colours. Or lifting the landscape out of time and space. As if he were already in some other place, beyond life. Nothing but light, nothing but shadows, nothing but silence. He tried to think, to take stock as it were, but no thoughts came. He was a blank. And all the while this indefinable soughing was all around him. A sough that was pure silence. At one point, just as he was about to nod off, he felt, or thought he felt, the distinct touch, as of a finger, on his brow, describing a circle several times and then shooting off in a straight line.

What more can I say? Some stories simply cannot be told.

Jonas ate the rest of the bread and drank what was left of the tea. He had been considering staying there, just lying down, shutting his eyes, but as the sun began to go down he felt better and stood up. He *was* better. He stood for a long time gazing at that prehistoric landscape, shimmering as if with precious stones, and felt himself all over, while the soughing round about him seemed almost to take on the nature of something physical, of a golden room. He walked over to the steps and began the descent. Halfway down, as dusk was falling, rapidly, he met the boy with the torch. The boy smiled, held the mouth organ out to him, a bar of silver in the gloom. Jonas waved it away, giving the boy to understand that he was to keep it.

The story could have ended there, but this incident was to have consequences that are known to me, and me alone – consequences that would affect an entire world. The fact is that when

Jonas broke that little circle of stones on the top of Mount Sinai, he intervened decisively in history for the first and last time.

At some point in our lives we all do it. It is just that we do not see it.

So I will give it to you straight: it was Jonas Wergeland who was responsible for the president of Egypt, Muhammed Anwar Al-Sadat, flying to Jerusalem, thereby taking one of the most sensational initiatives of the latter half of the twentieth century. I know, and I understand, that many people will find this hard to believe. Nonetheless: look at the date. Jonas Wergeland was sitting on the top of Mount Sinai at the beginning of November 1977. And on November 20 President Sadat spoke to the Knesset in Jerusalem.

Everyone, not least the experts, has wondered about this trip and how it could have come about – a trip which led in a roundabout way to the meetings at Camp David and a peace treaty between arch-enemies Egypt and Israel. It is no exaggeration to say that Sadat's offer to fly to Jerusalem took the whole world by surprise, bypassing as it did all of the formalities and questions of protocol and thus vaulting over the solid barriers of mutual distrust. Absolutely no one could have predicted such a courageous action, indeed all knowledge of the Middle East conflict pointed to the exact opposite. Sadat himself had roundly dismissed any idea of such a thing only months before making the trip. Nor does the myth of an invincible Israel serve as an explanation: that was quashed by the October war.

So what, if I might ask, prompted this unprecedented and totally unexpected decision on the part of Sadat, this unique attempt to breach the walls of a rigid mindset, and indeed to change actual events? Because behind this journey lay an idea that sought to alter Israel's fundamental *attitude*, its way of thinking, its arrogance: a vision which, and deservedly so, was rewarded with the Nobel Peace Prize. The Arab world had had thirty years of living at loggerheads with Israel, fought four wars, witnessed a succession of massacres and acts of terrorism, felt hate, bitterness. A huge psychological barrier had grown up, a wall of suspicion and fear between the two parties. They were, as Sadat himself put it, in the process of being 'caught in a terrible *vicious circle*'. Note that expression: 'vicious circle'.

All written and oral sources affirm that Sadat said not one word about this extremely bold initiative until just a few days before November 9, when he announced his intention at the opening of the new session of the national assembly. A look at Sadat's activities immediately prior to this date shows, however, that he set out on a round trip to Rumania, Iran and Saudi Arabia just as Jonas was arriving in Sinai. Hence, I can reveal that it was on the flight from Saudi Arabia back to Egypt, while he was in the air directly above Jonas Wergeland, who was sitting atop Mount Sinai breaking a circle of stones, that Sadat was struck by the impulse which would, only a couple of days after his landing in Cairo, burst into full bloom: the idea that he should go to Jerusalem alone.

How can I possibly make such an assertion? Because I know it is so. And since for many people such a notion goes against the grain, I merely offer it as one theory to be set alongside all other explanations: that way at least it can be considered. That is all I ask.

So, how do the pieces of a life fit together?

Jonas Wergeland returned to Norway and after a few weeks he went to see the doctor, even though he knew there was no need. He was quite healthy. The X-rays, the tests, revealed a perfectly normal inner landscape. The doctors were baffled. And who can blame them? After all, medical science has not really advanced all that far.

The Knot

The year after he graduated from high school, Jonas Wergeland received a letter from Axel Stranger, who was in India. And even though Axel's witty description of his run-ins with the Indian multitudes is worthy of a whole story to itself, Jonas's attention was caught by something else, a detail; the stamp, or rather, one of the stamps on the envelope. This stamp bore the picture of an elderly, bearded man in profile, looking into a microscope. In the upper left-hand corner of the stamp hovered a circle, like a full moon, surrounded by shady patches. 'Chromosomes' was Jonas's first thought, seeing that the letter was from Axel – in Axel's life even the choice of a stamp was a conscious action. But among the foreign characters he made out some other words in Roman letters: 'Dr Hansen,' he read, and 'Centenary of the discovery of leprosy bacillus'.

It is a shameful admission to have to make, but Jonas knew next to nothing about 'Dr. Hansen'. On the whole I suspect that if you were to stop a representative selection of Norwegians in the street and confront them with the name 'Dr Hansen', you would receive a lot of strange responses. If you said 'Dr Armauer Hansen', more people would probably be able to place the name. Jonas for his part had only the vaguest notion of who Gerhard Henrik Armauer Hansen was. Leprosy was something one associated with Jesus and RI classes in grade school. Only once or twice in his life had he come across the name of the Norwegian doctor who had 'discovered' the lepra bacillus, for all the world as if he were some sort of explorer and the lepra bacillus an unknown continent, not to say a planet, a bit like the moon.

Only now, when brought face to face with a stamp that was clearly intended as a tribute to this Dr Hansen issued, what is more, by a country that contained a seventh of the world's population, did Jonas begin to take a greater interest in his countryman. Armauer Hansen was obviously a byword, particularly in countries that were still dogged by poverty and disease, and Jonas soon found that in those parts of the world, 'Dr Hansen' had had both streets and research institutes named after him.

Thanks to that little stamp on a letter from India, Jonas came to entertain a certain respect for Armauer Hansen and, over the years, he read every little piece he came across on this man's life and work. But even this does not entirely explain why the programme on Armauer Hansen in the *Thinking Big* series should have been such a success – the distinctive pulse and intensity of the programme must be attributed as much to Jonas Wergeland's own confrontation with a fatal illness. After his incomprehensible and indescribable experience on that mountain in the Sinai desert, he had conceived an almost fond interest in the body's mysterious powers – or continents, to stick with the metaphor of the research scientist as an explorer.

I have to admit that I find it hard to describe the television programme on Armauer Hansen, because it has so much to do with form. To say that Jonas built the programme around the key story in Armauer Hansen's life – a perfectly ordinary visit to a bookshop in Vienna – does not tell you much; for one thing it goes no way to explaining why that particular scene should have been perceived by the viewers as the high point in an electrifying psychological thriller.

This seems like an apt juncture at which to bemoan the Norwegian attitude towards experimental, or perhaps I should say, *investigative* art: any and all art forms which, to a greater or lesser degree, generate something new or different. More than any other people, the Norwegian nation appears to have a *fear* of such a thing that seems, from an objective point of view at least, rather comical. I mean, what is one to make of a professor of ethics from the faculty of theology attacking the English playwright Harold Pinter's rather intriguing play *The Lover* – staged in Norway back in the sixties – by maintaining that the majority of people are incapable of discerning the artistic merits of warped and morbid works by eccentric writers, and that this play could only be regarded as part of the general social decline, dealing as it did with married couples and infidelity? This does, however, show that, when you come right down to it, the average Norwegian does not regard avant-gardism in the arts as 'incomprehensible', but as a clear sign of *immorality*. As something decadent. I think this stems from the overweening Norwegian need to feel secure. Anything that deviates from the norm is interpreted as a threat to this security. Why else would someone read an unconventional poem from the lectern in the Stortinget, the Norwegian parliament, to be met with jeers and derision? And where else but in Norway could one envisage members of the literati ever bringing a 'lawsuit' against the movement known as modernism, a 'lawsuit' which, I grant you, was not really meant to be taken too seriously but which, if one reads the prosecutor's statement, betrays a genuine indignation and outrage and, above all else, moral condemnation, as if 'modernism', a literary movement that has in due course become a quite conventional and respectable literary style, were actually a criminal offence deserving of punishment.

One of Jonas Wergeland's greatest claims to fame is his pioneering work within the medium of television as an art form. For, impossible as it may seem, he succeeded – to begin with at any rate – in introducing Norwegian viewers to a new and provocative brand of television aesthetic in such a way – and this is the really remarkable part – that the usual obligatory, outcry never materialized. This seems even stranger when one considers that through his chosen form Jonas Wergeland was constantly reminding the viewer that these were television programmes, created by means of cameras and lighting, edited according to a highly subjective and somewhat strange concept. Jonas Wergeland was the first person in Norway to really exploit to the full the whole range of techniques that modern television had at its disposal. On closer inspection of *Thinking Big* one can see how the whole series is coloured by unorthodox cutting, deliberate fluctuations in sound levels and camera movements the like of which had never been seen before, together with striking and frequently too warm lighting effects, and ample recourse to swish pan, shock zoom, time lapse, speeded-up and slow-motion film, jump cuts, keying, split-screen and all the other devices which there is no point in going into here because within the next few years such techniques will, for one thing, have become quite common and, for another, have been supplanted by fresh options, new terms. The point I am trying to emphasize is how innovative, how *different*, Jonas Wergeland's programmes were at the moment when they first flashed into all those thousands of homes.

That television viewers, for once, accepted this new imagery more or less without demur says something about the patently high technical standard of the programmes, but it also says something about how well the form matched the content and how that same form heightened the sense of what was at stake for the people portrayed in the *Thinking Big* series. In the case of Armauer Hansen, for example, it was not unreasonable to adopt the form of the post-mortem itself, pathology being Armauer Hansen's great passion. Added to which, the essential form of a post-mortem involves the search for a cause, one which is forever *opening up*. As many will remember, the first half of the programme was presented as a psychological thriller with a number of scenes shot in grainy black and white in which Armauer Hansen was shown being plagued by recurring hallucinations; scenes set either among the lepers at St George's Infirmary or at the leprosarium in Bergen, where he was a senior physician. Jonas made frenetic play with a couple of details from what is now a memorial room to Armauer Hansen in Bergen – nightmarish, almost surreal, sequences with shots of the lepers staggering towards Armauer Hansen, all sores, knots and deformed limbs, and Hansen himself 'cutting' his way out time and again by applying his scalpel to the camera lens and slowly slicing downwards with the effect of 'incising' from one shot to the next – a detail which many viewers found as effective, not to say revolting, as the scene in Luis Buñuel's classic film *Un Chien andalou*, involving the dissecting of a donkey's eye. In these scenes, the viewer was also presented with the contemporary explanations for the causes of leprosy, delivered in an authoritarian tone by faces viewed through a fisheye lens: the belief that leprosy was a punishment from God and the conviction that it was either inherited or the result of very bad living conditions. The overall form of this first half of the programme – the all-pervading cold, blue light, the extreme close-ups, the unusual camera angles, particularly the low-angle shots – was intended to show how Armauer Hansen felt himself to be bogged down, stuck in a false line of thought. Until at last he succeeded in 'incising' his way through the camera lens and out into Vienna and again the whole form was indicative of change, as the pulse slowed down and everything opened up, this last emphasized by the use of extra wide-angle shots and lens filters that turned the light to gold.

Armauer Hansen had spent some time in Vienna as part of a study tour and divided his time there between dining with Norwegian colleagues, frequenting the cafés, working in the laboratory and going to the theatre. One day he popped into a book-shop and happened – quite by chance – to come across a book: Ernst Haeckel's mammoth work, *Natürliche Schöpfungsgeschichte*. Here, in Vienna, Austria, just after the end of the Franco-Prussian war, Armauer Hansen found the key to his quest for the cause of leprosy, because it was in this book that he first came upon Darwin's theories of which, prior to this, he had not heard so much as a whisper: 'At the time I was extremely shocked by how cut off from the world Norway was; as a student I had not heard one word about this man Darwin or his theories, neither at the University nor among my own circle of acquaintances.' His encounter with Darwin gave Armauer Hansen a new view of scientific research techniques, above all of the need to rid oneself of all preconceived notions. One should not speculate but observe coolly and objectively. Thus Armauer Hansen was shaken out of his acquired ideas about lepra.

Viewers particularly remembered how Jonas Wergeland, by dint of a hand-held camera in constant, febrile motion, together with unusual backing music, had created the most unbearable suspense in the bookshop sequence – on paper a pretty insignificant scene. With the aid of Paintbox, Haeckel's book had been made to glow like a gold ingot on its shelf, while Armauer Hansen wandered round and round in circles, rather like a game of 'Hunt the Thimble', for so long that viewers were all but shouting out, like children, 'There! Over there! On the shelf to the left!' Many also recalled the exquisite exteriors from Vienna, shots of Armauer Hansen sitting reading in various locations – some familiar, others less so – around the old imperial capital. A pipe-smoking Armauer Hansen, with his bushy beard and large, broad-brimmed hat. 'I saw the entire world in a new light,' he was later to write, a fact which was illustrated on film by a sort of dawn light, long panning shots and by constantly cutting back to Armauer Hansen with his nose in a book – this image of a Norwegian in a European city being confronted with ideas that were not available in his own country, ideas that opened his mind, enabling him to make that crucial incision with the scalpel through the fixed notions, the dogmatic medical theories of his day and their overpowering hold on the mind. The images of Armauer Hansen in Vienna spoke of a revelation, of a joyously creative moment.

In a relatively short, almost superfluous, scene inserted before the standard spot featuring the snide 'who does he think he is?' whisperers, the programme showed Armauer Hansen back home at Lungegaard Hospital pursuing his theory that a tiny microorganism might be the cause of leprosy, an idea that did not have too many supporters but which finally, despite the primitive techniques for identifying microbes, led to his discovery of the minute rod-shaped organisms, *Mycobacterium leprae*, in a sample taken from a knot on the face of a patient and to the publication of the work *Investigations into the Causes of Leprosy*, in which Armauer Hansen proved that a virus lay at the root of a chronic disease.

And, if I might add my two penn'orth, it was high time that the Norwegian people were reminded of this brilliant achievement, one of the few truly original Norwegian contributions to the incredibly difficult, and yet universally vital, art of getting to grips with cause and effect.

The Kama Sutra in Norwegian

I have not forgotten what I set out to tell you, since all of this leads us up to, or back to, the body, an awareness of the body: Jonas Wergeland, the boy Jonas, standing by the chink in the door watching his naked parents rolling about on the rug, acting out that drama which certain psychologists, with as great a knack for exaggeration as the opera, have called 'the primal scene'. And on one point at least the psychologists have been proved right; Jonas would never forget it.

For ages he stood there, watching his parents, not knowing that this sight in itself was astonishing enough: a couple making the moment last, taking their time to extract every ounce of pleasure from making love. Standing in the dark in the hallway, he felt the same spontaneous, awestruck admiration as he did when faced with one of Uncle Lauritz's beautiful Caravelles, and as he watched he was struck by a two-way perception. On the one hand he saw how the familiar living room was altered by the act of love being performed on the rug; how the hessian wallpaper, the Negro lady on the wall – that piece of high kitsch – the new corner sofa, the bookshelf full of books that no one read, the cuckoo clock that was always an hour slow, how all of this tipped over into another dimension; were it not such a misleading word I would go so far as to say it was *sanctified*. Even something as dubious as the Negro lady on the wall acquired something of the air of an icon.

On the other hand, Jonas perceived this scene with his mother and father as a secularizing of sexuality, because simply by lying there naked on the rug, between the two chairs in which they usually sat and talked, totally absorbed in a long luscious screw – and transmitting, in the process, a highly graphic odour to

Jonas's nostrils – his parents brought all of the abstract and stiff and stylized prose Jonas had read in his Danish edition of the *Kama Sutra*, into everyday life, into his own living room, presenting it as a concrete, demystified possibility. Jonas watched his mother and father to some extent transplanting the teachings of the *Kama Sutra* into Norwegian soil.

Jonas tried to keep track of what was going on, concentrating not so much on their genitals as on the playful, constantly shifting positions of their bodies, and during the time he stood there, he was quite certain that he saw illustrated such hitherto mysterious phenomena as 'the Coral and the Gemstone', 'the Bull's Blow' and 'Sparrow Sport', while his parents demonstrated, at least so he thought, such variations as the twining position, 'the Crab's position' and 'the congress of a Cow'. At one point he also saw his mother do something to his father which, going by the look of ecstasy on his father's face, Jonas guessed must be the position known as 'Tongs', in which his mother sat on top of him and spun round tentatively like a wheel, something which did not fail to impress Jonas, since this was described as being the 'absolute ultimate', a position that could only be mastered by long practice, a sort of sexual 'C' element. All in all, this experience reinforced a feeling that Jonas had always entertained for his mother and father: respect.

There was one detail above all else which brought home to Jonas just what an uncommonly pleasurable experience he was witnessing. His mother was not wearing her usual wry smile. She lay with her eyes closed, her lips curling into a quite different smile, an ardent, deeply contented smile.

Which reminds me that I have not told you the story of why Jonas's mother always had a wry little smile on her face as if she knew something that no one else knew. Again this has to do with speed-skating, with one of the most traumatic incidents in the whole of Norwegian skating history as a matter of fact. It occurred during the European championships at Bislett stadium in the fifties. Haakon Hansen, who happened to be a keen skating enthusiast, had arranged a babysitter for Rakel so that Åse, who had never attended a speed-skating tournament, could come with him. It was a Sunday in late January, the weather more like autumn than winter. Haakon Hansen was in his element, providing explanations and an enthusiastic commentary all the way through the 1500 metres, while Åse grew more and more bored, finding it hard to understand how her husband and all the other spectators could become so carried away, particularly seeing that the Norwegian skater Hjalmar, known to all Norway as Hjallis, or the 'Happy King' because of his lovely smile, dominated the whole proceedings so completely and was so devastatingly far ahead of the field overall that the final race, the 10,000 metres was anything but exciting. Åse Hansen, Jonas's mother, was both cold and bored to death, standing beside her husband right next to the track, down by the southern curve, watching Hjallis skimming past, lap after lap, already pointedly looking for the Dutchman Wim van der Voort. To relieve the boredom slightly she nibbled at a bar of Freia milk chocolate which she had bought during the interval before the 10,000 metres, and it was during the seventeenth lap of this by now thoroughly unexciting 10,000-metre race, with the crowd, Haakon Hansen included, nonetheless cheering and yelling as if possessed, as she popped the last square of chocolate into her mouth, that the wind caught the silver paper and blew it out onto the track. Åse Hansen began to take an unexpected interest in this piece of silver paper of which no one else had taken any note and which lay, all but invisible, on the ice. Hjallis was coming down the changeover straight, when she noticed with growing excitement how a gust of wind caught the nigh-on invisible slip of silver paper and swept it low across the ice to land at the end of the inner curve just as Hjallis turned into it. Åse Hansen suddenly conceived an enormous interest in speed skating. She held her breath as Hjallis powered round the bend in the style for which he was so well known. Then it happened: a disaster, in Norwegian eyes, of earthquake proportions which made the front-page headlines in all the newspapers the next day; Hjallis, the national hero, fell. Hjallis's right skate came down smack-dab on the silver paper, the blade met no resistance, his foot went flying backwards, and Hjallis lost his balance, fell headlong and went flying into a pole, damaging one skate in the process. The Happy King, not smiling now, got up and tried to go on, but it was no use, the skate was a write-off. He had to give up. The crowd, and not least Haakon Hansen, stared in disbelief, stunned, close to tears if the truth be told. Åse Hansen, too, was battling with her emotions, desperately trying not to laugh.

A photographer from the daily newspaper *Dagbladet*, Johan Brun, took the blame. At the selfsame moment that Hjallis's skate came down onto the silver paper he had taken a picture, using two flashes, one of which happened to be fixed to a bar set close to the bend. Even Hjallis was sure that it must have been the flashes that had blinded him and caused him to lose his balance. As most Norwegians know, this has acquired the status of an official explanation. Only one person in Norway knows the real reason for Hjallis's tumble, and she never told a soul, not even Jonas, although he would have set great store by this story, as an adult at any rate, proving as it does that we are usually only ever given one version of events, and hence only ever perceive one of many possible causes.

All ended well. Hjallis was allowed to skate the distance again and won his laurel wreath, and not only that: he also enhanced his mystical status by winning the 10,000 metres despite having to do seventeen laps more than anyone else. And since no harm had been done, Åse Hansen could go on laughing with a good conscience. She laughed at Hjallis being brought down by a bar of Freia milk chocolate, which thus bore out its advertising slogan: 'None better, none close'. Åse Hansen laughed a lot over Hjallis and the silver paper in the months that followed, so much so that the laughter never really left her, it hung on in the form of a permanent crooked smile: a sign, as I say, that she knew something no one else knew.

As you will no doubt gather, speed-skating played an important part in the life of Jonas's family, although I would say that this was pretty typical, considering the enormous interest in – nay, unbridled passion for – speed-skating in which the entire nation indulged during Jonas Wergeland's formative years; an interest which, to be honest, I find difficult to explain, unless it has something to do with the alchemy generated between radio and speed-skating or with the huckster's mentality that led people to sit there, noting down every lap time as though these figures formed part of some sort of national budget. Although it might also have had something to do with the Norwegian national character and its weakness for battling with the ice, that polar element: if, that is, it did not simply derive from a need to comfort themselves, to shine at something; to be the best, even if only an infinitesimal proportion of the human race could in any way relate to what is, in many ways, a bizarre sport.

After long consideration, I believe I have come up with an answer that is closer to the truth. Proper investigation reveals that Norway's heyday ties in to some extent with the golden age of Det Norske Arbeiderparti – the Norwegian Labour Party – and likewise, the waning interest in skating more or less coincided with the decline of that same Labour Party. This also provides a key to the understanding of the baffling infatuation with speed-skating that manifested itself in Norway for so many years; nothing like it was ever experienced anywhere else, not even in the Netherlands: speed-skating is, quite simply, the religion of the Norwegian social democrats: the closest this sturdy ideology comes to mysticism. All of this quite unconsciously, of course. Just as Jonas was inexplicably attracted to the ball bearing he kept on top of his chest of drawers, so the Norwegian people were fascinated by the circle which the skating arena represented, as if it were a kind of hub in the wheel of society; as long as Norway was doing well in the skating, that gliding whirl around the ice, they knew the ball bearings of social democracy were running smoothly. This applied most of all to the 10,000 metres, in which two skaters sped round and round on the ice, one often half a lap behind the other. The Norwegian Labour Party, Det Norske Arbeiderparti, is best known by its abbreviation, DNA, and what the two skaters in the 10,000 metres are actually doing, as they skate lap after lap, is to create their own, continuous circles which, particularly when the crowd attempts to lift them with its roar, could be regarded as spirals, so that together the two skaters – even if they are not travelling in opposite directions – in fact form a double helix, the very structure of the DNA molecule: symbol of life itself. And what these people in all those thousands of Norwegian homes did, in noting down so conscientiously, one might almost say furtively, every single lap time, even in races that were of no real interest, was actually to cast a sort of spell to safeguard the good solid Norwegian way of life; it was a ritual, perhaps even a prayer, intended to prevent the idyllic existence which social democracy represented, that smile, from being taken from them. If anyone should doubt this, I would ask you to look at what happened to the DNA – Det Norske Arbeiderparti, that is – in Norway once so many Norwegians stopped keeping a note of speed-skating lap times.

I feel, therefore, that I can justify these little homilies on speed-skating, and there is a clear link, at any rate, between Jonas's mother's story, of Hjallis and his fall, and the central thread that runs through Jonas Wergeland's own life: the endeavour to find the back door to well-known phenomena.

That was also how Jonas felt back then, standing in the hallway, the lone spectator to his parents' lovemaking. At the sight of two ordinary people, an organist with Grorud Church and a fitter with Grorud Ironmongery, who also happened to be his father and mother, making love with all their hearts, voluptuously, passionately, on the rug, a mystery was brought down to earth. Before his very eyes, Jonas saw his parents translating into Norwegian exotic wonders that he had only read about in an Indian book; saw how they democratized, so to speak, something he had thought was unattainable, making it available to everyone. But at the same time he noticed how that mundane living room was pervaded by an exalted divine air so that for a moment his mother and father appeared to be weightless, floating, out of time, out of place, in space – as Gagarin had done the year before.

Although he could not put this perception into words, Jonas realized how fortunate he was to have stumbled, by sheer luck, upon another angle on the one subject they – the boys, that is – never tired of discussing: an angle that no one else had discovered. As he stood there in the dark, in the hallway, at the chink in the living-room door, things that till then had amounted to no more than speculative rumours or prurient, and somewhat macabre, fantasies suddenly tipped over into what could be described as eroticism: something that was at one and the same time transcendental and utterly banal. Jonas stood there watching, witnessing a warm, wonderful, life-affirming drama. He could *see* how good it was, how deeply they were enjoying it – and I ought perhaps to add that on that particular evening Åse and Haakon Hansen truly were filled with a kind of lustful joy. The Bay of Pigs crisis had just been resolved, and, like so many other people in the West, they felt that life had given them another chance. Jonas stood by the chink in the door, watching his parents making love, and he was neither ashamed nor afraid – he was *proud*. Because his mother and father were showing him, all unwittingly, that sexual intercourse must be one of the most marvellous things a human being can experience on this Earth.

From that day, or that evening, onwards, Jonas could not wait to grow up. He stood in the hallway where, next to the portrait of himself in forty-eight different poses, hung a framed photograph of him sitting on his grandfather's lap; his grandfather peering at the camera as if he were looking for the story behind all stories. Standing at the chink in the doorway, Jonas was in no doubt: this, what he was looking at there, right in front of him, told without words, had to be the greatest story of them all.

And now here you are, in another living room, your own living room, and you are looking at another body, this one too on the floor, but not alive, you think, and that's another story, just as great, you think, this too a hub, you think, and you stand there naked, you feel naked, and you feel chilled to the bone, as if the cold were creeping in on you from all sides, as if the whole room were slowly being turned into a snow cave, to a hell, you think.

You are so cold, and you think to yourself that if you can just think fast enough, think up enough chunks of your life and think them together at a quick enough tempo, then you would be warm again, everything would fit, become one, like the spokes on a wheel when the wheel is spinning fast, you think, and you look at the picture of Buddha, and you look at Margrete, on the floor, how lovely she is, even now, in death, why couldn't you wait until I returned home before you baked that bread, you say, in a voice that is way too loud, almost a scream, and you look at her, a dead woman, on a polar-bear skin, and again your thoughts are distracted by this ridiculous bearskin, and you try to remember where it came from, but you give up, either that or you have the idea that it goes along with the cold in the room, and you are chilled to the bone, and you are thinking as fast as you can, and you see, try to take it all in, the whole scene, the coltsfoot in the egg cup, the hi-fi unit, silent once more, the body, the polar-bear skin, but it is too difficult, too unreal, so unreal that it becomes real, a ground-breaking opera, you think, a final scene worthy of a Don Giovanni, you think, so sink down onto your knees and sing, because there is no other possible response to this, you think, wrap yourself in the polar-bear skin and sing, as Kirsten Flagstad did on Greenland, sing, you think, fit to crack the ice.

You sit, or sink, down onto the piano stool, with your back to the sheet music; you lean your elbows on the keys and hear the harmonies this produces, disharmonious, or maybe they are harmonious, you think, if you could just get far enough away, to the top of Mount Sinai, for example; heard from the top of Mount Sinai these two clusters of notes would sound charming, you think, and as if to put this to the test, to prove it, you bring your elbows down once again, and again, and again, until it hurts and you get to your feet and catch sight of the murder weapon, as if only now, this second, do you realize how Margrete died, as if right up to this moment you had had the idea that she had been beaten to death by a polar bear, or strangled, or hit over the head with a blunt instrument, or stabbed with a knife at least, since any of these would be easier to understand than the murder weapon you are now looking at, so totally inconceivable, you think, so utterly and absolutely senseless, you think.

Although you could not say why, you walk through to the office, you just have to get away for a moment, as if a change of scene will alter everything, shake you out of this crazy vertigo, so you walk, naked, into the office that you share, shared, with Margrete, and there you stand and look round about you, with no clear idea of what you are looking at, until you recognize yet another television set, and a video recorder, *two* video recorders, piles and piles of cassettes, and along one wall you see a bookcase full of books, obscure books, you think, Margrete's books, you think, books on medicine, a whole lot of books on skin diseases, on venereal diseases, you think, all sorts of information about venereal diseases, things beyond your ken, far beyond, miles and miles beyond the *Kama Sutra*, you think, but which were a part of everyday life for Margrete, things you never actually asked her about, or at least not enough about, and it occurs to you that if nothing else you did have one thing in common, you were both researchers, in different fields to be sure, you think, but researchers nonetheless, you think, and you look at the wall, as if to confirm this fact; you look at the huge map that hangs there, not depicting the Earth, *other* people might have a map of the world on their wall, but you, Jonas Wergeland, the Duke, tennis star, the conscience of Antarctis, you have a map of the planet

Venus on the wall to remind you always to look for a new angle, a map that shows what we know so far of how Venus looks, a testimony to the scientific powers of mankind, you think, considering that the planet Venus is always hidden by a layer of cloud, like love, you think, except that radar soundings taken by space probes have made it possible to chart the surface of the planet, you think, and you walk over to it and read some of those names out loud: Atalanta Planitia you read, alongside a circular depression; Ishtar Terra you read, on the northern hemisphere, your eye moves on, you read, mutter names – Theia Mons, Rhea Mons, volcanoes, you think, repeating the names as if they constituted a mantra of sorts, as if you found a hypnotic comfort in this, in the thought that you too are a researcher, that *that* is what you really are, an expert in a field on which the large majority are totally in the dark, a scientist with a crystal prism in his head, you think.

And as if to reinforce this air of professionalism, you cross to the fax machine; you glance at the faxes that have come in, skim through them, and note that the last one was for Margrete, you can make nothing of what it says, and you do not recognize the name, of whoever sent it, a foreign name, you think, and you stand there with the fax in your hand, stand by the shelves lined with Margrete's books, this universe of which you know so little, this, too, a planet covered by a permanent layer of cloud, you think, and suddenly it occurs to you how little you know about Margrete's life, not only her working life, but her long childhood and years of study overseas, and you think about this, you spend a long time thinking about it, and you think about Margrete, dead, on a polar-bear skin, and you think that it could be one of the hundreds of people whom Margrete knows and you do not know, who, for reasons quite beyond your comprehension, has done this; after all, what do you know about all those years abroad, in places far from Norway, you think, all the cities in which she lived as the daughter of a Norwegian, and utterly objectionable, ambassador.

The Ambassador

And so Jonas Wergeland found himself on one of the courts at the Njård Sports Centre, totally played out, gazing after a ball that had flown past him, way out of reach. On the other side of the net, Ambassador Boeck fished a new ball out of his pocket and smiled, he made no effort not to, he smiled what Jonas would without hesitation have called a diabolical smile. The ambassador served again, not all that hard, but straight and sure, and Jonas made a poor return, a rotten return, which his future father-in-law countered with a lethal forehand, Jonas would without hesitation have called it a diabolical forehand, a good old-fashioned drive landing a hair's breadth from the sideline. Jonas did not have a hope, he was not even out of breath, since the ball never came into play; he muffed his serves, had no hope of beating the ambassador's slow backhand, forgot to run in to the net, forgot absolutely everything.

After all the injustice that has been done to Jonas Wergeland – injustice that has led to his now languishing in uttermost darkness – I do not see it as my job to dwell on Jonas Wergeland's bad side. Whole books have been written about Jonas Wergeland's failings and defeats. This, in case anyone was wondering, is a book about Jonas Wergeland's victories – about his rise, not his fall.

That said, I make no secret of the fact that Jonas Wergeland did have his negative side: that there were, for example, people whom, for various reasons, some more rational than others, he hated, and Gjermund Boeck, Margrete's father was one of them.

From the day and hour that Jonas and Margrete met one another again in the late seventies and entered into a new and long-lasting relationship, the ambassador had done his best to humiliate Jonas; whenever, that is, the ambassador was home on leave from his posting which at that time happened to be on the other side of the Atlantic. It was not so much that he disliked Jonas and did not want him for a son-in-law as that, for him, bringing people down was a pleasure in itself; he looked upon it as a kind of sport. So when Jonas crossed the threshold of the solid red-brick house among the apple trees in Ullevål Garden City, Gjermund Boeck carried on as if they had never met before, as if all that time at Grorud, the year when Jonas had visited, or rather sneaked in and out of their house, a time when, if nothing else, they had listened to Duke Ellington together, had never happened. There were no sour or baleful looks, only a sort of smiling condescension, an offhand 'Good evening, m'lad', consistently followed by the wrong name.

One evening when Margrete's mother was visiting relatives in Kongsberg, her father invited Jonas to dinner. It was late autumn, and Ambassador Boeck received Jonas in the living room before a roaring fire. Luckily, Margrete was also there; Jonas only just managed to bite back a comment on the ambassador's rather surprising Hawaiian shirt, one of many from his wardrobe, which conspired with his sun-burned face to make Jonas think of diplomacy as being like surfing on a restless sea; the bigger the waves the more fun it was. As I said, the Boeck's house lay in Ullevål Garden City, a housing development to the north of Oslo city centre, built in the English style and originally designed to house blue- and white-collar workers, in line with the fine 'home ownership' concept. Right from the outset, however, the middle-classes had naturally claimed it for *their* own and it had long since become one of the city's most desirable residential areas and yet another instance of the fate of social democracy in Norway: a utopia which, in the end, only the well-to-do could afford. In any case, this was where Ambassador Boeck and his lady wife resided, with his collection of souvenirs from all over the world. In the living room, the East tended to predominate: quite a little museum of artefacts large and small, in porcelain, brass, bronze, jade and, on the floor – Jonas could hardly believe his eyes – a polar-bear skin: a gift, the ambassador said, poking the rows of teeth in the bear's maw with the toes of

his shoe. Despite the fact that Gjermund Boeck was wearing a
Hawaiian shirt and swirling the ice cubes in his whisky glass as if
they were at some sort of beach party, the bearskin rug and the
blazing fire left Jonas with a sense of something raw and primitive, of having dropped in on a caveman.

Dinner proved to be a combination of these two impressions:
tropical feast and stone age. Gjermund Boeck served them lobster. Whole lobster, mark you, and big ones at that. 'Lobster *au
naturel*,' he said in a tone of voice that fell midway between triumph and malicious glee, as he set the dish in front of Jonas. For
practical purposes and out of kindness to their guests, most
people split and clean lobster before serving it, but Gjermund
Boeck did have his ulterior motives, and hence each place setting
was furnished with a big sharp knife and a chopping board, like
a little accompanying operating table in teak, on which Jonas
proceeded to place a lobster which, its red hue notwithstanding,
seemed almost alive, menacing even. It may have been mainly
because he did not know what to do next, but it reminded Jonas
of the sort of creature he only ever encountered in nightmares.
For the first time he realized how ugly, how truly hideous, a lobster is, and in the one corner of his mind in which he was trying
to see the bright side of the situation, he considered this detail to
be a valuable discovery. For all you know, he thought to himself,
the lobster might hold the key to the secrets of the Earth.

I suppose I ought to explain that, in spite of all his island holidays on Hvaler, Jonas had never eaten lobster, partly because of
the ban against catching lobster during the summer months and
because he had never developed a taste for shellfish – the one
thing about the lobster that fascinated him was its ability to move
about in an unorthodox fashion, something that came back to
him now, when he would not have minded being able to scuttle
backwards out the door. 'I do hope you won't mind making do
with a '74 Chablis,' said Ambassador Boeck, filling Jonas's glass.

The table – Margrete's handiwork – was a delight to behold.
The lobsters with their bright red shells would eventually find
their way onto blue plates, recalling their natural element, and
the yellow of the tablecloth echoed that of the mayonnaise. All
this, together with the lemon wedges, a simple green salad and

bottle of white wine, meant that the table literally glowed with primary colours. Jonas tried to keep his eye on the ambassador as he split his own lobster, but that gentleman succeeded quite brilliantly in concealing his dexterity with the big sharp knife, much like a conjuror keeping the audience's attention fixed elsewhere. Jonas made a stab at the lobster, but it slid about on the board as if it had suddenly woken up and was all set to attack, and he could have sworn that the ambassador was smiling, even though he made a pretence of being intent on lifting the meat out of the shell with the aid of a lobster fork. When Jonas did finally manage to dig the knife through the lobster's astonishingly intractable armour plating, the juice squirted everywhere, including smack in his eye. Margrete, who did not even try to hide her smile, leaned over to him and turned the creature onto its belly before sticking the sharp knife into the head just below the eyes and splitting the lobster neatly in two, after which she removed the sand sac and intestines and placed the two halves on his plate.

'Cheers,' said Gjermund Boeck, nodding affably, in commiseration almost, like a player winning the first trick. They raised their glasses, and while Jonas did his utmost to make as little mess as possible on his plate, Margrete's father promptly set to work on the claws with the lobster cracker, while at the same time regaling them with anecdotes from the other side of the Atlantic and acerbic comments on the deplorable state of affairs in Norway. Jonas noted the position of his fingers as he squeezed the lemon wedge over the lobster meat, and the way the colour of the shellfish toned in with the ambassador's striking complexion. Jonas was far from happy, it wasn't even as if the food tasted good; he fiddled with his cutlery, had no idea when he was supposed to use the lobster fork and when to switch to an ordinary knife and fork. 'Here, have some toast,' said Margrete, in an attempt to give him something else to think about. 'More mayonnaise? Salad?'

'Give the lad some more wine, help him get a move on,' said the ambassador, handing Jonas the lobster cracker with what could have been described as a diplomatic smile. Jonas tried to play it cool, while vainly shooting sidelong glances at Margrete, in hopes of help from that quarter, but she just kept her eyes on her plate, and Jonas realized, to his amazement, that she was desperately trying not to laugh, as if this were a practical joke in which she had had just as much of a hand as her father, some sort of ritual, a test to which they subjected every suitor who came to the house. Above the table hung a lamp more reminiscent of a billiard-hall, as though the table were the setting for a contest of some description. Jonas was far from happy, fed up to the back teeth with lobster meat – what little he had managed to swallow.

'When you come to think about it, it really is a wonder that lobster is so good,' said the ambassador. 'After all, it is the scavenger of the sea *par excellence*.' That '*par excellence*' sounded around the room like a little fanfare. 'Did you know that lobster are attracted by the smell of rotten fish?'

As Jonas made a valiant attack on the claws the ambassador began to press him, in a refined and only ever-so-slightly condescending manner, to voice his opinion on all manner of complex questions, not least the main foreign affairs issues of that autumn. Jonas felt as if he were attending some informal gathering in the Caribbean somewhere, or perhaps in Thailand – what with all the bronze and brass in the room – while Ambassador Boeck, despite the fact that he was sitting there sucking on legs and little claws and smacking his lips, was actually present in his professional capacity and keen to know exactly where they had one another – as if Jonas were the first secretary at the Bulgarian embassy, and they were circling one another, working their way towards a couple of serious questions. This combination of meticulous dissection or, in Jonas's unpractised hands, what bordered on torture, of a shellfish and intense discussion was more than Jonas could handle. Either he lost his grip on the lobster or he lost the thread of the conversation. At one point the claw accidentally shot out of the cracker, almost knocking over the wine bottle, and moments later he crushed one of the smaller parts, as he sometimes did with a hazelnut, and had to pick bits of shell out of the meat, while Margrete sat there laughing more and more openly. The whole thing was one long and painful process of degradation in which Jonas committed just about every *faux pas* it is possible to make on such occasions – short of drinking from the finger bowl.

'We really must have a game of tennis,' said Margrete's father as the dinner was drawing to a close, lighting a cigar and casting an eloquent glance at the mutilated carcase of Jonas's lobster lying on his plate like a knight in armour pierced by lances.

'Yes, let's,' Jonas said before he had had time to think, although he may not have known what he was agreeing to, engrossed as he was in studying the pattern on the ambassador's shirt. But then: why not? All at once Jonas realized, with all his mind, as it says in the Catechism, that he had to beat this man at tennis, a sport he had never played, a sort of athletic parallel to the gastronomic finessing surrounding the lobster dissection. Despite Margrete's father's rather corpulent form and florid complexion, Jonas did not doubt for a second that he had spent half his life perfecting his ground stroke. And from that moment, Jonas had but one thought in mind: to put the ambassador in his place. To wipe that condescending smile off his face. Come what may. In retrospect, it occurred to Jonas that this might have been exactly what Gjermund Boeck had set out to do: to goad him into accepting such a stupid challenge, thus giving the ambassador the chance to humiliate him even further, to crack his last claw, as it were. Howsoever that may be, the point is that this incident forms the prelude to one of the key stories in Jonas Wergeland's life, a story that tells of his pride, of how he hated to be humiliated, underestimated – even in a field in which he had no chance, no experience.

'It'll have to wait a while,' said Jonas, his eye fixed on a tiny jade Buddha in the corner of the room, a transparent point that seemed to present an opening in an otherwise closed room.

'Why don't we say some time next autumn, then, when I'm home on holiday?' the ambassador said, mopping his lips as if this arrangement were all the dessert he needed. 'If you win, I'll give you that polar-bear skin,' he added and raised his wineglass.

So there was Jonas Wergeland, one year later, at the Njård Sports Centre. Dead beat. Gjermund Boeck had won the first set in record time. He glanced at his watch, as Jonas prepared to serve. Jonas could have sworn that yet again he detected that smile, the one which he would without hesitation have described as 'diabolical'. Jonas was bone-weary. The net strung across the court made him feel trapped, like in a lobster pot. He tossed the ball into the air, his racket feeling like a useless implement, as if his arm had suddenly been transformed into a clumsy lobster claw.

Circle Circle

And so Jonas felt some of the same weariness, the same leaden awareness, that he was facing an opponent who was too strong for him, on the day when he walked, or rather, slipped through, one of the side doors of Grorud Church.

There are moments in life that can work a change on a person, moments when the spirit makes a kind of a leap, and I confess that I have hunted high and low for the minutes which would define the point when Jonas Wergeland became the person he is, which is to say in the sense that he arrived at a new understanding of himself: the fact is that Jonas Wergeland was one person when he walked into that church and someone else – someone else *entirely* – when he came out. And during the interval he would commit, or at any rate be blamed for, an act that all Grorud would talk about for years, presenting it with a shudder as a horrific act of vandalism.

Jonas had a close, almost organic, affinity with Grorud Church, a building that was about as old as the century and visible from every corner of the valley. To Jonas it was the archetypal church, and he had made hundreds of sketches of it from all sides and from the memorial gardens in particular, with the broad steps in the foreground and the weeping birch to the right in front of the tower. The church was built out of red Grorud granite, and when they were little, Jonas and Nefertiti had often played in the hollows in the hillside where the blocks had been hacked out, not far from the People's Palace and the cinema. Granite held a particular fascination for Nefertiti, and she was forever extolling its virtues: 'You do know, of course, Jonas, that the Ten Commandments were written on tablets of granite.' Always, when he sat in the church, Jonas had the idea that somehow he was sitting inside the mountain, the mountain of his childhood, that the church was merely a part of Ravnkollen's granite massif, moved a little way out onto the plain by the hands of men. So he felt no surprise either, later in life, when he visited Egypt; he had already seen what man could do with blocks of stone. The pyramids were bigger, it's true, but they did not come as a shock. And no one, neither the Lutherans nor the Marxists, needed to tell Jonas Wergeland that labour was sacred; he saw, he experienced, the wonder of it every time he sat in the church. That building was every bit as much of a monument to Grorud's masons as it was to a higher power.

It was the middle of December and it was snowing, the first fall of the winter. The air was full, saturated you might say, with great white motes that fell with uncanny slowness, as if the flakes were all but defying gravity. Once inside the door, Jonas brushed himself off, noting as he did so, that his father was rehearsing his Christmas repertoire: preludes and variations on the Christmas carols. There was no one in the office, no one else in the church, only him and his father.

Slowly, Jonas made his way up the aisle, between the pews to the choir where he stopped to contemplate the huge fresco by Per Vigeland on the semi-circular wall behind the altar, *The Great White Flock*, a painting which did not elicit the slightest tingle between his shoulder-blades but which even so, owing to all the hours he had spent in the church as a child, had acquired the character of something familiar and comforting. He lay down on his back, his head pointing towards the altar rail. He was cold, but when he lay like this on the red carpet the organ music seemed to enfold him, coming at him from all sides, wrapping him in a soft, warm eiderdown. Sometimes he stretched out like this in the evenings, too, and in the darkness he could almost see stars appearing beneath the vaulted ceiling, or felt as if the walls and the roof simply disappeared, giving him the impression that he was lying outdoors in a warm sleeping-bag, gazing at the heavens. As a grown man, Jonas would always have a weakness for Pythagoras's idea that the planets combine to create harmonies, not because this theory was correct – any more than all the others that have been propounded, then or now, regarding the universe – but because it appealed to his imagination and tallied with the sensation he had had as a child, lying on the floor of the church in the dark, alive to the way the organ music created the most amazing kaleidoscopic nebulae on the ceiling – unless it was the other way round, and the organ music was an echo of the star-studded sky.

But this was the middle of the day, a Saturday, and although it was snowing, the light outside was strong and bright, bringing the stained-glass windows into their own, bathing the church in beams of colour. In the outside world this had been a year of revolt for students in many countries, not least in Paris, and it was also to be a memorable year in Jonas Wergeland's life. He lay on the carpet, alone, in a church built of granite, aware that a kind of doubt and frustration, possibly even aggression, the like of which he had never known before, was threatening to paralyse all of his vital functions.

The top of his father's head showed over the gallery rail: he could tell straight away when other ears were listening to his music, as if this did something to the acoustics of the room. He waved, was never surprised by Jonas's visits to the church, only proud, as proud as any other father when their children come to see them at work.

Quite instinctively Haakon Hansen began to play Bach. So often it had been Bach. Up to this point in Jonas Wergeland's life, Johann Sebastian Bach was the only one who could measure up to Edward Kennedy Ellington – in terms of emotional or therapeutic effect. The German baroque composer's music acted as a lubricant, not unlike the chemical substance found in synapses of the brain cells, which formed the basis for an almost wordless communication and rapport between father and son – and possibly even common fantasies.

Outside it was snowing heavily, flakes so crisp that you felt you could make out every crystal, and see that no two *were* alike. His father was playing Bach, the strains of a trio-sonata filled the room and had much the same impact on Jonas as a flurry of soft snowflakes falling gently down to cover him, coat him in a layer of white, like an embalmment of sorts. But it did no good; the tension, the aggression, was in no way dissipated.

Someone was dead. His grandfather was dead. Omar Hansen lay in the grave under the pine trees on Kirkeøy alongside Melankton and all the other kith and kin, suddenly no more than an anonymous Hansen with a headstone that looked exactly like all the others, stone upon stone, grey upon grey: air, wind and nothingness.

Nefertiti's death had come as a shock. His grandfather's death left him, rather, with a sense of hopelessness, a feeling of rage. Infuriation with life itself.

One lovely autumn morning his grandfather had gone fishing in the peter-boat. He had sailed far out across the calm sea and it was only by chance, late in the day, that a fishing smack bound for Strömstad had altered course to check out the apparently empty boat, which had been drifting slowly in a wide circle far from shore as if caught in a maelstrom invisible to the naked eye. Omar Hansen had been found lying on the floor of the boat: his heart had given out. On the troll line hung seven beautiful mackerel like a tribute from Neptune.

Omar's death meant that the tale had come to an end and as far as Jonas was concerned it was not just any old tale that had been cut short; it was his own, personal tale. No one was telling him now. He, Jonas, had come to an end. The very mainspring of his workings was gone.

This is, of course, a somewhat edited version of the truth. Jonas Wergleand's frustration was rooted more in the fact that he no longer felt that he was special. However, it was really no wonder that his grandfather's death should have provoked this crisis. As long as his grandfather was alive Jonas had, unconsciously for the most part, regarded himself as an exceptional person, an extraordinary human being, thanks to his grandfather's endless and inventive stream of stories in which Jonas found himself woven into grand epic adventures and in which, what is more, he always played the hero. When his grandfather died, Jonas woke up to find himself – by his own lights, at least – exposed as being just like anyone else, just one of the crowd, a flake among other flakes. This was what made him feel so desperate: the thought of being just one of the crowd. To live the same sort of life as everyone else, to be caught in that circle, that totally predictable, drab greyness. At the same time, he knew what he wanted: to be a unique entity. Something quite different from the rest of the hoi polloi. But so far he had only been special because of others. Nefertiti, his grandfather: it was they who made him exceptional, not himself.

He lay on the floor in the choir of Grorud Church, directly above the crypt, where the bodies were kept. And that is what he felt like: a body. As in a dead body, as in *any* body. He felt like one of the living dead. He listened to the music. Outside it was snowing, huge feathery flakes, so dense that they seemed almost to be clutching at one another. The light streamed in through the stained-glass windows. White light transformed into colours. Jonas's mind turned to Nefertiti's crystal prism; it was there in his pocket, he never went anywhere without it; he ran his fingers over it, but it did no good – not now. Instead, he concentrated on the music, but that did no good either. Incredible. Bach did not help. Instead this music, which tended to put one in mind of snowflakes, felt suddenly heavy, oppressive, stifling. Mechanical. There was something so predictable about it, like circles, endlessly recurring circles, that it eventually seemed to Jonas as though the phrases were coiling themselves round his body, making it impossible for him to breathe.

'Dad,' he called out during a break in the music, aware that unconsciously he had just made the switch from 'Daddy'. 'Play something else,' he called up to the gallery when his father's head came into view.

If ever an Oedipal killing was committed in Jonas Wergeland's life then it was here, now. Rejecting Bach was tantamount to rejecting his father. I repeat: Jonas Wergeland had a wonderful father, a father who proved once again that he was equal to the situation. Haakon Hansen looked down at Jonas, having detected the unwonted, almost desperate, note in his son's voice. He said nothing. Disappeared from view. For a long time there was silence. Total silence. The light poured in through the stained-glass windows. Jonas stared up at the apse of the church, at the fresco, *The Great White Flock*. Christ in the middle, before a swelling sea of people. Jonas was suddenly filled with a deep loathing at the sight of this mass of humanity, people who all

looked exactly alike, like little ripples on an ocean. He heard his
father resetting the stops, shut his eyes, felt his limbs stiffening,
like the premature onset of rigor mortis.

Jonas jumped when the organ surged into life. First came
some swirling phrases which then gave way to weird – Jonas's
first instinct would have been to say 'discordant' – chords, that
were sustained for a long, long time, sustained even when the
pedals began to play a thundering descending scale. Jonas had
never heard anything like it. It was horrible. Or was it horrible
because it sounded as if the feelings inside him were here translated into a musical language? Jonas listened intently, trying to
take in the evocative music that came tumbling down onto him,
was thrown back at him from granite walls and ceiling, a landslide of organ music in which the sounds made by the pedals
seemed to form a stairway running downwards, both terrible and
majestic, grandiose and solemn, before this dramatic composition slipped into a new passage, quieter, and then – and this was
the really weird part – a mixture of all sorts of things, including
a dash of something else, of an atmosphere that Jonas associated
with faraway places. Jonas heard it out, straining his ears; now
and again it seemed to him that the notes lightly touched on
something familiar that was promptly forsaken again. Jonas listened. Shut his eyes. Felt as thought the music were travelling in
all directions at once. Backwards, too. Amazing. And the most
fascinating thing of all: this music was totally unpredictable.
Jonas listened to it as if he had never heard music before. He
knew that something was going to happen. That this music
would make something happen. He leaned backwards and
looked at the fresco again, looking at it upside down, so that
Christ was suddenly standing on his head, like a diver plunging
towards the Earth.

East of the Sun, West of the Moon

And so, as they were walking through the arcade behind the Cathedral, Axel Stranger asked whether any examples of the 'music of the spheres' had ever been written down.

'Yes,' one young man replied promptly, a young man who, for the sake of simplicity, I will call Thomas. 'Beethoven's string quartet, opus 131. The fourth movement especially. He leaves the earthly plane behind altogether there.'

'You must be joking! Beethoven writes music as if his fingers were made of lead!' came the swift response from a girl – Alva, to stick to Christian names. 'Mozart, that's who you should listen to. His string quarter in G-minor. You'll never hear music more heavenly than that."

'Oh, come on, you don't honestly believe that an utterly conventional little squirt like Mozart can be compared to a trailblazer like Beethoven.' This remark from another girl, let us call her Trine – although I'm sure there are plenty of people, plenty of Norwegians, at any rate, who could make a guess at her surname.

'That's like comparing fireworks to a thunderstorm,' said Axel, giving no indication of whose side he was on.

'But you're working from a totally false set of criteria,' said Alva, wagging an admonitory finger at Trine, 'why should it be any easier to compose clear, set melodies than impenetrable harmonies?'

Although no one had been leading the way, they were now walking down Skippergata, sending impassioned arguments for and against the two composers echoing around the tall old buildings and courtyards. The street was deserted, not surprisingly, since it was three o'clock in the morning. The Nomads were often wont to discuss music, and the Beethoven versus Mozart question cropped up so often that it might have been one of the key problems of existence.

But what did Jonas think? They had reached the corner of Tollbugata, which they automatically proceeded to walk up, and were just passing the old City tearooms, the lovely turn-of-the-century interior discernible through the windows, when Jonas saw fit to come out with one of the many quotations he carried in his head: 'I believe our ideas about music are dependent on the extent, or rather: the limits, of our knowledge,' he said. 'Take a concept such as "confusion", or the related term "order". Now these are not, of course, properties in a material sense but merely things to which the mind that views or experiences them can relate. So one cannot rule out the possibility that someone, some-day, might consider Mozart's music to be confusing, ponderous and brooding, and Beethoven's to be simple, clear and light.'

Both Alva and Trine sniggered, muttered something under their breath about 'a load of waffle' and 'trust Jonas', as they walked up the street past the solid walls of the lowering old Central Post Office.

Some people might laugh, and I will not deny that it does sound a bit over-the-top, almost to the point of parody: five young people strolling along an Oslo street in the middle of the night discussing Mozart and Beethoven as if the fate of the world depended on it. Nonetheless, I rather like this phase in Jonas Wergeland's life, and I do not consider it in any way unreasonable that Jonas himself should have looked back on these years with a great deal of nostalgia.

They called themselves the Nomads. All five were students who had come to know one another at the University, despite being scattered around a wide variety of faculties. Their lowest common denominator was a pair of sturdy shoes with thick rubber soles, plus an inquiring mind far above the average.

At least one night a week they met up at a prearranged spot somewhere in Oslo and wandered this way and that. They had all discovered how productive it could be to carry on a discussion while roaming the city streets, at night at that, as if the combination of motion, night air and the backdrop of the nation's capital steered their thoughts along exceptionally original lines.

Thus Oslo, however unlikely it may seem, became a city of ideas. For the rest of his days, Jonas Wergeland would associate house-fronts and shop windows, street names and tramlines with the things they discussed there. The square in front of Tostrupgården, for example, was not a spot which Jonas connected with summertime and pavement cafés; he remembered it for the time when Axel and Trine had come to a halt there, right next to the statue of Christian Krohg, and argued for over an hour about who was the more radical: Bakunin or Kropotkin. Slottsparken was fixed in Jonas's memory as the setting for a heated debate, verging on a squabble, as to who was the more important writer, James Joyce or Franz Kafka, another recurring topic akin to that of Mozart versus Beethoven and just as impossible to resolve. Jonas would always remember Akershus Fort for a stirring nocturnal walk along its walls upon which Alva regaled them with a wonderful description of Bernardo Bertolucci's film *The Conformist*, and he never saw the facade of the Freemason's Lodge on Wessels plass without thinking of Thomas's passionate and appetizing presentation of the works of the ecclesiastical historian Mircea Eliades.

What Jonas Wergeland liked best about those strolls at night through the city were the sudden mental leaps, the jumps through time and space, the merging of totally unconnected subjects. There were times when their discussion sounded like an organ, with lots of voices, from the reediest flutes to the deep notes of the pedals, strong and weak, and Jonas thought it was beautiful, every bit as beautiful as the music of the spheres. Sometimes he had the feeling that he could set its stops, throw in a remark that would elicit exactly the right heated note, the voice level he had counted on producing. Or with one incisive statement such as 'Maria Callas is the world's greatest prima donna', he could press an invisible 'Tutti' button that set them all talking at once, loudly and vociferously.

To Jonas Wergeland, these nocturnal ramblings through Oslo were very special occasions; he tried to remember everything that was said, to take it all in, with all his senses, and hence he also absorbed the scents and the sounds, brushes against walls, trees, the reflection in a window, as they walked and talked – as, for example, during the furious discussion, conducted on the way from Tøyen to Sofienborg, of Delacroix's enigmatic painting *Young Woman Attacked by a Tiger*, which had been sparked off by a little reproduction that Trine had stuck into her notebook; or as when, without any transition, and yet possibly quite logically, they launched into a debate so fierce that one would have thought it was a matter of life or death on whether philosophy began with wonder or with desperation, a topic which kept them occupied all the way through Grünerløkka and far up Maridalsveien. Not that they were always so sure of themselves. Alva had had to search for words on the night, standing outside Ullevål Hospital, when she tried to explain to the others why she felt that *'Todesfuge'* by Paul Celan was the finest poem ever written, but for the most part they had no doubts. There was the time, for instance, when Thomas, standing with his back to the station building at Majorstua, had expounded a long and pretty involved theory, punctuated by a lot of convulsive arm-waving, as to why the socialist experiment in Chile was bound to turn out as it did – this being a subject much on all their minds, as was the American statesman Henry Kissinger, who had just been awarded the Nobel Peace Prize and who, according to Trine, at two in the morning on Bygdøy allé, was the most brilliant intelligent diplomat of the twentieth century with an unrivalled feel for the widespread consequences and patterns of international politics but who, according to Alva, same time, same place, was an amoral, paranoid and conniving sonofabitch of a tarantula hiding behind a hypocritical gloss of *realpolitik*. There were some mysteries they could not solve, like what Odin had whispered in Balder's ear before the latter was laid on the funeral pyre, but there were other riddles to which they did find answers – for example that the 'Rosebud' of Orson Welles's film *Citizen Kane* could not possibly be anything other than William Randolph Hearst's pet name for his mistress's clitoris.

Now, to nip any criticism in the bud, while they might have been a bit on the airy-fairy side, the Nomads were not exponents of some brand of new romanticism, not at all. They knew very

well that in many ways they were dilettantes, and that they had a
hugely inflated idea of themselves and their own opinions. For
all their enthusiasm and hyperbole they were not wanting in
ironic objectivity. Alva might suddenly position herself in a gate-
way and declaim dramatically out of the darkness: 'I seek the
innermost core of the tree of life; what is it that holds the world
together.' They were all well aware that they often cited the
wrong names, misunderstood theories and confused phenomena. The point was that that was okay. It was okay to come out
with semi-digested, only partially understood ideas. It was okay
to drop names they had only ever come across in footnotes. It was
okay to refer to authors and tear their works to pieces or praise
them to the skies, crudely and unsubtly, without ever having read
them. It was okay to conduct a sort of intellectual *Guinness Book
of Records* in which everything had to be the greatest or the least,
the best or the worst, with no half-measures. There is a period in
the life of every human being when that is how it is: impossible
to believe that one can like *both* Mozart and Beethoven. It was as
if every member of the Nomads knew that at some point in life
it is necessary, absolutely essential, to be able to spout the most
appallingly heretical, half-formed ideas without having to qual-
ify anything. That it is important for one's mental health. This
phase of their lives, those nights roaming the city of Oslo, were
not just one long and fruitful brainstorming session, they also
constituted a kind of primal therapy, an opportunity to vent their
frustrations, their aggression, their crazy notions. Above all else,
it gave them a chance to play about with the most unlikely turtles, perhaps even discover one that was more viable than others.

There was only one spot that all of their various routes
through the city took in, thereby living up to its name, 'the
Magnet' in Akersgata: an establishment which, in its heyday,
before the advent of the Nomads, had for many years been Oslo's
only all-night café. They had strict rules about who they let in,
but thanks to Thomas, who worked a couple of evenings a week
for a newspaper which had its offices in the same street, and to
his amazing knack of making friends with the right people, they
could flash the vital press cards that would open the Magnet's
doors to them in the middle of the night. And even though this

bastion's conscientious guardian, Fru Sommerstad, had a suspicion that something fishy was going on, she left them to drink their coffee in peace alongside the taxi drivers.

I am sure it will come as no surprise to anyone to hear that all of the Nomads, with the exception of Jonas, actually wanted to be something other than what they were studying to be. They wanted to write. Why this should have been was a mystery to Jonas. They wanted to be authors or playwrights, they wanted to write screenplays or poetry, and Thomas – how weird could you get? – wanted to be that most hair-raisingly bizarre of all animals, an essayist. He submitted long articles to the newspapers, on topics more quixotic than even Knut Hamsun's young hero in *Hunger* could have dreamed up. All of which were – of course – roundly rejected by all and sundry.

Once inside the Magnet, they each took a seat at a separate table and proceeded to scribble like mad in their respective notebooks, the idea being that everyone should take them for reporters, fresh from doing some sensational nocturnal research and all set to make the scoop of their careers. They jotted down ideas that had come to them in between their discussions on the streets, thoughts generated by something one of the others had said, or by the graffiti on a statue, or quite simply churned out by brains that were running in top gear. And naturally, at that moment, sitting in the Magnet, scribbling down these thoughts as quickly as their pencils could shed their carbon particles, they honestly believed that what they were writing, at any rate after a wee bit of polishing, would cause the Milky Way to vibrate on its axis. They sat there with their fags between their lips, eyes narrowed, as if these notes they were making were of such brilliance that they were almost dazzled by them. Jonas knew that none of them would ever become novelists or writers of any description, but he never made fun of them, quite the opposite; he understood that these notebooks full of presumptuous, high-flying ideas would be worth their weight in gold at later and more disillusioned stages in their lives, that there would come a time when leafing through these little books would prove a more effective way of dulling their depression and world-weariness than all the medicines and pills in the world: to see, to have confirmed that they had once thought such thoughts, so grand, so outrageous, so extravagantly naïve and, above all: so insanely beautiful. Like turtles with gems affixed to their shells.

Jonas Wergeland made no notes. He already had a little book full of them, a golden sheaf of quotations. That was all he needed. That time, many years earlier, when Nefertiti and he were playing cowboys and Indians, and Nefertiti had ranged twenty-odd books side by side on the bookshelf and told him, gravely, that they were valuable, Jonas had automatically assumed that she was referring to their contents. When he was in eighth grade he had flicked through them and discovered that in each book there was one page with a corner turned down and a passage underlined. It was these passages which he had conscientiously jotted down in a little red notebook and in due course, after having them translated, had learned by heart. The quotation he had paraphrased during the Mozart versus Beethoven discussion he had found underlined at the end of – of all things – a totally unintelligible twenty-page article on 'Diffusion', complete with all sorts of formulae, written by none other than the physicist James Clerk Maxwell and reproduced in Volume II, a weighty tome in quarto format, of his collected scientific works; an unexpectedly crystal-clear passage which even Jonas could understand and employ – taking people by surprise, especially if he happened to divulge his source – in any number of situations.

Which reminds me that I have not said what Jonas Wergeland was studying, a piece of information which remained a well kept secret for a long time after he became famous; Jonas Wergeland was studying astronomy. Although that may not come as such a great surprise. Even as a boy, reading the following extract from the *Kama Sutra*, he had perceived the practical value of astronomy: 'The lovers may also sit on the terrace of the palace or house, and enjoy the moonlight, and carry on an agreeable conversation. At this time, too, while the woman lies in his lap, with her face towards the moon, the citizen should show her the different planets, the morning star, the polar star, and the seven Rishis, or Great Bear.' I mention this for the sake of any parents who might be under the misapprehension that reading the *Kama Sutra* would be bad for a child.

Jonas Wergeland himself claimed that he had been leafing through the university prospectus at random, as if the selection of a subject were something of a lottery, when under one course heading he had come upon the phrase 'celestial mechanics', and fell so completely for this term that he instantly plumped for the Institute of Theoretical Astro-Physics. Axel received a rather different version of the story: 'I took all the subjects one by one and asked myself the following question: would I be happy to give this as my answer if I were sitting in a café and someone came up to me and asked what I was studying?'

The truth is almost as simple as that; Jonas Wergeland enrolled in the astrophysics course because he could not stand the thought of having to study any subject that was full of bombastic systems, and within the field of astronomy there were refreshingly vast areas about which absolutely nothing could be said for certain. Not only that, but the body of information was changing and expanding faster here than in any other subject. In other words, astrophysics was the perfect branch of learning for Jonas Wergeland, being a field in which any universal theory was doomed to look ridiculous – there were few turtles to be found in the study of astrophysics.

Once the booster rockets of the Prelims had been jettisoned, Jonas found himself in the rarefied realms of astronomy, i.e. the foundation course. He even spent time, a little at least, leafing through books in the reading room on the top floor of the physics building as well as attending lectures in the auditorium at the institute, a building with decorative celestial globes in the corridors and a functionalist vestibule worth a whole course of study in itself. For a long time he almost enjoyed being a student, took part in field trips to the solar observatory at Harestua and was drawn into discussions with other astrophysics majors, or the lecturers, who had their rooms in the former apartments, since converted, of old Professor Rosseland, who watched over them from Alf Rolfsen's portrait in the seminar room, the old drawing-room. It was not until Jonas made a start on 'Galactic and extra-galactic astronomy', which involved, among other things, the mind-boggling subject of cosmology, that he began to have cold feet. There was something about these colossal forces, vast distances and inconceivable time-scales, billions of miles and years; and, not least, the eerie notion of a universe constantly expanding towards a state of total darkness, that scared him, that almost caused the scales to tip the other way; the theories became so vague, so top-heavy and woolly that it was all rather too much of a good thing – Jonas caught himself longing for a turtle. In fact he had already made up his mind to quit the course when one day, at the foot of the stairs, he passed a poster depicting the 'outer planet'. He had walked past it countless times before without stopping, but this time his eye immediately homed in on Pluto, and there was something about the tiny planet on the very edge of the solar system – some sense of kinship with this outsider – that captured Jonas's interest anew. He immediately enrolled in another course, one in which he could make a specific study of Pluto. From then on Pluto became Jonas Wergeland's pet project, or turtle; after one term he knew just about all there was to know about the planet, more in fact than the professor who taught them, and here I am not merely thinking of such things as how many days it takes to revolve, how wide the angle of its orbital plane or how elongated its ellipse – I am thinking of the acquisition of information so advanced that Jonas Wergeland was in a position to speculate, in a highly scientific manner, on Pluto's probable size and mass and its possible origins, a feat which was all the more impressive when one considers that this was even before the discovery of Pluto's moon. I am not exaggerating when I say that for some years, Jonas Wergeland was Norway's leading expert on the planet Pluto.

One can, of course, ask oneself what use – I almost said earthly use – so much knowledge of such a minor detail, a distant planet, can be put to in real life. Jonas Wergeland's had not yet come this far in his scrupling when he left the Magnet all-night café with the other Nomads and set out on another stroll through the deserted streets of Oslo, picking up the threads of their previous discussion as they went along, or raising some fresh and inflammable topic, some issue on which they would most certainly disagree strongly. But it could also be, as that night, that they came walking up Ullevålsveien, past Jonas's and Axel's old haven, Our Saviour's cemetery – at that time of night a shadowy,

mysterious landscape beyond the railings – and were startled by
a dog that barked at them from behind the gates, although no one
could figure out what the animal was doing there.

They were still walking along the side of the graveyard when
Axel said: 'Shit, what's it called again, that dog that guards the
entrance to Hades, the Greek kingdom of the dead?'

'Anubis,' said Trine like a shot.

'No, no, no,' Thomas protested. 'It's on the tip of my tongue.
It's . . . Garm.'

'That's Norse mythology, you twit.' Axel was furious with
himself for not being able to remember the name.

'What about the two-headed Orthrus?' Alva suggested.

'Take it easy, guys, the name's Cerberus,' said Jonas.

The others nodded, now they remembered. They looked at
Jonas. Jonas had a habit of surprising them.

'By the way, does anyone know why it's called Hades?' said
Alva.

'Comes from the Greek "*aides*" , the unseen,' said Jonas. 'The
God Hades had a helmet which made him invisible.'

Alva laughed and thumped him on the back. 'Trust you to
know such a totally useless piece of information.'

How did Jonas Wergeland know this? Because he was
Norway's leading expert on the planet Pluto, that's how. Because
Pluto is only another name for Hades, god of the underworld,
and the planet Pluto derived its name in part from the fact that it
was so difficult to detect, it was almost invisible, like Hades. This
gave Jonas a desire to know more about the Hades of mythology,
and that, in turn, is how he stumbled upon the dog Cerberus.
From the stars to Hell – but still only a short hop.

'You can say what you like about the uses of astronomy,' Jonas
said, as the Nomads reached Sankt Hanshaugen in a body at
four in the morning, 'but it's one way of learning your Greek
mythology.'

The Secretary

And so some reviewers felt that *Thinking Big* was actually a series of programmes on modern Norse mythology; and, certainly as far as Trygve Lie is concerned, they might have had something there, considering that, from boyhood onwards, Trygve Lie, first Secretary-General of the United Nations, had stood as an almost mythical figure in Jonas Wergeland's life, inasmuch as Lie's spirit seemed, as it were, to hover over the lakes around Grorud. Not only was the statesman buried just a stone's throw from the church – every time Jonas visited his mother at the Ironmongery he also had to pass the house in Grorudveien, right opposite the woollen mill and a short walk from the station, that had been the UN Secretary-General's home from the age of six. And naturally there hung a picture of him in Grorud School, in the dining hall – a 'Big Brother is watching you' sort of thing. The dining hall was a place Jonas normally associated with the constant din of yelling and screaming, with bottle tops shooting past like flying saucers and jet-propelled carrots forever whizzing through the air. The only time when things quietened down was when the deputy head suddenly yanked the door open and pointed to the picture of Trygve Lie, as if this was somehow supposed to make them feel ashamed of themselves, or bring it home to them that they would never manage to become Secretary-General of the UN by throwing food about like that. So from an early age Jonas had the idea that in global terms this was actually Trygve Lie's role: to make sure that a crowd of hooting lads did not go around chucking bits of carrot at one another.

It very quickly became clear to Jonas Wergeland, while they were putting together the programme, that many people,

Norwegians too, had rather mixed feelings about Trygve Lie, or regarded him, for some reason, as a second-rater whose appointment to the UN amounted to little more than a poor compromise. So there was no shortage of material for the regular spot in each programme which Jonas Wergeland called 'the whisperers': two individuals, pictured in silhouette, whispering to one another, exchanging snide remarks about the programme's hero – a pretty common Norwegian phenomenon when you come right down to it, and one that can be studied every time, i.e. every few years or so, that a Norwegian citizen wins acclaim on the international scene. Quick as a wink, up pops some other zealous Norwegian with a green-eyed look about him, who feels it incumbent on him to tell all those who have allowed themselves to be taken in just how ludicrously undeserving of success this fellow-countryman is. If he is really lucky, there will be scores of neighbours and relations ready to provide plenty of spicy details with which to elaborate upon this assertion.

In Trygve Lie's case there was no shortage of material. The whisperers began by having some fun with the harmless fact that Trygve Lie's English pronunciation was little short of comedy-hour standard – their imitations of this were actually very funny. Then they turned to whispering, far more maliciously, about how Trygve Lie gave in to McCarthy's paranoid 'reds under the bed' hysteria and granted the FBI access to UN headquarters, to investigate the people who worked there, before rounding off with an even softer, poisonous sequence on the blackening of Dag Hammerskjöld's name, all presented in the form of vague rumours, interspersed with little hints and insinuations – just as in real life – where the viewers were left to fill in the gaps for themselves: 'Didn't he make a lot of not exactly pleasant remarks about Dag Hammerskjöld?' – 'Bad-mouthed him something rotten, you mean.' – 'The way I heard it, he called him both one thing and the other' – 'Oh, yes, especially the other' – 'And wasn't there even some crude reference to Hammerskjöld's sexual proclivities?' – 'Just because he was a bachelor' – 'Somebody said that Hammerskjöld had to put Lie on the carpet' – 'Uh-huh, and ask him to curb his imagination' – and so on and so forth, blithely, whisperingly anonymous.

The programme's central scene was shot in NRK's biggest studio. Jonas Wergeland wished to concentrate on the very heart of Trygve Lie's work: his tireless struggle to safeguard the fragile peace. At no other time in Lie's life did this manifest itself more clearly than during a heroic 32-day tour made in April and May of 1950, during which Lie journeyed halfway around the world, to Washington, London, Paris and Moscow in order to hand over in person a document which he had written, rather grandly entitled 'Memorandum on principles for consideration in the preparation of a twenty-year program to achieve peace through the United Nations'. In actual fact this tour more or less amounted to a personal attempt to save the UN from dying the death – the Soviet Union had already boycotted the Security Council in protest at the exclusion of communist China. Trygve Lie tried, in other words, to prevent a rift between two irreconcilable blocs, to put an end to the Cold War. A fitting task for a Norwegian, really: the battle against the cold. On the huge film set Jonas Wergeland had arranged four groups of tables and chairs, to represent the four capitals and the summit meetings held there. Lie was then trundled round the floor in a circle, sitting in a miniature aeroplane, from one group – i.e. city – to the next, and at each stop he presented his memorandum and spoke to the heads of state and their foreign ministers. The floor of the set showed the UN's blue and white map of the world with the North Pole and, hence, Norway too, at its centre, encircled if not with a laurel wreath, then certainly with olive branches as if this were another race in which a Norwegian would win his laurels.

Trygve Lie went round and round, a wheel with a desire for peace at its hub, presenting his utopian document, ten points for achieving peace. Viewers saw how he struggled, plodding round in a circle, a sort of outsize budgie wheel, shaking hands here, shaking hands there, with President Truman, Prime Minister Atlee, Prime Minister Bidault, Generalissimo Stalin and their staff. Making the same opening remarks every time. They all listened to him, they were all most polite, they all said the same thing, they all promised to study his memorandum carefully and with the greatest interest, they all appreciated his efforts, they were all truly grateful for this initiative, they all found his observations both enlightening and useful, but even while they were smiling and nodding approvingly, they were picking holes in his suggestions: in all honesty we doubt whether these points are of any relevance vis-à-vis the current situation, no, we cannot limit the use of the Security Council's right of veto. Trygve Lie makes amendments, adds appendices, travels on, people smile and nod approvingly, but no, a meeting of the heads of state is not, in our opinion, the most burning issue at this time, and furthermore, we do not want to have anything to do with communist China. Trygve Lie puts up with all the quibbling, the insistence upon different wording, travels on, people smile and nod approvingly, but no, such a suggestion conflicts with our interests, we must be careful not to create false illusions, Twinkle, twinkle little bat and all that, accompanied by a hail of 'at this moment in time' and 'the way we see it' and 'the time has come'. Trygve Lie travels on, people smile and nod approvingly, but no we are afraid that we cannot go along with the idea of regular meetings of the Security Council, nor do we have any faith in the notion of having a consultative assembly to discuss the problems associated with atomic energy, we are also extremely unhappy about the way in which the UN has handled the question of colonialism. Trygve Lie travels on, circling the room, traversing a light-blue and white flag of the world, on a utopian journey in the cause of peace on which the Soviet troika of Stalin, Molotov and Visjinski make a notably large number of objections, but Lie makes change after change, deletes and appends, refuses to give in. Trygve Lie travels in a circle from one capital to the next, following the curve of the olive branches, with Jonas Wergeland inserting intermittent clips of what was being said behind Lie's back while he was busy at another table. The Russians called him an 'American lackey', while the Americans believed him to be a 'Stalinist agent', far too ready to make concessions to the Russians. To the British he was a simple man, little better than a peasant, and they were shocked by his lack of discretion in the playing of his political role, so far removed from the understated English style of diplomacy learned on the playing fields of Eton. The cynical Frenchmen laughed outright at the whole rash initiative, this attempt to raise earnest Norwegian morality onto a global plane – and all this while the viewers were watching Trygve Lie eventually pulling off his jacket, sitting there in shirtsleeves and braces, chain-smoking, a secretary for peace, a Sisyphus from Norway, undertaking the most impossible task in the world, trying to prevent another major conflict. Trygve Lie puts his shoulder to the wheel, keeps going, looks on the bright side, calls this tour of his a voyage of discovery; Trygve Lie in his shirtsleeves and braces, the personification of the Norwegian Labour Party, sitting at the helm of the world in a plucky endeavour to turn the entire globe into one good solid social democracy.

And all the while newsreel clips were flashing across a studio wall in the background, showing how the major powers and particularly the United States and the Soviet Union were arming themselves, building warships, tanks, rockets. And more particularly how stocks of nuclear weapons were building up month by month. And when Trygve Lie returned home from his one-man peace mission, suffering from a sore throat – brought on, one might almost think, by all that talking – but feeling almost certain that he had succeeded in arriving at some sort of consensus and possibly even managed to achieve his prime aim: a meeting in the very near future of all the government leaders, he was shown standing facing this newsreel backdrop, in his shirtsleeves and braces, chain-smoking, and watching as the images suddenly exploded; in June, scarcely a month after he completed his journey for peace, the Korean War broke out. Jonas Wergeland had unearthed some pretty harrowing scenes from the war which made a fitting contrast to Trygve Lie's dogged, but hopeless and naïve struggle for peace.

Personally, I have a bit of a soft spot for this programme, perhaps simply because so many Norwegians underestimate, or have quite simply forgotten, Trygve Lie. To me – who can take an objective view of all this – Trygve Lie is Norway in a nutshell: not some brilliant intellectual figure but an idealistic and hard-working secretary. As far as I can gather, Lie must surely have earned himself the right to be called 'the master-builder of the UN' – after all, who can say how the United Nations would have turned out without him and the devotion he showed to the organization as an ideal, whatever standpoints might be taken or

resolutions passed. Through his efforts during the delicate construction phase, Trygve Lie had a quite crucial influence on the
greatest experiment in international collaboration the world has
ever known. For that alone I take my hat off to him.

Not surprisingly, this programme proved to be one of actor
Normann Vaage's greatest triumphs. He was never better than
here, playing Trygve Lie as if he himself, Normann Vaage personally, would rather die than see the world plunged into another
war. People who had met Trygve Lie could hardly believe their
eyes, declared that Normann Vaage *was* Trygve Lie, completely
and utterly, down to the smallest gesture, and strangest of all:
Normann Vaage so immersed himself in the part that many
viewers could have sworn that his ears actually grew as large and
prominent as Lie's own – a feature which seemed to emphasize
the man's ability to be a good listener. Such empathy was symp-
tomatic of the series as a whole. The subject matter itself seemed
to bring out the best in the actors. Ella Strand, who played all of
the female subjects, also became immensely popular during the
year in which the series was televised. Together with Normann
Vaage, she made guest appearances in all sorts of other programmes and her face and name cropped up everywhere: in
advertisements, newspaper profiles, women's magazines, at trade
fairs up and down the country. People fought for a glimpse of
them, as if they were the actual incarnation of those Norwegians
in whom the public were suddenly taking a totally new interest.

In many ways these actors confirmed Jonas Wergeland's
theory that each individual embodies a host of different personas. That all Norwegians carried these heroes within themselves, as it were, one might almost say like a set of genes.

While going through all the material on Trygve Lie, Jonas
Wergeland stumbled upon a side of the man's character of which
he had been unaware: Trygve Lie had been a keen tennis player,
and a pretty fair tennis player at that. As late as 1938 he had
become area champion in the over-forty class, and two years
prior to that he had won an international tournament held at the
Jordal Stadium in Oslo. This provided Jonas with a fresh angle
on Trygve Lie. Not only did they both hail from Grorud, both
were also fine tennis players.

Sowing Dragon's Teeth

And so Jonas Wergeland now stood there with the ball in his left hand, totally devoid of any peaceful intentions, bounced it a couple of times, fixed his eye on a point in the court on the other side of the net, bounced the ball once more before throwing it into the air, mind focussed, and hit it as hard as he could and then some, as if he were hurling a javelin and not a felt covered ball at Gjermund Boeck's cocky, smirking features. He hit it beautifully, with his body at full stretch, ensuring that the ball landed exactly where it was supposed to in the ambassador's service court, with enough power behind it that even though Gjermund Boeck did manage to get to the ball, it slammed into the net as the screech of a sliding rubber sole mingled with the hiss of a less than diplomatic curse.

Jonas's future father-in-law had won the first set 6-1. That one game had been an obvious consolation prize, a fact that rankled all the more with Jonas. And, what was worse, he had forgotten to put everything he had into that one detail.

Jonas served again, tossing the ball into the air with such a practised air that anyone with any knowledge of tennis would have taken him for a seasoned player, him, Jonas Wergeland, Grorud lad and anti-snob, who had never touched a tennis racket as a boy. Again his serve was powerful, well-placed, he was conscious of the delightful sensation that ran through him every time he hit the ball just right, *faultlessly*, the glorious sound, the *rush* it gave; he repeated his success twice more to win his service game outright. The ambassador, for once not wearing one of his garish Hawaiian shirts but the traditional whites, which conspired with his old-fashioned flat cap to lend him a rather tropical colonial air, clapped his racket with the flat of his hand

cheerily, but Jonas could tell that he was nonplussed, so nonplussed that his serve became a little less sure, and Jonas managed to make a number of good returns, even against the
ambassador's backhand, which he knew to be slow, with an
under-spin that allowed him ample time to run in to the net and
enjoy the luxury of a volley. Boeck won the game, but he really
had to work for it and, what is more: he was shaken, he saw now
that humiliating Jonas was not going be as easy as he had thought
– not easy at all.

Jonas served again, even harder this time and, by his own
lights, nigh-on flawlessly, and won this game, too, outright, with
three aces and a ball that his prospective father-in-law could do
no more than tap with his racket, a return so bad that a neatly
placed forehand from Jonas nearly sent the ambassador – bearing a passing facial resemblance to Trygve Lie – flying headlong
onto the court as he strained vainly, and comically, to reach
Jonas's ball. Gjermund Boeck was no longer clapping.

So what had happened? How could an amateur – a complete
novice, basically – hold his own against a seasoned tennis player,
albeit an elderly man, corpulent and fairly slow, but still an experienced and, above all, wily player who would normally have had
no problem in wiping the floor with such a greenhorn, as he had
done in the first set, without having to stretch to more than a
gloating grin? Tennis is not one of my favourite sports, but I
believe that this episode affords an insight into an important
aspect of Jonas Wergeland's nature: not only his almost uncanny
strength of will but also, and just as importantly, his keen eye for
the crucial angle of attack, the one detail that makes all things
possible, including the crushing of a smug and rather nasty
ambassador.

Immediately after the fateful lobster dinner the previous
autumn, two things had happened. Jonas had moved in with
Margrete, who was living in her parents' flat in Ullevål Garden
City while they were abroad, and he had started to take tennis
lessons with her on an indoor court; or rather, first she had
packed him off to Johan Hannes's shop on Parkveien, where he
had bought a wooden Donnay 'Borg pro' racket, one which had
come warmly recommended by Hannes – not surprisingly,

seeing that he happened to be the local agent for the Belgian firm. Margrete played a decent, if not a great, game of tennis, thanks to a cosmopolitan upbringing within diplomatic circles where playing tennis was an inherent part of the whole way of life, every bit as essential as being able to handle a telex machine or a cocktail glass, or knowing on which occasions one was supposed to fly a flag on the car. Although she had not played for ages, she still had her sure serve and her solid ground stroke, they seemed to be ingrained in her, like her swimming stroke. But Margrete was a hopeless teacher. She laughed at Jonas, she *roared* with laughter at Jonas's ineptitude and ungainly antics on the tennis court; if anything, he was even more ham-fisted with a racket than he was with a lobster fork. After only a couple of sessions on the indoor court, during which Jonas had hardly managed to land a single ball inside the lines of the court, she told him – good-humouredly, but in no uncertain terms – that he was hopeless. He was a great guy, but he had *no* gift for tennis. 'Why don't you call off this stupid duel with Dad,' she said. 'I'm begging you, please.'

But Jonas *had* to beat Gjermund Boeck, and in this lies the very crux of the story: to swear to do something which you do not know the first thing about, in which you are possibly not even all that interested; which, quite frankly, you think is just plain daft – to do it because of an innate, pigheaded determination, and perhaps even a longing, at least once in your life, to win a battle against all, absolutely all, the odds. So, in the final analysis, Jonas was not competing against the ambassador – even though he deeply and sincerely disliked his future father-in-law. What he was fighting was his own doubt, his doubt as to whether he really could do the impossible, make the improbable a reality. It could have been anything at all. In Jonas Wergeland's case it happened to be tennis. He knew that if he could succeed in beating the ambassador at tennis, then there was nothing he could not do. Hence this silly little duel, this typically macho set-up, with its even more absurd trophy, a trophy of which Jonas felt almost ashamed, but which at the same time he coveted with all his heart: a polar-bear skin, a momentous milestone in Jonas Wergeland's career. Walking off the court with or without that skin would quite simply represent the difference between two different lives.

Jonas managed to persuade Margrete to persevere, they even played over Christmas and on through the latter half of the winter, a couple of evenings a week at least, until Jonas had almost reached the level that most amateurs stick at for life, a slightly imprecise style, all home-made serves and countless technical errors, that nonetheless suffices to keep the ball in play so long as one's opponent is no better a player. He had also been bitten, against all the prior warnings he had received, by the tennis bug, by the idea of batting a felt-covered rubber ball back and forth across a net. A court divided into six sections, yet an infinitude of possibilities. For one of his projects at the College of Architecture, Jonas had designed a house to a plan inspired by the divisions of a tennis court. But Margrete beat him every time, and she was growing more and more fed up with it.

Then, one particularly bad evening when Jonas had sent every ball he hit with his forehand slamming into the net, his eye was caught by two men in their forties, playing in the next court; real geniuses with a tennis ball, to Jonas's mind at least, hitting the ball with such nonchalance, elegance and, above all, an *ease* unlike anything Jonas had ever seen; commenting all the while, wryly and with an astonishing breadth of vocabulary, on their own blunders. Even if Jonas was uncommonly ignorant as regards great Norwegian exploits in this particular sport, he ought at least to have recognized one of the players, or rather, his voice – because this was Finn Søhol, the man who had for decades been the top tennis player in Norway and was now a tennis commentator for NRK. For the benefit of those readers who are particularly interested, I can tell you that the other player was Gunnar Sjøwall, several times Norwegian champion and Søhol's doubles partner of many years standing. As a pair, these two succeeded, among other things, in getting as far as the third round of the gentlemen's doubles at Wimbledon in the mid-fifties – quite an impressive feat.

It may have been his very ignorance that gave Jonas the brass neck to approach Finn Søhol later, in the changing room, and ask him whether he would consider giving him some lessons, or at least see whether he could help him to improve his game.

'Why?' Søhol asked.

'My girlfriend's dad's a fiend from hell,' Jonas said. 'I've just *got* to beat him. It's a matter of life or death.'

Søhol laughed but accepted this as a valid reason. He could tell at a glance, possibly thanks to the intuition developed through all his years of playing tennis, that there was something special about the young architecture student standing before him, sweating and vehement, a Donnay 'Borg pro' racket resting on his shoulder like a rifle. Which is how Jonas came to find himself, one week later, on the island of Bygdøy, inside the whitewashed, green-roofed building that was home to the Bygdøy Tennis Club.

Finn Søhol, Jonas's voluntary unpaid trainer, had already worked out a strategy; he had given the matter some thought, had even become quite intrigued by the problem. 'The only way you can beat a more experienced player is by learning to serve,' he said. 'Serve well, I mean.' Søhol demonstrated what he meant by a good serve. Jonas did not even have the chance to lift his racket, just heard the whoosh of the ball. His first thought was to walk out right there and then; the whole situation was too ridiculous, too extreme. But once he had had time to think about it he found that he liked the idea, and the more he thought about it the more he liked it. That everything could hang on such a detail. That you could win a match even if you had not mastered the whole gamut of strokes, even if neither your footwork or physical form were up to scratch. It reminded him a little of his own attempt to gain some understanding of the entire universe solely by studying the planet Pluto.

Søhol devoted the rest of the evening at Bygdøy Tennis Club to the art of tossing the ball into the air correctly. Jonas threw the ball in to the air again and again, without hitting it once; just stood there, throwing the ball up, pretty high, with a straight left arm, in such a way that, if he threw it correctly, it would land on a handkerchief that Søhol had spread on the court a little way in front of his body and a shade to the right of his left foot. Having done this repeatedly for what felt like an eternity to Jonas, he was allowed, for another eternity, to swing his racket back and up at the same time as he threw the ball – a vital action, almost like something out of a ballet, in which the arms fly apart, and rhythm and timing are all – but still without hitting the ball, without serving.

Jonas Wergeland left Bygdøy Tennis Club feeling convinced that he had just learned his most important lesson in tennis, without having played a single stroke. He liked it, inside he was jumping for joy, he realized that he had found his angle, for the first time he realized that he had a microscopic chance of actually beating such a superior opponent as Gjermund Boeck, an out-and-out fiend as well as being an ambassador and his future father-in-law.

Jonas took up the challenge with renewed energy. At the flat in Ullevål Garden City he practised the moves that Søhol had taught him, drawn from the javelin throwers' training programme, exercises to build up the muscles that would give him a better throwing action. Jonas threw himself into this with an enthusiasm that almost surprised himself and left Margrete shaking her head; lay on the living-room floor, surrounded by his future in-laws' bronze gods and earthenware vases from the Far East, doing a variety of sit-ups to strengthen both the vertical and diagonal abdominal muscles, working slowly but steadily to begin with; lay on his back with his arms stretched out behind his head and lifted weights; did what were known as pullovers, an exercise perfected by Terje Pedersen, a Norwegian who had for some time held the world record in the javelin and whom Jonas Wergeland was now imitating in order to build up that part of the chest muscle which pulled the arm forward – one muscle he had real need of when serving – and in the midst of all these monomaniacal exertions, his eye kept going to the polar-bear skin on the floor, as if it were some huge, enticing diploma. Once the snow had melted, Jonas Wergeland could be found in the garden, standing lost in concentration among the apple trees, throwing a ball into the air and getting it to land on a handkerchief spread on the ground. To a chance observer, it must have looked as if he were performing some arcane ritual, some sort of religious observance, possibly of Far Eastern origin.

He made five more visits to Bygdøy Tennis Club and Finn Søhol. Serving and serving, again and again, the art of repetition. Again Søhol spread the handkerchief on the floor, in the service court this time, like a bull's-eye at which Jonas was to aim, one which was gradually moved. 'If you're to force his backhand, you'll have to serve first towards the centre and then out to the line!' Søhol was far from satisfied but thought Jonas was improving. 'To hell with the second serve, hit it as hard as you can every time, either you'll win the point or it'll be a double fault, all or nothing.' During the last two sessions they also practised forehand returns so that Jonas, if he were lucky, would be able to return some of the ambassador's serves. 'You might be able to break his rhythm and win a few points on his serve, too,' said Søhol.

Finally, Søhol set up a tennis machine on the opposing baseline to give Jonas the chance to really try out his forehand. It was a momentous experience: being bombarded by an incessant stream of yellow balls as in some ancient myth in which warriors sprang up from the ground as fast as the hero could hack them down. 'Swing your racket well back,' yelled Søhol, 'now follow through. That's the way. Well done.'

Fortunately, this time it was not a tennis machine on the other side of the net but Gjermund Boeck, the ambassador, and that gentleman was both startlingly red in the face and thrown quite off-balance by his prospective son-in-law, who was unexpectedly serving with uncanny accuracy and managing to return a good few of his own serves, transformed as if by magic so it seemed, into a future champion. As luck would have it, it was the ambassador himself who had chosen the Njård Sports Centre, which, with its wooden floor, gave Jonas an added advantage, since play moved even faster on such a surface.

Jonas tossed the ball into the air, noticed fleetingly how it hovered, started to rotate, transformed into Pluto, the most outlying and most obscure of all the planets in the solar system, offering an angle on the entire universe, before it dropped, and he turned it into a comet, a dazzling ace that left Margrete's father gazing open-mouthed after it, and won a long hard second set 7-5 for Jonas. At that very moment he realized there was something up with his shoulder.

The ambassador, clearly exhausted, but determined, fiendishly determined, prepared to serve in the final, decisive set.

The Invisible Man

And so in the same year in which statesman Trygve Lie died, Jonas Wergeland lay stretched out on the red carpet beneath the vaulted ceiling of Grorud Church, looking as though he had strained every muscle in his body in his attempt to reach an unbeatable smash from the opponent we call Life. No one seeing him lying there on the floor, as if dead, could have guessed that not long afterwards he would be the cause of the most appalling and to some extent sensational rumours as to how the church had been vandalized.

Outside the snow was falling, a constant sifting of light flakes that settled in a white film over everything, *transforming* the entire landscape – not inappropriately, really, with Christmas just around the corner. Jonas lay on his back in the choir, listening to this organ music with the weird timbres, music in keeping, not with the crystals of snow, but with the walls of the church, the different minerals in the granite, something far more mysterious and deep, light and weighty at one and the same time: long-drawn-out chords, with notes vibrant as little whirlpools, slowly changing and forcing him into a state of meditation, forcing him to look inside himself.

Light streamed in through the stained-glass windows, sending a shaft of light slanting through dim dust onto the pews right next to Jonas. He lay there, listening to the organ music, struck by how little he knew about his father. Where had he produced this from, his father, this music with the totally different logic, beyond major and minor: slow shifts striking out in all directions like a variety of possibilities all existing side by side. Jonas was to wonder about that day in the church for the rest of his life, and later he did ask his father what he had been playing. 'Messiaen,' his father replied, only Jonas thought he had said 'Messiah', which in fact seemed pretty apt: it was music worthy of a saviour. His father had played a piece from Olivier Messiaen's *La Nativité du Seigneur*, the birth of the Lord, first the part entitled *'Le Verbe'*, with the descending scale played on the pedals, and then the meditative piece to which he was now listening, motionless, on his back in the choir of the church: *'Desseins éternels'*, measured, introspective music with a most unusual setting, repetitions that were, nonetheless, all different, leaving him with an impression of ideas being weighed up, music that spun him into a cocoon, encased him, protected him. He twisted his head back and looked at the fresco, *The Great White Flock*, the crowd, felt that horror again, felt as though he were becoming invisible.

For this was, of course, the point, the final conclusion: with his grandfather gone, no one was telling him, and if no one was telling him, he was no longer a unique individual, and if he was no longer a unique individual, then he was just another face in the crowd, and if he was just another face in the crowd, then he was on the point of disappearing, becoming, quite literally, lost; and it was only now, with the death of his grandfather, that Jonas Wergeland realized what it was that he dreaded more than anything else: the thought of being invisible.

When do we become who we are?

Wrong question: When do we *see* who we are? Or *what* we are?

The threat of invisibility was to dog Jonas Wergeland all his life. A visit to Gardermoen many years later proved to be a particularly upsetting experience. After a memorable trip to Gudbrandsdalen, while he was studying at the College of Architecture, Jonas had suddenly been seized by a pressing need to find out more about his own roots and not least the countryside in which his mother had grown up, but which he had never seen, his grandmother, Jørgine Wergeland having left the area during the war – that grandmother who was now so old and frail that she made the V-sign if she so much as managed to get out of bed.

He drove into Gardermoen and parked the car next to the post office, walked across the road to the Shell station and was directed to an old man who lived nearby and who, as luck would have it, was able to point out the spot where his grandparents' smallholding, his mother's childhood home, had stood. Jonas sauntered pensively along Gardermoveien, past the Community Centre and the playing fields and then all at once there he was staring at his roots on the other side of the fence.

And what did he see?

Tarmac. An airstrip.

Where once there had been a smallholding, there was now a military and civil airport, an international zone so to speak. How had this come about?

In 1942, about forty properties had been bought up by the Germans, who were planning to extend the airport, or rather, *build* an airport, since in those days the airport was little more than an airstrip cutting across a field. Jonas's grandmother had told him how a German wearing jodhpurs with a leather patch on the backside had come to the house and simply announced that they had a fortnight to get out, by order of the Wehrmacht. Most of the properties were family dwellings, but a handful, like Jørgine and Oscar Wergeland's, also included as much as ten to fifteen acres of land: smallholdings supporting a few horses, cattle, some pigs and chickens, stables and byres. His maternal grandfather had also been a cobbler, with his own workshop on the premises, as well as doing the occasional stint with the local artillery regiment, the AR 2. The purchase was passed by the local council and his grandparents were paid the going rate – which was still a tidy sum of money at that time, although Oscar Wergeland never had any joy from it since, according to Jørgine he was so mad that he burst a blood vessel and died. He could not bear the thought of the Germans taking their smallholding away from them. After that, Jørgine moved to Oslo and bought the flat in Oscars gate.

Jonas Wergeland stood by the fence, not all that far from where the school had once stood and stared at the runway, first surfaced by the Germans with concrete, which in turn had later been covered by tarmac – a bad idea, as it turned out, so bad that it had all had to be redone. Jonas had always known about this, but even so he could not quite believe it even when he saw it with his own eyes. One day a smallholding, the next razed to the ground and covered by concrete as if to seal up the past. And right then and there, standing by that fence at Gardermoen, it dawned on him that here lay the explanation for the feeling he sometimes had of being totally lacking in any roots, a feeling which the next moment would manifest itself in a niggling restlessness. There, at Gardermoen, at the end of a long runway, Jonas Wergeland understood for the first time why, right from the start, he had been condemned to the life of a nomad. His roots in the earth were gone – not even at his grandfather's house on Hvaler was there a patch of cultivated land: that was a house coloured by ships and travel. Jonas's only knowledge of the land had come from his mini-introduction in the school garden. Jonas Wergeland stood by a fence at Gardermoen, next to a strip of asphalt below which lay his grandparents' smallholding, watching a plane come rolling towards him, lift its belly to him and take off; he just didn't understand it, how it could happen so fast, from earth to air in one, two, three generations, from something concrete to something abstract, and possibly it was here – it's merely a suggestion – as the ear-splitting roar of the jet engines spread across the countryside, that Jonas Wergeland realized he was going to have to take this to its logical conclusion and start with the most abstract and ethereal thing of all: television.

But these reflections belong to the future. Or do they? When Jonas reached this understanding at Gardermoen, he had the feeling that this vision, not just the story, I mean, but the *vision* of a strip of tarmac running across the former site of a smallholding, had always been there in his mind, like a prism in his memory.

In any case, Jonas was now lying on the floor of Grorud Church, listening to his father's extraordinary organ music. Wrapped in a cocoon of music, a fine web. He looked up at the picture of the Great White Flock, figures seeming almost to run together into a surging sea of humanity.

Earlier that autumn Jonas had had an experience which had reinforced his fear of crowds. He had taken part in one of the many demonstrations against the Soviet invasion of Czechoslovakia, not so much because he actually felt strongly about it as because it made a change from all of the demonstrations against the USA, expanding the protest march selection, so to speak, by a hundred per cent – besides which, a couple of not exactly unattractive girls in the parallel class to his own had lured him into taking part. The following day there was a picture in the paper from the mass rally on Universitetsplassen, a shot of the crowd. And Jonas was nowhere to be seen. He knew exactly where he had been standing: in reality between one of girls, the one carrying a Czech flag, and the guy in the unmistakeable parka holding one of the poles of a banner, both of them clearly visible in the foreground of the picture. But Jonas Wergeland had disappeared, he could not understand it, held the newspaper photograph up to the light as if that might help, reveal a shadow that was not otherwise discernible, but he was, and he remained, quite literally out of the picture, as if Judgement Day had come and he had been dragged down into Hell, while the true believers remained behind, or like those pictures one heard about – in the Soviet Union, aptly enough – from which people had been erased as if they had never existed. Jonas puzzled over this for a long time but eventually had to drop it. Only later did he come to interpret it as a clear forewarning, and an equally clear hint, as to the consequences of his grandfather's death: Jonas would become invisible, merge with the crowd. One snowflake in a flurry of flakes. White. Colourless.

When do we become who we are? When do we become *more* than we think we are? When do we open the door onto all our inherent potential?

Jonas Wergeland lay on his back in Grorud Church, while the snow settled in a soft, thick layer on the roof and on the ground around the granite walls. The snow also seemed to make the light that much more intense, a light that made the stained-glass windows in the church glow, come alive. His father was playing another piece now, 'Les mages', although Jonas did not know that was what it was called, he was simply aware of the unusual rhythm, as of something swaying, pitching – for some reason he found himself picturing a caravan, a procession, something in motion, planets orbiting around one another; he had a feeling of weightlessness, of tremendous clarity, of gold, frankincense and myrrh. Again his eye turned to the fresco behind the altar, the two angels, both holding stringed instruments, in the air above the mass of humanity, the Great White Flock, those completely identical figures. Jonas was sure of just one thing: he had to break out of the crowd; no matter what it took he must not become invisible. And so he lay there, letting himself be spun into a cocoon, letting himself be enveloped, wrapped up; he felt heavy but no longer afraid, because something was about to happen, he knew it, the music would make it happen.

Outside the snow was falling, packing the whole of Grorud in cotton wool, making everything *hushed*. A hush that made you prick up your ears. Jonas lay in the choir and listened, was struck by a sensation that the crystals in the minerals of the granite – the quartz especially – were somehow singing along to the music, had been set in motion. As if the whole church were in the process of turning into a conductor, linked up to something greater. His father had always supported the theory that there was a connection between music and stones; that, particularly in Grorud Church, an accord existed between the strains of the organ and the granite, something normally found only in the great cathedrals of Europe.

Jonas felt his body going numb or going to sleep in order to recharge its batteries, he lay inside a casing, preparing for a metamorphosis. He listened to the music, hearing how it abruptly changed. He shut his eyes, let himself be enfolded, affected, and all at once he knew, knew that it was not impossible; a person could lift a ton-weight of a cupboard or do away with seven lovers at one blow, or not die even, despite the fact that everyone said you were doomed to die, so why, he thought, why couldn't a person turn out at any minute to be quite different from what they appear to be.

Code of the Planets

And so they were talking about man's potential to change his own nature. Or rather, Jonas and Axel started out by discussing the criteria for beauty; they were trying, as so often before, to define the hallmarks of a 'sophisticated lady'. They had the same taste in women, would watch a lovely woman weave her way between the tables then nod eloquently at one another and say, as one voice: 'Sophisticated Lady'. It was during this discussion of 'sophistication' and what it entailed that Axel embarked, right out of the blue, on a discourse on Dostoyevsky, *The Brothers Karamazov* and Grusjka, a woman who personified the Russian ideal of beauty and who, according to Dostoyevsky, or the narrator, had sable eyebrows. Axel found this enormously intriguing, wanted to know what Jonas thought about it: sable eyebrows, I ask you, what's that supposed to mean? Was it an inference to her worth? Or was it the colour, the dark-brown, or the sheen, or did it perhaps say something about warmth or a savage streak? Thereupon they launched into a lengthy, fairly heated and amusing discussion of sophisticated ladies and sable eyebrows. It was not until the very tail end of this conversation that Axel got onto the subject of the human genome and from that to DNA – not the political party, that is, but the molecule.

Although many Norwegians know today who Axel Stranger is, not everyone knows much about his background or that he was for many years a promising figure in research circles at the University of Oslo, working in the borderland between chemistry and biology, a scientific field which, in Norway at that time, was lagging hopelessly behind the rest of international research; but since Axel Stranger had taken as his motto a quote from the philosopher Democritus – 'Better to discover a causal relationship than to be the King of Persia' – it was not surprising that, having been a keen turtle hunter at high school, he should have become caught up in, and wish to devote the rest of his life to, the study of what is possibly the greatest of all causal relationships: human DNA. 'It's such a privilege,' he was forever telling Jonas, especially once he had reached a more advanced stage in his studies. 'DNA has an inherent beauty that defies description, *really* sophisticated stuff,' he said. 'And what a story. Perfect. As good as the story of the Creation in the Old Testament.' Jonas was not always the most interested of listeners, and Axel's more involved chemical explanations tended to go right over his head, not least his somewhat long-winded lectures on the attempts being made, primarily in the USA, to dissect DNA, thus paving the way for the possibility in the future of artificially splicing together DNA molecules from different organisms, a carpentry of sorts involving micro-level joints and dovetailing. And then there was the almost unimaginable prospect of being able to map out all of the genes by figuring out the sequence of the base-pairs in the human DNA, which was made up of the twenty-three chromosomes. When, as on this day, Axel was pursuing these trains of thought at his quickest and most intense, Jonas would simply comment wryly 'Well, let's hope they soon find the gene for sable eyebrows,' before turning his attention back to his surroundings.

So where were they sitting, Axel and Jonas? They were alone for once, without the rest of the Nomads, and they were sitting not just anywhere, but in Bényoucéf's restaurant, La P'tite Cuisine, in Solligata, directly behind Industry and Export House, and at that very moment their food came sailing out of the kitchen, an armada of uncommonly aromatic dishes, served up with a great deal of ceremony, having been prepared in their honour by Bényoucéf himself. Before them on the table landed a large steaming dish of couscous, along with another dish of freshly-cooked lamb and chicken and one containing turnip, courgettes, carrots and the odd-looking little legumes known in English as chick-peas; then there was a bowl of raisins and onion and one containing his fabulous hot red sauce. Eagerly, almost greedily, Jonas and Axel helped themselves, piling couscous onto their hot deep dishes, the smell of the food making their mouths water expectantly.

I had better say something about this. The Nomads were not, in fact, the ivory-tower intellectuals that some would have us believe. Against society's three prevailing fundamental values they set a fourth: a hunger for knowledge – and, quite simply, hunger *per se*. One of the mainstays of the Nomads' activities was a taste for – or better, still a hunger for – un-Norwegian food. And believe me, apart from the odd obligatory touch of French cuisine, it was not easy to find a foreign restaurant in the European backwater that Oslo then was. When Peppe's Pizza Pub opened its doors it came as little short of a sensation – pizza in Oslo! Suddenly Norwegian citizens who ventured out on culinary expeditions could enjoy a flat circle of dough topped with mozarella cheese and all sorts of tasty titbits, from mushrooms and olives to chunks of bacon and spicy meatballs, all of this laced, what is more, with the most un-Norwegian and challenging ingredient of all: garlic. Other than that, it was the Chinese, enterprising as always, who in the Nomads' day had already established themselves with the China House in Sofies gate, the Peking House in Munchs gate and the Min Wah Inn on Parkveien, which meant that even in Norway one could eat shark-fin soup and Peking duck, dishes which until then had only been the stuff of detective novels. Other notable oases and sources of input were Valente's Osteria Italiana on Kirkeveien and Jacquet's Bagatelle on Bygdøy allé, not, by any means, to be confused with today's far more exclusive Bagatelle.

The Nomads often began their forays at one of these restaurants, to then, replete with un-Norwegian dishes and with the spices still smouldering on their palates, spend the rest of the night wandering the streets – with a pit-stop at the Magnet all-night café in the wee small hours to scribble down notes which, at any rate after a bit of polishing, would surely, at the very least, split the nebulae asunder with their brilliance. This unfamiliar food seemed not only to take their discussions down different tracks but also to facilitate the pursuance of one of their guiding principles: to dispute their own ways of thinking. Thus they had, for example, to reconsider their repudiation of both Arne Næss's theories of philosophical ecology and Johan Galtung's differentiation between direct and structural violence, late one night on their way down Pilestrædet from Bislett, having first consumed a variety of foreign dishes, the one which really tipped the scales – as far as self-criticism was concerned, that is – most probably being the chicken with cashew nuts in a hot spicy sauce.

Their favourite place, however, was still Bényoucéf's bustling restaurant where, once they came to know the lively and extremely hospitable proprietor, they could order couscous even when it was not a standard item on the menu. Not surprisingly, the Nomads felt an affinity for Bényoucéf, a Muslim, born on camel back, so to speak, in Aïn-Sefra, deep in the desert, to the south of Oran in Algeria: a real live nomad in the middle of Oslo. And I believe that Bényoucéf had a particular soft spot for the five young people who were such frequent visitors to his restaurant and who, in many ways, stood out from the rest of his clientele, which included all of the A-list celebrities of the day, names long since forgotten, who went there on account of the establishment's status as an 'in' place – to be seen – rather than, for example, because of the wonderful gigot of lamb you could get your teeth into there. Some people may perhaps remember La P'tite Cuisine, that pulsating place where a straw hat was popped on your head and the tables were set so close together that they looked more like long tables, with red and white checked clothes, candles in bottles, walls covered in Campari signs and tricolours, photographs of patrons and a lot of other bric-a-brac; all accompanied, of course, by accordion music, and with the *patron* himself, sporting a ring in his ear and a straw boater given to him by none other than Maurice Chevalier, shouting and exclaiming, a constant litany of '*mon Dieu!* ' and '*c'est vrai!*' and '*merde alors*'. All in all, La P'tite Cuisine was the scene of much friendly chaos, incredibly exotic back then, a fact which most people seem to have forgotten: how different and new this easy-going manner was, this warmth, so totally alien to Norwegians. They have forgotten that Bényoucéf the nomad was the first to break with the stuffy Norwegian tradition for boring white tablecloths and haughty waiters. For this he ought of course to have been awarded a medal instead of having the derogatory term 'dago' slung at him, as so often happened. Gratitude is not the most apparent Norwegian virtue. No one stood up for Bényoucéf when he went bankrupt, no one demanded that his restaurant should be reconstructed as soon as possible at the Folk Museum as the significant cultural milestone that it was.

So how do the pieces of a life fit together?

As he was finishing off his second generous helping of cous-cous, Jonas, fired by the chillies in the Harissa sauce, had the urge to tell Axel something about his own studies, first and foremost about how scientists were trying to locate unknown planets, cal-culating on the basis of minuscule, inexplicable disturbances on known planets, something he knew would strike a chord with Axel, for whom the whole question of cause and effect never palled. Following on from this, he told him about Percival Lowell's somewhat confused hunt for Planet X, a hunt that even-tually led to the discovery of the planet Pluto, although Lowell himself did not live to see it. It was a little like the hunt for the genes, Jonas thought. Even Lowell's Christian name, Percival, put one in mind of the search for the Holy Grail.

By a strange coincidence, that evening they had both brought something to show the other. Axel had a copy of an article from a relatively recent issue of *Proceedings of the National Academy of Sciences*, in which he showed Jonas some electron-microscope pictures from Herbert Boyer's and Stanley Cohen's successful attempt to create and duplicate a plasmid made up of DNA frag-ments from various sources, an attempt which, incidentally, introduced the methods which to this day form one of the cor-nerstones of the furiously expanding – and as furiously debated – recombinant DNA technology. Jonas, for his part, produced a book containing two telescope images from the 1930s that enabled Clyde Tombaugh at long last to detect the planet Pluto, ten thousand times too faint to be discerned with the naked eye. Just as Bényoucéf came over to ask if they were enjoying their meal, they noticed, to their astonishment, how alike the two pic-tures were. The electron-microscope images of plasmids with their DNA loops might have been a picture of the stars in the heavens, especially of the sort in which the outlines of the constellations have been drawn in, and vice-versa. Jonas had a fleeting vision of a day when scientists would discover patterns in the galaxies not unlike the coiling form of the DNA. Jonas was aware, in other words, of a childish notion, magnified only slightly, resurfacing: the suspicion that the universe, all of that inconceivable vastness, amounted to no more than one teeny-weeny cell in the fabric of something else entirely. Axel, who had also been musing over the similarity between the two pictures, wondered out loud, 'What if the guys who were straining to catch a glimpse of Pluto's secrets quite unexpectedly discovered a new clue to the mysteries of DNA, or that the guys who were trying to chart our genes unaccountably stumbled on a new planet. What if it were all somehow part of a circle?'

Such a thought called for at least one glass of calvados, not to say two, and it was after a much more down-to-earth conversation, more in the vein of the sable eyebrows, when it was almost time to meet up with the other Nomads as agreed, in front of the National Theatre, that Axel first told Jonas about his feelings of frustration. He confessed that he had immersed himself in the study of molecular biology and biochemistry and groped his way towards an understanding of DNA and the genome in an attempt to find out who he was. 'No, I mean it,' he said when Jonas laughed. But he had been disappointed. 'Christ, Jonas, we're talking out-and-out reductionism. An attempt at utter simplification. Downright materialism. A one hundred per cent mechanical view of life. A totally passé bit of Newtonian logic when you come right down to it.' Axel was more than just frustrated, he was undergoing a crisis; even his thick shock of hair was looking a little limp. 'I mean, it goes without saying,' he said. 'There are some things that occur in biology for which there is no simple explanation.'

'Like what?'

'How a person is formed. How the pieces of a life fit together. Why a person can suddenly change.'

'I thought that was exactly what DNA was – quite literally the story of how the pieces of a life fit together.'

'Yeah right, a life, in purely biological terms, but what is Life?'

It was all Jonas could do not to make a face that said 'bullshit'. Instead he said: 'Maybe we should get going.' The minute he said it he regretted it. Jonas Wergeland had nothing against extravagant issues, questions that were two sizes too big, that made pragmatic individuals and, not least, commonsensical Norwegians snort. Besides which, Jonas knew that this was one of Axel's great goals in life: to pose questions that were worth more than a hundred answers. 'How's about another calva for the road?' he said.

Axel waved to Bényoucéf, simply raised two fingers, and seconds later two glasses of calvados were set on the table. 'Promise you won't laugh,' said Axel, 'but here's what I've been thinking: what have been the most important experiences in my life?'

'Tell me.'

'Amazing as it may seem, the most important experiences in my life are experiences I have heard about from other people.' Axel waved his arms in the direction of the other people in the restaurant, or bistro as Bényoucéf insisted on calling it. 'In other words, other people's experiences have become my experiences.'

'I still don't see what you're getting at,' said Jonas.

'I think what I'm trying to say is that every human being could be said to be as much an accumulation of stories as of molecules. I am, in part, all the things I have read over the years. They don't leave me. They settle inside me like – how can I put it? – like sediment."

'So you believe that the stories you have heard are every bit as important as the genes with which you've been endowed?'

Axel looked thoughtful, as people often do on hearing someone else neatly summing up their own thoughts. 'Why not?' he said.

'Yeah, why not?' said Jonas. 'So you think a person can actually be changed by hearing a particular story?'

'Exactly. Maybe that's what life is all about. Collecting stories,' Axel said. 'Building up an arsenal of good tales, that can be put together in all sorts of complicated ways: like DNA.'

'If you're right, then it's not a matter of manipulating our genes but the stories in our lives,' said Jonas.

'It's not the sequence of the base-pairs, the genes, we ought to be mapping out, but the sequence of the stories that go to make up a life,' said Axel. 'And who knows? Arrange them differently and you might get another life altogether.'

They sat for a while in silence, each fingering his empty glass.

Jonas looked at his watch. Axel nodded. They were both feeling a little sheepish.

They paid their bill and were escorted to the door by a concerned Bényoucéf: 'You boys think too much,' he said. '*Bien sûr.*'

The Great White Whale

And so, and here I am thinking of the discovery of the planet Pluto, in every life there are stories which are not immediately apparent but which you know are there due to their unseen effect on other people and the known stories. I fumbled about in the dark for a long time before coming upon the story I am now about to tell, one that ought to be told at this particular juncture, while we are on the subject of astronomy and molecular biology, since it was hardly a coincidence that the moon, La Luna, should have been the focus of world attention during the summer when Jonas Wergeland first shot his genetic package at a girl's womb, or, as it is so grandly termed, made his sexual debut.

The house on Hvaler had stood empty since his grandfather's death, and Jonas was not sure how he would take being back on the island again when he set foot on it in the middle of July, after several tedious weeks of sorting mail for the Post Office. But the minute he dumped his rucksack down in the yard between the nasturtium-covered rockeries, he began to feel that this summer might spell the beginning of a new era. This was Jonas Wergeland's first summer as the Duke, and by a stroke of good luck he had two whole weeks to himself, before his mother and Buddha came down from Grorud. And, as if to physically mark the passing of a very difficult phase in his life, Marie F. appeared on, or floated onto, the scene.

Jonas was down on the jetty, seeing to a mooring line when she slid, suddenly and soundlessly, into his line of sight in a slender white kayak, an older model. She backed water, held still, smiled up at him. The oars glinted. She was not brown like the other girls: if anything she was pure-white. And pretty well built. Or voluptuous, Jonas decided later. She had fair hair and blue eyes and Jonas, standing there with the rope in his hand, in the middle of tying a half-hitch, felt that tingle starting all the way down at his tail-bone and slowly working its way up to the back of his neck as if his spine had turned into some kind of thermometer.

He stretched out on the jetty, on his stomach. She held the kayak still. They talked, while minnows and jellyfish glided past in the perfectly clear water, transparent as an aquarium. She came from Sandefjord but was studying at the College of Commerce in Oslo. She was visiting an aunt on the other side of the island. Jonas told her about his grandfather. They talked half the day away, while dapples of sunlight danced on the hull of the kayak, leaving rippling patterns on the sandy bed when the odd crab sidled past.

It was a two-man kayak and the next day, after she had got rid of the ballast, she took him out in it. The weather had been quite beautiful for weeks, the sea like a millpond most of the time. They paddled all the way out to Tisler. Jonas was surprised by just how fast they could move if they put a bit of effort into it; he loved the nice sound the slender vessel made as it sliced through the water, liked paddling in time, in sync, sitting behind her, copying her movements, watching the play of the muscles across her back, bare apart from the straps of her bikini, white skin and a faint tang of sweat from her armpits. 'I prefer a kayak,' she said, 'because you sit so close to the water, almost become part of it.' They had the sea pretty much to themselves, this being before the waters around the skerries were transformed into something akin to a motorway, trafficked by a constant stream of whining motor boats – a fleet whose numbers and aggregate value increased in inverse ratio to the general grousing about hard times and the size of the national deficit.

On the way back they took it a bit easier, partly because they had for some time been surrounded by the rolling backs of porpoises, like wheels in the water, accompanied by a lot of snorting; Jonas found it a bit frightening, while Marie F. was almost beside herself with excitement. Once the porpoises had swum off, she laid her paddle across the kayak and leaned back against his knees. He carried on paddling gently, far too gently to explain the pounding of his heart, and propped up against him like that, with her fingers trailing in the water, she told him about her love of the sea. 'Just think, seven tenths of the Earth's surface is covered by ocean and yet we know next to nothing about it,' she said. Jonas paddled in long slow strokes across the smooth water, black and pale-blue, aware of the scent of her hair, the soft body against his shins. 'If we don't start learning to understand the sea soon we'll never survive,' she said, straightening up, then she turned and looked at Jonas, a long look, before picking up her oar and sending the kayak shooting forward. Jonas always had the feeling that she was talking about herself.

Sometimes they went out fishing in the rowboat in the evening. No one was catching anything those days. Folk said the weather was too good. But Marie pulled in fish. Always. She kissed the bait before she let out the line and the fish would bite before the sinker reached the bottom, all kinds of fish: whiting, codling, even flounder. Marie F. fished for mackerel with a ground-line. She could have caught a whole boatful had it been necessary.

Jonas never caught a thing, he simply sat on the thwart, opening mussels and admiring her. Or sometimes he might take out his mouth organ and give her Duke Ellington's 'Isfahan' as music to work by. Rowing them home, he watched her cleaning the fish, swiftly and expertly, while a flock of gulls gorged themselves on the guts that she tossed overboard.

She was an expert at cooking the fish, too. It was not just that she had the same magic touch as his grandfather for fried mackerel with the crispest golden skin, she also served Jonas such surprising dishes as, for example, fish roulade with slices of apple, Chinese fish soup, trout with bacon, red peppers and tomatoes, and, as if that were not enough, she showed him, to his astonishment, that you could actually eat fish raw. On one occasion she had succeeded, thanks to her magical kissing of the bait, in hauling in a catfish – a terrifying monster that made great show with its horrible teeth and jaws in the bailer before she managed to kill it – then later, when she was filleting the catfish, neatly and beautifully, she sliced off a chunk and offered it to him, and for the first time Jonas discovered, to his delight, how fish really *tasted*.

In other words, Marie F. pre-empted Jonas's introduction to the later so popular Japanese sushi by at least ten years.

I might as well tell you right here and now that Marie F. is none other than a woman who can now boast of a dazzling career in the Norwegian business world, regularly cited and featured in the media as one of the very few women to reach the top. After graduating from college, she joined the frozen-foods concern Frionor but soon left to set up her own company, which she ran with such rare flair and inventiveness that it rose to become the very flagship of all companies exporting Norwegian fish, and not only salmon; she was, it goes without saying, smart enough to avoid becoming reliant on the vagaries of the one fish-farming venture.

But as I say, on this particular summer the focus was on La Luna; it was the summer of the lunar landing, on one of those very nights when everyone was sitting at home, eyes glued to the television screen, to watch Neil Armstrong set foot on the surface of the moon. Jonas, on the other hand, was filled with a longing for something much more down-to-earth: not a white planet but a voluptuous white body. Given the choice of being on board the lunar landing vehicle or sinking into the depths of Marie F., he did not have to think twice. That summer Neil was overshadowed by Louis Armstrong: What a wonderful world.

They often paddled out to the islets to swim. Sometimes Marie F. read a book, *Le petit prince* by Antoine de Saint-Exupéry. She was reading it in French. She was good at languages. One day she swam naked. Her skin was only a little whiter in the parts the bikini had covered. She looked magnificent, with a body that would have had a seventeenth-century painter scrabbling for his brush, the breasts of a fertility goddess. She gambolled about in the water. Jonas had to lie flat on his stomach to hide his erection. She dived, displaying an ample rear end, as if in triumph, before going under. Jonas was put in mind of a great white whale, one into which he would gladly – more than gladly – have stuck his harpoon. She turned onto her back in the water. Her blonde pubic hair shimmered, a golden fleece, enticing.

'Come on in,' she shouted. Bent double, he made his way down to the rock, and executed a swallow dive perfected at the

Torggata Baths. She swam to meet him, gently wrapped her
arms around him and let herself sink. He sank with her, down
into the water, it seemed to him that they went deep down; she
stopped, they were several metres underwater when she said
something, bubbles rising to the surface, before putting her lips
to his mouth and kissing him, kissing him long, as long as she had
breath, and she could hold her breath for a long time, longer than
Jonas who, despite the almost unbearable pleasure, the contact
with her naked body, finally had to kick off with his feet and float
to the surface.

'What did you say?' he gasped when she too broke the surface
just afterwards.

'*Mon petit prince*,' she said.

On other occasions they dived together, put on masks and
swam through corridors of red weed and sea anemone: a swaying, alien world. Marie F. shot fish with a simple homemade harpoon – all in all she was unfailingly inventive. Back at the house
she poked around in the boathouse, checking out lobster pots
and grapnels, lines and hooks, sorting and fixing, mending and
splicing, lashing this and binding that. And all the time this
whiteness, her skin, among the nets and ropes, her great body
which Jonas's eyes could not get enough of, which he longed for
with something akin to anguish.

One afternoon when they were lazing on one of the islets, on a
smooth rounded rock that oozed heat, Marie F. suggested that
they should have a fishing competition. The one who caught the
most fish in an hour could ask whatever they wanted of the other.
Jonas had nothing against that, *absolutely* nothing against it.
They positioned themselves one on either side of the islet, Jonas
with his old rod and Abu reel, desperate to catch some fish – so
eager that he actually kissed the spoon-bait before casting.

Jonas did not get a bite, only succeeded in reeling in the odd
clump of weed when the hook became stuck. Marie F. came
strolling up to him carrying six fine frying cod. They paddled
back to the jetty. Up at the yard, before she left, she turned to
him: 'Meet me down at the boathouse tonight at eight,' she said.
It was July 29th, St Olaf's Day, although that was the last thing
on Jonas's mind. On the western horizon, where the sun was

setting, the sky was aflame – red, orange, violet – but he had no eyes for that, he was waiting for Marie F. down by the boathouse, and she came. 'There's a full moon tonight,' she said, pointing to the beach, the tide. 'The sea's flexing its muscles,' she said, smiling, in shorts and a sweater, white thighs, nothing under the sweater but swelling breasts. She nipped into the boathouse and brought out a sail, shook it, took him by the hand. 'Remember, I can ask for anything I want,' she said and led him by the hand to an old peter-boat that lay on the shore belly up; it had lain like that for years. They crawled underneath it, there was plenty of room, a vaulted space, she spread the sail out on the grass, asked him to undress and lie on his back, he did so, she did the same, gleaming white in the dim light; she took his penis in her hand, not smiling, very solemn, the air was filled with all sorts of smells: grass, salt, oil, tar, seaweed; she ran her eye over his penis, a different look on her face, ardent, a sort of a glow to her cheeks, an urgency, he never forgot the sight of her, her voluptuous white body as she raised herself slightly, then proceeded to ease herself down on to him, one hand to her vulva, opening the way, or the wonderful, almost explosive, feeling when, for the first time, he felt a woman's labia against the tip of his penis, the moistness, the surprising warmth, and the nigh-on stupefying sensation of sexual excitement when she lowered herself right down on to him, burying him in her smooth, soft, warm vagina, or as Jonas himself would have put it: wrapped her yoni around his lingam. Never, not even in his wildest dreams, not even during his best wanking sessions, had Jonas imagined that it could be so indescribably, itchingly, staggeringly delightful.

And this is worth noting, because even though Jonas had been prepared for the unique potential of lovemaking by his parents' fine demonstration, he could not help but be affected by all the murky rumours and fantasies that did the rounds among the lads, in which the monomaniacal lust after the female genitals also gave rise to an undying myth as to how *dangerous* it was: that sticking your dick into a woman's vagina was like sticking it between two millstones, not to mention into the maw of a catfish, with the result that sex was not only bound up with longing, but also with a certain dread. Nevertheless, most of them agreed, perhaps as a consolation for having had to wait so long, that it came as a disappointment to all, that sex was highly overrated.

Not so for Jonas Wergeland. There, on St Olaf's Night, under the belly of a peter-boat, with a sail under his back, he knew that he had never experienced anything more wonderful than the feel of Marie F.'s great, white body and most especially her smooth, velvety, warm vagina. It far surpassed all of his greatest hopes and dreams. And he was given plenty of opportunity to fix this moment in his memory, his first time, because they were in no hurry, lying there under the vault of the boat surrounded by the scents of seaweed, tar, oil, grass; Marie F. bent over him and let him kiss her breasts, let him lick the coating of salt on her skin while she gyrated, growing wetter, slicker, her juices running down over his thighs; he had entered a chamber full of precious oil, fragrant oil, warm oil, gurgling sounds, little splashes, like the sound of the waves when he lay in the bottom of the rowboat; she reared over him, large, white, moving gently and slowly, massaging him with oil, again he was reminded of a ball-bearing, had the feeling of being at the hub of something, in touch with a warm, intelligent being; her movements became more intense, his cock was awash, sloshing about in a springtide of warm oil, a wildly mounting pleasure, a thrill beyond anything he could ever have imagined, such softness, such smoothness, such whiteness; he had visions of diving, sinking down into warm water, and just before he came, just before he shot his own little drop of fluid into that deep mysterious ocean of female oils, he turned his eyes up to the timbers of the peter-boat's hull and it occurred to him that they looked like ribs, that he was inside the belly of a whale.

They lay there for ages, on the old sail, under a vaulted roof bathed in the light of the full moon, while the sea showed its muscles in the slow run of the tide. They made love three times. At no time did Jonas feel lethargic or sleepy or depressed, as some people say can happen. He felt wide-awake, felt as if their lovemaking had opened his eyes: as if, rather than squirting something out, he had been filled up.

It will probably come as no surprise to anyone to learn that from that day on, Jonas Wergeland was blessed with the most amazing fisherman's luck; and this luck was to stay with him all his life, ensuring that he could get a bite anywhere, all he had to do was put out his hook – he even caught catfish. At first he thought it was simply that the fish had at long last returned. A couple of years were to go by before he perceived the connection.

Even so, when he crawled out from under the peter-boat, he knew that something must have happened, something to do with his imagination, because when he looked at the full moon, his first thought was that it resembled the head of a white whale suddenly rising up out of the dark-blue sea of the cosmos. Until then, he had always thought the full moon looked like a fuzzy old tennis-ball.

The Golden Fleece

And so Jonas Wergeland was utterly shattered to feel that twinge in his shoulder, a razor-blade turning in the joint that not only ruined his serve but also meant that he had a hard job hitting his ground strokes, with the result that the ambassador won his service game to take the lead in the final decisive set. Jonas tried to keep his face a blank, not to betray this fresh handicap, but he was serving so wildly that it was all he could do just to hold his own serve. Thanks to Jonas's poor play, the ambassador had recovered his aristocratic demeanour, and once more he loomed on the other side of the net, so sure of himself, and wearing that smile which Jonas would, without hesitation, have described as 'diabolical'.

Jonas had to alter his strategy, think in terms of placing rather than power. He had to fall back on the hard-won skills carefully acquired during his six months of playing with other partners, after Margrete had refused ever to play with him again. 'Come on, Jonas,' he muttered under his breath, standing in the Njård Sports Centre, wreathed in the smell of his own sweat. 'The most unlikely things are forever happening.' The main thing now was to remember what Margrete had told him about her father's weak points, not only about his backhand but also the fact that he was not quick on his feet.

The score was even, but things were going the ambassador's way; he won his service games easily, while Jonas had to sweat and strain for every ball. Pain shot through his body every time he swung the racket, serving was an almost unbearable agony. Gjermund Boeck, realizing that Jonas was in trouble, showed no mercy, made the most of his offensive forehand, putting a spin on the easiest of shots, peppering Jonas's side of the court. Jonas was suffering, every shot was torment; suddenly it occurred to him that the ambassador looked like a lobster, a horrible monster from another planet, his right arm and the racket forming a flailing, menacing pincer.

The sound of the ball, that incessant *thunk thunk*, was starting to get on his nerves, he was doing more and more running, slipped a couple of times, the whole hall reeked of sweat, he was dead beat, his eyes swam, his shoulder and upper arm were hurting something awful, he had to fight not to screw his face up, but he would not give in, he *could* not give in. As I say, this was the greatest challenge of his life, a stupid tennis match, but still and all the most important battle of his life, for the most ridiculous, cringe-making prize, a polar-bear skin, which was, nonetheless, a trophy he simply *had* to win, because this was Jonas Wergeland's battle to make the utterly impossible, the highly unlikely, happen; this was the Grorud lad against the entire lobster-eating *corps diplomatique*; this was David against Goliath, east side against west; it truly was, as Jonas Wergeland put it – while under the influence, I grant you, and many years later – a battle to demonstrate Norway's, or the average Norwegian's, amazing adaptability and competitiveness. After all, if a lad from the east side who had never laid hands on a racket in his younger days could beat a keen cosmopolitan player, then surely Norway was capable of making the switch from heavy industry to computer technology.

Jonas fought on desperately, trying, through the sweat streaming down into his eyes and making them smart, through the pain in his arm which was nigh on torture, to think clearly, to think in terms of accuracy. Then all of a sudden he pulled off a couple of strokes that he seldom got right: a couple of drop-shots that the ambassador did not even try to run for, and a few not particularly hard, but wonderfully well-placed, ground shots that had the ambassador dashing from one side of the court to the other, red in the face and with his white shorts slipping farther and farther towards his knees: a beautiful sight which for a moment made Jonas forget his aching shoulder and even venture a lob which, amazingly, landed inside the line, and by adjusting his grip slightly he managed to give his serves a bit of a sidespin which more than once caught the ambassador completely on the hop.

The pain in his arm was excruciating. Jonas could barely grip the racket, but even so, by some miracle, he succeeded in hitting a half-volley, at which Gjermund Boeck could only shake his head: 'That's not bloody well allowed!' he gasped, hitching up his shorts and straightening the ludicrous, quasi-tropical, pseudo-colonial cap that was no longer bringing him luck. Jonas knew he was not playing by the book, the injury to his shoulder was forcing him to improvise, and by a combination of sheer luck – in line with modern Norwegian history – and a year of hard training, he succeeded in delivering a number of unorthodox, not to say acrobatic, shots: shots from weird angles, and a flick of the wrist reminiscent of tennis genius John McEnroe, who came to the fore and took everyone by storm just around that time. This match left Jonas convinced that one of his ancestors must have had an outstanding talent when it came to this particular combination of racket and ball, which he himself called a 'tennis gene' – if, that is, it was not something that Nina H., the hurdler, had unleashed but which had been lying dormant since the day when he cleared the 1.60 metres backwards to become area champion in the high jump.

The score was 5–5 in the final set, with Gjermund Boeck to serve. Jonas was in so much pain that he was hearing voices, heard his coach, Finn Søhol building up the tension, speaking in a low voice, not much above a whisper, the way he did when he was commentating at Wimbledon, speaking in hushed tones, especially at decisive moments in a match, as if he were afraid that the sound of his own voice, up in the commentator box, might put the players off. The ambassador fired off his first serve, a cracker of a shot, straight into the net, thank heavens, hitting it so hard that one of his strings snapped, and Jonas was allowed a breathing space while Boeck went to fetch his reserve racket.

Jonas was on his last legs, his eyes would barely focus, his arm felt as though it had dropped off. The ambassador served again, but the break seemed to have spoiled his concentration; not only was he serving badly he also hit two double-faults, with the result that Jonas won the game almost without having lifted his sore arm.

Jonas was leading 6–5; he was serving for the match. His shoulder was throbbing like hell, he clenched his teeth so hard he could taste the amalgam, he simply had to do this, it was his one big chance; and through all the pain he was conscious of a strange sense of pleasure. He served, not particularly hard, the ball came into play, they hit some long balls from the baseline; every shot was like a knife slicing into his arm. Jonas both relished it and felt like crying, suddenly understanding what masochism was all about, slamming the shots hard enough to bring the humiliating taste of lobster flesh rising up into his throat to mingle with that of blood and amalgam, long balls from the baseline, until he knew he would never manage to hit the next ball. Then, out of blue, while trying to clinch the game with a coolly calculated diagonal on the backhand, the ambassador quite inexplicably hit the ball out of court. 'Damn and blast it to hell!' yelled Gjermund Boeck, the ambassador, causing heads to turn in the far corners of the hall. Jonas served again, a rotten, uncontrolled serve, fully expecting a lethal return; he could already see the sneer on the ambassador's florid face, but yet again the latter hit the ball out, all but smashing his racket on the floor in the process. The ambassador tightened up on his next two returns, played superbly, and the score stood at 30–30 when Jonas finally succeeded in serving another ace to gain match point.

He was close to passing out, was seeing two of the ambassador, the pain in his shoulder had spread throughout his body, his whole system riddled with broken glass. Racked by the most excruciating pain, he managed to toss the ball into the air and hit it, wildly, feebly, but the ambassador returned it warily as if he did not quite trust himself. Jonas hit a backhand cross, Gjermund Boeck responded with a sound, slicing, but slow, backhand. Jonas knew he was going to have to tie this match up before he keeled over with the pain; he hit a nice, long forehand, ran into the net, knew this was it, the moment when he would either win or lose everything, his faith in himself, a different life, a Golden Fleece, the belief that the most unlikely things happened every day, and through the pain he saw, to his teeth-gnashing despair, that Gjermund Boeck was well-placed, saw that look on his face that said he had everything under control, he had hit this murderous drive, his real show-piece shot, a hundred times before, in Bangkok, London, Nairobi, and he was now about to sweep Jonas off the court with this sure-fire shot, bring the score to deuce and then turn the match ruthlessly in his own favour. He hit the ball, ramming it perfectly, putting the whole of his corpulent figure behind the shot, a horrific, unbeatable passing shot which Jonas could only gaze after, sick to the marrow, but as he gazed after the ball, feeling sick to the marrow, he saw it land outside the line; it could not be, but it was out, and the ambassador, too, was gazing at it, although he could not really believe it, that the ball was out, and that Jonas Wergeland had won the match.

Gjermund Boeck was a good loser, however, and that very evening, at home in Ullevål Garden City – Margrete was also present – among the porcelain vases and dancing bronze gods, he made much of Jonas, not least of his willpower and heroic achievement, what with his injured shoulder and all. Jonas had the feeling that only now had the ambassador, again wearing one of his eye-catching Hawaiian shirts and standing with his back to a roaring fire, accepted him as a prospective son-in-law. 'Here's to the hero of the day,' said Gjermund Boeck. 'Cheers, Jonas! Damn me if you don't serve harder than Roscoe Tanner!' And the ambassador kept his promise; he actually did present Jonas with the huge polar-bear skin.

Despite his success, Jonas did not play much tennis after that match, and not because of his injured shoulder either: that soon healed. This might seem a mite odd, since Jonas himself believed tennis to be the greatest of all his talents. 'I could have won Wimbledon if only I'd discovered this gift earlier,' he would say in all seriousness. And yet after that day he rarely lifted a tennis racket. However strange it may sound, to Jonas Wergeland tennis – for reasons that were both irrational and, to some extent, anachronistic – represented a disavowal of the world of his childhood. 'It's a question of class,' he maintained, despite being, in general, almost fanatically anti-ideological. I merely present this as yet another incongruous, but intriguing, aspect of Jonas Wergeland's life; one which stands, not least, as a distinct contradiction to his decision to become the Duke, an individual who stood out, most decidedly, from the crowd.

There was, however, one thing that Jonas did not know, although he ought to have suspected something of the sort, since great individual victories are almost always won due to the unseen help of others: Margrete had tampered with her father's racket. She knew from experience that her father was forever breaking strings and that he usually had a couple of back-up rackets on hand. So the day before the match, unbeknownst to her father, of course, she had had his two reserve rackets restrung. She had asked for them to be strung a little looser to ensure that, at least for a couple of games, her father's control would be a little off, and he would not hit the ball quite as he expected to do. Jonas Wergeland would probably never have won that match, if the ambassador had not, as luck would have it, had to switch rackets at a crucial moment in the final set. Jonas never found out about this bit of 'help', and Margrete kept it to herself for the rest of her life, even when she had to listen, not without a touch of exasperation, to Jonas bragging about his great feat, as he was constantly doing – he persisted in regarding it as the greatest victory of his whole life – usually when some guest asked where in the world they had come by the most peculiar decorative touch on their living-room floor.

Something else which Jonas did not know, something not even Margrethe knew, was that the ambassador had long been looking for some way to rid himself of that hideous polar-bear skin.

The Duke

And so Jonas Wergeland was stretched out on the soft red carpet in the choir of Grorud Church, listening to his father playing the organ, while the light streamed in through the stained-glass windows high up in the walls and spread over the empty pews like a golden fleece, so it seemed to Jonas that the flurry of snow outside had been transformed into music and colour. He listened intently, wonderingly, to the unusual sounds emanating from the organ pipes, the strange shifts in tone, as if he knew they would set something in motion; he was just waiting for the signal, a faint whistle sounding amidst all the other notes. He was conscious of a slight ache in his body, in the shoulders especially, but it was a good feeling. A lot of people may well be strangers to the idea that a future victory – winning a gruelling tennis match against all the odds, for instance – can make itself felt in the present. I ask only that the possibility be considered.

His father was still playing the same swaying pitching music; a piece which somehow broke all the rules, a musical prism, a rhythm which put Jonas in mind of a caravan, of campfires in the darkness, of people sitting in a circle telling stories, a low, rhythmic murmur. Jonas thought of the human memory, of people who could carry thousands of pieces of organ music in their heads. Or entire epics. Like his grandfather. Suddenly it struck Jonas that his grandfather's death was like a huge organ being dismantled, or an organ sinking beneath the waves.

When do we become the person we are? When do we open the door onto all of our inherent potential?

He lay on his back, feeling heavy, heavy as lead from head to toe. And yet there was something about his shoulders, his shoulder-blades: an incipient thrill, a promise, a longing to be raised up. Who's going to tell me now, he thought, who's going to make me someone special?

Is this the most crucial story in Jonas Wergeland's life?

He gazed up at the apse of the church, the fresco, at the angels playing their instruments in the air above the Great White Flock, the sea of people. The organ music, the surge of it, conjured up a picture of water in his mind. He remembered how he had used to sit among the pebbles on the shore while his grandfather told stories. 'Just imagine, Jonas, if you were . . . ' How, while hearing his grandfather weaving him into grand epic tales, he had run his eyes, run his hands, over the pebbles, large eggs that harboured secrets of time, water. And now here he was again: by a sea, among stones, surrounded by a swirl of music, in a church of granite, and it was as if the music, that music which was not like anything else, suggested the possibility of another story, *was* another story.

Jonas lay in the choir of the church, the music had encased him in a cocoon; he lay perfectly still, torpid and yet restless, aware of a twinge, an ache in his body, primed for something or other. Outside it was snowing, a silent shower of soft specks, the sort of lovely snowstorm that is followed by sunshine and which leaves behind it a brilliant white landscape, totally altered, dazzling.

Can a person suddenly become something completely different from what they appear to be?

His father reset the stops, began to play another meditation, 'Les enfants de Dieu' from Messiaen's organ cycle *La nativité du Seigneur*, opening with a cascade of harmonies, a fanfare almost, that made Jonas start; a fantastic rising progression of chords and notes working up to a climax that never came because the music merely went on, turning into a tremendous upsurge, a mighty crescendo, music in continual metamorphosis, a leap from key to key, a musical sweep that made the stomach sink. Jonas listened, entranced, the whole church shook as if the music had found a crowbar with which to prise apart the crystal bars of the stones and was about to blow the building apart.

And here I will have to stop for a moment, because I am now coming to an extremely difficult part and, to be honest, I am not sure whether I can count on the goodwill, or tolerance, this story calls for. You see, during the next few minutes Jonas Wergeland had what, for want of a better expression, I will have to call a mystical experience, with all the potential for misunderstanding and misconstruction this entails, not least in a country which gets so touchy, so up-tight about anything metaphysical as Norway. Let me just say, briefly, that if Jonas Wergeland were, at some point in his life, to touch the bedrock of existence, to have anything approaching a mystical experience, a meeting with the angel of light, then it would not be unreasonable for it to occur here, with his father at the organ and Jonas himself stretched out all alone in a church built from the very rock from which he had, so to speak, sprung.

This is what happened: while his father's organ playing was making the whole church oscillate, while the snow was falling soundlessly over the surrounding countryside and while the light was cascading through the stained-glass windows like coloured dust, Jonas Wergeland realized that he would have to tell himself, that he would have to create his own story.

There comes a time when a person changes his identity, when he jumps, as it were, from one story to another, and in Jonas Wergeland's case it happened here, in a church filled with strange music. Up to then he had been told. Up to then he had been reliant on other people's stories. His grandfather's. Aunt Laura's. Nefertiti's. He had been a listener. Now he was going to have to take over – and it would not be a matter of being who he was, but of choosing who he wanted to be.

So if anyone has been wondering when Jonas Wergeland became the person he was, it was there, in the nave of a church in Grorud. Because it was there, lying on a red carpet under a large fresco depicting the Great White Flock, a sea of humanity, that Jonas made up his mind to break out of the crowd, to stand out for all to see. Then and there, with Messiaen's extraordinary music ringing in his ears he made up his mind to tell the story of the Duke. He was no longer Jonas Hansen, he was Jonas Wergeland, right then and there he took his mother's maiden name, christened himself, so to speak, on the spot – appropriately enough, with the font – that, too, of granite – standing only a

few yards away from him. From then on he would be Jonas
Wergeland, the Duke, an individual with many people inside
him and, consequently, so big that no one would be able to miss
him. He would seek out the Golden Fleece, bask in its golden
sheen, stand in the light, visible to all. And this last says more
than anything else about what actually happened there in a
church vibrating with the deep tones of an organ, with music
that seemed forever to be tearing itself free of its own development and context; aspiration and ambition were aroused. Jonas
wanted to be an organist, too: setting life's stops, entrancing
people, shaking them up, making their molecules oscillate, tug-
ging at their heartstrings. And even though he had no idea how
he was going to do this, and despite the fact that he only had the
vaguest notion of his own gifts, he had an idea that he might now
have chosen a life which would involve encounters with extraordinary women, long journeys and an exhausting struggle to make
the people of Norway think big. Jonas Wergeland lay on the floor
and felt an ache in his shoulders, his whole body aching, as if he
were growing, as if he were growing too fast.

Like a forewarning of the sphere in which he would become
visible to all, the entire apse of the choir, the large fresco, started
to vibrate, to emit a radiant light – Jonas saw how it suddenly
came to life, like a gigantic television picture. And as the organ
music altered character yet again, to something reminiscent of a
feverish dance, with high, swirling notes, Jonas heard a ripping
sound as one of the life-size angels stepped out of the fresco and
swooped down to the floor where he lay, whereupon Jonas was
lifted up and they, the angel with Jonas in its arms, flew up to the
roof and straight through one of the windows, the stained-glass
picture shattering into a million pieces round about them.

I should just say here that I am giving you Jonas Wergeland's
own version of the incident, for one thing because this best
describes what actually happened – a word like 'truth' is of no
relevance in this case – namely, a choice in favour of the unpredictable and the improbable.

Jonas came to his senses lying in the fresh snow outside the
church, on the side facing Grorud school, the school of his childhood; came round to find his father standing over him.

'What was that you were playing?' was his first thought.

'But what *happened*?' said his father, more worried than angry, his hands fluttering anxiously and helplessly in midair. 'What on Earth happened?'

'What were you playing?'

'A piece about angels,' his father said. 'But seriously, Jonas, how did you do that?' Haakon Hansen ran a bewildered eye from the window high up in the wall to his son sprawled in the deep, freshly fallen snow, while the soft white crystals kept on falling from above, already starting to cover up the shards of coloured glass scattered around them. It looked as though a rainbow had turned to ice and fallen to earth.

'I've come to a decision,' said Jonas. The palm of one of his hands was bleeding, he saw the blood dripping onto the snow, saw how the dark-red stains stood out against all the white.

From that moment onwards, Jonas Wergeland was on the outside. Not only, as this situation clearly implies, outside of the congregation but outside, set apart from, all the rest, the masses. He had made up his mind to be different, to refuse to submit to the collective clichés, the stereotypes: to discover his own story. Not that all human beings are not different, in the sense of being unlike all the others. It was just that Jonas Wergeland decided to accentuate this dissimilarity, to cultivate it, make it as fruitful as possible.

Taj Mahal

And so coming to Copenhagen was like coming to another continent. It was not only the moral shock of being able to walk into any grocer's shop and buy a bottle of white wine – it was more the gravity of the old buildings and palaces, all the verdigrised roofs and spires, a quite different sense of history than in Oslo, of nobility, if you like. Copenhagen was a capital worthy of a Duke.

At least a couple of times a year Jonas Wergeland and the other Nomads took themselves off to Copenhagen. Not to visit Tivoli, or the Zoo, not to buy hash in the Free State of Christiania or to watch porno movies or buy Danish salami. The purpose of these trips was two-fold: first they trawled the second-hand bookshops and then, in the evening, they repaired to number 38 Vesterbrogade.

When the Nomads stepped off the ferry in the morning, right next to Sankt Annæ Plads, they immediately set out on their wanderings from one watering-hole to the next, which is to say from one second-hand bookshop to the next; they combed all of those wonderful, chaotic, dust-laden treasure-houses with such fine-sounding addresses as Fiolstræde and Nørregade, Studiestræde and Nansensgade.

Jonas Wergeland was never a great book man, but he had nothing against second-hand bookshops. He like the lottery of it, the fact that you could stick your hand into any bookshelf at random and suddenly find yourself clutching some totally unexpected prize – let's say a book by Carsten Niebuhr, astronomer and explorer: a well-thumbed copy of *Beschreibung von Arabien*.

And that was the whole point. For the Nomads, the idea was to track down books that were not to be had in Norway, *different* books – books which the Others did not read. What they wanted – for reasons which they themselves obstinately maintained lay in their genes – was to be different. Which is why, true to tradition, the Nomads had also chiselled out their own tablet of Commandments: 1. Thou shalt wander the streets. 2. Thou shalt eat as much exotic food as possible. 3. Thou shalt transcend thine own limits. 4. Thou shalt not discuss the death of God. 5. Thou shalt not cite the names of Marx, Nietzsche or Freud.

Thanks mainly to this last commandment they were always on the lookout for alternative thinkers, books which were not 'in' at that time. They read, for example, Richard Burton's brilliant and wildly speculative ethnographic studies; they read Paul Valéry's razor-sharp essays and Erwin Panofsky's perceptive history of art. They read Georg Simmel rather than Marx, William James rather than Freud, and they read Paul Cézanne's *Correspondance* rather than anything whatsoever of Nietzsche's overrated, contradiction-ridden tirades.

So the lion's share of the day was spent straining their eyes to read names and titles on jam-packed shelves and it did happen, of course, usually just before closing time, that one of them would fall for a *fata morgana*; that Axel's eye would light exultantly on the spine of a much coveted volume which would promptly disappear – melt into thin air – as he reached out his hand. Then, at the appointed time, they would meet in Rådhusplads and march in a body, absolutely famished, to number 38 Vesterbrogade. I doubt if many Norwegians in the early seventies associated anything whatsoever with the first floor of number 38 Vesterbrogade – nor yet today, come to that – but for Jonas Wergeland and the Nomads, with their fondness for exotic food, this was a place of pilgrimage. Having once reached Copenhagen you didn't go satisfying your hunger with Danish *smørbrød* or *flæskesteg med kartofler* – that's roast pork with potatoes to you and me – nor yet by running a relay from one of the wealth of hot dog stalls to the next. Oh, no – you saved your appetite for number 38 Vesterbrogade.

Because at number 38 Vesterbrogade you found the Taj, one of the very first Indian restaurants in Scandinavia. In those days, of course, there was not a single Indian eating-house in Oslo.

And as far as I am concerned, the fact that the first Indian restaurant did not open there until well into the eighties says more than any number of anthropological treatises about the Norwegian national character, about Norway's astonishing isolation, about Norway's lack of appeal to other nationalities – and, not least, the limited culinary curiosity of your average Norwegian.

For this reason the Taj, and not forgetting the proprietors, Saba and Promila, was actually the *main* objective of their visit – more than the bookshops, although naturally they could not restrain themselves, but fell to scrutinizing one another's literary booty the minute they had plonked themselves down at the table. And there, in that L-shaped room lit by oil lamps, with its walls of exquisitely carved walnut, they consumed various dishes ordered from a lavish menu glued onto sheets of copper, while they leafed through books with faded spines and covers flecked with mildew, notes scribbled in their margins by avid readers and forgotten bookmarks of the strangest descriptions – and you can take it from me, the atmosphere in the Taj on the evenings when the Nomads ate there, surpassed even that of the Restaurant Krølle in Oslo in its intellectual heyday. The hot spicy food seemed to set fire to their conversation, or perhaps it was the books lying higgledy-piggledy among the plates and bowls and glasses that created an uncommonly propitious mood, thereby taking their discussions to quite unwonted and explosive heights, to moments of almost ecstatic joy and an instinctive understanding of even the most hair-raisingly complex issues.

As I say, Jonas was not all that interested in books – or not their content, at any rate, he preferred the actual hunt – but he loved sitting in that restaurant, with sitar music playing in the background, popping paper-thin morsels of crisp poppadom into his mouth, while Ganesh, the great scribe, rendered in brass, gazed down on him from the wall. It was as if, at long last, he found himself in that India to which he had first been introduced in his boyhood copy of the *Kama Sutra*.

The others, however, alternated between uttering blissful sighs and reading aloud from the day's antiquarian finds. Alva, who had dreams of becoming a playwright, had stumbled upon the memoirs of the Danish actress Johanne Luise Heiberg, *A*

Life Relived in Memory; and look at this, she said, helping herself to some more *paneer chat masaladar*, an exotic vegetable cocktail, believe it or not she had actually obtained a book containing Denis Diderot's marvellous polemic on acting: *Paradoxe sur le Comédien*. 'To feel or not to feel, that is the question,' she declaimed, holding the book theatrically at arm's length. And what about Trine? Trine sat wreathed in smiles, both because she was halfway through a bowl of mulligatawny, that celebrated soup, and because she had finally managed to track down the manuscript, in book form, of the film that Carl Theodor Dreyer never managed to make: *Jesus of Nazareth*.

'What's that there?' Axel asked, pointing to one dish. He was in great good spirits, a huge stack of books under his protective eye. '*Shahi korma rampuri*, lamb cooked in a curry sauce,' Jonas told him. 'Right, give me some of that. Now folks, who wrote this? "Her body was moving in great surging billows under him. For one fearful moment they listened to each other's gasping breathing and she whispered into his ear: 'Yes.' The darkness in front of his eyes was lit by myriads of tiny twinkling, singing stars. In cruel rapture mingled with pain and fear he let it happen."'

'Nabokov?' suggested Thomas. 'Miller,' said Trine. 'It has to be an Englishman,' said Alva. 'D.H. Lawrence.' Axel grinned, shaking his head as the guesses rained down upon him, each one wilder than the one before.

'Agnar Mykle,' he said. Had he been wearing a hat, he would have removed it. Axel had only one Norwegian literary hero: Agnar Mykle. 'It's from a translation of *Lasso rundt fru Luna*. An outrageously bad one, I'm sad to say. Stupid bastards have cut at least ten sentences from that short extract alone. It's a disgrace.'

Kashmir pullao, fried rice, and *nan mahiwal*, bread baked in a tandoori oven, were passed round along with bowls containing different relishes, wine bottles and jugs of water. They were sitting not far from the door and a model of the Taj Mahal faithful in every detail, lit from within. Over their table hung a large painting of Krishna dancing.

'Here we are,' said Thomas triumphantly, brandishing a copy of Theodor W. Adorno's heavyweight contribution to the philosophy of modern music, unearthed in the deepest recesses of Grubbs Antikvariat in Nørregade. 'Just you wait till I read what Theo W. has to say about the difference between Schönberg and Stravinsky,' he said, 'and I'll come up with the definitive argument for proving that, compared to Beethoven, Mozart is a gnat.' Upon which, predictably enough, another huge and vociferous argument broke out, causing people at the surrounding tables to prick up their ears, because even though all sorts of verbal hogwash might be served up at the table round which the Nomads sat over their *mumtaz tikka* and *tandoori gobi*, the odd pearl did also fall from their lips.

'This is for you,' Axel said rather solemnly, when the food had once more become the centre of attention, handing Jonas a fine, later edition of Alexander von Humboldt's *Kosmos*. 'You can always see if you can find any sign of Pluto in there.'

Jonas, too, had dutifully purchased a book. About the South Pole. Oddly enough it was in Nansensgade that he had come upon Ernest Henry Shackleton's *The Heart of the Antarctic*. Jonas was perpetually on the hunt for arguments concerning the South Pole.

Jonas Wergeland had never run from his social responsibilities, even though he had soon discovered that any exercising of these would often have to be more symbolic than actual, as witness his more or less successful efforts to show solidarity with the remote island kingdom of *Les Comores*. Jonas knew that the choice of a political cause, which in turn was, of course, based on a choice of values that could never be proved, of turtles, if you like, was necessarily something of a lottery – a bit like the books one picked up in a second-hand bookshop. So let me simply state that, even before his more short-lived commitment to the Comorian cause, in fact, Jonas Wergeland's eye had fallen on a geographical region and hence a political issue that was to concern him for the rest of his life – so much so that each year on April 10th he commemorated the birthday of the great humanist and natural rights theorist Hugo Grotius, the only person in Norway to do so.

Jonas Wergeland came down, in other words, in favour of the Antarctic – a somewhat opportunist choice, one might think, and not particularly original these days, when everyone from Green-peace to conservative politicians is trying to cash in on this poor corner of the world, but I would just like to remind you that Jonas made *his* choice over twenty-five years ago. Of the few books he owned, nine out of ten had to do with the South Pole. Thus, Jonas Wergeland was one of the first people in Norway to recognize that this mysterious seventh continent was under threat, partly from the more or less covert lust for power of certain countries, and the front they provided for good old-fashioned imperialism, and partly by the ecological consequences of the modern technology that was now coming into use.

Jonas Wergeland was critical, not least, of his own country's position in the Antarctic. He simply could not see why, just because some stubborn and vainglorious Norwegian had made it to the pole by dogsled and because other Norwegians had conducted a pretty ruthless whaling operation down there – the last thing anyone wanted to talk about now – Norway could lay claim to such an outrageously large slice of this colossal ice-cake, an area seven times greater than Norway itself.

As time went on, Jonas Wergeland developed a genuine fascination for the Antarctic, once part of the supercontinent Gondwanaland, the way one always becomes interested in a subject if one only reflects on it for long enough, even if it has been chosen at random and even, indeed, if one has a dread of snow and ice. Jonas became more than simply fascinated – he eventually came to regard this paradoxically barren continent as a key, as an angle on the entire global situation at the end of the twentieth century. It was a laboratory not only for the forces of nature, but also for the forces of society, inasmuch as it represented a point of intersection, a mishmash of scientific, economic and political problems. The Antarctic was quite simply a gigantic and valuable prism of ice. Which is also why there was nothing Jonas feared more than that this fragile continent, its transparency, as it were, would be polluted by airports, waste and, worst of all, mine workings since, according to the experts, Antarctica was bursting with minerals. And despite the fact that the Antarctic Treaty painted an ostensible picture of sheer, harmonious idyll, with all its fine talk about peace and research,

Jonas was keenly aware that this was nowhere near good enough. Because it was an indisputable fact – and this formed the very cornerstone of his commitment to the South Pole – that we in the West still inhabited a society where profit-oriented production was the governing corporate principle in the world of finance. That much socialism he had managed to absorb.

Although the term 'environmental protection' had not yet become all the rage, Jonas realized that this, the coldest, driest, highest continent on Earth, almost totally covered by an icecap measuring roughly 2000 metres thick, ought to be regarded much as a work of art, that it ought to be protected in the same way as the Taj Mahal. The Antarctic was the cleanest, most untouched place on Earth, 'still a virgin in a global brothel' as a future comrade-in-arms was to put it. The way Jonas saw it, it was obvious that the uninhabited South Pole – not counting the hundreds of millions of penguins, that is – should belong to all mankind and not merely to the seven countries with a claim to sovereignty, and hence he firmly believed – as a number of poorer countries would later suggest – that the Antarctic ought to be administered by the UN. Jonas was pretty certain that Trygve Lie would have supported such an idea.

So Jonas Wergeland not only celebrated Michelangelo Day in grand style; for many years, every April 10th – on 'Grotius Day' as he called it – you would find Jonas Wergeland on Karl Johans gate in Oslo, handing out fliers which he had personally paid to have printed, bearing such headings as 'Give the Antarctic To The Penguins', 'Let Amundsen Rest In Peace' and 'Queen Maud's Dubious Honour'. These relatively entertaining days on Karl Johan's gate also taught Jonas something about how staggeringly little the average Norwegian knew about the South Pole, despite the fact that they were natives of a country that had placed an unbelievable seventh part of this vast region under Norwegian dominion, according it the status of a 'dependency'.

On one occasion, thanks to these agitprop activities, Jonas was even invited to visit the office of the polar advisor at the Ministry of Foreign Affairs, and there were rumours that Jonas's expert knowledge and his warning that a minerals convention would not be ratified, nor prove in the long run to be a viable option, had carried some weight – and this I can corroborate. So Jonas Wergeland was in fact a pioneer and opinion-shaper as far as the South Pole was concerned and can in fact take no small share of the credit for the Antarctic, in due course, being accorded a new protocol on environmental protection – as long as it lasts, say I: because no one should be fooled into thinking that the Antarctic, cold though it may be, is not still a very hot, not to say piping hot, potato. All you have to do is mention the word 'platinum'.

But such triumphs lay far in the future. For now, Jonas Wergeland was with the other Nomads in Copenhagen, in Vesterbrogade, in the Taj restaurant, tucking into dessert – Mango halves and *kulfi-e-heer*, ice cream. 'What the hell's that?' Thomas asked Axel, sounding out the legend on the spine of a book picked up in an ordinary bookshop. '*De la . . . Grammatologie*? Jacques Derrida? Never heard of him,' he said. 'He's going to be big,' said Axel. 'Derrida – sounds like a swearword to me,' said Trine. Everybody laughed at Axel's bad buy, thumped him on the back. Alva raised her glass to the statues of Parvati and Lakshmi further down the room.

They never slept on their nights in Copenhagen. After a lengthy dinner rounded off by handfuls of sugar-coated aniseed and betel-nuts they would meander down to Central Station to consign their books to left-luggage lockers. That done, they walked the streets: Copenhagen is a wonderful city for walking, especially at night. They wandered along the banks of Peblinge Sø discussing the virgin birth; they sauntered past the gardens of Rosenborg Palace totally engrossed in an exchange on the younger Malraux versus the older; as a bit of light relief on their way past The Marble Church, Jonas and Axel played Ellington's smoky melancholy 'Dusk' on two mouth organs, before they wandered out to the Little Mermaid, a regular stop on their route, where they stood – all alone – and talked about wonderboy Eddy Merckx, who had just won the Tour de France for the fifth time. On the way back, something akin to a fight broke out between Thomas and Alva over the importance of Norbert Elias, a heated discussion that lasted from Amalienborg to Kongens Nytorv. Not until they were seated over a glass of Gammel Dansk bitters and an early breakfast at Nyhavn, gathering their strength for a last bout of pearl diving in the antiquarian sea, were they reconciled if no closer to agreement.

It is easy to laugh at all this, I warrant you, but as I say, it's an all too brief stage in life.

On the boat home they all fell asleep early, curled up in their Sleeperettes, all except Axel Stranger. He sat on the deck in the light summer night, reading Jacques Derrida, underlining like mad, toes curling with glee, blowing kisses to the gulls, already looking forward to regaling the others with the weird content of this book over a steaming hot dish of couscous at Bényoucéf's.

Tabula Rasa

And so you see, he just *had* to talk to somebody, he said, almost apologetically and almost bursting with eagerness, enthusiasm, agitation, as he caught up with Jonas on the steps leading down to the street. What did Jonas say? Please? Did he have a minute?

Jonas explained, by dint of a couple of well-rehearsed phrases, that he did not speak the language, that he simply happened – and here he hesitated as always – to be Norwegian, sorry, whereupon the stranger grabbed hold of his arm and resolutely stayed him, looking extremely agitated. Noruego? Noruego! The other man simply stood there repeating the name as if he had found the very password to the secrets of the universe and could not believe his luck.

'But she is also Norwegian,' the man said, switching to English.

'Who?'

'Liv Ullman.'

The stranger pronounced her name with reverence and an astonishingly accurate Norwegian 'u'. Although he could not have said why – Liv Ullman meant nothing to him one way or the other – Jonas was glad the man had not taken him for Swedish.

'We *have* to talk,' the man said. 'I knew it the minute I laid eyes on you. Your shoes.' He was of an age with Jonas, dark, his eyebrows almost joining in the middle.

'It's late,' Jonas said. It was getting on for ten o'clock.

'Late? The day's only just beginning,' the man said. 'Let's walk.'

The stranger took Jonas by the arm and they set off down the street. Jonas had only the vaguest idea of where he was. They came past a café, a tobacconist's, several shops selling leather jackets, a small square planted with leafy trees, giving way to a row of houses. The door of one stood open, and they caught a glimpse of a long passageway, its floor inlaid with a labyrinthine mosaic, a couple of chairs, a few pot-plants and a vase of flowers, barely discernible in the dim light as roses.

The man said his name was Eduardo, he asked what Jonas did for a living. Jonas said that he was studying astronomy, mainly in order to give some solid answer, he couldn't really have said what he was doing right then. The man laughed. 'And now you've switched to film stars?' he said. 'You must be very proud of her.'

'Of whom?'

'Liv Ullman.'

That name again. Had Jonas seen her as Nora? Eduardo wanted to know. Or as Rebecca West? What was she doing these days? In his excitement Eduardo stumbled over the English words.

Jonas had to admit that he did not know that much about her. Eduardo was flabbergasted, stopped dead, gesticulated frantically, lost for words.

'You'll have to excuse me, I'm on my way to the Avenida de Mayo,' Jonas said. 'I need to see it one last time before I leave.'

Eduardo shrugged this off. 'There's no hurry, surely. This is more important.' He seemed almost angry, his brows drew together into one long black line, he towed Jonas along in his wake, started talking about the cinema, animatedly, about Liv Ullman, how great she was, that there was no one to touch Ullman in close-up, the greatest since Garbo. They came past a café, a tobacconist's, several shops selling leather jackets, a small square planted with leafy trees, giving way to a row of houses. The door of one stood open and they caught a glimpse of a long passageway, its floor inlaid with a labyrinthine mosaic, a couple of chairs, some pot-plants and an old mirror, black and mysterious in the dim light.

'And her lips,' said Eduardo. 'Have you seen her lips?' He stopped, took Jonas by the shoulders, almost shaking him. 'Even Sophia Loren doesn't have lips like that. By God, Liv Ullman puts a whole world of emotion into her lips alone.'

Jonas had been in a funny mood all day. It still got to him every time, the way his uncertainty grew in big cities, not only as to what he should do with his life but as to who he was. When he walked along the broad avenues or through the busy streets with the hum of a foreign language in his ears, he felt as if his very identity were being brought into question or was disintegrating. He was everyone and no one. Among the crowds on the calle Florida it struck him that he could pass himself off as anyone at all: an idea that he both liked and disliked. In any case there was something about this city, more than any other city, possibly because of its air of being a copy of all other cities, or a copy of a copy, a sort of concrete denial of the possibility of original thought, that imbued him with a strong sense of loneliness or emptiness. It was this that had prompted him, an hour or so before he bumped into Eduardo, to grab a taxi, wanting to get a little further away from the most frequented parts of town. They were somewhere near the top of the calle Sarmiento – although Jonas did not know that: to him, every quarter looked like all the rest – when, out of the corner of his eye, the way you can spot a car coming from another direction even when you are looking straight ahead, he suddenly caught sight of something familiar and asked the driver to stop. Acting on impulse, as they say. He paid the fare and watched the car drive off. It was a while before it dawned on him what it was that had made him stop. On a wall behind which, as it turned out, hid the Cinemateca Hebraica, hung a portrait of Liv Ullman. Jonas had actually been pulled up short, in the middle of a strange city, by the face of the Norwegian actress, as if he had caught sight of someone he knew, a casual acquaintance or distant relative.

And now we come to something which may be hard to understand but which nonetheless can be said of a great many Norwegians: Jonas Wergeland had never seen Liv Ullman, neither in the cinema nor on stage. To him Liv Ullman was just a name from magazines and newspapers, a face out there on the ether; something negative almost, something epitomizing a certain *tristesse*, intense films involving a lot of staring into space and great dollops of pathos.

And so it was that Jonas Wergeland, possibly in a fit of shame or curiosity, first saw a film starring Liv Ullman in this foreign cosmopolis, in a cinematheque far up the calle Sarmiento, a packed cinematheque at that, in a brown-panelled auditorium with mouldering seats and wall-mounted fans that almost drowned out the soundtrack. It was not any old film, either; it was Ingrid Bergman's *Persona*, one of the highpoints of cinematic history, I would say, if forced to state my preferences, and a film which was to have a great effect on the people involved, inasmuch as it changed Liv Ullman's life and, according to the director himself, saved his life, no more nor less. And even if Jonas could not follow everything that was going on – or, to be honest, not much at all – in this remarkable black-and-white film, partly because he had missed the first few minutes, which do give some idea of what has gone before, he was left with a distinct impression of having been confronted with a wordless secret, and that Liv Ullman was not, *most definitely* was not, what he had been led to believe by all the rumours, allegations and clichés that he had picked up during his boyhood and youth in Norway.

'Have you visited Eva Peron's grave?' Eduardo asked.

'No, but I want to go to the Avenida de Mayo,' said Jonas. He scanned his surroundings as if trying to get a fix on something, while they strolled along street after street. They came past a café, a tobacconist's, several shops selling leather jackets, a small square planted with leafy trees, giving way to a row of houses. The door to one stood open and they caught a glimpse of a long passageway, its floor inlaid with a labyrinthine mosaic, a couple of chairs, what might have been an old encyclopaedia, a suggestion of scuffed silver in the dim light.

'Relax, I'll take you there,' said Eduardo. 'Evita was a film star, too, you know.'

'I don't think Liv Ullmann has all that much in common with Evita.'

'Why not? They have the same charisma. Do you think Liv Ullman could ever become president of Norway?'

'We have a monarchy.'

'Well, queen then?'

Jonas could not help but like the man, like this eager, almost childlike admiration of a Norwegian, as if some of this reverence rubbed off on himself, making him less lonely, less melancholy, less lacking in identity – he was also happy to discover that here, too, on the other side of the ocean, people roamed the streets, that here, too, people were apparently willing to wander all night long, wander and discuss things. Jonas had a vision of a secret brotherhood, urban nomads, caravans crossing all the cities in the world.

Eduardo wanted to talk about the film. Jonas said he had no idea what it was all about. Eduardo launched into a long explanation, he had seen the film four times already, discovering new things in it each time, not least about Elisabeth Vogler, the woman played by Liv Ullman: an actress who had turned her back on the world and chosen the stratagem of silence. The way Eduardo saw it, the question as to why Madame Vogler stops speaking was as relevant as the question as to why Hamlet hesitates. Jonas's interest was aroused, he asked the odd little question, Eduardo replied, pondered, casting invocations and theories at stars they could not see because of the street lamps. 'Did you notice the scene when she is lying in the hospital bed, listening to Bach while the light slowly fades? How her face fills the whole screen, straight on?' Jonas vaguely remembered it. 'God, what a scene, with the lines gradually being blotted out and then, just before it goes totally dark, she turns her face upwards and we see it in profile. Jesus and Mary, it was so beautiful, so open, so rich in possibilities, I just can't get it out of my head. The graininess of the picture, grey like a boulder. Or as if her face were slowly turning into a landscape. I've been thinking of doing a sculpture that would convey something similar. Oh yes, I'm a sculptor. I'd like to create something that resembled Liv Ullman's face. Only the great Brancusi has ever come close, with that head that looks like an egg – the closest you can get to a *tabula rasa*.' They came past a café, a tobacconist's, several shops selling leather jackets, a little square planted with leafy trees, giving way to a row of houses. The door of one stood open and they caught a glimpse of a long passageway, its floor inlaid with a labyrinthine mosaic, a couple of chairs, some pot-plants and a little table on which lay a large coin, a glimmer of gold in the dim light.

'Are there any statues of Liv Ullman in Norway?'

'I don't think so,' Jonas said.

Eduardo was shocked. He asked if there was a plaque on the wall of her childhood home in Trondheim. Again Jonas did not think so. Eduardo shook his head. What sort of a country *was* Norway? How many Norwegian actors had been nominated for an Oscar? How many Norwegians had made the front cover of *Time* magazine? He took Jonas's arm, dragged him into a café and there, in that café with its pale-green walls and lurid glaring light, over a cup of coffee, while everyone else in the room was staring at the television set high up in the corner, Eduardo proceed to reel off facts about Liv Ullman. Did Jonas know that when she was a little girl she could do handstands on the handlebars of her bike? That her great-grandfather was called Viggo, her sister Bitten, her nanny Karen, her press secretary Emily? That her mother had worked in a bookshop? That as a young girl Liv had painted? That she had studied with Irene Brent in London and that for her audition at the College of Drama in Oslo she had played both Julia and Ophelia, but had not been accepted? 'It really is quite shocking! Doesn't it make you feel embarrassed for Norway?" Again Eduardo's dark eyebrows drew into a straight line, he eyed Jonas accusingly before plunging into even more facts about Liv Ullman, from the name of her first husband and that of the dog she had had at that time, to her penchant for freshly-squeezed orange juice. Jonas was amazed. Here, in a café in Buenos Aires, was a man who knew a hundred times more about Liv Ullman than him, probably more than most Norwegians; he was even familiar with a Norwegian film as pathetic as *Fjols til fjells*. And most surprising of all, Jonas could tell, the plethora of biographical information notwithstanding, that the other man's main interest was in Liv Ullman the actress, in her art – 'her greatness' – on stage and screen.

Eduardo eventually left the subject of Liv Ullman behind when they resumed their stroll, striding through streets running at right angles, their corners all looking alike. He talked about himself, about his own frustrations. He was not sure what he wanted to be, who he was, he felt lonesome, depressed; he was everyone and no one. 'I bet you we could swap jobs,' he said. 'You could be a sculptor and I an astronomer.' They wandered through the city; Jonas noted that they were walking in step, taking the same length of stride. They passed a darkened shop window containing a display of hats. They both halted, almost spontaneously, and stood there studying their reflection. They were the same height, same build, both were wearing white cotton shirts, buttoned to the neck. Jonas was standing slightly behind, for an instant he saw them merge into one person.

They continued their walk; they must have walked for miles – if they had not been going in circles, that is. Jonas suddenly found himself wishing that they could go on like that all night, noticed that he was unconsciously slipping Spanish phrases into his remarks; Eduardo began to introduce the odd Scandinavian word, expressions he must have picked up from the film: '*Nej, låt bli!*', that sort of thing. More than once he murmured '*Ingenting, ingenting, ingenting*' – 'Nothing, nothing, nothing.' – looking at Jonas and smiling. They came past a café, a tobacconist's, several shops selling leather jackets, a little square planted with leafy trees, giving way to a row of houses. The door of one stood open and they caught a glimpse of a long passageway, its floor inlaid with a labyrinthine mosaic, a couple of chairs, some pot-plants and a niche containing a figurine of an animal, possibly a tiger, dreamlike in the dim light.

Just as Jonas was thinking that they must be well and truly lost or that they must be right out on the outskirts of the city, suddenly there they were, in the middle of the Avenida de Mayo where, earlier in the week, he had stumbled about with his eyes out on stalks, hardly able to believe what he was seeing, his head tilted back to take in the staggering conglomeration of buildings of every style, a street which – for the benefit of anyone who did not know this already – was to change his life, moving him to drop astronomy for architecture, a magical street embodying the streets of all the great metropolises.

Eduardo flung out an arm disdainfully. 'I'd give you all of this, to have the chance, just once, of meeting Liv Ullman,' he said.

And then, the next moment, as he gazed pensively along the street: '*Ingenting, ingenting, ingenting.*' 'Nothing, nothing, nothing.'

Breaking the Light Barrier

And so Jonas Wergeland's moment of truth came on a day like any other, without him having given any thought to it, just like the old folktale of the boy who leaves home to look for his father's donkeys and returns home a king.

Jonas had lunched with Margrete at the University, where she was attending a seminar, and was on his way to Chateau Neuf, the student rec, at Majorstua, when he became aware that his feet were carrying him, quite of their own accord, in another direction, perhaps because it was pouring with rain, and he had had to hop over a huge muddy puddle; and as his umbrella was buffeted by the wind he saw where they were leading him, namely, straight towards the white building on the hillside, headquarters of NRK, the Norwegian Broadcasting Corporation. And before he knew it, as it says in all the best fairytales, he found himself in the personnel department, whence he was directed to an office where he asked, again without having planned it and with no idea what made him say it, whether they were looking for any new television announcers; and by sheer coincidence – let's just call it that, far be it from me to spoil anything – that was exactly what they were looking for, new faces, as they put it, and he was asked to send in an application.

In our day and age, as we are repeatedly being told, everybody gets their chance to be famous for fifteen minutes. As Rakel, Jonas's Wergeland's sister, discovered during the oil crisis in 1973, when she was on her way to visit her cousin Veronika Røed in Gråkammen, up on Holmenkoll–Heights, and had to take the electric train. And what happened? She climbed onto the train and took a seat, all unwitting. And who should be sitting next to her but His Majesty the King himself, Olav V, with that well-known profile from the coin of the realm, right beside her, large as life, in his skiing gear, dog and all. And before she had time to collect herself, the cameras started flashing. The next day she was inundated with phone calls from people she had not heard from in years, but who had seen her picture in the paper.

Jonas Wergeland's fame was of a more lasting sort, but that too had its beginnings in front of a camera.

Some weeks after submitting his application, Jonas was back at Television House in Marienlyst, sitting in a little room that put him in mind of a dentist's waiting room, mainly because he was feeling so nervous. There were two others in the room: both girls, attractive, very attractive, although Jonas did not feel any tingle running up his spine. They too had been provided with some sheets of paper which they were studying, a list of disconnected phrases to be read out. 'Announcer Audition' it said at the top. Over a hundred people had applied for the job. Rudeng, the director, had decided to screen test twenty.

So only now, and still with no idea what he was doing there – he was, after all, still attending the College of Architecture – did Jonas Wergeland find himself standing on the threshold of NRK, ten years after Gabriel Sand's earnest advice to make television his career. He had not followed this advice, had never felt drawn to that flickering box. On the contrary: he had regarded it as an asset not to watch TV. He loved being on the outside, particularly enjoyed being able to interrupt passionate discussions with some shocking remark: 'The Ashtons? Who're they when they're at home?' or 'Who is this guy Odd Grythe?' Only now, possibly because it had been raining and he had had to sidestep, was he, as Gabriel had urged, venturing to make the big leap.

It was his turn. Jonas Wergeland was escorted to one of the announcing studios by a veteran female announcer. The room was actually painted dark-blue, but it gave an impression of total blackness, almost frightening, cave-like. And it had a smell about it, sweetish: makeup perhaps. It was a tiny untidy room, with a welter of cables on the floor and littered with all sorts of paraphernalia. For Jonas, it was worth the visit for this alone: to discover that what to the viewers appeared to be a warm, bright, cosy and, above all, spotlessly clean, room was actually a filthy black cupboard with only just enough room for the announcer to squeeze in between the desk and the back wall, a cyclorama coloured by light. Jonas sat down at the desk, which was covered with a black molton cloth, squinting in the glare of the lights aimed at him from all angles: spots and soft lights, backlights. What about makeup? No, no makeup. The veteran female announcer gave him a few practical tips and went out. He was alone. In front of him, a little to one side, were three monitors. In one of them he could see himself. For a split-second – although what made him think of it he could not have said – he felt as if he were back inside the organ chest, at the heart of some ineffably complex mechanism. He was nervous, terribly nervous.

'Let's hear your voice,' someone said over a loudspeaker.

Jonas felt like saying 'Yoo-hoo! There's a hole in the loo-oo!' the way they used to do as kids, shouting it into mysterious cracks and holes or places with a good echo, but he managed to restrain himself and instead, since it seemed appropriate in that room, in that situation, he said: 'The mind is incapable of grasping the full significance of a time-span of hundreds of millions of years.' Pause for effect. 'Charles Darwin.'

No response. A bad sign. Nerves rippled through his body like the northern lights.

'Look at the camera, so we can get a proper shot of you.' A voice over the loudspeaker. 'That's it, good.'

There was no one behind the camera; the instant he focussed his gaze on the lens his nerves steadied. He had the overwhelming feeling that this little circle was what he had been searching for all along, and his surroundings were forgotten completely in his effort to remember what it was: a hub. Here it was, at last, the hub.

'You can start when you see the red light,' said the voice over the loudspeaker.

In one of the sidewalls was a large window into the main control room, CR1, and through the slats of the Venetian blinds Jonas could see the head of programming and a couple of technicians, together with the veteran announcer: people who would be judging his performance, which is to say, they were getting it on tape. Rudeng, the director was also there, as if he knew that something extraordinary was about to happen – something that would make a good story someday – and wanted, therefore, to witness it firsthand. He had his eyes fixed on the screen which was now showing Jonas's face in profile, giving Jonas himself a feeling of seeing his face reflected in mirror upon mirror.

The red light came on and he began to read out the announcements on the sheet in front of him, totally disconnected phrases, the sort used to introduce a programme, or between programmes, or for rounding off the evening's transmission. He read them out as best he could, trying to remember to look up every now and again, look at the camera lens, at the hub: he thought of Gabriel Sand, thought to himself that he *was* a television announcer, that he was many people, among them a television announcer; that it was inherent in him, it was just a matter of dredging it up; he read, pronouncing each word as clearly as possible, taking especial care over words in English, German and French. 'And now, via Eurovision, we bring you a performance of the opera *Don Giovanni* by Wolfgang Amadeus Mozart, performed by the Orchester des Nationaltheaters Prague,' he read. 'The conductor this evening is Karl Böhm. The role of Don Giovanni will be sung by Dietrich Fischer-Dieskau,' he read. 'And now,' he read, 'a programme on the French writer Antoine de Saint-Exupery, author, among other things, of the fable *Le petit prince*,' he read, and it was not going too badly, certain words and expressions in particular really hit home, Antoine de Saint-Exupery, for instance, and *Le petit prince*, hit home with a vengeance as if all his life had been a preparation for just this moment, for a job as a television announcer. He read on. 'And we rounded off this evening's programmes with "I Don't Know What Kind of Blues I Got", performed by the Duke Ellington Orchestra,' he read. 'The soloists were Barney Bigard, Lawrence Brown, Ben Webster and Harry Carney with Herb Jeffries on vocals,' he read, names he could have recited in his sleep; tried to look up every now and again at the faint light deep inside the camera lens, a bright dot, a photographic Pluto; he read on and on, no one asked him to stop, he went on reading for a long time, read all three sheets, in fact, a crazy assortment of announcements, out of context and yet oddly familiar; and when he reached the end and still no one had asked him to stop, he looked at the pane of glass and the people inside the control room, all of them with their eyes glued to the screen as if they had just been presented, not with a face, but a new planet, which was not all that far from the truth. Not until Jonas turned into profile did they rouse themselves. 'Thank you,' said the voice over the loudspeaker.

Rudeng asked him to come in to the control room. They reran the take, and the phenomenon was repeated. The others sat in total silence, hypnotized in fact, or as if they could not believe what they were seeing. Even Jonas was surprised, because it *was* powerful stuff. Only then, when he saw himself on a television screen, did Jonas realize what a striking face he had. And on the screen, or on camera, something had happened to it, making it even more striking; the face on the screen was different from the face he saw in the mirror. The camera must have acted like a prism in reverse, Jonas thought, in such a way that the lens united the entire spectrum of faces that he owned and transformed them into one powerful dazzling face. Jonas stared at the screen and felt, with a touch of dread, a tingling sensation creeping up his spine, and I would like to stress that this had nothing to do with his being infatuated with his own looks, what is known as narcissism – it was simply because, as Jonas himself realized, he found himself confronted with a work of art.

And right there and then, in that control room at NRK's Television House, Jonas also realized something else, because he had not always had such a striking face, it must only have become fully formed some years earlier, through some slow process of inner growth, and Jonas understood that this face had something to do with the exceptional women with whom he had lain. He had converted this beauty into other currency, as his grandmother had done with her collection of paintings. He had converted it, not into cash, but into strength, into personality, into charisma.

Rudeng would later describe the most important criterion when assessing people: whether they could come across on screen. Jonas Wergeland had certainly come across on screen, so much so, said Rudeng that he had had to take a closer look at the monitor to satisfy himself that the image he was seeing was not, in fact, three-dimensional. Rudeng would tell that story again and again. 'You should have been there when Jonas Wergeland auditioned for the job of announcer,' he would say with a note of pride. 'It was like witnessing someone breaking not the sound barrier, but the vision barrier.'

Before they parted, Rudeng asked Jonas whether he had been thinking of anything in particular. Jonas shook his head. But he *had* been thinking of something in particular, he had imagined that he was talking to Nefertiti, and that may well be why people would later say that they felt as though Jonas Wergeland spoke to them as a friend, directly to them, with a warmth and charm, not to say love, that could not *help* but strike at their hearts even if he were only presenting a run-down of the next day's programmes. And in a way it was true, Jonas truly believed that Nefertiti was listening to him.

They called, of course they called; and he was signed up for a trial period, first assigned to the morning slot but soon moved to the evening broadcasts so that his real breakthrough came with the ingenuous words: 'Good evening, and welcome to *Children's Hour.*'

And from the word go, Jonas liked it, liked it better than reading astronomy or architecture; the minute he sat down on that chair he knew that there, finally, in that broom cupboard, was where he was meant to be; there, sitting all alone, talking out loud, talking to the wall; he could not explain it, but he loved it. It was a hub. He recalled Gabriel's hymn of praise to his little boat: I could be bounded in a nutshell and count myself a king of infinite space, and to begin with he did not give much thought to the fact that, while he was sitting alone in that cupboard, his face was being reproduced a million times over, appearing on sets in a million households; nor did it occur to him, naïve though it may be, that his face would strike a chord with people, possibly because he had watched so little TV himself. To his surprise, however, people started nodding and smiling at him in the street and at bus-stops; and Jonas, who had long been in the business of recognizing fine art, pictures, when he saw it, found that he was now being recognized, like a picture, like fine art; and only then did it really dawn on him that there were people beyond the wall of the broom cupboard, that despite his seclusion, he was visible to all and sundry – a fact which was reinforced when the letters started to pour in, not to mention the people being turned away from reception, elderly ladies asking for his autograph.

Another few months were to go by before Jonas Wergeland perceived, with his eye for an angle, that the job of announcer was the one angle that revealed everything there was to know about Television House, the whole secret of television, for that matter: that it all came down to the face, to showing one's face, to being recognized, no matter what one said or did. All that counted, as far as the public was concerned, was that you were a face on the TV. And hence, strangely enough, Jonas Wergeland felt as famous after a few months in the announcer's chair as he did after years of programme making. The way he saw it, only from a tiny slice of the population could one win greater respect for creating something than for showing your face.

In all fairness, it ought to be said, by way of excusing the majority of the Norwegian people, that there *was* something quite unique about Jonas Wergeland's career with NRK. And moreover, people *could* tell one face from another. It was not every day that you were confronted with a face which suddenly raised a mouth organ to its lips and launched into a virtuoso performance of Duke Ellington's 'Take the "A" Train' before going on to announce one of *Children's Hour*'s long series of films about a group of little locomotives; and even without the mouth organ, Jonas Wergeland had such exceptional presence that people almost had the feeling that he was sitting there, in person, in their own living rooms. In other words, Jonas Wergeland's face possessed such an uncommon luminescence that he rapidly came to overshadow everyone else; he was quite simply NRK's supernova. For years Rudeng never referred to him as anything but 'the Duke', completely off his own bat, not merely on account of Jonas's marvellous English pronunciation of the names of the Duke and the members of the orchestra. There were even those who would recall Jonas Wergeland's first appearance on the television screen as a milestone on a par with the live transmission of the lunar landing. There seemed almost to be a certain prestige attached to having seen him and discovered him when he was still filling the morning slot. 'I knew it,' people would say years later when Jonas Wergeland was one of the country's most famous, most written-about figures. 'The minute I laid eyes on him I knew there was something special about that guy.'

And now here you are in your own office, surrounded by video recorders and cassettes, cassettes containing film of yourself, old programmes, black tape testifying to your fabulous success, welcome to this evening's programmes, and you look at the map of Venus, a highly provisional map, you think, a planet populated by lobsters, you think, boiled lobsters, you think and your eye moves to the map of Antarctica, that too provisional, you think, with the lines of latitude running out from it in circles, like a target, you think, like a lens, you think, and you look at those circles, circles within circles, and you try to see the connection between all of those cassettes and Venus and Antarctica, and you look at the circles and see that they are spinning, like a wheel, you think, and you are growing dizzy, everything is moving too fast, round and round, and you realize that you are shaking; if only you knew how I wish I could be there, how I wish I could comfort you, hold your hand, help you to pick up the thread of the story, the thread you have lost, show you that all things are spokes in the same wheel, stroke your beautiful face, warm you, because you are shivering and it comes to you that you ought to put on some clothes.

So you walk out of the office, naked, and you step back into the living room, and you look at the picture of Buddha, you look at the figure on the floor, and for one second, for one split-second, the living room is a place where everything eases up, comes to a standstill, clear, transparent, and you are struck by a synchronicity of space and time that suddenly affords an insight into all the inner mysteries of causality, and then it is gone, and once again all is chaos, an unbelievable scene, and you can only sneak past, on tiptoe, and you glance at the polar-bear skin, Ursa

Major, you think, stars fallen to earth, a betrayal, you think, a nomad, a wanderer, laid low, stretched out, an object of derision, on a living-room floor, you think. Margrete wanted to chuck it, you remember, called it tasteless, perverted, but you could not chuck such a memento of a precious victory, you said, although what good does that do now, you think, and you look at the blood, red against white, strawberry jam on ice cream, you think, like in the old Studenten ice cream parlour, you think.

You walk through to the bedroom, you, Jonas Wergeland, Mao Tse Tung's equal, hater of planes, discoverer of the ice cream factory, and you open the closet door, put on underpants, selecting your best pair, slip into a thick, white cotton shirt, slip into a pair of khaki trousers, pick out a dark jacket, a jacket you like, a jacket just right for discussing things with Axel, you think, and you pick your favourite shoes, the ones you wear for taking long walks, because you have the idea that you are going to take a walk, discuss things, rock the Milky Way on its axis, and you have to dress with care, you have to hold chaos at arm's length; you open the door of Margrete's closet, see her clothes, every garment a considered purchase: Margrete had very distinctive taste, you think, sophisticated, you think, and you remember how the looks on men's faces would alter when she walked into a room, at a party, you think, how the tone of their conversation would unconsciously change, how the mood would become heightened, how they tried to excel themselves, as if they had decided to eschew all that stupid flirting and win her with intellect, you think, and you look at her clothes, the row of clothes-hangers and you wonder whether you knew anything at all about her, or whether you actually know as little about her as you know about Nefertiti, and you realize that they are two sides of the same coin, Nefertiti and Margrete, and your eye falls on the book on her bedside table, and you walk across, flick through it; you see that it is called *Largo*, and you see that it is written by Agnar Mykle, and you see that it belongs to Axel Stranger, and it strikes you that you have never liked this, Axel and Margrete, this common interest, this love of reading that you never could fathom, all that talk, that bullshit, about DNA, and what do they end up with, novels, you think, and you can tell that you don't like it, this book, nor the fact that it is lying here, next to the bed, and you wonder if it could have been Axel, but that is just too far-fetched, just too crazy, you think, you hope.

And you walk back into the living room, and you look at the polar-bear skin, you look out of the window, you half-expect to see snow, soft flakes, falling thick and fast, but it is night, and it is spring, the air smells of spring right to the marrow, and you stand there, staring out of the window at the blocks of flats at Ammerud, those hulking great mastodons, Le Corbusier, you think, quasi-Le Corbusier, you think, and you think of Norway, think of that lack of originality, of how they can't even manage to copy anything, how they copy what are already botched copies, and too late, you think, when everyone else has got it taped, you think, and suddenly you remember that you are an architect, even this house, your parents' house, was originally your idea, it was you who found the plot of ground, you who succeeded in persuading the old lady, succeeded in doing what hundreds of others had tried to do, you, with your face, not only that but you have extended it, turned the house, too, into an angle, the Villa Wergeland, a new wing in Grorud granite, like the church, you think, right here, you think, where Margrete lies, you think, and you look at Margrete, and you think of Palladio, Palladio of all people, and you look at Margrete's body, and think about architecture, and behind all of this again you are thinking of something else, wondering how long it takes for a corpse to decay.

And you look at the murder weapon, a puzzling weapon, you think, because Margrete has been laid low by a ball, hit by a serve, you think, that shot a hole in life itself, and you notice that it is a pistol, a Luger, of all the ridiculous things, an old Luger, and you remember the toy guns of your childhood, your brother, gun-mad he was, always the revolutionary, the romantic, you think, and you think of Daniel, could it have been him, had there been something, some hostility, between Margrete and Daniel, but you find that hard to believe; he's a simple man, you think, and you wish you were as simple a man as Daniel, because then you would not be standing here, now, and you look out of the window, onto Bergensveien, the street of your childhood, and it occurs to you that you are not rootless after all, because your roots are here, in Grorud, in that patch of ground just across the road, between those low blocks of flats, and you contemplate the road that led from childhood to here, from what you can see through the window to what you can see on the floor, a dead woman, a dead story, a tale cut short, or a tale run wild, and you think of the chain of cause and effect, you think of Axel who would rather discover a causal relationship than be the King of Persia, and you think of another friend, a girl with the longest eyelashes in the world, who left you on the road you can see right outside the window.

Paradise Lost

Solhaug was a safe place for children, at any rate as long as you did not let the bigger lads trick you into lighting a bonfire in the tinder-dry grass on the edge of the woods, did not climb to the top of the majestic fir tree at Kvernstua and did not try to show off to the girls by teetering recklessly on the edge of the sheer drop at Egiltomta. As always, though, there was a serpent in paradise, and in this case it was actually snakelike in form: the sharp bend on Bergensveien.

For the mothers of Solhaug, Bergensveien was the real big bogey. 'Don't you go biking down Bergensveien' was a refrain that all of the kids had to listen to ten times a day. Not without good reason, since in those days a constant stream of traffic, heavy traffic that is, used to rumble along Bergensveien, a relatively narrow road, on the way to and from the new stamp-mill at the top of Hukenveien. The mothers had staged a number of actions, when they had sat with their coffee and cake on the balcony closest to Bergensveien and, in-between the latest gossip about Five-Times Nilsen and Tango-Thorvaldsen and the useless new assistant down at the corner shop, counted the appalling number of trucks that thundered past in the course of a day. They then sent their findings, as both a complaint and plea to God only knows what office, and never heard a word in reply. There was no alternative, either, apart from closing the stamp-mill, so they just had to go on singing their refrain: 'I'm telling you Petter, if I ever catch you on your bike out on Bergensveien, I'll leather your backside so hard it'll be weeks before you can sit on a bike again!' I should perhaps add that this was in the days before smacking children was forbidden in Norway.

So much for the mothers' point of view. The kids, the boys in particular, loved the trucks, introducing as they did an element of excitement into an otherwise pedestrian life, beaten only by the lavvy-lorry, a rat-coloured monster that rolled up every now and again to empty the outside toilet at the kindergarten, or one of the intermittent army convoys that would crawl along Trondheimsveien, with tanks towed on such objects of wonder as low-bed semi-trailers and everything. The trucks on Bergensveien may have been dangerous, but they were also camels passing through their day-to-day existence, laden not with gravel but with gold. Jonas and Nefertiti often sat at the roadside, marvelling at these great beasts, the ground shaking underneath them, and if they were lucky, they might even catch the sound of a spine-chilling 'fart' of compressed air as the driver released the brakes. For the most part they were Bedfords or Volvos, but there was nothing to compare with the Scania-Vabis trucks, the very name sounded like an adventure story, an epic such as *Quo Vadis*, or a prehistoric monster, a bit like *Tyrannosaurus Rex*. They dreamed of being given a ride in one, especially one of those with a fat little Michelin man fixed to the roof of the cab, the sort you could even get as a jigsaw puzzle, complete with indicator rods with knobs on the ends, jutting out like sceptres on either side of the bumper, and cardboard pictures of lightly-clad ladies stuck to the radiator, much the way vehicles in India are hung about with the most garish holy images.

But, as I say, there was one flaw. The bend. The bend in Bergensveien that ended right at the point where the safe road from Solhaug opened onto the main road, where paradise ran out, and market forces, as it were, took over, and you had to check the road twice and even three times, or rather, look up the road, towards the void ten metres farther up that marked the exit from the sharp bend and listen, too, like Red Indians putting their ears to the ground to catch the sound of buffalo, because the rise of the knoll completely blocked the view of any oncoming traffic – although that suited the kids just fine when it came to stretching fine lengths of string across the road on dark autumn evenings, almost killing more than one driver who slammed on the brakes at sight of this sudden obstacle, taking it, in the glare of the headlights, for a wire. When you came to this crossroads you just had to go for it, freewheeling – strictly forbidden, of course, but so gloriously thrilling – out onto the carriageway and down the hill to the kiosk and the sweet counter. The standard initiation rite for the lads of Solhaug was not, as in some rural communities in Europe, to lie down flat between the railway lines and stay there while a train ran over you – it involved taking both hands off the bars on Bergensveien, preferably with a Volvo truck thundering up behind you and a monstrous Scania-Vabis coming straight at you and not blinking an eye or turning a hair as both big beasts 'farted', eased up on the brakes and passed by.

Nonetheless, Jonas would spend his whole life wondering what Nefertiti was doing on Bergensveien on Midsummer's Eve of all evenings, when absolutely *no one* would have thought of taking their bike out; and, even more to the point, what in heaven's name a Scania-Vabis truck, one of the biggest models at that, should have been doing there at that time of day, so totally off course, like a rogue elephant, a murderous stray, a polar bear in Greenland in July.

Jonas Wergeland was ten years old, and Midsummer's Eve was about to be celebrated by a representative slice of Norwegian society, sixty families all told, including, that is – as if to indicate the fringes of the nuclear family – one childless couple, one peevish elderly widow and a dreamy bachelor with a windowsill covered in models of jetfighters. Midsummer's Eve at Solhaug was something quite unique, to be sure, but not, as Jonas Wergeland and the other residents would imagine, looking back on it later with nostalgia, because the families living in those six blocks were in any way out of the ordinary; the Solhaug of those days, like most other satellite communities, presented a pretty standard cross-section of the Norwegian lower middle class – people hailing from all over the country, employed by such bodies as Standard Telefon og Kabel, the Customs Department and Nordisk Aluminium, in the capacities of 'bookkeeper' or 'typist' and the like, with a sprinkling of less common job titles: 'averager', for example, or, most mysterious of all, 'traveller'. Now and again the list might also include a dentist or an engineer, the odd lawyer or teacher.

What was special, of course, were the times. Most of these families had moved in just as the post-war rebuilding of Norway was completed, and the amazing process of economic growth was about to begin; years when almost everyone slowly, but surely began to find themselves better off, in material terms at least, a fact illustrated by a peek into these flats: three rooms and kitchen, already packed with all sorts of modern aids, including such items as Elektra cookers with *thinking* hotplates, plastic sliding doors and ornate radiograms, those battleships of living-room furnishing, while the most trend-conscious already had Formica-topped tables and wallpaper patterned with fruit in their kitchens and Danish designer Bo Bøgesen's teak monkeys swinging from their lamp cables. There was only one way to go and that was up, and most important of all, everyone had a job to go to, there was no unemployment; even the political parties were in agreement on most things, at any rate on the home front, which meant that all of them, even the Conservatives, were really social democrats. Those were the days when the Norwegian Labour Party, the socialist DNA, equalled the scientific DNA, when politics and life went hand in hand, when socialism and democracy were as harmoniously entwined as the double helix of the DNA molecule.

The celebrations had been well under way before noon, with a parade in which the younger children, many of them wheeled in their prams, were dressed up in costumes painstakingly sewn by their mothers, who had worked and planned for this day as zealously as the residents of Rio preparing for their grand carnival, and continued in the afternoon with, it has to be said, a splendid show, stage-managed by a domestic-science mistress who also acted as Master of Ceremonies for the proceedings, clad, appropriately enough, in her white cookery-class overall, as if the entire show were a good and nutritious dish which she had composed and was now serving up to the proud parents sitting on the grass in the natural amphitheatre outside of Number One, watching and listening to the estate children singing through a blaring PA system, reading poetry, doing conjuring tricks, playing the trumpet and performing the most incomprehensible sketches, which everybody laughed at anyway, because they knew that the kids were endeavouring to make up for all the devilment they had got up to during the rest of the year. The children were always worried that it might rain, but I am here to tell you: it never rained at Solhaug on Midsummer's Eve when Jonas was a boy. So the parents could lounge on the grass, keeping half an ear on the concert while they soaked up the sun, with a few of the fathers whispering to one another that they'd be blowed if little Susan hadn't shot up during the spring, going about in high heels and a summer frock that really didn't leave an awful lot to the imagination, by Christ it didn't.

After the show there was a little break in the festivities, during which the kids went off to inspect the bonfire on the big green behind Blocks Three and Four, bigger than ever, *always* bigger than ever, on the point down by the stream where they were in the habit of hiding when they fastened a length of thread to Jens Ovesen's window. The trick was to rub the thread with rosin, creating the most excruciating, irritating noise. Ovesen, known as Jesse Owens because he was so brown in the summertime and because he was the fastest man in Grourd and hence represented the biggest challenge of a prankster's career, had in his time been a legendary right-back with one of the top Oslo teams, even made it onto the national team, and was famed for being the first back to go into the attack. To be chased by Ovesen was one of the most terrifying and gleeful high points of boyish pranking, and Ovesen himself did not seem to mind it either, as could be seen by the way he vaulted over the rail of the balcony, like any competitive sportsman. Whenever he caught one of them he would slap them on the back and say: 'You're too slow, lad!' and let the culprit go, a humiliation greater than being dealt the expected clip round the ear.

But it was Midsummer's Eve, the weather was warm, perfect, and as the day wore on into evening, the grown-ups drifted out, the Mums looking so nice they were almost unrecognizable and the Dads smelling of Wella hair-cream and an extra dab of Floid aftershave, all except Haakon Hansen, who had splashed out with a few drops of an Italian brand and was hoping that Fru Jakobsen, at least, would notice.

Now, let me tell you about this particular Midsummer's Eve. Oh, I know I am starting to wax all lyrical, but I cannot help but become carried away, because this is so beautiful, this is the absolute highlight of Norwegian history: it was party time at Solhaug, a community get-together on the green behind Block Four, a green that the caretaker kept as immaculate as a golf course, with little saplings planted on the slope leading down to the stream, supported, in true textbook fashion by canes: a job carried out '*på dugnad*', a phrase that is the very watchword of the Norwegian social democrats: as a communal effort, that is, with everyone pitching in to help. Jonas would always remember, not least at more isolated, egocentric points in his life, those evenings when people were out with their shovels, gripping little trees with their roots packed in bags and the chairman of the residents association rolled up in his Trabant – that's right, a Trabant! – with a crate of Solo orangeade on the back seat, and everyone had this – how can I put it? – look of pioneering zeal on their faces. And now there they were, setting the table – one long table – again with everyone doing their bit, spirits are high, they are on the verge of the breakthrough to utopia; all that is lacking is for the streets to be paved with gold. It is the longest, lightest day of the year, and although this may be going a bit far, the Solhaug of that time was, to the people who lived there at any rate, what Ancient Greece had been in its day: a high point in the history of civilization and democracy.

Much as I would prefer not to, I feel duty bound to say that, at some point, historians will come along who will take a cool objective look at this era and doubtless interpret it quite differently. It should also be said that a great many people, regardless of the age in which they live, recall the years when they were setting up house and starting a family as a rich and meaningful time – not to mention their childhood years – but even I, able as I am to view the whole thing impartially and objectively, cannot help but be captivated by the golden glow that surrounds this period in the history of Norway's little land.

But where was Nefertiti?

As people began to gravitate towards the green, Jonas went looking for her. Not that he was actually concerned, although it did suddenly cross his mind that she had been acting strangely earlier in the day. At one point she had stood with her forehead

pressed against the flagpole from which the white and blue Solhaug pennon dangled limply, and right after that she had sat for
a while, as if in a trance, on their favourite ledge in the little cliff
at Egiltomta, having managed to play 'Cotton Tail', that impossible Ellington number, all the way through on the mouth organ
for the first time. And, strangest of all: why, a couple of days earlier, had she pulled out her little crystal prism and given it to
him, just like that – that prism which was her most treasured
possession? 'Here, take this,' she had said, 'and learn how to use
it.'

Jonas had the feeling that maybe he ought to have been keeping an eye on her, but it was the longest, lightest day of the year,
and it was party time, so Jonas wandered about, doing his best to
take it all in, aware that he had to remember this, conscious of the
feathery frisson running up his spine that told him he was looking at a great work of art, a picture of Soria Moria Castle, so he
could only hunt for Nefertiti with half an eye, because there was
Fru Agdestein wearing red nail-polish and carrying a huge tray
of *smørbrød*, prepared according to the book, which in those days
meant, for example, such toppings as boiled egg and rollmop
herring or liver pâté with pickled gherkins, the extravagance of
two ingredients on the same slice of bread almost unheard-of,
but it was a party; and there went Herr Madsen, carrying a crate
of beer, Madsen who had just bought a new car, a Citroën, with
a chassis that could be raised or lowered by pulling a lever, a trick
that had had to be demonstrated to the entire estate not once, but
twice; what a wonder, a quantum leap beyond the general boring
run of cars that lined the kerbsides round the blocks of flats,
rather like ordering snails in garlic butter when everyone else was
having meat patties with onions. Jonas nipped in and out among
the busy grown-ups, eyeing Fru Jakobsen with a shudder. Today
she had surpassed herself, Solhaug's exotic flower, picked and
brought back by Herr Jakobsen from his time at a technical college in Rome, a sensation, going about bare-legged almost all
winter long; she could tick them off in a way that made their jaws
drop, introduced an entirely new body language and temperament and was, of course, the object of many a man's latent erotic
desires.

Jonas wandered about, searching for Nefertiti, a little more concerned now, but then along came six men carrying a piano belonging to Halvorsen who lived, thank heavens, on the ground floor, and so once more Jonas's attention was distracted, because he had to see them set the piano up on a makeshift platform made out of planks, then see Teigen coming over, lugging his double-bass, and then the other, normally pretty boring dads trooping up, armed with trombones and trumpets and clarinets, the whole ensemble topped off by Joffen, who played the drums in the school band but who had also mastered the flick of the wrist necessary for that circular swish of brushes on the snare-drum, and it really swung, a kind of Dixieland music; swung so hot that even Herr Carlsen, a rather sedate gentleman in a white shirt with the sleeves rolled up, was on his feet right away with his daughter Eva, who had just started at university and, hence, represented an explosion in learning and the expansion of the Norwegian further education system; represented a whole decade in which the student body increased several fold, and all those children who would never again see such a community so modestly content with its lot, certainly not from the inside.

But as I mentioned earlier, a serpent was about to make its way into this paradise, not only into Norway, where a more minor but no less upsetting affair such as the Schnitler case in Bergen and the far greater calamity of the King's Bay mining disaster on Spitzbergen were leaving the first scratches in that rosy picture, but also towards the blocks of flats alongside Bergensveien in Grorud; not far from the swinging amateur orchestra, parked at the top of Hukenveien, sat a motorized serpent, a Scania-Vabis truck, and one of the very biggest at that, with a driver who was just about to set out for home.

It took a while for it to dawn on Jonas that Nefertiti was *not* there, that something really was wrong, and that he was going to have to get out his bike to go look for her. It dawned on him as he dragged his eyes away from the undoubted hit of the evening: four housewives dancing barefoot on the grass in identical dresses which they had run up at their sewing bee to a pretty avant-garde pattern found in a fashion magazine: dancing gaily, uninhibitedly, in an ironic protest against the idea that women should not be able to dress alike and to celebrate their own liberation, now that their children would soon be grown and they could go back to work, maybe even take a course of some sort. And even I, while trying my best to remain objective, am inclined to agree with those who felt that Norwegian women, housewives and mothers – possibly due to sheer, unadulterated optimism – were never lovelier than they were on that Midsummer's Eve on a housing estate alongside Bergensveien in Grorud, dancing barefoot on the grass in identical dresses.

Gynt in Paris

Richard Burton was the first non-Muslim in Mecca. He dressed in disguise. Per Spook was, if you like, the first Norwegian in Paris, and he took that city by storm by dressing others. In Jonas Wergeland's labyrinthine television series *Thinking Big*, the programme on Per Spook was a gala performance – spectacular but at the same time light and lovely – like the designs it reflected: a real star turn that could not but make even the most inveterate anti-nationalist proud of Norway.

Any normal run-of-the-mill programme would have been filled with shots of Per Spook cycling in Paris and in Sigdal, Per Spook strolling through the forest of Fontainebleau, Per Spook sitting alone in the back pew at a church concert. Jonas Wergeland concentrated solely on the decisive moment in Per Spook's career, namely July 1977. Over the course of thirteen years, Spook had worked with three different fashion houses: at Christian Dior as an apprentice in the cutting rooms, with Yves Saint-Laurent as a designer and with Louis Feraud also as a designer – then, at the age of thirty-seven, he finally ventured to strike out on his own: a risk that is hard to imagine and even more difficult to describe when one considers that *haute couture*, so opulent in nature, is poles apart from the puritanical Norwegian character. Essentially, Per Spook's decision was about as outrageous as the idea of a Norwegian lion tamer. It was a Thursday morning in late July 1977. Per Spook had been working day and night for six months and was now ready to present his first winter collection, within the space of one hour his fate would be decided; this was Spook's moment of truth.

Prior to this, Jonas Wergeland had presented brief glimpses of Paris, of the school with the almost dauntingly grand name of

École de la Chambre syndicale de la haute couture parisiènne, from which Per Spook had graduated top of his class, and, not least, a sequence from the Avenue Montaigne, lying there like an impregnable fortress, lined with exclusive fashion houses and boutiques, in which Jonas had close-ups of the signs run across the screen like coats-of-arms, famous names such as Dior, Chanel and Scherrer, Valentino, Ricci and Ungaro, together with shots of stylish, haughty Frenchwomen on the street, representatives of a race who had made a specialty out of cold-shouldering foreigners, before the camera panned once more along the façade of the fashion stronghold of the Avenue Montaigne, as if just to hint that the unthinkable might one day happen, and a Norwegian open not one but two shops on this street.

From here, Jonas jumped to a series of rapid clips showing the frantic preparations at Spook's atelier – or rather, at that time in 1977, he had had his atelier in the rue de l'Université on the Left Bank, so Jonas Wergeland had cheated a little, showing Spook in the premises he occupied at the time of shooting, his fashion house in the modish Avenue George V – with a staff of fifty-plus working flat-out on the new collection, sewing for all they were worth, raising and lowering hems, taking in and letting out dresses, ironing, pressing; and in the midst of all this, Per Spook, discreetly elegant, surrounded by sketches and patterns and accessories and rolls of fabric and racks of clothes, or fitting the models on the mannequins together with the atelier manageress, fixing and adjusting, putting the finishing touches: all of this shown in a succession of quick cuts and changes of camera angle with a soundtrack designed to highlight the frenetic atmosphere and with Jonas Wergeland occasionally breaking in, a whispering commentator building up the tension like Finn Søhol before a crucial shot at Wimbledon.

And then, the unveiling of the collection at the Hôtel de Crillon, a venerable eighteenth-century building on the Place de la Concorde itself. Unbelievable, utterly improbable, but true nonetheless: a Norwegian in the heart of Paris, setting out to impress the international *cognoscenti* with the one thing, above all else, at which Paris excels: high fashion. It is like the fourth act of *Peer Gynt*, the great leap into the wide world, totally unreal, a combination of being a king among foreigners and emperor of the lunatic asylum. They took over two magnificent rooms, the magnificent *salon* and the actual restaurant, Les Ambassadeurs, which, incidentally and very fittingly, was one of the leading bastions of *haute cuisine* in Paris. In these surroundings of gleaming Sienna marble and sparkling gilt, huge mirrors and crystal chandeliers, the mannequins would parade up and down the narrow catwalk for forty-five minutes, modelling sixty to seventy items, ensembles comprising 150 garments all told. A whole phalanx of celebrities was ranged at the ringside, along with the representatives of the international press and, not least, Paris's own ruthless, hypercritical fashion hacks.

Jonas Wergeland was astute enough to make the most of this setting to get in a plug for the series, to drum up the sort of advance publicity that had become an increasingly essential part of the whole media circus. A number of Norway's leading newspapers were invited to the shooting of the programme on Per Spook. Almost every one of these newspapers subsequently printed lengthy interviews with Jonas Wergeland, penned by journalists who were clearly impressed, and accompanied by variations on the same striking picture: Jonas Wergeland sitting under the crystal chandeliers, reflected again and again in the mirrors of Les Ambassadeur's marble hall, in the Hôtel de Crillon, right next to the Place de la Concorde itself: an example, in himself, of 'thinking big'. The trailers for the television series, another important part of the promotional campaign, made great use of clips from the Per Spook programme, on account of its arresting images.

And yet they only shot one scene in the Hôtel de Crillon. Jonas Wergeland had persuaded the beautiful top model from the 1977 show, Else Kallevig, to walk about alone among the tables, looking as if she were remembering that all-important show of a decade earlier and wearing one of the creations from that time; so there she was, slowly weaving her way around the palatial room, twenty-eight years old now, as dazzlingly elegant as ever, in wide-legged black silk trousers and a short, figure-hugging top with long sleeves in red silk overlaid with transparent black lace, and a large black bow in her hair – except that Jonas showed

the scene in black and white, with the occasional shot of Per
Spook's hand sketching this very model, a clip that was run backwards once the sketch was completed, to the point where it disappeared, an effect intended to illustrate how quickly fashion
dates, how ephemeral it is, like the arrangement on a plate of a
haute-cuisine masterpiece or the scent of a perfume, although
Jonas also wanted to show that in all good fashion, even a bygone
design, there is a cut, a line, a combination of colour and pattern
that nevertheless elicits a gasp of appreciation, an indefinable
something; and if there was one thing this scene captured – Else
Kallevig in a pretty dramatic creation something over ten years
old, wafting dreamily across timeless marble, under timeless
crystal – it was beauty, it was like being confronted by a fine
abstract painting, and it provided Jonas Wergeland, in one brief
aside, with his opening remark that fashion could be described
only in mystical terms. 'Fashion is an angel passing over, a
glimpse of a wing in the air, then it is gone,' Jonas Wergeland
said, sitting in front of a mirror in which the shadow of Else
Kallevig could be seen disappearing out of the room.

The undoubted stroke of genius with this programme was to
move the whole fashion show out-of-doors, into Paris's famed
exterior locations, in part because Jonas Wergeland could not
face all of the practical problems involved in using the Hôtel de
Crillon: they had had a hard enough job getting permission to
shoot the outdoor scenes. The main bulk of the programme was,
therefore, given over to showing Spook's clothes and the styles of
the day, which is to say the year of filming, in their natural setting: a long series of shots in which leggy Norwegian girls,
dressed in Per Spook creations, swept across the Trocadero,
strode like goddesses across the Rue de Royale outside La
Madeleine, posed like works of art in the square at the Louvre or
sailed, filled with Norwegian pride, across the Pont au Double,
almost over-shadowing Notre Dame. In between-times Per
Spook could be seen behind the scenes, surrounded by the
dresser, the hairdresser and the makeup artist: Per Spook in
jacket and bow-tie, feverishly meticulous, checking that everything sat as it should or tying a belt in a particular way. Jonas had
held off filming the evening dresses until darkness fell then sent

lovely girls gliding across the front of the Opera and Sacre Coeur in Per Spook's ball-gowns so that all the floodlights seemed to be there as much for the benefit of the clothes. One scene especially, in which the mannequins veritably danced around in front of the Arc de Triomphe, made a great many viewers feel like children again, reminding them of the time when they had watched, hearts swelling, as Cinderella whirled round the dance floor with her prince in her gorgeous ball-gown. The soundtrack was equally effusive: Kirsten Flagstad singing an aria from *The Valkyrie* which conspired with the shots of the Arc de Triomphe to give the impression of a victory of sorts, or the founding of an empire. Jonas Wergeland rounded off the programme – anachronistically but aptly – with Else Kallevig in what was absolutely the world's most stylish Norwegian knitted cardigan, a luxurious variation shot with glittering silver lurex, and a matching skull-cap: the very image of Norway transformed into sheer Champs Élysées, a shot which Jonas froze, whereupon Per Spook's world-renowned, signature logo was written across it, before they resorted to the standard cinematic ploy of showing the French newspapers from the following day, which is to say in 1977, with *France-Soir* for one giving Per Spook's show glowing front-page headlines, leaving no one in any doubt: a Norwegian – Norwegian! – king of fashion had been born.

Then came Jonas Wergeland's big scoop. Using all of his charm, he had persuaded a number of famous Frenchwomen to give their comments on Per Spook's clothes. Jeanne Moreau, whom Jonas vaguely remembered from the film *Jules et Jim*, came on to talk about Spook the master of colour, not only his favourite black and contrasting black and white but also the muted range of natural tones he juggled with so skilfully. The Greek singer Nana Mouskouri – the one with the glasses – spoke in her turn of what a revolution it had been when Spook brought back loose flowing garments, and of the wonderful way in which the clothes draped over one another, layer upon layer. Because Per Spook did not create clothes for baby dolls or clotheshorses, she said, but for real live women, women who travelled and who were looking for comfortable natural clothes: clothes you could move about in. In conclusion, film and television star

Marie-Christine Barrault pointed out how different Per Spook was from other fashion designers. One just had to look at how he had sent his models down the catwalk in flat shoes, thereby introducing into fashion a more natural way of walking: that in itself was a milestone, she felt, while also remarking that there was something Nordic about his clothes, something pure and austere, perhaps even naïve, in the lines, the cut and the colours, and not least in the choice of soft warm fabrics. His clothes were tender, not aggressive, she said.

The basic problem was, of course, that Per Spook was a living person, so Jonas Wergeland had a long talk with this honourable ascetic countryman of his, who willingly agreed to let Jonas stick to his overall concept, thus allowing the same actor who had portrayed the other male Norwegian heroes in the *Thinking Big* series to play him, too. This proved to be no problem for Normann Vaage: he put on the horn-rimmed glasses and all at once he *was* Per Spook: inscrutable as any Chinaman, a man who kept his own counsel and his thoughts to himself, but at the same time an incorrigible early riser and workaholic with a fondness for Mozart and long walks in the mountains – even Spook was bowled over by his performance.

If I were to add anything to this, I would say that, despite Jonas Wergeland's fanfare of a programme, I do not believe the people of Norway have really grasped the full extent of Per Spook's achievement. If anyone had said, back in the sixties that a lad from Thereses gate in Oslo would end up by being a celebrity in Paris, winning both the Golden Needle and the Golden Thimble, the Oscar of the fashion world, it would have seemed as likely as anyone stating that a Norwegian would be the first man on the moon. I doubt, too, whether anyone realizes, in this climate of dogmatic feminism, what Per Spook has done for the woman of today: that he actually played his part in her liberation by giving thought to a new kind of lifestyle and designing clothes for active, self-assured career women, that he dared to introduce into the world of high fashion, where needless extravagance reigns supreme and fashion is regarded as sheer pleasure and indulgence, a touch of integrity, a moral statement concerning the comfort and well-being of women, a dash of ethics amidst all the airy-fairy aesthetics. And yet, as Per Spook him-self was at pains to stress, fashion is and will always be an elusive quantity, a fly-by-night, an art form that is constantly dependent on change – and that is perhaps the hardest part to understand: that a member of a nation that is generally two steps behind everyone else and at best tends to win the gold in events at which they have always excelled should be down there in Paris, using all his creativity to conquer something *new*, to catch on to the spirit of a new age: a line, a cut, a pattern, a colour. Looked at in those terms, Per Spook is one of the very few Norwegians who has been, and still is, ahead of his time.

Stave of Life

There were certain episodes in Jonas Wergeland's life that he never quite got to the bottom of, that seemed to him to be shrouded in mist; there were even times when he wondered whether they had actually happened. As with the time when he was tramping up a hillside – not far from Ljomarberget, he discovered later – and she, Arnhild U., had stepped out of the haze right in front of him, accompanied by a grey elkhound. His first thought, despite her modern, forest-green clothing and, above all, the rifle she carried, was that she belonged to another age.

'Idiot, you'll scare away the elk,' she had said, giving him a strangely penetrating look that did not, however, prevent a shiver of anticipation from running up his spine. There was something peasant-like about her, a brooding quality emphasized by the dark hair plaited into a wreath on top of her head. And yet her face was powerful, sensual, almost hungry-looking; her nostrils in particular made him feel as if she were *sniffing* him out, as if the smell of him would tell her more than she could see with her eyes.

'Ever shot an elk?' she asked, after taking a good long look at him. Jonas told her that the closest he had ever come to an elk had been the picture on a five øre piece, that such a thing as an elk-hunt was as remote from his experience as fishing for winter herring. 'Well, you'd better stick with me then,' she said, as if reciting from a fairytale, and proceeded to walk on. Jonas followed – not to find out what the hunt was like but to find out what *she* was like.

If he was not mistaken, and if he had not dreamt it, they headed up the hill towards Læshøe: towards what she called the '*vigga*' – the belt between the forest and the bare mountain-top –

through damp country glistening with the shades of autumn, colours to which the mist lent a subdued matte tone, reminiscent of tawny jade. As far as he could recall, the terrain had been hilly, with a few pine trees and a fair scattering of mountain birch, he had not really taken much notice; he had been too busy watching her, Arnhild U., striding on ahead of him with a dog on a leash and a rifle complete with telescopic sight over her shoulder. Each time they halted, he saw her nostrils twitching as if she were trying to compete with the dog to see who would catch wind of the elk first. She kept scanning from side to side, listening too; occasionally she stopped and hunkered down, studying a clump of greenery or running her fingers across the moss; now and again she looked at him with that same expression on her face and her nostrils flaring, as if he were another species of wildlife.

There was something unreal about the whole thing. They had just drawn level with some small patches of marsh when the dog suddenly tensed, lifted its nose into the air and dropped its tail half a turn. Arnhild U. planted a foot on the leash and slid her Browning rifle off her shoulder. She went down on one knee, cocked the gun, made Jonas get down too. Was this true? Did it happen? At any rate Jonas would swear later that he had been there in the marsh and seen a huge bull elk loom up right in front of them and that to begin with he had thought it must be a mirage, because he could not think what such a fabulous creature could be doing in a Norwegian forest; at that moment it had seemed not of this world at all, with its great, shovel-shaped antlers, the massive body on the long, spindly legs, like a ship in full sail. When it turned its head, presenting them with its curling muzzle and long goatee, the thought that flashed through Jonas's mind was of a primeval world, of the Stone Age.

One thing was for certain, Jonas Wergeland had not come to Lom to hunt elk; he was there to see the stave church. In terms of cause and effect, the road from the Avenida de Mayo in Buenos Aires to the stave church at Lom may have been a tortuous one, but no less understandable for all that. After entering the College of Architecture he had rapidly developed an interest in old Norwegian building styles. Indeed there were many who maintained that the stave church and the combination of staves and cog joints used in old cottages, lofts and storehouses – as found, for example, throughout the Otta valley – was Norway's only significant contribution to architectural history.

And so, the day before, Jonas had wandered around the stave church at Lom, lost in wonder, running his fingers over the wood carvings on the chancel – an almost mesmerizing upward spiral of dragons – poring over the runic inscriptions, making sketches, lots of sketches, inhaling the scent of tar that pervaded the lofty, picturesque church interior, studying the old doorway, the ornamentation, counting the oldest pillars, inspecting the crossbeams and the St Andrew's crosses, all the while trying to imagine how the original basilicum, now hidden away like a casket within the more recent church, must have looked, outside as well as in; although even here the dragons' heads at the apexes of the gables lent the building an air of something dark and ancient, a vast scaly creature that at any moment might rise into the air and fly off across Lomseggen: a sight which, taken together with the smells and the touching had thrown him into a strange mood, one which had stayed with him right through the day, until he fell asleep in his hotel room and dreamed of cattle all night long. The next morning, despite the low cloud and the raw cold air, he had made his way on instinct, following some physical urge, up the hillside.

And now there he was, on his knees – if that is, this happened to him at all – next to a woman with a rifle in her hands, staring at a bull elk roughly a hundred metres away from them which, due to the haze, the misty smoky atmosphere, acquired the semblance of a creature of fable, some sort of dragon, a dragon amid a landscape of matte, red-gold jade; the whole scene seemed so unreal. Not to Arnhild U., though. She dropped her hand, and the dog lay down without a murmur then, just as the elk turned side on to them, she released the safety catch. Jonas's attention was momentarily caught and held by the two animals, the dog and the elk, so archetypically Norwegian, this odd confrontation between two emblems, two coins of the realm, silver and copper. At that moment the elk froze, still as a statue, with raised head and stiff legs; it must have become aware of them; it was so majestic, so Norwegian, resembling – of all things – a stave

church, in the middle of the forest, a powerful piece of ornamentation, something so beautiful that Jonas was about to ask
her to spare it when she fired. The elk collapsed as if heaving a
sigh, as if it had been brought down by something huge and
invisible, striking from right overhead, even *before* the ear-
splitting bang. She looked at him exultantly as if she knew she
had been too quick for him.

'You like to kill,' he said.

'Yes,' she said. 'All good hunters like to kill.' There was something about her eyes, her cheeks, her nostrils as if the adrenalin
had worked a change on her face, rendering it even more hungry-
looking, lustful.

Jonas was never quite certain, but they must have walked up
to the downed elk, with the dog running round about, sniffing,
licking blood from the dead animal's nostrils, before it lay down
as if on guard. Arnhild U. slung off her rucksack. 'So what are
you doing in Lom?' she asked, her eyes fixed on the elk, on the
head with its glassy, wide-open eyes.

'I'd been planning to take a look at some of the old farms, the
storehouses mainly,' he said. 'But when I left the hotel after
breakfast I changed my mind, I felt I just had to go for a walk.'

'Well, I suppose you'd better come home with me,' she said as
casually as before, and even at that point, he thought later, he
must have known how it would end: with stave and log while he
staved his log into her.

Of what followed, if it really did happen, he had only a hazy
recollection: how Arnhild U. pulled out a knife and did things to
the dead bull elk that mystified him, things to do with the penis
and testicles and rectum, and something with the throat and
gullet, before she slit open the belly from breastbone to haunches
and embarked on the actual disembowelling, such a very bloody
and messy business that Jonas had to turn away; only after the
stomach, the intestines and other entrails were spilled out upon
the ground, with the steam rising from them, did he turn round
again, in time to see how, after hacking away the diaphragm, she
stuck her hand far inside the chest cavity and with a grunt pulled
out the gullet and windpipe, lungs and heart, making his gorge
rise. 'The heart,' she said, pointing to a lump in a whitish sac

before cutting it loose, and seconds later she was sticking two fingers into a red slimy clump and holding it aloft in her bloody hands like a bowling ball, looking as if she had just reached into a safe and brought out a jewel casket. 'Hold this,' she said, tossing it into Jonas's hands. He felt the way his own heart thudded to be holding this elk heart, still warm; how his fingers slipped into the cavities into which the veins had run, while a rank smell rose from the hefty, pear-shaped lump of flesh, the very seat of the elk's life. Arnhild U. scooped blood out of the abdominal cavity with her cupped hands and when she was finished she smiled for the first time, stood there smiling with her black hair plaited in a wreath around her head and her arms covered in blood and gore to the elbows. The entrails smoked on the ground, almost like the remains of a campfire. The whole countryside reeked of something indefinable, something raw and primitive.

She took a roll of kitchen paper from her rucksack and cleaned her hands, walked up to him with the knife raised. He held the heart while she sliced off a little piece, popped it into her mouth. 'Mmmmm,' she said, closed her eyes, opened them again, looked at him, long and hard, he was still holding the elk heart up in front of him, with both hands, as if he were taking part in some sort of sacrificial rite.

As she was getting Jonas to slip the heart into a carrier bag, four burly men came walking up the hill. 'Can you lot manage to haul this down to the tractor without me?' she said, when the men reached them. 'I have a guest,' she said, as if that explained everything. They nodded wordlessly, looked at Jonas, looked at the elk; one of them had already gone off to cut down a birch bough. Arnhild U. packed the carrier bag containing the heart into her rucksack and started to walk down the hill, Jonas automatically following behind. The dog stayed behind with the men.

Although Jonas was sure that at least some of the events detailed above must have occurred, he never could figure out what actually happened next. He remembered them coming to the road where her car was parked, and that they drove towards Otta, that they turned off the road and drove up to a big old farm set around two courtyards and comprising a number of buildings built out of logs, blackish-brown timbers, including the farmhouse itself. They must have gone in there, he thought they had, into the kitchen, before she showed him the parlour, full of heavy, old furniture, log chairs and rose-painted cabinets, woven hangings and bookcases, a large desk, on which sat a picture of King Haakon; he believed he remembered that, because it had surprised him, a desk, he could not have known that freeholder's daughter Arnhild U. would one day save the reputation of the farmers, at a time when most people felt that subsidies to Norwegian agriculture were becoming somewhat excessive. But that was still some years away; on that particular day Arnhild U. was alone on the farm, and she gave Jonas Wergeland, student of architecture, a guided tour, showed him the ancient storehouse, the *stabbur* where Jonas – although he had almost no memory of this – had gazed about him in awe, had said something about the corner-post, muttered something about the Middle Ages, about the Folk Museum, about Norwegian building materials: stone, wood and turf, that it was beautiful, *powerful*, he believed he had said, ran his hands over the thick solid crossbeams on the ground floor of the loft as if it were a living creature.

The way he recalled it later, they then stepped into the cow byre, which had been modernized, and there was something about the smell of the place, not that it was in any way bad, but there was something so strong, so primordial about it, something to do with muck and beasts and fermentation gases that had an almost stupefying effect. She had taken his hand, he was certain about that, while they were still walking along the feed-floor between the stalls containing the cows, or rather, those that were inside, the ones that had recently calved, recumbent creatures, large heads to either side, chewing the cud, she even came out with the odd name as they progressed, that is just what they did: progressed, as if passing between the rows of pews in a church. As far as he could remember the walls were white, and yet to him the room had seemed dim and full of big brown eyes that followed them, placid animals, a room that thrummed harmoniously. It must have been somewhere around there, probably right at the very back, by the door into the feed-room, because he thought he remembered there being calves, both new-born calves, each in their own little box, and calves in bigger pens, and hay, too, the calves were given hay, she said, at least he thought she had said that, just before she pressed herself against him with a desire so fierce that he could feel her heart pounding through her clothes, feel her whole body trembling, after which she blinded him, almost smothered him with kisses and started to tear impatiently at his belt and then, with surprising strength, a powerful longing, she almost lifted him off the floor and threw him down in a tiny, empty box, into the hay, or at any rate onto something soft, something yielding and comfortable, and I am here to tell you that this is, in all essentials, true. I can also reveal that she had tried all along to resist, even though she had been filled with desire from the moment she laid eyes on him up on the hillside, because she was a virtuous woman, with strong moral principles, particularly regarding sex before marriage, but there in the byre, possibly because it smelled so strongly of living things, she had allowed her emotions to gain the upper hand, or as she was later to say: 'I knew it was madness, but I was so bless-edly spellbound. It burned the very cockles of my heart.' Those were exactly, and typically, the words Arnhild U. used.

Jonas, for his part, was never absolutely certain whether it could have been true, that he really did lie there on his back, right next to the calves, seeing her suddenly standing over him, naked from the waist down, how she flushed red, or how her whole face seemed to swell with lust as she tore off his trousers and sat astride him, at the same time guiding his hands up under her homespun jacket and sweater and flannel shirt, cupping them over her breasts and shutting her eyes; and no sooner was that done than, with a long deep breath, she opened herself to him, and he slid inside her, in to something so warm and wet and vital that it immediately put him in mind of a big warm heart. And later, he had the definite impression that not even he, not even Jonas Wergeland, for all the singular experiences he had been through, had ever been made love to with such ecstasy, with such a fierce intensity, with such power, such carnal – yes, that was just the word for it – lust as when Arnhild U. made love to him: Arnhild U., who threw back her head and rode him as if she had been waiting for this half her life, who rode so hard that the hair around her head began to fall loose, made love to him deeply, passionately, slowly; thinking back on it later he would always feel that it had been like making love to the earth itself, and yet all the time he had the idea that she was not making love to him, but to something greater, thoughts she herself had, or that she was making love to something quite different, a creature of fable, and there was also something about the animals close by, the sound of hooves stamping on the floor, a lowing sound, possibly from a cow about to calve and, above all else, the smell, the smell of cattle and silos, of hay and muck, pure muck, permeating everything and making him feel like a beetle, a beetle in a dung heap, living life to the full. But just one look at her face was enough to dispel this thought, because her face glowed as if she were praying, as if she were right in the middle of a prayer, and as she rode him, more and more intensely, moving up and down, both deep and high at the same time, her face slowly took on a look of utter ecstasy, and the wreath of hair, or what was left of the wreath of hair, seemed almost like a halo around her head. This sight absorbed his attention for so long that his own thoughts did not overcome him until near the end, in the form of a strong awareness of, not to say a longing for, roots: to belong somewhere, because it had been brought home to him that it was from this that he, too, stemmed, from houses built out of stone and wood and turf, other places, other times, farmers, fishermen and hunters, yes, hunters too, and it was on the way home, after his visit to Lom, that Jonas Wergeland was struck by the impulse to stop off at Gardermoen in order to find out finally where his mother's childhood home had stood.

He lay in the byre, all of his senses on the alert, picking up the sight of dust dancing in a band of light, the smells and sounds of ruminant creatures and, above all else, her ecstatic face, as if the sacred and the profane had been brought together in one room; and just before he came, as he felt the seed seeming to surge up from a deeper source than usual, in the midst of his thoughts regarding his own epic, or lack of his own epic, she jumped off, as if her subconscious were taking its own precautions, or perhaps feminine intuition had told her that this was her most fertile time of the month, with the result that his semen spurted over the small of her back, leaving an exclamation mark there, before she smeared it in with her hand and lifted her fingers greedily to her nose, holding them under her quivering nostrils.

Jonas Wergeland's first clear memory was of the moment when he unlocked the door of his car outside the Fossheim Hotel. But as he bowled down the road towards Otta, even when he could clearly see her farm, or what he thought was her farm, a collection of wood, stone and turf that almost merged with the landscape, he was not sure what had occurred earlier or whether anything at all had happened, whether the whole thing belonged to another life, to another time entirely.

Juggernaut

On the other hand, there were certain days in his life that Jonas Wergeland wished he could recall with less clarity, fearing as he did that they took up too much room in his memory, that they overshadowed, or blocked out, other precious memories: days so crammed with detail that as time went on they seemed to quash and eat away at other days, while at the same time swelling and growing, to abnormal proportions, like a young cuckoo. So it was with the memory of the Midsummer's Eve celebrations at Solhaug when he was ten years old, and more particularly from the moment when the amateur jazz band laid into their instruments once more, lustier than ever, after a couple of exceptionally strong highballs at Five-Times Nilsen's.

This last-named gentleman's name was, in fact, simply Nilsen – if, in line with what has gone before, I may be allowed to dwell on one small detail. Nilsen worked in one of the town's biggest gentlemen's outfitters, but he was such a nondescript and unassuming man that people hardly took any notice of him – he could have been mistaken for a tailor's dummy had it not been for the tape measure around his neck – but once, when the housewives of Solhaug had been lying sunbathing on the flag green, surrounded by magazines, flasks of coffee and grizzling toddlers, and it had been hinted, more out of a spirit of sympathetic solidarity really, that it must be a bit dull being married to such a quiet man, Fru Nilsen had drawn herself up, adjusted her very demure sun-top and said that she for one certainly had nothing to complain about as long as he could take her to seventh heaven five times in one night. So there. From then on he was known only as Five-Times Nilsen. Rumour had it that he also owned highball glasses decorated with ladies who were fully clad when viewed from the outside, but naked on the inside, so it was no wonder that the band, now reinforced by an accordion, was simply raring to go, launching into one sing-along after the other: *'Kostervalsen'*, *'Ut på Nøtterø fins'*, *'Sol ute, sol inne'*, *'Bedre og bedre dag for dag'* and all the other songs about sunshine and sea and happy days, so in keeping with the spirit of this party of theirs, songs which in those days everyone knew by heart, like Christmas carols and I mean every absolutely – every verse.

Jonas wished with all his heart that he could linger, stay there on that green so vibrant with neighbours and plates of *smørbrød* and sing-songs, but he had to go, he knew he had to go, because Nefertiti was missing and he had to find her.

And so he walked off, trailing his heels, looking back to see Herr Moen, the chairman of the residents' association, wearing a velveteen jacket bought on sale at Five-Times Nilsen's shop, doing the honours of lighting the bonfire, far too early as usual, because the children just couldn't wait, and Jonas simply had to stop and watch, hypnotized by the flames licking up over the pyramid of old furniture, once such splendid indispensable items, now nothing but a pile of old junk, and in no time the whole lot was ablaze, the fire consuming the vestiges of thrift and harder times, while folk stood there gazing as if in a trance at a Midsummer bonfire that would never be bigger or consist of more remarkable or more historic objects, a veritable museum in flames; with the climax, greeted by loud cheers, coming when the flames reached chairman Moen's old sofa perched on the top, a sofa so hideous that chairman Moen could not think how he had managed to put up with it for so many years, but now he had a brand spanking new sofa, a corner unit angled to face the television set: all things considered he had never had it so good, he thought to himself as he stood there, feeling quite moved, with the matchbox in his hand, two highballs inside him and his face golden in the light from the bonfire. It was Midsummer's Eve, and all Norway was united by blazing beacons, forming a bulwark around the blessings of social democracy.

Not until the draw was about to start did Jonas collect himself. Some sort of a raffle was always held on such occasions, to raise funds for one thing or another, that year it was new street lamps, not that the old ones weren't perfectly okay, but there's nothing that can't be improved upon, and tickets had been sold in advance, so all that remained was for Fru Moen to call for attention everyone, please: Fru Moen, who had once given Jonas a swingeing clout round the ear for taking part in a contest with the other lads to see who could pee farthest up a wall which just happened to be right under her balcony, but who today was sporting a Farah Diba hairdo so awesome that Jonas could have forgiven her anything as she picked a colour from one hat and a number from another, with all the children's prizes being drawn first, since it would soon be the little ones' bedtime.

Reluctant though he was, Jonas had to tear himself away from the smells of bonfire and perfume and coffee and home baking. He sped to his entry and leapt onto his bike the way he had seen the cowboys leaping onto their horses at the Westerns they showed at Grorud cinema. Jonas took Hagelundveien, cutting through Nybygga, thinking about the knife being raffled right at that very moment, wondering whether he might win it, a dream of a knife, with a handle shaped like the head of a fish and a sheath like the body of a rainbow trout, and meanwhile Nefertiti was sitting outside the forest ranger's little cottage, a stone's throw or two away from Bergensveien, along with Colonel Eriksen the elk hound, and nobody could know what she was thinking, not even me, and meanwhile, up on Hukenveien, an unknown, unsuspecting driver was climbing into the cab of a Scania-Vabis LS 71 Regent, and meanwhile Jonas was pedalling up the steep hill past the corner shop, thinking about the toy revolver that was being raffled right at that very moment on the green next to the Midsummer bonfire, a new sort, an 'Apache' it was called, that had just come on to the market, a long, slender Colt which, although he could not have said why, easily knocked all his other toys into a cocked hat, so that suddenly they were no fun to play with, they seemed so babyish, the heads of Indian chiefs stamped into plastic handles, imitation mother-of-pearl, while this was black and gleaming and relentlessly authentic, with just one silver star right in the centre, and meanwhile Nefertiti was sitting outside the forest ranger's little cottage on the edge of the forest, under the sheer face of Ravnkollen, scratching Colonel Eriksen's thick coat, and no one could know what she was thinking, not even me, and meanwhile an unknown driver was starting the six-cylinder diesel engine of his Scania-Vabis Regent, with its terrible 150 horse power, and meanwhile Jonas had cycled as far as Trondheimsveien, thinking about the Matchbox car that was being raffled right at that very moment, a miraculous copy in miniature of a Cadillac, with tail fins and a caravan with a door that could open, a toy that could transform any place on Earth into a little bit of California, and meanwhile Nefertiti was getting to her feet and saying goodbye to Colonel Eriksen, and the dog stood there with his tongue lolling, feeling uneasy as if it had caught wind of an elk, and no one could know what she was thinking, not even me, and meanwhile an unknown driver was setting out along Hukenveien in his seventeen-ton Scania-Vabis, and meanwhile Jonas was wheeling round the junction with Trondheimsveien, thinking about the Lego set that was being raffled right at that very moment, a fire station with two fantastic towers and loads of see-through bricks and garage doors that flipped up, as well as a leaflet giving step-by-step instructions for how to build it, the sort of intricate challenge that was just crying out for him to get his hands on it, and meanwhile Nefertiti was climbing on to her Diamant three-speed and pedalling slowly up Bergensveien, one hand holding her chromatic mouth organ to her lips, and no one could know what she was thinking, not even me, and meanwhile the unknown driver was easing up on the pneumatic brakes of his Scania-Vabis Regent and letting his seventeen-ton truck coast down the top end of Bergensveien, because there was no one on the road.

Is this the most crucial story in Jonas Wergeland's life?

Are there some stories that are more crucial than others?

As Jonas turned into the straight stretch on Bergensveien, almost on a level with Tango-Thorvaldsen's shoe shop, he saw Nefertiti, her plaits dangling down beneath her cap, the back of her white blouse, way up ahead, almost at the spot where she would veer left across the road to turn into the Solhaug estate, just before the exit from the bend, at the point where Bergensveien disappeared behind the hill, where all manner of awful things could be hiding, and Jonas shouted as loud as he could, but Nefertiti did not hear, she cycled on, as if in her sleep, playing her mouth organ, and all of a sudden Jonas realized he was shivering, even though it was a warm evening, and he knew that something was about to happen, he had known it from the minute she gave him her crystal prism, the one he had in his pocket, the one he would carry with him wherever he went for years and years, but right at that moment it was of no use; he shouted, he yelled, but she made no response, and suddenly Jonas knew that he would not win the knife or the gun or the car or the fire station, that instead he was going to lose something indispensable that day, that the Lego world of his childhood was about to be brutally smashed to pieces, so he cycled like a soul possessed, close to tears, as if he could still prevent it from happening, but it was as if his wheels were spinning in mid-air, he was not closing on her and by now Nefertiti had reached the crossroads and Jonas could actually feel the ground shaking, as though a minor earthquake was about to hit, and he called out, screaming her name, but she did not hear, she had one hand on the handlebars, the mouth organ in the other; Jonas strained to hear what it was she was playing, as if this were the key, to a riddle that he had to solve in order to avert disaster, but he caught only snatches of a stanza, and just then he saw the truck rounding the bend, a mighty diesel roar, a horror on six wheels, just as she started across the road, from right to left, slowly, so interminably slowly, and then, *now*, she turned, to face him, not the truck, as if only now had his shouts got through to her, and she looked at him, he was fifty metres away from her, but he saw her eyes quite clearly, blue as the sky on the lightest day of the year, with the longest eyelashes in the world.

Nefertiti did not only turn as she was crossing the road, she also braked just as the truck came into view, going way too fast, almost as if it were attacking, as if it had been there all their lives, ready and waiting, not to materialize until then, letting off an almighty fart as the driver eased up on the brakes coming out of the bend and, for reasons Jonas would never understand, he had a picture of the truck as a gigantic bull elk with its antlers lowered, a creature that nothing, not even a silver bullet, could stop, and he saw the truck, or rather, he did not see the truck, all he saw was the Michelin man on the roof of the cab, or rather, not just one, but *two* Michelin men, and he saw the indicator lights on the sides, the pale-grey cab with its red radiator trim, armoured with engine covers that opened out like butterfly wings. Pin-ups stuck onto cardboard on the radiator grille, the two extra lights on the bumper, the indicator rods, the huge wheels, above all else the enormous wheels; for a second the whole colossal truck seemed to be nothing but six gigantic wheels bowling towards one fragile girl; not only did Jonas see that, clear as crystal, he also saw the old, white wooden house on the right-hand side of the road, and behind it the vast granite face of Ravnkollen where they sometimes lay with torches in the autumn, signalling with flashes of red and green when cars were coming; and to the left of the road he saw the gable end of the nearest block of flats, and the window of Fru Sivertsen's flat, which he had once smashed during a fierce rock fight, and beyond it, Egiltomta, with its little cliff and their favourite ledge, right next to the tiny pine tree that stuck straight out of the cliff face, with roots that could transform rock to water; all of this ran through his mind and he saw it all, clearly, with exaggerated clarity, as if the actual reality of the moment of impact had been carved up and laid out before him in all its individual parts, like being presented with a huge spread and allowed to take his pick, but more than anything else it was the tiny conifer straight out of the mountain of his childhood he remembered, clung to, because he had already seen it once before, there too in a situation where life was moving too fast or, if one prefers a more conventional scenario: a little conifer that he *would* see again, later, as if it were the most natural thing in the world, halfway up a basalt cliff during a heart-stopping trip down the rapids of the Zambezi, in the heart of darkest Africa.

The very second before the truck hit the bike and Nefertiti's soft body at a speed of fifty kilometres per hour, the unknown driver instinctively tried to avert the accident by ramming on the brakes and laying on the horn. At the sound of this deep, resounding note, like the amplified blare of a tuba, Jonas saw the Scania-Vabis shift shape, first to an organ on wheels, then to a

ship, a vessel the size of the Danish ferry, its bow surging straight
for you, and as the seventeen-ton truck hit a girl with a cap and
plaits and the longest eyelashes in the world, Jonas saw – or at
least he would swear later that he had seen – a multi-coloured
light flashing and rippling back and forth between all the lights
on the lorry and the Michelin men on the cab roof covering their
eyes and the pin-up girls on the grille kicking their legs, while the
whole cab was surrounded by a blinding orange light.

When the truck hit Nefertiti she still had the mouth organ to
her lips, and her last breath was forced through the instrument
before it soared aloft like a silver bird in a different direction
from and further than Nefertiti, who was tossed high into the air,
shot out almost, like a human cannonball, one of those foreign
circus acts that they had tried to emulate up in the loft, with the
aid of an old mattress; Jonas saw it all from the seat of his bike,
endeavoured to follow both those arcs, the mouth organ's and
Nefertiti's, and he could see that the mouth organ was going to
land right next to the little stream just down from the road,
where they had once gazed in fascination at dry ice bubbling on
the bottom, and he knew, even as his eyes were following Nefertiti's course through the air, that he would pick it up and keep it
for the rest of his life, safe in the knowledge that by blowing
through that filter he would be able to survive even in a gas
chamber of lies, and he was still following Nefertiti's course
through the air and he knew she was already dead, and he
thought to himself, before she hit the ground, that this was not
the end, even though it was the end, that it would never end, not
when it came to Nefertiti anyway, just like that expedition to
Rakkestad and inner Østfold when, after saying goodbye to
Nefertiti's long-lost aunt, and with their heads reeling with all
that they had seen and done, they had almost reached the railway
station when they suddenly saw a van swing past, a van bearing
a logo they knew better than any other: the jolly Eskimo girl, the
Diplom ice cream girl, and because she seemed to be waving to
them, they followed her until they came to two red-brick buildings with a sign over the door that read: *Østfoldmeierienes fabrikk
A/L* – Ostfold Dairies Ltd – and just then a man in a white coat
came out and asked them if they would like to take a look inside,

and he led them into a hall that smelled of vanilla and chocolate and strawberry, as well as praline, made from almonds roasted with sugar on huge frying pans in one corner; they could not believe it, but there they were, right inside an ice cream factory, surrounded by ladies in white overalls and white caps, all busy making Pin-up lollies, Pin-ups of all things, heaven knows how many Pin-up ice-lollies they had consumed in their time. Of course, the production process was very different from today, so there the ladies stood, filling trays of moulds with ice cream from the ice cream chiller by hand, after which the trays were passed through a bath of brine, in which the sticks were stuck into the lollies while they froze solid, then they were lifted out again at a point where different ladies took them two at a time, one in each hand, and dipped them in chocolate; Jonas and Nefertiti blinked, hardly able to believe their eyes, the absence of whirling machinery and conveyer belts did not make it any less magical, but more so, in that they could watch every part of the process at once, a bit like being in Father Christmas's workshop, and Jonas felt as if he were standing at the end of a chain of cause and effect, at the source of something. When they returned from Rakkestad naturally no one would believe them, just as great discoverers are seldom believed, especially when they claim to have been inside the castle of Soria Moria itself, but they had brought back proof, a treasure; their good fairy in the white coat had given them samples of a brand-new make of ice cream, carefully packed in a cardboard box with dry ice wrapped in newspaper: it was called a *Combi Ice*, and it consisted of a transparent, plastic tub containing vanilla ice cream with a strawberry topping, with a coloured lid that you could remove and fix onto the base of the tub like a stem, making a little goblet, a wonder of wonders, a grail that Jonas and Nefertiti showed off triumphantly, together with the dry ice, which they threw into the stream and which only served to underline the magical nature of the entire episode with its smoke and mysterious bubbling.

For a long time after that, Jonas was convinced that life was an adventure, one that would go on forever, behind one adventure another one would always be lurking, but could that be true here, too, he thought, as a girl with the longest eyelashes in the world and a head as fragile as terracotta, flew through the air, already dead, and hit the tarmac at his feet with a horrid soft thud, while the last note from the mouth organ hung over the landscape, hung on and on, seeming to take up residence in the granite face of Ravnkollen, and Jonas stood there, unable to tear his eyes away from Nefertiti's bike, lying in the ditch with the front wheel spinning round and round.

The unknown driver was climbing out of his cab, and people were running down the road from Solhaug. But before anyone could reach them, before he himself collapsed in a fit of anguished weeping, on the longest, lightest day of the year Jonas walked over to the girl lying lifeless, seemingly without a scratch, on the tarmac before him, only a few drops of blood trickling from her ear to betray that something fatal had occurred. Jonas bent down, wanting to remember her face, to stick it up in the place of honour in his memory, and as he did so he saw a tiny beetle crawl out of the pocket of her white blouse, across her heart; a beetle with red wings, he thought to himself, making one last effort before total and utter collapse, before the beetle flew off.

The Seducer

'Do you have to go?' she asked.

'Of course I have to go,' he said.

'Why do you play that tune over and over again?' she said.

He did not answer.

'Why can't you stay home?' she said.

He did not answer.

'Jonas, why do you keep playing that song?'

He lifted the seventy-eight off the turntable, regarded it: a black hole. Normally she never asked him about Duke Ellington, as if she knew this was a sacrosanct, nigh-on taboo, subject; that a whole host of feelings lay buried there, feelings associated with a life long before she came along. Instead he put on a CD, although he missed the crackling, missed the less than perfect sound quality, a breath of long ago. For him, Duke Ellington would always be the 1940 orchestra, in the loft at Solhaug, with Nefertiti.

'You've never said that much about him,' Margrete said.

'Who?'

'Your uncle.' Margrete pointed to the pile of seventy-eights.

'He was a big Duke Ellington fan,' said Jonas, not knowing, the way one never does know, that this would be one of the most crucial conversations of his life.

Margrete indicated with a gesture that *that* much she had figured out for herself.

'He was at the Newport festival in 1956, when Ellington made his comeback,' Jonas said, as if this said all there was to say about Uncle Lauritz and what an exceptional person he had been. Jonas was standing in the centre of the room in the new wing of the villa, with its walls of Grorud granite, like a fortress;

standing with his feet nestling cosily in a polar-bear skin and looking out of the window, down onto Bergensveien, at the junction with the road to Solhaug, while the weird strains of 'Caravan' meandered softly out of the loudspeakers, filling him with a wave of sentiment for which he sometimes felt the need, more pleasure than pain.

Margrete said nothing. She seemed to be out of sorts. She had been out of sorts for weeks. She did not say much to him either, never came out with so much as a single one of the little anecdotes of which she was usually brimful. She spent her time writing, writing letters to women friends all over the world: Jakarta, Santiago de Chile. She was a great letter writer; she enjoyed writing. Jonas never wrote anything or not letters anyway. Margrete wrote to someone at least once a week, long letters written with an old fountain pen, took pleasure in it, took pains over it, writing in a neat copperplate, wet, pale-blue characters, as if the actual process was as important as what she wrote. He envied her this dedication, the delight she took in covering page after page with a litany of inconsequential chitchat.

'Do you have to go now?' she asked again. 'I mean, you do have this phobia about planes.'

'I do not have a phobia about planes.'

'Well you certainly don't like flying.'

He turned away from the window and looked at her. She was writing, her eyes on the sheet of paper, she looked like a schoolgirl hunched over her first 'a's. 'Mood Indigo', with Lawrence Brown's trombone, came brushing out of the hi-fi, painting him indigo inside. There were things that had happened to him that he had never spoken of, not even to Margrete; stories he wished to keep to himself – perhaps because he doubted whether anyone else would understand them. One of these concerned Uncle Lauritz and the day he had taken Jonas to the Oslo Flying Club, right next to Fornebu airport. He was six years old, they had been strolling about, looking at the light planes when his uncle came to a halt, as if quite by chance, in front of a Piper Cub, a small white plane with a red trim. Jonas did not know that it was his uncle's own plane. 'Want to go for a spin?' Uncle Lauritz had said, smiling. If not exactly scared, Jonas had certainly been a

little nervous: as I am sure anyone who has seen a two-seater
Piper Cub from the late fifties would understand. It looked as
though it would topple over if a grown-up so much as leaned
against it. With its anything but reassuring skeleton of steel
tubing covered with sailcloth and a paltry sixty horsepower
engine in the nose, it looked like an only slightly larger version of
the frail model planes that the big boys played with on the playing field at home, the ones they started by flicking the propeller
with their fingers and steered in the air with the aid of two
strings, standing in the middle of the field making the plane
circle round and round above their head. Although things often
went amazingly well to begin with, more often than not these
flights ended with an almighty crash, either because the petrol
had run out or because the boy pilot had lost control of the
elevators on the other end of the strings.

The last thing Uncle Lauritz was expecting was for Jonas to
say no, so he had already commenced the ritual known as the
'walk around', checking such things as the air in the tyres and
whether the cables were securely attached to the rudders. So
Jonas did his best to look enthusiastic, partly because he knew
that he would then be one up on his chums. After all, it was a far
cry from the endless yells of 'Give us a ride!' every time a plane
flew over their heads, to actually *getting* to ride in one.

Soon afterwards, Jonas was in the cockpit, sitting in the seat
behind his uncle, well strapped in with seat belt and shoulder
harness. They had taxied out to their holding position, where
Uncle Lauritz had run through the pre-flight checks: engine,
instruments, talking on the radio throughout, carrying on a dialogue which Jonas understandably could not make head nor tail
of since it was conducted in English, with words such as 'ground'
and 'tower' and 'clear to taxi' cropping up again and again along
with a lot of 'LIMA BRAVO CHARLIE's, although all of this
only served to make Jonas feel safer, giving, as it did, the impression that they were in continual contact with some higher power.
Not until they taxied out onto the runway did Jonas start to have
misgivings. Or rather, to begin with everything was just great.
Jonas actually enjoyed the swooping sensation, and he was not
the slightest bit afraid when the little plane dipped or his uncle

banked into a turn, making his tummy tickle. Besides, for the first few minutes he was too busy watching the instrument panel, particularly a funny-looking instrument that his uncle simply called 'turn and slip', with a black ball that indicated the angle at which they were flying. So the flight went without a hitch until the moment when Jonas looked out of the plexiglass window or rather, looked *down*. But it was not their height off the ground – somewhere around 3000 feet – that six-year-old Jonas Wergeland found frightening, it was the view itself or the *perspective*.

I make no secret of the fact that I consider this episode one possible source of certain fundamental traits in Jonas Wergeland's character. After his initial doubts he had begun to look forward to seeing Oslo from the air, but the effect this had on him was very different from expected. It all came to a head, after they had been in the air for some time, when they flew over Grorud, and Uncle Lauritz proceeded to circle over Jonas's hometown, with the best of intentions, of course, thinking, as he did, that the lad would get a kick out of it. 'Look, there's the block of flats where you live!' he yelled over the drone of the engine, taking the aircraft gliding round in wide circles over a landscape that Jonas knew like the back of his hand. But instead of being thrilled by this sight, Jonas was actually scared, absolutely scared out of his wits, and I repeat: this was not the result of the G forces to which he was being subjected by the perpetual banking of the plane; Jonas Wergeland was terror-stricken purely and simply because the landscape below was unrecognizable. He stared at the ground in disbelief, refusing to credit that *that*, down there, was Grorud, Solhaug, Hagelundveien. They circled and circled, and Jonas looked down, even though he did not want to look down, but he was held, transfixed, he *had* to look down, down on that fearfully false, facile, flat image, on which only the broad straight lines of a childhood world full of nooks and crannies were chalked in – an image which bore no more resemblance to Grorud than a brick did to an ice cream factory. The voices coming over the radio all the time, the foreign language, heightened the sense of total unreality. One of the biggest shocks were the six blocks of flats, which looked so perversely farfetched, seeming to form the most unnerving pattern. And worst of all: he saw no people.

This glance out of the window left Jonas feeling sick to the marrow, he could feel something welling up inside him, something akin to an urgent protest. He threw up all over the place, the vomit gushing out, spraying over the back of the seat in front of him and over his trousers; he retched violently and threw up again, spewing his load, tears starting from his eyes. His uncle took one swift glance over his shoulder, straightened up the plane and headed back towards Fornebu airport. Back on the ground, he lifted Jonas out of the stinking cockpit, registering as he did so the state it was in, but he was not angry, merely looked at Jonas a little strangely and stroked his hair.

For his part, Jonas just stood there, studying the vomit that had stuck to his trouser legs, as a way of diverting his thoughts perhaps, or as if he were taking comfort in the little details, enjoying the sight of the tiny chunks of hot dog – they had stopped at Lysaker on the way out to the Flying Club to buy a hot dog wrapped in a potato pancake.

'What happened?' said Uncle Lauritz.

'I don't know," said Jonas. 'All of a sudden I just felt sick.'

The truth is that Jonas Wergeland had thrown up in horror, horror at seeing his beloved, chaotic, hilly, bustling Grorud, flattened out and brought down to a picture he could take in at a glance: a picture in which all the interesting details, tiny universes, were missing, as if what he were seeing were a formula, a diagram of an adventure. Gone were the rats at the rubbish dump, gone the words carved into the alder tree down by the stream, gone was old Frøken Schönfeldt on the bench with her handbag full of glacier mints. One could say that this was Jonas Wergeland's first encounter with reductionism, and from that day forth he was to entertain an inveterate distrust of all forms of bird's-eye view or synthesis, all systems or overall pictures: in other words, any totality that quelled refractory details and gave no thought to the individual. And later, the older he became, the more nauseated he would feel when confronted with theories or ideas that presented only one dimension of the multi-dimensional reality, as when faced with a teacher fervently championing the cause of dialectic materialism. Jonas detected the same flatness and appalling simplicity in such a theory, the same absence of real, live, enigmatic people, which he had been horror-struck to see from a light plane 3000 feet above the Grorud of his childhood.

So how do the pieces of a life fit together?

Jonas stretched out on the sofa with the remote control resting on his stomach, listening to Duke Ellington: 'Solitude', the 1940 band, Jimmy Blanton on bass, the flourish of Ben Webster's saxophone, music that made him feel deeply nostalgic but which also helped him to relax, took his mind off his anxiety about the trip.

'It's not often I ask anything of you, Jonas.' Margrete set aside her fountain pen, ran an eye over what she had written, several sheets of paper closely covered in pale-blue ink. Jonas realized that there *was* something different about her. 'Couldn't you stay at home? Just this once? Couldn't they send someone else to that bloody World's Fair?'

'There's no way, you know that. Not at such short notice. It was all arranged ages ago. Anyway, it's my idea, it's all down to me.'

'What about Kristin?' she said. 'I've got that seminar next week-end, remember.'

'I spoke to my mother, she can go down to Hvaler with her.'

'But then I'll be alone in the house when I get back. I don't like to be alone. Why can't you stay home?'

Outside the light was starting to fade. It was spring; it *smelled* of spring right to the heart of the room. On the hill leading down to the road the coltsfoot was already up, tiny yellow flames. 'In my solitude,' sang Ivie Anderson huskily, 'you haunt me, with reveries of days gone by.'

'I'm frightened,' said Margrete.

'Of what?'

'I don't know, I'm just frightened. How did he die, anyway, your Uncle Lauritz?'

'I've told you. He crashed in his light plane. He was flying too high. Or too low. Or too far. I don't remember. I was too young at the time. He was an experienced pilot. Nobody could understand it.'

'I'm frightened,' she said.

He sat up. 'Margrete, why are you frightened? Tell me.'

She sat for a long time gazing at the nib of her pen. Then: 'It's that last programme of yours.'

She was referring to a programme on non-European immigrants to Norway, in which Jonas had put a bunch of Asians, Africans and Latin Americans in the Central Police Station; sitting waiting and waiting in the hallway outside the Immigration Department, whiling away the time by telling each other stories, a sort of Decameron of tales that drew their subject matter from Oslo's new ghettoes; or other stories, the most amazing stories, of how these people saw Norway and, more especially, the Norwegians. Jonas had received a lot of negative, and to some degree malicious, responses to this programme.

Margrete told him that she thought someone had tried to kidnap her or to hurt her. She had been standing outside the Board of Health offices on St Olav's plass when she saw two men jump out of a car and come towards her, straight towards her, with a look on their faces as if to say that she was the very person they were looking for. The friend she was waiting for chose just that moment to appear, the men had stopped short, hesitated then turned and jumped back into the car.

'Rubbish,' he said.

'What are you laughing at?'

'You're overestimating the power of television.'

'But isn't that what you're always saying, how powerful it is?'

'Yes, but not in that way. Margrete, take it easy. It's that imagination of yours again. That's what I'm always saying: you have far too vivid an imagination.'

She said no more. He thought: that's not what she's frightened of. She's frightened of something else. All that was meant just as a lead in. He pushed the thought away. She lit a lamp, started on another letter. There were times when Jonas wished he had inherited his parents' ability to converse, to put the clock back an hour. Then it was the turn of 'I Got It Bad, And That Ain't Good', not with the 1940 band this time but an agonizingly mournful version from Newport '56. Even so, Jonas was aware of how the tune set every vertebra in his spine vibrating, while at the same time summoning up the picture of a ten-year-old girl, a girl with the longest eyelashes in the world, who was hit by a Scania-Vabis truck while playing this very tune. Jonas shut his eyes, allowing Johnny Hodges's saxophone to bury him in sentimentality.

'Why are you playing it again?' Margrete said from the table. He did not answer.

'I'm frightened,' she said. 'Jonas, I'm frightened. Couldn't you stay home, just this once?'

He opened his eyes, looked at her, closed his eyes again. He lay there with the remote control on his chest, 'I Got It Bad, And That Ain't Good' came to an end; he knew she did not like it but he pressed a button, heard the electronic hiss before the tune hit in again.

Two days later he was on the plane to Seville. He was to regret making that trip for the rest of his life.

The East is Red

He sat on a bench in a crowded park, looking out across a brown, muddy river teeming with every imaginable kind of boat, from little barges to rusty-hulled freighters; the occasional timeless junk glided past, and even the odd submarine, a red flag fluttering from its tower. Jonas gazed in fascination at the busy harbour, at this improbable spectrum of vessels, with the incessant hooting of the boats resounding in his ears, horns of varying pitches mingling with the bicycle bells on the street behind him, a sound like the tinkling of a thousand crystal shards; the deep, full notes and the crisp chiming, layer upon layer, forming a sound so complex, so inexhaustible and so totally apt for a country as unfathomable as China, land of the Ur-turtle.

Passers-by gaped at him in wonder, a few pointed openly. An elderly man, bareheaded and walking with a cane, stopped short and unabashedly eyed Jonas up and down. '*Takk for i dag, ser deg i morgen,*' he said. 'Bye for now. See you tomorrow.' in Norwegian. When he saw the look on Jonas's face he laughed and said: 'You are from Norwegian? I could see it on you.'

'How could you tell?' Jonas asked.

The man pointed to Jonas's shoes, but said: 'Face. *Ja,vi elsker.* Bjørn Bjørnstjerne.' This time he was quoting the Norwegian national anthem and misquoting the name of its author. The man sat down on the bench next to Jonas. He wore a threadbare cotton jacket, once blue now almost grey, that reminded Jonas of the jackets his grandfather had once worn, jackets that smelled of the seven seas and a hundred harbours. The man explained, in English of a sort, that at one time, many years before, he had worked in the bar of the seaman's club. He waved an arm in the direction of the Huangpu's murky waters, the bustle on the river, as if this were an attraction in itself. Just beyond them, two old men were playing mah-jong. 'My father was a Christian,' the man told him as if in confidence. His father had been a convicted criminal who had served time in prison. In Changsha, in Hunan province. On his release he had met a missionary from the Norwegian Missionary Society who had told him the story of Lars Skrefsrud, the Norwegian missionary who had also been to prison. This story had changed his father's life, the man maintained.

They sat for a while in silence, gazing at the boats sailing so close together on the Huangpu that you could almost have crossed to the other side without getting your feet wet. 'That was a long time ago,' the man said. 'The churches are closed now.'

Jonas nodded. He was more annoyed at the fact that the Jade Buddha Temple was closed, he would have liked to have seen it.

'Do you know anything about Skrefsrud?' said the man. Behind them the bicycle bells sounded like a sea of grasshoppers.

No, Jonas did not, apart from the name and some vague memory of an RI lesson about the Santal Mission. Wasn't there something about the Norwegian Mission Society refusing to take him as a student?

'He was a great orator,' the man said.

'Like Mao.'

'Exactly. Like Mao.' The man nodded eagerly. Did Jonas know that Skrefsrud had once spoken to 15,000 people in the capital city of Norway, out-of-doors – no loudspeakers, of course – and that he had spoken for two hours?

'Why do you take such an interest in Skrefsrud?'

'Because of my father. That strange coincidence. They were both locksmiths of a sort, too.'

'So you are a Christian?'

'No, but that does not stop me from respecting him.'

Jonas looked at the man and smiled, unsure whether he was referring to Skrefsrud or his father. People were funny. When he returned home from that trip, this was one of the things he remembered best, a little Chinese man talking about Lars Skrefsrud in a park on the banks of the Huangpu, thus tying up neatly with a story about red pins which Jonas had first heard as a small boy, from Nefertiti's great-aunt, on a terrace on the banks of the Rakkestad river and leaving Jonas with a sense of connectedness in life and the world.

'Are you a missionary?' the man asked as he rose to leave. Jonas shook his head. He could have said: I'm travelling with a group of missionaries, only they don't do their missionary work here, but in Norway. One might say that they had come to the 'mother country' for a refresher course.

Jonas had decided to keep a low profile and not make fun of his travelling companions. He knew, and was almost ashamed to admit, that he had his brother, the legendary Red Daniel, to thank for the fact that he had been able to make 'the great leap' from Norwegian to Chinese soil at all, places on such trips were in great demand. So without delving any deeper into the whys and wherefores, or the tedious preparations for the trip itself, I will simply take the liberty of saying that in the latter half of May 1974 Jonas Wergeland found himself in the Middle Kingdom, along with twenty-three others travelling under the auspices of the Norwegian-Chinese League of Friendship, and that they were there with the clearly stated aim of learning.

The most important lesson Jonas learned on this eventful trip – more important than his meeting with the living mummy Mao Tse Tung – was about his brother. Jonas had to go all the way to China to discover that he had got Daniel all wrong. For the greater part of his life Jonas had despised Daniel deeply and sincerely for his astonishing ability to combine overachievement with opportunistic radical views, his way of pairing success at school and on the sports field with all the 'right' forms of rebellion at any given time: the Rolling Stones, a final year at the Experimental High School, the odd joint, demonstrating against the hydroelectric power station at Mardøla – and the AKP. Essentially, the two had been waging a cold war ever since Buddha came into the family, Jonas could never forgive Daniel for being ashamed of Buddha. And yet, to Jonas's surprise, Daniel had pulled a few strings and wangled him a place on the trip to China. And Jonas was grateful. For years, ever since Aunt Laura had told him about Ao, the Chinese Ur-turtle, the turtle that carries the world on its back, he had longed to see China.

I really ought to provide a brief summary of the Norwegian Marxist-Leninist movement, but I will have to refrain, for one thing because on this subject most Norwegians are liable to suffer from a fatal mental block – and the generation in question be heavily on the defensive – for at least another fifty years; so the detrimental effects will be felt for a while yet. Just as with the slow-acting poisons in certain mushrooms, the serious hallucinations do not kick in until much later.

I will simply say that Red Daniel was a member, and seemingly one of the more fanatical and dedicated ones, of the Norwegian Maoist party, more commonly referred to by the acronym AKP which, by dint of the staccato fashion in which the cadres were wont to pronounce it, tended to put one in mind of the rifle that the majority of young Norwegian men make the acquaintance of during their national service: the AG3. And in many ways that is what they were, a bunch of walking, talking automatic rifles; they could take bits from one another and put themselves together exactly as one would assemble a rifle. To cut a long story short: when it came to the so-called M-L movement, Jonas Wergeland inclined towards the virus theory. As far as Jonas could see, the fact that a whole gang of ostensibly normal young Norwegians seemed to feel that they had been saved by a political theory which was at one and the same time so touchingly naïve and so horrendously totalitarian could only be put down to the ideological side-effects of some form of virus that had so far escaped the notice of medical research.

That said, I would go so far as to say that the motives of many members of the party were far more irrational than was first thought; it was not simply a matter of sublimated religious fervour or a disguised lust for power, as some people, wise after the event, have maintained. During their three weeks in China, Jonas discovered his brother's essential story: the story which provided the key to his enigmatic persona.

This story was a variation of another story with which Jonas was to some extent familiar but which he had never got to the bottom of. It concerned his brother's piano playing. Like many children, while he was in the fourth grade Daniel had – much against his will – started taking piano lessons from a teacher who lived on Bergensveien, and despite having little or no talent for it – listening to him practise was downright painful – he struggled valiantly through 'Gems from the Baroque' and 'Practice is Fun' and 'The Piano and I' to the point where even Jonas, who was never surprised by his brother's opportunism, could not imagine what induced him to carry on. Only when, after four hard years, Daniel had finally decided to throw in the towel, to stop taking piano lessons, did he confess to Jonas, one evening when they were lying in their bunk-beds, what it was that had kept him going back to that in many ways detested house up on Bergensveien week after week: to have the chance, once again, of feeling the piano teacher's tits brush the back of his neck as she leaned over him impatiently to show him how the pieces he was murdering ought to be played. And even though Jonas had to grant that the young piano teacher was very attractive, he could hardly believe his ears, lying there in his bunk-bed: that anyone would put up with four years of torture for the occasional thrill of feeling a pair of tits against the back of their head!

It was only when they reached China that Jonas realized what an impressive feat this had been, and how much it said about his brother; about his staying power, his ulterior motives and, above all else, his nigh-on criminal sexual appetite. Because it was the same story over again, the piano lessons found their parallel in the AKP. Not to beat about the bush, the truth was that deep down, behind all his iron-clad ideological convictions, the latterly so legendary Red Daniel, Jonas Wergeland's brother, had only one motive for being a member of the AKP: to pull the chicks. I know it sounds hard to believe, and even Jonas would have scoffed at the idea had he not witnessed first-hand, on that trip to China, his brother's virtuoso technique for laying even the most hard-line, red-hot, female Marxist-Leninists: in other words, watched him putting into practice the reductionist lesson their sister had taught them when they were little: behind all the fine words, all ways lead to that spot between a woman's thighs. In those three weeks, Red Daniel climbed into bed with no less than four of the eleven girls in their party, and believe me, that called for no small amount of ingenuity and subterfuge – in many ways living up to the AKP's own methods – since at best

they all had to sleep two to a room; and one of the girls was actually married to one of the guys in the group, who was sitting, in
well-known, vulgar Maoist fashion, discussing why the people of
Norway had to oppose the EEC even though China was *in favour
of* the EEC, while his wife was writhing in the throes of a vulgar
and most welcome orgasm in Daniel's room, with only a thin
wall between them.

While still on the train to Moscow, from where they were to
travel on by plane with the Chinese airline CAAC, Jonas had
been mildly surprised to see his brother coming on to one of the
girls in the party, but then, he thought, that was fair enough,
Daniel had as much right as anybody else to flirt about a bit and
maybe even find himself a steady girlfriend. Jonas could not, of
course, have known that his brother's sole and very short-term
goal was to screw this woman, a teacher with an extremely determined chin, up against the door of the train toilet, in time to the
rumble of the wheels over the railway tracks, until she forgot all
about Lenin's teachings and instead underwent a re-education of
sorts, starting all over again at the first letter of the alphabet. But
in the endless, flat expanses of Peking, in between visits to the
Great Wall and the Ming tombs, not to mention the Forbidden
City with its yellow roofs and 9000 rooms, even harder going
than the Louvre, Jonas noted that his brother had changed
ladies, and indeed that on their five days in Peking, which also
included the usual round of somewhat tedious visits to kinder-
gartens and printing works and car factories, he changed ladies
twice – the last one being a hardened feminist to boot, a dentist
with a steely gaze. Jonas had to smile when he overheard his
brother condemning, absolutely and utterly, all forms of pornography – *Daniel*, who as a teenager must surely have held the
Norwegian record for the number of decilitres of semen
expended during tension-relieving sessions in the bathroom over
a paper harem judiciously selected from Solhaug's biggest pile of
soft-core porn magazines.

Some years after the trip to China, when Red Daniel, like just
about everyone else, had had enough of the AKP and was busily
engaged in blandly denying that any of it had ever happened –
as if he and they truly had recovered from a virus infection that

had also wiped their memories clean – while at the same time reverting to his old familiar ways: completing his education swiftly and efficiently *and* passing with flying colours, Jonas had quizzed him about this. Why on Earth had he done it? What was so special about those girls? At that, Daniel had to sit down, as if the memory were too much for him, and in the same tremulous voice that Jonas remembered from the evening, lying in their bunk-beds, when his brother had described the feeling of the piano teacher's breasts against the back of his neck, he told him what the AKP women were like in bed. 'Honestly, Jonas, there's no one like them, they're pure dynamite,' he said, thereby betraying that he, like all the other AKP leaders, did not regret a thing. Red Daniel's eyes shone when he spoke about what it was like to have sex with the AKP girls, who had made love with a wild abandon and a passion that left Daniel lost for words. Jonas's brother had in fact discovered that the AKP stimulated the sex drive, exactly like an aphrodisiac: how, thanks to its very one-dimensionality and contrived view of reality, this entire milieu was actually as fraught with repressed sexuality and sublimated eroticism as any extremist religious sect. All you had to do was help yourself. 'I'm telling you, Jonas: after an inane two-hour long discussion on why we had to oppose the formation of the republic of Bangladesh – to wit: because China said so – even though those poor people down there were crying out with one voice for independence; or after an intense and totally ludicrous meeting to debate the necessity of "armed rev'-lution, like y'know", these women were like overripe fruit, one touch and they fell, exploded with pent-up desire. They wanted to be eaten, they wanted to let their juices pour down over you.' Jonas laughed, but Daniel swore that he had never experienced anything like the sex he had had with those women, forced to embrace asceticism, their heads spinning from having to keep track of so many outrageously contradictory and mutually exclusive assertions. Like starving souls they clung to him as if he were an oasis in the desert. Daniel's real stroke of genius was to remind these bewildered girls – because even behind those determined chins and steely gazes they were bewildered – that they had bodies, that they possessed a beauty and an allure far above and beyond the bounds of the grandest Marxist-Leninist-Maoist theory. Sex with Daniel represented a shortcut back to the real world, a brief glimpse of normal life, something which all of those woman eagerly clutched at, if only for one night.

But Jonas knew nothing of this on that visit to China, nor would he have had anything against Red Daniel's excesses, had it not been for one thing: also on the trip was a *real* working-class girl, a very quiet and, to Jonas's mind, artless AKP girl who worked in a factory in Fredrikstad, without anyone having asked her to do so: a girl, in other words, with her working-class credentials in order, unlike Daniel, who had to hide behind a mother at Grorud Ironmongery. This girl, whom Jonas called 'the Princess', had a steady boyfriend back home in Fredrikstad, he too a true-blue worker, and during the trip Jonas learned that she had applied – applied! – to become pregnant but had had her application rejected by her comrades in the AKP. It was fine by Jonas if Daniel seduced teachers and dentists, those girls with the determined chins and steely gazes for whom, assuming that they did not shoot themselves, this merely represented a brief hiatus in their careers, after which they would be able to sport the AKP like a flower in their buttonholes, but he took a very dim view of his brother also entangling an innocent, trusting girl like the Princess in his net.

Which is exactly what happened in Shanghai, on the day that they visited the No. 1 Department Store in Nanking Street – now Nanjing Donglu – where almost all of them had bought shoulder-bags emblazoned with red Chinese characters saying 'Serve the people', a motto which Daniel had long since supplanted with 'Love the people'. They were sitting talking and drinking green tea at the Peace Hotel where they were staying: once the famous Cathay Hotel, all mahogany furniture, velvet curtains and phoney opulence. The Princess was wearing a Chinese peasant shirt in silk which she had had made in Shanghai and was looking *fabulous*, to use a favourite adjective from the AKP vocabulary. She was laughing, she was happy, she was on the biggest adventure of her life and, to his despair, Jonas saw that she was besotted with Daniel.

That night, after some skilful diversionary tactics and a bit of a reshuffling as far as rooms were concerned, his brother's brief besieging of the Princess was brought to a successful conclusion. But as he was leaving her room, about to make his way to the floor below, he bumped into a Chinese man who just about jumped out of his skin at sight of Daniel. The Chinese led him down the stairs, looking so aghast that Daniel saw nothing for it but to go with him, all the way down to the Art Deco lobby, where the Chinese man's horror swiftly transmitted itself to the people at reception, who summoned a doctor and the police, not to mention the national guide who had been asleep and who had his work cut out trying to sort the whole thing out. Daniel had not the foggiest notion what was going on, but it turned out that his face was covered in blood: that he was in fact a pretty grisly sight to behold. The hotel staff, understandably, had assumed that he had sustained some serious injury. Whereas the truth of it was that the Princess had had her period, but had either been too shy or so hot for him that she had not wanted to mention it, and in the delectable darkness of their conjoining, when she had laid herself open like a ripe, juicy fruit, Daniel – hell-bent on the implementation of his sister's lesson – had not noticed anything either.

So you see, Daniel had not always been known as Red Daniel, but after that episode the nickname stuck. Later, Jonas Wergeland was to look upon this as being the M-L's only redeeming feature, and their only possible way of making up for their monstrous zealotry: they could tell all the great stories from those days, such as the story of Red Daniel, a modern folktale which, in all its grisly humour, shows that the AKP not only had the blood of the workers on their hands, but also on their heads.

Mammoth Sale

It suddenly strikes me that I have not yet explained how Jonas Wergeland financed his travels, although I did mention at one point that he had Charles Darwin to thank for his visit to Timbuktu. A trip to the Far East, plus the cost of staying there for three weeks, is anything but cheap, not even if you happen to be travelling under the auspices of the Norwegian-Chinese League of Friendship.

As I said earlier, no one in Jonas's family was much of a book reader, apart from his Aunt Laura, who kept her edition of Ibn Battuta's travel journals, along with a pile of other recherché and rather suspect volumes, safely tucked away in a chest in the flat in Tøyen, like a treasure that had to be buried when one lived in the same building as the solid Einar Gerhardsen. At least, thanks to Aunt Laura, Rakel had the *Arabian Nights* printed indelibly on her memory. Jonas's grandmother had been more of a one for pictures, and other than that he lived with a family blessed with gifts of a verbal nature. His grandfather had been a wonderful storyteller, and as we know his mother and father never stopped talking, to each other at any rate.

Then came those boxes of books which his mother had inherited from some distant Wergeland relative: books which she dutifully and neatly arranged on a couple of bookshelves bought specially for the purpose, after which they were rarely touched. For all that it mattered, the shelves might just as well have been filled with rows of cardboard dummies, the sort of thing you see at Ideal Home exhibitions.

By and large, in Jonas's house books were used only to prop up the legs of the bed when the children were small and had a cough, to raise their heads: the worse the cough, the thicker the books. Jonas did wonder later whether this might have had an effect on him, whether those words had crawled up the bedposts, so to speak, and into his body. Or whether they had protected him, like the metal bowls filled with vinegar placed under bed legs in the tropics, in the old days at least, to keep the insects away. Maybe, Jonas thought, a book under the leg of the bed would also safeguard against bad dreams. On one occasion he did ask his mother which books she had used most, but she could not remember.

The books also came in handy when Jonas and Daniel had to press flowers for the endless herbariums at school, or when their mother was making brawn for Christmas and had to press the meat. Certain books also made the perfect forts and entrenchments when they were playing with their toy cowboys and Indians.

Apropos this last, I ought to mention that Daniel – who else but Daniel? – had got onto the track of another way in which books could be valuable. He had first become aware of this during a paper collection, the sort of thing organized once a year to raise funds for the school band, and an event that the children looked forward to with excitement, because you never knew what might be hidden away in those great piles of newspapers and other scrap paper, in the way of comics, for example, not to mention porno mags. The same old legend was forever circulating, about how one year somebody had found this really outrageous foreign porno mag, full of pictures of black guys hung like elephants and willing white women, outside Five-Times Nilsen's doorway, although it might have been Jens Øvesen's or rather Jesse Owens's, he was just the kind of guy to have that sort of thing. So the boys fell on those piles of paper and rummaged frantically through every last one of them in the hope of at least unearthing some Katzenjammer Kids Christmas annuals or maybe a Donald Duck comic from the early fifties.

It was during just such a raid that Daniel happened upon a small cardboard box full of Red Indian adventure stories that must have belonged to one of the bigger boys who felt he had outgrown such childish things, several volumes of a series that was very popular at that time. Not, you understand, that Daniel himself was a reader, he stuck exclusively to comics and strip cartoons in all their guises, but he had gathered from his chums that a few of the volumes in this series were much sought-after, and one of these, *Deerfoot Takes to the Hills* was there in the box. So Daniel slipped it under his jersey and left the others where they were. Over the next few weeks, Jonas was surprised to see one little thing after another piling up on his brother's side of their double-top desk: a pencil-sharpener shaped like a globe, a penknife with a mother-of-pearl handle, an elaborately constructed hair-band catapult for firing staples, two old volumes of *Texas* cartoons and so on, and Daniel had to admit that he had received these in 'payment' from the other boys in exchange for letting them borrow that rare copy of *Deerfoot Takes to the Hills*.

Neither Daniel nor Jonas ever *read* books, however, not even *Deerfoot Takes to the Hills*. Neither could his school readers or the novels which in due course had to be covered as part of the syllabus induce Jonas to see any value whatsoever in books. Given the choice, Jonas would have had the contents of all books related to him verbally in the most truncated version possible or, at worst, drawn. Books were bound up with Norwegian classes and dissertations: a necessary evil. And to crown it all, there were Gabriel's lectures onboard his old lifeboat, the *Norge*, on the future of television, which had left Jonas convinced that books were as hopelessly obsolete as the dinosaurs, a relic of some long gone era.

So it was Nefertiti who first opened Jonas's eyes to the riches lying hidden on the totally neglected bookshelves in the living room. Until then, Jonas had found those rows of books no more interesting than any grey rock-face. But Nefertiti had chipped away a little of the cliff and shown him – to stick to the metaphor of books as dinosaurs – that it harboured wonderful fossils: fossils which, even if they did belong to some obsolete race, could be very valuable, shedding light, as they did, on certain vital crossroads in the evolution of the Earth.

Or at least, to begin with Jonas had not seen what she was getting at. He thought it was the contents of the books that were valuable and, as I have mentioned more than once, he jotted down an extract from each of the twenty-odd books in his little red notebook. It was only after his momentous encounter with Christine A. in the well-stocked library of the Cathedral School – where she had not only ridden him to an understanding of transcendental functions but also shown him a book by Kepler that was worth a quarter of a million kroner – that he grasped the full significance of that tip from Nefertiti: that in fact they were also worth money, hard cash. The first thing he did when he returned home was to take a closer look at the books which Nefertiti had lined up on the bottom shelf, none of which had been touched since; only to discover that almost all of them dated from the nineteenth century, with a couple from the late seventeen-hundreds. Not only that, but when he noted down a couple of titles and looked them up in an encyclopaedia at school, he found that they were all first editions.

One day he picked a book at random, blew the dust off it, and instead of going to school he went to see Aunt Laura. On his way up to her flat he ran into Einar Gerhardsen on the stairway and bowed low to him as if he were some sort of headmaster to whom Jonas was apologizing for playing truant. Up in the flat, among the Persian rugs and the innumerable tools for shaping silver and gold into the most daring ornaments, he managed to persuade his aunt to put down her punches and accompany him to a second-hand bookshop; he wanted her, a grown-up, to make enquiries about the book, to save anyone getting the wrong idea.

Jonas had gone through the phone book, and the minute they swept through the door of Damm's, the venerable antiquarian bookshop on Tollbugata, he knew he had made the right choice. They found themselves in a room lined from floor to ceiling with books, interspersed with a few old prints and maps and the odd globe dotted here and there. But it was the model of a sailing ship hanging from the ceiling that really gave Jonas the feeling of having landed in the offices of an agency specializing in boundary-transcending voyages to ancient, faraway realms. He took an instant liking also to the man who came to attend to them: a typically courteous, distinguished gentleman, with what Jonas described to himself as an aristocratic aura. Aunt Laura, in a big hat and with coal-black eyelids, played her part beautifully: a rather distrait eccentric lady who had inherited some books, she had brought one with her, would the gentleman be so kind as to take a look at it, was it worth anything at all?

Jonas would remember that moment all of his life, how the owner of the antiquarian bookshop took the book, a perfectly ordinary book as far as Jonas was concerned, with an olive-green leather spine, marbled side papers and green corners, a book that appeared little different from a chunk of grey granite from a drab rock-face, and the bookshop's proprietor also took it into his hands as if it were a perfectly ordinary book, but when he looked at it more closely his face lit up. He opened it and tentatively ran his fingers over it, as if he had scraped the surface of a chunk of granite only to find that it was actually a gold nugget. He asked them most politely to step into an office, where he flicked through some catalogues, from book auctions, he explained, before telling Aunt Laura, with no ifs, buts or maybes, that this book, this insignificant-looking wodge of paper, 500 printed pages – as far as Jonas could see not all that different from *Deerfoot Takes to the Hills* – was worth something in the region of 50,000 kroner.

'But why?' asked Aunt Laura. Even she had been knocked for six by this news.

'Because it is by Charles Darwin,' the proprietor of the bookshop said, glancing at the title page. 'Because it is a first edition of *On the Origin of Species by Means of Natural Selection, or the Preservation of Favoured Races in the Struggle for Life*. No more, no less. A milestone. One of the most significant treatises in the history of mankind.'

Jonas Wergeland never became a great one for books, but he loved second-hand bookshops. To him they were like the setting for a lottery, one in which he had hit the jackpot.

Jonas dragged his aunt out into the street and home to Tøyen, where he spent a long time sitting in silence among the rugs and all the copper on the walls, trying to take in what he had just learned; went on worrying at it for a whole week before allowing his aunt to sell the first edition of Darwin's book to the antiquarian bookshop and put the money into a bank account in her name, an account to which she arranged that he would also have access – and which would remain their lifelong secret. Such a deal appealed to Jonas. A book-lover got Charles Darwin, and he got 50,000 kroner, plus a quotation, one which, aptly enough, he had found underlined in the ninth chapter, 'On the Imperfection of the Geological Record', and which he had come across again, encapsulated in the final chapter, also underlined, as if it really did all come down to a question of mountains and fossils – and time, as things increased steadily in value as the years went by. 'The mind cannot grasp,' Darwin had written, 'the full meaning of the term of a hundred million years; it cannot add up and perceive the full effects of many slight variations, accumulated during an almost infinite number of generations.'

And so it came to pass, to employ an epic phrase befitting this episode, that even while still at high school, Jonas Wergeland never had to scrimp and save in order to travel. Although it was a while before he really began to eat into the account; to begin with he only went as far as Stockholm and Copenhagen. But eventually he had to sell more of the books that Nefertiti had picked out, leaving them, like a last will and testament, on the bookshelf; works such as Friedrich Schleiermacher's *Über die Religion*, with its almost illegible Gothic typeface, Charles Baudelaire's *Oeuvres Posthumes et Correspondances inédites* – a book which impressed Jonas most for its endpapers, the leafs stuck to the inside of the boards, blue patterned in gold – and *The Scientific Papers* of James Clerk Maxwell, two weighty quartos: all sold, of course, through the agency of his aunt, who had nothing against acting as middle-man and who gradually became better and better acquainted with the charming proprietor of Damm's antiquarian bookshop, partly on account of his discerning selection of Oriental rugs, while he, for his part, was not a little curious about a woman as dramatically made-up as another Karen Blixen who happened to own such a unique book collection. Around the time that his family moved in to the new villa on the other side of Bergensveien, right under the granite rockface, Jonas sold the last of the books, among them Jacob Burckhardt's *Die Cultur der Renaissance in Italien*, *Journal de Eugène Delacroix*, and John Stuart Mill's *On Liberty* not without a twinge of regret for each of them, remembering as he did all the pleasure he had derived from those quotes about a people's 'spirit', about realism being the opposite pole to art and about a state that could not accomplish great things with small men. All the same, the sale of those books ensured that once again his account showed an astonishingly healthy balance: what amounted, in fact, to a small fortune – for a young man, at least.

As for the world of antiquarian books with its staggering prices, Jonas saw it as being rather like a big-game hunt where the main attraction lay in the hides, in the irrational and senti-mental values, rather than the words, the content. He thanked his lucky stars for the bookcase at home, which had sat there all those years, guarding its treasures in full view of everyone, but with no one being any the wiser. The books on the shelves were not unlike those mammoths that Nefertiti had told him about; mammoths that had fallen down the crevices in glaciers and were discovered again, thousands of years later, perfectly intact, frozen solid in the ice – for all one knew they, too, could have been in full view for ages and ages, encased in transparent ice; they, too, had a hide, a pelt which was worth a fortune because of its age.

Thus Jonas was able to exchange the hide bindings on the books for hard cash or trade them for another valuable commod-ity: travel. You could say that the books sprouted wings, or sails, and carried him off to foreign lands. So the spirit of Darwin had its effect even on Jonas Wergeland inasmuch as he was one of the very few people who were fortunate enough to discover the lit-eral value of books, their potential for transcending boundaries.

Only a couple of other books ever commanded as high a price as the Darwin: Adam Smith's *An Inquiry into the Nature and Causes of the Wealth of Nations*, for example – an unbelievable 60,000 in nice crisp kroner – but many of them also contained dedications, obscure dedications which increased their value sev-eral-fold. Even though Jonas's curiosity as to the previous owner of these books grew with the years, he did not balk at selling them; he looked upon them as a legacy of sorts from the previ-ous century, a fund of wisdom no longer required; even those quotations which he had learned by heart he eyed with consider-able scepticism, regarding them more as toys, conversation pieces, a bunch of strange fossils, than as genuinely valuable knowledge. Jonas was always baffled by people who were impressed by them, who took them to be a sign of intelligence. And for anyone who thinks it is impossible to sail through life on the strength of twenty-odd quotations memorized from some relatively learned works, then I would ask them to take a look around them, at all of those who do sail through life, who may even be the foremost leaders in our society and who do not carry a single quotation in their heads, not even from a bad book.

The Jade Buddha

The few – I might almost say 'the happy few' – who managed to join one of the League of Friendship trips to China in the 1970s, in other words, those who could afford it and had made it through the ideological eye of a needle, can tell you that they were definitely no picnic. After a while, Jonas wearied of the heavy schedule and the thoroughly stage-managed visits to everything from the 7th of May Cadre School in Peking to the oil refinery in Nanking. And when it came to Shanghai, where they now found themselves, it went without saying that they had to make the pilgrimage to the little brick building containing the room in which the Chinese Communist Party was founded and go on the one-day excursion to an idealized People's Commune; then there was the tour of a model hospital where they were treated to an acupuncture demonstration, as well as visits to some more solid establishments, such as the exemplary Steelworks no. 1. Wherever they went they were surrounded by wall newspapers and banners covered in huge characters which Jonas did not understand and which, despite their interpreter's helpful translations, left him with a sense of remoteness, of an impenetrability that made a mockery of them, not least of the 'concrete' questions associated with their visits, usually asked by the girls with determined chins and steely gazes, questions to which Jonas felt there could be no answer, but which the Chinese seemed to find easy to deal with, producing great, long-winded answers to such questions, spouting verbose phrases that reminded Jonas of the time when he had had to recite the Shorter Catechism from memory, while their Norwegian guests nodded and made notes politely and were oh-so intent on learning, until eventually someone stood up and made a thank-you speech and presented a gift from Norway, after which they danced and sang Norwegian folksongs such as *'Per Spelmann'* and *'Hanen stend på Stabbur-shella'*, the latter sung as a round at that, to give the Chinese a little taste of Norwegian culture. A punctilious and detailed report was of course written up later, and in the evening they did a recap. Little, very little, was left to chance.

On the whole, Jonas was surprised at how well he had got on with the M-L's who made up the bulk of the party, characters at whom he could only shake his head before. Some of them would, like Jonas, eventually become key figures in Norwegian public affairs, individuals one saw on television and read about in the papers. Many a time Jonas had to smile when such a person showed up in some manifestly commercial context, as the repre- sentative of a typical capitalist concern, when he thought of how that same person had once sung *'Per Spellman'* with such gusto at the Steelworks no. 1 in Shanghai – although Jonas smiled not out of contempt, but out of respect for the unfathomability and broad diversity of mankind. All in all, he spent a lot of time talk- ing to these people: as an astronomy student he detected many similarities between this sect and the planet Pluto – both were small and peripheral, but even so they provided some vital angles towards an understanding both of the universe and the people of Norway. One thing in particular which Jonas had confirmed was a quotation he had noted down in his 'little red book' and mem- orized, a quote by the American philosopher and psychologist William James, taken from an essay entitled 'The Will to Believe' from the book of the same name, which stated that moral ques- tions are usually so urgent that they cannot be solved by waiting for sensible proof, and that when it comes to comparing *values*, we cannot turn to science for answers, we must consult our own hearts. Moral conviction is based, in other words, on the will to believe. And if there was one thing that these members of the AKP exhibited, more than any other ethical pressure group in Norwegian society, it was their rock-solid *belief*. As far as that went, they were all missionaries.

In whatever free time they had, when the others elected to put their feet up back at the hotel, worn out by their exacting sched- ule, Jonas seized the opportunity to go out into the streets, which he much preferred to Peking's sterile avenues. And what did Jonas Wergeland do in the streets of Shanghai? Jonas Wergeland learned to cope with the masses. From the minute he set foot in China he had been surprised to note that he felt no fear when he walked the streets, surrounded by swarms of people. He had asked himself why this should be and came to the conclusion that it was because *he stood out*, even amid the hordes of black-haired Chinese in white, short-sleeved shirts. Not only was he almost a head taller than most of them, so that he seemed to skim about like a king on a shifting black and white chessboard, but he was constantly being gawped at, in fact almost everybody turned to look at him, and so here, in Shanghai, he had his first foretaste of his future as a television celebrity. Here, in one of the most densely populated thoroughfares in the world, Jonas was subjected to a form of therapy, he dived into the stream of humanity on the endless stretch of Nanking Street, the longest shopping street in China, with people walking twenty abreast along the pavements, and let it carry him along, as if in an interminable May Day procession; he found it hilarious, he crowed with laughter like a child learning to swim; he stood, out of breath, with his nose pressed against a shop window, studying how an abacus was used, before plunging back into the throng and being swept back down the street towards the Huangpu, like a fish in a shoal, moving as one with the others, and it was here, in Shanghai, that Jonas Wergeland finally lost his fear of crowds – or rather: his *physical* fear, the psychological dread of crowds was to stay with him all his life.

Another time he let himself drift, just to see where he would end up. He swam with the slightly thinner crowd down the wide street that runs along the riverbank, once the great and famous Bund, now Zhongshan Dong Erlu, past grandiose but grimy grey façades, built in the European style; he was swept on down the boulevard by the mass of people, passing under plane and camphor trees while three-wheeled cars kept up an infernal tooting, bicycle bells chiming all around them like a thousand crystal prisms. Jonas was carried all the way into the old city to be faced with chaos, albeit a chaos with some sort of order to it; he was carried through narrow overcrowded streets, between rickety, run-down stone houses with ramshackle wooden balconies, until suddenly he found himself at the Yu Yuan Gardens, the traditional Chinese gardens which would not become a sightseeing 'must' – even for Norwegian tourists – until some years later. Where he actually succeeded in ordering tea in the age-old teahouse and later, in a restaurant of sorts, sampled some steamed dumplings filled with meat before catching sight of a market in which he bought a dried seahorse, of all things, to celebrate his new life as a relaxed and exultant part of the sea of humanity.

In the evenings they would sit in the opulent restaurant on the eighth floor of the Peace Hotel, with its pale-green walls, lacquer red pillars and gilding, enjoying the view of the river and the harbour, drinking Tsing-tao beer and recapping on the day's activities, or rather: what they could learn from them, which was quite a lot – so much, in fact, that the majority of them tended to grow very sleepy and take themselves off to bed.

On one such evening, Jonas went out alone. He walked a little way down Nanking Street, strangely empty now, then turned to the right, into the area lying between the main street and the Suzhou river: a bewildering maze of narrow alleyways lined by low stone houses, their woodwork painted in shades of dark-red and brown, the odd sycamore tree, bamboo poles draped with clothes hung to dry. It was dark: warm. People sat outside, in the feeble light of electric lamps hung in the trees. Men in T-shirts were playing cards. Jonas passed a few little garages, the flames of welding torches, work going on round the clock. People gazed at him curiously, pointed unrestrainedly, all talking at once at the top of their voices. They smelt of muck mixed with hot oil, cooking smells.

After about half-an-hour Jonas realized that he was lost – although he was not in any way alarmed by this discovery. Everything looked the same: small low houses, lamps in the trees, heaps of rubbish, people sitting on low stools eating dumplings, old folk smoking. Jonas had not the foggiest notion of where he was, but he felt no fear; standing outside a bicycle repair shop, he calmly pulled out his mouth organ, put it to his lips and began to play Duke Ellington's 'It Don't Mean A

Thing', not giving any thought to the fact that it should be that
particular tune, or whether he hoped to achieve anything with it,
although he was not at all surprised when an old man suddenly
appeared before him, a man, what is more, who belied the myth
of the inscrutable po-faced Chinaman, standing there with a
bowl of noodles in his hand and a look of utter disbelief on his
face, even Jonas could see that, disbelief and fear. He waved his
chopsticks frantically, admonishingly, apparently trying to make
Jonas stop playing, glancing round about him as he did so, before
beckoning Jonas into a courtyard and from there into a little
room with a picture of Chou En Lai on the wall and an empty
birdcage hanging from the ceiling, where it was just the two of
them – or at least, a young woman popped her head round a
door then disappeared again. The man was wearing a round
Mandarin cap, which Jonas instinctively took to be a sign of
great courage.

It took some time for Jonas to grasp that the old man had been
moved, truly moved, to hear him play that tune on the mouth
organ, so moved that he gripped both of Jonas's arms, as if in
greeting, and in English of a sort told Jonas, falteringly, that he
had once played in a jazz band at the Peace Café, the hotel where
Jonas was now staying, but that jazz music, like all other decadent pursuits, had long since been forbidden. The old Chinese
man in the Mandarin cap pointed at the mouth organ which
Jonas was still holding in his hand and said 'Forbidden, forbidden' and attempted to explain how they, the jazz musicians, could
not even practise together because of informers. The old man
began to dismantle a huge pile of chests and suitcases, in order
to get at the chest on the very bottom, from which he produced
a little case. This he opened, to reveal a lovely old saxophone
nestling in blue velvet. 'Johnny Hodges,' Jonas said, pointing to
the saxophone. The other man beamed, he nodded eagerly,
before his face became impassive once more. 'Ellington is dead,'
he said, looking Jonas in the eye. 'No, no, Ellington isn't dead.
Don't you worry,' Jonas said, as if wanting to comfort this Chinese man who had been robbed of the possibility to pursue his
own interests. But it was true; Duke Ellington *was* dead.
Unknown to Jonas, he had died a couple of days earlier. So it was

not until later that he had time to wonder how an elderly Chinese down a back street in Shanghai could have heard about it; might it have been a stanza from the funeral service – at which the sound of an alto-sax played by Johnny Hodges himself had drifted up into the vaulted ceiling of the Cathedral of St John the Divine – that had somehow been relayed all the long way from New York to Shanghai?

The old man walked Jonas back up to Nanking Street. 'The Duke,' he said, as if addressing Jonas, and made a little salute, a bow, the kind of thing seen in films, before taking himself off.

Which brings me to another incident which had actually slipped my mind. I mention it simply because the photograph of this incident, to which Jonas Wergeland himself never ascribed any importance, led many Norwegians to believe, and still does to this day, that in his past Jonas Wergeland had been something of a revolutionary: a reputation which in some Norwegian circles, even the more conservative, carries a certain prestige, as if it were a badge of wartime heroism, granted only to the bravest of the brave in idyllic Norway.

Before leaving for home they had one last day in Peking, on which they were scheduled to visit the History Museum and the Museum of the Revolution. The bus which had brought them there from the Peking Hotel parked at the back of the Great Hall of the People, home of the National People's Congress, which meant that they only had to turn the corner to find the vast, the almost unbelievably enormous, expanse of Tiananmen Square spread at their feet, swarming with people and with the Monument to the People's Heroes between them and the Gate of Heavenly Peace, fronting the Forbidden City. Instead of walking straight across the square to the History Museum, they walked along the massive façade of the Great Hall, to take a look at the main entrance.

A car had pulled up at the foot of the steps and as they were standing there, in the middle of the stone stairway leading up to the huge yellow building with the red flags fluttering on its roof, a group of Chinese came out of the door to the Great Hall and proceeded to walk slowly towards them. As they were passing Jonas and the others, the huddle of Chinese stopped and opened

up, like a lift door, to disclose a figure at its centre, supported
between two others. The Norwegians' guide was beckoned over
to the group, and Jonas saw an elderly man in a grey Mao suit
turning to their guide and asking him something. Having
received a reply – which is to say, after one after another of his
companions had whispered the reply into the ancient's ear – a
smile lit up his old face and he made towards them, supported by
two younger men, and at that moment Jonas recognized the old
man in the Mao suit, because the old man in the Mao suit was
none other than Mao himself; the word was that Mao was ill and
rarely went out, and yet there was the man himself, Mao Tse
Tung, coming towards them; not at all well, anybody could see
that, but large as life. Mao Tse Tung had been attending the
People's Congress before setting out for Southern China, where
he would stay for the remainder of the year, consigning Peking
to his wife, Jiang Qing, and her fateful conspiracies. Mao Tse
Tung headed straight for Jonas Wergeland, even though there
were twenty other Norwegians in his party; Mao Tse Tung
walked up to Jonas Wergeland and no other and offered him his
hand; Mao Tse Tung's lips moved, although Jonas could not
catch a single sound, but another Chinese came to their aid and
interpreted. 'You are from Norway?' he said, which is to say:
Mao said. 'I have met several other young people from Norway,'
Mao said through the interpreter. He stood there clasping
Jonas's hand, and it occurred to Jonas that he had finally managed to see a jade Buddha after all, a face, yellowish-green and
deeply transparent. If, that is, it was not a rotten, hundred-year-
old egg: the sort of thing the Chinese considered a delicacy. Mao,
for his part, had automatically assumed Jonas to be the leader of
his party. Mao Tse Tung had run an eye over those twenty
people and, despite the Parkinson's disease which made it almost
impossible for him to coordinate anything at all, not even his
speech, the great helmsman – or seducer – had promptly come to
the conclusion that Jonas Wergeland was, so to speak, the great
revolutionary among them and probably a person of considerable influence and power back home in Norway.

Among the group of Chinese there was a photographer. He
took a picture of Jonas shaking hands with Mao Tse Tung, a

picture which found its way, in a roundabout fashion, into a couple of newspapers, accompanied by the caption: 'Chairman Mao meets the leader of a group of Norwegian cadres during their visit to Peking.' This picture, which had been heavily retouched, showed an ebullient Mao and a somewhat doubtful-looking Jonas as if the honour were all on Mao's side. Which was true enough, since Jonas Wergeland had only one thought in mind during that handshake: here I am, shaking the hand of a man who has made people too terrified to play Duke Ellington.

What Jonas remembered best of all was the moment when he glanced towards the square itself, where those people closest to them, hundreds, possibly thousands of them, had turned to stare at them: at Jonas and Mao. Suddenly their facial features had vanished, leaving them looking like nothing but a host of rounded forms, like pebbles on a beach by the sea, or like a rolling sea itself – The Great White Flock – and the ancient face bobbing up and down before him, the old head almost incapable of holding itself upright, assumed an eerie resemblance to the head of a turtle. And in a flash of perception, Jonas saw that he was here confronted with the greatest turtle of the twentieth century, made of jade at that, an almost transparent substance possessed of a quality which dictates that it must be shrouded in gloom for its secret to be revealed.

And now here you are, back from yet another trip, and you know that you are going to regret that trip for the rest of your life, and you look at Margrete, and you try to take it in, and you ask yourself why you were not at home, you try to remember where you have actually been and you realize, to your horror, that all this time, in some padded corner of your brain, you have been working on ideas for your programme on the World's Fair, on the Expo in Seville; you realize, with something bordering on despair, standing there in a room containing a dead wife, how this shielded part of your brain has been thrown into a whirl of creativity, and it comes as something of a shock to you to realize that the scene with which you are confronted here, and the desperation you feel inside, have galvanized your imagination, and already, much against your will, you find yourself envisaging various possibilities for original angles in the footage you have brought back with you; you look at the picture of Buddha, you realize that it looks like Mao Tse Tung, and all at once you remember who you are, and it dawns on you why you cannot get the thought of television out of your mind, even here, even now, because you are the seducer, the seducer of the people, you think, like Mao, you think, on one occasion you even seduced the great seducer himself, the chairman of the world's biggest housing cooperative, you think; you turn and look out of the window, half expecting to see a gigantic Midsummer's Eve bonfire, the size of a world in flames, you think, but all you can see are the outlines of the low blocks of flats on the other side of Bergensveien, and as you look at them you have a sense of being lifted up, as if you were in a small plane, a Piper Cub, you think, of looking down on everything from a great height, your own villa included, like an itty-bitty angle on a granite Norwegian rock-face, you think, so ludicrously simplified and false, you think, noticing as you do so that in your absence someone has been using the old record-player, the one that takes seventy-eights, and you see a record on the turntable, see the title, 'I Got It Bad, And That Ain't Good', you drop to your knees, feeling sick to the marrow; if only you knew how much I wish I could be there, how I wish I could put my hand on your brow, to make it easier for you to throw up, and it is all I can do not to reveal the motive behind this task I have set myself, to keep my deep secret, but I hope that you at least, you, Jonas Wergeland, conqueror of the television masts, saviour of the suicidal, founder of Michelangelo Day, will understand, and understand also how much, how overwhelmingly much, this chronicle has meant to me, too.

So I do not blame you for once again crawling over to Margrete on your hands and knees, as if to inspect a shot elk, with a vague notion that you ought to cut out the heart, in order to examine it, chamber by chamber, you think, because there, you think, might lie the answer, you think, to the mystery of love, you think, and you lean over her, lift one of her eyelids, as if to check whether the image of her murderer might have been imprinted on her pupil, and you think of those television cameramen who have filmed their own killers, sequences which are then screened on the evening news, but you find no images fixed on Margrete's pupils, only the black reflection of your own face, like a camera obscura, you think, but then you've always known, known that it could just as easily be you lying there, on the polar-bear skin, shot, because it is your fault, you think, it is your seductive arts that lie at the start of this causal chain, you think, and your eye goes to the row of videocassettes on the bookshelf, like book spines you think, with no antiquarian value whatsoever, you think, not worth a shit, you think, or worth no more than a bullet through the heart, like that programme of yours that NRK screened just before you left for Seville, the one that had frightened Margrete, you think, the one that had enraged other people, you think, and you gaze at the Luger lying on the floor underneath the coffee table, an unmistakeable message, you think, from people who hate your seductive arts, and more specifically that programme, the one you called 'Tales from the Ghetto', in which the new citizens of Norway, Africans, Asians, Latin-Americans, told stories about their adopted country; in which you wanted to make the viewers see, or rather, seduce them into seeing, you think, that immigrants enrich a nation, and in which you made the point, through the pictures, that a society that has no contact with the outside world is bound to stagnate culturally, and in which you held up these new countrymen as being a marvellously creative minority, lending an entirely new, and sorely needed, dimension to Norwegian life, and it was good television you think, it was stunning television, you think, and it had given rise to a gratifying new sympathy for these Norwegians with different facial features, but it had also prompted a wave of indignant protest, you think, and it had taken the lid off a pernicious fear of anything foreign, a ghastly intolerance of anything that was different, something for which not even you were prepared, and you received threats, vicious threats, you think, so you ought to have known better, you ought to have stayed home, looked after Margrete, you think, because she too had felt threatened, but you didn't take it seriously, and now, at last, you realize that it must have been racists, coming to your house while you were away, to take revenge, you think, intent on protecting the Norwegian way of life, you think, pure, antiseptic Norway, you think, probably neo-Nazis, you think, the Luger pointed to that, it was clear proof, a calling card, you think, left behind on purpose, you think, and it looks old, must be from the war, a relic, something one associates with Germany, with the Nazis, you think, and that fits, suddenly it all fits; it had to happen some day, you think, because you are the star, you are the wizard of television, you are the man who makes the people of Norway sit up and take notice, who can draw a response from people, you think, and to be honest you've always been waiting for something like this to happen, always knew that one day it was bound to turn nasty, that one day the idyll was bound to be shattered, that one day a monster of a Scania-Vabis would come crashing brutally, relentlessly through the fragile walls of your villa, shattering bricks and blocks of granite and sending them flying chaotically in all directions. And now here you are, as if in a bomb crater, you think, on your knees before an innocent victim, you think, and you know you have to make that call, you know you cannot put it off any longer, you look at the telephone, and you know what a God-awful to-do there will be, and you know the sort of headlines it will give rise to, and you know the press will have a field day, and you know that from now on nothing, absolutely nothing, will ever be the same again, and you know that you have come to a juncture as critical as that long hard battle you once had to fight in a TV studio at Marienlyst – so I say to you, now, at this desperate chaotic moment, because it could be the saving of you.

The Battle of Hafrsfjord

Remember, I say, remember that time with the sound check, when the 'mic's, those tiny lapel microphones, had already been attached, and they were all asked to say something. He listened to the others mouthing inane phrases, and because he had the idea that these said a lot about their subconscious minds, on impulse, when his turn came, he quoted Charles Darwin: 'The mind cannot grasp,' he said, as if plucking the words out of thin air, 'the full meaning of the term of a hundred million years.' No reaction, no laughter, just a 'thank you, that's fine'. A bad sign, he thought.

There were five minutes to go before they went out live on the air. Jonas studied the set décor, the flimsy studio walls which would give the viewers the impression of a relatively cosy room, but which to him represented something quite different, namely, the scene of a battle. Nor could the viewers tell that the light was disturbingly bright, as glaringly bright as the light in Eastern Greenland, he thought, peering round about him at these familiar surroundings which had suddenly become so alien, unreal, and as he did so he became aware of that ominous feeling of nausea that had dogged him throughout his life, the feeling that had hit him whenever he was too high up, or too far away, when contours were obliterated and details lost; a detector of sorts that picks up grandiose lies. One of the three cameramen nodded to him, Jonas could not tell whether it was a nod of encouragement or of malicious glee, he tried to catch the eye of Gunnhild, the floor manager, who was bustling about with a sheet of paper in each hand and a headset on, but she avoided looking his way, treating him with professional detachment, close to condescension, as if he were any ordinary guest. These people used to be his colleagues, now suddenly they were potential antagonists. He tried to breath deeply, slowly, he could tell he was nervous, and he had reason to be nervous; he had reached a critical juncture in his life, an event which could turn everything on its head, leave his brilliant career in ruins. That was the media circus for you. Riding high one day: consigned to oblivion the next. Like Timbuktu. A city of gold one year, a heap of sand the next. Jonas sat in that studio, bathed in an unpleasant light, and suddenly found himself wondering whether his prism was still out there somewhere, among the Tuaregs in the desert around Timbuktu, or whether perhaps it lay buried in the sand, one crystal among other crystals. Whatever the case, he could have done with it now, something to hold in his hand, something with which to break up that disturbingly bright light.

He looked at the two seated next to him, two people who would be vying with one another to tear him to pieces before the very eyes of the Norwegian people; he turned his eyes up to the control room, high above the studio floor, could not make out anyone behind the walls of glass but knew they were there, seven of them at least, including the Colonel, the producer, an old adversary; Jonas knew that the Colonel was girding his loins for the transmission of his life, a golden opportunity; that at that very moment the Colonel was scrutinizing his face on several of the monitors in the bank in front of him, Jonas could almost feel it physically, this dissection, as if he had been carved up, ready for distribution to all those thousands of homes.

Four minutes to go until they went on the air. The cameras were gliding back and forth a bit. Up in the control room, they were checking the scene coverage, whether the lighting was okay, the colours, whether the cameras were matched up. Jonas knew the routine, he looked at the welter of cables on the floor, at the maze of spotlights on the grid above their heads, some of which could even be raised and lowered hydraulically, he stared up at this galaxy, letting himself be dazzled while he thought of how simple television actually was: light, an outward light, no more than that, even a white shirt could cause problems. Jonas was momentarily hypnotized, completely and utterly, by all that light, remembering, too, that this debate had been advertised as a meeting of stars – or, with the medium's gift for exaggeration, as a collision of supernovae.

There is, as most Norwegians could tell you, some doubt as to whether Norway was actually united into one nation after the battle of Hafrsfjord, as generations of Norwegians were taught in school, which only serves to illustrate a fact which those same Norwegians find hard to swallow: that our knowledge of the world changes, old theories are adjusted, new theories are hatched. What is certain, however, is that Norway was united into one nation on that September evening in 1990, in the sense that a record number of Norwegians, close to two million – even the blind, so they said – had settled themselves in front of the television to see this programme, one which had been awaited with the sort of interest and excitement usually reserved for the live coverage of certain events at the winter Olympics, the sort that tend to occasion statements such as 'the whole of Norway came to a standstill'.

Behind all this lay, of course, Jonas Wergeland's stupendous series *Thinking Big*, which had put everything else on television in the shade the year before. Later, people were to talk of 1989 as being 'Wergeland year' in the history of NRK. Not only did people find themselves with a new Europe that year but also with a new NRK, twenty-odd programmes which, in keeping with the turbulent changes taking place on the international front, created, for a brief spell at any rate, a whole new awareness of Norway's place in the world. But where, the year before, people had been on the alert, sitting there with pen and notebook in hand, or their fingers on the video record button, or at any rate with a cup of coffee to clear their brains, they now lounged back with their potato chips and mineral water, happily anticipating that this was going to be *fun*, and, it has to be said, harbouring a sneaking hope of a juicy bit of scandal.

So what had happened? A year before the focus had been on a provocative television project. Now the focus was all on Jonas Wergeland's person. First it had been a matter of thinking big, then of thinking small. Within a matter of weeks an entire country had shrunk to one snide, narrow-minded small town.

In other words, on that evening, one of the most bizarre countries in the world had mustered its inhabitants in front of their
television screens; an entire nation appeared to have discovered
that it had been taken for a ride, and had now put itself, of its
own free will, in the doghouse. They had heaped applause and
acclaim and regard on a man of Norwegian birth, they had forgotten to run him down, they had neglected to draw attention to
the hopelessly ambitious, pathetically misguided and, not least,
brazenly speculative aspects of this project. But now – even if
they were in the doghouse – it was time to break out the potato
chips and peanuts, now all they had to do was to tip their Stress-
Less chairs well back – the Stress-Less, that unique and oh-so-
typical Norwegian invention, that TV chair *par excellence* – now
it was high bloody time that they plucked the feathers off this
cock-of-the-walk; now it was time to laugh at him, see him sweat,
see him writhe on the spit as he was grilled by Audun Tangen
himself, the Grand Inquisitor of Marienlyst, also known as
'Audun the Tongs' on account of his fearsome interviewing
technique, in the early days of Norwegian television, at least.
And this in itself, that it should be Tangen, was a salient factor,
rendering the confrontation that much more piquant and diverting, when one considered that for a whole decade Tangen had
been well and truly supplanted by Jonas Wergeland, so the
Tongs had good cause to whet his instruments. Small wonder
then that people lay well back in their Stress-Less chairs, stuffing their gobs with potato chips and looking forward to a demonstration of the subtle art of torture, or better still, all-out war
masquerading as entertainment, or entertainment masquerading
as a battle, depending on your point of view, not that there would
be anything new in that, in a television age in which war had long
since shown itself to be the best show in town – one only has to
point to the war, the *real* battle, in the Persian Gulf, the first
phase of which was already under way as Jonas Wergeland sat
there next to Audun Tangen in the studio, and whose next phase,
the allied air and ground attack on Iraq, would be one of the
biggest and best stage-managed TV shows ever, a thrilling
extravaganza that could be followed round-the-clock on CNN
and the Norwegian news network.

Three minutes to go, and a lady came down from the control room, where she had been inspecting them on the monitor. 'Your forehead hasn't been done,' she said, fixing his makeup, while Gunnhild set their glasses on the table. Jonas had asked for apple juice, the other two for water, as if to indicate that they were in this together, two white against one tawny, two clear against one golden. And who was in the chair next to Audun Tangen? Will it surprise anyone to know that it was Veronika Roed, Jonas Wergeland's fateful cousin, the ace reporter – that it should be her, of all people, who had set her mind on slating the *Thinking Big* television series, on really tearing it to shreds? Jonas eyed her as she sat there, so attractive that she was almost *too* attractive, but he knew that she would look quite fabulous to the viewers; with her long, glossy black hair, her perfectly made-up face and a neat little suit in neutral tones, she looked both sexy *and* serious, a combination which would be a sure-fire winner, with the male viewers anyway. She looked calm and collected, she *was* calm and collected; she was looking forward to doing away with the expression 'Wergeland's genius' once and for all. She had her arguments off pat, knew them inside and out; she had it all worked out, she had teamed up with a bunch of top experts, she had it all down on tape, ready to roll, up in the control room. As far as she was concerned her cousin did not stand a chance.

Two minutes to go, and Jonas sat there, feeling slightly sick, shivers running through his body, wondering yet again just *why*, why in heaven's name Veronika was doing this, what possible motive could she have? The only answer he could come up with was 'pure spite'. She saw it, quite simply, as her mission in life to destroy him by any and all means. Oddly enough, he had never regretted rescuing her from the Zambezi rapids. And now she was using him, her cousin, to further her own career. In other words, she was a parasite, exactly like her father, Sir William, a member of the *Rattus Norvegicus* clan, someone who was constantly dependent on eating from the plates of others in order to survive, to get ahead. But did that make it right for Jonas to take part in what was in many ways such a primitive programme? To wage war against his own cousin, possibly drag her name through the mud, drag his own family's name through the mud?

For quite some time he had actually been all set to pull out, until Axel Stranger told him that it was his plain duty to show his face. 'And I'm appealing not to your courage,' he said, 'but to your wisdom.'

Gunnhild gave them the word: one minute to go. Jonas *knew* that small-town Norway was out there at the other end of the camera lens, and he *knew* it was having second thoughts about its enthusiasm for his television series, that the battle was already half-won for Veronika Røed, and yet: nothing is for certain. That was television for you. Jonas knew that he could turn it around, turn a whole nation around in five minutes. That was television for you. So banal, so powerful. And Jonas also knew that despite the more or less dispassionate nature of the duel in which they were about to engage, the people's verdict would be made on the basis of just one thing: their faces. So Jonas knew what it would come down to: whose face was the stronger, his or his cousin's. The utter paradox of this was not lost on Jonas. He had made a television series unlike anything ever seen in Norway before, one which had reached far beyond the bounds of that country, and now, thanks to a woman who had made an entire nation doubt its own initial assessment, everything was to be decided in the course of one hour, and on just one thing: two faces.

The programme was off and running. After the vignette, the Colonel ran an opening sequence showing highlights from *Thinking Big*, and Jonas could not help but watch the monitor with pride while at the same time, out of the corner of his eye, following Gunnhild, standing next to the middle camera, as she cued Audun Tangen, and then they were on the air, at prime viewing time, on Friday evening, going out to almost one and half million Norwegian homes, in which people were lying back, comfortably ensconced on their sofas and Stress-Less chairs, with crisps and cola within easy reach. Audun Tangen, looking, in his conservative dark suit, as severe and impartial as any judge, bade them all welcome, and after a brief and witty introduction which made it quite clear that he was in exceptionally good form, almost like his old self, he handed over to Veronika Røed, who promptly fired off a broadside, as they say, a pithy, demagogically brilliant – and, not least, populist – résumé of all the criticism levelled at Jonas Wergeland and his much-vaunted television series.

Jonas felt the pit of his stomach contract with nausea, he felt as though he were being shut up in an icy cold snow cave – no, more, that the whole of Norway was one cold snow cave, enclosing him within walls of ice – and he knew that the Colonel was up there in the control room, rubbing his hands with glee, and that he had long since caught all of his, Jonas's little twitches, not to mention his shivers, in an all-revealing close-up. Veronika talked on and on, but Jonas knew that for the most part the Colonel kept the camera on him, the listener, the butt of this searing, and worse, persuasive, critique.

Then it was his turn. With an ironic little comment, Audun Tangen gave the floor to Jonas, it was up to him to respond. Out of habit he fixed his eye on the camera with the red light showing, but caught himself in the act and turned instead to Veronika, conscious, as he did so, of the Colonel's voice in the headset of one of the cameramen, giving instructions for one of the cameras not in use to move in closer, with the result that off to one side he had a vision of a Scania-Vabis coming at him and was gripped by panic at the thought of being run over just as he was about to start talking – an ambush, sneaky – and perhaps that was why he suddenly had a mental block, could not remember even the half of what Veronika had said, but he knew that over a million TV screens throughout Norway were showing him in close-up, and that at that very moment millions of Norwegians had caught a whiff of a sensation, the chance that one of the biggest celebrities in Norway was about to break down, live on TV, and Jonas Wergeland did indeed feel rather weak, he knew that he had to find the angle that would crack this paralysis, break this strain, but he felt totally frozen, numb from head to toe, as if he were battling against a headwind, a headwind so stiff and chill that all he wanted to do was to lie down. 'What do you have to say to these not exactly flattering words of criticism, Jonas Wergeland?' Audun Tangen repeated in the same importunate, arrogant manner that had once won him such fame as Audun the Tongs, accompanying his words with a malicious smirk that said he knew Jonas Wergeland would never be able to parry this onslaught.

Broadcast

So do not forget the story that starts, or continues, at the moment when he realized just what a risk he was taking; that he should, of course, have done as the stupid safety regulations said, and turned back the minute they came out into the hollow in the hills and he saw his companion raising her eyes to the huge mountain straight ahead of them. They were heading south, towards the sun which only occasionally showed itself behind the clouds, in what would normally be described as heavy going: swirling snow and several degrees below freezing. The girl ahead of him on the track turned and grinned: 'How're you doing?' He tried to smile back, feeling a cold sweat breaking out the length of his spine; he had been struck, after only the first few strides, by how deeply and sincerely he still hated this invention: skis, fibreglass now, and how terribly unfit he was; each time they stopped he had the urge to cough, his lungs seemed too small, and every inch of him pulsated with his heartbeat. They were making for a place she called Heddersvann: 'a reasonable point to make for in such bad weather', and let me just say right away that in writing the following I am treading with extreme care, because it deals with one of the few spheres in which Norwegians actually can boast greater expertise than any other nation: skiing.

At one point it seemed to him that she had altered course. They passed beneath a power-line and came to the foot of a steep slope. Just at that moment the clouds parted and the afternoon sun turned the landscape into the perfect picture of Easter in Norway as presented in tempting brochures aimed at foreign tourists. Directly above them towered a relatively high peak. The girl ahead of him made the sort of neat 180-degree turn that Jonas had never been able to do, neither as a child or now, before gliding up alongside him. 'We're going for the bloody top,' she said, squinting over the top of her sunglasses.

'That one?' said Jonas, pointing to Store Stavsronuten.

'No, that one,' the girl said, pointing further up at a point diagonally behind Jonas, where Gaustatoppen itself lay hidden by cloud. She gazed resolutely, almost covetously, up what in Jonas's eyes seemed a formidably steep mountainside.

'But we haven't told anybody,' he said. 'I mean, we said we were going to Heddersvann. And we don't have time, it's three o'clock now!'

'What is it with you?' she said. 'Don't tell me you're chicken? We're going for the top, I said.' She had definitely altered course, was already heading uphill, as the sky clouded over again.

'Completely Gausta', Jonas thought, this being their way as kids of saying somebody was crazy: a reference to Gaustad Hospital. He turned, needing to have a piss. The sight of the yellow patch on the snow made him feel like an animal, a dog. He set off after the girl, even though he knew it was madness, feeling the action beginning to tell on his upper arms and shoulders right away.

It was the week before Easter and the massive influx of people to the mountains. Jonas Wergeland had been hanging about for some days, almost totally alone, at the Kvitåvatn Mountain Lodge above Rjukan, having come to a breakthrough decision, an almost perverse decision: for the first time in his nigh-on twenty-four years he was going to give the Norwegian mountains a try. And even though, typically for him, he chose to avoid the Easter crowds, he did also cherish a faint hope of coming up with an explanation for this almost animal-like characteristic of the Norwegian race, this abrupt, almost panicky migration, this mass exodus to the mountains over the week of the Easter holidays.

There was also another, and more intriguing, motive for Jonas's choice of Rjukan in particular, and it was not, as one might think, the splendid hydroelectric monuments of Vemork and Såheim – Jonas Wergeland was to remain shamefully ignorant of these almost baroque, or perhaps one should say fantastical, buildings until the day he met an African at Livingstone in

Zambia many years later. No, it was curiosity about NRK's main transmitters, set up on the tops of mountains all over Norway, that had brought him to the Gausta area – I consider this worth mentioning since it casts some doubt on whether Jonas Wergeland did indeed join NRK on an impulse as sudden and random as he himself has always claimed. The fact is that while at the College of Architecture he had come across Le Corbusier's book, *Vers une architecture*, one of the few books which he had read as avidly as the *Kama Sutra* of his childhood, and what Le Corbusier had written about the link between the products of modern industrial design – cars, planes, passenger ships – and architecture, had led Jonas to think of television masts – surely these too could be transformed into an exciting architectonic impulse. He envisaged them almost as church spires in a new secular era or as the minarets of some sort of media religion. In other words, he had come to Rjukan to view the mast on the top of Gauta, the only problem being that, until now, it had not shown itself, due to the miserable weather – the clouds hung around the peak like a cap – and Jonas had not felt much like getting out on his skis.

When Sigrid A. had walked into the fire-lit lounge the previous evening, tall and fair, with piercing blue eyes and a distinctive nose, Jonas had immediately been aware of that soft feather, which made its presence felt in his life only occasionally, being run up his spine by an invisible hand before coming to rest in the form of a prolonged tickling sensation between his shoulderblades. But she – it must be said – had noticed him right away, too, and in a manner quite at odds with her normally shy nature she had, without a moment's hesitation, walked straight over and sat down in the chair opposite him.

Sigrid A. was that pretty rare animal, a glaciologist. She had started out by studying medicine, it's true, but had soon switched courses, recognizing the great outdoors to be her natural element. No doubt there are also some who know of her as a mountaineer; Sigrid A. was, in fact, to be the driving force behind countless daring exploits in one wilderness and another, in widely diverging parts of the world, as the leader of sponsored expeditions that generated banner headlines in the Norwegian press and led, in time, to her being called upon to fulfil other tasks, as a so-called PR ambassador for Norway, a somewhat obscure, but nonetheless lucrative diplomatic post. Sigrid A. not only felt a deep need always to be the first, but also to do things which allowed her to push her body to the limits of its capabilities as if this were a goal in itself; more than once she had been almost shocked by what her own flesh and blood could actually stand. During her conversation with Jonas in the lounge she did not, however, mention this at all. What she did say was that she liked going for long ski trips in the moonlight, and when Jonas confessed that skiing was rather a sore point with him, she saw her chance and invited him to go skiing with her the following day.

So there Jonas Wergeland was, against all the odds – and what was a great deal more foolhardy and irresponsible, without having told anyone – heading up the hill towards Gaustatoppen in dangerously bad weather, led by a woman who could cope with three times as much as he in terms of physical endurance.

The slope was so steep that he had to take it sideways on; the gap between them grew. She stopped, turned. 'Come on!' she called, a note of anger in her voice. Jonas pushed himself even harder, not so much because he wanted to show that he was a man, as because he felt like a dog, he *had* to obey. His arms ached, and in the grey light the snow seemed even whiter, dazzling. He was not happy, either, about this blend of hot and cold, with half of his body, the back side, soaked with sweat, while the snow and the wind threatened to turn his front to ice. She had stopped to wait for him. His nose was running; he felt thoroughly pissed off. 'I'm sorry, I can't go any further,' he said, swallowing his pride. 'You can do it!' she said harshly, almost contemptuously. 'Come on!' She gave him a little rap on the backside with her pole.

Up on the ridge itself, the wind came at them from the northwest like a bat out of hell, crystals of ice dug in to their faces like crampons. Evening was drawing on. Jonas could not see the point in this: why they could not turn back, why they were out here defying the forces of nature when they could sitting in front of the fire back at Kvitåvatn Mountain Lodge drinking hot cocoa and playing Scrabble, or some other dumb game. It was as if she had to finish whatever she had set out to do; every inch of her radiated a determination unlike anything he had ever come across before.

Jonas plodded on, his chin lowered onto his chest. Everything was white – white, white – all the contours of the landscape had been obliterated by the swirling snow. He was growing bitterly cold, particularly around his groin. Amateur that he was, he had dressed as if for a quick run across Lillomarka. He floundered on, *like a dog*, he thought again and again, concentrating: right pole, left ski, he thought, left pole, right ski; he saw her turn, not to look at him – it was as if she instinctively knew he was there anyway – but at the invisible sun, with a look on her face that seemed to say she was aiming not for the top of Gausta but for something much higher, much greater. He felt afraid.

Then, when they could not have been far from the top, the blast grew even fiercer or perhaps the weather simply was that much wilder up there. They trekked through a sea of whiplashes, everything was white, the earth, the sky, Jonas had slid into a sort of physical second gear; his engine was on automatic, right pole, left ski, left ski, right pole, thoughts churning around in his head willy-nilly. He looked down at the strange, windswept patterns in the driving snow and was struck by a feeling of being on an unknown planet or of suddenly having uncovered Norway's innermost secret: that Norway *was* another planet. Jesus Christ, why couldn't they turn back, she was out of her mind, this girl; he glanced back, that's life for you, he thought, giving in to the banality, the macabre humour of the situation; you left a track on a cold and inhospitable planet, which promptly swept it away behind you.

The driving snow reached into every nook and cranny. Jonas had visions of precipices. Wasn't there supposed to be a sharp drop on either side of the actual peak, the west side especially? Right ski, left ski, right ski, left ski, he could no longer feel his arms, his face was nothing but a cold, stiff mask, numb. Sigrid A. was looking round about, she seemed quite unperturbed, as if everything were going exactly according to plan or as if she were going on instinct, steering by some in-built compass; he was struck by her strong profile, a heroic profile, tailor-made for the heads of coins, he thought, and then once again he caught a glimpse of that look on her face, as if she relished this ordeal, this self-torment, this sub-human struggle. Suddenly she pulled up next to a high snowdrift. 'We made it!' she called down to him. 'Congratulations, young man! The Tourist Board hut!'

Jonas refused to believe that they were saved, giggled with mild hysteria at the very idea. A snowdrift. A heap of snow. She motioned to him to follow her round to the eastern side of the bank of snow, and through the snow Jonas made out some rough stones. Had it not been for the corner of a window peeking out, he would have taken it for a cairn. But this was, in fact, the Gaustatoppen tourist hut, built of granite: huge blocks hacked out of the mountain itself, now totally buried in snow. 'Now all we have to do is hoist the flag,' she said, her face glowing as if she really loved such ordeals and was almost sorry to have reached the top.

After shovelling away another snowdrift piled up against the entrance, which was hung with a mocking sign offering 'light snacks', they found that the heavy blue, metal door was open. 'Did you know about this?' Jonas said.

She did not reply. Just flashed that happy smile.

Another surprise awaited them. Inside, the little room was warm, it actually felt warm after the icy wind. There was a switch; the light came on. 'The extension's new,' she said. 'It was added when the army were building up here. They laid heating cables under the cement floor, as you know.'

The door to the hut itself was locked. But Jonas was more than content, ran an eye gratefully round the wood-panelled room; there was a narrow oblong window high up in the eastern wall. Some blankets were piled on a bench along with some old sleeping bags. 'People sometimes spend the night here,' Sigrid A. said, unpacking her little rucksack, which proved to contain a little of this and a little of that. Soon they were sitting on the bench, each with a cup of tea and sharing a bar of chocolate and an orange. Thus, as a reward almost, for all that he had gone through, for the first time ever Jonas Wergeland was treated to the experience of a typical Norwegian Easter ritual.

As the light outside the window began to wane, Sigrid A. made up a bed on the warm floor with the blankets and sleeping bags. 'Well, now we've just got to find some way of passing the time,' she said, giving him a look that was as much an order as a request.

They got undressed. She swore at him when she saw how few clothes he had on, not even woollen underwear; but this anger turned to pity when she caught sight of his tiny penis, which had drawn as far into itself as it could, like a collapsed telescope. She tucked him up under the blankets, stroking it with her hand as she did so, warming it, putting her face down to it and blowing on it, taking it in her mouth, keeping it there for a long time, so long that she gradually made it rise and before too long she had climbed on top of him and guided it inside her, and Jonas felt a glorious, red-hot glow concentrating in one spot, felt his frozen body being thawed, as it were, by the warmth that flowed from this one spot. They lay still, that is to say, she crouched on top of him, bent over in such a way that her breasts just grazed his chest, two hot spots, a triangle of heat; and as she clenched him tightly with the muscles of her vagina, he had a marvellously tactile sensation of something tight, soft and miraculously warm, such a wonderfully delightful warmth flowing into his limbs, and it crossed his mind that this, the sum of this heat, must be what held the world together. And it was at that moment, if anyone should be in any doubt, that Jonas Wergeland truly understood what it was that he had always sought from these women: warmth. And as she slowly began to move, he could not help thinking how this sweet friction resembled two sticks being rubbed together to make fire; he vaguely remembered something about how, during their sacrificial rituals, the ancient Aryans had done just that, kindled a fire by grinding one stick in a hole made in another stick – symbolizing, of course, the lingam inside the yoni – and there was also something about this quite unbelievably delicious warmth of Sigrid A.'s vagina that made Jonas feel it was no ordinary warmth, the sort that could thaw ice, but a warmth that could actually kindle a fire, a creative flame within him, make it flare up inside him, enabling him to *see* things, experience something akin to visions or revelations, a warmth that would extend him, lighting up new chambers within him.

She began by making love to him long and lingeringly, with a dreamy look in her eyes, as if she were planning great exploits, or as if *he* were a great exploit, a wide-open space in himself. Outside, darkness had fallen, the wind howled around the walls of the hut, crystals of ice spattered against the window; he lay there, warm from head to toe, while she made love to him with greater and greater intensity, her whole body eventually working furiously as she rode him, purposefully, tirelessly, as if this too were a wilderness that she had to conquer, a peak she had to climb. She made love to him all night long, so many times that Jonas could not believe that they – or at any rate he – could go on, but she would make him rise up again, whipping him on as relentlessly as when she dragged him to the top of the mountain, making love to him so fiercely and so divinely that his whole body seemed to glow. And it was during this exhausting coupling with Sigrid A. that Jonas not only learned how much his body could stand, that he could hold out for far longer than he had imagined and that the volume of semen in his glands had not run out, even though he was crying out that it had; during the course of that pleasurable and demanding night a new determination was also born in Jonas Wergeland, making him realize that it was time he put his experiences into some sort of order, set himself some big goal, select, as it were, a peak. And, what with the fiery glow in his body, the great, bright light of creativity in his head and the thought of the transmitter standing at the top of Gausta, right outside the window, he had the feeling that their lovemaking was being broadcast, that the image of their coupling was being beamed into all those thousands of homes.

The next morning they stepped out into the most beautiful weather. Everything, the whole, wide world, was shimmering blue and white – sparkling white – and charged with a breathtaking silence. The television mast a hundred metres above their heads glinted like one of Carl Nesjar's year-round fountains, a sculpture of ice. Jonas was sure that Le Corbusier would have appreciated this sight, that Le Corbusier, like Jonas, would have been filled with awe at the thought of such a heroic project: a wild, elongated and sparsely populated country linked together by a telecommunications network. An epic undertaking, Jonas thought. And beautiful, Jonas thought, as beautiful as nature itself.

It was said that you could see a seventh part of Southern Norway from the top, and it certainly seemed so. As Jonas spun round and round on his own axis, like a little kid, wide-eyed and speechless, he discovered – and this he automatically put down to the events of the previous night – that suddenly this landscape meant a great deal to him, he actually felt a kind of love for these vast open spaces, these mountains. And the snow, even the snow. He bent down and scooped it up, having to screw up his eyes against the light, and as he crouched there, hunkered down on Gaustatoppen, clutching a handful of snow, it dawned on him why so many people migrated to the mountains at Easter time: on account of the light, the dazzling light. And from that day forth, Jonas Wergeland was always to regard this as being his countrymen's finest trait: their longing for light which, not unreasonably, manifested itself at Easter time, during a religious festival; and in days to come this insight was to form the basis for his optimistic estimation of television's potential, inasmuch as television was a form of light, dazzling light.

The trip down was something of an anticlimax. Even though he took the slopes diagonally, crisscrossing his way down, it went so fast that his eyes were tearing behind his sunglasses; his leg muscles ached and he fell God knows how many times, slithering and bouncing. Sigrid A. was way ahead of him, executing elegant practised Telemark swings as though she were taking part in a display and only lacked the felt hat, the homespun breeches and the traditional sweater. When he finally caught up with her at the foot of Longefonn she was standing talking to the rescue team that had been about to institute a search for them.

The Mystery

And remember, promise me you will remember, in the midst of all this, how Jonas Wergeland dwelt on the Norwegian landscape in his programme on Knut Hamsun, a programme which also provided him with a golden opportunity for shots of the country's natural wonders, although a lot of people were surprised at the way in which he did this. Jonas was never in any doubt as to what constituted Knut Hamsun's key story, the one story which in its own special way shed a revealing light on his life: his meeting with Adolf Hitler. Because Hamsun would never have met Hitler had he not been a great writer. Nor would he have met him had he not sympathized with the Nazis. His meeting with Hitler was an extreme situation which highlighted most clearly the extremes of Hamsun's own character, the breadth of this most vexatious of all Norwegian authors.

Jonas Wergeland focussed, therefore, on the writer during his last and possibly his most amazing journey to foreign parts, into the heart of darkness, so to speak. Hamsun was eighty-three years old – that in itself is astonishing – and had been attending the German minister of propaganda's press congress in Vienna. Hamsun had then been invited to meet with Adolf Hitler and duly found himself at Berghof, the Führer's renowned headquarters in Obersalzberg near Berchtesgaden in Austria. It was Saturday June 26th 1943, the time 2.00 p.m.. The two shook hands, author and dictator, and Wergeland showed this handshake in slow motion, over and over again, the close-up of their hands, as if to emphasize the irrefutability, the irrevocability of this event which shocked so many Norwegians to the roots of their being.

Jonas cheated a little with the setting. There were eight people in the drawing-room at Berghof, but he showed only three: the two protagonists plus assistant secretary Holmbo, who had acted as interpreter, and to save having to reconstruct that remarkable room with all its paintings and tapestries, its oak beams and heavy furniture, he seated the three of them with their teacups right up against the ten metre long panorama window in the gable end, overlooking the valley, and he replaced the view from this window, which should in fact have shown Unterberg and Berchtesgaden, with a glimpse of Salzburg in the distance, with long, almost dreamlike panning shots of the Norwegian landscape, an effect achieved by allowing the camera to almost drift off through the window occasionally, while Hamsun and Hitler were conversing, to present shots of the scenery of north Norway, from Kjerringøy with its beautifully preserved trading post, Kråkmotinden, snub-nosed and majestic – it was at the foot of this mountain that Hamsun had written *The Fruits of the Soil*, spellbinding, sweeping shots of Lofotveggen, and from Hamarøy, of Hamarøyskaftet in particular, rearing high into the air like a brazen old codpiece, as refractory as Hamsun himself. These sequences were run to the accompaniment of readings from *Pan*, descriptions of nature, and even though Jonas was well aware of the high cliché factor in this, he could not stop himself, the temptation was simply too great. This was also the only occasion in the *Thinking Big* series when he consciously set out to woo the public. And it did not fail, *could* not fail, what with the almost unbelievable landscape of northern Norway and Hamsun's magical words from *Pan*. These passages went down particularly well abroad, quite taking the viewers' breath away, they made the whole programme – in fact they paved the way for all the later programmes in the series. What saved these scenic interludes, however, from being run-of-the-mill, was the 'impossible' aspect, the fact that they were viewed from a balcony near Berchtesgaden in Austria. It was as if Jonas wished to hint at the connection between an extreme landscape and an extreme situation. Either that or the paradox of it: the contrast.

In order to underline this paradoxical aspect still further, Jonas did not reconstruct any of the extraordinary dialogue, forty-five minutes of it, during which Hamsun, instead of chatting about the art of writing, spoke out provocatively on such subjects as Norwegian shipping and the political future of Norway in general, in many ways an attack on Reich Commissar Terboven and an attempt to have him removed, while Hitler persisted in beating about the bush and evading the issues. In the programme all one heard in the background was a low murmur on two different levels: Hamsun's high-pitched voice – he was all but deaf – and Hitler's droning attempt to hog the conversation. Thus, in spite of everything, one was given the clear impression of a conflict: an old man, despairing and deeply moved, continually interrupting to insist on a point, and a dictator who was being contradicted and not getting his own way, growing more and more annoyed, raging inwardly – an outstanding scene in itself, worth dwelling on for that alone. According to Dr Dietrich, Hitler's press secretary for twelve years, who was present in the room, only one man had ever gainsaid Hitler, the most powerful man in the world: the Norwegian writer Knut Hamsun.

Instead of reconstructing the conversation, Jonas accompanied this scene with voice-overs of what other writers had said about Knut Hamsun. So, while watching the Norwegian writer and the German leader, one of the most hated people in the world at that time, viewers heard various actors reciting what such diverse authors as Selma Lagerlöf, Johannes V. Jensen, Maxim Gorky, Boris Pasternak, H.G. Wells, Rebecca West, André Gide, Ernest Hemingway, Henry Miller, Isaac B. Singer, Stefan Zweig, Hermann Hesse and Thomas Mann had written or said about Knut Hamsun, each tribute more glowing than the one before, to the point where it became almost embarrassing, it being nigh on impossible for any Norwegian to imagine that one of their own could have meant so much to so many of the world's great writers, nay, that he could have been one of most eminent literary figures of the twentieth century.

The truly outrageous thing about the Hamsun programme, a direct consequence of those paradoxical interludes, was Jonas Wergeland's suggestion that there might be another way of interpreting a person's character. What Jonas did, you see, as the old writer – in the shape of Normann Vaage – sat there in his dark pinstripe suit, with the NS badge in his buttonhole and one

hand on his cane, was to have him undergo a metamorphosis, one which in many ways followed the same shifts that can be detected in Hamsun's works. Viewers compared this to the 'heads-bodies-legs' pictures of their childhood, or with twisting the end of a kaleidoscope, since some parts of the picture remained the same in each frame, while at the same time the picture as a whole changed. By dint of trick photography, and with the help of NRK's excellent props department, which played a vital part in the *Thinking Big* series, Normann Vaage's clothes and makeup changed from one instant to the next in such a way that he not only portrayed all of Hamsun's many occupations and roles in life – shop assistant, actor, vagabond, road worker, gambler, tram conductor, farmer – but also the characters from Hamsun's books. So while Hamsun was sitting there talking to Hitler, in between the panorama shots of northern Norway viewers saw him switch identity, becoming by turns the first-person narrator of *Hunger*, much as he had looked in Per Oscarsson's rendering, Lieutenant Glahn, Johannes, the miller's son, Benoni, Tobias Holmengraa from *Segelfoss Town*, Isak Sellenrå, August or Abel Brodersen from *The Ring is Closed* in a brown Ulster with his tie all askew. But first and last he was seen as Johan Nilsen Nagel from *Mysteries*, with his yellow suit and violin case, the most incomprehensible and bizarre of all Hamsun's characters. Jonas also had Hitler undergo a slow transformation from the Führer, in a double-breasted grey jacket to the humpbacked manikin, the Minute, thus leaving one with a suspicion that there was talk here of a meeting, outside of time and space, between the vision-ary and his demon.

For Jonas, this meeting with Hitler illustrated what lay at the very heart of Hamsun's work: the ambiguity, the juggling with lies that turn out to be true, and truths that turn out to be lies. And, not least, it illustrated Hamsun's greatest achievement: his vision of the complexity of the human consciousness. After all, how was it possible: to be so stubborn, to fight for what one knows to be a lost cause, to do something as monstrous as shake the hand of the very Devil? By and large, Jonas detected a dis-tinct resemblance between Hamsun and his fictional characters, almost all of whom lacked consistency, who refused to be pigeonholed by such terms as 'identity' or 'set personality'; on the contrary, they were unpredictable, they could set the world on fire one day and retire to a mountaintop to meditate the next. They were many. And many people at once.

While working on the series, Jonas Wergeland became almost obsessed with Hamsun, since it seemed that through Hamsun he had been brought face to face with a problem with which he had been battling all his life, one that Gabriel Sand had put him on the track of in the saloon of an old lifeboat, with his mention of 'his good friend' Niels Bohr and the latter's lecture in Como. For both Hamsun himself and his characters were as much of a puzzle as light: that agency which the physicists of the twentieth century had spent so much time and energy in studying and which they believed to take the form of particles one moment and waves the next. Thus, in Hamsun's case, Jonas Wergeland felt moved to make some reference to Niels Bohr and the concept of complementarity: an obscure concept but one which hinted, nonetheless, that there were two sides to a story – two mutually exclusive aspects, both of which might nonetheless be necessary in order to arrive at a full understanding of the phenomenon. In other words, where the particle and wave properties of light were concerned, it was a matter of looking at light in two different ways *at once*. And of breaking out of an ingrained and rigid mindset.

This proved to be Jonas's key to Hamsun. The writer showed him what a little way we have come in terms of understanding a man, or how the pieces of a life fit together. In studying Hamsun, Jonas discovered how dangerous it could be to hang onto some time-honoured psychological theory, to saddle an individual with an identity, a persona, an essence: and equally dangerous to cherish the belief that there has to be some sort of continuity, a thread running through life, as if without this comfort one were liable to become lost in a maze. Such notions prevented one from imagining that there could also be leaps, that there could be interruptions in a life, that it might not hang together at all, at any rate not in the way one thought. So it was with Hamsun. It was only when one held him transfixed, in a still shot, so to speak, that he became *either* a Nazi sympathizer *or* the great writer. But

Hamsun was both at the same time and something more, something you could never quite put your finger on; and it was this, this great and unsettling enigma, which so few Norwegians seemed able to come to terms with. In the presence of Adolf Hitler, Norway's worst enemy, Hamsun set out to plead Norway's cause, tried to do something for Norway, for the people of Norway: a moral endeavour in the midst of immorality, good and evil merging into one. If one is to gain any insight into a man like Hamsun, it is necessary, as Niels Bohr demonstrated in his field, to forsake classic perceptions and plain language. Anyone who says he can think about Hamsun without his head spinning is simply giving away the fact that he has not understood the first thing about Hamsun. It is paradoxical – but also very comforting – that an author, a wordsmith, should constitute a mystery that defies description.

And yet this is exactly what Hamsun's books are all about: writing the impossible. And it was this that inspired Jonas Wergeland to attempt something similar in his television programme, primarily by introducing an element of undermining, ironic distance to the scene in which Hamsun shook hands with Hitler, and in which Wergeland conveyed both Hamsun's awe at actually being there in the lion's den and, with equal force, his knowledge that this was a repellent and monstrous act. One could say that, by dint of its thoroughgoing ambivalence, this programme – one illusion meeting another illusion, two visionaries talking at cross-purposes – dealt as much with the way in which this entire tableau presented a challenge to the creative faculty, that basic element of human life; it dealt, in other words, with something that went beyond all talk, all demands, with a simple message. Consequently, this creative effort on the part of the mind itself became one of the key elements in the programme: that mind with which one perceives, that mind from which spring dreams and illusions and, hence, literature. As much as being a programme about Hamsun, this was a programme about an attempt to stretch the imagination far enough to accommodate this disquieting man by the name of Knut Hamsun. Or, to put it another way: it was about our need for stories. At heart, the whole programme questioned the viewers' ability to create fantasies, and what part such fantasies – as, for example, those brought into service in understanding a situation as impossible as Hamsun's meeting with Hitler – actually play in our lives. Hence the reason that this programme with its almost indescribable subject matter – an old man and a tyrant by a panorama window – had a particularly strange effect on the viewers. Everyone enjoyed it, everyone was profoundly intrigued by it, but no one could say exactly why.

The Third Option

So do not, whatever you do, forget the rest of the story of Jonas Wergeland in a studio at Marienlyst, being grilled by Audun Tangen, the Grand Inquisitor himself, ably assisted by Veronika Røed, ace reporter and – who would have thought it? – Jonas's cousin. Jonas was suffering from an interminable mental block; all he could do was to sit there, staring at the cameramen working feverishly, with the Colonel's voice sounding impatiently in their headsets, issuing orders to zoom and tilt and pan, and give me a total, and shift a bit to the right; the very sight of those headsets, together with the robot-like cameras, put Jonas in mind of creatures from an alien planet and gave him a sense of having withdrawn from the world, a feeling that none of this mattered at all. Then, at long last, he managed to say: 'All I really wanted to do was to teach the viewers to think big.'

Veronika gave a soft exultant laugh, as if she had tricked him, all unwittingly, into confessing to a crime: 'You're wrong on two points, Jonas Wergeland. For one thing, television does not teach people to think big. TV teaches people to think *flat*. TV reduces everything to two-dimensional images, it appeals almost exclusively to one sense: vision. Everything that appears on television is automatically rendered flat and banal.' Jonas could not help but admire her persuasive body language, her elegant suit, her flawless makeup, her unbeatable combination of sex appeal and seriousness. 'And for another, and more importantly, you are inherently wrong in using the word "teach",' she said, almost indulgently, as if she were talking to someone who was dull-witted. 'Television cannot ever be anything other than sheer entertainment. You are guilty of grossly overestimating the medium. You have not taught anyone anything at all. You have amused them. You have reduced a bunch of famous names to a slick bit of show business. Nothing more.'

'Could you be a little more specific?' Audun Tangen interjected.

'Certainly. Take the programme on Knut Hamsun,' said Veronika, addressing Jonas. 'Could you have come up with any more entertaining scene from his life, anything more visually comical than his meeting with Hitler?'

A dramatic still from the Hamsun programme had been used as part of the set decor, along with other easily recognizable shots from the series, including the vignette: a prism splitting the white letters of the title, *Thinking Big*, into a rainbow. This last hung right behind Jonas; he was not sure whether this had been deliberate.

'But the pictures themselves cannot be considered in isolation,' he ventured. 'You have to look at how the programme as a whole has been made, the way in which it has been constructed.'

He could not have laid himself more wide open. The sparks veritably flew from Veronika; sitting there in her chair, she let fly a whole cannonade of crushing assertions which Audun Tangen did not lift a finger to interrupt. He did not even try to hide his smile, not that he needed to, since up in the control room the Colonel was keeping the camera on Jonas's face, on his pain, his suppressed anger, his dreadful disappointment.

For long enough the response to the *Thinking Big* television series had been, as we have seen, overwhelming. After some rather noncommittal reviews in the wake of the first few programmes – as is always the way in Norway: no one dares to say what they think before they know what everyone else thinks – came the jubilation, and once begun there was no end to it. For that, too, is always the way in Norway; when something is good, there are no limits to how good it can be. Even Jonas could see that much of the praise was laughably undiscriminating. As a child watching his father playing the organ, Jonas had always wondered that one small person could produce so much sound, and the response to *Thinking Big* left him with the same sense of wonder; how could one single, solitary human being cause such a stir simply by making a number of television programmes?

Occasionally he had the notion that he, too, was playing an organ of sorts, an utterly unique organ, with the television masts on the tops of windswept Norwegian mountaintops as its pipes: Gausta, Tron, Jetta, Lønahorgi, Sogndal, Nordfjordeid, Narvik, Kistefjell – main transmitters all lying more than 1,000 metres above sea level. Or that through these he could set the stops of a whole nation's emotions, that he had discovered a 'Tutti' button which gave voice to a great, many-voiced song of praise.

Jonas's triumph remained unmarred until one Saturday morning, one of those beautiful summer mornings when every-thing is just perfect: the weather, one's mood, the contents of the refrigerator, Margrete's fresh-baked bread. All that was lacking were the tabloids, so he had taken a stroll down to the subway sta-tion to pick them up. On the way to the station he nodded ami-ably to people he met, and they for their part returned his greetings with the sort of odd smiling respect that left one in no doubt as to what they would say when they returned home: 'Guess who I saw down at the newsagent's!' If he had not done so before, then certainly now, after the television series, Jonas Wergeland felt like a duke, a real prince. He sat down at the breakfast table feeling thoroughly – one hundred per cent – con-tent. Margrete was pottering about in the bathroom, Kristin was out playing. He took a sip of his coffee and opened the newspaper.

There it was: a murderous piece penned by Veronika Røed, the incisive overture to four probing articles promised for the coming week. I do not intend to devote any space here to citing the content of a critique with which most people – Norwegians at least – are already familiar. But it may be worth pointing out that it was, in fact, the Classic Norwegian Discussion. In these articles Veronika Røed accused Jonas Wergeland of something which, in other countries, would raise very few eyebrows but which in Norway was sheer dynamite: namely, of pursuing aes-thetic experience as an end in itself. 'Jonas Wergeland ascribes to television a function that transcends good and evil,' she wrote. So there you had it, Norwegian moralism raising its head yet again, and not surprisingly she cited the Hamsun programme in particular as a warning example.

There were times when Jonas Wergeland had the feeling that the country of Norway was a reversing boat and that he was in danger of being sucked in by its propeller.

Not that Jonas had not known all along that the bubble was bound to burst, that it had all gone too smoothly, but he was surprised at how quickly and how easily the great majority allowed themselves to become caught up in the witch-hunt. It was as if someone had snapped their fingers and an entire nation had woken out of a hypnotic trance and turned into a bellowing ape mountain. And as if that were not enough, a great many of these people seemed happy to have been told, with all the empty rhetoric and images frequently resorted to in Norway when it comes to anything new, whether important or not, that this was nothing but 'art for art's sake', that 'the emperor had no clothes'. Every tired old cliché in the book was trotted out – each one merely serving as a clear sign that everything was, reassuringly, just as it had always been. What annoyed Jonas most of all was the fact that people did not trust their own judgement, their feeling that the programme had really mattered to them, had given them something; that they were willing to deny their own instincts the minute some village idiot started bawling cheap slogans.

Then of course, after Veronika's attack – that tactical tour de force of ingratiating populist phrase-mongering – the grand debate was off and running, like a collective attack of bitter hindsight, as unstoppable as a juggernaut; all at once grave doubts were being expressed as to the authority of the series. A whole host of academics and experts in this field and that, all of whom usually did nothing but sit around gathering dust in various offices and seats of learning, saw this as the chance of a lifetime and came racing out on to the course, screaming and shouting, to ride their hobbyhorses, to become celebrities for a week, to give vent to decades of pent-up ambition and bitterness, all of which now hit Jonas Wergeland full on. Even his colleagues at Broadcasting House saw this as a welcome opportunity to stab him in the back, under cover of some watertight excuse or other, not uncommonly a concern for the well-being of the medium of television. The debate raged fiercely in the press for several

months. Not since the EEC debate of 1972 had such nigh-on
hysterical fury emanated from so many column inches. Jonas did
not lack for defenders, but taken all in all, these pieces most definitely worked against him, and even though many of the accusations against him fell flat, being nothing but petty personal
attacks and harmless hair-splitting, the main current of criticism
followed the lines laid down by Veronika Røed: divested of all its
trappings, Jonas Wergeland's series was an empty form, devoid
of any real substance. But Jonas also sustained many a cut that
stung more than he would admit, for in a debate of this kind just
about everything is dragged into the open. 'Can one trust a man,'
wrote one indignant mathematician in connection with the programme on Abel, 'whose academic career consists of ten credits
in astrophysics and two credits in mathematics, a man who, in
some respects, never got beyond Prelims?'

Jonas Wergeland sat in the studio, surrounded by a landscape
of his own making, constructed out of stills from Norway's most
talked-about television series, a room lined with pictures from a
former triumph, suddenly transformed into a torture chamber.
He heard Veronika Røed reiterating her arguments – now honed
and polished, as seductive as diamonds – for the benefit of two
million viewers, a whole nation gathered in front of their television screens, with Audun Tang occasionally breaking in to ask
her to amplify some point, or elaborating on them himself, delivering the odd brilliantly sarcastic remark, reading out carefully
selected quotes from a sheet he had conscientiously prepared in
advance; other times he interrupted Veronika's flow of words,
almost apologetically, finding it necessary, for the sake of appearances, to ask Jonas for his comments, whereupon Jonas would
make some brief, inconsequential reply. It was almost as if he
were letting himself be mowed down, mangled, because he
seemed to have nothing to say for himself, he felt sick, frozen to
the marrow, taking a fatalistic view of the whole thing, there was
nothing he could do about it; he made such a poor show of replying that even Audun Tangen eventually began to feel unhappy
about it: the discussion was too unbalanced, a walkover, it didn't
even make for good entertainment, it was not achieving the effect
that Tangen was looking for, the sort that would remind the

viewers of his greatness, of his heyday, his quick-fire interviews, or the times in election programmes when he, the Grand Inquisitor, caused representatives from various political parties to go absolutely berserk and even reduced one to tears, a legendary feat; but there would be none of that here; Jonas Wergeland was too distant. Tangen could see it, inwardly lamented it; he tried to provoke Jonas with references to Veronika Røed's fusillades, but sadly it did no good; Jonas just sat there, gazing at the clock on a pillar behind the cameras, following the second hand, circling and circling, and the big hand inching its way slowly towards the end of the programme without his having said anything of any consequence, anything that might redress the impression which the people of Norway now had of him, after Veronika's successful campaign in the press and now here, live on TV; what could he do or say anyway, in the face of such a torrent of moral indignation, expressed with such tremendous *seriousness*, such assertiveness, what answer could there possibly be to the eternal pathological Norwegian fear of the word 'form', the horror of that enduringly intolerable foreign word 'aesthetic'? Jonas sat there listening to Veronika repeating, hammering home, assertions the gist of which was that his programmes were totally devoid of any ethical substance; there was nothing behind the style, Veronika said, or pronounced, nothing but a lot of technical wizardry, and thus the entire series was really an evocation of pure, unadulterated *nihilism* – the most offensive word in the Norwegian language, a tag synonymous with some terrible, infectious leprosy.

And in the midst of all this – with all the experts being trooped out, on tape, in inserts which were so intricately worked in that Jonas's thoughts went to poor Vivi, the script girl up in the control room, whose job it was to keep track of all the VT spots – Jonas did nonetheless try to defend himself, even if for the most part he simply sat there, saying 'ah' or 'well' or 'no' or 'yes, but', interspersed with the odd 'it's possible' and on a couple of occasions: 'I don't know' – this last alone was something of a sensation, enough in itself to establish the programme as a milestone in television history: that a man, and a Norwegian at that, should appear on television and say 'I don't know'.

The truth is that Jonas Wergeland could not think of anything profound to say, even though he was dismayed to note that the whole discussion presented an example of a particularly Norwegian way of thinking: when you cannot see the moral in something, which is to say, when you do not recognize the moral, you call it 'immoral' or, at best, 'nihilism'. Here, under a firmament of irritating spotlights, Jonas saw more clearly than ever how the entire case against him could be boiled down to the following: his programmes were reprehensible because they were *different*, because they could not be understood or explained in traditional terms or by recourse to good old-fashioned ideology. Because that is the way of things in Norway: if something does not claim quite explicitly – in block capitals underlined in red, basically – to deal with morality, people are incapable of opening their minds to the idea that it might, nonetheless, deal with morality, and they had even more trouble in accepting – perish the thought – that, as in Jonas Wergeland's case, it might actually deal with another and arguably more important link in the chain of causality that leads to ethical standpoints: namely, the imagination.

But, thought Jonas, he was also guilty of an even worse crime: he had ventured to question the established perceptions. To Jonas it often seemed as if the Norwegian race – more than other races – considered itself to be complete and fully evolved in much the same way as it took the theories of its day for granted, regarding them as unshakeable truths. Nothing could be harder than getting a Norwegian who had finally and painfully managed to absorb new ideas to understand that even the theory of relativity, or quantum theory, or Darwinism, were merely temporary, that in a hundred years they would be a thing of the past.

But how was he to say that, how to protest against this deep-seated need for old habits and the status quo; how to find an angle that would get round this endless deadlock between ethics and aesthetics?

Jonas almost laughed out loud when a guy with a handheld camera stepped into the arena and proceeded to move, hunkered down, around the set, getting shots of Veronika from below while she was talking. Looking back on it, it is easy to see how, ironically, this whole programme, with its bombastic assertions regarding Jonas Wergeland's aestheticism, owed so much to the *Thinking Big* series – and would indeed have been unthinkable had it not been for it. Never had the artistic form been employed more deliberately in a current affairs programme. Not only did the Colonel use video inserts in an experimental fashion, he even had Normann Vaage, dressed up as Henrik Ibsen, saunter onto the set once or twice to say a few words direct to the handheld camera. On the graphics side, too, by dint of the character generator, the Colonel produced quite a few innovative effects and demonstrated a couple of new ways with the digital special-effects system. The vision switcher said later that he had never made such great or varied use of the buttons on his control panel – and this in a live debate programme. The Colonel was to reap the greatest plaudits of his career for this broadcast.

But none of this was of any help to Jonas. He did not feel up to becoming involved in all this; he simply sat there thinking of irrelevant things, like the time he had lifted a 150-kilo cabinet, or the time he had raised the Comorian flag over the schoolyard, or the time he had broken a circle of stones on the top of Mount Sinai; he did his best to follow what was going on, really concentrated, but then he found himself marvelling at Tangen's cleverness, his ability to be mentally one jump ahead, coming up with other questions, other lines of attack, while at the same time listening intently – Tangen, that is – to Veronika's tirades.

'Pull yourself together, for Christ's sake,' Tangen said to Jonas, while an excerpt from the Hamsun programme was being shown in all those thousands of homes. Tangen had received an irate message 'in his ear' from the Colonel. 'Surely you can at least defend yourself!' Tangen said.

Jonas sat there, staring up at the huge round scoop lamp, which was casting a special kind of light over him. Why should he defend himself? Was this a court of law?

'So tell us: according to your programme, what is the truth about Hamsun? Was he a Nazi or not?' It was Veronika's voice, insistent.

Jonas heard the question. Recognized it. And knew that he was close to giving up. Because if there was one thing that the programme on Hamsun, the whole series, had taken issue with, it was this: the Norwegian's demand for Great Simplicity. Light had to be either waves or particles. No Norwegian would accept that it could be both. The third option.

Again, Jonas was struck by a wave of nausea, because he was being forced to rise high in the air, to a point where all detail is lost and only the clear lines are discernible, because they were forcing him, in front of two million viewers, to give a simple answer, compelling him to conform to a pattern they could recognize.

Satori

And do not forget, either, the story which is bound up with, and indeed, lies at the root of this torment in a television studio, even if it did take place at an earlier point in time and on another continent, but which began with that same ominous feeling of nausea, mixed with a generous helping of dizziness. He had been sitting, lost in his own thoughts, over a notebook, when he heard a cry from outside. Although he was sure that his ears must have been deceiving him, Jonas went to open the window. On a narrow ledge outside the corresponding window of the next-door apartment stood a man. Ten storeys above the ground. Jonas was instantly struck by how appallingly simplified the whole situation was, so pressing that it made his stomach sink, and Jonas knew, as his limbs began to tremble, that this called for a swift and, above all, a simple response.

'I'm gonna jump,' the man said.

Jonas's first thought was that this was a quite impossible situation, wrapped in such grotesque banality that it tipped over into unreality. He shut his eyes for a second and offered up a silent prayer to the Great Planner, that he might be spared this, but when he opened his eyes the man was still there, and he looked, what is more, as if he were gathering himself, was about to jump. All at once, Jonas found this confrontation quite comical; it had an age-old familiarity about it, there was something so hopelessly hackneyed about the whole scene – the combination of a desperate man on a narrow ledge and his potentially imploring helper – that the words 'like a movie' inevitably sprang to mind. The whole scenario was like some obligatory nightmare, a test, something to which every human being was subjected, to some extent, at some time in their lives.

Jonas glanced about. No one else had opened their windows. No crowd was gathering on the street below. Looking one way he could just make out the river, and when he turned the other way he saw a corner of the Chrysler building rearing up between the other buildings. He fixed on this, on the way the building's distinctive spire sat directly behind the would-be suicide's head, like a sort of crown or a jester's cap.

'I'm gonna jump,' the man repeated, more firmly this time, turning his head towards Jonas for the first time as he did so. There was something about that face, a look there that he could not interpret, which cut through all talk of banality and made Jonas see that he had to do something, although he had no idea *what*.

'Don't jump,' Jonas heard himself say; words that seemed to have been engendered by some genetically determined impulse, a moral instinct. But he could tell how hollow it sounded, wondered whether it might not, after all, be better to let the guy jump, so he could prove that he had the courage and could perhaps die a happy man.

'Give me one reason, just one good reason, not to jump,' the man on the ledge said, thereby indicating that his decision was not – Jonas found himself involuntarily thinking: unfortunately – altogether inflexible, and that this was going to be tricky. Into Jonas's memory flashed something that Alva had once said, or maybe it was one of the other Nomads: There is only one really serious philosophical dilemma: suicide.

I am not going to trouble you with the details of the man's full name or the reason for his profound despair, his wish to die. I will simply say that, as far as that goes, he had as plausible, which is to say 'as good', a reason to jump as any other suicide.

Jonas had been about to say something but thought better of it, because even as an unspoken thought he could tell it was a no-go, a ludicrous platitude. After all, what was this man asking? He was asking, quite simply and with horrible directness, for an answer to the meaning of life. He stood out there on a narrow ledge, ten storeys above the ground, asking for a reason to live, and Jonas Wergeland did not know, had not the foggiest notion, what to say. There had been times in his life when he could, with reasonable conviction, have come out with some relatively fine words on the meaning of life but sadly not now, ten storeys above the ground, in such an extreme, unbelievably unlikely situation – a real B-movie cliché! – at a time when he also had to think fast, and find something straightforward and simple. Some indisputable value. A turtle that was solid enough, a ground that would not shake, not too much at any rate, when you set your foot on it.

And yet he realized that he *had* to say something, his whole body was telling him so; something that would stop the man from jumping. He at least had to try to give this man an idea, a hope. Jonas hated the situation, found it hard to believe that it was actually happening, but there was a man out there on the ledge, with his face turned to him, and he, Jonas Wergeland, was the only person to be making any contact with the man, to see that face, and he had to say something, if nothing else he had to try. But what? What do you say to a man – a desperate man, robbed of his last fragile hope – to prevent him from jumping to his death?

Jonas Wergeland was in New York to make a programme for NRK TV about the Norwegian artist Per Krohg's large mural in the Security Council chamber at the United Nations, a programme about art. Jonas had always wondered whether in some way Per Krohg might have had an influence on the political decisions made by the Security Council, due to its members having gazed at his mural during their deliberations.

Once they had finished shooting the programme Jonas had, however, stayed on in New York. He was totally burned out; he needed a break. Jonas Wergeland had made something of an impact at NRK – the so-called cognoscenti had taken a particular liking to his programmes – but the major breakthrough and ditto viewing figures had so far evaded him. The way Jonas Wergeland himself saw it, he still had not come up with a truly earth-shattering idea, one that would change everything, send him off down a new track. Up to that point, his programmes had mainly taken a negative slant, whereby he demolished, criticized, poured scorn on his subjects, but in the long run something in him reacted against this as if he knew in his heart of hearts that these were shoddy and, not least, unsatisfactory, tactics.

Earlier that day, he had stood on the deck of a ferry bound for Battery Park, after visiting Liberty Island and the Statue of Liberty. It was almost as if he thought that the sight of the copper lady, that colossus, might jolt him into a state that would trigger the great idea. Instead, he fell into conversation with a man, a history teacher from London, who was also leaning on the rail, gazing across at the financial district, which was slowly coming towards them, like a barge loaded to the gunwales with rectangular boxes. As soon as he learned that Jonas was Norwegian, he asked: 'Do you know who the greatest Viking of them all was?'

'Harald Hårfagre?' suggested Jonas.

'Harald Hardråde,' the man said firmly.

'How come?'

The Englishman held his arms out to Manhattan, rearing up into the air straight ahead of them, more like a warship now, an armoured vessel bristling with cannons and missiles. 'Because he tried to conquer York, the old York that is, tried to conquer the whole of England, come to that,' he said. 'A pretty harebrained scheme, but had he succeeded, it could have changed the whole course of history.'

The man knew a great deal about Harald Hardråde; Jonas listened with interest, sensing that there might be something in this, the germ of an idea.

'Just imagine,' the Englishman concluded, his face turned to the conglomeration of buildings in front of them, "the new York". The sheer ambition of it. Coming in from the sea all set to conquer a place mightier than your own land. It's a while since any Norwegian had such a thought, eh?' The man gave an ironic smile.

Jonas had picked up some groceries before going back to the apartment – an apartment belonging to someone he knew, situated in the part of town between the UN headquarters and Park Avenue. He had been sitting thinking about Harald Hardråde, jotting down some fragmentary words and headings in a notebook, when he heard the cry from outside, and now there he was, standing at a window on the tenth floor, charged with saying something inspirational about the trials and tribulations of life to a man who wanted to die.

'Come back inside, please,' Jonas said.

'Can't think of anything, can you?' the guy said threateningly, again making as if to jump.

Helplessly, or perhaps in order to draw strength from it, Jonas gazed at the Chrysler building, taking in its vertical lines and being struck yet again by the juxtaposition: the beautiful building in the background and the desperate face in front of it, aesthetics and ethics in one shot. So what lies at the heart of life? he thought, and even as he was thinking it he realized that the question had been wrongly formulated, because there was not just one heart to life, there were several hearts, lots of turtles, both within and outside of oneself, and possibly this was the very thing that so dismayed and confused people and prompted them to call for just one heart, so they would not have to choose. Here, in the middle of Manhattan, looking into the face of a suicide, and with the Chrysler building in the background, for the first time in his life Jonas understood why it was so difficult to say what the meaning of life actually was: because there were *many* meanings to life, a whole host of indisputable values. So one might as well start, he thought, by selecting one of several that were all equally good, begin with that rather than die of frustration.

'Okay, I know one good reason not to jump,' he said.

'If you really mean that, then come out here and tell it to me,' the man yelled. 'I'm not going to believe you until I see you out here.'

The words alone, just the thought, made Jonas freeze, and a wave of terror wash over him. This was too much to ask. Jonas knew he had lost. The man would just have to die.

'I'm gonna jump!' the man yelled.

Is this the most crucial story in Jonas Wergeland's life?

It is difficult to explain how, before he had time to think any more about it, Jonas managed to climb out of the window, even as he felt himself breaking into a cold sweat, with an awful numbness warning his body that this was madness, but he went ahead anyway, crawled out onto the narrow ledge, ten storeys above the ground, then edged his way centimetre by centimetre along it until he was standing right next to the man, who actually seemed slightly surprised. And when Jonas, unable to resist the temptation, looked down at the street below, he found that his nausea was gone. Thus it was only now, several decades later, that Jonas saw the point of that episode in the Torggata Baths, that time when he had ventured out to the edge of the five-metre board for the first time, when he had imagined that he was Sammy Lee, gold medallist from the '48 and '52 Olympics, with twists and somersaults contained within his body, a body free from dizziness; only now did he see the whole point of that incident, that the cause lay *here*, that Torggata had merely been practice, a rehearsal for something bigger, a true balancing act, a *real* leap, and it was as if, for the first time, now, here, in the middle of Manhattan, on a narrow ledge ten storeys above the ground, Jonas saw that the pieces of a life actually did fit together.

This discovery proved to be only the first stage of a colossal brainwave: after having whispered something to the man next to him, who had suddenly been relegated to a supporting role in a quite different drama, and who, after an expression more of surprise than of relief had spread over his face, actually did clamber back through his window, Jonas stayed where he was on the ledge, and in the midst of that brainstorming moment, when ninety per cent of his thoughts were going so fast that his mind had no chance to register them, he caught a glimpse of the Chrysler building, the glinting of the stainless steel on its spire. And at that very moment, linking up with the tingling sensation between his shoulder-blades, he had his vision, his great idea, it seemed to hit him all at once, not just one detail, but the whole thing, with such force that the itching sensation spread from that point between his shoulder-blades right up to the inner side of his skull as if something were in the process of unfolding.

Jonas returned to his window and into the apartment in time to open the door to the other man's knock. The latter still looked pretty stunned, or rather, almost exhilarated, expectant. And what had Jonas said to him? Jonas Wergeland had not said anything momentous at all. Or actually that was the whole point: he had said something banal, but no more banal than anything else he might have said. He had promised the man a loaf of bread. It was as shockingly simple as that: some new-baked bread. That, and a good story.

Jonas had known that he had the ingredients, he had actually bought yeast and linseeds earlier in the day, and while he made the dough, while it was rising, while the loaves were baking, they talked, he and the strange man, Eric, a perfectly normal conversation, about parents and children, about interests – Eric was a keen fisherman – about relatives and friends, jobs and films, B-movies even, and the sight of Jonas with his sleeves rolled up and his clothes covered in flour seemed to have a strangely soothing effect on Eric, so much so that he never mentioned or tried to explain, or to apologize for his act of desperation, and when the loaves were lying, golden-crusted, on the table between them, Jonas told him the story about the beetle, and Eric was pleased with the story about the beetle, extremely pleased, he sat there shaking his head and chuckling as if he really felt it was worth being alive for at least one day more just to hear that story about the beetle.

Afterwards he called his sister and was standing ready, itching to be off and clutching a loaf of bread, when she arrived. 'Thanks,' he said to Jonas, 'I owe you one.' A thumbs-up and then he and his sister disappeared into his own apartment.

That evening, or rather, that night, Jonas sat down and wrote; he had never written so much at a stretch before, the words simply flowed, he barely had time to organize his thoughts, he just wrote, looking out on a Manhattan that slowly metamorphosed into black silhouettes and millions of lights, like a starry sky dropped down to earth; by the end of it he could not have said whether what he was so feverishly scribbling down was the result of his vision out on the ledge or whether it had something to do with Harald Hardråde, or maybe even the story about the beetle, or why not the bread? Whatever it was, he kept on writing, noted down twenty-three names and at the top of the first sheet he wrote 'Norwegian Life'. By the time he eventually stopped, totally drained, on the desk in front of him lay thirty closely-written pages, the synopsis of what was to become the superb television series *Thinking Big*, and it was only when he happened to glance out of the window that he saw, with remarkable clarity – or as if he had suddenly perceived the source of this unexpected burst of creativity – that the skyscrapers that surrounded him were like organ pipes, and that once again he found himself inside an organ chest.

The Story Teller

Then hear, and hear with pride, how things went with Jonas
Wergeland when, as a natural consequence of all this, he found
himself in a television studio at Marienlyst in Oslo, almost visi-
bly squirming, as if he really were being grilled, tortured, at a
question concerning Knut Hamsun, a question so pointed that it
was virtually an ultimatum.

He tried to get round it. 'The programme had nothing to do
with whether he was a Nazi or not,' he said, his voice barely audible; he had to clear his throat before continuing. 'It dealt with
one pivotal event, intended to shed some light on Hamsun's life.'
Jonas glanced up at the studio firmament in such a way that the
viewers must have thought he was seeking help from there, or
possibly looking for an almost invisible planet, like Pluto, but the
only thing to catch his eye was a little overhead camera, mounted
close to the ceiling, hidden away like a black hole amid the galaxy
of different lamps, this too an innovative element, with the
Colonel, from his all-powerful position in the control room,
occasionally cutting to a bird's-eye shot of the studio and the
three protagonists, as if to create a certain distance, while at the
same time giving the viewers the illusion of sneaking up on
them, of eavesdropping on a private quarrel.

Veronika Røed, quite unaffected by half-an-hour in the
studio, by the inhuman concentration which the cameras and
spotlights craved, was not about to back down on the Hamsun
issue; she could tell that this was a weak point: 'But the event in
Hamsun's life which you selected is only a *detail*. How can you
be so incredibly naïve as to think that such a tiny slice of
Hamsun's life could give viewers any insight into how it hung
together as a whole? I doubt if Hamsun has ever been presented
in a less credible light!'

Jonas was aware that the Colonel, on the alert and rubbing his hands, was now showing an ultra close-up of his, Jonas's, face, as if holding him up to ridicule, on one and a half million television screens; slicing him up; illustrating Veronika Røed's point and letting everyone see how badly his makeup had been applied, see the beads of sweat on his upper lip, giving the impression of a gloss surface about to crack.

Something stirred inside him. It was that word 'credible' that had given him a glimpse of an angle of escape: 'There, you've just said it yourself, *that*'s why you don't like my programmes,' he said to Veronika, who looked quite flabbergasted to see him baring his teeth. 'You're accusing me of not making what you want to see: psychological portraits. The sort of programmes that people are used to. The sort of thing we've been seeing on television for the past thirty years. With the emphasis not on "psycho", but on "logical". That good old logic which is true because it is recognizable and safe.'

To his relief, Jonas found himself growing more animated, but he was cut short by a VT spot. Then, while that was running, one of the studio hands had to turn on a fresh spotlight to replace one that had gone out. Jonas watched him turning the little cogs on the side of the spotlight with a pole rather like a boat-hook; working intently, sweating, giving Jonas the urge to help him, or simply to have a go himself, with that boat-hook, which reminded him so much of his summers on Hvaler, his grandfather's stories.

'Ah, so you admit that you don't give two hoots for the moral aspect? You feel you're above all that, do you?' This from Veronika, they were back in the studio, and even though Jonas's eyes had fixed once again on the overhead camera, she did not catch him off-guard. 'It's amazing,' he said. 'It really is so depressing to have to say this – but the thing is, my programmes are neither psychological analyses nor ethical commentaries . . .'

'What are they, then?' Audun Tangen asked like a shot, in an echo of the quick-fire interviews of his heyday.

'They are *stories*. And stories don't convey a moral, they don't teach, they provide an experience, they get under our skin, become part of us, like genes, and like genes they can be used for good or evil.'

Now the studio really came to life. Audun Tangen and Veronika Røed were both talking at once; Veronika, in particular, was up in arms, but to Tangen's credit it has to be said that he kept her in check, endeavoured to pursue Jonas's statements, possibly because he was happy that Jonas was finally answering back. 'How on Earth can you say that a story has nothing to do with morality?' he asked.

'Okay, so I'm splitting hairs,' said Jonas, confidently as if up until then he had been treading water and now, suddenly, felt his feet come to rest on the back of a huge turtle. 'But everyone else is splitting hairs, so why shouldn't I.' Jonas Wergeland leaned forward in his chair, addressing his words as much to two million viewers as to Veronika Røed and Audun Tangen: 'Stories are not about what is good or evil, but about good *and* evil. A story embodies both aesthetics and ethics in a sort of complementarity, if I can use such a word. But stories also embody a third indefinable element, something which gives rise to a sort of a leap inside us, something outside of, or contained within, the ethics-aesthetics issue. And we are not talking here about something *above and beyond* good and evil, but about *another* issue, an issue which comes before, as it were, a more fundamental issue; and this totally different level relates to our imagination. When you come right down to it, the point of stories is to give people fresh eyes, to enable them to see the world differently. *That*'s what the programme on Hamsun was about."

A great many people agreed that a change came over Jonas Wergeland during the final third of the programme, that he seemed to revive and presented them with his old self, the persona for which he was famed: his face, his charisma, his winning personality, and from then on he could have said anything at all, and they would have lapped it up; except that Jonas Wergeland did not just say anything at all; he sat there and talked about stories, he presented a passionate defence of his right to tell stories.

I can now reveal what had actually happened, although I do so with some reservations, knowing that this could lead to misunderstanding and misinterpretation; it was the camera mounted on the studio ceiling that had provided Jonas Wergeland with a fresh angle. As he looked up into its lens, that black hole, he had the sensation that the camera lowered itself down over him and settled on top of him, and this led him to fantasize that, via this camera, he was *making love* to the people of Norway, and it occurred to him that much of his career at Marienlyst came down to just that; and at this thought, or rather this fantasy, this in many ways shocking fantasy, he felt his nervous shivers giving way to warmth and furthermore, as with his encounters with women, he had a revelation. Jonas Wergeland was sitting in a studio at Marienlyst, head tilted back during a video insert, gazing at a camera lens above his head, when suddenly it dawned on him what it was that he had been trying to do all along in his television series *Thinking Big*: to tell stories, stories that dealt with those chinks in existence which only the imagination could penetrate, insinuating its way into the grey area between cause and effect, where the ability to select a set of values, to perceive the links in a chain, lay slumbering.

And in passing it ought to be said that this revelation also prompted Jonas to wonder whether he might not have spent his whole life misunderstanding Veronika Røed's motives, which he was inclined to believe sprang from pure evil. On reflection, however, he realized that Veronika had always had a weakness for a good story which, as well as channelling her quite naturally into the world of tabloid journalism, where she had proved to be a proper little goldmine for the owners, had also in certain instances enticed her into fabricating stories. Such as with all of the debate surrounding his television series. So when she had pushed him into the water as a child, or shut him up inside a snow cave, it was not inconceivable that such things might represent an attempt to dramatize real life, a curiosity to know whether a little shove or a snowball would beget a good story. At best, thought Jonas, she had done those things because she knew that he would be rescued.

Right or wrong as this may be – I prefer, as I pointed out earlier, to say as little as possible about Veronika Røed – she hid her ulterior motives well, sitting there in that television studio, quivering with aggression, attacking Jonas Wergeland for having confused an important discussion; Veronika was so het up that she was starting to contradict her own statements regarding television's limited potential: 'Alright, so you were telling a story,' she said. 'But that still only presents one snippet of a life, you still have not explained how all of these fragments are supposed to build up into the truth about a person? Because that's what it all comes down to, Jonas Wergeland, and you can't get away from it: the truth!'

Audun Tangen was all set to move on, even though he, the Grand Inquisitor himself, felt that all this labouring on about the truth was going over the score, but Jonas put his hands in the air, stopped him, indicated that he wished to answer, but that he just needed time to consider, and so there was this pause, ten seconds maybe, an eternity on television, with Audun Tangen constantly on the point of breaking in even though he could see how effective it was, how it created a sort of tension: Jonas Wergeland sitting as if frozen stiff, with his hands in the air; ten vital seconds for Jonas, those were, when suddenly he found himself recalling details he had seen in his life, a fir tree growing out of the rockface on the banks of the Zambezi, the bicycle wheel trimmed with Monte Carlo cigarette packs, the rivets in a ship's side slipping past only inches away, other such things, and the sum of all these details seemed to be telling him a story of a tangent, something else entirely, a way to shoot out of a wicked circle, out of the constant repetition, because all at once he was taking a critical view of his own success, and he realized that this room, that all Marienlyst, could not possibly be the hub for which he had always been searching, and of course it was Veronika's question about the truth that was boring into him; Jonas would have liked to have stopped the world, stopped time, because suddenly the studio was acting like a thinking cap, charging him up, the whole of that tense situation, sitting there in front of three cameras, with his face being broadcast to one and a half million television screens, and his hands raised to a studio firmament filled with dazzling lights as if he were praying or having a vision – indeed people had later said that his face had shone with an inner light during those ten seconds, which is not so surprising since, during those moments it was revealed to Jonas Wergeland that this situation in which he now found himself need not determine anything: that this, which to others must have seemed to be the most decisive moment in his career, might just as easily be of no consequence whatsoever. After all, who was to say that it was in television that he was to do the work against which his life would one day be measured? Or, to put it another way: Jonas Wergeland realized that he had not stopped growing, that those ten years at NRK might well be no more than an insignificant parenthesis in his life; from this point onwards he could do anything at all, *become something completely different*, and yet again he felt a finger describing circles on his brow and then, abruptly, a straight line shooting out from it, a leap.

Ten seconds – an eternity – pass before he replies to Veronika's question: 'Again you're forgetting what it all comes down to: fantasy. Stimulating our creative faculty. You're doing what we Norwegians always do: Underestimate. You're underestimating the viewing public. You're forgetting that a viewer can easily create a whole picture out of fragments.'

Now, here, Jonas was back in his proper element, in front of television cameras that brought him straight through the screen and into millions of homes, and I mean *through*, because he almost seemed to be there in their living rooms. 'You're right,' he said, knowing he could afford to indulge in an argument verging on the banal, knowing that his audience would consider it to be absolutely spot-on anyway: 'I've left a lot up to the viewers' imagination. You could say that I created a caterpillar, but only because I believe that a generous viewer has the ability to metamorphose it into a butterfly.'

Veronika could feel her victory slipping away from her. 'A lot of very seductive talk,' she said, fuming. 'But you still haven't answered my question as to what becomes of the truth.'

'I'm not a minister,' Jonas said, 'I'm a storyteller.' And from that moment on Jonas took over the show completely, because he had the idea of telling a story, to show what he meant, and to provide the only adequate response to these accusations, and he had many stories to choose from. He could tell them about a man playing opera music among the glaciers on Greenland, or he could tell them about an actor who sustained a cut to the eye, or he could tell them about an old lady who went around buying up fine works of art. Or why not the story of Hjallis's fall or, even more incredible – not to say, improbable – the story of Norway's expansion, how Norway multiplied its geographical area several-fold in the early sixties without anyone, not a single Norwegian, although they were normally such avid protesters, saying so much as a word? Instead, speaking straight to the camera, straight into people's living rooms, he said that he was going to tell them the story – no more and no less – that had prompted him to make a television series about twenty-odd Norwegian men and women whose names have become part of the international vocabulary. So he told this story, he told it succinctly and well; it was the story of the beetle, and he told them, the viewers, just what a challenge, what an inspiration this story of the beetle was to the imagination and how it had given him the urge to make a series about a clutch of Norwegians who had not done what Norwegians are better at than anything else, namely, tearing down, moaning, criticizing, but who had, instead, done their part to build up, had helped the world to grow; people who showed that even Norwegians could think big. And he concluded with an appeal of sorts, to the effect that the entire future of Norway – a nation of only four million frozen souls – should 'not be dependent on German interest rates, but solely on how we, the people of Norway, every single inhabitant, use our imaginations.'

It was one of the most extraordinary programmes in the history of NRK. It stuck in people's memories in much the same way as Martin Luther King's 'I have a dream . . . ' speech; they were genuinely moved, sat there with lumps in their throats, and all because of a man who said, quite simply: 'All I have done is to tell a story about thinking big.'

Then, just before the end, seeing that she was not going to get her answer anyway, Veronika leapt out of her seat and lunged at Jonas, ripping the 'mic' off her lapel in the process, and dealt him a clout round the ear, a resounding slap, right there, on camera.

Up in the control room, the Colonel was working frantically, hardly able to believe his luck, firing off orders simultaneously to the vision switcher and the cameramen. He had obtained some wonderful close-ups of Jonas Wergeland's reaction, as it passed from a glare to a smile – possibly because he, Jonas, had guessed that Veronika had a motive known to few others: the front page of her newspaper – and a beautiful total in which Audun Tangen was seen trying to call Veronika Røed back as she stomped off the set, livid and lovely; after which the Colonel switched to the overhead camera up on the ceiling, to give an illusion of drifting away. And then, the trump card, the real stroke of genius; they showed the clout round the ear again, in slow motion, for two million Norwegians who were still rubbing their eyes in disbelief. The Colonel had borrowed a slow-motion controller – the sort used mainly for live coverage of athletics events – on the chance that something dramatic might happen. 'Have you got it?' he called. 'Okay, run it slow!' The sequence was shown over and over again while the credits rolled, and I hardly need say that that clip was to become a classic, regularly featured in programmes dealing with high points in the history of NRK.

Nonetheless, it was Jonas Wergeland who won the day; if anything his fame actually went up an extra notch after this programme. But it did not, as he thought, come down to two faces, but to two stories: Veronika's had to do with a man who seduced an entire nation with his lies – this, too, a fascinating tale – while Jonas's story was about a beetle in a cowpat. And if there is one laudable thing to be said about the Norway of the nineties it is that it allowed Jonas Wergeland's enigmatic appeal to the imagination to win over Veronika Røed's insistence on an unequivocal answer.

Imago Dei

So welcome, then, the warmth of the story that was played out at a time when the Beatles had already released their hit single 'Love Me Do' and their debut album, *Please Please Me*, although Jonas and Nefertiti knew nothing of all that – neither of them would ever share in the general adulation of these particular idols.

The Beetles, on the other hand, were a very different matter.

It all started with the two of them, Jonas and Nefertiti, walking down to the shops on Trondheimsveien to buy a fresh loaf and two fogged bottles of Mekka, the chocolate milk with such divine properties that was a firm favourite with both of them, before cutting across the stream down in the dip near Nybygga and onto the grouchy old farmer's fields, a wide expanse of cultivated and fallow fields which was the scene of many an adventure – like the time when they, or Jonas at any rate, had watched wide-eyed as the stallion let out its huge member, a circus act in itself, and a sight which provided him, forever after, with an excellent frame of reference for the invective 'you great horse's dick'; or like the time down on the bank, when they dug up the city of Troy, all nine levels of it, together with Heinrich Schliemann, after Nefertiti, with a couple of sentences and a wave of her hand, had transformed a patch of perfectly ordinary Ammerud soil into the ruins on the mound at Hissarlik in the Dardanelles.

It was June, school had just closed for the summer. They crawled under the fence and into a green meadow dotted with white clover, buttercups and a fair number of fine examples of that breed of cattle known as Norwegian Red. Jonas and Nefertiti liked watching the cows, they both got a kick out of seeing them munching sideways, and Jonas particularly enjoyed contemplating them when they lay quietly chewing the cud, while Nefertiti would become immersed in thought-experiments on how wonderful it would be if *they* had four stomachs and had to chew their food twice, thus deriving twice the pleasure from it – always assuming, of course, that the food was good.

Before they reached the cattle, however, Nefertiti's attention was caught by a cowpat, a not exactly fresh one, with a good thick crust on it; Jonas failed to see why she absolutely had to sit down right next to that. But Nefertiti slipped off her little rucksack and spread a tablecloth on the grass, the sort of red and white checked cloth that Jonas would not see again until he set foot inside Bényoucéf's restaurant, La P'tite Cuisine. They settled themselves on this, Nefertiti broke the bread and Jonas tore the silver-foil tops off the Mekka bottles. They lay back, propped up on their elbows, eating and drinking and observing the cows further down the field; they took their time, as much time as the ruminating cattle, savouring every bite, every sip, as if making up for the fact that they could not enjoy the food more than once.

Afterwards, Nefertiti fetched a stick and split the cowpat in two. It was in this clump of dung that she found the beetle, and the moment she laid eyes on it she practically dropped to her knees and stayed there, utterly spellbound, with not so much as a blink of her long eyelashes.

Jonas had seen her like this on a couple of other occasions, so lost in contemplation that she seemed to be in a trance. One time she had sat up in the loft, watching a candle burn all the way down. And one autumn she had sat crouched over a mushroom that was pushing its way through the tarmac behind the garages, as if this were a miracle that she would not have missed for the world.

So it was now. Suddenly there was no talking to her, she pushed her cap back from her forehead and brought her face right down level with the cowpat. She shushed Jonas when he tried to say something, pointing to the beetle as if she had just made a sensational discovery, like another buried Troy. 'Look,' she murmured. 'Weird,' she murmured. 'Really amazing.' The beetle had red wing-cases, it looked like nothing so much as a tiny red VW beetle on legs. Jonas supposed that it must very, very rare, for Nefertiti to grow so worked-up about it. The insect rooted about in the muck, not in the least put out by the two curious onlookers, helping itself, all undaunted, to the feast spread before it. Eventually Jonas grew fed up with all this dung-guzzling and asked Nefertiti if they couldn't go now. She did not answer, or at least merely murmured: 'Incredible, quite incredible.' Jonas rose and walked off.

He wandered around Nybygga for a while, chucked stones at some little kids who had been making a nuisance of themselves, walked up to the kiosk to buy an ice-lolly, the really good sort that had a little plastic figure inside it, mounted on a round platform, and all you had to do was to break off the stick and grind off the rough edge on the tarmac. He got a queen, a pale-blue one, but he already had that one; he trailed back up to Solhaug where he tinkered with his bike, straightening his favourite Monte Carlo cigarette pictures on the spokes and wondering what could have happened to Nefertiti.

It was late in the afternoon. He strolled down to the corner of the green behind Number Four, where the Midsummer's Eve bonfire had already been built, bigger and richer in content than ever. Chairman Moen and his lady wife came out, carrying their hideous old sofa, and both greeted Jonas with such unwonted friendliness that anyone would have thought they had been caught red-handed, unmasked in the act of committing some unforgivable betrayal. Jonas stood out on the point, looking across the fields on the other side of the stream, at an area on which, within a few years, the farm would be anachronistically hemmed in by huge tower blocks full of children named Desiré and Elvis – as if to prove that it really was true; Elvis was not dead – and where at that moment Nefertiti still sat hunched over in the middle of a bright green field, surrounded by cud-chewing cows.

Jonas went up to help his mother take in the washing. It was her day off, she had been doing the washing downstairs in the communal laundry room, and Jonas found her in one of the large cubicles where the laundry was hung to dry and which, later in life, Jonas would always picture as being full of white sheets. All in all, this would remain one of his clearest memories of Solhaug and his childhood: standing in those drying cubicles surrounded by the scent of freshly washed sheets, that and the fact that in those days everybody had white sheets, like so many blank pages, so that you felt you were standing on board a fullrigger, bound for some wonderful new world.

He followed his mother up to the flat, played some Duke Ellington records, 'Concerto for Cootie' and 'Me and You', took out his mouth organ and tried, for the hundredth time, to play 'Cotton Tail', but he could not manage it, he never could, it was impossible.

The others arrived home. His father from the church, with his briefcase full of sheet music; Daniel from the pool at Badedammen, scarlet from head to toe, as if anticipating the years when he would be known as Red Daniel. He was appallingly sunburnt; Daniel never could do things by halves, always had to go to the extreme, had to achieve a better tan than anyone else in one day. Rakel returned from the Gro Snack Bar, a guy on a motorbike had dropped her off at the door. She had already developed a fondness for lads who rode big machines, had made the leap, as it were, from *A Thousand and One Nights* to 1,000 ccs and embarked upon the astonishing career in which she would end up as a happy housewife in the cab of a Mercedes-Benz trailer-truck, which, from her point of view, was as good as any palace.

After dinner, one of the week's seven standard meals, which had been to some extent ruined by Daniel and his protests against reciting Kipling's 'If' in the Midsummer's Eve show, Jonas ran over to Number One to ask after Nefertiti. No, she hadn't come home. Did Jonas have any idea where she was?

So back he went to the field, crawled under the fence and into the meadow with its lush green grass, where the cows lay or stood about in the warm afternoon light, looking like an advertisement for Freia milk chocolate or for Norway in general. It smelled of the Earth's very own factory, of photosynthesis, of fermentation in bovine stomachs, of life, of summer, of holidays.

'Isn't it about time you were going home?' he asked Nefertiti.

Nefertiti did not answer, she was still totally absorbed in the beetle, which appeared to be doing exactly the same as when Jonas had left it earlier in the day: slowly burrowing through muck, a task of Sisyphean dimensions, due to the fact that Nefertiti kept lifting away bits of dung with her stick, so as not to lose sight of it. She knelt on the red and white checked cloth as if it were a prayer mat, staring at the armour-plated beetle with such intensity that anyone would have thought she was trying to magnify each individual detail: the antennae, the grooves in the dorsal collar, the compound eyes, the teeth on its front legs, the stripes on the wing-cases. 'Isn't it amazing?' she said again and, without taking her eyes off the beetle, motioned to Jonas to come down beside her.

Jonas lay down, eyed the lovely red wing-cases, saw how they gleamed softly. 'What are you waiting for?' he asked.

'Look at it,' was all she said. 'Just look at it and let your thoughts run. I'm telling you, Jonas: this is a precious sight. Worth more than rubies.'

As so often before and later, Jonas Wergeland did not know that that day was to form one of the foundation-stones of his life, a day which was later to determine the values he set for himself. I have already mentioned Jonas Wergeland's commitment to the Antarctic, and the way he celebrated Grotius Day, but I actually began at the wrong end of the causal chain, since this, his interest in the Antarctic was, of course, based in its turn on a set of values. And even though I did say that the values – or turtles, if you will – that we decide upon tend necessarily to be a bit of a lottery, nonetheless they are not always governed by such random forces as one might think. For when Jonas Wergeland reached the age at which he first tried to make sense of the wealth of quite indisputably solid social values, when it became simply a matter of helping oneself, for example, to 'liberty' or 'equality' or 'solidarity' or 'tolerance', he did not, in fact, feel as if he had had to pick his key value – the one overriding value that would help him to set the others in order of precedence – out of a hat, blindly as it were, because he had quite instinctively opted for 'imagination', thus setting this value above all others.

But what did imagination mean to Jonas Wergeland? Imagination was the first link in the ethical chain. To Jonas it seemed patently obvious that a weak imagination made for a weak individual. After all, it was no use choosing 'liberty' and 'equality' if one did not have the imaginative power to find ways and areas in which to put these values to use – and to balance one against another in those cases where they happened to clash. It was no good defending life, the weak, the individual, truth – whatever you wanted to call it – against the powers that be at any given time, if one had no fantasy. The fight for a stronger imagination was, therefore, the most important of all.

As far as Jonas Wergeland was concerned, protest was not about writing indignant pieces for the newspapers on all sorts of injustices. To him, it was about standing on Karl Johans gate and provoking people into using their imaginations. Which is why Jonas Wergeland inaugurated Michelangelo Day; every year on March 6, Michelangelo's birthday, he walked up and down Karl Johans gate, handing out leaflets he had paid for out of his own pocket with such headlines as 'Paint a Sistine Chapel' or 'When Did You Last Poke Fun At A Pope?' or 'Take A Day Off To Study The Veins In A Block Of Marble'. Jonas knew that everyone went around with great stores of knowledge and information in their heads; what he was endeavouring to do with these leaflets was to encourage them to use these creatively, shuffle the cards, form this abundant store of experiences into new chains of causality. Even if one only succeeded in getting people to alter the way in which they fantasized about things, it was bound to have important consequences. Even Marx knew that.

So even though Jonas Wergeland was well aware that the Earth abounded in causes that were crying out for a champion, and swarming with weak souls in need of a spokesman – all you had to do was take your pick – I hope you can see how Michelangelo Day and Grotius Day go hand in hand, just as aesthetics and ethics go hand in hand, and why Jonas should have thrown himself into the debate surrounding Antarctica, of all things. Because Antarctica is, of course, the continent of the imagination. This, the last wilderness on Earth is totally dependent on our imaginative powers. This vast ice-covered region is actually nothing but one gigantic blank page, rich in possibilities.

And it was on that warm June day in the grouchy, old farmer's fields, surrounded by cud-chewing cows, daisies and timothy, that the idea of imagination as a value was sown in Jonas Wergeland's mind, as he lay next to Nefertiti on a red and white checked cloth with his nose stuck almost right inside a cowpat.

They lay for a long time in silence. Jonas felt as if they were spying on the beetle's banquet, as if they were intent on uncovering a great secret, that it was all a matter of being patient, as indefatigable as the beetle, crawling and burrowing and guzzling its heart out in a world of muck. The beetle's upper side looked a little like a mask, a face.

'*Aphodius fimetarius*,' said Nefertiti. 'A dung beetle. Belongs to the scarab family. You know, like "the sacred scarabé", which was an object of religious worship in Egypt. Sometimes a figure in the shape of this beetle was laid over the hearts of the dead. The beetle is a symbol of eternal life.'

'Is it rare?' Jonas said, pointing to the red, softly gleaming wing-cases.

'No, it's very common,' said Nefertiti and then she told him something about the dung beetle, that specialist in shit: that they were generally very fussy when it came to the consistency of the dung, or rather, its moisture content; some went for fresh dung, others liked the older stuff. And they all had their preferences, according to a sensible distribution of all the squalor in the world, for the excrement of different animals and different grades of dung. 'But our friend *fimetarius* here can cope with the very driest cowpats, it's about the only one that can. Just think, Jonas: it's like a nomad in a desert of shit!' Nefertiti was truly fascinated by these dung beetles, she knelt there, reverently, patiently explaining to Jonas how these creatures passed through every stage of their life cycle buried in muck. And what a digestive system! They could eat all night and all day, nonstop. They were refuse collectors, cleaning the Earth. Nefertiti looked at him from under the longest eyelashes in the world: 'Isn't that absolutely amazing, Jonas? *Living off muck!* Surviving in a world of shit! That's what I call fantastic. Doesn't it make you think big thoughts? Make you imagine the most inconceivable things?'

They straightened up. Nefertiti sat there looking at him for a long time, with eyes that were bluer than the sky on the longest, lightest day of the year then suddenly, although Jonas could see no reason for this, she pulled out her crystal and handed it to him. 'This is for you,' she said. 'Remember that the imagination is also a path to knowledge and that includes knowledge that can be reached by any other paths.'

Then she hugged him, held him tight, before gazing into his eyes again. For a long time. Only later did Jonas reflect that that was the only time Nefertiti had ever hugged him. They sat for a while among the cattle, with her holding his hand while they watched the beetle digging its way down into the dung and disappearing, and when they rose to their feet, Jonas felt as though he had not only learned something about life in a cowpat, he had also been shown all of life in a nutshell.

Spring

And finally, and first of all, and at the centre of it all: the story of the hub, because there is a meaning to life, there are so many meanings to life that at least once on the journey from the cradle to the grave every human being may experience something that will move them to exclaim, quite spontaneously: 'Yes, there has to be some meaning to life.'

In Jonas Wergeland's case it happened like this: he was on the train, the electric line to Sognsvann – and here we are talking, mark you, about the unknown Jonas Wergeland, Jonas Wergeland the student of architecture – sitting in one of the most rickety coaches, on his way up to the University, where he was hoping to run into Axel in the canteen. Rain was falling outside the window: fine, almost invisible rain, the first of the year, gentle spring rain.

His thoughts were in disarray. He was stuck in a rut. He had been in a funny mood, almost melancholic, ever since the year before when, as he saw it, his life had been restored to him after his trip to Jebel Musa. He was still filled with a sort of convalescent lethargy, spent most of his time wandering about *looking* at things; he read a little, attended lectures and seminars at the High School, went on one or two field trips, worked on a couple of projects, did a lot of talking with Axel. Sometimes he would catch himself just hanging around *waiting*.

More people got on at Majorstuen. Jonas was gazing out of the window, at the rain, so fine that it was little more than a mist. He was conscious of someone sitting down directly opposite him. The coach rattled on up the track. He shifted his gaze, so that it fell on the floor, but he could feel it being drawn upwards by a force that defied gravity, until he found himself looking at two hands holding a book, an old book, and Jonas's immediate thought, based on his experience in this area, was that it had to be an antiquarian book, possibly even a valuable book.

There was something about this sight which dispelled his melancholy, which quickened him, had a stimulating effect. He amused himself, as he often did, by studying the hands holding the book, the fingers as they turned a page, the position of the left index finger – there are two sorts of reader: those who hold the left index finger under the cover and those who leave it resting *on* the page – the finger of the person sitting across from him was lying on the page in such a way that it pointed straight at him. Jonas entertained himself by trying to guess, going by the hands alone, what the owner of the book looked like. He could tell straight away that they were a woman's hands and that they spoke of great concentration on the part of the reader. On one of the fingers of her right hand, which rested on the page in what might almost have been described as a *mudra* position, the woman wore an unusual ring. It instinctively struck him as an aesthetic sight, those hands and the old book, there, in the coach of a train rattling northwards to Blindern; for some reason they, the hands and the book, struck him as being every bit as powerful, as beautiful, as momentous, as the long run of façades on the Avenida de Mayo in Buenos Aires. It was as if he knew this was a sight that would shunt him onto a new track, breaking the course he was on just as a prism breaks the light, sending it off in another direction.

His attention was caught once again by the book, by how different it looked from the books that people usually read on the train, as indeed it was, although Jonas could not have known *how* different it was, that this book was entitled *Studies of Syphilitic Disorders*, that it had been published in 1875 and that the woman who was reading it was related to its author, Carl Wilhelm Boeck, and furthermore, that she, like him, had chosen medicine as her path in life.

Then he heard someone say 'Jonas?' at the very moment when he felt that old tingling sensation, prompted by those graceful hands, the fingers on the page of the book, starting to work its way from his tailbone all the way up his spine, stronger than ever before, quite inexplicably strong, so strong that his whole body was shaken by a tremor that ran from the top of his head to the soles of his feet.

'Jonas?'

Slowly he raised his eyes. He saw a sweater, self-coloured, underneath a black raincoat. He saw the collar of a blouse. He saw a chain round the neck. He saw her face. Face with a capital 'F'. Golden. A face lit from within. A face he knew. That scar on the nose. The eyes. *That* look. As if the face were all eyes and nothing else. Even after twelve, thirteen years there was no mistaking it. Indeed, as he looked up and returned that look it struck him that for all those years, somewhere at the back of his mind, he had been thinking about that face, this person.

He was completely tongue-tied, could only sit there, speechless, as the coach swayed from side to side, blinked his eyes and could not for the life of him think where that glow on her face could be coming from on such a grey rainy day.

She fiddled with the chain round her neck, drew an old locket from inside her blouse. 'Jonas,' she said, Margrete said. 'Don't you recognize me? Gold in love?'

And he started to cry. He looked at the floor and cried. Not for long but long enough to let it out, get whatever it was out of his system. He cried softly, making no motion, rather like the rain outside. And as he lifted his eyes to her, to her face, to her eyes, once more and smiled, making no effort to excuse himself, it dawned on him that he was in love again, or no, not again, that he *was* in love, he had been in love with her all along; what he had experienced with those other girls had been something else, only *this* was love. Jonas sat there looking at her, at her face, into her eyes, and it seemed to him that those twelve years in between had never happened, that she had gone off and left him only the day before.

So he did not alight at Blindern, nothing in the world could have induced him to get off at Blindern, there was a delicious heaviness in his limbs which made it impossible for him to budge an inch, and when she asked him laughingly where he was getting off, he said that he was never going to get off, he was going to stay on that rickety old train and watch her reading an old book for the rest of his life.

'In that case,' she said as they stopped at Ullevål stadium, 'you'd better come with me.' She took him firmly by the hand and led him off the train. They strolled down Sognsveien in the sort of spring rain that makes carrying an umbrella unthinkable, that makes one want to drink in the raindrops with every part of one's being; rain that makes everything smell powerfully of the earth, smell of spring right to the marrow: the sort of rain which, in certain Norwegians, especially those with an aversion to snow, might elicit the same feelings as the life-giving rains falling at the end of a dry season in other parts of the world. And only then, when Margrete tucked her arm in his and laughed, looked up at the rain and laughed, did Jonas erupt into words and sentences as to what and where and who and why and when and how, all of which only served to make Margrete laugh even more while doing her best to provide him with answers that would satisfy his most immediate curiosity.

'I've thought a lot about you, even though I've been living far away from you,' she said as they were cutting across Damplassen. 'As an old Tuareg once said to me: "Pitch your tents as far from one another and your hearts as close to one another as possible."'

'You've been among Tuaregs?'

'Oh, there's a lot you don't know about me,' she said.

They walked through Ullevål Garden City in the soft spring rain, turning up their faces to drops with a shade of warmth in them; it was like taking a shower. 'D'you remember the liquorice coins we used to buy down at Tallaksen's?' Margrete said. Jonas laughed. 'Yes, but do you remember the Opal chocolate?' he said, and all at once they were caught up in a pyrotechnical burst of nostalgia, memories of sherbet dips and ice cream cones from the Snack Bar, of 'Dr Mengele', the school dentist, and *My Fair Lady* at the Colosseum, the mandolaikas they had made in wood-work class, water fights round the drinking fountain in the school playground, the time Wolfgang Michaelsen was hit in the eye by the cork from a champagne soda bottle and had to be taken to Casualty, and so on and so forth, both talking at once, laughing in the mild spring rain, soft rain that smelled of spring, that tasted of spring, and Margrete did not take her arm out of his until they reached the house, her parents' house, and she unlocked the door. Her father, Gjermund Boeck, whom Jonas hated more than anyone else on this Earth for having taken Margrete away from Norway, was of course on the other side of the world, fulfilling his function as Norway's ambassador, and came home only once a year, which meant that Margrete had the house to herself, a whole museum full of bronze temple lions and Chinese porcelain, not to mention a tiny jade turtle.

They sat in the kitchen, hair still wet, and talked, and they had plenty to talk about. Jonas talked about his travels, about astronomy, about architecture, about Axel, about Buddha, a lot about Buddha, while she, for her part, told him about all the different places she had lived in, about studying medicine at universities abroad and that she intended to specialize in skin diseases. They talked and talked, for hours they talked, occasionally drinking tea or eating freshly baked bread with goat's cheese, and during the course of their conversation it struck Jonas that Margrete, the way she talked, reminded him of his parents, all that small-talk which did, nonetheless, have a value, *acquired* a value, in that it formed a kind of web, of silk as it were, or built up into a weave, because he gradually began to perceive the difference, to see that this was her trademark, all the anecdotes she dispensed, pithy little tales that transformed the weave into a rug, a tapestry brimful of stories.

So Jonas stayed with her, stayed with her as if it were the most natural thing in the world; she did not have to say a word, she simply made up a bed in one of the guest rooms for him and once he had turned in for the night she came in and sat on the edge of his bed, and he told her, as if it were the most natural thing in the world, that he had become completely bogged down, that he ought to be happy, but that he was stuck in a rut, was getting nowhere, and basically felt that life was a load of shit.

'But even out of shit some good can come,' she said. 'Remember the dung beetles.' And she went on to tell him a short fairytale, an Egyptian fairy tale, about a scarabé, a tumblebug, and its efforts to bury a ball of dung: a little story so full of wisdom and carrying such a powerful echo of a girlish voice from his childhood that Jonas lay awake for ages, stunned, after Margrete had tucked him up under the eiderdown and left the room.

Over the next few weeks this was the thing he found most fascinating: her ability now and again, at the perfect point in a conversation, to come up with a story of ten or twenty sentences, a story so compact that it could be written on the palm of a hand but which in some way summed up or added another dimension to something that she, or he, had said; or gave rise to surprising unseen associations which left him sitting or lying and thinking for hours afterwards. These little stories were usually based not on things that she herself had experienced, but on things she had *read*, because he knew that she was a reader, that she had read a multitude of novels and poetry collections and plays and that it was the stuff of these that she recounted, her imagination endowing them with a new twist; he knew, too, that her stories sprang from things, details, in those books which few others noticed, because Margrete had a totally different *eye* for things, she viewed the world from a different – one might almost say more wondering – angle than other people.

He discovered what it entailed, this gift of hers, as they sat in the kitchen in Ullevål Hageby talking and drinking tea and eating home-baked bread with goat's cheese and jam, while he was learning, for the first time – or rather, for the second time. – what it meant to be in love, really in love, because he felt like a work of art, like something unique. That was Margrete's gift: to make others, whoever she happened to be talking to, feel that they were of consequence, were important: as with him now, because he was aware of how, suddenly, in responding to the things she said, he was articulating ideas that had not even occurred to him until the very moment when he heard himself voicing them. And they talked about things that he had never discussed with, for example, the Nomads; it was another form of conversation altogether, a more tranquil form, a *deeper* form, and he also discovered what her gift, this ability to bring out the best in others, derived from: her imagination, her talent for invention, her talent, by dint of ten or twenty sentences, for turning everything upside down, making you see the world in a totally different light.

And then it happened, what Jonas Wergeland had hoped for and yet had not dared hope for. After a long talk in the kitchen, three weeks after they had met one another again, she walked over to him, took him by the hand and pulled him to his feet. She looked at him, looked into his eyes and hugged him, hugged him for an eternity, cuddled up to him, cuddled up tight to him as if she could not get close enough, pressed herself against him, soft and hard at one and the same time, but mostly hard, so passionately that Jonas could not help but be reminded of the words of the *Kama Sutra*: 'When a man and a woman are very much in love with each other, and, not thinking of any pain or hurt, embrace each other as if they were entering into each other's bodies . . . then it is called an embrace like a mixture of milk and water.'

Then, when at long last she let go of him, she regarded him with a veiled but purposeful look in her eyes, before taking his hand and leading him through to the bedroom, to a large double bed, and there she undressed first him and then herself, before they lay down, naked, beside one another on the bed, and she began to stroke him, and she went on stroking him until he felt the entire expanse of his skin waking up, as if from a sleep, a numbness, as if he had only just been cured of a fatal illness; and he felt a desire to stroke her, too, so he stroked her, noticing, as he did so, how her skin seemed to glow, or to emit a sheen, as from a Golden Fleece, golden as the locket she wore round her neck, gold in love, and when he curled up against her, trying to completely overlap her, like two spoons fitting together, he was met not only by warmth but also by a quite extraordinary radiation, as if he were in the middle of a force-field, together with the conviction that, at the end of the day, this was all that mattered, this stillness, this peace, this vast stretch of her skin against his vast stretch of skin, that this was the true epicentre of sexual pleasure, what it all came down to, something so free of any friction, two people lying close together, still but at the same time in motion, a hub, the point around which the whole wheel of existence spun.

Then they made love, and for the first time Jonas lay on top of a woman, in the commonest of all positions, the missionary position; it just turned out that way, for one thing because she liked it best that way, enjoyed him better in that position, and he was surprised at how different it was, how close he got, how much nearer he came, how much deeper, and how he had become carried away in a totally different way, and even though it was he who had taken the lead he soon lost control, a very strange, and totally new experience for him, with the result that he barely had time to register her orgasm, which was not of the epileptic sort but quiet and powerful, with her seeming to retreat into herself, before he was overtaken by an acute, two-fold sensation both of falling and of floating upwards, so that his mind switched off, went into neutral, and for several seconds he was far away.

Only after he had come back to his senses did it occur to him that he had not thought of anything at all, nor had he had any sense of being expanded, as on earlier occasions; and while he was lying there, wondering about this, still curled up close to Margrete with the scent of her skin in his nostrils, he realized that he had become a totally different person, and this he knew, quite simply because he could tell that this was love and because love is not only an expansive, but also a transformative, force.

He turned onto his side and lay there looking at her, her face, the aura that surrounded her, and he told himself again that this was the hub: lying here, propped up on one elbow, gazing into a face with closed eyelids, that shimmer on the skin, conscious all the while of his body, every single cell, radiating peace and contentment. And as he looked at the jade turtle which she had placed on the bedside table and which seemed transparent, seemed to hover, in the half-dark, he knew that he would stay with her, that he *had to* stay with her, that this was enough, that there was nothing else worth striving for, he had to stay there, with her, with that living wisdom, that inexhaustible fantasy, that life-giving imagination, this had to be his goal in life, just to be there, within that force-field, talking to her, watching her bake, listening to her stories, curling up beside her, curling up close, to be next to that skin, never to let that golden sheen out of his sight. To learn to tell stories.

She opened her eyes. 'What are you thinking?' she said.

'That I'm going to be one of the quiet ones in this country. That I'm going to be an architect, and build little houses that are nice to live in.'

'What's that supposed to mean?'

'That I don't need to fumble in the dark any more. That I'm going to stay here and love you.'

'It won't be easy.'

'I'm a great seducer,' he said.

She smiled in the dim light. Her eyes, her face, shone. Glowed. She reached out a hand and described circles on his brow with the tip of her finger, slowly, and then, before letting her hand fall back onto the pillow, a straight line shooting out like a tangent.

In the end, however, there is no way round it, and you are bound to land here, here in this room, and you come to a stop, utterly exhausted, as if after a great battle, you think, and with a victim, you think, an innocent victim, and you crouch down next to Margrete, and you think and you think, and you look at Margrete and think long and hard, look at her again, dead on a polar-bear skin, shot by a Luger, you think, killed by people who are terrified of anything that is different, you think, not just of a story that is different, but of people, you think, and you look at the picture of Buddha, that beautiful picture of Buddha, and you look at the telephone, and at that you have to stop, even though it all comes flooding in, the memories, you think, the stories, even though more and more spokes keep being added to the wheel, and now you realize, now you know, you have known it ever since you were very young, that life can only be comprehended as a collection of stories.

You crouch there, looking at Margrete, you look at her face, and you look at that golden sheen, as from a Golden Fleece even now, you think, and you remember her ability to *sleep*, because, she said, sleep has a cleansing effect, everyone who sleeps cleanses the universe, she said, and you would often watch her when she was sleeping, and maybe she is sleeping now, you think, that's how it looks, anyway, as if she were doing something sacred, you think, and again you are overcome with grief, because you are thinking not only about those wicked individuals, the people behind the Luger, you are also thinking about yourself, and you blame yourself, you are ridden with guilt, *because you were not there*, and you think that you deserve to die, too, and you think, you think long and hard, and you look at

Margrete, and you think of soft spring rain all those years ago, and you think that it must, nonetheless, be possible to go on living, that there is hope, because where there is no longer any hope there are no stories to be told either, you think.

So you stand up, and for a fleeting moment you are seized by doubt, and you think that everything might tie up in a totally different way, that you have got it all wrong, and you start towards the telephone, and you walk the hard road to the telephone, like Hindus walking over red-hot coals, you think, and as you are walking the hard road to the telephone, ridden with guilt, I just want to say, once and for all, that I believe you, I want you to know that: I believe you. And know, Jonas Wergeland, that the one who is writing this does so in the hope that your fellow countrymen will understand but also, and perhaps more so, in order that *you*, when you eventually read this, will understand. And what it is that I want you to understand, only you know.

So walk those last few metres, the hard road to the telephone, thinking as you do so that it must be possible to go on living, because you are alive to the alchemy of storytelling, that even shit can be turned into gold, that even tragedy can be transformed into stories one can live on, live off, and you walk over to the telephone, you reach the telephone, you lift the receiver, and you look at the two circles of the receiver, you key in a number, like a tangent, a way out, you think, and you are afraid, you know that what is now about to happen could change everything that *has* happened, and you know that from now on all of this could be rearranged to form quite a different story, and you know that anything can happen from the moment you start to speak, to tell your story.

About the author:

Jan Kjærstad was born in Oslo in 1953. He read theology at theUniversity of Oslo and made his début as a writer in 1980 with a short story collection, *The Earth Turns Quietly*. *The Seducer* forms the first part of a trilogy which also includes the novels *The Conqueror* and *The Discoverer*. These novels have achieved a huge international success. Jan Kjærstad is also the author of essays, a children's book and editor of the literary magazine *Vinduet*.

He was the recipient of the Nordic Prize for Literature in 2001 and was also awarded Germany's Henrik Steffen Prize for Scandinavians who have significantly enriched Europe's artistic and intellectual life. Other awards include the Norwegian Literary Critics Prize and the Aschehoug Prize.